HENRY MILLER

THE OBELISK TRILOGY

TROPIC OF CANCER

TROPIC OF CAPRICORN

BLACK SPRING

THE NEW TRAVELLER'S COMPANION SERIES, NUMBER 41

TROPIC OF CANCER

SEPTEMBER 1934

TROPIC OF CAPRICORN

MAY 1939

BLACK SPRING

JUNE 1936

OLYMPIA PRESS.COM EDITION FIRST PUBLISHED AUGUST, 2004
REVISED EDITION, FEBRUARY 2005
COMPLETELY REDONE, 2008

ISBN: 1-59654-110-5

The Olympia Press. A Division of Disruptive Publishing, Inc.

TROPIC OF CANCER

Preface

Here is a book which, if such a thing were possible, might restore our appetite for the fundamental realities. The predominant note will seem one of bitterness, and bitterness there is, to the full. But there is also a wild extravagance, a mad gaiety, a verve, a gusto, at times almost a delirium. A continual oscillation between extremes, with bare stretches that taste like brass and leave the full flavor of emptiness. It is beyond optimism or pessimism. The author has given us the last frisson. *Pain has no more secret recesses.*

In a world grown paralyzed with introspection and constipated by delicate mental meals this brutal exposure of the substantial body comes as a vitalizing current of blood. The violence and obscenity are left unadulterated, as manifestation of the mystery and pain which ever accompanies the act of creation.

The restorative value of experience, prime source of wisdom and creation, is reasserted. There remain waste areas of unfinished thought and action, a bundle of shreds and fibers with which the over critical may strangle themselves. Referring to his Wilhelm Meister *Goethe once said: "People seek a central point: that is hard, and not even right. I should think a rich, manifold life, brought close to our eyes, would be enough without any express tendency; which, after all, is only for the intellect."*

The book is sustained on its own axis by the pure flux and rotation of events. Just as there is no central point, so also there is no question of heroism or of struggle since there is no question of will, but only an obedience to flow.

The gross caricatures are perhaps more vital, "more true to life," than the full portraits of the conventional novel for the reason that the individual today has no centrality and produces not the slightest illusion of wholeness. The characters are integrated to the false, cultural void in which we are drowning; thus is produced the illusion of chaos, to face which requires the ultimate courage.

The humiliations and defeats, given with a primitive honesty, end not in frustration, despair, or futility, but in hunger, an ecstatic, devouring hunger—for more life. *The poetic is discovered by stripping away the vestiture of art; by descending to what might be styled "a pre-artistic level" the durable skeleton of form which is hidden in the phenomena of disintegration reappears to be transfigured again in the ever-changing flesh of emotion. The scars are burned away—the scars left by the obstetricians of culture. Here is an artist who re-establishes the potency of illusion by gaping at the open wounds, by courting the stern, psychological reality which man seeks to avoid through recourse to the oblique symbolism of art. Here the symbols are laid bare, presented almost as naively and unblushingly by this over-civilized individual as by the well-rooted savage.*

It is no false primitivism which gives rise to this savage lyricism. It is not a retrogressive tendency, but a swing forward into unbeaten areas. To regard a naked book such as this with the same critical eye that is turned upon even such diverse types as Lawrence, Breton, Joyce and Celine is a mistake. Rather let us try to look at it with the eyes of a Patagonian for whom all that is sacred and taboo in our world is meaningless. For the adventure which has brought the author to the spiritual ends of the earth is the history of every artist who, in order to express himself, must traverse the intangible gridirons of his imaginary world. The air pockets, the alkali wastes, the crumbling monuments, the putrescent cadavers, the crazy jig and maggot dance, all this forms a grand fresco of our epoch, done with shattering phrases and loud, strident, hammer strokes.

If there is here revealed a capacity to shock, to startle the lifeless ones from their profound slumber, let us congratulate ourselves; for the tragedy of our world is precisely that nothing any longer is capable of rousing it from its lethargy. No more violent dreams, no refreshment, no awakening. In the anaesthesia produced by self-knowledge, life is passing, art is passing, slipping from us: we are drifting with time and our fight is with shadows. We need a blood transfusion.

And it is blood and flesh which are here given us. Drink, food, laughter, desire, passion, curiosity, the simple realities which nourish the roots of our highest and vaguest creations. The superstructure is lopped away. This book brings with it a wind that blows down the dead and hollow trees whose roots are withered and lost in the barren soil of our times. This book goes to the roots and digs under, digs for subterranean springs.

—Anais Nin 1934

I am living at the Villa Borghese. There is not a crumb of dirt anywhere, nor a chair misplaced. We are all alone here and we are dead.

Last night Boris discovered that he was lousy. I had to shave his armpits and even then the itching did not stop. How can one get lousy in a beautiful place like this? But no matter. We might never have known each other so intimately, Boris and I, had it not been for the lice.

Boris has just given me a summary of his views. He is a weather prophet. The weather will continue bad, he says. There will be more calamities, more death, more despair. Not the slightest indication of a change anywhere. The cancer of time is eating us away. Our heroes have killed themselves, or are killing themselves. The hero, then, is not Time, but Timelessness. We must get in step, a lock step, toward the prison of death. There is no escape. The weather will not change.

It is now the fall of my second year in Paris. I was sent here for a reason I have not yet been able to fathom.

I have no money, no resources, no hopes. I am the happiest man alive. A year ago, six months ago, I thought that I was an artist. I no longer think about it, I *am*. Everything that was literature has fallen from me. There are no more books to be written, thank God.

This then? This is not a book. This is libel, slander, defamation of character. This is not a book, in the ordinary sense of the word. No, this is a prolonged insult, a gob of spit in the face of Art, a kick in the pants to God, Man, Destiny, Time, Love, Beauty ... what you will. I am going to sing for you, a little off key perhaps, but I will sing. I will sing while you croak, I will dance over your dirty corpse....

To sing you must first open your mouth. You must have a pair of lungs, and a little knowledge of music. It is not necessary to have an accordion, or a guitar. The essential thing is to *want* to sing. This then is a song. I am singing.

It is to you, Tania, that I am singing. I wish that I could sing better, more melodiously, but then perhaps you would never have consented to listen to me. You have heard the others sing and they have left you cold. They sang too beautifully, or not beautifully enough.

It is the twenty-somethingth of October. I no longer keep track of the date. Would you say—my dream of the 14th November last? There are intervals, but they are between dreams, and there is no consciousness of them left. The world around me is dissolving, leaving here and there spots of time. The world is a cancer eating itself away.... I am thinking that when the great silence descends upon all and everywhere music will at last triumph. When into the womb of time everything is again withdrawn chaos will be restored and chaos is the score upon which reality is written. You, Tania, are my chaos. It is why I sing. It is not even I, it is the world dying, shedding the skin of time. I am still alive, kicking in your womb, a reality to write upon.

Dozing off. The physiology of love. The whale with his six-foot penis, in repose. The bat—*penis libre*. Animals with a bone in the penis. Hence, *a bone on*.... "Happily," says Gourmont, "the bony structure is lost in man." Happily? Yes, happily. Think of the human race walking around with a bone on. The kangaroo has a double penis—one for weekdays and one for holidays. Dozing. A letter from a female asking if I have found a title for my book. Title? To be sure: "Lovely Lesbians."

Your anecdotal life! A phrase of M. Borowski's. It is on Wednesdays that I have lunch with Borowski. His wife, who is a dried-up cow, officiates. She is studying English now— her favorite word is "filthy." You can see immediately what a pain in the ass the Borowskis are. But wait....

Borowski wears corduroy suits and plays the accordion. An invincible combination, especially when you consider that he is not a bad artist. He puts on that he is a Pole, but he is not, of course. He is a Jew, Borowski, and his father was a philatelist. In fact, almost all Montparnasse is Jewish, or half-Jewish, which is worse. There's Carl and Paula, and Cronstadt and Boris, and Tania and Sylvester, and Moldorf and Lucille. All except Fillmore. Henry Jordan Oswald turned out to be a Jew also. Louis Nichols is a Jew. Even Van Norden and Cherie are Jewish. Frances Blake is a Jew, or a Jewess. Titus is a Jew. The Jews then are snowing me under. I am writing this for my friend Carl whose father is a Jew. All this is important to understand.

Of them all the loveliest Jew is Tania, and for her sake I too would become a Jew. Why not? I already speak like a Jew. And I am as ugly as a Jew. Besides, who hates the Jews more than the Jew?

Twilight hour. Indian blue, water of glass, trees glistening and liquescent. The rails fall away into the canal at Jaures. The long caterpillar with lacquered sides dips like a roller coaster. It is not Paris. It is not Coney Island. It is a crepuscular melange of all the cities of Europe and Central America. The railroad yards below me, the tracks black, webby, not ordered by the engineer but cataclysmic in design, like those gaunt fissures in the polar ice which the camera registers in degrees of black.

Food is one of the things I enjoy tremendously. And in this beautiful Villa Borghese there is scarcely ever any evidence of food. It is positively appalling at times. I have asked Boris time and again to order bread for breakfast, but he always forgets. He goes out for breakfast, it seems. And when he comes back he is picking his teeth and there is a little *egg* hanging from his goatee. He eats in the restaurant out of consideration for me. He says it hurts to eat a big meal and have me watch him.

I like Van Norden but I do not share his opinion of himself. I do not agree, for instance, that he is a philosopher, or a thinker. He is cunt-struck, that's all. And he will never be a writer. Nor will Sylvester ever be a writer, though his name blaze in 50,000-candle-power red lights. The only writers about me for whom I have any respect, at present, are Carl and Boris. They are possessed. They glow inwardly with a white flame. They are mad and tone deaf. They are sufferers.

Moldorf, on the other hand, who suffers too in his peculiar way, is not mad. Moldorf is word drunk. He has no veins or blood vessels, no heart or kidneys. He is a portable trunk filled with innumerable drawers and in the drawers are labels written out in white ink, brown ink, red ink, blue ink, vermilion, saffron, mauve, sienna, apricot, turquoise, onyx, Anjou, herring, Corona, verdigris, gorgonzola....

I have moved the typewriter into the next room where I can see myself in the mirror as I write.

Tania is like Irene. She expects fat letters. But there is another Tania, a Tania like a big seed, who scatters pollen everywhere—or, let us say, a little bit of Tolstoy, a stable scene in which the fetus is dug up. Tania is a fever, too—*les votes urinaires,* Cafe de la Liberte, Place des Vosges, bright neckties on the Boulevard Montparnasse, dark bathrooms, Porto Sec, Abdullah cigarettes, the adagio sonata *Pathetique,* aural amplificators, anecdotal seances, burnt sienna breasts, heavy garters, what time is it, golden pheasants stuffed with chestnuts, taffeta fingers, vaporish twilights turning to ilex, acromegaly, cancer and delirium, warm veils, poker chips, carpets of blood and soft thighs. Tania says so that every one may hear: "I love him!" And while Boris scalds himself with whisky she says: "Sit down here! O Boris... *Russia*... what'll I do? I'm bursting with it!"

At night when I look at Boris' goatee lying on the pillow I get hysterical. O Tania, where now is that warm cunt of yours, those fat, heavy garters, those soft, bulging thighs? There is a bone in my prick six inches long. I will ream out every wrinkle in your cunt, Tania, big with seed. I will send you home to your Sylvester with an ache in your belly and your womb turned inside out. Your Sylvester! Yes, he knows how to build a fire, but I know how to inflame a cunt. I shoot hot bolts into you, Tania, I make your ovaries incandescent. Your Sylvester is a little jealous now? He feels something, does he? He feels the remnants of my big prick. I have set the shores a little wider, I have ironed out the wrinkles. After me you can take on stallions, bulls, rams, drakes, St. Bernards.

You can stuff toads, bats, lizards up your rectum. You can shit arpeggios if you like, or string a zither across your navel. I am fucking you, Tania, so that you'll stay fucked. And if you are afraid of being fucked publicly I will fuck you privately. I will tear off a few hairs from your cunt and paste them on Boris' chin. I will bite into your clitoris and spit out two franc pieces....

Indigo sky swept clear of fleecy clouds, gaunt trees infinitely extended, their black boughs gesticulating like a sleepwalker. Somber, spectral trees, their trunks pale as cigar ash. A silence supreme and altogether European. Shutters drawn, shops barred. A red glow here and there to mark a tryst. Brusque the facades, almost forbidding; immaculate except for the splotches of shadow cast by the trees. Passing by the Orangerie I am reminded of another Paris, the Paris of Maugham, of Gauguin, Paris of George Moore. I think of that terrible Spaniard who was then startling the world with his acrobatic leaps from style to style. I think of Spengler and of his terrible pronunciamentos, and I wonder if style, style in the grand manner, is done for. I say that my mind is occupied with these thoughts, but it is not true; it is only later, after I have crossed the Seine, after I have put behind me the carnival of lights, that I allow my mind to play with these ideas. For the moment I can think of nothing—except that I am a sentient being stabbed by the miracle of these waters that reflect a forgotten world. All along the banks the trees lean heavily over the tarnished mirror; when the wind rises and fills them with a rustling murmur they will shed a few tears and shiver as the water swirls by. I am suffocated by it. No one to whom I can communicate even a fraction of my feelings....

The trouble with Irene is that she has a valise instead of a cunt. She wants fat letters to shove in her valise. Immense, *avec des choses inouïes*. Llona now, she had a cunt. I know because she sent us some hairs from down below. Llona—a wild ass snuffing pleasure out of the wind. On every high hill she played the harlot—and sometimes in telephone booths and toilets. She bought a bed for King Carol and a shaving mug with his initials on it. She lay in Tottenham Court Road with her dress pulled up and fingered herself. She used candles, Roman candles, and door knobs. Not a prick in the land big enough for her... *not one*. Men went inside her and curled up. She wanted extension pricks, self-exploding rockets, hot boiling oil made of wax and creosote. She would cut off your prick and keep it inside her forever, if you gave her permission. One cunt out of a million, Llona! A laboratory cunt and no litmus paper that could take her color. She was a liar, too, this Llona. She never bought a bed for her King Carol. She crowned him with a whisky bottle and her tongue was full of lice and tomorrows. Poor Carol, he could only curl up inside her and die. She drew a breath and he fell out—like a dead clam.

Enormous, fat letters, *avec des choses inouïes*. A valise without straps. A hole without a key. She had a German mouth, French ears, Russian ass. Cunt international. When the flag waved it was red all the way back to the throat. You entered on the Boulevard Jules-Ferry and came out at the Porte de la Villette. You dropped your sweetbreads into the tumbrils—red tumbrils with two wheels, naturally. At the confluence of the Ourcq and Marne, where the water sluices through the dikes and lies like glass under the bridges. Llona is lying there now and the canal is full of glass and splinters; the mimosas weep, and there is a wet, foggy fart on the windowpanes. One cunt out of a million Llona! All cunt and a glass ass in which you can read the history of the Middle Ages.

It is the caricature of a man which Moldorf first presents. Thyroid eyes. Michelin lips. Voice like pea soup. Under his vest he carries a little pear. However you look at him it is always the same panorama: netsuke snuffbox, ivory handle, chess piece, fan, temple motif. He has fermented so long now that he is amorphous. Yeast despoiled of its vitamins. Vase without a rubber plant.

The females were sired twice in the ninth century, and again during the Renaissance. He was carried through the great dispersions under yellow bellies and white. Long before the Exodus a Tatar spat in his blood.

His dilemma is that of the dwarf. With his pineal eye he sees his silhouette projected on a screen of incommensurable size. His voice, synchronized to the shadow of a pinhead, intoxicates him. He hears a roar where others hear only a squeak.

There is his mind. It is an amphitheater in which the actor gives a protean performance. Moldorf, multiform and unerring, goes through his roles—clown, juggler, contortionist, priest, lecher, mountebank. The amphitheater is too small. He puts dynamite to it. The audience is drugged. He scotches it.

I am trying ineffectually to approach Moldorf. It is like trying to approach God, for Moldorf *is* God—he has never been anything else. I am merely putting down words....

I have had opinions about him which I have discarded; I have had other opinions which I am revising. I have pinned him down only to find that it was not a dung-beetle I had in my hands, but a dragonfly. He has offended me by his coarseness and then overwhelmed me with his delicacy. He has been voluble to the point of suffocation, then quiet as the Jordan.

When I see him trotting forward to greet me, his little paws outstretched, his eyes perspiring, I feel that I am meeting.... No, this is not the way to go about it!

"Comme un oeuf dansant sur un jet d'eau."

He has only one cane—a mediocre one. In his pocket scraps of paper containing prescriptions for *Weltschmerz*. He is cured now, and the little German girl who washed his feet is breaking her heart. It is like Mr. Nonentity toting his Gujarati dictionary everywhere. *"Inevitable for everyone"*—meaning, no doubt, *indispenensable.* Borowski would find all this incomprehensible. Borowski has a different cane for each day in the week, and one for Easter.

We have so many points in common that it is like looking at myself in a cracked mirror.

I have been looking over my manuscripts, pages scrawled with revisions. Pages of *literature.* This frightens me a little. It is so much like Moldorf. Only I am a Gentile, and Gentiles have a different way of suffering. They suffer without neuroses and, as Sylvester says, a man who has never been afflicted with a neurosis does not know the meaning of suffering.

I recall distinctly how I enjoyed my suffering. It was like taking a cub to bed with you. Once in a while he clawed you—and then you really were frightened. Ordinarily you had no fear—you could always turn him loose, or chop his head off.

There are people who cannot resist the desire to get into a cage with wild beasts and be mangled. They go in even without revolver or whip. Fear makes them fearless.... For the Jew the world is a cage filled with wild beasts. The door is locked and he is there without whip or revolver. His courage is so great that he does not even smell the dung in the corner. The spectators applaud but he does not hear. The drama, he thinks, is going on inside the cage. The cage, he thinks, is the world. Standing there alone and helpless, the door locked, he finds that the lions do not understand his language. Not one lion has ever heard of Spinoza. Spinoza? Why they can't even get their teeth into him. "Give us meat!" they roar, while he stands there petrified, his ideas frozen, his *Weltanschauung* a trapeze out of reach. A single blow of the lion's paw and his cosmogony is smashed.

The lions, too, are disappointed. They expected blood, bones, gristle, sinews. They chew and chew, but the words are chicle and chicle is indigestible. Chicle is a base over which you sprinkle sugar, pepsin, thyme, licorice. Chicle, when it is gathered by *chicleros,* is O.K. The *chicleros* came over on the ridge of a sunken continent. They brought with them an algebraic language. In the Arizona desert they met the Mongols of the North, glazed like eggplants. Time shortly after the earth had taken its gyroscopic lean—when the Gulf Stream was parting ways with the Japanese current. In the heart of the soil they found tufa rock. They embroidered the very bowels of the earth with their language. They ate one another's entrails and the forest closed in on them, on their bones and skulls, on their lace tufa. Their language was lost. Here and there one still finds the remnants of a menagerie, a brain plate covered with figures.

What has all this to do with you, Moldorf? The word in your mouth is anarchy. Say it, Moldorf, I am waiting for it. Nobody knows, when we shake hands, the rivers that pour through our sweat. Whilst you are framing your words, your lips half parted, the saliva gurgling in your cheeks, I have jumped halfway across Asia. Were I to take your cane, mediocre as it is, and poke a little hole in your side, I could collect enough material to fill the British Museum. We stand on five minutes and devour centuries. You are the sieve through which my anarchy strains, resolves itself into words. Behind the word is chaos. Each word a stripe, a bar, but there are not and never will be enough bars to make the mesh.

In my absence the window curtains have been hung.

They have the appearance of Tyrolean tablecloths dipped in lysol. The room sparkles. I sit on the bed in a daze, thinking about man before his birth. Suddenly bells begin to toll, a weird, unearthly music, as if I had been translated to the steppes of Central Asia. Some ring out with a long, lingering roll, some erupt drunkenly, maudlinly. And now it is quiet again, except for a last note that barely grazes the silence of the night—just a faint, high gong snuffed out like a flame.

I have made a silent compact with myself not to change a line of what I write. I am not interested in perfecting my thoughts, nor my actions. Beside the perfection of Turgenev I put the perfection of Dostoevski. (Is there anything more perfect than *The Eternal Husband?*) Here, then, in one and the same medium, we have two kinds of perfection. But in Van Gogh's letters there is a perfection beyond either of these. It is the triumph of the individual over art.

There is only one thing which interests me vitally now, and that is the recording of all that which is omitted in books. Nobody, so far as I can see, is making use of those elements in the air which give direction and motivation to our lives. Only the killers seem to be extracting from life some satisfactory measure of what they are putting into it. The age demands violence, but we are getting only abortive explosions. Revolutions are nipped in the bud, or else succeed too quickly. Passion is quickly exhausted. Men fall back on ideas, *comme d'habitude.* Nothing is proposed that can last more than twenty-four hours. We are living a million lives in the space of a generation. In the study of entomology, or of deep sea life, or cellular activity, we derive more ...

The telephone interrupts this thought which I should never have been able to complete. Someone is coming to rent the apartment....

It looks as though it were finished, my life at the Villa Borghese. Well, I'll take up these pages and move on. Things will happen elsewhere. Things are always happening. It seems wherever I go there is drama. People are like lice—they get under your skin and bury themselves there. You scratch and scratch until the blood comes, but you can't get permanently deloused. Everywhere I go people are making a mess of their lives. Everyone has his private tragedy. It's in the blood now—misfortune, ennui, grief, suicide. The atmosphere is saturated with disaster, frustration, futility. Scratch and scratch—until there's no skin left. However, the effect upon me is exhilarating. Instead of being discouraged, or depressed, I enjoy it. I am crying for more and more disasters, for bigger calamities, for grander failures. I want the whole world to be out of whack, I want everyone to scratch himself to death.

So fast and furiously am I compelled to live now that there is scarcely time to record even these fragmentary notes. After the telephone call, a gentleman and his wife arrived. I went upstairs to lie down during the transaction. Lay there wondering what my next move would be. Surely not to go back to the fairy's bed and toss about all night flicking bread crumbs with my toes. That puking little bastard! If there's anything worse than being a fairy it's being a miser. A timid, quaking little bugger who lived in constant fear of going broke some day—the 18th of March perhaps, or the 25th of May precisely. Coffee without milk or sugar. Bread without butter. Meat without gravy, or no meat at all. Without this and without that! That dirty little miser! Open the bureau drawer one day and find money hidden away in a sock. Over two thousand francs—and checks that he hadn't even cashed. Even that I wouldn't have minded so much if there weren't always coffee grounds in my beret and garbage on the floor, to say nothing of the cold cream jars and the greasy towels and the sink always stopped up. I tell you, the little bastard he smelled bad—except when he doused himself with cologne. His ears were dirty, his eyes were dirty, his ass was dirty. He was double-jointed, asthmatic, lousy, picayune, morbid. I could have forgiven him everything if only he had handed me a decent breakfast! But a man who has two thousand francs hidden away in a dirty sock and refuses to wear a clean shirt or smear a little butter over his bread, such a man is not just a fairy, nor even just a miser—he's an imbecile!

But that's neither here nor there, about the fairy. I'm keeping an ear open as to what's going on downstairs. It's a Mr. Wren and his wife who have called to look at the apartment. They're talking about taking it. Only *talking* about it, thank God. Mrs. Wren has a loose laugh—complications ahead. Now *Mister* Wren is talking. His voice is raucous, scraping, booming, a heavy blunt weapon that wedges its way through flesh and bone and cartilage.

Boris calls me down to be introduced. He is rubbing his hands, like a pawnbroker. They are talking about a story Mr. Wren wrote, a story about a spavined horse.

"But I thought Mr. Wren was a painter?"

"To be sure," says Boris, with a twinkle in his eye, "but in the wintertime he writes. And he writes well... remarkably well."

I try to induce Mr. Wren to talk, to say something, anything, to talk about the spavined horse, if necessary. But Mr. Wren is almost inarticulate. When he essays to speak of those dreary months with the pen he becomes unintelligible. Months and months he spends before setting a word to paper. (And there are only three months of winter!) What does he cogitate all those months and months of winter? So help me God, I can't see this guy as a writer. Yet Mrs. Wren says that when he sits down to it the stuff *just pours out.*

The talk drifts. It is difficult to follow Mr. Wren's mind because he says nothing. *He thinks as he goes along*—so Mrs. Wren puts it. Mrs. Wren puts everything about Mr. Wren in the loveliest light. "He thinks as he goes along"—very charming, charming indeed, as Borowski would say, but really very painful, particularly when the thinker is nothing but a spavined horse.

Boris hands me money to buy liquor. Going for the liquor I am already intoxicated. I know just how I'll begin when I get back to the house. Walking down the street it commences, the grand speech inside me that's gurgling like Mrs. Wren's loose laugh. Seems to me she had a slight edge on already. Listens beautifully when she's tight. Coming out of the wine shop I hear the urinal gurgling. Everything is loose and splashy. I want Mrs. Wren to listen....

Boris is rubbing his hands again. Mr. Wren is still stuttering and spluttering. I have a bottle between my legs and I'm shoving the corkscrew in. Mrs. Wren has her mouth parted expectantly. The wine is splashing between my legs, the sun is splashing through the bay window, and inside my veins there is a bubble and splash of a thousand crazy things that commence to gush out of me now pell-mell. I'm telling them everything that comes to mind, everything that was bottled up inside me and which Mrs. Wren's loose laugh has somehow released. With that bottle between my legs and the sun splashing through the window I experience once again the splendor of those miserable days when I first arrived in Paris, a bewildered, poverty-stricken individual who haunted the streets like a ghost at a banquet. Everything comes back to me in a rush—the toilets that wouldn't work, the prince who shined my shoes, the Cinema Splendide where I slept on the patron's overcoat, the bars in the window, the feeling of suffocation, the fat cockroaches, the drinking and carousing that went on between times, Rose Cannaque and Naples dying in the sunlight. Dancing the streets on an empty belly and now and then calling on strange people—Madame Delorme, for instance. How I ever got to Madame Delorme's, I can't imagine any more. But I got there, got inside somehow, past the butler, past the maid with her little white apron, got right inside the palace with my corduroy trousers and my hunting jacket—and not a button on my fly. Even now I can taste again the golden ambiance of that room where Madame Delorme sat upon a throne in her mannish rig, the goldfish in the bowls, the maps of the ancient world, the beautifully bound books; I can feel again her heavy hand resting upon my shoulder, frightening me a little with her heavy Lesbian air. More comfortable down below in that thick stew pouring into the Gare St. Lazare, the whores in the doorways, seltzer bottles on every table; a thick tide of semen flooding the gutters. Nothing better between five and seven than to be pushed around in that throng, to follow a leg or a beautiful bust, to move along with the tide and everything whirling in your brain. A weird sort of contentment in those days. No appointments, no invitations for dinner, no program, no dough. The golden period, when I had not a single friend. Each morning the dreary walk to the American Express, and each morning the inevitable answer from the clerk. Dashing here and there like a bedbug, gathering butts now and then, sometimes furtively, sometimes brazenly; sitting down on a bench and squeezing my guts to stop the gnawing, or walking through the Jardin des Tuileries and getting an erection looking at the dumb statues. Or wandering along the Seine at night, wandering and wandering, and going mad with the beauty of it, the trees leaning to, the broken images in the water, the rush of the current under the bloody lights of the bridges, the women sleeping in doorways, sleeping on newspapers, sleeping in the rain; everywhere the musty porches of the cathedrals and beggars and lice and old hags full of St. Vitus' dance; push-carts stacked up like wine barrels in the side streets, the smell of berries in the market place and the old church surrounded with vegetables and blue arc lights, the gutters slippery with garbage and women in satin pumps staggering through the filth and vermin at the end of an all-night souse. The Place St. Sulpice, so quiet and deserted, where toward midnight there came every night the woman with the busted umbrella and the crazy veil; every night she slept there on a bench under her torn umbrella, the ribs hanging down, her dress turning green, her bony fingers and the odor of decay oozing from her body; and in the morning I'd be sitting there myself, taking a quiet snooze in the sunshine, cursing the god-damned pigeons gathering up the crumbs everywhere. St. Sulpice! The fat belfries, the garish posters over the door, the candles flaming inside. The Square so beloved of Anatole France, with that drone and buzz from the altar, the splash of the fountain, the pigeons cooing, the crumbs disappearing like magic and only a dull rumbling in the hollow of the guts. Here I would sit day after day thinking of Germaine and that dirty little street near the Bastille where she lived, and that buzz-buzz going on behind the altar, the buses whizzing by, the sun beating down into the asphalt and the asphalt working into me and Germaine, into the asphalt and all Paris in the big fat belfries.

And it was down the Rue Bonaparte that only a year before Mona and I used to walk every night, after we had taken leave of Borowski. St. Sulpice not meaning much to me then, nor anything in Paris. Washed out with talk. Sick of faces. Fed up with cathedrals and squares and menageries and what not. Picking up a book in the red bedroom and the cane chair uncomfortable; tired of sitting on my ass all day long, tired of red wallpaper, tired of seeing so many people jabbering away about nothing. The red bedroom and the trunk always open; her gowns lying about in a delirium of disorder. The red bedroom with my galoshes and canes, the notebooks I never touched, the manuscripts lying cold and dead. Paris! Meaning the Cafe Select, the Dome, the Flea Market, the American Express. Paris! Meaning Borowski's canes, Borowski's hats, Borowski's *gouaches,* Borowski's pre-historic fish—and prehistoric jokes. In that Paris of '28 only one night stands out in my memory—the night before sailing for America. A rare night, with Borowski slightly pick-led and a little disgusted with me because I'm dancing with every slut in the place. But we're leaving in the morning! That's what I tell every cunt I grab hold of—*leaving in the morning!* That's what I'm telling the blonde with agate-colored eyes. And while I'm telling her she takes my hand and squeezes it between her legs. In the lavatory I stand before the bowl with a tremendous erection; it seems light and heavy at the same time, like a piece of lead with wings on it. And while I'm standing there like that two cunts sail in— Americans. I greet them cordially, prick in hand. They give me a wink and pass on. In the vestibule, as I'm buttoning my fly, I notice one of them waiting for her friend to come out of the can. The music is still playing and maybe Mona'll be coming to fetch me, or Borowski with his gold-knobbed cane, but I'm in her arms now and she has hold of me and I don't care who comes or what happens. We wriggle into the cabinet and there I stand her up, slap up against the wall, and I try to get it into her but it won't work and so we sit down on the seat and try it that way but it won't work either. No matter how we try it it won't work. And all the while she's got hold of my prick, she's clutching it like a life-saver, but it's no use, we're too hot, too eager. The music is still playing and so we waltz out of the cabinet into the vestibule again and as we're dancing there in the shithouse I come all over her beautiful gown and she's sore as hell about it. I stumble back to the table and there's Borowski with his ruddy face and Mona with her disapproving eye. And Borowski says "Let's all go to Brussels tomorrow," and we agree, and when we get back to the hotel I vomit all over the place, in the bed, in the washbowl, over the suits and gowns and the galoshes and canes and the notebooks I never touched and the manuscripts cold and dead. A few months later. The same hotel, the same room.

We look out on the courtyard where the bicycles are parked, and there is the little room up above, under the attic, where some smart young Alec played the phonograph all day long and repeated clever little things at the top of his voice. I say "we" but I'm getting ahead of myself, because Mona has been away a long time and it's just today that I'm meeting her at the Gare St. Lazare. Toward evening I'm standing there with my face squeezed between the bars, but there's no Mona, and I read the cable over again but it doesn't help any. I go back to the Quarter and just the same I put away a hearty meal. Strolling past the Dome a little later suddenly I see a pale, heavy face and burning eyes— and the little velvet suit that I always adore because under the soft velvet there were always her warm breasts, the marble legs, cool, firm, muscular. She rises up out of a sea of faces and embraces me, embraces me passionately—a thousand eyes, noses, fingers, legs, bottles, windows, purses, saucers all glaring at us and we in each other's arm oblivious. I sit down beside her and she talks—a flood of talk. Wild consumptive notes of hysteria, perversion, leprosy. I hear not a word because she is beautiful and I love her and now I am happy and willing to die.

We walk down the Rue du Chateau, looking for Eugene. Walk over the railroad bridge where I used to watch the trains pulling out and feel all sick inside wondering where the hell she could be. Everything soft and enchanting as we walk over the bridge. Smoke coming up between our legs, the tracks creaking, semaphores in our blood. I feel her body close to mine—all mine now—and I stop to rub my hands over the warm velvet. Everything around us is crumbling, crumbling and the warm body under the warm velvet is aching for me....

Back in the very same room and fifty francs to the good, thanks to Eugene. I look out on the court but the phonograph is silent. The trunk is open and her things are lying around everywhere just as before. She lies down on the bed with her clothes on. Once, twice, three times, four times... I'm afraid she'll go mad... in bed, under the blankets, how good to feel her body again! But for how long? Will it last this time? Already I have a presentiment that it won't.

She talks to me so feverishly—as if there will be no tomorrow. "Be quiet, Mona! Just look at me... *don't talk!*" Finally she drops off and I pull my arm from under her. My eyes close. Her body is there beside me... it will be there 'til morning surely.... It was in February I pulled out of the harbor in a blinding snowstorm. The last glimpse I had of her was in the window waving goodbye to me. A man standing on the other side of the street, at the corner, his hat pulled down over his eyes, his jowls resting on his lapels. A fetus watching me. A fetus with a cigar in its mouth. Mona at the window waving goodbye. White heavy face, hair streaming wild. And now it is a heavy bedroom, breathing regularly through the gills, sap still oozing from between her legs, a warm feline odor and her hair in my mouth. My eyes are closed. We breathe warmly into each other's mouth. Close together, America three thousand miles away. I never want to see it again. To have her here in bed with me, breathing on me, her hair in my mouth—I count that something of a miracle. Nothing can happen now 'til morning....

I wake from a deep slumber to look at her. A pale light is trickling in. I look at her beautiful wild hair. I feel something crawling down my neck. I look at her again, closely. Her hair is alive. I pull back the sheet—more of them. They are swarming over the pillow.

It is a little after daybreak. We pack hurriedly and sneak out of the hotel. The cafes are still closed. We walk, and as we walk we scratch ourselves. The day opens in milky whiteness, streaks of salmon-pink sky, snails leaving their shells. Paris. Paris. Everything happens here. Old, crumbling walls and the pleasant sound of water running in the urinals. Men licking their mustaches at the bar. Shutters going up with a bang and little streams purling in the gutters. *Amer Picon* in huge scarlet letters. *Zigzag.* Which way will we go and why or where or what?

Mona is hungry, her dress is thin. Nothing but evening wraps, bottles of perfume, barbaric earrings, bracelets, depilatories. We sit down in a billiard parlor on the Avenue du Maine and order hot coffee. The toilet is out of order. We shall have to sit some time before we can go to another hotel. Meanwhile we pick bedbugs out of each other's hair. Nervous. Mona is losing her temper. Must have a bath. Must have this. Must have that. Must, must, must... "How much money have you left?" Money! Forgot all about that.

Hotel des Etats-Unis. An *ascenseur.* We go to bed in broad daylight. When we get up it is dark and the first thing to do is to raise enough dough to send a cable to America. A cable to the fetus with the long juicy cigar in his mouth. Meanwhile there is the Spanish woman on the Boulevard Raspail—she's always good for a warm meal. By morning something will happen. At least we're going to bed together. No more bedbugs now. The rainy season has commenced. The sheets are immaculate....

A new life opening up for me at the Villa Borghese. Only ten o'clock and we have already had breakfast and been out for a walk. We have an Elsa here with us now. "Step softly for a few days," cautions Boris.

The day begins gloriously: a bright sky, a fresh wind, the houses newly washed. On our way to the Post Office Boris and I discussed the book. *The Last Book*—which is going to be written anonymously.

A new day is beginning. I felt it this morning as we stood before one of Dufresne's glistening canvases, a sort of *dejeuner intime* in the thirteenth century, *sans vin.* A fine, fleshy nude, solid, vibrant, pink as a fingernail, with glistening billows of flesh; all the secondary characteristics, and a few of the primary. A body that sings, that has the moisture of dawn. A still life, only nothing is still, nothing dead here. The table creaks with food; it is so heavy it is sliding out of the frame. A thirteenth century repast—with all the jungle notes that he has memorized so well. A family of gazelles and zebras nipping the fronds of the palms.

And now we have Elsa. She was playing for us this morning while we were in bed. *Step softly for a few days....* Good! Elsa is the maid and I am the guest. And Boris is the big cheese. A new drama is beginning. I'm laughing to myself as I write this. He knows what is going to happen, that lynx, Boris. He has a nose for things too.

Step softly ....

Boris is on pins and needles. At any moment now his wife may appear on the scene. She weighs well over 180 pounds, that wife of his. And Boris is only a handful. There you have the situation. He tries to explain it to me on our way home at night. It is so tragic and so ridiculous at the same time that I am obliged to stop now and then and laugh in his face. "Why do you laugh so?" he says gently, and then he commences himself, with that whimpering, hysterical note in his voice, like a helpless wretch who realizes suddenly that no matter how many frock coats he puts on he will never make a man. He wants to run away, to take a new name. "She can have everything, that cow, if only she leaves me alone," he whines. But first the apartment has to be rented, and the deeds signed, and a thousand other details for which his frock coat will come in handy. But the size of her!—that's what really worries him. If we were to find her suddenly standing on the doorstep when we arrive he would faint—that's how much he respects her!

And so we've got to go easy with Elsa for a while. Elsa is only there to make breakfast—and to show the apartment.

But Elsa is already undermining me. That German blood. Those melancholy songs. Coming down the stairs this morning, with the fresh coffee in my nostrils, I was humming softly.... *"Es war' so schon gewesen."* For breakfast, that. And in a little while the English boy upstairs with his Bach. As Elsa says—"he needs a woman." And Elsa needs something too. I can feel it. I didn't say anything to Boris about it, but while he was cleaning his teeth this morning Elsa was giving me an earful about Berlin, about the women who look so attractive from behind, and when they turn round—*wow, syphilis!*

It seems to me that Elsa looks at me rather wistfully. Something left over from the breakfast table. This afternoon we were writing, back to back, in the studio. She had begun a letter to her lover who is in Italy. The machine got jammed. Boris had gone to look at a cheap room he will take as soon as the apartment is rented. There was nothing for it but to make love to Elsa. She wanted it. And yet I felt a little sorry for her. She had only written the first line to her lover—I read it out of the corner of my eye as I bent over her. But it couldn't be helped. That damned German music, so melancholy, so sentimental. It undermined me. And then her beady little eyes, so hot and sorrowful at the same time.

After it was over I asked her to play something for me. She's a musician, Elsa, even though it sounded like broken pots and skulls clanking. She was weeping, too, as she played. I don't blame her. Everywhere the same thing, she says. Everywhere a man, and then she has to leave, and then there's an abortion and then a new job and then another man and nobody gives a fuck about her except to use her. All this after she's played Schumann for me—Schumann, that slobbery, sentimental German bastard! Somehow I feel sorry as hell for her and yet I don't give a damn. A cunt who can play as she does ought to have better sense than be tripped up by every guy with a big putz who happens to come along. But that Schumann gets into my blood. She's still sniffling, Elsa; but my mind is far away. I'm thinking of Tania and how she claws away at her adagio. I'm thinking of lots of things that are gone and buried. Thinking of a summer afternoon in Greenpoint when the Germans were romping over Belgium and we had not yet lost enough money to be concerned over the rape of a neutral country. A time when we were still innocent enough to listen to poets and to sit around a table in the twilight rapping for departed spirits. All that afternoon and evening the atmosphere is saturated with German music; the whole neighborhood is German, more German even than Germany. We were brought up on Schumann and Hugo Wolf and sauerkraut and kummel and potato dumplings. Toward evening we're sitting around a big table with the curtains drawn and some fool two-headed wench is rapping for Jesus Christ. We're holding hands under the table and the dame next to me has two fingers in my fly. And finally we lie on the floor, behind the piano, while someone sings a dreary song. The air is stifling and her breath is boozy. The pedal is moving up and down, stiffly, automatically, a crazy, futile movement, like a tower of dung that takes twenty-seven years to build but keeps perfect time. I pull her over me with the sounding board in my ears; the room is dark and the carpet is sticky with the kummel that has been spilled about. Suddenly it seems as if the dawn were coming: it is like water purling over ice and the ice is blue with a rising mist, glaciers sunk in emerald green, chamois and antelope, golden groupers, sea cows mooching along and the amber jack leaping over the Arctic rim....

Elsa is sitting in my lap. Her eyes are like little belly-buttons. I look at her large mouth, so wet and glistening, and I cover it. She is humming now.... *"Es war' so schon gewesen...."* Ah, Elsa, you don't know yet what that means to me, your *Trompeter von Sackingen.* German Singing Societies, Schwaben Hall, the Turnverein... *links um, rechts um...* and then a whack over the ass with the end of a rope.

Ah, the Germans! They take you all over like an omnibus. They give you indigestion. In the same night one cannot visit the morgue, the infirmary, the zoo, the signs of the zodiac, the limbos of philosophy, the caves of epistemology, the arcana of Freud and Stekel.... On the merry-go-round one doesn't get anywhere, whereas with the Germans one can go from Vega to Lope de Vega, all in one night, and come away as foolish as Parsifal.

As I say, the day began gloriously. It was only this morning that I became conscious again of this physical Paris of which I have been unaware for weeks. Perhaps it is because the book has begun to grow inside me. I am carrying it around with me everywhere. I walk through the streets big with child and the cops escort me across the street. Women get up to offer me their seats. Nobody pushes me rudely any more. I am pregnant. I waddle awkwardly, my big stomach pressed against the weight of the world.

It was this morning, on our way to the Post Office, that we gave the book its final imprimatur. We have evolved a new cosmogony of literature, Boris and I. It is to be a new Bible—*The Last Book.* All those who have anything to say will say it here—*anonymously.* We will exhaust the age. After us not another book—not for a generation, at least. Heretofore we had been digging in the dark, with nothing but instinct to guide us. Now we shall have a vessel in which to pour the vital fluid, a bomb which, when we throw it, will set off the world. We shall put into it enough to give the writers of tomorrow their plots, their dramas, their poems, their myths, their sciences. The world will be able to feed on it for a thousand years to come. It is colossal in its pretentiousness. The thought of it almost shatters us.

For a hundred years or more the world, *our* world, has been dying. And not one man, in these last hundred years or so, has been crazy enough to put a bomb up the asshole of creation and set it off. The world is rotting away, dying piecemeal. But it needs the *coup de grace,* it needs to be blown to smithereens. Not one of us is intact, and yet we have in us all the continents and the seas between the continents and the birds of the air. We are going to put it down—the evolution of this world which has died but which has not been buried. We are swimming on the face of time and all else has drowned, is drowning, or will drown. It will be enormous, the Book. There will be oceans of space in which to move about, to perambulate, to sing, to dance, to climb, to bathe, to leap somersaults, to whine, to rape, to murder. A cathedral, a veritable cathedral, in the building of which everybody will assist who has lost his identity. There will be masses for the dead, prayers, confessions, hymns, a moaning and a chattering, a sort of murderous insouciance; there will be rose windows and gargoyles and acolytes and pallbearers. You can bring your horses in and gallop through the aisles. You can butt your head against the walk—they won't give. You can pray in any language you choose, or you can curl up outside and go to sleep. It will last a thousand years, at least, this cathedral, and there will be no replica, for the builders will be dead and the formula too. We will have postcards made and organize tours. We will build a town around it and set up a free commune. We have no need for genius—genius is dead. We have need for strong hands, for spirits who are willing to give up the ghost and put on flesh....

The day is moving along at a fine tempo. I am up on the balcony at Tania's place. The drama is going on down below in the drawing room. The dramatist is sick and from above his scalp looks more scabrous than ever. His hair is made of straw. His ideas are straw. His wife too is straw, though still a little damp. The whole house is made of straw. Here I am up on the balcony, waiting for Boris to arrive. My last problem—*breakfast*—is gone. I have simplified everything. If there are any new problems I can carry them in my rucksack, along with my dirty wash. I am throwing away all my sous. What need have I for money? I am a writing machine. The last screw has been added. The thing flows. Between me and the machine there is no estrangement. I am the machine....

They have not told me yet what the new drama is about, but I can sense it. They are trying to get rid of me. Yet here I am for my dinner, even a little earlier than they expected. I have informed them where to sit, what to do. I ask them politely if I shall be disturbing them, but what I really mean, and they know it well, is—*will you be disturbing me?* No, you blissful cockroaches, you are not disturbing me. You are *nourishing* me. I see you sitting there close together and I know there is a chasm between you. Your nearness is the nearness of planets. I am the void between you. If I withdraw there will be no void for you to swim in.

Tarda is in a hostile mood—I can feel it. She resents my being filled with anything but herself. She knows by the very caliber of my excitement that her value is reduced to zero. She knows that I did not come this evening to fertilize her. She knows there is something germinating inside me which will destroy her. She is slow to realize, but she is realizing it...

Sylvester looks more content. He will embrace her this evening at the dinner table. Even now he is reading my manuscript, preparing to inflame my ego, to set my ego against hers.

It will be a strange gathering this evening. The stage is being set. I hear the tinkle of the glasses. The wine is being brought out. There will be bumpers downed and Sylvester who is ill will come out of his illness.

It was only last night, at Cronstadt's, that we projected this setting. It was ordained that the women must suffer, that off-stage there should be more terror and violence, more disasters, more suffering, more woe and misery.

It is no accident that propels people like us to Paris. Paris is simply an artificial stage, a revolving stage that permits the spectator to glimpse all phases of the conflict. Of itself Paris initiates no dramas. They are begun elsewhere. Paris is simply an obstetrical instrument that tears the living embryo from the womb and puts it in the incubator. Paris is the cradle of artificial births. Rocking here in the cradle each one slips back into his soil: one dreams back to Berlin, New York, Chicago, Vienna, Minsk. Vienna is never more Vienna than in Paris. Everything is raised to apotheosis. The cradle gives up its babes and new ones take their places. You can read here on the walls where Zola lived and Balzac and Dante and Strindberg and everybody who ever was anything. Everyone has lived here some time or other. Nobody *dies* here....

They are talking downstairs. Their language is symbolic. The world "struggle" enters into it. Sylvester, the sick dramatist, is saying: "I am just reading the *Manifesto*." And Tania says—*"Whose?"* Yes, Tania, I heard you. I am up here writing about you and you divine it well. *Speak more,* that I may record you. For when we go to table I shall not be able to make any notes.... Suddenly Tania remarks: "There is no prominent hall in this place." Now what does that mean, if anything?

They are putting up pictures now. That, too, is to impress me. See, they wish to say, we are at home here, living the conjugal life. Making the home attractive. We will even argue a little about the pictures, for *your* benefit. And Tania remarks again: "How the eye deceives one!" Ah, Tania, what things you say! Go on, carry out this farce a little longer. I am here to get the dinner you promised me; I enjoy this comedy tremendously. And now Sylvester takes the lead. He is trying to explain one of Borowski's *gouaches.* "Come here, do you see? One of them is playing the guitar; the other is holding a girl in his lap." True, Sylvester. Very true. Borowski and his guitars! The girls in his lap! Only one never quite knows what it is he holds in his lap, or whether it is really a man playing the guitar....

Soon Moldorf will be trotting in on all fours and Boris with that helpless little laugh of his. There will be a golden pheasant for dinner and Anjou and short fat cigars. And Cronstadt, when he gets the latest news, will live a little harder, a little brighter, for five minutes; and then he will subside again into the humus of his ideology and perhaps a poem will be born, a big golden bell of a poem without a tongue.

Had to knock off for an hour or so. Another customer to look at the apartment. Upstairs the bloody Englishman is practicing his Bach. It is imperative now, when someone comes to look at the apartment, to run upstairs and ask the pianist to lay off for a while.

Elsa is telephoning the greengrocer. The plumber is putting a new seat on the toilet bowl. Whenever the doorbell rings Boris loses his equilibrium. In the excitement he has dropped his glasses; he is on his hands and knees, his frock coat is dragging the floor. It is a little like the Grand Guignol—the starving poet come to give the butcher's daughter lessons. Every time the phone rings the poet's mouth waters. Mallarme sounds like a sirloin steak, Victor Hugo like *foie de veau*. Elsa is ordering a delicate little lunch for Boris—"a nice juicy little pork chop," she says. I see a whole flock of pink hams lying cold on the marble, wonderful hams cushioned in white fat. I have a terrific hunger though we've only had breakfast a few minutes ago—it's the lunch that I'll have to skip. It's only Wednesdays that I eat lunch, thanks to Borowski. Elsa is still telephoning—she forgot to order a piece of bacon. "Yes, a nice little piece of bacon, not too fatty," she says... *Zut alors!* Throw in some sweetbreads, throw in some mountain oysters and some psst clams! Throw in some fried liverwurst while you're at it; I could gobble up the fifteen hundred plays of Lope de Vega in one sitting.

It is a beautiful woman who has come to look at the apartment. An American, of course. I stand at the window with my back to her watching a sparrow pecking at a fresh turd. Amazing how easily the sparrow is provided for. It is raining a bit and the drops are very big. I used to think a bird couldn't fly if its wings got wet. Amazing how these rich dames come to Paris and find all the swell studios. A little talent and a big purse. If it rains they have a chance to display their brand new slickers. Food is nothing: sometimes they're so busy gadding about that they haven't time for lunch. Just a little sandwich, a wafer, at the Cafe de la Paix or the Ritz Bar. "For the daughters of gentlefolk only"—that's what it says at the old studio of Puvis de Chavannes. Happened to pass there the other day. Rich American cunts with paint boxes slung over their shoulders. A little talent and a fat purse.

The sparrow is hopping frantically from one cobblestone to another. Truly herculean efforts, if you stop to examine closely. Everywhere there is food lying about—in the gutter, I mean. The beautiful American woman is inquiring about the toilet. The toilet! Let me show you, you velvet-snooted gazelle! The toilet, you say? *Par ici, Madame. N'oubliez pas que les places numerotees sont reservees aux mutiles de la guerre.*

Boris is rubbing his hands—he is putting the finishing touches to the deal. The dogs are barking in the courtyard; they bark like wolves. Upstairs Mrs. Melverness is moving the furniture around. She had nothing to do all day, she's bored; if she finds a crumb of dirt anywhere she cleans the whole house. There's a bunch of green grapes on the table and a bottle of wine—*vin de choix,* ten degrees. "Yes," says Boris. "I could make a washstand for you, just come here, please. Yes, this is the toilet. There is one upstairs too, of course. Yes, a thousand francs a month. You don't care much for Utrillo, you say? No, this is it. It needs a new washer, that's all...."

She's going in a minute now. Boris hasn't even introduced me this time. The son of a bitch! Whenever it's a rich cunt he forgets to introduce me. In a few minutes I'll be able to sit down again and type. Somehow I don't feel like it any more today. My spirit is dribbling away. She may come back in an hour or so and take the chair from under my ass. How the hell can a man write when he doesn't know where he's going to sit the next half-hour? If this rich bastard takes the place I won't even have a place to sleep. It's hard to know, when you're in such a jam, which is worse—not having a place to sleep or not having a place to work. One can sleep almost anywhere, but one must have a place to work. Even if it's not a masterpiece you're doing. Even a bad novel requires a chair to sit on and a bit of privacy. These rich cunts never think of a thing like that. Whenever they want to lower their soft behinds there's always a chair standing ready for them....

Last night we left Sylvester and his God sitting together before the hearth. Sylvester in his pajamas, Moldorf with a cigar between his lips. Sylvester is peeling an orange. He puts the peel on the couch cover. Moldorf draws closer to him. He asks permission to read again that brilliant parody, *The Gates of Heaven.* We are getting ready to go, Boris and I. We are too gay for this sickroom atmosphere. Tania is going with us. She is gay because she is going to escape. Boris is gay because the God in Moldorf is dead. I am gay because it is another act we are going to put on.

Moldorf's voice is reverent. "Can I stay with you, Sylvester, until you go to bed?" He has been staying with him for the last six days, buying medicine, running errands for Tania, comforting, consoling, guarding the portals against malevolent intruders like Boris and his scalawags. He is like a savage who has discovered that his idol was mutilated during the night. There he sits, at the idol's feet, with breadfruit and grease and jabber-wocky prayers. His voice goes out unctuously. His limbs are already paralyzed.

To Tania he speaks as if she were a priestess who had broken her vows. "You must make yourself worthy. Sylvester is your God." And while Sylvester is upstairs suffering (he has a little wheeze in the chest) the priest and the priestess devour the food. "You are polluting yourself," he says, the gravy dripping from his lips. He has the capacity for eating and suffering at the same time. While he fends off the dangerous ones he puts out his fat little paw and strokes Tania's hair. "I'm beginning to fall in love with you. You are like my Fanny."

In other respects it has been a fine day for Moldorf. A letter arrived from America. Moe is getting A's in everything. Murray is learning to ride the bicycle. The victrola was repaired. You can see from the expression on his face that there were other things in the letter besides report cards and velocipedes. You can be sure of it because this afternoon he bought 325 francs worth of jewelry for his Fanny. In addition he wrote her a twenty-page letter. The *garcon* brought him page after page, filled his fountain pen, served his coffee and cigars, fanned him a little when he perspired, brushed the crumbs from the table, lit his cigar when it went out, bought stamps for him, danced on him, pirouetted, salaamed... broke his spine damned near. The tip was fat. Bigger and fatter than a Corona Corona. Moldorf probably mentioned it in his diary. It was for Fanny's sake. The bracelet and the earrings, they were worth every sou he spent. Better to spend it on Fanny than waste it on little strumpets like Germaine and Odette. Yes, he told Tania so. He showed her his trunk. It is crammed with gifts—for Fanny, and for Moe and Murray.

"My Fanny is the most intelligent woman in the world. I have been searching and searching to find a flaw in her—but there's not one.

"She's perfect. I'll tell you what Fanny can do. She plays bridge like a shark; she's interested in Zionism; you give her an old hat, for instance, and see what she can do with it. A little twist here, a ribbon there, and *voila quel-que chose de beau!* Do you know what is perfect bliss? To sit beside Fanny, when Moe and Murray have gone to bed, and listen to the radio. She sits there so peacefully. I am rewarded for all my struggles and heartaches in just watching her. She listens intelligently. When I think of your stinking Montparnasse and then of my evenings in Bay Ridge with Fanny after a big meal, I tell you there is no comparison. A simple thing like food, the children, the soft lamps, and Fanny sitting there, a little tired, but cheerful, contented, heavy with bread... we just sit there for hours without saying a word. That's bliss!

"Today she writes me a letter—not one of those dull stock-report letters. She writes me from the heart, in language that even my little Murray could understand. She's delicate about everything, Fanny. She says that the children must continue their education but the expense worries her. It will cost a thousand bucks to send little Murray to school. Moe, of course, will get a scholarship. But little Murray, that little genius, Murray, what are we going to do about him? I wrote Fanny not to worry. Send Murray to school, I said. What's another thousand dollars? I'll make more money this year than ever before. I'll do it for little Murray—because he's a genius, that kid."

I should like to be there when Fanny opens the trunk. "See, Fanny, this is what I bought in Budapest from an old Jew.... This is what they wear in Bulgaria—it's pure wool.... This belonged to the Duke of something or other—no, you don't wind it, you put it in the sun.... This I want you to wear, Fanny, when we go to the Opera... wear it with that comb I showed you.... And this, Fanny, is something Tania picked up for me... she's a little bit on your type...."

And Fanny is sitting there on the settee, just as she was in the oleograph, with Moe on one side of her and little Murray, Murray the genius, on the other. Her fat legs are a little too short to reach the floor. Her eyes have a dull permanganate glow. Breasts like ripe red cabbage; they bobble a little when she leans forward. But the sad thing about her is that the juice has been cut off. She sits there like a dead storage battery; her face is out of plumb—it needs a little animation, a sudden spurt of juice to bring it back into focus. Moldorf is jumping around in front of her like a fat toad. His flesh quivers. He slips and it is difficult for him to roll over again on his belly. She prods him with her thick toes. His eyes protrude a little further, "Kick me again, Fanny, that was good." She gives him a good prod this time—it leaves a permanent dent in his paunch. His face is close to the carpet; the wattles are joggling in the nap of the rug. He livens up a bit, flips around, springs from furniture to furniture. "Fanny, you are marvelous!" He is sitting now on her shoulder. He bites a little piece from her ear, just a little tip from the lobe where it doesn't hurt. But she's still dead—all storage battery and no juice. He falls on her lap and lies there quivering like a toothache. He is all warm now and helpless. His belly glistens like a patent-leather shoe. In the sockets of his eyes a pair of fancy vest buttons. "Unbutton my eyes, Fanny, I want to see you better!" Fanny carries him to bed and drops a little hot wax over his eyes. She puts rings around his navel and a thermometer up his ass. She places him and he quivers again. Suddenly he's dwindled, shrunk completely out of sight. She searches all over for him, in her intestines, everywhere. Something is tickling her—she doesn't know where exactly. The bed is full of toads and fancy vest buttons. "Fanny, where are you?" Something is tickling her—she can't say where. The buttons are dropping off the bed. The toads are climbing the walls. A tickling and a tickling. "Fanny, take the wax out of my eyes! I want to look at you!" But Fanny is laughing, squirming with laughter. There is something inside her, tickling and tickling. She'll die laughing if she doesn't find it. "Fanny, the trunk is full of beautiful things. Fanny, do you hear me?" Fanny is laughing, laughing like a fat worm. Her belly is swollen with laughter. Her legs are getting blue. "O God, Morris, there is something tickling me.... I can't help it!"

Sunday! Left the Villa Borghese a little before noon, just as Boris was getting ready to sit down to lunch. I left out of a sense of delicacy, because it really pains Boris to see me sitting there in the studio with an empty belly. Why he doesn't invite me to lunch with him I don't know. He says he can't afford it, but that's no excuse. Anyway, I'm delicate about it. If it pains him to eat alone in my presence it would probably pain him more to share his meal with me. It's not my place to pry into his secret affairs.

Dropped in at the Cronstadts' and they were eating too. A young chicken with wild rice. Pretended that I had eaten already, but I could have torn the chicken from the baby's hands. This is not just false modesty—it's a kind of perversion, I'm thinking. Twice they asked me if I wouldn't join them. No! No! Wouldn't even accept a cup of coffee after the meal. I'm *delicat,* I am! On the way out I cast a lingering glance at the bones lying on the baby's plate—there was still meat on them.

Prowling around aimlessly. A beautiful day—so far. The Rue de Buci is alive, crawling. The bars wide open and the curbs lined with bicycles. All the meat and vegetable markets are in full swing. Arms loaded with truck bandaged in newspapers. A fine Catholic Sunday—in the morning, at least.

High noon and here I am standing on an empty belly at the confluence of all these crooked lanes that reek with the odor of food. Opposite me is the Hotel de Louisiane. A grim old hostelry known to the bad boys of the Rue de Buci in the good old days. Hotels and food, and I'm walking about like a leper with crabs gnawing at my entrails. On Sunday mornings there's a fever in the streets. Nothing like it anywhere, except perhaps on the

East Side, or down around Chatham Square. The Rue de l'Echaude is seething. The streets twist and turn, at every angle a fresh hive of activity. Long queues of people with vegetables under their arms, turning in here and there with crisp, sparkling appetites. Nothing but food, food, food. Makes one delirious.

Pass the Square de Furstenberg. Looks different now at high noon. The other night when I passed by it was deserted, bleak, spectral. In the middle of the square four black trees that have not yet begun to blossom. Intellectual trees, nourished by the paving stones. Like T. S. Eliot's verse. Here, by God, if Marie Laurencin ever brought her Lesbians out into the open, would be the place for them to commune. *Tres lesbienne ici.* Sterile, hybrid, dry as Boris' heart.

In the little garden adjoining the Eglise St. Germain are a few dismounted gargoyles. Monsters that jut forward with a terrifying plunge. On the benches other monsters—old people, idiots, cripples, epileptics. Snoozing there quietly, waiting for the dinner bell to ring. At the Galerie Zak across the way some imbecile has made a picture of the cosmos— *on the flat.* A painter's cosmos! Full of odds and ends, bric-a-bric. In the lower left-hand corner, however, there's an anchor—and a dinner bell. Salute! Salute! O Cosmos!

Still prowling around. Mid afternoon. Guts rattling. Beginning to rain now. Notre-Dame rises tomblike from the water. The gargoyles lean far out over the lace facade. They hang there like an *idee fixe* in the mind of a monomaniac. An old man with yellow whiskers approaches me. Has some Jaworski nonsense in his hand. Comes up to me with his head thrown back and the rain splashing in his face turns the golden sands to mud. Bookstore with some of Raoul Dufy's drawings in the window. Drawings of charwomen with rosebushes between their legs. A treatise on the philosophy of Joan Miro. The *philosophy,* mind you!

In the same window: *A Man Cut In Slices!* Chapter one: the man in the eyes of his family. Chapter two: the same in the eyes of his mistress. Chapter three:—No chapter three. Have to come back tomorrow for chapters three and four. Every day the window trimmer turns a fresh page. *A man cut in slices....* You can't imagine how furious I am not to have thought of a title like that! Where is this bloke who writes "the same in the eyes of his mistress ... the same in the eyes of ... the same ...?" Where is this guy? Who is he? I want to hug him. I wish to Christ I had had brains enough to think of a title like that— instead of *Crazy Cock* and the other fool things I invented. Well, fuck a duck! I congratulate him just the same.

I wish him luck with his fine title. Here's another slice for you—for your next book! Ring me up some day. I'm living at the Villa Borghese. We're all dead, or dying, or about to die. We need good titles. We need meat—slices and slices of meat—juicy tenderloins, porterhouse steaks, kidneys, mountain oysters, sweetbreads. Some day, when I'm standing at the corner of 42nd Street and Broadway, I'm going to remember this title and I'm going to put down everything that goes on in my noodle—caviar, rain drops, axle grease, vermicelli, liverwurst—slices and slices of it. And I'll tell no one why, after I had put everything down, I suddenly went home and chopped the baby to pieces. *Un acte gratuit pour vous, cher monsieur si bien coupe en tranches!*

How a man can wander about all day on an empty belly, and even get an erection once in a while, is one of those mysteries which are too easily explained by the "anatomists of the soul." On a Sunday afternoon, when the shutters are down and the proletariat possesses the street in a kind of dumb torpor, there are certain thoroughfares which remind one of nothing less than a big chancrous cock laid open longitudinally. And it is just these highways, the Rue St. Denis, for instance, or the Faubourg du Temple—which attract one irresistibly, much as in the old days, around Union Square or the upper reaches of the Bowery, one was drawn to the dime museums where in the show windows there were displayed wax reproductions of various organs of the body eaten away by syphilis and other venereal diseases. The city sprouts out like a huge organism diseased in every part, the beautiful thoroughfares only a little less repulsive because they have been drained of their pus.

At the Cite Nortier, somewhere near the Place du Combat, I pause a few minutes to drink in the full squalor of the scene. It is a rectangular court like many another which one glimpses through the low passageways that flank the old arteries of Paris. In the middle of the court is a clump of decrepit buildings which have so rotted away that they have collapsed on one another and formed a sort of intestinal embrace. The ground is uneven, the flagging slippery with slime. A sort of human dump heap which has been filled in with cinders and dry garbage. The sun is setting fast. The colors die. They shift from purple to dried blood, from nacre to bister, from cool dead grays to pigeon shit. Here and there a lopsided monster stands in the window blinking like an owl. There is the shrill squawk of children with pale faces and bony limbs, rickety little urchins marked with the forceps. A fetid odor seeps from the walls, the odor of a mildewed mattress. Europe—medieval, grotesque, monstrous: a symphony in B-mol. Directly across the street the Cine Combat offers its distinguished clientele *Metropolis*.

Coming away my mind reverts to a book that I was reading only the other day. "The town was a shambles; corpses, mangled by butchers and stripped by plunderers, lay thick in the streets; wolves sneaked from the suburbs to eat them; the black death and other plagues crept in to keep them company, and the English came marching on; the while the *danse macabre* whirled about the tombs in all the cemeteries...." Paris during the days of Charles the Silly! A lovely book! Refreshing, appetizing. I'm still enchanted by it. About the patrons and prodromes of the Renaissance I know little, but Madam Pimpernel, *la belle boulangere*, and Maitre Jehan Crapotte, *l'orfevre*, these occupy my spare thoughts still. Not forgetting Rodin, the evil genius of *The Wandering Jew*, who practiced his nefarious ways "until the day when he was en-flamed and outwitted by the octoroon Cecily." Sitting in the Square du Temple, musing over the doings of the horse knackers led by Jean Caboche, I have thought long and ruefully over the sad fate of Charles the Silly. A halfwit, who prowled about the halls of his Hotel St. Paul, garbed in the filthiest rags, eaten away by ulcers and vermin, gnawing a bone, when they flung him one, like a mangy dog. At the Rue des Lions I looked for the stones of the old menagerie where he once fed his pets. His only diversion, poor dolt, aside from those card games with his "low-born companion," Odette de Champdivers.

It was a Sunday afternoon, much like this, when I first met Germaine. I was strolling along the Boulevard Beaumarchais, rich by a hundred francs or so which my wife had frantically cabled from America. There was a touch of spring in the air, a poisonous, malefic spring that seemed to burst from the manholes. Night after night I had been coming back to this quarter, attracted by certain leprous streets which only revealed their sinister splendor when the light of day had oozed away and the whores commenced to take up their posts. The Rue du Pasteur-Wagner is one I recall in particular, corner of the Rue Amelot which hides behind the boulevard like a slumbering lizard. Here, at the neck of the bottle, so to speak, there was always a cluster of vultures who croaked and flapped their dirty wings, who reached out with sharp talons and plucked you into a doorway. Jolly, rapacious devils who didn't even give you time to button your pants when it was over. Led you into a little room off the street, a room without a window usually, and, sitting on the edge of the bed with skirts tucked up gave you a quick inspection, spat on your cock, and placed it for you. While you washed yourself another one stood at the door and, holding her victim by the hand, watched nonchalantly as you gave the finishing touches to your toilet.

Germaine was different. There was nothing to tell me so from her appearance. Nothing to distinguish her from the other trollops who met each afternoon and evening at the Cafe de l'Elephant. As I say, it was a spring day and the few francs my wife had scraped up to cable me were jingling in my pocket. I had a sort of vague premonition that I would not reach the Bastille without being taken in tow by one of these buzzards. Sauntering along the boulevard I had noticed her verging toward me with that curious trot-about air of a whore and the run-down heels and cheap jewelry and the pasty look of their kind which the rouge only accentuates. It was not difficult to come to terms with her. We sat in the back of the little *tabac* called L'Elephant and talked it over quickly. In a few minutes we were in a five franc room on the Rue Amelot, the curtains drawn and the covers thrown back. She didn't rush things, Germaine. She sat on the *bidet* soaping herself and talked to me pleasantly about this and that; she liked the knickerbockers I was wearing. *Tres chic!* she thought. They were once, but I had worn the seat out of them; fortunately the jacket covered my ass. As she stood up to dry herself, still talking to me pleasantly, suddenly she dropped the towel and, advancing toward me leisurely, she commenced rubbing her pussy affectionately, stroking it with her two hands, caressing it, patting it, patting it. There was something about her eloquence at that moment and the way she thrust that rosebush under my nose which remains unforgettable; she spoke of it as if it were some extraneous object which she had acquired at great cost, an object whose value had increased with time and which now she prized above everything in the world. Her words imbued it with a peculiar fragrance; it was no longer just her private organ, but a treasure, a magic, potent treasure, a God-given thing—and none the less so because she traded it day in and day out for a few pieces of silver. As she flung herself on the bed, with legs spread wide apart, she cupped it with her hands and stroked it some more, murmuring all the while in that hoarse, cracked voice of hers that it was good, beautiful, a treasure, a little treasure. And it *was* good, that little pussy of hers! That Sunday afternoon, with its poisonous breath of spring in the air, everything clicked again. As we stepped out of the hotel I looked her over again in the harsh light of day and I saw clearly what a whore she was—the gold teeth, the geranium in her hat, the run-down heels, etc., etc. Even the fact that she had wormed a dinner out of me and cigarettes and taxi hadn't the least disturbing effect upon me. I encouraged it, in fact. I liked her so well that after dinner we went back to the hotel again and took another shot at it. "For love," this time. And again that big, bushy thing of hers worked its bloom and magic. It began to have an independent existence—for me too. There was Germaine and there was that rosebush of hers. I liked them separately and I liked them together.

As I say, she was different, Germaine. Later, when she discovered my true circumstances, she treated me nobly—blew me to drinks, gave me credit, pawned my things, introduced me to her friends, and so on. She even apologized for not lending me money, which I understood quite well after her *maquereau* had been pointed out to me. Night after night I walked down the Boulevard Beaumarchais to the little *tabac* where they all congregated and I waited for her to stroll in and give me a few minutes of her precious time.

When some time later I came to write about Claude, it was not Claude that I was thinking of but Germaine.... "All the men she's been with and now you, just you, and barges going by, masts and hulls, the whole damned current of life flowing through you, through her, through all the guys behind you and after you, the flowers and the birds and the sun streaming in and the fragrance of it choking you, annihilating you." That was for Germaine! Claude was not the same, though I admired her tremendously—I even thought for a while that I loved her. Claude had a soul and a conscience; she had refinement, too, which is bad—in a whore. Claude always imparted a feeling of sadness; she left the impression, unwittingly, of course, that you were just one more added to the stream which fate had ordained to destroy her. *Unwittingly*, I say, because Claude was the last person in the world who would consciously create such an image in one's mind. She was too delicate, too sensitive for that. At bottom, Claude was just a good French girl of average breed and intelligence whom life had tricked somehow; something in her there was which was not tough enough to withstand the shock of daily experience. For her were meant those terrible words of Louis-Philippe, "and a night comes when all is over, when so many jaws have closed upon us that we no longer have the strength to stand, and our meat hangs upon our bodies, as though it had been masticated by every mouth." Germaine, on the other hand, was a whore from the cradle; she was thoroughly satisfied with her role, enjoyed it in fact, except when her stomach pinched or her shoes gave out, little surface things of no account, nothing that ate into her soul, nothing that created torment. *Ennui!* That was the worst she ever felt. Days there were, no doubt, when she had a bellyful, as we say—but no more than that! Most of the time she enjoyed it—or gave the illusion of enjoying it. It made a difference of course, whom she went with—or *came* with. But the principal thing was *a man*. A man! That was what she craved. A man with something between his legs that could tickle her, that could make her writhe in ecstasy, make her grab that bushy twat of hers with both hands and rub it joyfully, boastfully, proudly, with a sense of connection, a sense of life. That was the only place where she experienced any life— down there where she clutched herself with both hands.

Germaine was a whore all the way through, even down to her good heart, her whore's heart which is not really a good heart but a lazy one, an indifferent, flaccid heart that can be touched for a moment, a heart without reference to any fixed point within, a big, flaccid whore's heart that can detach itself for a moment from its true center. However vile and circumscribed was that world which she had created for herself, nevertheless she functioned in it superbly. And that in itself is a tonic thing. When, after we had become well acquainted, her companions would twit me, saying that I was in love with Germaine (a situation almost inconceivable to them), I would say: "Sure! Sure, I'm in love with her! And what's more, I'm going to be faithful to her!" A lie, of course, because I could no more think of loving Germaine than I could think of loving a spider; and if I *was* faithful, it was not to Germaine but to that bushy thing she carried between her legs. Whenever I looked at another woman I thought immediately of Germaine, of that flaming bush which she had left in my mind and which seemed imperishable. It gave me pleasure to sit on the *terrasse* of the little *tabac* and observe her as she plied her trade, observe her as she resorted to the same grimaces, the same tricks, with others as she had with me. "She's doing her job!"—that's how I felt about it, and it was with approbation that I regarded her transactions. Later, when I had taken up with Claude, and I saw her night after night sitting in her accustomed place, her round little buttocks chubbily ensconced in the plush settee, I felt a sort of inexpressible rebellion toward her; a whore, it seemed to me, had no right to be sitting there like a lady, waiting timidly for someone to approach and all the while abstemiously sipping her *chocolat*. Germaine was a hustler. She didn't wait for you to come to her—she went out and grabbed you. I remember so well the holes in her stockings, and the torn ragged shoes; I remember too how she stood at the bar and with blind, courageous defiance threw a strong drink down her stomach and marched out again.

A hustler! Perhaps it wasn't so pleasant to smell that boozy breath of hers, that breath compounded of weak coffee, cognac, *aperitifs*, Pernods and all the other stuff she guzzled between times, what to warm herself and what to summon up strength and courage, but the fire of it penetrated her, it glowed down there between her legs where women ought to glow, and there was established that circuit which makes one feel the earth under his legs again. When she lay there with her legs apart and moaning, even if she did moan that way for any and everybody, it was good, it was a proper show of feeling. She didn't stare up at the ceiling with a vacant look or count the bedbugs on the wallpaper; she kept her mind on her business, she talked about the things a man wants to hear when he's climbing over a woman. Whereas Claude—well, with Claude there was always a certain delicacy, even when she got under the sheets with you. And her delicacy offended. Who wants a *delicate* whore! Claude would even ask you to turn your face away when she squatted over the *bidet*. All wrong! A man, when he's burning up with passion, wants to see things; he wants to see *everything*, even how they make water. And while it's all very nice to know that a woman has a mind, literature coming from the cold corpse of a whore is the last thing to be served in bed. Germaine had the right idea: she was ignorant and lusty, she put her heart and soul into her work. She was a whore all the way through—and that was her virtue!

Easter came in like a frozen hare—but it was fairly warm in bed. Today it is lovely again and along the Champs-Elysees at twilight it is like an outdoor seraglio choked with dark-eyed houris. The trees are in full foliage and of a verdure so pure, so rich, that it seems as though they were still wet and glistening with dew. From the Palais du Louvre to the Etoile it is like a piece of music for the pianoforte. For five days I have not touched the typewriter nor looked at a book; nor have I had a single idea in my head except to go to the American Express. At nine this morning I was there, just as the doors were being opened, and again at one o'clock. No news. At four-thirty I dash out of the hotel, resolved to make a last-minute stab at it. Just as I turn the corner I brush against Walter Pach. Since he doesn't recognize me, and since I have nothing to say to him, I make no attempt to arrest him. Later, when I am stretching my legs in the Tuileries his figure reverts to mind. He was a little stooped, pensive, with a sort of serene yet reserved smile on his face. I wonder, as I look up at this softly enameled sky, so faintly tinted, which does not bulge today with heavy rain clouds but smiles like a piece of old china, I wonder what goes on in the mind of this man who translated the four thick volumes of the *History of Art* when he takes in this blissful cosmos with his drooping eye.

Along the Champs-Elysees, ideas pouring from me like sweat. I ought to be rich enough to have a secretary to whom I could dictate as I walk, because my best thoughts always come when I am away from the machine.

Walking along the Champs-Elysees I keep thinking of my really superb health. When I say "health" I mean optimism, to be truthful. Incurably optimistic! Still have one foot in the nineteenth century. I'm a bit retarded, like most Americans. Carl finds it disgusting, this optimism. "1 have only to talk about a meal," he say, "and you're radiant!" It's a fact. The mere thought of a meal—*another* meal—rejuvenates me. A meal! That means something to go on—a few solid hours of work, an erection possibly. I don't deny it. I have health, good solid, animal health. The only thing that stands between me and a future is a meal, *another* meal.

As for Carl, he's not himself these days. He's upset, his nerves are jangled. He says he's ill, and I believe him, but I don't feel badly about it.

I *can't*. In fact, it makes me laugh. And that offends him, of course. Everything wounds him—my laughter, my hunger, my persistence, my insouciance, *everything*. One day he wants to blow his brains out because he can't stand this lousy hole of a Europe any more; the next day he talks of going to Arizona "where they look you square in the eye."

"Do it!" I say. "Do one thing or the other, you bastard, but don't try to cloud my healthy eye with your melancholy breath!"

But that's just it! In Europe one gets used to doing nothing. You sit on your ass and whine all day. You get contaminated. You rot.

Fundamentally Carl is a snob, an aristocratic little prick who lives in a dementia praecox kingdom all his own. "I hate Paris!" he whines. "All these stupid people playing cards all day ... look at them! And the writing! What's the use of putting words together? I can be a writer without writing, can't I? What does it prove if I write a book? What do we want with books anyway? There are too many books already...."

My eye, but I've been all over that ground—years and years ago. I've lived out my melancholy youth. I don't give a fuck any more what's behind me, or what's ahead of me. I'm healthy. Incurably healthy. No sorrows, no regrets. No past, no future. The present is enough for me. Day by day. Today! *Le bel aujourd'hui!*

He has one day a week off, Carl, and on that day he's more miserable, if you can imagine it, than on any other day of the week. Though he professes to despise food, the only way he seems to enjoy himself on his day off is to order a big spread. Perhaps he does it for my benefit—I don't know, and I don't ask. If he chooses to add martyrdom to his list of vices, let him—it's O.K. with me. Anyway, last Tuesday, after squandering what he had on a big spread, he steers me to the Dome, the last place in the world I would seek on my day off. But one not only gets acquiescent here—one gets supine.

Standing at the Dome bar is Marlowe, soused to the ears. He's been on a bender, as he calls it, for the last five days. That means a continuous drunk, a peregrination from one bar to another, day and night without interruption, and finally a layoff at the American Hospital. Marlowe's bony emaciated face is nothing but a skull perforated by two deep sockets in which there are buried a pair of dead clams. His back is covered with sawdust— he has just had a little snooze in the water closet. In his coat pocket are the proofs for the next issue of his review, he was on his way to the printer with the proofs, it seems, when some one inveigled him to have a drink. He talks about it as though it happened months ago. He takes out the proofs and spreads them over the bar; they are full of coffee stains and dried spittle. He tries to read a poem which he had written in Greek, but the proofs are undecipherable. Then he decides to deliver a speech, in French, but the *gerant* puts a stop to it. Marlowe is piqued: his one ambition is to talk a French which even the *garcon* will understand. Of Old French he is a master; of the surrealists he has made excellent translations; but to say a simple thing like "get the hell out of here, you old prick!"—that is beyond him. Nobody understands Marlowe's French, not even the whores. For that matter, it's difficult enough to understand his English when he's under the weather. He blabbers and spits like a confirmed stutterer ... no sequence to his phrases. *"You pay!"* that's one thing he manages to get out clearly.

Even if he is fried to the hat some fine preservative instinct always warns Marlowe when it is time to act. If there is any doubt in his mind as to how the drinks are going to be paid he will be sure to put on a stunt. The usual one is to pretend that he is going blind. Carl knows all his tricks by now, and so when Marlowe suddenly claps his hands to his temples and begins to act it out Carl gives him a boot in the ass and says: "Come out of it, you sap! You don't have to do that with me!"

Whether it is a cunning piece of revenge or not, I don't know, but at any rate Marlowe is paying Carl back in good coin. Leaning over us confidentially he relates in a hoarse, croaking voice a piece of gossip which he picked up in the course of his peregrinations from bar to bar. Carl looks up in amazement. He's pale under the gills. Marlowe repeats the story with variations. Each time Carl wilts a little more. "But that's impossible!" he finally blurts out. "No it ain't!" croaks Marlowe. "You're gonna lose your job ... I got it straight." Carl looks at me in despair. "Is he shitting me, that bastard?" he murmurs in my ear. And then aloud—"What am I going to do now? I'll never find another job. It took me a year to land this one."

This, apparently, is all that Marlowe has been waiting to hear. At last he has found someone worse off than himself. "They be hard times!" he croaks, and his bony skull glows with a cold, electric fire.

Leaving the Dome Marlowe explains between hiccups that he's got to return to San Francisco. He seems genuinely touched now by Carl's helplessness. He proposes that Carl and I take over the review during his absence. "I can trust you, Carl," he says. And then suddenly he gets an attack, a real one this time. He almost collapses in the gutter. We haul him to a *bistro* at the Boulevard Edgar-Quinet and sit him down. This time he's really got It—a blinding headache that makes him squeal and grunt and rock himself to and fro like a dumb brute that's been struck by a sledge hammer. We spill a couple of Fernet-Brancas down his throat, lay him out on the bench and cover his eyes with his muffler. He lies there groaning. In a little while we hear him snoring.

"What about his proposition?" says Carl. "Should we take it up? He says he'll give me a thousand francs when he comes back. I know he won't, but what about it?" He looks at Marlowe sprawled out on the bench, lifts the muffler from his eyes, and puts it back again. Suddenly a mischievous grin lights up his face. "Listen, Joe," he says, beckoning me to move closer, "we'll take him up on it. We'll take his lousy review over and we'll fuck him good and proper."

"What do you mean by that?"

"Why we'll throw out all the other contributors and we'll fill it with our own shit—that's what!"

"Yeah, but what kind of shit?"

"Any kind... he won't be able to do anything about it. We'll fuck him good and prop-er. One good number and after that the magazine'll be finished. Are you game, Joe?"

Grinning and chuckling we lift Marlowe to his feet and haul him to Carl's room. When we turn on the lights there's a woman in the bed waiting for Carl. "I forgot all about her," says Carl. We turn the cunt loose and shove Marlowe into bed. In a minute or so there's a knock at the door. It's Van Nor den. He's all aflutter. Lost a plate of false teeth— at the Bal Negre, he thinks. Anyway, we get to bed, the four of us. Marlowe stinks like a smoked fish.

In the morning Marlowe and Van Norden leave to search for the false teeth. Marlowe is blubbering. He imagines they are *his* teeth.

It is my last dinner at the dramatist's home. They have just rented a new piano, a con-cert grand. I meet Sylvester coming out of the florist's with a rubber plant in his arms. He asks me if I would carry it for him while he goes for the cigars. One by one I've fucked myself out of all these free meals which I had planned so carefully. One by one the hus-bands turn against me, or the wives. As I walk along with the rubber plant in my arms I think of that night a few months back when the idea first occurred to me. I was sitting on a bench near the Coupole, fingering the wedding ring which I had tried to pawn off on a *garcon* at the Dome. He had offered me six francs for it and I was in a rage about it. But the belly was getting the upper hand. Ever since I left Mona I had worn the ring on my pinkie. It was so much a part of me that it had never occurred to me to sell it. It was one of those orange-blossom affairs in white gold. Worth a dollar and a half once, maybe more. For three years we went along without a wedding ring and then one day when I was going to the pier to meet Mona I happened to pass a jewelry window on Maiden Lane and the whole window was stuffed with wedding rings. When I got to the pier Mona was not to be seen. I waited for the last passenger to descend the gangplank, but no Mona. Finally I asked to be shown the passenger list. Her name was not on it. I slipped the wed-ding ring on my pinkie and there it stayed. Once I left it in a public bath, but then I got it back again. One of the orange blossoms had fallen off. Anyway, I was sitting there on the bench with my head down, twiddling the ring, when suddenly someone clapped me on the back. To make it brief, I got a meal and a few francs besides. And then it occurred to me, like a flash, that no one would refuse a man a meal if only he had the courage to demand it. I went immediately to a cafe and wrote a dozen letters. "Would you let me have dinner with you once a week? Tell me what day is most convenient for you." It worked like a charm. I was not only fed ... I was feasted. Every night I went home drunk. They could-n't do enough for me, these generous once-a-week souls. What happened to me between times was none of their affair. Now and then the thoughtful ones presented me with cig-arettes, or a little pin money. They were all obviously relieved when they realized that they would see me only once a week. And they were still more relieved when I said—"it won't be necessary any more." They never asked why. They congratulated me, and that was all. Often the reason was I had found a better host; I could afford to scratch off the ones who were a pain in the ass. But that thought never occurred to them. Finally I had a steady, solid program—a fixed schedule. On Tuesdays I knew it would be this kind of a meal and on Fridays that kind. Cronstadt, I knew, would have champagne for me and homemade apple pie. And Carl would invite me out, take me to a different restaurant each time, order rare wines, invite me to the theater afterward or take me to the Cirque Medrano. They were curious about one another, my hosts. Would ask me which place I liked best, who was the best cook, etc. I think I liked Cronstadt's joint best of all, perhaps because he chalked the meal up on the wall each time. Not that it eased my conscience to see what I owed him, because I had no intention of paying him back nor had he any illusions about being requited. No, it was the odd numbers which intrigued me. He used to figure it out to the last centime. If I was to pay in full I would have had to break a sou. His wife was a marvelous cook and she didn't give a fuck about those centimes Cronstadt added up. She took it out of me in carbon copies. A fact! If I hadn't any fresh carbons for her when I showed up, she was crestfallen. And for that I would have to take the little girl to the Luxembourg next day, play with her for two or three hours, a task which drove me wild because she spoke nothing but Hungarian and French. They were a queer lot on the whole, my hosts....

At Tania's I look down on the spread from the balcony. Moldorf is there, sitting beside his idol. He is warming his feet at the hearth, a monstrous look of gratitude in his watery eyes. Tania is running over the adagio. The adagio says very distinctly: no more words of love! I am at the fountain again, watching the turtles pissing green milk. Sylvester has just come back from Broadway with a heart full of love. All night I was lying on a bench outside the mall while the globe was sprayed with warm turtle piss and the horses stiffened with priapic fury galloped like mad without ever touching the ground. All night long I smell the lilacs in the little dark room where she is taking down her hair, the lilacs that I bought for her as she went to meet Sylvester. He came back with a heart full of love, she said, and the lilacs are in her hair, her mouth, they are choking her armpits. The room is swimming with love and turtle piss and warm lilacs and the horses are galloping like mad. In the morning dirty teeth and scum on the windowpanes; the little gate that leads to the mall is locked. People are going to work and the shutters are rattling like coats of mail. In the bookstore opposite the fountain is the story of Lake Chad, the silent lizards, the gorgeous gamboge tints. All the letters I wrote her, drunken ones with a blunt stub, crazy ones with bits of charcoal, little pieces from bench to bench, firecrackers, doilies, tutti-frutti; they will be going over them now, together, and he will compliment me one day. He will say, as he flicks his cigar ash: "Really, you write quite well. Let's see, you're a surrealist, aren't you?" Dry, brittle voice, teeth full of dandruff, solo for solar plexus, g for gaga.

Upon the balcony with the rubber plant and the adagio going on down below. The keys are black and white, then black, then white, then white and black. And you want to know if you can play something for me. Yes, play something with those big thumbs of yours. Play the adagio since that's the only goddamned thing you know. Play it, and then cut off your big thumbs.

That adagio! I don't know why she insists on playing it all the time. The old piano wasn't good enough for her; she had to rent a concert grand—for the adagio! When I see her big thumbs pressing the keyboard and that silly rubber plant beside me I feel like that madman of the North who threw his clothes away and, sitting naked in the wintry boughs, threw nuts down into the herring-frozen sea. There is something exasperating about this movement, something abortively melancholy about it, as if it had been written in lava, as if it had the color of lead and milk mixed. And Sylvester, with his head cocked to one side like an auctioneer, Sylvester says: "Play that other one you were practicing today." It's beautiful to have a smoking jacket, a good cigar and a wife who plays the piano.

So relaxing. So lenitive. Between the acts you go out for a smoke and a breath of fresh air. Yes, her fingers are very supple, extraordinary supple. She does batik work too. Would you like to try a Bulgarian cigarette? I say, pigeon breast, what's that other movement I like so well? The scherzo! Ah, yes, the scherzo! Excellent, the scherzo! Count Waldemar von Schwisseneinzug speaking. Cool, dandruff eyes. Halitosis. Gaudy socks. And croutons in the pea soup, if you please. We always have pea soup Friday nights. Won't you try a little red wine? The red wine goes with the meat, you know. A dry, crisp voice. Have a cigar, won't you? Yes, I like my work, but I don't attach any importance to it. My next play will involve a pluralistic conception of the universe. Revolving drums with calcium lights. O'Neill is dead. I think, dear, you should lift your foot from the pedal more frequently. Yes, that part is very nice... *very* nice, don't you think? Yes, the characters go around with microphones in their trousers. The locale is in Asia, because the atmospheric conditions are more conducive. Would you like to try a little Anjou? We bought it especially for you....

All through the meal this patter continues. It feels exactly as if he had taken out that circumcised dick of his and was peeing on us. Tania is bursting with the strain. Ever since he came back with a heart full of love this monologue has been going on. He talks while he's undressing, she tells me—a steady stream of warm piss, as though his bladder had been punctured. When I think of Tania crawling into bed with this busted bladder I get enraged. To think that a poor, withered bastard with those cheap Broadway plays up his sleeve should be pissing on the woman I love. Calling for red wine and revolving drums and croutons in his pea soup. The cheek of him! To think that he can lie beside that furnace I stoked for him and do nothing but make water! My God, man, you ought to get down on your knees and thank me. Don't you see that you have a *woman* in your house now? Can't you see she's bursting? You telling me with those strangulated adenoids of yours—"well now, I'll tell you... there's two ways of looking at that...." Fuck your two ways of looking at things! Fuck your pluralistic universe, and your Asiatic acoustics! Don't hand me your red wine or your Anjou ... hand *her* over ... she belongs to me! *You* go sit by the fountain, and let *me* smell the lilacs! Pick the dandruff out of your eyes... and take that damned adagio and wrap it in a pair of flannel pants! And the other little movement too ... all the little movements that you make with your weak bladder. You smile at me so confidently, so calculatingly. I'm flattering the ass off you, can't you tell? While I listen to your crap she's got her hand on me—but you don't see that. You think I like to suffer—that's my role, you say. O.K. Ask her about it! She'll tell you how I suffer. "You're cancer and delirium," she said over the phone the other day. She's got it now, the cancer and delirium, and soon you'll have to pick the scabs. Her veins are bursting, I tell you, and your talk is all sawdust. No matter how much you piss away you'll never plug up the holes. What did Mr. Wren say? *Words are loneliness.* I left a couple of words for you on the tablecloth last night—you covered them with your elbows.

He's put a fence around her as if she were a dirty, stinking bone of a saint. If he only had the courage to say "Take her!" perhaps a miracle would occur. Just that. *Take her!* and I swear everything would come out all right. Besides, maybe I wouldn't take her—did that ever occur to him, I wonder? Or I might take her for a while and hand her back, *improved.* But putting up a fence around her, that won't work. You can't put a fence around a human being. It ain't done any more.... You think, you poor, withered bastard, that I'm no good for her, that I might pollute her, desecrate her. You don't know how palatable is a polluted woman, how a change of semen can make a woman bloom! You think a heart full of love is enough, and perhaps it is, for the right woman, but you haven't got a heart any more ... you are nothing but a big, empty bladder. You are sharpening your teeth and cultivating your growl. You run at her heels like a watchdog and you piddle everywhere. She didn't take you for a watchdog... she took you for a poet. You were a poet once, she said. And now what are you? Courage, Sylvester, courage! Take the microphone out of your pants. Put your hind leg down and stop making water everywhere. Courage, I say, because she's ditched you already. She's contaminated, I tell you, and you might as well take down the fence. No use asking me politely if the coffee doesn't taste like carbolic acid: that won't scare me away. Put rat poison in the coffee, and a little ground glass. Make some boiling hot urine and drop a few nutmegs in it....

It is a communal life I have been living for the last few weeks. I have had to share myself with others, principally with some crazy Russians, a drunken Dutchman, and a big Bulgarian woman named Olga. Of the Russians there are chiefly Eugene and Anatole.

It was just a few days ago that Olga got out of the hospital where she had her tubes burned out and lost a little excess weight. However she doesn't look as if she had gone through much suffering. She weighs almost as much as a camel-backed locomotive; she drips with perspiration, has halitosis, and still wears her Circassian wig that looks like excelsior. She has two big warts on her chin from which there sprouts a clump of little hairs; she is growing a mustache.

The day after Olga was released from the hospital she commenced making shoes again. At six in the morning she is at her bench; she knocks out two pairs of shoes a day. Eugene complains that Olga is a burden, but the truth is that Olga is supporting Eugene and his wife with her two pairs of shoes a day. If Olga doesn't work there is no food. So everyone endeavors to pull Olga to bed on time, to give her enough food to keep going, etc.

Every meal starts off with soup. Whether it be onion soup, tomato soup, vegetable soup, or what not, the soup always tastes the same. Mostly it tastes as if a dish rag had been stewed in it—slightly sour, mildewed, scummy. I see Eugene hiding it away in the commode after the meal. It stays there, rotting away, until the next meal. The butter, too, is hidden away in the commode; after three days it tastes like the big toe of a cadaver.

The smell of rancid butter frying is not particularly appetizing, especially when the cooking is done in a room in which there is not the slightest form of ventilation. No sooner than I open the door I feel ill. But Eugene, as soon as he hears me coming, usually opens the shutters and pulls back the bedsheet which is strung up like a fishnet to keep out the sunlight. Poor Eugene! He looks about the room at the few sticks of furniture, at the dirty bed-sheets and the wash basin with the dirty water still in it, and he says: "I am a slave!" Every day he says it, not once, but a dozen times. And then he takes his guitar from the wall and sings.

But about the smell of rancid butter.... There are good associations too. When I think of this rancid butter I see myself standing in a little, old-world courtyard, a very smelly, very dreary courtyard. Through the cracks in the shutters strange figures peer out at me... old women with shawls, dwarfs, rat-faced pimps, bent Jews, *midinettes,* bearded idiots. They totter out into the courtyard to draw water or to rinse the slop pails. One day Eugene asked me if I would empty the pail for him. I took it to the corner of the yard. There was a hole in the ground and some dirty paper lying around the hole. The little well was slimy with excrement, which in English is *shit*. I tipped the pail and there was a foul, gurgling splash followed by another and unexpected splash. When I returned the soup was dished out. All through the meal I thought of my toothbrush—it is getting old and the bristles get caught in my teeth.

When I sit down to eat I always sit near the window. I am afraid to sit on the other side of the table—it is too close to the bed and the bed is crawling. I can see bloodstains on the gray sheets if I look that way, but I try not to look that way. I look out on the court-yard where they are rinsing the slop pails.

The meal is never complete without music. As soon as the cheese is passed around Eugene jumps up and reaches for the guitar which hangs over the bed. It is always the same song. He says he has fifteen or sixteen songs in his repertoire, but I have never heard more than three. His favorite is *Charmant poeme d'amour*. It is full of *angoisse* and *tristesse*.

In the afternoon we go to the cinema which is cool and dark. Eugene sits at the piano in the big pit and I sit on a bench up front. The house is empty, but Eugene sings as if he had for audience all the crowned heads of Europe. The garden door is open and the odor of wet leaves sops in and the rain blends with Eugene's *angoisse* and *tristesse*. At midnight, after the spectators have saturated the hall with perspiration and foul breaths, I return to sleep on a bench. The exit light, swimming in a halo of tobacco smoke, sheds a faint light on the lower corner of the asbestos curtain; I close my eyes every night on an artificial eye....

Standing in the courtyard with a glass eye; only half the world is intelligible. The stones are wet and mossy and in the crevices are black toads. A big door bars the entrance to the cellar; the steps are slippery and soiled with bat dung. The door bulges and sags, the hinges are falling off, but there is an enameled sign on it, in perfect condition, which says: "Be sure to close the door." Why close the door? I can't make it out. I look again at the sign but it is removed; in its place there is a pane of colored glass. I take out my artificial eye, spit on it and polish it with my handkerchief. A woman is sitting on a dais above an immense carved desk; she has a snake around her neck. The entire room is lined with books and strange fish swimming in colored globes; there are maps and charts on the wall, maps of Paris before the plague, maps of the antique world, of Knossos and Carthage, of Carthage before and after the salting. In the corner of the room I see an iron bedstead and on it a corpse is lying; the woman gets up wearily, removes the corpse from the bed and absent-mindedly throws it out the window. She returns to the huge carved desk, takes a goldfish from the bowl and swallows it. Slowly the room begins to revolve and one by one the continents slide into the sea; only the woman is left, but her body is a mass of geog-raphy. I lean out the window and the Eiffel Tower is fizzing champagne; it is built entire-ly of numbers and shrouded in black lace. The sewers are gurgling furiously. There are nothing but roofs everywhere, laid out with execrable geometric cunning.

I have been ejected from the world like a cartridge. A deep fog has settled down, the earth is smeared with frozen grease. I can feel the city palpitating, as if it were a heart just removed from a warm body. The windows of my hotel are festering and there is a thick, acrid stench as of chemicals burning. Looking into the Seine I see mud and desolation, street lamps drowning, men and women choking to death, the bridges covered with hous-es, slaughterhouses of love. A man is standing against a wall with an accordion strapped to his belly; his hands are cut off at the wrists, but the accordion writhes between his stumps like a sack of snakes. The universe has dwindled; it is only a block long and there are no stars, no trees, no rivers. The people who live here are dead; they make chairs which other people sit on in their dreams. In the middle of the street is a wheel and in the hub of the wheel a gallows is fixed. People already dead are trying frantically to mount the gallows, but the wheel is turning too fast....

Something was needed to put me right with myself. Last night I discovered it: *Papini.* It doesn't matter to me whether he's a chauvinist, a little Christer, or a near sighted pedant. As a failure he's marvelous....

The books he read—at eighteen! Not only Homer, Dante, Goethe, not only Aristotle, Plato, Epictetus, not only Rabelais, Cervantes, Swift, not only Walt Whitman, Edgar Allan Poe, Baudelaire, Villon, Carducci, Manzoni, Lope de Vega, not only Nietzsche, Schopenhauer, Kant, Hegel, Darwin, Spencer, Huxley—not only these but all the small fry in between. This on page 18. *Alors,* on page 232 he breaks down and confesses. I know nothing, he admits. I know the titles, I have compiled bibliographies, I have written critical essays, I have maligned and defamed.... I can talk for five minutes or for five days, but then I give out, I am squeezed dry.

Follows this: "Everybody wants to see me. Everybody insists on talking to me. People pester me and they pester others with inquiries about what I am doing. How am I? Am I quite well again? Do I still go for my walks in the country? Am I working? Have I finished my book? Will I begin another soon?

"A skinny monkey of a German wants me to translate his works. A wild-eyed Russian girl wants me to write an account of my life for her. An American lady wants the *very latest* news about me. An American gentleman will send his carriage to take me to dinner— just an intimate, confidential talk, you know. An old schoolmate and chum of mine, of ten years ago, wants me to read him all that I write as fast as I write it. A painter friend I know expects me to pose for him by the hour. A newspaperman wants my present address. An acquaintance, a mystic, inquires about the state of my soul; another, more practical, about the state of my pocketbook. The president of my club wonders if I will make a speech for the boys! A lady, spiritually inclined, hopes I will come to her house for tea as often as possible. She wants to have my opinion of Jesus Christ, and—what do I think of that new medium? ...

"Great God! what have I turned into? What right have you people to clutter up my life, steal my time, probe my soul, suckle my thoughts, have me for your companion, confidant, and information bureau? What do you take me for? Am I an entertainer on salary, required every evening to play an intellectual farce under your stupid noses? Am I a slave, bought and paid for, to crawl on my belly in front of you idlers and lay at your feet all that I do and all that I know? Am I a wench in a brothel who is called upon to lift her skirts or take off her chemise at the bidding of the first man in a tailored suit who comes along?

'I am a man who would live an heroic life and make the world more endurable in his own sight. If, in some moment of weakness, of relaxation, of need, I blow off steam—a bit of red-hot rage cooled off in words—a passionate dream, wrapped and tied in imagery— well, take it or leave it... *but don't bother me!*

"I am a free man—and I need my freedom. I need to be alone. I need to ponder my shame and my despair in seclusion; I need the sunshine and the paving stones of the streets without companions, without conversation, face to face with myself, with only the music of my heart for company. What do you want of me? When I have something to say, I put it in print. When I have something to give, I give it. Your prying curiosity turns my stomach! Your compliments humiliate me! Your tea poisons me! I owe nothing to any one. I would be responsible to God alone—if He existed!"

It seems to me that Papini misses something by a hair's breadth when he talks of the need to be alone. It is not difficult to be alone if you are poor and a failure. An artist is always alone—if he *is* an artist. No, what the artist needs is *loneliness*.

The artist, I call myself. So be it. A beautiful nap this afternoon that put velvet between my vertebrae. Generated enough ideas to last me three days. Chock-full of energy and nothing to do about it. Decide to go for a walk. In the street I change my mind. Decide to go to the movies. Can't go to the movies—short a few sous. A walk then. At every movie house I stop and look at the billboards, then at the price list. Cheap enough, these opium joints, but I'm short just a few sous. If it weren't so late I might go back and cash an empty bottle.

By the time I get to the Rue Amelie I've forgotten all about the movies. The Rue Amelie is one of my favorite streets. It is one of those streets which by good fortune the municipality has forgotten to pave. Huge cobblestones spreading convexly from one side of the street to the other. Only one block long and narrow. The Hotel Pretty is on this street. There is a little church, too, on the Rue Amelie. It looks as though it were made especially for the President of the Republic and his private family. It's good occasionally to see a modest little church. Paris is full of pompous cathedrals.

Pont Alexandre III. A great windswept space approaching the bridge. Gaunt, bare trees mathematically fixed in their iron grates; the gloom of the Invalides welling out of the dome and overflowing the dark streets adjacent to the Square. The morgue of poetry. They have him where they want him now, the great warrior, the last big man of Europe. He sleeps soundly in his granite bed. No fear of him turning over in his grave. The doors are well bolted, the lid is on tight. Sleep, Napoleon! It was not your ideas they wanted, it was only your corpse!

The river is still swollen, muddy, streaked with lights. I don't know what it is rushes up in me at the sight of this dark, swift-moving current, but a great exultation lifts me up, affirms the deep wish that is in me never to leave this land. I remember passing this way the other morning on my way to the American Express, knowing in advance that there would be no mail for me, no check, no cable, nothing, nothing. A wagon from the Galeries Lafayette was rumbling over the bridge. The rain had stopped and the sun breaking through the soapy clouds touched the glistening rubble of roofs with a cold fire. I recall now how the driver leaned out and looked up the river toward Passy way. Such a healthy, simple, approving glance, as if he were saying to himself: "Ah, spring is coming!" And God knows, when spring comes to Paris the humblest mortal alive must feel that he dwells in paradise. But it was not only this—it was the intimacy with which his eye rested upon the scene. It was *his* Paris. A man does not need to be rich, nor even a citizen, to feel this way about Paris. Paris is filled with poor people—the proudest and filthiest lot of beggars that ever walked the earth, it seems to me. And yet they give the illusion of being at home. It is that which distinguishes the Parisian from all other metropolitan souls.

When I think of New York I have a very different feeling. New York makes even a rich man feel his unimportance. New York is cold, glittering, malign. The buildings dominate. There is a sort of atomic frenzy to the activity going on; the more furious the pace, the more diminished the spirit. A constant ferment, but it might just as well be going on in a test tube. Nobody knows what it's all about. Nobody directs the energy. Stupendous. Bizarre. Baffling. A tremendous reactive urge, but absolutely uncoordinated.

When I think of this city where I was born and raised, this Manhattan that Whitman sang of, a blind, white rage licks my guts. New York! The white prisons, the sidewalks swarming with maggots, the breadlines, the opium joints that are built like palaces, the kikes that are there, the lepers, the thugs, and above all, the *ennui,* the monotony of faces, streets, legs, houses, skyscrapers, meals, posters, jobs, crimes, loves.... A whole city erected over a hollow pit of nothingness. Meaningless. Absolutely meaningless. And Forty-second Street! The top of the world, they call it. Where's the bottom then? You can walk along with your hands out and they'll put cinders in your cap. Rich or poor, they walk along with head thrown back and they almost break their necks looking up at their beautiful white prisons. They walk along like blind geese and the searchlights spray their empty faces with flecks of ecstasy.

"Life," said Emerson, "consists in what a man is thinking all day." If that be so, then my life is nothing but a big intestine. I not only think about food all day, but I dream about it at night.

But I don't ask to go back to America, to be put in double harness again, to work the treadmill. No, I prefer to be a poor man of Europe. God knows, I am poor enough; it only remains to be a man. Last week I thought the problem of living was about to be solved, thought I was on the way to becoming self-supporting. It happened that I ran across another Russian—Serge is his name. He lives in Suresnes where there is a little colony of *emigres* and run-down artists. Before the revolution Serge was a captain in the Imperial Guard; he stands six foot three in his stockinged feet and drinks vodka like a fish. His father was an admiral, or something like that, on the battleship "Potemkin."

I met Serge under rather peculiar circumstances. Sniffing about for food I found myself toward noon the other day in the neighborhood of the Folies-Bergere—the back entrance, that is to say, in the narrow little lane with an iron gate at one end. I was dawdling about the stage entrance, hoping vaguely for a casual brush with one of the butterflies, when an open truck pulls up to the sidewalk. Seeing me standing there with my hands in my pockets the driver, who was Serge, asks me if I would give him a hand unloading the iron barrels. When he learns that I am an American and that I'm broke he almost weeps with joy. He has been looking high and low for an English teacher, it seems. I help him roll the barrels of insecticide inside and I look my fill at the butterflies fluttering about the wings. The incident takes on strange proportions to me—the empty house, the sawdust dolls bouncing in the wings, the barrels of germicide, the battleship "Potemkin"—above all, Serge's gentleness. He is big and tender, a man every inch of him, but with a woman's heart.

In the cafe nearby—Cafe des Artistes—he proposes immediately to put me up; says he will put a mattress on the floor in the hallway. For the lessons he says he will give me a meal every day, a big Russian meal, or if for any reason the meal is lacking then five francs. It sounds wonderful to me—*wonderful.* The only question is, how will I get from Suresnes to the American Express every day?

Serge insists that we begin at once—he gives me the carfare to get out to Suresnes in the evening. I arrive a little before dinner, with my knapsack, in order to give Serge a lesson. There are some guests on hand already—seems as though they always eat in a crowd, everybody chipping in.

There are eight of us at the table—and three dogs. The dogs eat first. They eat oatmeal. Then we commence. We eat oatmeal too—as an hors d'oeuvre. *"Chez nous,"* says Serge, with a twinkle in his eye, *"c'est pour les chiens, les Quaker Oats. Ici pour le gentleman. Ca va."* After the oatmeal, mushroom soup and vegetables; after that bacon omelet, fruit, red wine, vodka, coffee, cigarettes. Not bad, the Russian meal. Everyone talks with his mouth full. Toward the end of the meal Serge's wife, who is a lazy slut of an Armenian, flops on the couch and begins to nibble bonbons. She fishes around in the box with her fat fingers, nibbles a tiny piece to see if there is any juice inside, and then throws it on the floor for the dogs.

The meal over, the guests rush away. They rush away precipitously, as if they feared a plague. Serge and I are left with the dogs—his wife has fallen asleep on the couch. Serge moves about unconcernedly, scraping the garbage for the dogs. "Dogs like very much," he says. "Very good for dogs. Little dog he has worms ... he is too young yet." He bends down to examine some white worms lying on the carpet between the dog's paws. Tries to explain about the worms in English, but his vocabulary is lacking. Finally he consults the dictionary. "Ah," he says, looking at me exultantly, *"tapeworms!"* My response is evidently not very intelligent. Serge is confused. He gets down on his hands and knees to examine them better. He picks one up and lays it on the table beside the fruit. "Huh, him not very beeg," he grunts. "Next lesson you learn me worms, no? You are gude teacher. I make progress with you...."

Lying on the mattress in the hallway the odor of the germicide stifles me. A pungent, acrid odor that seems to invade every pore of my body. The food begins to repeat on me—the Quaker Oats, the mushrooms, the bacon, the fried apples. I see the little tapeworm lying beside the fruit and all the varieties of worms that Serge drew on the tablecloth to explain what was the matter with the dog. I see the empty pit of the Folies-Bergere and in every crevice there are cockroaches and lice and bedbugs; I see people scratching themselves frantically, scratching and scratching until the blood comes. I see the worms crawling over the scenery like an army of red ants, devouring everything in sight. I see the chorus girls throwing away their gauze tunics and running through the aisles naked; I see the spectators in the pit throwing off their clothes also and scratching each other like monkeys.

I try to quiet myself. After all, this is a home I've found, and there's a meal waiting for me every day. And Serge is a brick, there's no doubt about that. But I can't sleep. It's like going to sleep in a morgue. The mattress is saturated with embalming fluid. It's a morgue for lice, bedbugs, cockroaches, tapeworms. I can't stand it. I *won't* stand it! After all I'm a man, not a louse.

In the morning I wait for Serge to load the truck. I ask him to take me in to Paris. I haven't the heart to tell him I'm leaving. I leave the knapsack behind, with the few things that were left me. When we get to the Place Pereire I jump out. No particular reason for getting off here. No particular reason for anything. *I'm free*—that's the main thing....

Light as a bird I flit about from one quarter to another. It's as though I had been released from prison. I look at the world with new eyes. Everything interests me profoundly. Even trifles. On the Rue du Faubourg Poissonniere I stop before the window of a physical culture establishment. There are photographs showing specimens of manhood "before and after." All frogs. Some of them are nude, except for a pince-nez or a beard. Can't understand how these birds fall for parallel bars and dumbbells. A frog should have just a wee bit of a paunch, like the Baron de Charlus. He should wear a beard and a pince-nez, but he should never be photographed in the nude. He should wear twinkling patent-leather boots and in the breast pocket of his sack coat there should be a white handker-chief protruding about three-quarters of an inch above the vent. If possible, he should have a red ribbon in his lapel, through the buttonhole. He should wear pajamas on going to bed.

Approaching the Place Clichy toward evening I pass the little whore with the wood-en stump who stands opposite the Gaumont Palace day in and day out. She doesn't look a day over eighteen. Has her regular customers, I suppose. After midnight she stands there in her black rig rooted to the spot. Back of her is the little alleyway that blazes like an inferno. Passing her now with a light heart she reminds me somehow of a goose tied to a stake, a goose with a diseased liver, so that the world may have its *pate de foie gras*. Must be strange taking that wooden stump to bed with you. One imagines all sorts of things—splinters, etc. However, every man to his taste!

Going down the Rue des Dames I bump into Peck-over, another poor devil who works on the paper. He complains of getting only three or four hours' sleep a night—has to get up at eight in the morning to work at a dentist's office. It isn't for the money he's doing it, so he explains—it's for to buy himself a set of false teeth. "It's hard to read proof when you're dropping with sleep," he says. "The wife, she thinks I've got a cinch of it. What would we do if you lost your job? she says." But Peckover doesn't give a damn about the job; it doesn't even allow him spending money. He has to save his cigarette butts and use them for pipe tobacco. His coat is held together with pins. He has halitosis and his hands sweat. And only three hours' sleep a night. "It's no way to treat a man," he says. "And that boss of mine, he bawls the piss out of me if I miss a semicolon." Speaking of his wife he adds: "That woman of mine, she's got no fucking gratitude, I tell you!"

In parting I manage to worm a franc fifty out of him. I try to squeeze another fifty centimes out of him but it s impossible. Anyway I've got enough for a coffee and *crois-sants*. Near the Gare St. Lazare there's a bar with reduced prices.

As luck would have it I find a ticket in the *lavabo* for a concert. Light as a feather now I go there to the Salle Gaveau. The usher looks ravaged because I overlook giving him his little tip. Every time he passes me he looks at me inquiringly, as if perhaps I will sudden-ly remember. It's so long since I've sat in the company of well-dressed people that I feel a bit panic-stricken. I can still smell the formaldehyde. Perhaps Serge makes deliveries here too. But nobody is scratching himself, thank God. A faint odor of perfume ... very faint. Even before the music begins there is that bored look on people's faces. A polite form of self-imposed torture, the concert. For a moment, when the conductor raps with his little wand, there is a tense spasm of concentration followed almost immediately by a general slump, a quiet vegetable sort of repose induced by the steady, uninterrupted drizzle from the orchestra. My mind is curiously alert; it's as though my skull had a thousand mirrors inside it. My nerves are taut, vibrant! the notes are like glass balls dancing on a million jets of water. I've never been to a concert before on such an empty belly. Nothing escapes me, not even the tiniest pin falling. It's as though I had no clothes on and every pore of my body was a window and all the windows open and the light flooding my gizzards. I can feel the light curving under the vault of my ribs and my ribs hang there over a hollow nave trembling with reverberations. How long this lasts I have no idea; I have lost all sense of time and place. After what seems like an eternity there follows an interval of semiconsciousness balanced by such a calm that I feel a great lake inside me, a lake of iridescent sheen, cool as jelly; and over this lake, rising in great swooping spirals, there emerge flocks of birds of passage with long slim legs and brilliant plumage. Flock after flock surge up from the cool, still surface of the lake and, passing under my clavicles, lose themselves in the white sea of space. And then slowly, very slowly, as if an old woman in a white cap were going the rounds of my body, slowly the windows are closed and my organs drop back into place. Suddenly the lights flare up and the man in the white box whom I had taken for a Turkish officer turns out to be a woman with a flowerpot on her head.

There is a buzz now and all those who want to cough, cough to their heart's content. There is the noise of feet shuffling and seats slamming, the steady, frittering noise of people moving about aimlessly, of people fluttering their programs and pretending to read and then dropping their programs and scuffling under their seats, thankful for even the slightest accident which will prevent them from asking themselves what they were thinking about because if they knew they were thinking about nothing they would go mad. In the harsh glare of the lights they look at each other vacuously and there is a strange tenseness with which they stare at one another. And the moment the conductor raps again they fall back into a cataleptic state—they scratch themselves unconsciously or they remember suddenly a show window in which there was displayed a scarf or a hat; they remember every detail of that window with amazing clarity, but where it was exactly, that they can't recall; and that bothers them, keeps them wide awake, restless, and they listen now with redoubled attention because they are wide awake and no matter how wonderful the music is they will not lose consciousness of that show window and that scarf that was hanging there, or the hat.

And this fierce attentiveness communicates itself; even the orchestra seems galvanized into an extraordinary alertness. The second number goes off like a top—so fast indeed that when suddenly the music ceases and the lights go up some are stuck in their seats like carrots, their jaws working convulsively, and if you suddenly shouted in their ear *Brahms, Beethoven, Mendeleev, Herzegovina,* they would answer without thinking—4, 967, 289.

By the time we get to the Debussy number the atmosphere is completely poisoned. I find myself wondering what it feels like, during intercourse, to be a woman—whether the pleasure is keener, etc. Try to imagine something penetrating my groin, but have only a vague sensation of pain. I try to focus, but the music is too slippery. I can think of nothing but a vase slowly turning and the figures dropping off into space. Finally there is only light turning, and how does light turn, I ask myself. The man next to me is sleeping soundly. He looks like a broker, with his big paunch and his waxed mustache. I like him thus. I like especially that big paunch and all that went into the making of it. Why shouldn't he sleep soundly? If he wants to listen he can always rustle up the price of a ticket. I notice that the better dressed they are the more soundly they sleep. They have an easy conscience, the rich. If a poor man dozes off, even for a few seconds, he feels mortified; he imagines that he has committed a crime against the composer.

In the Spanish number the house was electrified. Everybody sat on the edge of his seat—the drums woke them up. I thought when the drums started it would keep up forever. I expected to see people fall out of the boxes or throw their hats away. There was something heroic about it and he could have driven us stark mad, Ravel, if he had wanted to. But that's not Ravel. Suddenly it all died down. It was as if he remembered, in the midst of his antics, that he had on a cutaway suit. He arrested himself. A great mistake, in my humble opinion. Art consists in going the full length. If you start with the drums you have to end with dynamite, or TNT. Ravel sacrificed something for form, for a vegetable that people must digest before going to bed.

My thoughts are spreading. The music is slipping away from me, now that the drums have ceased. People everywhere are composed to order. Under the exit light is a Werther sunk in despair; he is leaning on his two elbows, his eyes are glazed. Near the door, huddled in a big cape, stands a Spaniard with a sombrero in his hand. He looks as if he were posing for the "Balzac" of Rodin. From the neck up he suggests Buffalo Bill. In the gallery opposite me, in the front row, sits a woman with her legs spread wide apart; she looks as though she had lockjaw, with her neck thrown back and dislocated. The woman with the red hat who is dozing over the rail—marvelous if she were to have a hemorrhage! if suddenly she spilled a bucketful on those stiff shirts below. Imagine these bloody no-accounts going home from the concert with blood on their dickies!

Sleep is the keynote. No one is listening any more. Impossible to think and listen. Impossible to dream even when the music itself is nothing but a dream. A woman with white gloves holds a swan in her lap. The legend is that when Leda was fecundated she gave birth to twins. Everybody is giving birth to something—everybody but the Lesbian in the upper tier. Her head is uptilted, her throat wide open; she is all alert and tingling with the shower of sparks that burst from the radium symphony. Jupiter is piercing her ears. Little phrases from California, whales with big fins, Zanzibar, the Alcazar. *When along the Guadalquivir there were a thousand mosques ashimmer.* Deep in the icebergs and the days all lilac. The Money Street with two white hitching posts. The gargoyles... the man with the Jaworski nonsense... the river lights ... the ...

In America I had a number of Hindu friends, some good, some bad, some indifferent. Circumstances had placed me in a position where fortunately I could be of aid to them; I secured jobs for them, I harbored them, and I fed them when necessary. They were very grateful, I must say; so much so, in fact that they made my life miserable with their attentions. Two of them were saints, if I know what a saint is; particularly Gupte who was found one morning with his throat cut from ear to ear. In a little boarding house in Greenwich Village he was found one morning stretched out stark naked on the bed, his flute beside him, and his throat gashed, as I say, from ear to ear. It was never discovered whether he had been murdered or whether he had committed suicide. But that's neither here nor there....

I'm thinking back to the chain of circumstances which has brought me finally to Nanantatee's place. Thinking how strange it is that I should have forgotten all about Nanantatee until the other day when lying in a shabby hotel room on the Rue Cels. I'm lying there on the iron bed thinking what a zero I have become, what a cipher, what a nullity, when bango! out pops the word: NONENTITY! That's what we called him in New York—Nonentity. *Mister* Nonentity.

I'm lying on the floor now in that gorgeous suite of rooms he boasted of when he was in New York. Nanantatee is playing the good Samaritan; he has given me a pair of itchy blankets, horse blankets they are, in which I curl up on the dusty floor. There are little jobs to do every hour of the day—that is, if I am foolish enough to remain indoors. In the morning he wakes me rudely in order to have me prepare the vegetables for his lunch: onions, garlic, beans, etc. His friend, Kepi, warns me not to eat the food—he says it's bad. Bad or good what difference? *Food!* That's all that matters. For a little food I am quite willing to sweep his carpets with a broken broom, to wash his clothes and to scrape the crumbs off the floor as soon as he has finished eating. He's become absolutely immaculate since my arrival: everything has to be dusted now, the chairs must be arranged a certain way, the clock must ring, the toilet must flush properly.... A crazy Hindu if ever there was one! And parsimonious as a string bean. I'll have a great laugh over it when I get out of his clutches, but just now I'm a prisoner, a man without caste, an untouchable....

If I fail to come back at night and roll up in the horse blankets he says to me on arriving: "Oh, so you didn't die then? I thought you had died." And though he knows I'm absolutely penniless he tells me every day about some cheap room he has just discovered in the neighborhood. "But I can't take a room yet, you know that," I say. And then, blinking his eyes like a Chink, he answers smoothly: "Oh, yes, I forgot that you had no money. I am always forgetting, Endree.... But when the cable comes... when Miss Mona sends you the money, then you will come with me to look for a room, eh?" And in the next breath he urges me to stay as long as I wish—"six months ... seven months, Endree ... you are very good for me here."

Nanantatee is one of the Hindus I never did anything for in America. He represented himself to me as a wealthy merchant, a pearl merchant, with a luxurious suite of rooms on the Rue Lafayette, Paris, a villa in Bombay, a bungalow in Darjeeling. I could see from first glance that he was a half-wit, but then half-wits sometimes have the genius to amass a fortune. I didn't know that he paid his hotel bill in New York by leaving a couple of fat pearls in the proprietor's hands. It seems amusing to me now that this little duck once swaggered about the lobby of that hotel in New York with an ebony cane, bossing the bellhops around, ordering luncheons for his guests, calling up the porter for theater tickets, renting a taxi by the day, etc., etc., all without a sou in his pocket. Just a string of fat pearls around his neck which he cashed one by one as time wore on. And the fatuous way he used to pat me on the back, thank me for being so good to the Hindu boys—"they are all very intelligent boys, Endree... very intelligent!" Telling me that the good lord so-and-so would repay me for my kindness. That explains now why they used to giggle so, these intelligent Hindu boys, when I suggested that they touch Nanantatee for a five-spot.

Curious now how the good lord so-and-so is requiting me for my benevolence. I'm nothing but a slave to this fat little duck. I'm at his beck and call continually. He needs me here—he tells me so to my face. When he goes to the crap-can he shouts: "Endree, bring me a pitcher of water, please. I must wipe myself." He wouldn't think of using toilet paper, Nanantatee. Must be against his religion. No, he calls for a pitcher of water and a rag. He's *delicate,* the fat little duck. Sometimes when I'm drinking a cup of pale tea in which he has dropped a rose leaf he comes alongside of me and lets a loud fart, right in my face. He never says "Excuse me!" The word must be missing from his Gujarati dictionary.

The day I arrived at Nanantatee's apartment he was in the act of performing his ablutions, that is to say, he was standing over a dirty bowl trying to work his crooked arm around toward the back of his neck. Beside the bowl was a brass goblet which he used to change the water. He requested me to be silent during the ceremony. I sat there silently, as I was bidden, and watched him as he sang and prayed and spat now and then into the washbowl. So this is the wonderful suite of rooms he talked about in New York! The Rue Lafayette! It sounded like an important street to me back there in New York. I thought only millionaires and pearl merchants inhabited the street. It sounds wonderful, the Rue Lafayette, when you're on the other side of the water. So does Fifth Avenue, when you're over here. One can't imagine what dumps there are on these swell streets. Anyway, here I am at last, sitting in the gorgeous suite of rooms on the Rue Lafayette. And this crazy duck with his crooked arm is going through the ritual of washing himself. The chair on which I'm sitting is broken, the bedstead is falling apart, the wallpaper is in tatters, there is an open valise under the bed crammed with dirty wash. From where I sit I can glance at the miserable courtyard down below where the aristocracy of the Rue Lafayette sit and smoke their clay pipes. I wonder now, as he chants the doxology, what that bungalow in Darjeeling looks like. It's interminable, his chanting and praying.

He explains to me that he is obliged to wash in a certain prescribed way—his religion demands it. But on Sundays he takes a bath in the tin tub—the Great I AM will wink at that, he says. When he's dressed he goes to the cupboard, kneels before a little idol on the third shelf, and repeats the mumbo jumbo. If you pray like that every day, he says, nothing will happen to you. The good lord what's his name never forgets an obedient servant. And then he shows me the crooked arm which he got in a taxi accident on a day doubtless when he had neglected to rehearse the complete song and dance. His arm looks like a broken compass; it's not an arm any more, but a knucklebone with a shank attached. Since the arm has been repaired he has developed a pair of swollen glands in the armpit— fat little glands, exactly like a dog's testicles. While bemoaning his plight he remembers suddenly that the doctor had recommended a more liberal diet. He begs me at once to sit down and make up a menu with plenty of fish and meat. "And what about oysters, Endree—for *le petit frere?*" But all this is only to make an impression on me. He hasn't the slightest intention of buying himself oysters, or meat, or fish. Not as long as I am there, at least. For the time being we are going to nourish ourselves on lentils and rice and all the dry foods he has stored away in the attic. And the butter he bought last week, that won't go to waste either. When he commences to cure the butter the smell is unbearable. I used to run out at first, when he started frying the butter, but now I stick it out. He'd be only too delighted if he could make me vomit up my meal—that would be something else to put away in the cupboard along with the dry bread and the moldy cheese and the little grease cakes that he makes himself out of the stale milk and the rancid butter.

For the last five years, so it seems, he hasn't done a stroke of work, hasn't turned over a penny. Business has gone to smash. He talks to me about pearls in the Indian ocean— big fat ones on which you can live for a lifetime. The Arabs are ruining the business, he says. But meanwhile he prays to the lord so-and-so every day, and that sustains him. He's on a marvelous footing with the deity: knows just how to cajole him, how to wheedle a few sous out of him. It's a pure commercial relationship. In exchange for the flummery before the cabinet every day he gets his ration of beans and garlic, to say nothing of the swollen testicles under his arm. He is confident that everything will turn out well in the end. The pearls will sell again some day, maybe five years hence, maybe twenty—when the Lord Boomaroom wishes it. "And when the business goes, Endree, you will get ten per cent—for writing the letters. But first Endree, you must write the letter to find out if we can get credit from India. It will take about six months for an answer, maybe seven months ... the boats are not fast in India." He has no conception of time at all, the little duck. When I ask him if he has slept well he will say: "Ah, yes, Endree, I sleep very well... I sleep sometimes ninety-two hours in three days."

Mornings he is usually too weak to do any work. His arm! That poor broken crutch of an arm! I wonder sometimes when I see him twisting it around the back of his neck how he will ever get it into place again. If it weren't for that little paunch he carries he'd remind me of one of those contortionists at the Cirque Medrano. All he needs is to break a leg. When he sees me sweeping the carpet, when he sees what a cloud of dust I raise, he begins to cluck like a pygmy. "Good! Very good, Endree. And now I will pick up the knots." That means that there are a few crumbs of dust which I have overlooked; it is a polite way he has of being sarcastic.

Afternoons there are always a few cronies from the pearl market dropping in to pay him a visit. They're all very suave, butter-tongued bastards with soft, doelike eyes; they sit around the table drinking the perfumed tea with a loud hissing noise while Nanantatee jumps up and down like a jack-in-the-box or points to a crumb on the floor and says in his smooth slippery voice—"Will you please to pick that up, Endree." When the guests arrive he goes unctuously to the cupboard and gets out the dry crusts of bread which he toasted maybe a week ago and which taste strongly now of the moldy wood. Not a crumb is thrown away. If the bread gets too sour he takes it downstairs to the concierge who, so he says, has been very kind to him. According to him, the concierge is delighted to get the stale bread—she makes bread pudding with it.

One day my friend Anatole came to see me. Nanantatee was delighted. Insisted that Anatole stay for tea. Insisted that he try little grease cakes and the stale bread. "You must come every day," he says, "and teach me Russian. Fine language, Russian ... I want to speak it. How do you say that again, Endree—*borsht?* You will write that down for me, please, Endree...." And I must write it on the typewriter, no less, so that he can observe my technique. He bought the typewriter, after he had collected on the bad arm, because the doctor recommended it as a good exercise. But he got tired of the typewriter shortly—it was an *English* typewriter.

When he learned that Anatole played the mandolin he said: "Very good! You must come every day and teach me the music. I will buy a mandolin as soon as business is better. It is good for my arm." The next day he borrows a phonograph from the concierge. "You will please teach me to dance, Endree. My stomach is too big." I am hoping that he will buy a porterhouse steak some day so that I can say to him: "You will please bite it for me, *Mister* Nonentity. My teeth are not strong!"

As I said a moment ago, ever since my arrival he has become extraordinarily meticulous. "Yesterday," he says, "you made three mistakes, Endree. First, you forgot to close the toilet door and so all night it makes boom-boom; second, you left the kitchen window open and so the window is cracked this morning. And you forgot to put out the milk bottle! Always you will put out the milk bottle please, before you go to bed, and in the morning you will please bring in the bread."

Every day his friend Kepi drops in to see if any visitors have arrived from India. He waits for Nanantatee to go out and then he scurries to the cupboard and devours the sticks of bread that are hidden away in a glass jar. The food is no good, he insists, but he puts it away like a rat. Kepi is a scrounger, a sort of human tick who fastens himself to the hide of even the poorest compatriot. From Kepi's standpoint they are all nabobs. For a Manila cheroot and the price of a drink he will suck any Hindu's ass. A Hindu's, mind you, but not an Englishman's. He has the address of every whorehouse in Paris, and the rates. Even from the ten franc joints he gets his little commission. And he knows the shortest way to any place you want to go. He will ask you first if you want to go by taxi; if you say no, he will suggest the bus, and if that is too high then the streetcar or the metro. Or he will offer to walk you there and save a franc or two, knowing very well that it will be necessary to pass a *tabac* on the way and that you will please be so good as to buy me a little cheroot.

Kepi is interesting, in a way, because he has absolutely no ambition except to get a fuck every night. Every penny he makes, and they are damned few, he squanders in the dance halls. He has a wife and eight children in Bombay, but that does not prevent him from proposing marriage to any little *femme de chambre* who is stupid and credulous enough to be taken in by him. He has a little room on the Rue Condorcet for which he pays sixty francs a month. He papered it all himself. Very proud of it, too. He uses violet-colored ink in his fountain pen because it lasts longer. He shines his own shoes, presses his own pants, does his own laundry. For a little cigar, a cheroot, if you please, he will escort you all over Paris. If you stop to look at a shirt or a collar button his eyes flash. "Don't buy it here," he will say. "They ask too much. I will show you a cheaper place." And before you have time to think about it he will whisk you away and deposit you before another show window where there are the same ties and shirts and collar buttons—maybe it's the very same store! but you don't know the difference. When Kepi hears that you want to buy something his soul becomes animated. He will ask you so many questions and drag you to so many places that you are bound to get thirsty and ask him to have a drink, whereupon you will discover to your amazement that you are again standing in a *tabac*—maybe the same *tabac!*—and Kepi is saying again in that small unctuous voice: "Will you please be so good as to buy me a little cheroot?" No matter what you propose doing, even if it's only to walk around the corner, Kepi will economize for you. Kepi will show you the shortest way, the cheapest place, the biggest dish, because whatever you have to do you *must* pass a *tabac*, and whether there is a revolution or a lockout or a quarantine Kepi must be at the Moulin Rouge or the Olympia or the Ange Rouge when the music strikes up.

The other day he brought a book for me to read. It was about a famous suit between a holy man and the editor of an Indian paper. The editor, it seems had openly accused the holy man of leading a scandalous life; he went further, and accused the holy man of being diseased. Kepi says it must have been the great French pox, but Nanantatee avers that it was the Japanese clap. For Nanantatee everything has to be a little exaggerated. At any rate, says Nanantatee cheerily: "You will please tell me what it says, Endree. I can't read the book—it hurts my arm." Then, by way of encouraging me—"it is a fine book about the fucking, Endree. Kepi has brought it for you. He thinks about nothing but the girls. So many girls he fucks—just like Krishna. We don't believe in that business, Endree...."

A little later he takes me upstairs to the attic which is loaded down with tin cans and crap from India wrapped in burlap and firecracker paper. "Here is where I bring the girls," he says. And then rather wistfully: "I am not a very good fucker, Endree. I don't screw the girls any more. I hold them in my arms and I say the words. I like only to say the words now." It isn't necessary to listen any further: I know that he is going to tell me about his arm. I can see him lying there with that broken hinge dangling from the side of the bed. But to my surprise he adds: "I am no good for the fucking, Endree. I never was a very good fucker. My brother, he is good! Three times a day, every day! And Kepi, he is good—just like Krishna."

His mind is fixed now on the "fucking business." Downstairs, in the little room where he kneels before the open cabinet, he explains to me how it was when he was rich and his wife and the children were here. On holidays he would take his wife to the House of All Nations and hire a room for the night. Every room was appointed in a different style. His wife liked it there very much. "A wonderful place for the fucking, Endree. I know all the rooms...."

The walls of the little room in which we are sitting are crammed with photographs. Every branch of the family is represented, it is like a cross section of the Indian empire. For the most part the members of this genealogical tree look like withered leaves: the women are frail and they have a startled, frightened look in their eyes: the men have a keen, intelligent look, like educated chimpanzees. They are all there, about ninety of them, with their white bullocks, their dung cakes, their skinny legs, their old-fashioned spectacles; in the background, now and then, one catches a glimpse of the parched soil, of a crumbling pediment, of an idol with crooked arms, a sort of human centipede. There is something so fantastic, so incongruous about this gallery that one is reminded inevitably of the great spawn of temples which stretch from the Himalayas to the tip of Ceylon, a vast jumble of architecture, staggering in beauty and at the same time monstrous, hideously monstrous because the fecundity which seethes and ferments in the myriad ramifications of design seems to have exhausted the very soil of India itself. Looking at the seething hive of figures which swarm the facades of the temples one is overwhelmed by the potency of these dark, handsome peoples who mingled their mysterious streams in a sexual embrace that has lasted thirty centuries or more. These frail men and women with piercing eyes who stare out of the photographs seem like the emaciated shadows of those virile, massive figures who incarnated themselves in stone and fresco from one end of India to the other in order that the heroic myths of the races who here intermingled should remain forever entwined in the hearts of their countrymen. When I look at only a fragment of these spacious dreams of stone, these toppling, sluggish edifices studded with gems, coagulated with human sperm, I am overwhelmed by the dazzling splendor of those imaginative flights which enabled half a billion people of diverse origins to thus incarnate the most fugitive expressions of their longing.

It is a strange, inexplicable medley of feelings which assails me now as Nanantatee prattles on about the sister who died in childbirth. There she is on the wall, a frail, timid thing of twelve or thirteen clinging to the arm of a dotard. At ten years of age she was given in wedlock to this old roue who had already buried five wives. She had seven children, only one of whom survived her. She was given to the aged gorilla in order to keep the pearls in the family. As she was passing away, so Nanantatee puts it, she whispered to the doctor: "I am tired of this fucking.... I don't want to fuck any more, doctor." As he relates this to me he scratches his head solemnly with his withered arm. "The fucking business is bad, Endree," he says. "But I will give you a word that will always make you lucky; you must say it every day, over and over, a million times you must say it. It is the best word there is, Endree ... say it now... OOMAHARUMOOMA!"

"OOMARABOO...."

"No, Endree... like this... OOMAHARU-MOOMA!"

"OOMAMABOOMBA...."

"No, Endree... like this...."

... But what with the murky light, the botchy print, the tattered cover, the jigjagged page, the fumbling fingers, the fox-trotting fleas, the lie-a-bed lice, the scum on his tongue, the drop in his eye, the lump in his throat, the drink in his bottle, the itch in his palm, the wail of his wind, the grief from his breath, the fog of his brainfag, the tick of his conscience, the height of his rage, the gush of his fundament, the fire in his gorge, the tickle of his tail, the rats in his garret, the hullabaloo and the dust in his ears, since it took him a month to steal a march, he was hard-set to memorize more than a word a week.

I suppose I would never have gotten out of Nanantatee's clutches if fate hadn't intervened. One night, as luck would have it, Kepi asked me if I wouldn't take one of his clients to a whorehouse nearby. The young man had just come from India and he had not very much money to spend. He was one of Gandhi's men, one of that little band who made the historic march to the sea during the salt trouble. A very gay disciple of Gandhi's I must say, despite the vows of abstinence he had taken. Evidently he hadn't looked at a woman for ages. It was all I could do to get him as far as the Rue Laferriere; he was like a dog with his tongue hanging out. And a pompous, vain little devil to boot! He had decked himself out in a corduroy suit, a beret, a cane, a Windsor tie; he had bought himself two fountain pens, a kodak, and some fancy underwear. The money he was spending was a gift from the merchants of Bombay; they were sending him to England to spread the gospel of Gandhi.

Once inside Miss Hamilton's joint he began to lose his *sang-froid*. When suddenly he found himself surrounded by a bevy of naked women he looked at me in consternation. "Pick one out," I said. "You can have your choice." He had become so rattled that he could scarcely look at them. "You do it for me," he murmured, blushing violently. I looked them over coolly and picked out a plump young wench who seemed full of feathers. We sat down in the reception room and waited for the drinks. The madam wanted to know why I didn't take a girl also. "Yes, you take one too," said the young Hindu. "I don't want to be alone with her." So the girls were brought in again and I chose one for myself, a rather tall, thin one with melancholy eyes. We were left alone, the four of us, in the reception room. After a few moments my young Gandhi leans over and whispers something in my ear. "Sure, if you like her better, take her," I said, and so, rather awkwardly and considerably embarrassed, I explained to the girls that we would like to switch. I saw at once that we had made a *faux pas,* but by now my young friend had became gay and lecherous and nothing would do but to get upstairs quickly and have it over with.

We took adjoining rooms with a connecting door between. I think my companion had in mind to make another switch once he had satisfied his sharp, gnawing hunger. At any rate, no sooner had the girls left the room to prepare themselves than I hear him knocking on the door. "Where is the toilet, please?" he asks. Not thinking that it was anything serious I urge him to do in the *bidet.* The girls return with towels in their hands. I hear him giggling in the next room.

As I'm putting on my pants suddenly I hear a commotion in the next room. The girl is bawling him out, calling him a pig, a dirty little pig. I can't imagine what he has done to warrant such an outburst. I'm standing there with one foot in my trousers listening attentively. He's trying to explain to her in English, raising his voice louder and louder until it becomes a shriek.

I hear a door slam and in another moment the madam bursts into my room, her face as red as a beet, her arms gesticulating wildly. "You ought to be ashamed of yourself," she screams, "bringing a man like that to my place! He's a barbarian... he's a pig... he's a...!" My companion is standing behind her, in the doorway, a look of utmost discomfiture on his face.

"What did you do?" I ask.

"What did he do?" yells the madam. "I'll show you.... Come here!" And grabbing me by the arm she drags me into the next room. "There! There!" she screams, pointing to the *bidet.*

"Come on, let's get out," says the Hindu boy.

"Wait a minute, you can't get out as easily as all that."

The madam is standing by the *bidet,* fuming and spitting. The girls are standing there too, with towels in their hands. The five of us are standing there looking at the *bidet.* There are two enormous turds floating in the water. The madam bends down and puts a towel over it. "Frightful! Frightful!" she wails. "Never have I seen anything like this! A pig! A dirty little pig!"

The Hindu boy looks at me reproachfully. "You should have told me!" he says. "I didn't know it wouldn't go down. I asked you where to go and you told me to use that." He is almost in tears.

Finally the madam takes me to one side. She has become a little more reasonable now. After all, it was a mistake. Perhaps the gentlemen would like to come downstairs and order another drink—f or the girls. It was a great shock to the girls. They are not used to such things. And if the good gentlemen will be so kind as to remember the *femme de chambre....* It is not so pretty for the *femme de chambre* —that mess, that ugly mess. She shrugs her shoulders and winks her eye. A lamentable incident. But an accident. If the gentlemen will wait here a few moments the maid will bring the drinks. Would the gentlemen like to have some champagne? Yes?

"I'd like to get out of here," says the Hindu boy weakly.

"Don't feel so badly about it," says the madam. "It is all over now. Mistakes will happen sometimes. Next time you will ask for the toilet." She goes on about the toilet—one on every floor, it seems. And a bathroom too.

"I have lots of English clients," she says. "They are all gentlemen. The gentleman is a Hindu? Charming people, the Hindus. So intelligent. So handsome."

When we get into the street the charming young gentleman is almost weeping. He is sorry now that he bought a corduroy suit and the cane and the fountain pens. He talks about the eight vows that he took, the control of the palate, etc. On the march to Dandi even a plate of ice cream it was forbidden to take. He tells me about the spinning wheel— how the little band of Satyagrahis imitated the devotion of their master. He relates with pride how he walked beside the master and conversed with him. I have the illusion of being in the presence of one of the twelve disciples.

During the next few days we see a good deal of each other; there are interviews to be arranged with the newspaper men and lectures to be given to the Hindus of Paris. It is amazing to see how these spineless devils order one another about; amazing also to see how ineffectual they are in all that concerns practical affairs. And the jealousy and the intrigues, the petty, sordid rivalries. Wherever there are ten Hindus together there is India with her sects and schisms, her racial, lingual, religious, political antagonisms. In the person of Gandhi they are experiencing for a brief moment the miracle of unity, but when he goes there will be a crash, an utter relapse into that strife and chaos so characteristic of the Indian people.

The young Hindu, of course, is optimistic. He has been to America and he has been contaminated by the cheap idealism of the Americans, contaminated by the ubiquitous bathtub, the five-and-ten-cent store bric-a-brac, the bustle, the efficiency, the machinery, the high wages, the free libraries, etc., etc. His ideal would be to Americanize India. He is not at all pleased with Gandhi's retrogressive mania. *Forward,* he says, just like a YMCA man. As I listen to his tales of America I see how absurd it is to expect of Gandhi that miracle which will deroute the trend of destiny. India's enemy is not England, but America. India's enemy is the time spirit, the hand which cannot be turned back. Nothing will avail to offset this virus which is poisoning the whole world. America is the very incarnation of doom. She will drag the whole world down to the bottomless pit.

He thinks the Americans are a very gullible people. He tells me about the credulous souls who succored him there—the Quakers, the Unitarians, the Theosophists, the New Thoughters, the Seventh-day Adventists, etc. He knew where to sail his boat, this bright young man. He knew how to make the tears come to his eyes at the right moment; he knew how to take up a collection, how to appeal to the minister's wife, how to make love to the mother and daughter at the same time. To look at him you would think him a saint. And he is a saint, in the modem fashion; a contaminated saint who talks in one breath of love, brotherhood, bathtubs, sanitation, efficiency, etc.

The last night of his sojourn in Paris is given up to "the fucking business." He has had a full program all day—conferences, cablegrams, interviews, photographs for the newspapers, affectionate farewells, advice to the faithful, etc., etc. At dinner time he decides to lay aside his troubles. He orders champagne with the meal, he snaps his fingers at the *garcon* and behaves in general like the boorish little peasant that he is. And since he has had a bellyful of all the good places he suggests now that I show him something more primitive. He would like to go to a very cheap place, order two or three girls at once. I steer him along the Boulevard de la Chapelle, warning him all the while to be careful of his pocketbook. Around Aubervilliers we duck into a cheap dive and immediately we've got a flock of them on our hands. In a few minutes he's dancing with a naked wench, a huge blonde with creases in her jowls. I can see her ass reflected a dozen times in the mirrors that line the room—and those dark, bony fingers of his clutching her tenaciously. The table is full of beer glasses, the mechanical piano is wheezing and gasping. The girls who are unoccupied are sitting placidly on the leather benches, scratching themselves peacefully just like a family of chimpanzees. There is a sort of subdued pandemonium in the air, a note of repressed violence, as if the awaited explosion required the advent of some utterly minute detail, something microscopic but thoroughly unpremeditated, completely unexpected. In that sort of half-reverie which permits one to participate in an event and yet remain quite aloof, the little detail which was lacking began obscurely but insistently to coagulate, to assume a freakish, crystalline form, like the frost which gathers on the windowpane. And like those frost patterns which seem so bizarre, so utterly free and fantastic in design, but which are nevertheless determined by the most rigid laws, so this sensation which commenced to take form inside me seemed also to be giving obedience to ineluctable laws. My whole being was responding to the dictates of an ambiance which it had never before experienced; that which I could call myself seemed to be contracting, condensing, shrinking from the stale, customary boundaries of the flesh whose perimeter knew only the modulations of the nerve ends.

And the more substantial, the more solid the core of me became, the more delicate and extravagant appeared the close, palpable reality out of which I was being squeezed. In the measure that I became more and more metallic, in the same measure the scene before my eyes became inflated. The state of tension was so finely drawn now that the introduction of a single foreign particle, even a microscopic particle, as I say, would have shattered everything. For the fraction of a second perhaps I experienced that utter clarity which the epileptic, it is said, is given to know. In that moment I lost completely the illusion of time and space: the world unfurled its drama simultaneously along a meridian which had no axis. In this sort of hair-trigger eternity I felt that everything was justified, supremely justified; I felt the wars inside me that had left behind this pulp and wrack; I felt the crimes that were seething here to emerge tomorrow in blatant screamers; I felt the misery that was grinding itself out with pestle and mortar, the long dull misery that dribbles away in dirty handkerchiefs. On the meridian of time there is no injustice: there is only the poetry of motion creating the illusion of truth and drama. If at any moment anywhere one comes face to face with the absolute, that great sympathy which makes men like Gautama and Jesus seem divine freezes away; the monstrous thing is not that men have created roses out of this dung heap, but that, for some reason or other, they should *want* roses. For some reason or other man looks for the miracle, and to accomplish it he will wade through blood. He will debauch himself with ideas, he will reduce himself to a shadow if for only one second of his life he can close his eyes to the hideousness of reality. Everything is endured—disgrace, humiliation, poverty, war, crime, *ennui*—in the belief that overnight something will occur, a miracle, which will render life tolerable. And all the while a meter is running inside and there is no hand that can reach in there and shut it off. All the while someone is eating the bread of life and drinking the wine, some dirty fat cockroach of a priest who hides away in the cellar guzzling it, while up above in the light of the street a phantom host touches the lips and the blood is pale as water. And out of the endless torment and misery no miracle comes forth, no microscopic vestige even of relief. Only ideas, pale, attenuated ideas which have to be fattened by slaughter; ideas which come forth like bile, like the guts of a pig when the carcass is ripped open.

And so I think what a miracle it would be if this miracle which man attends eternally should turn out to be nothing more than these two enormous turds which the faithful disciple dropped in the *bidet*. What if at the last moment, when the banquet table is set and the cymbals clash, there should appear suddenly, and wholly without warning, a silver platter on which even the blind could see that there is nothing more, and nothing less, than two enormous lumps of shit. That, I believe would be more miraculous than anything which man has looked forward to. It would be miraculous because it would be undreamed of. It would be more miraculous than even the wildest dream because *anybody* could imagine the possibility but nobody ever has, and probably nobody ever again will.

Somehow the realization that nothing was to be hoped for had a salutary effect upon me. For weeks and months, for years, in fact, all my life I had been looking forward to something happening, some extrinsic event that would alter my life, and now suddenly, inspired by the absolute hopelessness of everything, I felt relieved, felt as though a great burden had been lifted from my shoulders. At dawn I parted company with the young Hindu, after touching him for a few francs, enough for a room. Walking toward Montparnasse I decided to let myself drift with the tide, to make not the least resistance to fate, no matter in what form it presented itself. Nothing that had happened to me thus far had been sufficient to destroy me; nothing had been destroyed except my illusions. I myself was intact. The world was intact. Tomorrow there might be a revolution, a plague, an earthquake; tomorrow there might not be left a single soul to whom one could turn for sympathy, for aid, for faith. It seemed to me that the great calamity had already manifested itself, that I could be no more truly alone than at this very moment. I made up my mind that I would hold on to nothing, that I would expect nothing, that henceforth I would live as an animal, a beast of prey, a rover, a plunderer. Even if war were declared, and it were my lot to go, I would grab the bayonet and plunge it, plunge it up to the hilt. And if rape were the order of the day then rape I would, and with a vengeance. At this very moment, in the quiet dawn of a new day, was not the earth giddy with crime and distress? Had one single element of man's nature been altered, vitally, fundamentally altered, by the incessant march of history? By what he calls the better part of his nature, man has been betrayed, that is all. At the extreme limits of his spiritual being man finds himself again naked as a savage. When he finds God, as it were, he has been picked clean: he is a skeleton. One must burrow into life again in order to put on flesh. The word must become flesh; the soul thirsts. On whatever crumb my eye fastens, I will pounce and devour. If to live is the paramount thing, then I will live, even if I must become a cannibal. Heretofore I have been trying to save my precious hide, trying to preserve the few pieces of meat that hid my bones. I am done with that. I have reached the limits of endurance. My back is to the wall; I can retreat no further. As far as history goes I am dead. If there is something beyond I shall have to bounce back. I have found God, but he is insufficient. I am only spiritually dead. Physically I am alive. Morally I am free. The world which I have departed is a menagerie. The dawn is breaking on a new world, a jungle world in which the lean spirits roam with sharp claws. If I am a hyena I am a lean and hungry one: I go forth to fatten myself.

At one-thirty I called on Van Norden, as per agreement. He had warned me that if he didn't answer it would mean that he was sleeping with someone, probably his Georgia cunt.

Anyway, there he was, tucked away comfortably, but with an air of weariness as usual. He wakes up cursing himself, or cursing the job, or cursing life. He wakes up utterly bored and discomfited, chagrined to think that he did not die overnight.

I sit down by the window and give him what encouragement I can. It is tedious work. One has to actually coax him out of bed. Mornings—he means by mornings anywhere between one and five p.m.—mornings, as I say, he gives himself up to reveries. Mostly it

THE OBELISK TRILOGY   51

is about the past he dreams. About his "cunts." He endeavors to recall how they felt, what they said to him at certain critical moments, where he laid them, and so on. And as he lies there, grinning and cursing, he manipulates his fingers in that curious, bored way of his, as though to convey the impression that his disgust is too great for words. Over the bedstead hangs a douche bag which he keeps for emergencies—for the *virgins* whom he tracks down like a sleuth. Even after he has slept with one of these mythical creatures he will still refer to her as a virgin, and almost never by name. "My virgin," he will say, just as he says "my Georgia cunt." When he goes to the toilet he says: "If my Georgia cunt calls tell her to wait. Say I said so. And listen, you can have her if you like. I'm tired of her."

He takes a squint at the weather and heaves a deep sigh. If it's rainy he says: "God damn this fucking climate, it makes one morbid." And if the sun is shining brightly he says: "God damn that fucking sun, it makes you blind!" As he starts to shave he suddenly remembers that there is no clean towel. "God damn this fucking hotel, they're too stingy to give you a clean towel every day!" No matter what he does or where he goes things are out of joint. Either it's the fucking country or the fucking job, or else it's some fucking cunt who's put him on the blink.

"My teeth are all rotten," he says, gargling his throat. "It's the fucking bread they give you to eat here." He opens his mouth wide and pulls his lower lip down. "See that? Pulled out six teeth yesterday. Soon I'll have to get another plate. That's what you get working for a living. When I was on the bum I had all my teeth, my eyes were bright and clear. Look at me now! It's a wonder I can make a cunt any more. Jesus, what I'd like is to find some rich cunt—like that cute little prick, Carl. Did he ever show you the letters she sends him? Who is she, do you know? He wouldn't tell me her name, the bastard ... he's afraid I might take her away from him." He gargles his throat again and then takes a long look at the cavities. "You're lucky," he says ruefully. "You've got friends, at least. I haven't anybody, except that cute little prick who drives me bats about his rich cunt."

"Listen," he says, "do you happen to know a cunt by the name of Norma? She hangs around the Dome all day. I think she's queer. I had her up here yesterday, tickling her ass. She wouldn't let me do a thing. I had her on the bed.... I even had her drawers off ... and then I got disgusted. Jesus, I can't bother struggling that way any more. It isn't worth it. Either they do or they don't—it's foolish to waste time wrestling with them. While you're struggling with a little bitch like that there may be a dozen cunts on the *terrasse* just dying to be laid. It's a fact. They all come over here to get laid. They think it's sinful here... *the poor boobs!* Some of these schoolteachers from out West, they're honestly virgins ... I mean it! They sit around on their can all day thinking about it. You don't have to work over them very much. They're dying for it. I had a married woman the other day who told me she hadn't had a lay for six months. Can you imagine that? Jesus, she was hot! I thought she'd tear the cock off me. And groaning all the time. *"Do you? Do you?"* She kept saying that all the time, like she was nuts. And do you know what that bitch wanted to do? She wanted to move in here. Imagine that! Asking me if I loved her. I didn't even know her name. I never know their names... I don't want to. The married ones! Christ, if you saw all the married cunts I bring up here you'd never have any more illusions. They're worse than the virgins, the married ones. They don't wait for you to start things—they fish it out for you themselves. And then they talk about love afterwards. It's disgusting. I tell you, I'm actually beginning to hate cunt!"

He looks out the window again. It's drizzling. It's been drizzling this way for the last five days.

"Are we going to the Dome, Joe?" I call him Joe because he calls me Joe. When Carl is with us he is Joe too. Everybody is Joe because it's easier that way. It's also a pleasant reminder not to take yourself too seriously. Anyway, Joe doesn't want to go to the Dome—he owes too much money there. He wants to go to the Coupole. Wants to take a little walk first around the block.

"But it's raining, Joe."

"I know, but what the hell! I've got to have my constitutional. I've got to wash the dirt out of my belly." When he says this I have the impression that the whole world is wrapped up there inside his belly, and that it's rotting there.

As he's putting on his things he falls back again into a semi-comatose state. He stands there with one arm in his coat sleeve and his hat on assways and he begins to dream aloud—about the Riviera, about the sun, about lazing one's life away. "All I ask of life," he says, "is a bunch of books, a bunch of dreams, and a bunch of cunt." As he mumbles this meditatively he looks at me with the softest, the most insidious smile. "Do you like that smile?" he says. And then disgustedly—"Jesus, if I could only find some rich cunt to smile at that way!"

"Only a rich cunt can save me now," he says with an air of utmost weariness. "One gets tired of chasing after new cunts all the time. It gets mechanical. The trouble is, you see, I can't fall in love. I'm too much of an egoist. Women only help me to dream, that's all. It's a vice, like drink or opium. I've got to have a new one every day; if I don't I get morbid. I think too much. Sometimes I'm amazed at myself, how quick I pull it off—and how little it really means. I do it automatically like. Sometimes I'm not thinking about a woman at all, but suddenly I notice a woman looking at me and then, bango! it starts all over again. Before I know what I'm doing I've got her up to the room. I don't even remember what I say to them. I bring them up to the room, give them a pat on the ass, and before I know what it's all about it's over. It's like a dream.... Do you know what I mean?"

He hasn't much use for the French girls. Can't stand them. "Either they want money or they want you to marry them. At bottom they're all whores. I'd rather wrestle with a virgin," he says. "They give you a little illusion. They put up a fight at least." Just the same, as we glance over the *terrasse* there is hardly a whore in sight whom he hasn't fucked at some time or other. Standing at the bar he points them out to me, one by one, goes over them anatomically, describes their good points and their bad. "They're all frigid," he says. And then begins to mold his hands, thinking of the nice, juicy virgins who are just dying for it.

In the midst of his reveries he suddenly arrests himself, and grabbing my arm excitedly, he points to a whale of a woman who is just lowering herself into a seat. "There's my Danish cunt," he grunts. "See that ass? *Danish.* How that woman loves it! She just begs me for it. Come over here ... look at her now, from the side! Look at that ass, will you? It's enormous. I tell you, when she climbs over me I can hardly get my arms around it. It blots out the whole world. She makes me feel like a little bug crawling inside her. I don't know why I fall for her—I suppose it's that ass. It's so incongruous like. And the creases in it! You can't forget an ass like that. It's a fact... a solid fact. The others, they may bore you, or they may give you a moment's illusion, but this one—with her ass!—zowie, you can't obliterate her... it's like going to bed with a monument on top of you."

The Danish cunt seems to have electrified him. He's lost all his sluggishness now. His eyes are popping out of his head. And of course one thing reminds him of another. He wants to get out of the fucking hotel because the noise bothers him. He wants to write a book too so as to have something to occupy his mind. But then the goddamned job stands in the way. "It takes it out of you, that fucking job! I don't want to write about Montparnasse.... I want to write my life, my thoughts. I want to get the dirt out of my belly.... Listen, get that one over there! I had her a long time ago. She used to be down near Les Halles. A funny bitch. She lay on the edge of the bed and pulled her dress up. Ever try it that way? Not bad. She didn't hurry me either. She just lay back and played with her hat while I slugged away at her. And when I come she says sort of bored like— 'Are you through?' Like it didn't make any difference at all. Of course, it doesn't make any difference, I know that goddamn well... but the cold-blooded way she had ... I sort of liked it... it was fascinating, you know? When she goes to wipe herself she begins to sing. Going out of the hotel she was still singing. Didn't even say *Au revoir!* Walks off swinging her hat and humming to herself like. That's a whore for you! A good lay though. I think I liked her better than my virgin. There's something depraved about screwing a woman who doesn't give a fuck about it. It heats your blood...." And then, after a moment's medita-tion—"Can you imagine what she'd be like if she had any feelings?"

"Listen," he says, "I want you to come to the Club with me tomorrow afternoon ... there's a dance on."

"I can't tomorrow, Joe. I promised to help Carl out...."

"Listen, forget that prick! I want you to do me a favor. It's like this"—he commences to mold his hands again. "I've got a cunt lined up... she promised to stay with me on my night off. But I'm not positive about her yet. She's got a mother, you see ... some shit of a painter, she chews my ear off every time I see her. I think the truth is, the mother's jeal-ous. I don't think she'd mind so much if I gave her a lay first. You know how it is.... Anyway, I thought maybe you wouldn't mind taking the mother... she's not so bad ... if I hadn't seen the daughter I might have considered her myself. The daughter's nice and young, fresh like, you know what I mean? There's a clean smell to her...."

"Listen, Joe, you'd better find somebody else...." "Aw, don't take it like that! I know how you feel about it. It's only a little favor I'm asking you to do for me. I don't know to get rid of the old hen. I thought first I'd get drunk and ditch her—but I don't think the young one'd like that. They're sentimental like. They come from Minnesota or somewhere. Anyway, come around tomorrow and wake me up, will you? Otherwise I'll oversleep. And besides, I want you to help me find a room. You know I'm helpless. Find me a room in a quiet street, somewhere near here. I've got to stay around here... I've got credit here. Listen, promise me you'll do that for me. I'll buy you a meal now and then. Come around anyway, because I go nuts talking to these foolish cunts. I want to talk to you about Havelock Ellis. Jesus, I've had the book out for three weeks now and I haven't looked at it. You sort of rot here. Would you believe it, I've never been to the Louvre—nor the Comedie-Francaise. Is it worth going to those joints? Still, it sort of takes your mind off things, I suppose. What do you do with yourself all day? Don't you get bored? What do you do for a lay? Listen ... come here! Don't run away yet... I'm lonely. Do you know some-thing—if this keeps up another year I'll go nuts. I've got to get out of this fucking coun-try. There's nothing for me here. I know it's lousy now, in America, but just the same.... You go queer over here ... all these cheap shits sitting on their ass all day bragging about their work and none of them is worth a stinking damn. They're all failures—that's why they come over here. Listen, Joe, don't you ever get homesick? You're a funny guy... you seem to like it over here. What do you see in it?... I wish you'd tell me. I wish to Christ I could stop thinking about myself. I'm all twisted up inside ... it's like a knot in there.... Listen, I know I'm boring the shit out of you, but I've got to talk to someone. I can't talk to those guys upstairs... you know what those bastards are like ... they all take a byline. And Carl, the little prick, he's so goddamned selfish. I'm an egotist, but I'm not selfish. There's a difference. I'm a neurotic, I guess. I can't stop thinking about myself. It isn't that I think myself so important.... I simply can't think about anything else, that's all. If I could fall in love with a woman that might help some. But I can't find a woman who interests me. I'm in a mess, you can see that can't you? What do you advise me to do? What would you do in my place? Listen, I don't want to hold you back any longer, but wake me up tomorrow— at one-thirty—will you? I'll give you something extra if you'll shine my shoes. And listen, if you've got an extra shirt, a clean one, bring it along, will you? Shit, I'm grinding my balls off on that job, and it doesn't even give me a clean shirt. They've got us over here like a bunch of niggers. Ah, well, shit! I'm going to take a walk ... wash the dirt out of my belly. Don't forget, *tomorrow!*"

For six months or more it's been going on, this correspondence with the rich cunt, Irene. Recently I've been reporting to Carl every day in order to bring the affair to a head, because as far as Irene is concerned this thing could go on indefinitely. In the last few days there's been a perfect avalanche of letters exchanged; the last letter we dispatched was almost forty pages long, and written in three languages. It was a potpourri, the last letter— tag ends of old novels, slices from the Sunday supplement, reconstructed versions of old letters to Llona and Tania, garbled transliterations of Rabelais and Petronius—in short, we exhausted ourselves. Finally Irene decides to come out of her shell. Finally a letter arrives giving a rendezvous at her hotel. Carl is pissing in his pants. It's one thing to write letters to a woman you don't know; it's another thing entirely to call on her and make love to her. At the last moment he's quaking so that I almost fear I'll have to substitute for him. When we get out of the taxi in front of her hotel he's trembling so much that I have to walk him around the block first. He's already had two Pernods, but they haven't made the slightest impression on him. The sight of the hotel itself is enough to crush him: it's a pretentious place with one of those huge empty lobbies in which Englishwomen sit for hours with a blank look. In order to make sure that he wouldn't run away I stood by while the porter telephoned to announce him. Irene was there, and she was waiting for him. As he got into the lift he threw me a last despairing glance, one of those mute appeals which a dog makes when you put a noose around its neck. Going through the revolving door I thought of Van Norden....

I go back to the hotel and wait for a telephone call. He's only got an hour's time and he's promised to let me know the results before going to work. I look over the carbons of the letters we sent her. I try to imagine the situation as it actually is, but it's beyond me. Her letters are much better than ours—they're sincere, that's plain. By now they've sized each other up. I wonder if he's still pissing in his pants.

The telephone rings. His voice sounds queer, squeaky, as though he were frightened and jubilant at the same time. He asks me to substitute for him at the office. "Tell the bastard anything! Tell him I'm dying...."

"Listen, Carl... can you tell me ...?"

"Hello! Are you Henry Miller?" It's a woman's voice. It's Irene. She's saying hello to me. Her voice sounds beautiful over the phone ... beautiful. For a moment I'm in a perfect panic. I don't know what to say to her. I'd like to say: "Listen, Irene, I think you are beautiful... I think you're *wonderful.*" I'd like to say one true thing to her, no matter how silly it would sound, because now that I hear her voice everything is changed. But before I can gather my wits Carl is on the phone again and he's saying in that queer squeaky voice: "She likes you, Joe. I told her all about you...."

At the office I have to hold copy for Van Norden. When it comes time for the break he pulls me aside. He looks glum and ravaged.

"So he's dying, is he, the little prick? Listen, what's the lowdown on this?"

"I think he went to see his rich cunt," I answer calmly.

"*What!* You mean he called on her?" He seems beside himself. "Listen, where does she live? What's her name?" I pretend ignorance. "Listen," he says, "you're a decent guy. Why the hell don't you let me in on this racket?"

In order to appease him I promise finally that I'll tell him everything as soon as I get the details from Carl. I can hardly wait myself until I see Carl.

Around noon next day I knock at his door. He's up already and lathering his beard. Can't tell a thing from the expression on his face. Can't even tell whether he's going to tell me the truth. The sun is streaming in through the open window, the birds are chirping, and yet somehow, why it is I don't know, the room seems more barren and poverty-stricken than ever. The floor is slathered with lather, and on the rack there are the two dirty towels which are never changed. And somehow Carl isn't changed either, and that puzzles me more than anything.

This morning the whole world ought to be changed, for bad or good, but changed, radically changed. And yet Carl is standing there lathering his face and not a single detail is altered.

"Sit down ... sit down there on the bed," he says. "You're going to hear everything... but wait first... wait a little." He commences to lather his face again, and then to hone his razor. He even remarks about the water... no hot water again.

"Listen, Carl, I'm on tenterhooks. You can torture me afterward, if you like, but tell me now, tell me one thing ... was it good or bad?"

He turns away from the mirror with brush in hand and gives me a strange smile. "Wait! I'm going to tell you everything...."

"That means it was a failure."

"No," he says, drawing out his words. "It wasn't a failure, and it wasn't a success either.... By the way, did you fix it up for me at the office? What did you tell them?"

I see it's no use trying to pull it out of him. When he gets good and ready he'll tell me. Not before. I lie back on the bed, silent as a clam. He goes on shaving.

Suddenly, apropos of nothing at all, he begins to talk—disconnectedly at first, and then more and more clearly, emphatically, resolutely. It's a struggle to get it out, but he seems determined to relate everything; he acts as if he were getting something off his conscience. He even reminds me of the look he gave me as he was going up the elevator shaft. He dwells on that lingeringly, as though to imply that everything were contained in that last moment, as though, if he had the power to alter things, he would never have put foot outside the elevator.

She was in her dressing sack when he called. There was a bucket of champagne on the dresser. The room was rather dark and her voice was lovely. He gives me all the details about the room, the champagne, how the *garcon* opened it, the noise it made, the way her dressing sack rustled when she came forward to greet him—he tells me everything but what I want to hear.

It was about eight when he called on her. At eight-thirty he was nervous, thinking about the job. "It was about nine when I called you, wasn't it?" he says.

"Yes, about that."

"I was nervous, see...."

"I know that. Go on...."

I don't know whether to believe him or not, especially after those letters we concoct-ed. I don't even know whether I've heard him accurately, because what he's telling me sounds utterly fantastic. And yet it sounds true too, knowing the sort of guy he is. And then I remember his voice over the telephone, that strange mixture of fright and jubila-tion. But why isn't he more jubilant now? He keeps smiling all the time, smiling like a rosy little bedbug that has had its fill. "It was nine o'clock," he says once again, "when I called you up, wasn't it?" I nod my head wearily. Yes, it was nine o'clock. He is certain now that it was nine o'clock because he remembers having taken out his watch. Anyway, when he looked at his watch again it was ten o'clock. At ten o'clock she was lying on the divan with her boobies in her hands. That's the way he gives it to me—in driblets. At eleven o'clock it was all settled; they were going to run away, to Borneo. Fuck the husband! one never loved him anyway. She would never have written the first letter if the husband wasn't old and passionless. "And then she says to me: 'But listen, dear, how do you know you won't get tired of me?' "

At this I burst out laughing. This sounds preposterous to me, I can't help it.

"And you said?"

"What did you expect me to say? I said: 'How could anyone ever grow tired of *you?*'"

And then he describes to me what happened after that, how he bent down and kissed her breasts, and how, after he had kissed them fervidly, he stuffed them back into her cor-sage, or whatever it is they call these things. And after that another *coupe* of champagne.

Around midnight the *garcon* arrives with beer and sandwiches—caviar sandwiches. And all the while, so he says, he has been dying to take a leak. He had one hard on, but it faded out. All the while his bladder is fit to burst, but he imagines, the cute little prick that he is, that the situation calls for delicacy.

At one-thirty she's for hiring a carriage and driving through the Bois. He has only one thought in his head—how to take a leak? "I love you ... I adore you," he says. "I'll go anywhere you say—Istanbul, Singapore, Honolulu. Only I must go now.... It's getting late."

He tells me all this in his dirty little room, with the sun pouring in and the birds chirping away Like mad. I don't yet know whether she was beautiful or not. He doesn't know himself, the imbecile. He rather thinks she wasn't. The room was dark and then there was the champagne and his nerves all frazzled.

"But you ought to know something about her—if this isn't all a goddamned lie!"

"Wait a minute," he says. "Wait... let me think! No, she wasn't beautiful. I'm sure of that now. She had a streak of gray hair over her forehead ... I remember that. But that wouldn't be so bad—I had almost forgotten it you see. No, it was her arms—they were thin... they were thin and brittle." He begins to pace back and forth.—Suddenly he stops dead. "If she were only ten years younger!" he exclaims. "If she were ten years younger I might overlook the streak of gray hair... and even the brittle arms. But she's too old. You see, with a cunt like that every year counts now. She won't be just one year older next year—she'll be ten years older. Another year hence and she'll be twenty years older. And I'll be getting younger looking all the time—at least for another five years...."

"But how did it end?" I interrupt.

"That's just it... it didn't end. I promised to see her Tuesday around five o'clock. That's bad, you know! There were lines in her face which will look much worse in daylight. I suppose she wants me to fuck her Tuesday. Fucking in the daytime—you don't do it with a cunt like that. Especially in a hotel like that. I'd rather do it on my night off ... but Tuesday's not my night off. And that's not all. I promised her a letter in the meantime. How am I going to write her a letter now? I haven't anything to say.... Shit! If only she were ten years younger. Do you think I should go with her... to Borneo or wherever it is she wants to take me? What would I do with a rich cunt like that on my hands? I don't know how to shoot. I am afraid of guns and all that sort of thing. Besides, she'll be wanting me to fuck her night and day... nothing but hunting and fucking all the time ... I can't do it!"

"Maybe it won't be so bad as you think. She'll buy you ties and all sorts of things...."

Maybe you'll come along with us, eh? I told her all about you...."

"Did you tell her I was poor? Did you tell her I needed things?"

I told her everything. Shit, everything would be fine, if she were just a few years younger. She said she was turning forty. That means fifty or sixty. It's like fucking your own mother ... you can't do it... it's impossible."

"But she must have had some attractiveness... you were kissing her breasts, you said."

"Kissing her breasts—what's that? Besides it was dark, I'm telling you."

Putting on his pants a button falls off. "Look at that, will you. It's falling apart, the goddamned suit. I've worn it for seven years now.... I never paid for it either.

It was a good suit once, but it stinks now. And that cunt would buy me suits too, all I wanted most likely. But that's what I don't like, having a woman shell out for me. I never did that in my life. That's *your* idea. I'd rather live alone. Shit, this is a good room isn't it? What's wrong with it? It's a damned sight better than her room, isn't it? I don't like her fine hotel. I'm against hotels like that. I told her so. She said she didn't care where she lived... said she'd come and live with me if I wanted her to. Can you picture her moving in here with her big trunks and her hatboxes and all that crap she drags around with her? She has too many things—too many dresses and bottles and all that. It's like a clinic, her room. If she gets a little scratch on her finger it's serious. And then she has to be massaged and her hair has to be waved and she mustn't eat this and she mustn't eat that. Listen, Joe, she'd be all right if she were just a little younger. You can forgive a young cunt anything. A young cunt doesn't have to have any brains. They're better without brains. But an old cunt, even if she's brilliant, even if she's the most charming woman in the world, nothing makes any difference. A young cunt is an investment; an old cunt is a dead loss. All they can do for you is buy you things. But that doesn't put meat on their arms or juice between the legs. She isn't bad, Irene. In fact, I think you'd like her. With you it's different. You don't have to fuck her. You can afford to like her. Maybe you wouldn't like all those dresses and the bottles and what not, but you could be tolerant. She wouldn't bore you, that I can tell you. She's even interesting, I might say. But she's withered. Her breasts are all right yet—but her arms! I told her I'd bring you around some day. I talked a lot about you.... I didn't know what to say to her. Maybe you'd like her, especially when she's dressed. I don't know...."

"Listen, she's rich, you say? I'll like her! I don't care how old she is, so long as she's not a hag...."

"She's not a hag! What are you talking about? She's charming, I tell you. She talks well. She looks well too... only her arms...."

"All right, if that's how it is, *I'll* fuck her—if you don't want to. Tell her that. Be subtle about it, though. With a woman like that you've got to do things slowly. You bring me around and let things work out for themselves. Praise the shit out of me. Act jealous like.... Shit, maybe we'll fuck her together ... and we'll go places and we'll eat together ... and we'll drive and hunt and wear nice things. If she wants to go to Borneo let her take us along. I don't know how to shoot either, but that doesn't matter. She doesn't care about that either. She just wants to be fucked that's all. You're talking about her arms all the time. You don't have to look at her arms all the time, do you? Look at this bedspread! Look at the mirror! Do you call this living? Do you want to go on being delicate and live like a louse all your life? You can't even pay your hotel bill... and you've got a job too. This is no way to live. I don't care if she's seventy years old—it's better than this...."

"Listen, Joe, you fuck her for me... then everything'll be fine. Maybe I'll fuck her once in a while too... on my night off. It's four days now since I've had a good shit. There's something sticking to me, like grapes...."

"You've got the piles, that's what."

"My hair's falling out too... and I ought to see the dentist. I feel as though I were falling apart. I told her what a good guy you are.... You'll do things for me, eh? You're not too delicate, eh? If we go to Borneo I won't have hemorrhoids any more. Maybe I'll develop something else... something worse ... fever perhaps ... or cholera. Shit, it's better to die of a good disease like that than to piss your life away on a newspaper with grapes up your ass and buttons falling off your pants. I'd like to be rich, even if it were only for a week, and then go to a hospital with a good disease, a fatal one, and have flowers in the room and nurses dancing around and telegrams coming. They take good care of you if you're rich. They wash you with cotton batting and they comb your hair for you. Shit, I know all that. Maybe I'd be lucky and not die at all. Maybe I'd be a cripple all my life ... maybe I'd be paralyzed and have to sit in a wheelchair. But then I'd be taken care of just the same... even if I had no more money. If you're an invalid—a *real* one—they don't let you starve. And you get a clean bed to lie in ... and they change the towels every day. This way nobody gives a fuck about you, especially if you have a job. They think a man should be happy if he's got a job. What would you rather do—be a cripple all your life, or have a job ... or marry a rich cunt? You'd rather marry a rich cunt, I can see that. You only think about food. But supposing you married her and then you couldn't get a hard on any more—that happens sometimes—what would you do then? You'd be at her mercy. You'd have to eat out of her hand, like a little poodle dog. You'd like that, would you? Or maybe you don't think of those things? *I think of everything.* I think of the suits I'd pick out and the places

I'd like to go to, but I also think of the other thing. That's the important thing. What good are the fancy ties and the fine suits if you can't get a hard on any more? You couldn't even betray her—because she'd be on your heels all the time. No, the best thing would be to marry her and then get a disease right away. Only not syphilis. Cholera, let's say, or yellow fever. So that if a miracle did happen and your life was spared you'd be a cripple for the rest of your days. Then you wouldn't have to worry about fucking her any more, and you wouldn't have to worry about the rent either. She'd probably buy you a fine wheelchair with rubber tires and all sorts of levers and what not. You might even be able to use your hands—I mean enough to be able to write. Or you could have a secretary, for that matter. That's it—that's the best solution for a writer. What does a guy want with his arms and legs? He doesn't need arms and legs to write with. He needs security ... peace... protection. All those heroes who parade in wheelchairs—it's too bad they're not writers. If you could only be sure, when you go to war, that you'd have only your legs blown off ... if you could be sure of that I'd say let's have a war tomorrow. I wouldn't give a fuck about the medals— they could keep the medals. All I'd want is a good wheelchair and three meals a day. Then I'd give them something to read, those pricks."

The following day, at one-thirty, I call on Van Norden. It's his day off, or rather his night off. He has left word with Carl that I am to help him move today.

I find him in a state of unusual depression. He hasn't slept a wink all night, he tells me. There's something on his mind, something that's eating him up. It isn't long before I discover what it is; he's been waiting impatiently for me to arrive in order to spill it.

"That guy," he begins, meaning Carl, "that guy's an artist. He described every detail minutely. He told it to me with such accuracy that I know it's all a goddamned lie... but I can't dismiss it from my mind. You know how my mind works!"

He interrupts himself to inquire if Carl has told me the whole story. There isn't the least suspicion in his mind that Carl may have told me one thing and him another. He seems to think that the story was invented expressly to torture him. He doesn't seem to mind so much that it's a fabrication. It's the "images" as he says, which Carl left in his mind, that get him. The images are real, even if the whole story is false. And besides, the fact that there actually is a rich cunt on the scene and that Carl actually paid her a visit, that's undeniable. What actually happened is secondary; he takes it for granted that Carl put the boots to her. But what drives him desperate is the thought that what Carl has described to him might have been *possible.*

"It's just like that guy," he says, "to tell me he put it to her six or seven times. I know that's a lot of shit and I don't mind that so much, but when he tells me that she hired a carriage and drove him out to the Bois and that they used the husband's fur coat for a blanket, that's too much. I suppose he told you about the chauffeur waiting respectfully ... and listen, did he tell you how the engine purred all the time? Jesus, he built that up won-derfully. It's just like him to think of a detail like that... it's one of those little details which makes a thing psychologically real... you can't get it out of your head afterward. And he tells it to me so smoothly, so naturally.... I wonder, did he think it up in advance or did it just pop out of his head like that, spontaneously? He's such a cute little liar you can't walk away from him... it's like he's writing you a letter, one of those flowerpots that he makes overnight. I don't understand how a guy can write such letters ... I don't get the mentality behind it... it's a form of masturbation ... what do you think?"

But before I have an opportunity to venture an opinion, or even to laugh in his face, Van Norden goes on with his monologue.

"Listen, I suppose he told you everything ... did he tell you how he stood on the balcony in the moonlight and kissed her? That sounds banal when you repeat it, but the way that guy describes it... I can just see the little prick standing there with the woman in his arms and already he's writing another letter to her, another flowerpot about the roof tops and all that crap he steals from his French authors. That guy never says a thing that's original, I found that out. You have to get a clue like ... find out whom he's been reading lately ... and it's hard to do that because he's so damned secretive. Listen, if I didn't know that you went there with him, I wouldn't believe that the woman existed. A guy like that could write letters to himself. And yet he's lucky... he's so damned tiny, so frail, so romantic looking, that women fall for him now and then... they sort of adopt him... they feel sorry for him, I guess. And some cunts like to receive flowerpots ... it makes them feel important.... But this woman's an intelligent woman, so he says. You ought to know... you've seen her letters. What do you suppose a woman like that saw in him? I can understand her falling for the letters... but how do you suppose she felt when she *saw* him?

"But listen, all that's beside the point. What I'm getting at is the way he tells it to me. You know how he embroiders things... well, after that scene on the balcony—he gives me that like an hors d'oeuvre, you know—after that, so he says, they went inside and he unbuttoned her pajamas. What are you smiling for? Was he shitting me about that?"

"No, no! You're giving it to me exactly as he told me. Go ahead..."

"After that"—here Van Nor den has to smile himself—"after that, mind you, he tells me how she sat in the chair with her legs up ... not a stitch on ... and he's sitting on the floor looking up at her, telling her how beautiful she looks... did he tell you that she looked like a Matisse? ... Wait a minute ... I'd like to remember exactly what he said. He had some cute little phrase there about an odalisque... what the hell's an odalisque anyway? He said it in French, that's why it's hard to remember the fucking thing ... but it sounded good. It sounded just like the sort of thing he might say. And she probably thought it was original with him ... I suppose she thinks he's a poet or something. But listen, all this is nothing ... I make allowance for his imagination. It's what happened after that that drives me crazy. All night long I've been tossing about, playing with these images he left in my mind. I can't get it out of my head. It sounds so real to me that if it didn't happen I could strangle the bastard. A guy has no right to invent things like that. Or else he's diseased....

"What I'm getting at is that moment when, he says, he got down on his knees and with those two skinny fingers of his he spread her cunt open. You remember that? He says she was sitting there with her legs dangling over the arms of the chair and suddenly, he says, he got an inspiration. This was after he had given her a couple of lays already... after he had made that little spiel about Matisse. He gets down on his knees—*get this!*—and with his two fingers ... just the tips of them, mind you ... he opens the little petals ... *squish-squish* ... just like that. A sticky little sound ... almost inaudible. *Squish-squish!* Jesus, I've been hearing it all night long! And then he says—as if that weren't enough for me—then he tells me he buried his head in her muff. And when he did that, so help me Christ, if she didn't swing her legs around his neck and lock him there. *That finished me!* Imagine it! Imagine a fine, sensitive woman like that swinging her legs around *his neck!* There's something poisonous about it. It's so fantastic that it sounds convincing. If he had only told me about the champagne and the ride in the Bois and even that scene on the balcony I could have dismissed it. But this thing is so incredible that it doesn't sound like a he any more. I can't believe that he ever read anything like that anywhere, and I can't see what could have put the idea into his head unless there was some truth in it. With a little prick like that, you know, anything can happen. He may not have fucked her at all, but she may have let him diddle her ... you never know with these rich cunts what they might expect you to do...." When he finally pulls himself out of bed and starts to shave the afternoon is already well advanced. I've finally succeeded in switching his mind to other things, to the moving principally. The maid comes in to see if he's ready—he's supposed to have vacated the room by noon. He's just in the act of slipping into his trousers. I'm a little surprised that he doesn't excuse himself, or turn away. Seeing him standing there nonchalantly buttoning his fly as he gives her orders I begin to titter. "Don't mind her," he says, throwing her a look of supreme contempt, "she's just a big sow. Give her a pinch in the ass, if you like. She won't say anything." And then addressing her, in English, he says. "Come here, you bitch, put your hand on this!" At this I can't restrain myself any longer. I burst out laughing, a fit of hysterical laughter which infects the maid also, though she doesn't know what it's all about. The maid commences to take down the pictures and the photographs, mostly of himself, which line the walls. *"You,"* he says, jerking his thumb, "come here! Here's something to remember me by"—ripping a photograph off the wall—"when I go you can wipe your ass with it. See," he says, turning to me, "she's a dumb bitch. She wouldn't look any more intelligent if I said it in French." The maid stands there with her mouth open; she is evidently convinced that he is cracked. "Hey!" he yells at her as if she were hard of hearing. "Hey, *you!* Yes, *you!* Like this...!" and he takes the photograph, his own photograph, and wipes his ass with it. *"Comme ça!* Savvy? You've got to draw pictures for her," he says, thrusting his lower lip forward in absolute disgust.

He watches her helplessly as she throws his things into the big valises. "Here, put these in too," he says, handing her a toothbrush and the douche bag. Half of his belongings are lying on the floor. The valises are crammed full and there is nowhere to put the paintings and the books and the bottles that are half empty. "Sit down a minute," he says. "We've got plenty of time. We've got to think this thing out. If you hadn't come around I'd never have gotten out of here. You see how helpless I am. Don't let me forget to take the bulbs out... they belong to me. That wastebasket belongs to me too. They expect you to live like pigs, these bastards." The maid has gone downstairs to get some twine.... "Wait 'til you see ... she'll charge me for the twine even if it's only three sous. They wouldn't sew a button on your pants here without charging for it. The lousy, dirty scroungers!" He takes a bottle of Calvados from the mantelpiece and nods to me to grab the other. "No use carrying these to the new place. Let's finish them off now. But don't give *her* a drink! That bastard, I wouldn't leave her a piece of toilet paper. I'd like to ruin the joint before I go. Listen... piss on the floor, if you like. I wish I could take a crap in the bureau drawer." He feels so utterly disgusted with himself and everything else that he doesn't know what to do by way of venting his feelings. He walks over to the bed with the bottle in his hand and pulling back the covers he sprinkles Calvados over the mattress. Not content with that he digs his heel into the mattress. Unfortunately there's no mud on his heels. Finally he takes the sheet and cleans his shoes with it. "That'll give them something to do," he mutters vengefully. Then, taking a good swig, he throws his head back and gargles his throat, and after he's gargled it good and proper he spits it out on the mirror. "There, you cheap bastards! Wipe that off when I go!" He walks back and forth mumbling to himself. Seeing his torn socks lying on the floor he picks them up and tears them to bits. The paintings enrage him too. He picks one up—a portrait of himself done by some Lesbian he knew and he puts his foot through it. "That bitch! You know what she had the nerve to ask me? She asked me to turn over my cunts to her after I was through with them. She never gave me a sou for writing her up. She thought I honestly admired her work. I wouldn't have gotten that painting out of her if I hadn't promised to fix her up with that cunt from Minnesota. She was nuts about her ... used to follow us around like a dog in heat... we couldn't get rid of the bitch! She bothered the life out of me. I got so that I was almost afraid to bring a cunt up here for fear that she'd bust in on me. I used to creep up here like a burglar and lock the door behind me as soon as I got inside.... She and that Georgia cunt—they drive me nuts. The one is always in heat and the other is always hungry. I hate fucking a woman who's hungry. It's like you push a feed inside her and then you push it out again.... Jesus, that reminds me of something... where did I put that blue ointment? That's important. Did you ever have those things? It's worse than having a dose. And I don't know where I got them from either. I've had so many women up here in the last week or so I've lost track of them. Funny too, because they all smelled so fresh. But you know how it is...."

The maid has piled his things up on the sidewalk. The *patron* looks on with a surly air. When everything has been loaded into the taxi there is only room for one of us inside. As soon as we commence to roll Van Norden gets out a newspaper and starts bundling up his pots and pans; in the new place all cooking is strictly forbidden. By the time we reach our destination all his luggage has come undone; it wouldn't be quite so embarrassing if the madam had not stuck her head out of the doorway just as we rolled up. "My God!" she exclaims, "what in the devil is all this? What does it mean?" Van Norden is so intimidated that he can think of nothing more to say than *"C'est moi... c'est moi, madame!"* And turning to me he mumbles savagely: "That cluck! Did you notice her face? She's going to make it hard for me."

The hotel lies back of a dingy passage and forms a rectangle very much on the order of a modern penitentiary. The *bureau* is large and gloomy, despite the brilliant reflections from the tile walls. There are bird cages hanging in the windows and little enamel signs everywhere begging the guests in an obsolete language not to do this and not to forget that. It is almost immaculately clean but absolutely poverty-stricken, threadbare, woebegone. The upholstered chairs are held together with wired thongs; they remind one unpleasantly of the electric chair. The room he is going to occupy is on the fifth floor. As we climb the stairs Van Norden informs me that Maupassant once lived here. And in the same breath remarks that there is a peculiar odor in the hall. On the fifth floor a few windowpanes are missing; we stand a moment gazing at the tenants across the court. It is getting toward dinner time and people are straggling back to their rooms with that weary, dejected air which comes from earning a living honestly. Most of the windows are wide open: the dingy rooms have the appearance of so many yawning mouths. The occupants of the rooms are yawning too, or else scratching themselves. They move about listlessly and apparently without much purpose; they might just as well be lunatics.

As we turn down the corridor toward room 57, a door suddenly opens in front of us and an old hag with matted hair and the eyes of a maniac peers out. She startles us so that we stand transfixed. For a full minute the three of us stand there powerless to move or even to make an intelligent gesture. Back of the old hag I can see a kitchen table and on it lies a baby all undressed, a puny little brat no bigger than a plucked chicken. Finally the old one picks up a slop pail by her side and makes a move forward. We stand aside to let her pass and as the door closes behind her the baby lets out a piercing scream. It is room 56, and between *56* and 57 is the toilet where the old hag is emptying her slops.

Ever since we have mounted the stairs Van Norden has kept silence. But his looks are eloquent. When he opens the door of 57 I have for a fleeting moment the sensation of going mad. A huge mirror covered with green gauze and tipped at an angle of 45 degrees hangs directly opposite the entrance over a baby carriage which is filled with books. Van Norden doesn't even crack a smile; instead he walks nonchalantly over to the baby carriage and picking up a book begins to skim it through, much as a man would enter the public library and go unthinkingly to the rack nearest to hand. And perhaps this would not seem so ludicrous to me if I had not espied at the same time a pair of handle bars resting in the corner. They look so absolutely peaceful and contented, as if they had been dozing there for years, that suddenly it seems to me as if we had been standing in this room, in exactly this position, for an incalculably long time, that it was a pose we had struck in a dream from which we never emerged, a dream which the least gesture, the wink of an eye even, will shatter. But more remarkable still is the remembrance that suddenly floats up of an actual dream which occurred only the other night, a dream in which I saw Van Norden in just such a corner as is occupied now by the handle bars, only instead of the handle bars there was a woman crouching with her legs drawn up. I see him standing over the woman with that alert, eager look in his eye which comes when he wants something badly. The street in which this is going on is blurred—only the angle made by the two walls is clear, and the cowering figure of the woman. I can see him going at her in that quick, animal way of his, reckless of what's going on about him, determined only to have his way. And a look in his eyes as though to say—"you can kill me afterwards, but just let me get it in... I've got to get it in!" And there he is, bent over her, their heads knocking against the wall, he has such a tremendous erection that it's simply impossible to get it in her. Suddenly, with that disgusted air which he knows so well how to summon, he picks himself up and adjusts his clothes. He is about to walk away when suddenly he notices that his penis is lying on the sidewalk. It is about the size of a sawed-off broomstick. He picks it up nonchalantly and slings it under his arm. As he walks off I notice two huge bulbs, like tulip bulbs, dangling from the end of the broomstick, and I can hear him muttering to himself "flowerpots ... flowerpots."

The *garcon* arrives panting and sweating. Van Norden looks at him uncomprehendingly. The madam now marches in and, walking straight up to Van Norden, she takes the book out of his hand, thrusts it in the baby carriage, and, without saying a word, wheels the baby carriage into the hallway.

"This is a bughouse," says Van Norden, smiling distressedly. It is such a faint, indescribable smile that for a moment the dream feeling comes back and it seems to me that we are standing at the end of a long corridor at the end of which is a corrugated mirror. And down this corridor, swinging his distress like a dingy lantern, Van Norden staggers, staggers in and out as here and there a door opens and a hand yanks him, or a hoof pushes him out. And the further off he wanders the more lugubrious is his distress; he wears it like a lantern which the cyclists hold between their teeth on a night when the pavement is wet and slippery. In and out of the dingy rooms he wanders, and when he sits down the chair collapses, when he opens his valise there is only a toothbrush inside. In every room there is a mirror before which he stands attentively and chews his rage, and from the constant chewing, from the grumbling and mumbling and the muttering and cursing his jaws have gotten unhinged and they sag badly and, when he rubs his beard, pieces of his jaw crumble away and he's so disgusted with himself that he stamps on his own jaw, grinds it to bits with his big heels.

Meanwhile the luggage is being hauled in. And things begin to look crazier even than before—particularly when he attaches his exerciser to the bedstead and begins his Sandow exercises. "I like this place," he says, smiling at the *garcon*. He takes his coat and vest off. The *garcon* is watching him with a puzzled air; he has a valise in one hand and the douche bag in the other. I'm standing apart in the antechamber holding the mirror with the green gauze. Not a single object seems to possess a practical use. The antechamber itself seems useless, a sort of vestibule to a barn. It is exactly the same sort of sensation which I get when I enter the Comedie-Frangaise or the Palais-Royal Theatre; it is a world of bric-a-brac, of trap doors, of arms and busts and waxed floors, of candelabras and men in armor, of statues without eyes and love letters lying in glass cases. Something is going on, but it makes no sense; it's like finishing the half-empty bottle of Calvados because there's no room in the valise.

Climbing up the stairs, as I said a moment ago, he had mentioned the fact that Maupassant used to live here. The coincidence seems to have made an impression upon him. He would like to believe that it was in this very room that Maupassant gave birth to some of those gruesome tales on which his reputation rests. "They lived like pigs, those poor bastards," he says. We are sitting at the round table in a pair of comfortable old armchairs that have been trussed up with thongs and braces; the bed is right beside us, so close indeed that we can put our feet on it. The *armoire* stands in a corner behind us, also conveniently within reach. Van Norden has emptied his dirty wash on the table; we sit there with our feet buried in his dirty socks and shirts and smoke contentedly. The sordid-ness of the place seems to have worked a spell on him: he is content here. When I get up to switch on the light he suggests that we play a game of cards before going out to eat. And so we sit there by the window, with the dirty wash strewn over the floor and the Sandow exerciser hanging from the chandelier, and we play a few rounds of two-handed pinochle. Van Norden has put away his pipe and packed a wad of snuff on the underside of his lower lip. Now and then he spits out of the window, big healthy gobs of brown juice which resound with a smack on the pavement below. He seems content now.

"In America," he says, "you wouldn't dream of living in a joint like this. Even when I was on the bum I slept in better rooms than this. But here it seems natural—it's like the books you read. If I ever go back there I'll forget all about this life, just like you forget a bad dream. I'll probably take up the old life again just where I left off ... if I ever get back. Sometimes I lie in bed dreaming about the past and it's so vivid to me that I have to shake myself in order to realize where I am. Especially when I have a woman beside me; a woman can set me off better than anything. That's all I want of them—to forget myself. Sometimes I get so lost in my reveries that I can't remember the name of the cunt or where I picked her up. That's funny, eh? It's good to have a fresh warm body beside you when you wake up in the morning. It gives you a clean feeling. You get spiritual like... until they start pulling that mushy crap about love et cetera. Why do all these cunts talk about love so much, can you tell me that? A good lay isn't enough for them apparently... they want your soul too...."

Now this word soul, which pops up frequently in Van Norden's soliloquies, used to have a droll effect upon me at first. Whenever I heard the word soul from his lips I would get hysterical; somehow it seemed like a false coin, more particularly because it was usually accompanied by a gob of brown juice which left a trickle down the corner of his mouth. And as I never hesitated to laugh in his face it happened invariably that when this little word bobbed up Van Norden would pause just long enough for me to burst into a cackle and then, as if nothing had happened, he would resume his monologue, repeating the word more and more frequently and each time with a more caressing emphasis. It was the soul of him that women were trying to possess—that he made clear to me. He has explained it over and over again, but he comes back to it afresh each time like a paranoiac to his obsession. In a sense Van Norden is mad, of that I'm convinced. His one fear is to be left alone, and this fear is so deep and so persistent that even when he is on top of a woman, even when he has welded himself to her, he cannot escape the prison which he has created for himself. "I try all sorts of things," he explains to me. "I even count sometimes, or I begin to think of a problem in philosophy, but it doesn't work. It's like I'm two people, and one of them is watching me all the time. I get so goddamned mad at myself that I could kill myself... and in a way, that's what I do every time I have an orgasm. For one second like I obliterate myself. There's not even one me then... there's nothing... not even the cunt. It's like receiving communion. Honest, I mean that. For a few seconds afterward I have a fine spiritual glow... and maybe it would continue that way indefinitely— how can you tell?—if it weren't for the fact that there's a woman beside you and then the douche bag and the water running... all those little details that make you desperately self-conscious, desperately lonely. And for that one moment of freedom you have to listen to all that love crap ... it drives me nuts sometimes ... I want to kick them out immediately ... I do now and then. But that doesn't keep them away. They like it, in fact. The less you notice them the more they chase after you. There's something perverse about women... they're all masochists at heart."

"But what is it you want of a woman, then?" I demand.

He begins to mold his hands; his lower lip droops. He looks completely frustrated. When eventually he succeeds in stammering out a few broken phrases it's with the conviction that behind his words lies an overwhelming futility. "I want to be able to surrender myself to a woman," he blurts out. "I want her to take me out of myself. But to do that, she's got to be better than I am; she's got to have a mind, not just a cunt. She's got to make me believe that I need her, that I can't live without her. Find me a cunt like that, will you? If you could do that I'd give you my job. I wouldn't care then what happened to me: I wouldn't need a job or friends or books or anything. If she could only make me believe that there was something more important on earth than myself. Jesus, I hate myself! But I hate these bastardly cunts even more—because they're none of them any good.

"You think I like myself," he continues. "That shows how little you know about me. I know I'm a great guy.... I wouldn't have these problems if there weren't something to me. But what eats me up is that I can't express myself. People think I'm a cunt-chaser. That's how shallow they are, these high brows who sit on the *terrasse* all day chewing the psychologic cud.... That's not so bad, eh—psychologic cud? Write it down for me. I'll use it in my column next week.... By the way, did you ever read Stekel? Is he any good? It looks like nothing but case histories to me. I wish to Christ I could get up enough nerve to visit an analyst ... a good one, I mean. I don't want to see these little shysters with goatees and frock coats, like your friend Boris. How do you manage to tolerate those guys? Don't they bore you stiff? You talk to anybody, I notice. You don't give a goddamn. Maybe you're right. I wish I weren't so damned critical. But these dirty little Jews who hang around the Dome, Jesus, they give me the creeps. They sound just like textbooks. If I could talk to you every day maybe I could get things off my chest. You're a good listener. I know you don't give a damn about me, but you're patient. And you don't have any theories to exploit. I suppose you put it all down afterward in that notebook of yours. Listen, I don't mind what you say about me, but don't make me out to be a cunt-chaser—it's too simple. Some day I'll write a book about myself, about my thoughts. I don't mean just a piece of introspective analysis ... I mean that I'll lay myself down on the operating table and I'll expose my whole guts... every goddamned thing. Has anybody ever done that before?—What the hell are you smiling at? Does it sound naif?"

I'm smiling because whenever we touch on the subject of this book which he is going to write some day things assume an incongruous aspect. He has only to say "my book" and immediately the world shrinks to the private dimensions of Van Norden and Co. The book must be absolutely original, absolutely perfect. That is why, among other things, it is impossible for him to get started on it. As soon as he gets an idea he begins to question it. He remembers that Dostoevski used it, or Hamsun, or somebody else. "I'm not saying that I want to be better than them, but I want to be different," he explains. And so, instead of tackling his book, he reads one author after another in order to make absolutely certain that he is not going to tread on their private property. And the more he reads the more disdainful he becomes. None of them are satisfying; none of them arrive at that degree of perfection which he has imposed on himself. And forgetting completely that he has not written as much as a chapter he talks about them condescendingly, quite as though there existed a shelf of books bearing his name, books which everyone is familiar with and the titles of which it is therefore superfluous to mention. Though he has never overtly lied about this fact, nevertheless it is obvious that the people whom he buttonholes in order to air his private philosophy, his criticism, and his grievances, take it for granted that behind his loose remarks there stands a solid body of work. Especially the young and foolish virgins whom he lures to his room on the pretext of reading to them his poems, or on the still better pretext of asking their advice. Without the least feeling of guilt or self-consciousness he will hand them a piece of soiled paper on which he has scribbled a few lines—the basis of a new poem, as he puts it—and with absolute seriousness demand of them an honest expression of opinion. As they usually have nothing to give by way of comment, wholly bewildered as they are by the utter senselessness of the lines, Van Norden seizes the occasion to expound to them his view of art, a view, needless to say, which is spontaneously created to suit the event. So expert has he become in this role that the transition from Ezra Pound's cantos to the bed is made as simply and naturally as a modulation from one key to another; in fact, if it were not made there would be a discord, which is what happens now and then when he makes a mistake as regards those nitwits whom he refers to as "push-overs." Naturally, constituted as he is, it is with reluctance that he refers to these fatal errors of judgment. But when he does bring himself to confess to an error of this kind it is with absolute frankness; in fact, he seems to derive a perverse pleasure in dwelling upon his inaptitude. There is one woman, for example, whom he has been trying to make for almost ten years now—first in America, and finally here in Paris. It is the only person of the opposite sex with whom he has a cordial, friendly relationship.

They seem not only to like each other, but to understand each other. At first it seemed to me that if he could really make this creature his problem might be solved. All the elements for a successful union were there—except the fundamental one. Bessie was almost as unusual in her way as himself. She had as little concern about giving herself to a man as she has about the dessert which follows the meal. Usually she singled out the object of her choice and made the proposition herself. She was not bad-looking, nor could one say that she was good-looking either. She had a fine body, that was the chief thing—and she liked it, as they say.

They were so chummy, these two, that sometimes, in order to gratify her curiosity (and also in the vain hope of inspiring her by his prowess), Van Norden would arrange to hide her in his closet during one of his seances. After is was over Bessie would emerge from her hiding place and they would discuss the matter casually, that is to say, with an almost total indifference to everything except "technique." Technique was one of her favorite terms, at least in those discussions which I was privileged to enjoy. "What's wrong with my technique?" he would say. And Bessie would answer: "You're too crude. If you ever expect to make me you've got to become more subtle."

There was such a perfect understanding between them, as I say, that often when I called for Van Norden at one-thirty, I would find Bessie sitting on the bed, the covers thrown back and Van Norden inviting her to stroke his penis... "just a few silken strokes," he would say, "so as I'll have the courage to get up." Or else he would urge her to blow on it, or failing that, he would grab hold of himself and shake it like a dinner bell, the two of them laughing fit to die. "I'll never make this bitch," he would say. "She has no respect for me. That's what I get for taking her into my confidence." And then abruptly he might add: "What do you make of that blonde I showed you yesterday?" Talking to Bessie, of course. And Bessie would jeer at him, telling him he had no taste. "Aw, don't give me that line," he would say. And then playfully, perhaps for the thousandth time, because by now it had become a standing joke between them—"Listen, Bessie, what about a quick lay? Just one little lay ... no." And when this had passed off in the usual manner he would add, in the same tone: "Well, what about *him?* Why don't you give *him* a lay?"

The whole point about Bessie was that she couldn't, or just wouldn't, regard herself as a lay. She talked about passion, as if it were a brand new word. She was passionate about things, even a little thing like a lay. She had to put her soul into it.

"I get passionate too sometimes," Van Norden would say.

"Oh, *you,*" says Bessie. "You're just a worn-out satyr. You don't know the meaning of passion. When you get an erection you think you're passionate."

"All right, maybe it's not passion... bur you can't get passionate without having an erection, that's true isn't it?"

All this about Bessie, and the other women whom he drags to his room day in and out, occupies my thoughts as we walk to the restaurant. I have adjusted myself so well to his monologues that without interrupting my own reveries I make whatever comment is required automatically, the moment I hear his voice die out. It is a duet, and like most duets moreover in that one listens attentively only for the signal which announces the advent of one's own voice. As it is his night off, and as I have promised to keep him company, I have already dulled myself to his queries. I know that before the evening is over I shall be thoroughly exhausted; if I am lucky, that is, if I can worm a few francs out of him on some pretext or other, I will duck him the moment he goes to the toilet. But he knows

my propensity for slipping away, and, instead of being insulted, he simply provides against
the possibility by guarding his sous. If I ask him for money to buy cigarettes he insists on
going with me to purchase them. He will not be left alone, not for a second. Even when
he has succeeded in grabbing off a woman, even then he is terrified to be left alone with
her. If it were possible he would have me sit in the room while he puts on the performance. It would be like asking me to wait while he took a shave.

On his night off Van Norden generally manages to have at least fifty francs in his
pocket, a circumstance which does not prevent him from making a touch whenever he
encounters a prospect. "Hello," he says, "give me twenty francs ... I need it." He has a way
of looking panic-stricken at the same time. And if he meets with a rebuff he becomes
insulting. "Well, you can buy a drink at least." And when he gets his drink he says more
graciously—"Listen give me five francs then... give me *two* francs...." We go from bar to
bar looking for a little excitement and always accumulating a few more francs.

At the Coupole we stumble into a drunk from the newspaper. One of the upstairs
guys. There's just been an accident at the office, he informs us. One of the proofreaders
fell down the elevator shaft. Not expected to live.

At first Van Norden is shocked, deeply shocked. But when he learns that it was
Peckover, the Englishman, he looks relieved. "The poor bastard," he says, "he's better off
dead than alive. He just got his false teeth the other day too...."

The allusion to the false teeth moves the man upstairs to tears. He relates in a slobbery way a little incident connected with the accident. He is upset about it, more upset
about this little incident than about the catastrophe itself. It seems that Peckover, when he
hit the bottom of the shaft, regained consciousness before anyone could reach him.
Despite the fact that his legs were broken and his ribs busted, he had managed to rise to
all fours and grope about for his false teeth. In the ambulance he was crying out in his
delirium for the teeth he had lost. The incident was pathetic and ludicrous at the same
time. The guy from upstairs hardly knew whether to laugh or to weep as he related it. It
was a delicate moment because with a drunk like that, one false move and he'd crash a bottle over your skull. He had never been particularly friendly with Peckover—as a matter of
fact, he had scarcely ever set foot in the proofreading department: there was an invisible
wall like between the guys upstairs and the guys down below. But now, since he had felt
the touch of death, he wanted to display his comradeship. He wanted to weep, if possible,
to show that he was a regular guy. And Joe and I, who knew Peckover well and who knew
also that he wasn't worth a good goddamn, even a few tears, we felt annoyed with this
drunken sentimentality. We wanted to tell him so too, but with a guy like that you can't
afford to be honest; you have to buy a wreath and go to the funeral and pretend that you're
miserable. And you have to congratulate him too for the delicate obituary he's written.
He'll be carrying his delicate little obituary around with him for months, praising the shit
out of himself for the way he handled the situation. We felt all that, Joe and I, without
saying a word to each other. We just stood there and listened with a murderous, silent contempt. And as soon as we could break away we did so; we left him there at the bar blubbering to himself over his Pernod.

Once out of his sight we began to laugh hysterically. The false teeth! No matter what
we said about the poor devil, and we said some good things about him too, we always came
back to the false teeth. There are people in this world who cut such a grotesque figure that
even death renders them ridiculous. And the more horrible the death the more ridiculous

they seem. It's no use trying to invest the end with a little dignity—you have to be a liar and a hypocrite to discover anything tragic in their going. And since we didn't have to put on a false front we could laugh about the incident to our heart's content. We laughed all night about it, and in between times we vented our scorn and disgust for the guys upstairs, the fatheads who were trying to persuade themselves, no doubt, that Peckover was a fine fellow and that his death was a catastrophe. All sorts of funny recollections came to our minds—the semicolons that he overlooked and for which they bawled the piss out of him. They made his life miserable with their fucking little semicolons and the fractions which he always got wrong. They were even going to fire him once because he came to work with a boozy breath. They despised him because he always looked so miserable and because he had eczema and dandruff. He was just a nobody, as far as they were concerned, but, now that he was dead, they would all chip in lustily and buy him a huge wreath and they'd put his name in big type in the obituary column. Anything to throw a little reflection on themselves; they'd make him out to be a *big* shit if they could. But unfortunately, with Peckover, there was little they could invent about him. He was a zero, and even the fact that he was dead wouldn't add a cipher to his name.

"There's only one good aspect to it," says Joe. "You may get his job. And if you have any luck, maybe you'll fall down the elevator shaft and break your neck too. We'll buy you a nice wreath, I promise you that."

Toward dawn we're sitting on the *terrasse* of the Dome. We've forgotten about poor Peckover long ago. We've had a little excitement at the Bal Negre and Joe's mind has slipped back to the eternal preoccupation: cunt. It's at this hour, when his night off is almost concluded, that his restlessness mounts to a fever pitch. He thinks of the women he passed up earlier in the evening and of the steady ones he might have had for the asking, if it weren't that he was fed up with them. He is reminded inevitably of his Georgia cunt—she's been hounding him lately, begging him to take her in, at least until she can find herself a job. "I don't mind giving her a feed once in a while," he says, "but I couldn't take her on as a steady thing... she'd ruin it for my other cunts." What gripes him most about her is that she doesn't put on any flesh. "It's like taking a skeleton to bed with you," he says. "The other night I took her on—out of pity—and what do you think the crazy bitch had done to herself? She had shaved it clean ... not a speck of hair on it. Did you ever have a woman who shaved her twat? It's repulsive, ain't it? And it's funny, too. Sort of mad like. It doesn't look like a twat any more: it's like a dead clam or something." He describes to me how, his curiosity aroused, he got out of bed and searched for his flashlight. "I made her hold it open and I trained the flashlight on it. You should have seen me ... it was comical. I got so worked up about it that I forgot all about her. I never in my life looked at a cunt so seriously. You'd imagine I'd never seen one before. And the more I looked at it the less interesting it became. It only goes to show you there's nothing to it after all, especially when it's shaved. It's the hair that makes it mysterious. That's why a statue leaves you cold. Only once I saw a real cunt on a statue—that was by Rodin. You ought to see it some time ... she has her legs spread wide apart.... I don't think there was any head on it. Just a cunt you might say. Jesus, it looked ghastly. The thing is this—they all look alike. When you look at them with their clothes on you imagine all sorts of things: you give them an individuality like, which they haven't got, of course. There's just a crack there between the legs and you get all steamed up about it—you don't even look at it half the time. You know it's there and all you think about is getting your ramrod inside; it's as though your penis did the thinking for you. It's an illusion! You get all burned up about nothing ... about a crack with hair on it, or without hair. It's so absolutely meaningless that it fascinated me to look at it. I must have studied it for ten minutes or more. When you look at it that way, sort of detached like, you get funny notions in your head. All that mystery about sex and then you discover that it's nothing—just a blank. Wouldn't it be funny if you found a harmonica inside ... or a calendar? But there's nothing there... nothing at all. It's disgusting. It almost drove me mad.... Listen, do you know what I did afterwards? I gave her a quick lay and then I turned my back on her. Yeah, I picked up a book and I read. You can get some thing out of a book, even a bad book ... but a cunt, it's just sheer loss of time...."

It just so happened that as he was concluding his speech a whore gave us the eye. Without the slightest transition he says to me abruptly: "Would you like to give her a tumble? It won't cost much... she'll take the two of us on." And without waiting for a reply he staggers to his feet and goes over to her. In a few minutes he comes back. "It's all fixed," he says. "Finish your beer. She's hungry. There's nothing doing any more at this hour... she'll take the both of us for fifteen francs. We'll go to my room ... it'll be cheaper."

On the way to the hotel the girl is shivering so that we have to stop and buy her a coffee. She's a rather gentle sort of creature and not at all bad to look at. She evidently knows Van Norden, knows there's nothing to expect from him but the fifteen francs. "You haven't got any dough," he says, mumbling to me under his breath. As I haven't a centime in my pocket I don't quite see the point of this, until he bursts out: "For Christ's sake, remember that we're broke. Don't get tenderhearted when we get upstairs. She's going to ask you for a little extra—I know this cunt! I could get her for ten francs, if I wanted to. There's no use spoiling them...."

"*Il est mechant, celui-la,*" she says to me, gathering the drift of his remarks in her dull way.

"*Non, il n'est pas mechant, il est tres gentil.*"

She shakes her head laughingly. "*Je le connais bien, ce type.*" And then she commences a hard luck story, about the hospital and the back rent and the baby in the country. But she doesn't overdo it. She knows that our ears are stopped; but the misery is there inside her, like a stone, and there's no room for any other thoughts. She isn't trying to make an appeal to our sympathies—she's just shifting this big weight inside her from one place to another. I rather like her. I hope to Christ she hasn't got a disease....

In the room she goes about her preparations mechanically. "There isn't a crust of bread about by any chance?" she inquires, as she squats over the *bidet.* Van Norden laughs at this. "Here, take a drink," he says, shoving a bottle at her. She doesn't want anything to drink; her stomach's already on the bum, she complains.

"That's just a line with her," says Van Norden. "Don't let her work on your sympathies. Just the same, I wish she'd talk about something else. How the hell can you get up any passion when you've got a starving cunt on your hands?"

Precisely! We haven't any passion either of us. And as for her, one might as well expect her to produce a diamond necklace as to show a spark of passion. But there's the fifteen francs and something has to be done about it. It's like a state of war: the moment the condition is precipitated nobody thinks about anything but peace, about getting it over with.

And yet nobody has the courage to lay down his arms, to say, "I'm fed up with it... I'm through." No, there's fifteen francs somewhere, which nobody gives a damn about any more and which nobody is going to get in the end anyhow, but the fifteen francs is like the primal cause of things and rather than listen to one's own voice, rather than walk out on the primal cause, one surrenders to the situation, one goes on butchering and butchering and the more cowardly one feels the more heroically does he behave, until a day when the bottom drops out and suddenly all the guns are silenced and the stretcher-bearers pick up the maimed and bleeding heroes and pin medals on their chest. Then one has the rest of his life to think about the fifteen francs. One hasn't any eyes or arms or legs, but he has the consolation of dreaming for the rest of his days about the fifteen francs which everybody has forgotten.

It's exactly like a state of war—I can't get it out of my head. The way she works over me, to blow a spark of passion into me, makes me think what a damned poor soldier I'd be if I was ever silly enough to be trapped like this and dragged to the front. I know for my part that I'd surrender everything, honor included, in order to get out of the mess. I haven't any stomach for it, and that's all there is to it. But she's got her mind set on the fifteen francs and if I don't want to fight about it she's going to make me fight. But you can't put fight into a man's guts if he hasn't any fight in him. There are some of us so cowardly that you can't ever make heroes of us, not even if you frighten us to death. We know too much, maybe. There are some of us who don't live in the moment, who live a little ahead, or a little behind. My mind is on the peace treaty all the time. I can't forget that it was the fifteen francs which started all the trouble. Fifteen francs! What does fifteen francs mean to me, particularly since it's not my fifteen francs?

Van Norden seems to have a more normal attitude about it. He doesn't care a rap about the fifteen francs either now; it's the situation itself which intrigues him. It seems to call for a show of mettle—his manhood is involved. The fifteen francs are lost, whether we succeed or not. There's something more involved—not just manhood perhaps, but will. It's like a man in the trenches again: he doesn't know any more why he should go on living, because if he escapes now he'll only be caught later, but he goes on just the same, and even though he has the soul of a cockroach and has admitted as much to himself, give him a gun or a knife or even just his bare nails, and he'll go on slaughtering and slaughtering, he'd slaughter a million men rather than stop and ask himself why.

As I watch Van Norden tackle her, it seems to me that I'm looking at a machine whose cogs have slipped. Left to themselves, they could go on this way forever, grinding and slipping, without ever anything happening. Until a hand shuts the motor off. The sight of them coupled like a pair of goats without the least spark of passion, grinding and grinding away for no reason except the fifteen francs, washes away every bit of feeling I have except the inhuman one of satisfying my curiosity. The girl is lying on the edge of the bed and Van Norden is bent over her like a satyr with his two feet solidly planted on the floor. I am sitting on a chair behind him, watching their movements with a cool, scientific detachment; it doesn't matter to me if it should last forever. It's like watching one of those crazy machines which throw the newspaper out, millions and billions and trillions of them with their meaningless headlines. The machine seems more sensible, crazy as it is, and more fascinating to watch, than the human beings and the events which produced it. My interest in Van Norden and the girl is nil; if I could sit like this and watch every single performance going on at this minute all over the world my interest would be even less than nil. I wouldn't be able to differentiate between this phenomenon and the rain falling or a volcano erupting. As long as that spark of passion is missing there is no human significance in the performance. The machine is better to watch. And these two are like a machine which has slipped its cogs. It needs the touch of a human hand to set it right. It needs a mechanic.

I get down on my knees behind Van Norden and I examine the machine more attentively. The girl throws her head on one side and gives me a despairing look. "It's no use," she says. "It's impossible." Upon which Van Norden sets to work with renewed energy, just like an old billy goat. He's such an obstinate cuss that he'll break his horns rather than give up. And he's getting sore now because I'm tickling him in the rump.

"For God's sake, Joe, give it up! You'll kill the poor girl."

"Leave me alone," he grunts. "I almost got it in that time."

The posture and the determined way in which he blurts this out suddenly bring to my mind, for the second time, the remembrance of my dream. Only now it seems as though that broomstick, which he had so nonchalantly slung under his arm, as he walked away, is lost forever. It is like the sequel to the dream—the same Van Norden, but minus the primal cause. He's like a hero come back from the war, a poor maimed bastard living out the reality of his dreams. Wherever he sits himself the chair collapses; whatever door he enters the room is empty; whatever he puts in his mouth leaves a bad taste. Everything is just the same as it was before; the elements are unchanged, the dream is no different than the reality. Only, between the time he went to sleep and the time he woke up, his body was stolen. He's like a machine throwing out newspapers, millions and billions of them every day, and the front page is loaded with catastrophes, with riots, murders, explosions, collisions, but he doesn't feel anything. If somebody doesn't turn the switch off he'll never know what it means to die; you can't die if your own proper body has been stolen. You can get over a cunt and work away like a billy goat until eternity; you can go to the trenches and be blown to bits; nothing will create that spark of passion if there isn't the intervention of a human hand. Somebody has to put his hand into the machine and let it be wrenched off if the cogs are to mesh again. Somebody has to do this without hope of reward, without concern over the fifteen francs; somebody whose chest is so thin that a medal would make him hunchbacked. And somebody has to throw a feed into a starving cunt without fear of pushing it out again. Otherwise this show'll go on forever. There's no way out of the mess....

After sucking the boss's ass for a whole week—it's the thing to do here—I managed to land Peckover's job. He died all right, the poor devil, a few hours after he hit the bottom of the shaft. And just as I predicted, they gave him a fine funeral, with solemn mass, huge wreaths, and everything. *Tout compris.* And after the ceremonies they regaled themselves, the upstairs guys, at a *bistro.* It was too bad Peckover couldn't have had just a little snack—he would have appreciated it so much to sit with the men upstairs and hear his own name mentioned so frequently.

I must say, right at the start, that I haven't a thing to complain about. It's like being in a lunatic asylum, with permission to masturbate for the rest of your life. The world is brought right under my nose and all that is requested of me is to punctuate the calamities. There is nothing in which these slick guys upstairs do not put their fingers: no joy, no misery passes unnoticed. They live among the hard facts of life, reality, as it is called. It is the reality of a swamp and they are the frogs who have nothing better to do than to croak. The more they croak the more real life becomes. Lawyer, priest, doctor, politician, newspaper-man—these are the quacks who have their fingers on the pulse of the world. A constant atmosphere of calamity. It's marvelous. It's as if the barometer never changed, as if the flag were always at half-mast. One can see now how the idea of heaven takes hold of men's consciousness, how it gains ground even when all the props have been knocked from under it. There must be another world beside this swamp in which everything is dumped pell-mell. It's hard to imagine what it can be like, this heaven that men dream about. A frog's heaven, no doubt. Miasma, scum, pond lilies, stagnant water. Sit on a lily pad unmolested and croak all day. Something like that, I imagine.

They have a wonderful therapeutic effect upon me, these catastrophes which I proofread. Imagine a state of perfect immunity, a charmed existence, a life of absolute security in the midst of poison bacilli. Nothing touches me, neither earthquakes nor explosions nor riots nor famine nor collisions nor wars nor revolutions. I am inoculated against every disease, every calamity, every sorrow and misery. It's the culmination of a life of fortitude. Seated at my little niche all the poisons which the world gives off each day pass through my hands. Not even a fingernail gets stained. I am absolutely immune. I am even better off than a laboratory attendant, because there are no bad odors here, just the smell of lead burning. The world can blow up—I'll be here just the same to put in a comma or a semicolon. I may even touch a little over time, for with an event like that there's bound to be a final extra. When the world blows up and the final edition has gone to press the proofreaders will quietly gather up all commas, semicolons, hyphens, asterisks, brackets, parentheses, periods, exclamation marks, etc. and put them in a little box over the editorial chair. *Comme ca tout est regle....*

None of my companions seem to understand why I appear so contented. They grumble all the time, they have ambitions, they want to show their pride and spleen. A good proofreader has no ambitions, no pride, no spleen. A good proofreader is a little like God Almighty, he's in the world but not of it. He's for Sundays only. Sunday is his night off. On Sundays he steps down from his pedestal and shows his ass to the faithful. Once a week he listens in on all the private grief and misery of the world; it's enough to last him for the rest of the week. The rest of the week he remains in the frozen winter marshes, an absolute, an impeccable absolute, with only a vaccination mark to distinguish him from the immense void.

The greatest calamity for a proofreader is the threat of losing his job. When we get together in the break the question that sends a shiver down our spines is: what'll you do if you lose your job? For the man in the paddock, whose duty it is to sweep up manure, the supreme terror is the possibility of a world without horses. To tell him that it is disgusting to spend one's life shoveling up hot turds is a piece of imbecility. A man can get to love shit if his livelihood depends on it, if his happiness is involved.

This life which, if I were still a man with pride, honor, ambition and so forth, would seem like the bottom rung of degradation, I welcome now, as an invalid welcomes death. It's a negative reality, just like death—a sort of heaven without the pain and terror of dying. In this chthonian world the only thing of importance is orthography and punctuation. It doesn't matter what the nature of the calamity is, only whether it is spelled right. Everything is on one level, whether it be the latest fashion for evening gowns, a new battleship, a plague, a high explosive, an astronomic discovery, a bank run, a railroad wreck, a bull market, a hundred-to-one shot, an execution, a stick-up, an assassination, or what.

Nothing escapes the proofreader's eye, but nothing penetrates his bulletproof vest. To the Hindoo Agha Mir, Madam Scheer (formerly Miss Esteve) writes saying she is quite satisfied with his work." I was married June 6th and I thank you. We are very happy and I hope that thanks to your power it will be so forever. I am sending you by telegraph money order the sum of ... to reward you...." The Hindoo Agha Mir foretells your future and reads all your thoughts in a precise and inexplicable way. He will advise you, will help you rid yourself of all your worries and troubles of all kinds, etc. *Call or write 20 Avenue MacMahon, Paris.*

He reads all your thoughts in a marvelous way! I take it that means without exception, from the most trivial thoughts to the most shameless. He must have a lot of time on his hands, this Agha Mir. Or does he only concentrate on the thoughts of those who send money by telegraph money order? In the same edition I notice a headline announcing that "the universe is expanding so fast it may burst" and underneath it is the photograph of a splitting headache. And then there is a spiel about the pearl, signed Tecla. The oyster produces both, he informs all and sundry. Both the "wild" or Oriental pearl, and the "cultured" pearl. On the same day, at the Cathedral of Trier, the Germans are exhibiting the Coat of Christ; it's the first time it's been taken out of the moth balls in forty-two years. Nothing said about the pants and vest. In Salzburg, also the same day, two mice were born in a man's stomach, believe it or not. A famous movie actress is shown with her legs crossed: she is taking a rest in Hyde Park, and underneath a well-known painter remarks "I'll admit that Mrs. Coolidge has such charm and personality that she would have been one of the 12 famous Americans, even had her husband not been President." From an interview with Mr. Humhal, of Vienna, I glean the following..."Before I stop," said Mr. Humhal, "I'd like to say that faultless cut and fit does not suffice; the proof of good tailoring is seen in the wearing. A suit must bend to the body, yet keep its line when the wearer is walking or sitting." And whenever there is an explosion in a coal mine—a *British* coal mine—notice please that the King and Queen always send their condolences promptly, *by telegraph.* And they always attend the important races, though the other day, according to the copy, it was at the Derby, I believe, "heavy rains began to fall, much to the surprise of the King and Queen." More heart-rending, however, is an item like this: "It is claimed in Italy that the persecutions are not against the Church, but nevertheless they are conducted against the most exquisite parts of the Church. It is claimed that they are not against the Pope, but they are against the very heart and eyes of the Pope."

I had to travel precisely all around the world to find just such a comfortable, agreeable niche as this. It seems incredible almost. How could I have foreseen, in America, with all those firecrackers they put up your ass to give you pep and courage, that the ideal position for a man of my temperament was to look for orthographic mistakes? Over there you think of nothing but becoming President of the United States some day. Potentially every man is Presidential timber. Here it's different. Here every man is potentially a zero. If you become something or somebody it is an accident, a miracle. The chances are a thousand to one that you will never leave your native village. The chances are a thousand to one that you'll have your legs shot off or your eyes blown out. Unless the miracle happens and you find yourself a general or a rear admiral.

But it's just because the chances are all against you, just because there is so little hope, that life is sweet over here. Day by day. No yesterdays and no tomorrows. The barometer never changes, the flag is always at half-mast. You wear a piece of black crepe on your arm, you have a little ribbon in your buttonhole, and, if you are lucky enough to afford it, you buy yourself a pair of artificial lightweight limbs, aluminum preferably. Which does not prevent you from enjoying an *aperitif* or looking at the animals in the zoo or flirting with the vultures who sail up and down the boulevards always on the alert for fresh carrion. Time passes. If you're a stranger and your papers are in order you can expose yourself to infection without fear of being contaminated. It is better, if possible, to have a proofreader's job. *Comme ca, tout s'arrange.* That means, that if you happen to be strolling home at three in the morning and you are intercepted by the bicycle cops, you can snap your fingers at them. In the morning, when the market is in swing, you can buy Belgian eggs, at fifty centimes apiece. A proofreader doesn't get up usually until noon, or a little after. It's well to choose a hotel near a cinema, because if you have a tendency to oversleep the bells will wake you up in time for the matinee. Or if you can't find a hotel near a cinema, choose one near a cemetery, it comes to the same thing. Above all, never despair. *Il ne faut jamais desesperer.*

Which is what I try to din into Carl and Van Norden every night. A world without hope, but no despair. It's as though I had been converted to a new religion, as though I were making an annual novena every night to Our Lady of Solace. I can't imagine what there would be to gain if I were made editor of the paper, or even President of the United States. I'm up a blind alley, and it's cosy and comfortable. With a piece of copy in my hand I listen to the music around me, the hum and drone of voices, the tinkle of the linotype machines, as if there were a thousand silver bracelets passing through a wringer; now and then a rat scurries past our feet or a cockroach descends the wall in front of us, moving nimbly and gingerly on his delicate legs. The events of the day are slid under your nose, quietly, unostentatiously, "with, now and then, a by-line to mark the presence of a human hand, an ego, a touch of vanity. The procession passes serenely, like a cortege entering the cemetery gates. The paper under the copy desk is so thick that it almost feels like a carpet with a soft nap. Under Van Norden's desk it is stained with brown juice. Around eleven o'clock the peanut vendor arrives, a half-wit of an Armenian who is also content with his lot in life.

Now and then I get a cablegram from Mona saying that she's arriving on the next boat. "Letter following," it always says. It's been going on like this for nine months, but I never see her name in the list of boat arrivals, nor does the *garcon* ever bring me a letter on a silver platter. I haven't any more expectations in that direction either. If she ever does arrive she can look for me downstairs, just behind the lavatory. She'll probably tell me right away that it's unsanitary. That's the first thing that strikes an American woman about Europe—that it's unsanitary. Impossible for them to conceive of a paradise without modern plumbing. If they find a bedbug they want to write a letter immediately to the chamber of commerce. How am I ever going to explain to her that I'm contented here? She'll say I've become a degenerate. I know her line from beginning to end. She'll want to look for a studio with a garden attached—and a bathtub to be sure. She wants to be poor in a romantic way. I know her. But I'm prepared for her this time.

There are days, nevertheless, when the sun is out and I get off the beaten path and think about her hungrily. Now and then, despite my grim satisfaction, I get to thinking about another way of life, get to wondering if it would make a difference having a young, restless creature by my side. The trouble is I can hardly remember what she looks like, nor even how it feels to have my arms around her. Everything that belongs to the past seems to have fallen into the sea; I have memories, but the images have lost their vividness, they seem dead and desultory, like time-bitten mummies stuck in a quagmire. If I try to recall my life in New York I get a few splintered fragments, nightmarish and covered with verdigris. It seems as if my own proper existence had come to an end somewhere, just where exactly I can't make out. I'm not an American any more, nor a New Yorker, and even less a European, or a Parisian. I haven't any allegiance, any responsibilities, any hatreds, any worries, any prejudices, any passion. I'm neither for nor against. I'm a neutral.

When we walk home of a night, the three of us, it often happens after the first spasms of disgust that we get to talking about the condition of things with that enthusiasm which only those who bear no active part in life can muster. What seems strange to me sometimes, when I crawl into bed, is that all this enthusiasm is engendered just to kill time, just to annihilate the three-quarters of an hour which it requires to walk from the office to Montparnasse. We might have the most brilliant, the most feasible ideas for the amelioration of this or that, but there is no vehicle to hitch them to. And what is more strange is that the absence of any relationship between ideas and living causes us no anguish, no discomfort. We have become so adjusted that, if tomorrow we were ordered to walk on our hands, we would do so without the slightest protest. Provided, of course, that the paper came out as usual. And that we touched our pay regularly. Otherwise nothing matters. Nothing. We have become Orientalized. We have become coolies, white-collar coolies, silenced by a handful of rice each day. A special feature in American skulls, I was reading the other day, is the presence of the epactal bone, or *os Incae,* in the occiput. The presence of this bone, so the savant went on to say, is due to a persistence of the transverse occipital suture which is usually closed in fetal life. Hence it is a sign of arrested development and indicative of an inferior race. "The average cubical capacity of the American skull," so he went on to say, "falls below that of the white, and rises above that of the black race. Taking both sexes, the Parisians of today have a cranial capacity of 1,448 cubic centimeters; the Negroes 1,344 centimeters; the American Indians 1,376." From all of which I deduce nothing because I am an American and not an Indian. But it's cute to explain things that way, by a bone, an *os Incae,* for example. It doesn't disturb his theory at all to admit that single examples of Indian skulls have yielded the extraordinary capacity of 1,920 cubic centimeters, a cranial capacity not exceeded in any other race. What I note with satisfaction is that the Parisians, of both sexes, seem to have a normal cranial capacity. The transverse occipital suture is evidently not so persistent with them. They know how to enjoy an *aperitif* and they don't worry if the houses are unpainted. There's nothing extraordinary about their skulls, so far as cranial indices go. There must be some other explanation for the art of living which they have brought to such a degree of perfection.

At Monsieur Paul's, the *bistro* across the way, there is a back room reserved for the newspapermen where we can eat on credit. It is a pleasant little room with sawdust on the floor and flies in season and out. When I say that it is reserved for the newspapermen I don't mean to imply that we eat in privacy; on the contrary, it means that we have the privilege of associating with the whores and pimps who form the more substantial element of Monsieur Paul's clientele. The arrangement suits the guys upstairs to a T, because they're always on the lookout for tail, and even those who have a steady little French girl are not averse to making a switch now and then. The principal thing is not to get a dose; at times it would seem as if an epidemic had swept the office, or perhaps it might be explained by the fact that they all sleep with the same woman. Anyhow, it's gratifying to observe how miserable they can look when they are obliged to sit beside a pimp who, despite the little hardships of his profession, lives a life of luxury by comparison.

I'm thinking particularly now of one tall, blonde fellow who delivers the Havas messages by bicycle. He is always a little late for his meal, always perspiring profusely and his face covered with grime. He has a fine, awkward way of strolling in, saluting everybody with two fingers and making a beeline for the sink which is just between the toilet and the kitchen. As he wipes his face he gives the edibles a quick inspection; if he sees a nice steak lying on the slab he picks it up and sniffs it, or he will dip the ladle into the big pot and try a mouthful of soup. He's like a fine bloodhound, his nose to the ground all the time. The preliminaries over, having made peepee and blown his nose vigorously, he walks nonchalantly over to his wench and gives her a big, smacking kiss together with an affectionate pat on the rump. Her, the wench, I've never seen look anything but immaculate—even at three a.m., after an evening's work. She looks exactly as if she had just stepped out of a Turkish bath. It's a pleasure to look at such healthy brutes, to see such repose, such affection, such appetite as they display. It's the evening meal I'm speaking of now, the little snack that she takes before entering upon her duties. In a little while she will be obliged to take leave of her big blonde brute, to flop somewhere on the boulevard and sip her *digestif.* If the job is irksome or wearing or exhaustive, she certainly doesn't show it. When the big fellow arrives, hungry as a wolf, she puts her arms around him and kisses him hungrily—his eyes, nose, cheeks, hair, the back of his neck... she'd kiss his ass if it could be done publicly. She's grateful to him, that's evident. She's no wage slave. All through the meal she laughs convulsively. You wouldn't think she had a care in the world. And now and then, by way of affection, she gives him a resounding slap in the face, such a whack as would knock a proofreader spinning.

They don't seem to be aware of anything but themselves and the food that they pack away in shovelsful. Such perfect contentment, such harmony, such mutual understanding, it drives Van Norden crazy to watch them. Especially when she slips her hand in the big fellow's fly and caresses it, to which he generally responds by grabbing her teat and squeezing it playfully.

There is another couple who arrive usually about the same time and they behave just like two married people. They have their spats, they wash their linen in public and after they've made things disagreeable for themselves and everybody else, after threats and curses and reproaches and recriminations, they make up for it by billing and cooing, just like a pair of turtle doves. Lucienne, as he calls her, is a heavy platinum blonde with a cruel, saturnine air. She has a full underlip which she chews venomously when her temper runs away with her. And a cold, beady eye, a sort of faded china blue, which makes him sweat when she fixes him with it. But she's a good sort, Lucienne, despite the condor-like profile which she presents to us when the squabbling begins. Her bag is always full of dough, and if she deals it out cautiously, it is only because she doesn't want to encourage him in his bad habits. He has a weak character; that is, if one takes Lucienne's tirades seriously. He will spend fifty francs of an evening while waiting for her to get through. When the waitress comes to take his order he has no appetite. "Ah, you're not hungry again!" growls Lucienne. "Humpf! You were waiting for me, I suppose, on the Faubourg Montmartre. You had a good time, I hope, while I slaved for you. *Speak, imbecile, where were you?*"

When she flares up like that, when she gets enraged, he looks up at her timidly and then, as if he had decided that silence was the best course, he lets his head drop and he fiddles with his napkin. But this little gesture, which she knows so well and which of course is secretly pleasing to her because she is convinced now that he is guilty, only increases Lucienne's anger. *"Speak, imbecile!"* she shrieks. And with a squeaky, timid little voice he explains to her woefully that while waiting for her he got so hungry that he was obliged to stop off for a sandwich and a glass of beer. It was just enough to ruin his appetite—he says it dolefully, though it's apparent that food just now is the least of his worries. "But"—and he tries to make his voice sound more convincing—"I was waiting for you all the time," he blurts out.

"Liar!" she screams. "Liar! Ah, fortunately, I too am a liar... a *good liar.* You make me ill with your petty little lies. Why don't you tell me a big lie?"

He hangs his head again and absent-mindedly he gathers a few crumbs and puts them to his mouth. Whereupon she slaps his hand. "Don't do that! You make me tired. You're such an imbecile. Liar! Just you wait! I have more to say. I am a liar too, but I am not an imbecile."

In a little while, however, they are sitting close together, their hands locked, and she is murmuring softly: "Ah, my little rabbit, it is hard to leave you now. Come here, kiss me! What are you going to do this evening? Tell me the truth, my little one.... I am sorry that I have such an ugly temper." He kisses her timidly, just like a little bunny with long pink ears; gives her a little peck on the lips as if he were nibbling a cabbage leaf. And at the same time his bright round eyes fall caressingly on her purse which is lying open beside her on the bench. He is only waiting for the moment when he can graciously give her the slip; he is itching to get away, to sit down in some quiet cafe on the Rue du Faubourg Montmartre.

I know him, the innocent little devil, with his round, frightened eyes of a rabbit. And I know what a devil's street is the Faubourg Montmartre with its brass plates and rubber goods, the lights twinkling all night and sex running through the street like a sewer. To walk from the Rue Lafayette to the boulevard is like running the gauntlet; they attach themselves to you like barnacles, they eat into you like ants, they coax, wheedle, cajole, implore, beseech, they try it out in German, English, Spanish, they show you their torn hearts and their busted shoes, and long after you've chopped the tentacles away, long after the fizz and sizzle has died out, the fragrance of the *lavabo* clings to your nostrils—it is the odor of the *Parfum de Danse* whose effectiveness is guaranteed only for a distance of twenty centimeters. One could piss away a whole lifetime in that little stretch between the boulevard and the Rue Lafayette. Every bar is alive, throbbing, the dice loaded; the cashiers are perched like vultures on their high stools and the money they handle has a human stink to it. There is no equivalent in the Banque de France for the blood money that passes currency here, the money that glistens with human sweat, that passes like a forest fire from hand to hand and leaves behind it a smoke and stench. A man who can walk through the Faubourg Montmartre at night without panting or sweating, without a prayer or a curse on his lips, a man like that has no balls, and if he has, then he ought to be castrated.

Supposing the timid little rabbit does spend fifty francs of an evening while waiting for his Lucienne? Supposing he does get hungry and buy a sandwich and a glass of beer, or stop and chat with somebody else's trollop? You think he ought to be weary of that round night after night? You think it ought to weigh on him, oppress him, bore him to death? You don't think that a pimp is inhuman, I hope? A pimp has his private grief and misery too, don't you forget. Perhaps he would like nothing better than to stand on the corner every night with a pair of white dogs and watch them piddle. Perhaps he would like it if, when he opened the door, he would see her there reading the *Paris-Soir,* her eyes already a little heavy with sleep. Perhaps it isn't so wonderful, when he bends over his Lucienne, to taste another man's breath. Better maybe to have only three francs in your pocket and a pair of white dogs that piddle on the corner than to taste those bruised lips. Bet you, when she squeezes him tight, when she begs for that little package of love which only he knows how to deliver, bet you he fights like a thousand devils to pump it up, to wipe out that regiment that has marched between her legs. Maybe when he takes her body and practices a new tune, maybe it isn't all passion and curiosity with him, but a fight in the dark, a fight single-handed against the army that rushed the gates, the army that walked over her, trampled her, that left her with such a devouring hunger that not even a Rudolph Valentino could appease. When I listen to the reproaches that are leveled against a girl like Lucienne, when I hear her being denigrated or despised because she is cold and mercenary, because she is too mechanical, or because she's in too great a hurry, or because this or because that, I say to myself, hold on there bozo, not so fast! Remember that you're far back in the procession; remember that a whole army corps has laid siege to her, that she's been laid waste, plundered and pillaged. I say to myself, listen, bozo, don't begrudge the fifty francs you hand her because you know her pimp is pissing it away in the Faubourg Montmartre. It's *her* money and *her* pimp. It's blood money. It's money that'll never be taken out of circulation because there's nothing in the Banque de France to redeem it with.

That's how I think about it often when I'm seated in my little niche juggling the Havas reports or untangling the cables from Chicago, London and Montreal. In between the rubber and silk markets and the Winnipeg grains there oozes a little of the fizz and sizzle of the Faubourg Montmartre. When the bonds go weak and spongy and the pivotals balk and the volatiles effervesce, when the grain market slips and slides and the bulls commence to roar, when every fucking calamity, every ad, every sport item and fashion article, every boat arrival, every travelogue, every tag of gossip has been punctuated, checked, revised, pegged and wrung through the silver bracelets, when I hear the front page being hammered into whack and see the frogs dancing around like drunken squibs, I think of Lucienne sailing down the boulevard with her wings outstretched, a huge silver condor suspended over the sluggish tide of traffic, a strange bird from the tips of the Andes with a rose-white belly and a tenacious little knob. Sometimes I walk home alone and I follow her through the dark streets, follow her through the court of the Louvre, over the Pont des Arts, through the arcade, through the fents and slits, the somnolence, the drugged whiteness, the grill of the Luxembourg, the tangled boughs, the snores and groans, the green slats, the strum and tinkle, the points of the stars, the spangles, the jetties, the blue and white striped awnings that she brushed with the tips of her wings.

In the blue of an electric dawn the peanut shells look wan and crumpled; along the beach at Montparnasse the water lilies bend and break. When the tide is on the ebb and only a few syphilitic mermaids are left stranded in the muck, the Dome looks like a shooting gallery that's been struck by a cyclone. Everything is slowly dribbling back to the sewer. For about an hour there is a deathlike calm during which the vomit is mopped up. Suddenly the trees begin to screech. From one end of the boulevard to the other a demented song rises up. It is like the signal that announces the close of the exchange. What hopes there were are swept up. The moment has come to void the last bagful of urine. The day is sneaking in like a leper....

One of the things to guard against when you work nights is not to break your schedule; if you don't get to bed before the birds begin to screech it's useless to go to bed at all. This morning, having nothing better to do, I visited the *Jardin des Plantes*. Marvelous pelicans here from Chapultepec and peacocks with studded fans that look at you with silly eyes. Suddenly it began to rain.

Returning to Montparnasse in the bus I noticed a little French woman opposite me who sat stiff and erect as if she were getting ready to preen herself. She sat on the edge of the seat as if she feared to crush her gorgeous tail. Marvelous, I thought, if suddenly she shook herself and from her *derriere* there sprung open a huge studded fan with long silken plumes.

At the Cafe de l'Avenue, where I stop for a bite, a woman with a swollen stomach tries to interest me in her condition. She would like me to go to a room with her and while away an hour or two. It is the first time I have ever been propositioned by a pregnant woman: I am almost tempted to try it. As soon as the baby is born and handed over to the authorities she will go back to her trade, she says. She makes hats. Observing that my interest is waning she takes my hand and puts it on her abdomen. I feel some-thing stirring inside. It takes my appetite away.

I have never seen a place like Paris for varieties of sexual provender. As soon as a woman loses a front tooth or an eye or a leg she goes on the loose. In America she'd starve to death if she had nothing to recommend her but a mutilation. Here it is different. A missing tooth or a nose eaten away or a fallen womb, any misfortune that aggravates the natural homeliness of the female, seems to be regarded as an added spice, a stimulant for the jaded appetites of the male.

I am speaking naturally of that world which is peculiar to the big cities, the world of men and women whose last drop of juice has been squeezed out by the machine—the martyrs of modern progress. It is this mass of bones and collar buttons which the painter finds so difficult to put flesh on.

It is only later, in the afternoon, when I find myself in an art gallery on the Rue de Seze, surrounded by the men and women of Matisse, that I am drawn back again to the proper precincts of the human world. On the threshold of that big hall whose walls are now ablaze, I pause a moment to recover from the shock which one experiences when the habitual gray of the world is rent asunder and the color of life splashes forth in song and poem. I find myself in a world so natural, so complete, that I am lost. I have the sensation of being immersed in the very plexus of life, focal from whatever place, position or attitude I take my stance. Lost as when once I sank into the quick of a budding grove and seated in the dining room of that enormous world of Balbec, I caught for the first time the profound meaning of those interior stills which manifest their presence through the exorcism of sight and touch. Standing on the threshold of that world which Matisse has created I re-experienced the power of that revelation which had permitted Proust to so deform the picture of life that only those who, like himself, are sensible to the alchemy of sound and sense, are capable of transforming the negative reality of life into the substantial and significant outlines of art. Only those who can admit the light into their gizzards can translate what is there in the heart. Vividly now I recall how the glint and sparkle of light caroming from the massive chandeliers splintered and ran blood, flecking the tips of the waves that beat monotonously on the dull gold outside the windows. On the beach, masts and chimneys interlaced, and like a fuliginous shadow the figure of Albertine gliding through the surf, fusing into the mysterious quick and prism of a protoplasmic realm, uniting her shadow to the dream and harbinger of death. With the close of day, pain rising like a mist from the earth, sorrow closing in, shuttering the endless vista of sea and sky. Two waxen hands lying listlessly on the bedspread and along the pale veins the fluted murmur of a shell repeating the legend of its birth.

In every poem by Matisse there is the history of a particle of human flesh which refused the consummation of death. The whole run of flesh, from hair to nails, expresses the miracle of breathing, as if the inner eye, in its thirst for a greater reality, had converted the pores of the flesh into hungry seeing mouths. By whatever vision one passes there is the odor and the sound of voyage. It is impossible to gaze at even a corner of his dreams without feeling the lift of the wave and the cool of flying spray. He stands at the helm peering with steady blue eyes into the portfolio of time. Into what distant corners has he not thrown his long, slanting gaze? Looking down the vast promontory of his nose he has beheld everything—the Cordilleras falling away into the Pacific, the history of the Diaspora done in vellum, shutters fluting the froufrou of the beach, the piano curving like a conch, corollas giving out diapasons of light, chameleons squirming under the book press, seraglios expiring in oceans of dust, music is suing like fire from the hidden chromosphere of pain, spore and madrepore fructifying the earth, navels vomiting their bright spawn of anguish…. He is a bright sage, a dancing seer who, with a sweep of the brush, removes the ugly scaffold to which the body of man is chained by the incontrovertible facts of life. He it is, if any man today possesses the gift, who knows where to dissolve the human figure, who has the courage to sacrifice an harmonious line in order to detect the rhythm and murmur of the blood, who takes the light that has been refracted inside him and lets it flood the keyboard of color. Behind the minutiae, the chaos, the mockery of life, he detects the invisible pattern; he announces his discoveries in the metaphysical pigment of space. No searching for formulae, no crucifixion of ideas, no compulsion other than to create. Even as the world goes to smash there is one man who remains at the core, who becomes more solidly fixed and anchored, more centrifugal as the process of dissolution quickens.

More and more the world resembles an entomologist's dream. The earth is moving out of its orbit, the axis has shifted; from the north the snow blows down in huge knife-blue drifts. A new ice age is setting in, the transverse sutures are closing up and everywhere throughout the corn belt the fetal world is dying, turning to dead mastoid. Inch by inch the deltas are drying out and the river beds are smooth as glass. A new day is dawning, a metallurgical day, when the earth shall clink with showers of bright yellow ore. As the thermometer drops, the form of the world grows blurred; osmosis there still is, and here and there articulation, but at the periphery the veins are all varicose, at the periphery the light waves bend and the sun bleeds like a broken rectum.

At the very hub of this wheel which is falling apart, is Matisse. And he will keep on rolling until everything that has gone to make up the wheel has disintegrated. He has already rolled over a goodly portion of the globe, over Persia and India and China, and like a magnet he has attached to himself microscopic particles from Kurd, Baluchistan, Timbuktu, Somaliland, Angkor, Tierra del Fuego. The odalisques he has studded with malachite and jasper, their flesh veiled with a thousand eyes, perfumed eyes dipped in the sperm of whales. Wherever a breeze stirs there are breasts as cool as jelly, white pigeons come to flutter and rut in the ice-blue veins of the Himalayas.

The wallpaper with which the men of science have covered the world of reality is falling to tatters. The grand whorehouse which they have made of life requires no decoration; it is essential only that the drains function adequately. Beauty, that feline beauty which has us by the balls in America, is finished. To fathom the new reality it is first necessary to dismantle the drains, to lay open the gangrened ducts which compose the genitourinary system that supplies the excreta of art. The odor of the day is permanganate and formaldehyde. The drains are clogged with strangled embryos.

The world of Matisse is still beautiful in an old-fashioned bedroom way. There is not a ball bearing in evidence, nor a boiler plate, nor a piston, nor a monkey wrench. It is the same old world that went gaily to the Bois in the pastoral days of wine and fornication. I find it soothing and refreshing to move amongst these creatures with live, breathing pores whose background is stable and solid as light itself. I feel it poignantly when I walk along the Boulevard de la Madeleine and the whores rustle beside me, when just to glance at them causes me to tremble. Is it because they are exotic or well-nourished? No, it is rare to find a beautiful woman along the Boulevard de la Madeleine. But in Matisse, in the exploration of his brush, there is the trembling glitter of a world which demands only the presence of the female to crystallize the most fugitive aspirations. To come upon a woman offering herself outside a urinal, where there are advertised cigarette papers, rum, acrobats, horse races, where the heavy foliage of the trees breaks the heavy mass of walls and roofs, is an experience that begins where the boundaries of the known world leave off. In the evening now and then, skirting the cemetery walls, I stumble upon the phantom odalisques of Matisse fastened to the trees, their tangled manes drenched with sap. A few feet away, removed by incalculable eons of time, lies the prone and mummy-swathed ghost of Baudelaire, of a whole world that will belch no more. In the dusky corners of cafes are men and women with hands locked, their loins slather-flecked; nearby stands the *garcon* with his apron full of sous, waiting patiently for the entr'acte in order to fall upon his wife and gouge her. Even as the world falls apart the Paris that belongs to Matisse shudders with bright, gasping orgasms, the air itself is steady with a stagnant sperm, the trees tangled like hair. On its wobbly axle the wheel rolls steadily downhill; there are no brakes, no ball bearings, no balloon tires. The wheel is falling apart, but the revolution is intact....

Out of a clear sky there comes one day a letter from Boris whom I have not seen for months and months. It is a strange document and I don't pretend to understand it all clearly. "What happened between us—at any rate, as far as I go—is that you touched me, touched my life, that is, at the one point where I am still alive: my death. By the emotional flow I went through another immersion. I lived again, alive. No longer by reminiscence, as I do with others, but alive."

That's how it began. Not a word of greeting, no date, no address. Written in a thin, pompous scrawl on ruled paper torn out of a blank book. "That is why, whether you like me or not—deep down I rather think you hate me—you are very close to me. By you I know how I died: I see myself dying again: I *am* dying. That is something. More than to be dead simply. That may be the reason why I am so afraid to see you: you may have played the trick on me, and died. Things happen so fast nowadays."

I'm reading it over, line by line, standing by the stones. It sounds nutty to me, all this palaver about life and death and things happening so fast. Nothing is happening that I can see, except the usual calamities on the front page. He's been living all by himself for the last six months, tucked away in a cheap little room—probably holding telepathic communication with Cronstadt. He talks about the line falling back, the sector evacuated, and so on and so forth, as though he were dug into a trench and writing a report to headquarters. He probably had his frock coat on when he sat down to pen this missive, and he probably rubbed his hands a few times as he used to do when a customer was calling to rent the apartment. "The reason I wanted you to commit suicide ..." he begins again. At that I burst out laughing. He used to walk up and down with one hand stuck in the tail flap of his frock coat at the Villa Borghese, or at Cronstadt's—wherever there was deck space, as it were—and reel off this nonsense about living and dying to his heart's content. I never understood a word of it, I must confess, but it was a good show and, being a Gentile, I was naturally interested in what went on in that menagerie of a brainpan. Sometimes he would lie on his couch full length, exhausted by the surge of ideas that swept through his noodle. His feet just grazed the bookrack where he kept his Plato and Spinoza—he couldn't understand why I had no use for them. I must say he made them sound interesting, though what it was all about I hadn't the least idea. Sometimes I would glance at a volume furtively, to check up on these wild ideas which he imputed to them—but the connection was frail, tenuous. He had a language all his own, Boris, that is, when I had him alone; but when I listened to Cronstadt it seemed to me that Boris had plagiarized his wonderful ideas. They talked a sort of higher mathematics, these two. Nothing of flesh and blood ever crept in; it was weird, ghostly, ghoulishly abstract. When they got on to the dying business it sounded a little more concrete: after all, a cleaver or a meat ax has to have a handle. I enjoyed those sessions immensely. It was the first time in my life that death had ever seemed fascinating to me—all these abstract deaths which involved a bloodless sort of agony. Now and then they would compliment me on being alive, but in such a way that I felt embarrassed. They made me feel that I was alive in the nineteenth century, a sort of atavistic remnant, a romantic shred, a soulful Pithecanthropus erectus. Boris especially seemed to get a great kick out of touching me; he wanted me to be alive so that he could die to his heart's content. You would think that all those millions in the street were nothing but dead cows the way he looked at me and touched me. But the letter ... I'm forgetting the letter....

"The reason why I wanted you to commit suicide that evening at the Cronstadts', when Moldorf became God, was that I was very close to you then. Perhaps closer than I shall ever be. And I was afraid, terribly afraid, that some day you'd go back on me, die on my hands. And I would be left high and dry with my idea of you simply, and nothing to sustain it. I should never forgive you for that."

Perhaps you can visualize him saying a thing like that! Myself it's not clear what his idea of me was, or at any rate, it's clear that I was just pure idea, an idea that kept itself alive without food. He never attached much importance, Boris, to the food problem. He tried to nourish me with ideas. Everything was idea. Just the same, when he had his heart set on renting the apartment, he wouldn't forget to put a new washer in the toilet. Anyway, he didn't want me to die on his hands. "You must be life for me to the very end," so he writes. "That is the only way in which you can sustain my idea of you. Because you have gotten, as you see, tied up with something so vital to me, I do not think I shall ever shake you off. Nor do I wish to. I want you to live more vitally every day, as I am dead. That is why, when I speak of you to others, I am just a bit ashamed. It's hard to talk of one's self so intimately."

You would imagine perhaps that he was anxious to see me, or that he would like to know what I was doing—but no, not a line about the concrete or the personal, except in this living-dying language, nothing but this little message from the trenches, this whiff of poison gas to apprise all and sundry that the war was still on. I sometimes ask myself how it happens that I attract nothing but crackbrained individuals, neurasthenics, neurotics, psychopaths—and Jews especially. There must be something in a healthy Gentile that excites the Jewish mind, like when he sees sour black bread. There was Moldorf, for example, who had made himself God, according to Boris and Cronstadt. He positively hated me, the little viper—yet he couldn't stay away from me. He came round regularly for his little dose of insults—it was like a tonic to him. In the beginning, it's true, I was lenient with him; after all, he was paying me to listen to him. And though I never displayed much sympathy I knew how to be silent when it involved a meal and a little pin money. After a while, however, seeing what a masochist he was, I permitted myself to laugh in his face now and then; that was like a whip for him, it made the grief and agony gush forth with renewed vigor. And perhaps everything would have gone smoothly between us if he had not felt it his duty to protect Tania. But Tania being a Jewess, that brought up a moral question. He wanted me to stick to Mlle. Claude for whom, I must admit, I had a genuine affection. He even gave me money occasionally to sleep with her. Until he realized that I was a hopeless lecher.

I mention Tania now because she's just got back from Russia—just a few days ago. Sylvester remained behind to worm his way into a job. He's given up literature entirely. He's dedicated himself to the new Utopia. Tania wants me to go back there with her, to the Crimea preferably, and start a new life. We had a fine drinking bout up in Carl's room the other day discussing the possibilities. I wanted to know what I could do for a living back there—if I could be a proofreader, for example. She said I didn't need to worry about what I would do—they would find a job for me as long as I was earnest and sincere. I tried to look earnest, but I only succeeded in looking pathetic. They don't want to see sad faces in Russia; they want you to be cheerful, enthusiastic, light-hearted, optimistic. It sounded very much like America to me. I wasn't born with this kind of enthusiasm. I didn't let on to her, of course, but secretly I was praying to be left alone, to go back to my little niche, and to stay there until the war breaks. All this hocus-pocus about Russia disturbed me a little. She got so excited about it, Tania, that we finished almost a half dozen bottles of *vin ordinaire*. Carl was jumping about like a cockroach. He has just enough Jew in him to lose his head over an idea like Russia. Nothing would do but to marry us off—immediately. "Hitch up!" he says, "you have nothing to lose!" And then he pretends to run a little errand so that we can pull off a fast one. And while she wanted it all right, Tania, still that Russia business had gotten so solidly planted in her skull that she pissed the interval away chewing my ear off, which made me somewhat grumpy and ill at ease. Anyway, we had to think about eating and getting to the office, so we piled into a taxi on the Boulevard Edgar-Quinet, just a stone's throw away from the cemetery, and off we whizzed. It was just a nice hour to spin through Paris in an open cab, and the wine rolling around in our tanks made it seem even more lovely than usual. Carl was sitting opposite us, on the *strapontin,* his face as red as a beet. He was happy, the poor bastard, thinking what a glorious new life he would lead on the other side of Europe. And at the same time he felt a bit wistful, too— I could see that. He didn't really want to leave Paris, any more than I did. Paris hadn't been good to him, any more than it had to me, or to anybody, for that matter, but when you've suffered and endured things here it's then that Paris takes hold of you, grabs you by the balls, you might say, like some lovesick bitch who'd rather die than let you get out of her hands. That's how it looked to him, I could see that. Rolling over the Seine he had a big foolish grin on his face and he looked around at the buildings and the statues as though he were seeing them in a dream. To me it was like a dream too: I had my hand in Tania's bosom and I was squeezing her titties with all my might and I noticed the water under the bridges and the barges and Notre-Dame down below, just like the post cards show it, and I was thinking drunkenly to myself that's how one gets fucked, but I was sly about it too and I knew I wouldn't ever trade all this whirling about my head for Russia or heaven or anything on earth. It was a fine afternoon, I was thinking to myself, and soon we'd be pushing a feed down our bellies and what could we order as a special treat, some good heavy wine that would drown out all this Russia business. With a woman like Tania, full of sap and everything, they don't give a damn what happens to you once they get an idea in their heads. Let them go far enough and they'll pull the pants off you, right in the taxi. It was grand though, milling through the traffic, our faces all smudged with rouge and the wine gurgling like a sewer inside us, especially when we swung into the Rue Laffitte which is just wide enough to frame the little temple at the end of the street and above it the Sacre-Coeur, a kind of exotic jumble of architecture, a lucid French idea that gouges right through your drunkenness and leaves you swimming helplessly in the past, in a fluid dream that makes you wide awake and yet doesn't jar your nerves.

With Tania back on the scene, a steady job, the drunken talk about Russia, the walks home at night, and Paris in full summer, life seems to lift its head a little higher. That's why perhaps, a letter such as Boris sent me seems absolutely cockeyed. Most every day I meet Tania around five o'clock, to have a Porto with her, as she calls it. Met her take me to places I've never seen before, the swell bars around the Champs-Elysees where the sound of jazz and baby voices crooning seems to soak right through the mahogany wood-work. Even when you go to the *lavabo* these pulpy, sappy strains pursue you, come float-ing into the cabinet through the ventilators and make life all soap and iridescent bubbles. And whether it's because Sylvester is away and she feels free now, or whatever it is, Tania certainly tries to behave like an angel. "You treated me lousy just before I went away," she says to me one day. "Why did you want to act that way? I never did anything to hurt you, did I?" We were getting sentimental, what with the soft lights and that creamy, mahogany music seeping through the place. It was getting near time to go to work and we hadn't eaten yet. The stubs were lying there in front of us—six francs, four-fifty, seven francs, two-fifty—I was counting them up mechanically and wondering too at the same time if I would like it better being a bartender. Often like that, when she was talking to me, gush-ing about Russia, the future, love, and all that crap, I'd get to thinking about the most irrel-evant things, about shining shoes or being a lavatory attendant, particularly I suppose because it was so cosy in these joints that she dragged me to and it never occurred to me that I'd be stone sober and perhaps old and bent... no, I imagined always that the future, however modest, would be in just this sort of ambiance, with the same tunes playing through my head and the glasses clinking and behind every shapely ass a trail of perfume a yard wide that would take the stink out of life, even downstairs in the *lavabo*.

The strange thing is it never spoiled me trotting around to the swell bars with her like that. It was hard to leave her, certainly. I used to lead her around to the porch of a church near the office and standing there in the dark we'd take a last embrace, she whispering to me "Jesus, what am I going to do now?" She wanted me to quit the job so as I could make love night and day; she didn't even care about Russia any more, just so long as we were together. But the moment I left her my head cleared. It was another kind of music, not so croony but good just the same, which greeted my ears when I pushed through the swinging door. And another kind of perfume, not just a yard wide, but omnipresent, a sort of sweat and patchouli that seemed to come from the machines. Coming in with a skinful, as I usually did, it was like dropping suddenly to a low altitude. Generally I made a beeline for the toilet—that braced me up rather. It was a little cooler there, or else the sound of water running made it seem so. It was always a cold douche, the toilet. It was real. Before you got inside you had to pass a line of Frenchmen peeling off their clothes. Ugh! but they stank, those devils! And they were well paid for it, too. But there they were, stripped down, some in long underwear, some with beards, most of them pale, skinny rats with lead in their veins. Inside the toilet you could take an inventory of their idle thoughts. The walls were crowded with sketches and epithets, all of them jocosely obscene, easy to understand, and on the whole rather jolly and sympathetic. It must have required a ladder to reach certain spots, but I suppose it was worth while doing it even looking at it from just the psychological viewpoint. Sometimes, as I stood there taking a leak, I wondered what an impression it would make on those swell dames whom I observed passing in and out of the beautiful lavatories on the Champs-Elysees. I wondered if they would carry their tails so high if they could see what was thought of an ass here. In their world, no doubt, everything was gauze and velvet—or they made you think so with the fine scents they gave out, swishing past you. Some of them hadn't always been such fine ladies either; some of them swished up and down like that just to advertise their trade. And maybe, when they were left alone with themselves, when they talked out loud in the privacy of their boudoirs, maybe some strange things fell out of their mouths too; because in that world, just as in every world, the greater part of what happens is just muck and filth, sordid as any garbage can, only they are lucky enough to be able to put covers over the can.

As I say, that afternoon life with Tarda never had any bad effect upon me. Once in a while I'd get too much of a skinful and I'd have to stick my finger down my throat—because it's hard to read proof when you're not all there. It requires more concentration to detect a missing comma than to epitomize Nietzsche's philosophy. You can be brilliant sometimes, when you're drunk, but brilliance is out of place in the proofreading department. Dates, fractions, semicolons—these are the things that count. And these are the things that are most difficult to track down when your mind is all ablaze. Now and then I made some bad blunders, and if it weren't that I had learned how to kiss the boss's ass, I would have been fired, that's certain. I even got a letter one day from the big mogul upstairs, a guy I never even met, so high up he was, and between a few sarcastic phrases about my more than ordinary intelligence, he hinted pretty plainly that I'd better learn my place and toe the mark or there'd be what's what to pay. Frankly, that scared the shit out of me. After that I never used a polysyllabic word in conversation; in fact, I hardly ever opened my trap all night. I played the high-grade moron, which is what they wanted of us. Now and then, to sort of flatter the boss, I'd go up to him and ask politely what such and such a word might mean. He liked that. He was a sort of dictionary and timetable, that guy. No matter how much beer he guzzled during the break—and he made his own private breaks too, seeing as how he was running the show—you could never trip him up on a date or a definition. He was born to the job. My only regret was that I knew too much. It leaked out now and then, despite all the precautions I took. If I happened to come to work with a book under my arm this boss of ours would notice it, and if it were a good book it made him venomous. But I never did anything intentionally to displease him; I liked the job too well to put a noose around my neck. Just the same it's hard to talk to a man when you have nothing in common with him; you betray yourself, even if you use only monosyllabic words. He knew goddamn well, the boss, that I didn't take the least bit of interest in his yarns; and yet, explain it how you will, it gave him pleasure to wean me away from my dreams and fill me full of dates and historical events. It was his way of taking revenge, I suppose.

The result was that I developed a bit of a neurosis. As soon as I hit the air I became extravagant. It wouldn't matter what the subject of conversation happened to be, as we started back to Montparnasse in the early morning, I'd soon turn the fire hose on it, squelch it, in order to trot out my perverted dreams. I liked best talking about those things which none of us knew anything about. I had cultivated a mild sort of insanity, echolalia, I think it's called. All the tag ends of a night's proofing danced on the tip of my tongue. *Dalmatia*—I had held copy on an ad for that beautiful jeweled resort. All right, *Dalmatia*. You take a train and in the morning your pores are perspiring and the grapes are bursting their skins. I could reel it off about Dalmatia from the grand boulevard to Cardinal Mazarin's palace, further, if I chose to. I don't even know where it is on the map, and I don't want to know ever, but at three in the morning with all that lead in your veins and your clothes saturated with sweat and patchouli and the clink of bracelets passing through the wringer and those beer yarns that I was braced for, little things like geography, costume, speech, architecture don't mean a goddamn thing. Dalmatia belongs to a certain hour of the night when those high gongs are snuffed out and the court of the Louvre seems so wonderfully ridiculous that you feel like weeping for no reason at all, just because it's so beautifully silent, so empty, so totally unlike the front page and the guys upstairs rolling the dice. With that little piece of Dalmatia resting on my throbbing nerves like a cold knife blade I could experience the most wonderful sensations of voyage. And the funny thing is again that I could travel all around the globe but America would never enter my mind; it was even further lost than a lost continent, because with the lost continents I felt some mysterious attachment, whereas with America I felt nothing at all. Now and then, it's true, I did think of Mona, not as of a person in a definite aura of time and space, but separately, detached, as though she had blown up into a great cloudlike form that blotted out the past. I couldn't allow myself to think about her very long; if I had I would have jumped off the bridge. It's strange. I had become so reconciled to this life without her, and yet if I thought about her only for a minute it was enough to pierce the bone and marrow of my contentment and shove me back again into the agonizing gutter of my wretched past. For seven years I went about, day and night, with only one thing on my mind—*her*. Were there a Christian so faithful to his God as I was to her we would all be Jesus Christs today. Day and night I thought of her, even when I was deceiving her. And now sometimes, in the very midst of things, sometimes when I feel that I am absolutely free of it all, suddenly, in rounding a corner perhaps, there will bob up a little square, a few trees and a bench, a deserted spot where we stood and had it out, where we drove each other crazy with bitter, jealous scenes. Always some deserted spot, like the Place de l'Estrapade, for example, or those dingy, mournful streets off the Mosque or along that open tomb of an Avenue de Breteuil which at ten o'clock in the evening is so silent, so dead, that it makes one think of murder or suicide, anything that might create a vestige of human drama. When I realize that she is gone, perhaps gone forever, a great void opens up and I feel that I am falling, falling, falling into deep, black space. And this is worse than tears, deeper than regret or pain or sorrow; it is the abyss into which Satan was plunged. There is no climbing back, no ray of light, no sound of human voice or human touch of hand.

How many thousand times, in walking through the streets at night, have I wondered if the day would ever come again when she would be at my side: all those yearning looks I bestowed on the buildings and statues, I had looked at them so hungrily, so desperately, that by now my thoughts must have become a part of the very buildings and statues, they must be saturated with my anguish. I could not help but reflect also that when we had walked side by side through these mournful, dingy streets now so saturated with my dream and longing, she had observed nothing, felt nothing: they were like any other streets to her, a little more sordid perhaps, and that is all. She wouldn't remember that at a certain corner I had stopped to pick up her hairpin, or that, when I bent down to tie her laces, I remarked the spot on which her foot had rested and that it would remain there forever, even after the cathedrals had been demolished and the whole Latin civilization wiped out forever and ever.

Walking down the Rue Lhomond one night in a fit of unusual anguish and desolation, certain things were revealed to me with poignant clarity. Whether it was that I had so often walked this street in bitterness and despair or whether it was the remembrance of a phrase which she had dropped one night as we stood at the Place Lucien-Herr I do not know. "Why don't you show me that Paris," she said, "that you have written about?" One thing I know, that at the recollection of these words I suddenly realized the impossibility of ever revealing to her that Paris which I had gotten to know, the Paris whose *arrondissements* are undefined, a Paris that has never existed except by virtue of my loneliness, my hunger for her. Such a huge Paris! It would take a lifetime to explore it again. This Paris, to which I alone had the key, hardly lends itself to a tour, even with the best of intentions; it is a Paris that has to be lived, that has to be experienced each day in a thousand different forms of torture, a Paris that grows inside you like a cancer, and grows and grows until you are eaten away by it.

Stumbling down the Rue Mouffetard, with these reflections stirring in my brain, I recalled another strange item out of the past, out of that guidebook whose leaves she had asked me to turn but which, because the covers were so heavy, I then found impossible to pry open. For no reason at all—because at the moment my thoughts were occupied with Salavin in whose sacred precincts I was now meandering—for no reason at all, I say, there came to mind the recollection of a day when, inspired by the plaque which I passed day in and day out, I impulsively entered the Pension Orfila and asked to see the room Strindberg had occupied. Up to that time nothing very terrible had befallen me, though I had already lost all my worldly possessions and had known what it was to walk the streets in hunger and in fear of the police. Up to then I had not found a single friend in Paris, a circumstance which was not so much depressing as bewildering, for wherever I have roamed in this world the easiest thing for me to discover has been a friend. But in reality, nothing very terrible had happened to me yet. One can live without friends, as one can live without love, or even without money, that supposed *sine qua non*. One can live in Paris—I discovered that!—on just grief and anguish. A bitter nourishment—perhaps the best there is for certain people. At any rate, I had not yet come to the end of my rope. I was only flirting with disaster. I had time and sentiment enough to spare to peep into other people's lives, to dally with the dead stuff of romance which, however morbid it may be, when it is wrapped between the covers of a book, seems deliciously remote and anonymous. As I was leaving the place I was conscious of an ironic smile hovering over my lips, as though I were saying to myself "Not yet, the Pension Orfila!"

Since then, of course, I have learned what every madman in Paris discovers sooner or later; that there are no ready-made infernos for the tormented.

It seems to me I understand a little better now why she took such huge delight in reading Strindberg. I can see her looking up from her book after reading a *delicious* passage, and, with tears of laughter in her eyes, saying to me: "You're just as mad as he was... you *want* to be punished!" What a delight that must be to the sadist when she discovers her own proper masochist! When she bites herself, as it were, to test the sharpness of her teeth. In those days, when I first knew her, she was saturated with Strindberg. That wild carnival of maggots which he reveled in, that eternal duel of the sexes, that spiderish ferocity which had endeared him to the sodden oafs of the northland, it was that which had brought us together. We came together in a dance of death and so quickly was I sucked down into the vortex that when I came to the surface again I could not recognize the world. When I found myself loose the music had ceased; the carnival was over and I had been picked clean....

After leaving the Pension Orfila that afternoon I went to the library and there, after bathing in the Ganges and pondering over the signs of the zodiac, I began to reflect on the meaning of that inferno which Strindberg had so mercilessly depicted. And, as I ruminated, it began to grow clear to me, the mystery of his pilgrimage, the flight which the poet makes over the face of the earth and then, as if he had been ordained to re-enact a lost drama, the heroic descent to the very bowels of the earth, the dark and fearsome sojourn in the belly of the whale, the bloody struggle to liberate himself, to emerge clean of the past, a bright, gory sun god cast up on an alien shore. It was no mystery to me any longer why he and others (Dante, Rabelais, Van Gogh, etc., etc.) had made their pilgrimage to Paris. I understood then why it is that Paris attracts the tortured, the hallucinated, the great maniacs of love. I understood why it is that here, at the very hub of the wheel, one can embrace the most fantastic, the most impossible theories, without finding them in the least strange; it is here that one reads again the books of his youth and the enigmas take on new meanings, one for every white hair. One walks the streets knowing that he is mad, possessed, because it is only too obvious that these cold, indifferent faces are the visages of one's keepers. Here all boundaries fade away and the world reveals itself for the mad slaughterhouse that it is. The treadmill stretches away to infinitude, the hatches are closed down tight, logic runs rampant, with bloody cleaver flashing. The air is chill and stagnant, the language apocalyptic. Not an exit sign anywhere; no issue save death. A blind alley at the end of which is a scaffold.

An eternal city, Paris! More eternal than Rome, more splendorous than Nineveh. The very navel of the world to which, like a blind and faltering idiot, one crawls back on hands and knees. And like a cork that has drifted to the dead center of the ocean, one floats here in the scum and wrack of the seas, listless, hopeless, heedless even of a passing Columbus. The cradles of civilization are the putrid sinks of the world, the charnel house to which the stinking wombs confide their bloody packages of flesh and bone.

The streets were my refuge. And no man can understand the glamor of the streets until he is obliged to take refuge in them, until he has become a straw that is tossed here and there by every zephyr that blows. One passes along a street on a wintry day and, seeing a dog for sale, one is moved to tears. While across the way, cheerful as a cemetery, stands a miserable hut that calls itself "Hotel du Tombeau des Lapins." That makes one laugh, laugh fit to die. Until one notices that there are hotels everywhere, for rabbits, dogs, lice, emperors, cabinet ministers, pawnbrokers, horse knackers, and so on. And almost every other one is an "Hotel de l'Avenir." Which makes one more hysterical still. So many hotels of the future! No hotels in the past participle, no subjunctive modes, no conjunctivitis. Everything is hoary, grisly, bristling with merriment, swollen with the future, like a gumboil. Drunk with this lecherous eczema of the future, I stagger over to the Place Violet, the colors all mauve and slate, the doorways so low that only dwarfs and goblins could hobble in; over the dull cranium of Zola the chimneys are belching pure coke, while the Madonna of Sandwiches listens with cabbage ears to the bubbling of the gas tanks, those beautiful bloated toads which squat by the roadside.

Why do I suddenly recollect the Passage des Thermopyles? Because that day a woman addressed her puppy in the apocalyptic language of the slaughterhouse, and the little bitch, she understood what this greasy slut of a midwife was saying. How that depressed me! More even than the sight of those whimpering curs that were being sold on the Rue Brancion, because it was not the dogs which filled me so with pity, but the huge iron railing, those rusty spikes which seemed to stand between me and my rightful life. In the pleasant little lane near the Abattoir de Vaugirard (Abattoir Hippophagique), which is called the Rue des Perichaux, I had noticed here and there signs of blood. Just as Strindberg in his madness had recognized omens and portents in the very flagging of the Pension Orfila, so, as I wandered aimlessly through this muddy lane bespattered with blood, fragments of the past detached themselves and floated listlessly before my eyes, taunting me with the direst forebodings. I saw my own blood being spilled, the muddy road stained with it, as far back as I could remember, from the very beginning doubtless. One is ejected into the world like a dirty little mummy; the roads are slippery with blood and no one knows why it should be so. Each one is traveling his own way and, though the earth be rotting with good things, there is no time to pluck the fruits; the procession scrambles toward the exit sign, and such a panic is there, such a sweat to escape, that the weak and the helpless are trampled into the mud and their cries are unheard.

My world of human beings had perished; I was utterly alone in the world and for friends I had the streets, and the streets spoke to me in that sad, bitter language compounded of human misery, yearning, regret, failure, wasted effort. Passing under the viaduct along the Rue Broca, one night after I had been informed that Mona was ill and starving, I suddenly recalled that it was here in the squalor and gloom of this sunken street, terrorized perhaps by a premonition of the future, that Mona clung to me and with a quivering voice begged me to promise that I would never leave her, never, no matter what happened. And, only a few days later, I stood on the platform of the Gare St. Lazare and I watched the train pull out, the train that was bearing her away; she was leaning out of the window, just as she had leaned out of the window when I left her in New York, and there was that same, sad, inscrutable smile on her face, that last-minute look which is intended to convey so much, but which is only a mask that is twisted by a vacant smile. Only a few days before, she had clung to me desperately and then something happened, something which is not even clear to me now, and of her own volition she boarded the train and she was looking at me again with that sad, enigmatic smile which baffles me, which is unjust, unnatural, which I distrust with all my soul. And now it is I, standing in the shadow of the viaduct, who reach out for her, who cling to her desperately and there is that same inexplicable smile on my lips, the mask that I have clamped down over my grief. I can stand here and smile vacantly, and no matter how fervid my prayers, no matter how desperate my longing, there is an ocean between us; there she will stay and starve, and here I shall walk from one street to the next, the hot tears scalding my face.

It is that sort of cruelty which is embedded in the streets; it is *that* which stares out from the walls and terrifies us when suddenly we respond to a nameless fear, when suddenly our souls are invaded by a sickening panic. It is *that* which gives the lampposts their ghoulish twists, which makes them beckon to us and lure us to their strangling grip; it is *that* which makes certain houses appear like the guardians of secret crimes and their blind windows like the empty sockets of eyes that have seen too much. It is that sort of thing, written into the human physiognomy of the streets which makes me flee when overhead I suddenly see inscribed "Impasse Satan." That which makes me shudder when at the very entrance to the Mosque I observe that it is written: "Mondays and Thursdays *tuberculosis;* Wednesdays and Fridays *syphilis.*" In every Metro station there are grinning skulls that greet you with *"Defendez-vous contre la syphilis!"* Wherever there are walls, there are posters with bright venomous crabs heralding the approach of cancer. No matter where you go, no matter what you touch, there is cancer and syphilis. It is written in the sky; it flames and dances, like an evil portent. It has eaten into our souls and we are nothing but a dead thing like the moon.

I think it was the Fourth of July when they took the chair from under my ass again. Not a word of warning. One of the big muck-a-mucks from the other side of the water had decided to make economies; cutting down on proofreaders and helpless little *dactylos* enabled him to pay the expenses of his trips back and forth and the palatial quarters he occupied at the Ritz. After paying what little debts I had accumulated among the linotype operators and a goodwill token at the *bistro* across the way, in order to preserve my credit, there was scarcely anything left out of my final pay. I had to notify the *patron* of the hotel that I would be leaving; I didn't tell him why because he'd have worried about his measly two hundred francs.

"What'll you do if you lose your job?" That was the phrase that rang in my ears continually. *Ca y est maintenant! Ausgespielt!* Nothing to do but to get down into the street again, walk, hang around, sit on benches, kill time. By now, of course, my face was familiar in Montparnasse; for a while I could pretend that I was still working on the paper. That would make it a little easier to bum a breakfast or a dinner. It was summertime and the tourists were pouring in. I had schemes up my sleeve for mulcting them. "What'll you do.... ?" Well, I wouldn't starve, that's one thing. If I should do nothing else but concentrate on food that would prevent me from falling to pieces. For a week or two I could still go to Monsieur Paul's and have a square meal every evening; he wouldn't know whether I was working or not. The main thing is to eat. Trust to Providence for the rest!

Naturally, I kept my ears open for anything that sounded like a little dough. And I cultivated a whole new set of acquaintances—bores whom I had sedulously avoided heretofore, drunks whom I loathed, artists who had a little money, Guggenheim-prize men, etc. It's not hard to make friends when you squat on a *terrasse* twelve hours a day. You get to know every sot in Montparnasse. They cling to you like lice, even if you have nothing to offer them but your ears.

Now that I had lost my job Carl and Van Norden had a new phrase for me: "What if your wife should arrive now?" Well, what of it? Two mouths to feed, instead of one. I'd have a companion in misery. And, if she hadn't lost her good looks, I'd probably do better in double harness than alone: the world never permits a good-looking woman to starve. Tania I couldn't depend on to do much for me; she was sending money to Sylvester. I had thought at first that she might let me share her room, but she was afraid of compromising herself; besides, she had to be nice to her boss.

The first people to turn to when you're down and out are the Jews. I had three of them on my hands almost at once. Sympathetic souls. One of them was a retired fur merchant who had an itch to see his name in the papers; he proposed that I write a series of articles under his name for a Jewish daily in New York. I had to scout around the Dome and the Coupole searching for prominent Jews. The first man I picked on was a celebrated mathematician; he couldn't speak a word of English. I had to write about the theory of shock from the diagrams he left on the paper napkins; I had to describe the movements of the astral bodies and demolish the Einsteinian conception at the same time. All for twenty-five francs. When I saw my articles in the newspaper I couldn't read them; but they looked impressive, just the same, especially with the pseudonym of the fur merchant attached.

I did a lot of pseudonymous writing during this period. When the big new whore-house opened up on the Boulevard Edgar-Quinet, I got a little rake-off, for writing the pamphlets. That is to say, a bottle of champagne and a free fuck in one of the Egyptian rooms. If I succeeded in bringing a client I was to get my commission, just like Kepi got his in the old days. One night I brought Van Norden; he was going to let me earn a little money by enjoying himself upstairs. But when the *madame* learned that he was a news-paperman she wouldn't hear of taking money from him; it was a bottle of champagne again and a free fuck. I got nothing out of it. As a matter of fact, I had to write the story for him because he couldn't think how to get round the subject without mentioning the kind of place it was. One thing after another like that. I was getting fucked good and prop-er.

The worst job of all was a thesis I undertook to write for a deaf and dumb psycholo-gist. A treatise on the care of crippled children. My head was full of diseases and braces and workbenches and fresh air theories; it took about six weeks off and on, and then, to rub it in, I had to proofread the goddamned thing. It was in French, such a French as I've never in my life seen or heard. But it brought me in a good breakfast every day, an American breakfast, with orange juice, oatmeal, cream, coffee, now and then ham and eggs for a change. It was the only period of my Paris days that I ever indulged in a decent breakfast, thanks to the crippled children of Rockaway Beach, the East Side, and all the coves and inlets bordering on these sore points.

Then one day I fell in with a photographer; he was making a collection of the slimy joints of Paris for some degenerate in Munich. He wanted to know if I would pose for him with my pants down, and in other ways. I thought of those skinny little runts, who look like bellhops and messenger boys, that one sees on pornographic post cards in little bookshop windows occasionally, the mysterious phantoms who inhabit the Rue de la Lune and other malodorous quarters of the city. I didn't like very much the idea of advertising my physiog in the company of these elite. But, since I was assured that the photographs were for a strictly private collection, and since it was destined for Munich, I gave my consent. When you're not in your home town you can permit yourself little liberties, particularly for such a worthy motive as earning your daily bread. After all, I hadn't been so squeamish, come to think of it, even in New York. There were nights when I was so damned desperate, back there, that I had to go out right in my own neighborhood and panhandle.

We didn't go to the show places familiar to the tourists, but to the little joints where the atmosphere was more congenial, where we could play a game of cards in the afternoon before getting down to work. He was a good companion, the photographer. He knew the city inside out, the walls particularly; he talked to me about Goethe often, and the days of the Hohenstaufen, and the massacre of the Jews during the reign of the Black Death. Interesting subjects, and always related in some obscure way to the things he was doing. He had ideas for scenarios too, astounding ideas, but nobody had the courage to execute them. The sight of a horse, split open like a saloon door, would inspire him to talk of Dante or Leonardo da Vinci or Rembrandt; from the slaughterhouse at Villette he would jump into a cab and rush me to the Trocadero Museum, in order to point out a skull or a mummy that had fascinated him. We explored the 5th, the 13th, the 19th and the 20th *arrondissements* thoroughly. Our favorite resting places were lugubrious little spots such as the Place Nationale, Place des Peupliers, Place de la Contrescarpe, Place Paul-Verlaine. Many of these places were already familiar to me, but all of them I now saw in a different light owing to the rare flavor of his conversation. If today I should happen to stroll down the Rue du Chateau-des-Rentiers, for example, inhaling the fetid stench of the hospital beds with which the 13th *arrondissement* reeks, my nostrils would undoubtedly expand with pleasure, because, compounded with that odor of stale piss and formaldehyde, there would be the odors of our imaginative voyages through the charnel house of Europe which the Black Death had created.

Through him I got to know a spiritual-minded individual named Kruger, who was a sculptor and painter. Kruger took a shine to me for some reason or other; it was impossible to get away from him once he discovered that I was willing to listen to his "esoteric" ideas. There are people in this world for whom the word "esoteric" seems to act as a divine ichor. Like "settled" for Herr Peeperkorn of the *Magic Mountain*. Kruger was one of those saints who have gone wrong, a masochist, an anal type whose law is scrupulousness, rectitude and conscientiousness, who on an off day would knock a man's teeth down his throat without a qualm. He seemed to think I was ripe to move on to another plane, "a *higher* plane," as he put it. I was ready to move on to any plane he designated, provided that one didn't eat less or drink less. He chewed my head off about the "threadsoul," the "causal body," "ablation," the Upanishads, Plotinus, Krishnamurti, "the Karmic vesture of the soul," "the nirvanic consciousness," all that flapdoodle which blows out of the East like a breath from the plague. Sometimes he would go into a trance and talk about his previous incarnations, how he imagined them to be, at least. Or he would relate his dreams which, so far as I could see, were thoroughly insipid, prosaic, hardly worth even the attention of a Freudian, but, for him, there were vast esoteric marvels hidden in their depths which I had to aid him to decipher. He had turned himself inside out, like a coat whose nap is worn off.

Little by little, as I gained his confidence, I wormed my way into his heart. I had him at such a point that he would come running after me, in the street, to inquire if he could lend me a few francs. He wanted to hold me together in order to survive the transition to a higher plane. I acted like a pear that is ripening on the tree. Now and then I had relapses and I would confess my need for more earthly nourishment—a visit to the Sphinx or the Rue St. Apolline where I knew he repaired in weak moments when the demands of the flesh had become too vehement.

As a painter he was nil; as a sculptor less than nil. He was a good housekeeper, that I'll say for him. And an economical one to boot. Nothing went to waste, not even the paper that the meat was wrapped in. Friday nights he threw open his studio to his fellow artists; there was always plenty to drink and good sandwiches, and if by chance there was anything left over I would come round the next day to polish it off.

Back of the Bal Bullier was another studio I got into the habit of frequenting—the studio of Mark Swift. If he was not a genius he was certainly an eccentric, this caustic Irishman. He had for a model a Jewess whom he had been living with for years; he was now tired of her and was searching for a pretext to get rid of her. But as he had eaten up the dowry which she had originally brought with her, he was puzzled as to how to disembarrass himself of her without making restitution. The simplest thing was to so antagonize her that she would choose starvation rather than support his cruelties.

She was rather a fine person, his mistress; the worst that one could say against her was that she had lost her shape, *and* her ability to support him any longer. She was a painter herself and, among those who professed to know, it was said that she had far more talent than he. But no matter how miserable he made life for her she was just; she would never allow anyone to say that he was not a great painter. It was because he really has genius, she said, that he was such a rotten individual. One never saw her canvases on the wall—only his. Her things were stuck away in the kitchen. Once it happened, in my presence, that someone insisted on seeing her work. The result was painful. "You see this figure," said Swift, pointing to one of her canvases with his big foot. "The man standing in the doorway there is just about to go out for a leak. He won't be able to find his way back because his head is on wrong.... Now take that nude over there.... It was all right until she started to paint the cunt. I don't know what she was thinking about, but she made it so big that her brush slipped and she couldn't get it out again."

By way of showing us what a nude ought to be like he hauls out a huge canvas which he had recently completed. It was a picture of *her,* a splendid piece of vengeance inspired by a guilty conscience. The work of a madman—vicious, petty, malign, brilliant. You had the feeling that he had spied on her through the keyhole, that he had caught her in an off moment, when she was picking her nose absent-mindedly, or scratching her ass. She at there on the horsehair sofa, in a room without ventilation, an enormous room without a window; it might as well have been the anterior lobe of the pineal gland. Back of her ran the zigzag stairs leading to the balcony; they were covered with a bilious-green carpet, such green as could only emanate from a universe that had been pooped out. The most prominent thing was her buttocks, which were lopsided and full of scabs; she seemed to have slightly raised her ass from the sofa, as if to let a loud fart. Her face he had idealized: it looked sweet and virginal, pure as a cough drop. But her bosom was distended, swollen with sewer gas; she seemed to be swimming in a menstrual sea, an enlarged fetus with the dull, syrupy look of an angel.

Nevertheless one couldn't help but like him. He was an indefatigable worker, a man who hadn't a single thought in his head but paint. And cunning as a lynx withal. It was he who put it into my head to cultivate the friendship of Fillmore, a young man in the diplomatic service who had found his way into the little group that surrounded Kruger and Swift. "Let him help you," he aid. "He doesn't know what to do with his money."

When one spends what he has on himself, when one has a thoroughly good time with his own money, people are apt to say "he doesn't know what to do with his money." For my part, I don't see any better use to which one can put money. About such individuals one can't say that they're generous or stingy. They put money into circulation—that's the principal thing. Fillmore knew that his days in France were limited; he was determined to enjoy them. And as one always enjoys himself better in the company of a friend it was only natural that he should turn to one like myself, who had plenty of time on his hands, for that companionship which he needed. People said he was a bore, and so he was, I suppose, but when you're in need of food you can put up with worse things than being bored. After all, despite the fact that he talked incessantly, and usually about himself or the authors whom he admired slavishly—such birds as Anatole France and Joseph Conrad—he nevertheless made my nights interesting in other ways. He liked to dance, he liked good wines, and he liked women. That he liked Byron also, and Victor Hugo, one could forgive; he was only a few years out of college and he had plenty of time ahead of him to be cured of such tastes. What he had that I liked was a sense of adventure.

We got even better acquainted, more intimate, I might say, due to a peculiar incident that occurred during my brief sojourn with Kruger. It happened just after the arrival of Collins, a sailor whom Fillmore had got to know on the way over from America. The three of us used to meet regularly on the *terrasse* of the Rotonde before going to dinner. It was always Pernod, a drink which put Collins in good humor and provided a base, as it were, for the wine and beer and *fines,* etc., which had to be guzzled afterward. All during Collins's stay in Paris I lived like a duke; nothing but fowl and good vintages and desserts that I hadn't even heard of before. A month of this regimen and I should have been obliged to go to Baden-Baden or Vichy or Aix-les-Bains. Meanwhile Kruger was putting me up at his studio. I was getting to be a nuisance because I never showed up before three a.m. and it was difficult to rout me out of bed before noon. Overtly Kruger never uttered a word of reproach but his manner indicated plainly enough that I was becoming a bum.

One day I was taken ill. The rich diet was taking effect upon me. I don't know what ailed me, but I couldn't get out of bed. I had lost all my stamina, and with it whatever courage I possessed. Kruger had to look after me, had to make broths for me, and so on. It was a trying period for him, more particularly because he was just on the verge of giving an important exhibition at his studio, a private showing to some wealthy connoisseurs from whom he was expecting aid. The cot on which I lay was in the studio; there was no other room to put me in.

The morning of the day he was to give his exhibition, Kruger awoke thoroughly disgruntled. If I had been able to stand on my feet I know he would have given me a clout in the jaw and kicked me out. But I was prostrate, and weak as a cat. He tried to coax me out of bed, with the idea of locking me up in the kitchen upon the arrival of his visitors. I realized that I was making a mess of it for him. People can't look at pictures and statues with enthusiasm when a man is dying before their eyes. Kruger honestly thought I was dying. So did I. That's why, despite my feelings of guilt, I couldn't muster any enthusiasm when he proposed calling for the ambulance and having me shipped to the American Hospital. I wanted to die there, comfortably, right in the studio; I didn't want to be urged to get up and find a better place to die in. I didn't care where I died, really, so long as it wasn't necessary to get up.

When he heard me talk this way Kruger became alarmed. Worse than having a sick man in his studio should the visitors arrive, was to have a dead man. That would completely ruin his prospects, slim as they were. He didn't put it that way to me, of course, but I could see from his agitation that that was what worried him. And that made me stubborn. I refused to let him call the hospital. I refused to let him call a doctor. I refused everything.

He got so angry with me finally that, despite my protestations, he began to dress me. I was too weak to resist. All I could do was to murmur weakly—"you bastard you!" Though it was warm outdoors I was shivering like a dog. After he had completely dressed me he flung an overcoat over me and slipped outside to telephone. "I won't go! I won't go!" I kept saying but he simply slammed the door on me. He came back in a few minutes and, without addressing a word to me, busied himself about the studio. Last minute preparations. In a little while there was a knock on the door. It was Fillmore. Collins was waiting downstairs, he informed me.

The two of them, Fillmore and Kruger, slipped their arms under me and hoisted me to my feet. As they dragged me to the elevator Kruger softened up. "It's for your own good," he said. "And besides, it wouldn't be fair to me. You know what a struggle I've had all these years. You ought to think about me too." He was actually on the point of tears.

Wretched and miserable as I felt, his words almost made me smile. He was considerably older than I, and even though he was a rotten painter, a rotten artist all the way through, he deserved a break—at least once in a lifetime.

"I don't hold it against you," I muttered. "I understand how it is."

"You know I always liked you," he responded. "When you get better you can come back here again... you can stay as long as you like."

"Sure, I know.... I'm not going to croak yet," I managed to get out.

Somehow, when I saw Collins down below my spirits revived. If ever any one seemed to be thoroughly alive, healthy, joyous, magnanimous, it was he. He picked me up as if I were a doll and laid me out on the seat of the cab—gently too, which I appreciated after the way Kruger had manhandled me.

When we drove up to the hotel—the hotel that Collins was stopping at—there was a bit of a discussion with the proprietor, during which I lay stretched out on the sofa in the *bureau*. I could hear Collins saying to the *patron* that it was nothing ... just a little breakdown ... be all right in a few days. I saw him put a crisp bill in the man's hands and then, turning swiftly and lithely, he came back to where I was and said: "Come on, buck up! Don't let him think you're croaking." And with that, he yanked me to my feet and, bracing me with one arm, escorted me to the elevator.

Don't let him think you're croaking! Obviously it was bad taste to die on people's hands. One should die in the bosom of his family, in private, as it were. His words were encouraging. I began to see it all as a bad joke. Upstairs, with the door closed, they undressed me and put me between the sheets. "You can't die now, goddamn it!" said Collins warmly. "You'll put me in a hole.... Besides, what the hell's the matter with you? Can't stand good living? Keep your chin up! You'll be eating a porterhouse steak in a day or two. You think you're ill! Wait, by Jesus until you get a dose of syphilis! That's something to make you worry...." And he began to relate, in a humorous way, his trip down the Yangtze Kiang, with hair falling out and teeth rotting away. In the feeble state that I was in, the yarn that he spun had an extraordinary soothing effect upon me. It took me completely out of myself. He had guts, this guy. Perhaps he put it on a bit thick, for my benefit, but I wasn't listening to him critically at the moment. I was all ears and eyes. I saw the dirty yellow mouth or the river, the lights going up at Hankow, the sea of yellow faces, the sampans shooting down through the gorges and the rapids flaming with the sulfurous breath of the dragon. What a story! The coolies swarming around the boat each day, dredging for the garbage that was flung overboard, Tom Slattery rising up on his deathbed to take a last look at the lights of Hankow, the beautiful Eurasian who lay in a dark room and filled his veins with poison, the monotony of blue jackets and yellow faces, millions and millions of them hollowed out by famine, ravaged by disease, subsisting on rats and dogs and roots, chewing the grass off the earth, devouring their own children. It was hard to imagine that this man's body had once been a mass of sores, that he had been shunned like a leper; his voice was so quiet and gentle, it was as though his spirit had been cleansed by all the suffering he had endured. As he reached for his drink his face grew more and more soft and his words actually seemed to caress me. And all the while China hanging over us like Fate itself. A China rotting away, crumbling to dust like a huge dinosaur, yet preserving to the very end the glamor, the enchantment, the mystery, the cruelty of her hoary legends.

I could no longer follow his story; my mind had slipped back to a Fourth of July when I bought my first package of firecrackers and with it the long pieces of punk which break so easily, the punk that you blow on to get a good red glow, the punk whose smell sticks to your fingers for days and makes you dream of strange things. The Fourth of July the streets are littered with bright red paper stamped with black and gold figures and everywhere there are tiny firecrackers which have the most curious intestines; packages and packages of them, all strung together by their thin, flat, little gutstrings, the color of human brains. All day long there is the smell of powder and punk and the gold dust from the bright red wrappers sticks to your fingers. One never thinks of China, but it is there all the time on the tips of your fingers and it makes your nose itchy; and long afterward, when you have forgotten almost what a firecracker smells like, you wake up one day with gold leaf choking you and the broken pieces of punk waft back their pungent odor and the bright red wrappers give you a nostalgia for a people and a soil you have never known, but which is in your blood, mysteriously there in your blood, like the sense of time or space, a fugitive, constant value to which you turn more and more as you get old, which you try to seize with your mind, but ineffectually, because in everything Chinese there is wisdom and mystery and you can never grasp it with two hands or with your mind but you must let it rub off, let it stick to your fingers, let it slowly infiltrate your veins.

A few weeks later, upon receipt of a pressing invitation from Collins who had returned to Le Havre, Fillmore and I boarded the train one morning, prepared to spend the weekend with him. It was the first time I had been outside of Paris since my arrival here. We were in fine fettle, drinking Anjou all the way to the coast. Collins had given us the address of a bar where we were to meet; it was a place called Jimmie's Bar, which everyone in Le Havre was supposed to know.

We got into an open barouche at the station and started on a brisk trot for the rendezvous; there was still a half bottle of Anjou left which we polished off as we rode along. Le Havre looked gay, sunny; the air was bracing, with that strong salty tang which almost made me homesick for New York. There were masts and hulls cropping up everywhere, bright bits of bunting, big open squares and high-ceilinged cafes such as one only sees in the provinces. A fine impression immediately; the city was welcoming us with open arms.

Before we ever reached the bar we saw Collins coming down the street on a trot, heading for the station, no doubt, and a little late as usual. Fillmore immediately suggested a Pernod; we were all slapping each other on the back, laughing and spitting, drunk already from the sunshine and the salt sea air. Collins seemed undecided about the Pernod at first. He had a little dose of clap, he informed us. Nothing very serious—"a strain" most likely. He showed us a bottle he had in his pocket—"Venetienne" it was called, if I remember rightly. The sailors' remedy for clap.

We stopped off at a restaurant to have a little snack before repairing to Jimmie's place. It was a huge tavern with big, smoky rafters and tables creaking with food. We drank copiously of the wines that Collins recommended. Then we sat down on a terrasse and had coffee and liqueurs. Collins was talking about the Baron de Charlus, a man after his own heart, he said. For almost a year now he had been staying at Le Havre, going through the money that he had accumulated during his bootlegging days. His tastes were simple— food, drink, women and books. And a private bath! That he insisted on.

We were still talking about the Baron de Charlus when we arrived at Jimmie's Bar. It was late in the afternoon and the place was just beginning to fill up. Jimmie was there, his face red as a beet, and beside him was his spouse, a fine buxom Frenchwoman with glittering eyes. We were given a marvelous reception all around. There were Pernods in front of us again, the gramophone was shrieking, people were jabbering away in English and French and Dutch and Norwegian and Spanish, and Jimmie and his wife, both of them looking very brisk and dapper, were slapping and kissing each other heartily and raising their glasses and clinking them—altogether such a bubble and blabber of merriment that you felt like pulling off your clothes and doing a war dance. The women at the bar had gathered around like flies. If we were friends of Collins that meant we were rich. It didn't matter that we had come in our old clothes; all *Anglais* dressed like that. I hadn't a sou in my pocket, which didn't matter, of course, since I was the guest of honor. Nevertheless I felt somewhat embarrassed with two stunning-looking whores hanging on my arms waiting for me to order something. I decided to take the bull by the horns. You couldn't tell any more which drinks were on the house and which were to be paid for. I had to be a *gentleman,* even if I didn't have a sou in my pocket.

Yvette—that was Jimmie's wife—was extraordinarily gracious and friendly with us. She was preparing a little spread in our honor. It would take a little while yet. We were not to get too drunk—she wanted us to enjoy the meal. The gramophone was going like wild and Fillmore had begun to dance with a beautiful mulatto who had on a tight velvet dress that revealed all her charms. Collins slipped over to my side and whispered a few words about the girl at my side. "The *madame* will invite her to dinner," he said, "if you'd like to have her." She was an ex-whore who owned a beautiful home on the outskirts of the city. The mistress of a sea captain now. He was away and there was nothing to fear. "If she likes you she'll invite you to stay with her," he added.

That was enough for me. I turned at once to Marcelle and began to flatter the ass off her. We stood at the corner of the bar, pretending to dance, and mauled each other ferociously. Jimmie gave me a big horse-wink and nodded his head approvingly. She was a lascivious bitch, this Marcelle, and pleasant at the same time. She soon got rid of the other girl, I noticed, and then we settled down for a long and intimate conversation which was interrupted unfortunately by the announcement that dinner was ready.

There were about twenty of us at the table, and Marcelle and I were placed at one end opposite Jimmie and his wife. It began with the popping of champagne corks and was quickly followed by drunken speeches, during the course of which Marcelle and I played with each other under the table. When it came my turn to stand up and deliver a few words I had to hold the napkin in front of me. It was painful and exhilarating at the same time. I had to cut the speech very short because Marcelle was tickling me in the crotch all the while.

The dinner lasted until almost midnight. I was looking forward to spending the night with Marcelle in that beautiful home up on the cliff. But it was not to be. Collins had planned to show us about and I couldn't very well refuse. "Don't worry about her," he said. "You'll have a bellyful of it before you leave. Tell her to wait here for you until we get back."

She was a bit peeved at this, Marcelle, but when we informed her that we had several days ahead of us she brightened up. When we got outdoors Fillmore very solemnly took us by the arm and said he had a little confession to make. He looked pale and worried.

"Well, what is it?" said Collins cheerfully. "Spit it out!"

Fillmore couldn't spit it out like that, all at once. He hemmed and hawed and finally he blurted out—"Well, when I went to the closet just a minute ago I noticed something...."

"Then you've got it!" said Collins triumphantly, and with that he flourished the bottle of "Venetienne." "Don't go to a doctor," he added venomously. "They'll bleed you to death, the greedy bastards. And don't stop drinking either. That's all hooey. Take this twice a day... shake it well before using. And nothing's worse than worry, do you understand? Come on now. I'll give you a syringe and some permanganate when we get back."

And so we started out into the night, down toward the waterfront where there was the sound of music and shouts and drunken oaths, Collins talking quietly all the while about this and that, about a boy he had fallen in love with, and the devil's time he had to get out of the scrape when the parents got wise to it. From that he switched back to the Baron de Charlus and then to Kurtz who had gone up the river and got lost. His favorite theme. I liked the way Collins moved against this background of literature continuously; it was like a millionaire who never stepped out of his Rolls Royce. There was no intermediate realm for him between reality and ideas. When we entered the whorehouse on the Quai Voltaire, after he had flung himself on the divan and rung for girls and for drinks, he was still paddling up the river with Kurtz, and only when the girls had flopped on the bed beside him and stuffed his mouth with kisses did he cease his divagations. Then, as if he had suddenly realized where he was, he turned to the old mother who ran the place and gave her an eloquent spiel about his two friends who had come down from Paris express-

ly to see the joint. There were about half a dozen girls in the room, all naked and all beautiful to look at, I must say. They hopped about like birds while the three of us tried to
maintain a conversation with the grandmother. Finally the latter excused herself and told
us to make ourselves at home. I was altogether taken in by her, so sweet and amiable she
was, so thoroughly gentle and maternal. And what manners! If she had been a little
younger I would have made overtures to her. Certainly you would not have thought that
we were in a "den of vice," as it is called.

Anyway we stayed there an hour or so, and as I was the only one in condition to enjoy
the privileges of the house, Collins and Fillmore remained downstairs chattering with the
girls. When I returned I found the two of them stretched out on the bed; the girls had
formed a semicircle about the bed and were singing with the most angelic voices the chorus of *Roses in Picardy*. We were sentimentally depressed when we left the house—
Fillmore particularly. Collins swiftly steered us to a rough joint which was packed with
drunken sailors on shore leave and there we sat awhile enjoying the homosexual rout that
was in full swing. When we sallied out we had to pass through the red-light district where
there were more grandmothers with shawls about their necks sitting on the doorsteps fanning themselves and nodding pleasantly to the passers-by. All such good-looking, kindly
souls, as if they were keeping guard over a nursery. Little groups of sailors came swinging
along and pushed their way noisily inside the gaudy joints. Sex everywhere: it was slop-
ping over, a neap tide that swept the props from under the city. We piddled along at the
edge of the basin where everything was jumbled and tangled; you had the impression that
all these ships, these trawlers and yachts and schooners and barges, had been blown ashore
by a violent storm.

In the space of forty-eight hours so many things had happened that it seemed as if
we had been in Le Havre a month or more. We were planning to leave early Monday
morning, as Fillmore had to be back on the job. We spent Sunday drinking and carousing, clap or no clap. That afternoon Collins confided to us that he was thinking of returning to his ranch in Idaho; he hadn't been home for eight years and he wanted to have a
look at the mountains again before making another voyage East. We were sitting in a
whorehouse at the time, waiting for a girl to appear; he had promised to slip her some
cocaine. He was fed up with Le Havre, he told us. Too many vultures hanging around his
neck. Besides, Jimmie's wife had fallen in love with him and she was making things hot
for him with her jealous fits. There was a scene almost every night. She had been on her
good behavior since we arrived, but it wouldn't last, he promised us. She was particularly
jealous of a Russian girl who came to the bar now and then when she got tight. A trou-
blemaker. On top of it all he was desperately in love with this boy whom he had told us
about the first day. "A boy can break your heart," he said. "He's so damned beautiful! And
so cruel!" We had to laugh at this. It sounded preposterous. But Collins was in earnest.

Around midnight Sunday Fillmore and I retired; we had been given a room upstairs
over the bar. It was sultry as the devil, not a breath of air stirring. Through the open windows we could hear them shouting downstairs and the gramophone going continually. All
of a sudden a storm broke—a regular cloudburst. And between the thunderclaps and the
squalls that lashed the window-panes there came to our ears the sound of another storm
raging downstairs at the bar. It sounded frightfully close and sinister; the women were
shrieking at the tops of their lungs, bottles were crashing, tables were upset and there was
that familiar, nauseating thud that the human body makes when it crashes to the floor.

About six o'clock Collins stuck his head in the door. His face was all plastered and one arm was stuck in a sling. He had a big grin on his face.

"Just as I told you," he said. "She broke loose last night. Suppose you heard the racket?"

We got dressed quickly and went downstairs to say good-bye to Jimmie. The place was completely demolished, not a bottle left standing, not a chair that wasn't broken. The mirror and the show window were smashed to bits. Jimmie was making himself an eggnog.

On the way to the station we pieced the story together. The Russian girl had dropped in after we toddled off to bed and Yvette had insulted her promptly, without even waiting for an excuse. They had commenced to pull each other's hair and in the midst of it a big Swede had stepped in and given the Russian girl a sound slap in the jaw—to bring her to her senses. That started the fireworks. Collins wanted to know what right this big stiff had to interfere in a private quarrel. He got a poke in the jaw for an answer, a good one that sent him flying to the other end of the bar. "Serves you right!" screamed Yvette, taking advantage of the occasion to swing a bottle at the Russian girl's head. And at that moment the thunderstorm broke loose. For a while there was a regular pandemonium, the women all hysterical and hungry to seize the opportunity to pay off private grudges. Nothing like a nice barroom brawl... so easy to stick a knife in a man's back or club him with a bottle when he's lying under a table. The poor Swede found himself in a hornet's nest; everyone in the place hated him, particularly his shipmates. They wanted to see him done in. And so they locked the door and pushing the tables aside they made a little space in front of the bar where the two of them could have it out. And they had it out! They had to carry the poor devil to the hospital when it was over. Collins had come off rather lucky—nothing more than a sprained wrist and a couple of fingers out of joint, a bloody nose and a black eye. Just a few scratches, as he put it. But if he ever signed up with that Swede he was going to murder him. It wasn't finished yet. He promised us that.

And that wasn't the end of the fracas either. After that Yvette had to go out and get liquored up at another bar. She had been insulted and she was going to put an end to things. And so she hires a taxi and orders the driver to ride out to the edge of the cliff overlooking the water. She was going to kill herself, that's what she was going to do. But then she was so drunk that when she tumbled out of the cab she began to weep and before any one could stop her she had begun to peel her clothes off. The driver brought her home that way, half-naked, and when Jimmie saw the condition she was in he was so furious with her that he took his razor strop and he belted the piss out of her, and she liked it, the bitch that she was. "Do it some more!" she begged, down on her knees as she was and clutching him around the legs with her two arms. But Jimmie had enough of it. "You're a dirty old sow!" he said and with his foot he gave her a shove in the guts that took the wind out of her—and a bit of her sexy nonsense too.

It was high time we were leaving. The city looked different in the early morning light. The last thing we talked about, as we stood there waiting for the train to pull out, was Idaho. The three of us were Americans. We came from different places, each of us, but we had something in common—a whole lot, I might say. We were getting sentimental, as Americans do when it comes time to part. We were getting quite foolish about the cows and sheep and the big open spaces where men are men and all that crap. If a boat had swung along instead of the train we'd have hopped aboard and said good-bye to it all. But

Collins was never to see America again, as I learned later; and Fillmore... well, Fillmore had to take his punishment too, in a way that none of us could have suspected then. It's best to keep America just like that, always in the background, a sort of picture post card which you look at in a weak moment. Like that, you imagine it's always there waiting for you, unchanged, unspoiled, a big patriotic open space with cows and sheep and tender-hearted men ready to bugger everything in sight, man, woman or beast. It doesn't exist, America. It's a name you give to an abstract idea....

Paris is like a whore. From a distance she seems ravishing, you can't wait until you have her in your arms. And five minutes later you feel empty, disgusted with yourself. You feel tricked.

I returned to Paris with money in my pocket—a few hundred francs, which Collins had shoved in my pocket just as I was boarding the train. It was enough to pay for a room and at least a week's good rations. It was more than I had had in my hands at one time for several years. I felt elated, as though perhaps a new life was opening before me. I wanted to conserve it too, so I looked up a cheap hotel over a bakery on the Rue du Chateau, just off the Rue de Vanves, a place that Eugene had pointed out to me once. A few yards away was the bridge that spans the Montparnasse tracks. A familiar quarter.

I could have had a room for a hundred francs a month, a room without any conveniences to be sure—without even a window—and perhaps I would have taken it, just to be sure of a place to flop for a while, had it not been for the fact that in order to reach this room I would have been obliged to first pass through the room of a blind man. The thought of passing his bed every night had a most depressing effect upon me. I decided to look elsewhere. I went over to the Rue Cels, just behind the cemetery, and I looked at a sort of rat trap there with balconies running around the courtyard. There were birdcages suspended from the balcony too, all along the lower tier. A cheerful sight perhaps, but to me it seemed like the public ward ma hospital. The proprietor didn't seem to have all his wits either. I decided to wait for the night, to have a good look around, and then choose some attractive little joint in a quiet side street.

At dinnertime I spent fifteen francs for a meal, just about twice the amount I had planned to allot myself. That made me so wretched that I wouldn't allow myself to sit down for a coffee, even despite the fact that it had begun to drizzle. No, I would walk about a bit and then go quietly to bed, at a reasonable hour. I was already miserable, trying to husband my resources this way. I had never in my life done it; it wasn't in my nature.

Finally it began to come down in bucketsful. I was glad. That would give me the excuse I needed to duck somewhere and stretch my legs out. It was still too early to go to bed. I began to quicken my pace, heading back toward the Boulevard Raspail. Suddenly a woman comes up to me and stops me, right in the pouring rain. She wants to know what time it is. I told her I didn't have a watch. And then she bursts out, just like this: "Oh, my good sir, do you speak English by chance?" I nod my head. It's coming down in torrents now. "Perhaps, my dear good man, you would be so kind as to take me to a cafe. It is raining so and I haven't the money to sit down anywhere. You will excuse me, my dear sir, but you have such a kind face... I knew you were English right away." And with this she smiles at me, a strange, half-demented smile. "Perhaps you could give me a little advice, dear sir. I am all alone in the world... my God, it is terrible to have no money...."

This "dear sir" and "kind sir" and "my good man," etc., had me on the verge of hysteria. I felt sorry for her and yet I had to laugh. I did laugh. I laughed right in her face. And then she laughed too, a weird, high-pitched laugh, off key, an altogether unexpected piece of cachinnation. I caught her by the arm and we made a bolt for it to the nearest cafe. She was still giggling when we entered the *bistro*. "My dear good sir," she began again, "perhaps you think I am not telling you the truth. I am a good girl... I come of a good family. Only"—and here she gave me that wan, broken smile again—"only I am so misfortunate as not to have a place to sit down." At this I began to laugh again. I couldn't help it—the phrases she used, the strange accent, the crazy hat she had on, that demented smile....

"Listen," I interrupted, "what nationality are you?"

"I'm English," she replied. "That is, I was born in Poland, but my father is Irish."

'So that makes you English?"

"Yes," she said, and she began to giggle again, sheepishly, and with a pretense of being coy.

"I suppose you know a nice little hotel where you could take me?" I said this, not because I had any intention of going with her, but just to spare her the usual preliminaries.

"Oh, my dear sir," she said, as though I had made the most grievous error, "I'm sure you don't mean that! I'm not that kind of a girl. You were joking with me, I can see that. You're so good... you have such a kind face. I would not dare to speak to a Frenchman as I did to you. They insult you right away...."

She went on in this vein for some time. I wanted to break away from her. But she didn't want to be left alone. She was afraid—her papers were not in order. Wouldn't I be good enough to walk her to her hotel? Perhaps I could "lend" her fifteen or twenty francs, to quiet the *patron*? I walked her to the hotel where she said she was stopping and I put a fifty franc bill in her hand. Either she was very clever, or very innocent—it's hard to tell sometimes—but, at any rate, she wanted me to wait until she ran to the *bistro* for change. I told her not to bother. And with that she seized my hand impulsively and raised it to her lips. I was flabbergasted. I felt like giving her every damned thing I had. That touched me, that crazy little gesture. I thought to myself, it's good to be rich once in a while, just to get a new thrill like that. Just the same, I didn't lose my head. Fifty francs! That was quite enough to squander on a rainy night. As I walked off she waved to me with that crazy little bonnet which she didn't know how to wear. It was as though we were old playmates. I felt foolish and giddy. "My dear kind sir... you have such a gentle face... you are so good, etc." I felt like a saint.

When you feel all puffed up inside it isn't so easy to go to bed right away. You feel as though you ought to atone for such unexpected bursts of goodness. Passing the "Jungle" I caught a glimpse of the dance floor; women with bare backs and ropes of pearls choking them—or so it looked—were wiggling their beautiful bottoms at me. Walked right up to the bar and ordered a *coupe* of champagne. When the music stopped, a beautiful blonde—she looked like a Norwegian—took a seat right beside me. The place wasn't as crowded or as gay as it had appeared from outside. There were only a half dozen couples in the place—they must have all been dancing at once. I ordered another *coupe* of champagne in order not to let my courage dribble away.

When I got up to dance with the blonde there was no one on the floor but us. Any other time I would have been self-conscious, but the champagne and the way she clung to me, the dimmed lights and the solid feeling of security which the few hundred francs gave me, well.... We had another dance together, a sort of private exhibition, and then we fell into conversation. She had begun to weep—that was how it started. I thought possibly she had had too much to drink, so I pretended not to be concerned. And meanwhile I was looking around to see if there was any other timber available. But the place was thoroughly deserted.

The thing to do when you're trapped is to breeze—at once. If you don't, you're lost. What retained me, oddly enough, was the thought of paying for a hat check a second time. One always lets himself in for it because of a trifle.

The reason she was weeping, I discovered soon enough, was because she had just buried her child. She wasn't Norwegian either, but French, and a midwife to boot. A chic midwife, I must say, even with the tears running down her face. I asked her if a little drink would help to console her, whereupon she very promptly ordered a whisky and tossed it off in the wink of an eye. "Would you like another?" I suggested gently. She thought she would, she felt so rotten, so terribly dejected. She thought she would like a package of Camels too. "No, wait a minute," she said, "I think I'd rather have *les* Pall Mall." Have what you like, I thought, but stop weeping, for Christ's sake, it gives me the willies. I jerked her to her feet for another dance. On her feet she seemed to be another person. Maybe grief makes one more lecherous, I don't know. I murmured something about breaking away. "Where to?" she said eagerly. "Oh, anywhere. Some quiet place where we can talk."

I went to the toilet and counted the money over again. I hid the hundred franc notes in my fob pocket and kept a fifty franc note and the loose change in my trousers pocket. I went back to the bar determined to talk turkey.

She made it easier for me because she herself introduced the subject. She was in difficulties. It was not only that she had just lost her child, but her mother was home, ill, very ill, and there was the doctor to pay and medicine to be bought, and so on and so forth. I didn't believe a word of it, of course. And since I had to find a hotel for myself, I suggested that she come along with me and stay the night. A little economy there, I thought to myself. But she wouldn't do that. She insisted on going home, said she had an apartment to herself—and besides she had to look after her mother. On reflection I decided that it would be still cheaper sleeping at her place, so I said yes and let's go immediately. Before going, however, I decided it was best to let her know just how I stood, so that there wouldn't be any squawking at the last minute. I thought she was going to faint when I told her how much I had in my pocket. "The likes of it!" she said. Highly insulted she was. I thought there would be a scene.... Undaunted, however, I stood my ground. "Very well, then, I'll leave you," I said quietly. "Perhaps I've made a mistake."

"I should say you have!" she exclaimed, but clutching me by the sleeve at the same time. *"Ecoute, cheri... sois raisonnable!"* When I heard that all my confidence was restored. I knew that it would be merely a question of promising her a little extra and everything would be O.K. "All right," I said wearily, "I'll be nice to you, you'll see."

"You were lying to me, then?" she said.

"Yes," I smiled, "I was just lying...."

Before I had even put my hat on she had hailed a cab. I heard her give the Boulevard de Clichy for an address. That was more than the price of room, I thought to myself. Oh well, there was time yet... we'd see. I don't know how it started any more but soon she was raving to me about Henry Bordeaux. I have yet to meet a whore who doesn't know of Henry Bordeaux! But this one was genuinely inspired; her language was beautiful now, so tender, so discerning, that I was debating how much to give her. It seemed to me that I had heard her say—"*quand il n'y aura plus de temps."* It sounded like that, anyway. In the state I was in, a phrase like that was worth a hundred francs. I wondered if it was her own or if she had pulled it from Henry Bordeaux. Little matter. It was just the right phrase with which to roll up to the foot of Montmartre. "Good evening, mother," I was saying to myself, "daughter and I will look after you—*quand il n'y aura plus de temps!"* She was going to show me her diploma, too, I remembered that.

She was all aflutter, once the door had closed behind us. Distracted. Wringing her hands and striking Sarah Bernhardt poses, half undressed too, and pausing between times to urge me to hurry, to get undressed, to do this and do that. Finally, when she had stripped down and was poking about with a chemise in her hand, searching for her kimono, I caught hold of her and gave her a good squeeze. She had a look of anguish on her face when I released her. "My God! My God! I must go downstairs and have a look at mother!" she exclaimed. "You can take a bath if you like, *cheri.* There! I'll be back in a few minutes." At the door I embraced her again. I was in my underclothes and I had a tremendous erection. Somehow all this anguish and excitement, all the grief and histrionics, only whetted my appetite. Perhaps she was just going downstairs to quiet her *maquereau.* I had a feeling that something unusual was happening, some sort of drama which I would read about in the morning paper. I gave the place a quick inspection. There were two rooms and a bath, not badly furnished. Rather coquettish. There was her diploma on the wall— "first class," as they all read. And there was the photograph of a child, a little girl with beautiful locks, on the dresser. I put the water on for a bath, and then I changed my mind. If something were to happen and I were found in the tub ... I didn't like the idea. I paced back and forth, getting more and more uneasy as the minutes rolled by.

When she returned she was even more upset than before. "She's going to die ... she's going to die!" she kept wailing. For a moment I was almost on the point of leaving. How the hell can you climb over a woman when her mother's dying downstairs, perhaps right beneath you? I put my arms around her, half in sympathy and half determined to get what I had come for. As we stood thus she murmured, as if in real distress, her need for the money I had promised her. It was for *"maman."* Shit, I didn't have the heart to haggle about a few francs at the moment. I walked over to the chair where my clothes were lying and I wiggled a hundred franc note out of my fob pocket, carefully keeping my back turned to her just the same. And, as a further precaution, I placed my pants on the side of the bed where I knew I was going to flop. The hundred francs wasn't altogether satisfactory to her, but I could see from the feeble way that she protested that it was quite enough. Then, with an energy that astonished me, she flung off her kimono and jumped into bed. As soon as I had put my arms around her and pulled her to me she reached for the switch and out went the lights. She embraced me passionately, and she groaned as all French cunts do when they get you in bed. She was getting me frightfully roused with her carrying on; that business of turning out the lights was a new one to me ... it seemed like the real thing. But I was suspicious too, and as soon as I could manage conveniently I put my hands out to feel if my trousers were still there on the chair.

I thought we were settled for the night. The bed felt very comfortable, softer than the average hotel bed—and the sheets were clean, I had noticed that. If only she wouldn't squirm so! You would think she hadn't slept with a man for a month. I wanted to stretch it out. I wanted full value for my hundred francs. But she was mumbling all sorts of things in that crazy bed language which goes to your blood even more rapidly when it's in the dark. I was putting up a stiff fight, but it was impossible with her groaning and gasping going on, and her muttering: *"Vite cheri! Vite cheri! Oh, c'est bon! Oh, oh! Vite, vite, cheri!"* I tried to count but it was like a fire alarm going off. *"Vite, cheri!"* and this time she gave such a gasping shudder that bango! I heard the stars chiming and there was my hundred francs gone and the fifty that I had forgotten all about and the lights were on again and with the same alacrity that she had bounced into bed she was bouncing out again and grunting and squealing like an old sow. I lay back and puffed a cigarette, gazing ruefully at my pants the while; they were terribly wrinkled. In a moment she was back again, wrapping the kimono around her, and telling me in that agitated way which was getting on my nerves that I should make myself at home. "I'm going downstairs to see mother," she said. *"Mais faites comme chez vous, cheri. Je reviens tout de suite."*

After a quarter of an hour had passed I began to feel thoroughly restless. I went inside and I read through a letter that was lying on the table. It was nothing of any account—a love letter. In the bathroom I examined all the bottles on the shelf; she had everything a woman requires to make herself smell beautiful. I was still hoping that she would come back and give me another fifty francs' worth. But time dragged on and there was no sign of her. I began to grow alarmed. Perhaps there *was* someone dying downstairs. Absent-mindedly, out of a sense of self-preservation, I suppose, I began to put my things on. As I was buckling my belt it came to me like a flash how she had stuffed the hundred franc note into her purse. In the excitement of the moment she had thrust the purse in the wardrobe, on the upper shelf. I remembered the gesture she made—standing on her tiptoes and reaching for the shelf. It didn't take me a minute to open the wardrobe and feel around for the purse. It was still there. I opened it hurriedly and saw my hundred franc note lying snugly between the silk coverlets. I put the purse back just as it was, slipped into my coat and shoes, and then I went to the landing and listened intently. I couldn't hear a sound. Where she had gone to, Christ only knows. In a jiffy I was back at the wardrobe and fumbling with her purse. I pocketed the hundred francs and all the loose change besides. Then, closing the door silently, I tiptoed down the stairs and when once I had hit the street I walked just as fast as my legs would carry me. At the Cafe Boudon I stopped for a bite. The whores there having a gay time pelting a fat man who had fallen asleep over his meal. He was sound asleep; snoring, in fact, and yet his jaws were working away mechanically. The place was in an uproar. There were shouts of "All aboard!" and then a concerted banging of knives and forks. He opened his eyes for a moment, blinked stupidly, and then his head rolled forward again on his chest. I put the hundred franc bill carefully away in my fob pocket and counted the change. The din around me was increasing and I had difficulty to recall exactly whether I had seen "first-class" on her diploma or not. It bothered me. About her mother I didn't give a damn. I hoped she had croaked by now. It would be strange if what she had said were true. Too good to believe. *Vite cheri... vite, vite!* And the other half-wit with her "my good sir" and "you have such a kind face"! I wondered if she had really taken a room in that hotel we stopped by.

It was along the close of summer when Fillmore invited me to come and live with him. He had a studio apartment overlooking the cavalry barracks just off the Place Dupleix. We had seen a lot of each other since the little trip to Le Havre. If it hadn't been for Fillmore I don't know where I should be today—dead, most likely.

"I would have asked you long before," he said, "if it hadn't been for that little bitch Jackie. I didn't know how to get her off my hands."

I had to smile. It was always like that with Fillmore. He had a genius for attracting homeless bitches. Anyway, Jackie had finally cleared out of her own accord.

The rainy season was coming on, the long, dreary stretch of grease and fog and squirts of rain that make you damp and miserable. An execrable place in the winter, Paris! A climate that eats into your soul, that leaves you bare as the Labrador coast. I noticed with some anxiety that the only means of heating the place was the little stove in the studio. However, it was still comfortable. And the view from the studio window was superb.

In the morning Fillmore would shake me roughly and leave a ten franc note on the pillow. As soon as he had gone I would settle back for a final snooze. Sometimes I would lie abed 'til noon. There was nothing pressing, except to finish the book, and that didn't worry me much because I was already convinced that nobody would accept it anyway. Nevertheless, Fillmore was much impressed by it. When he arrived in the evening with a bottle under his arm the first thing he did was to go to the table and see how many pages I had knocked off. At first I enjoyed this show of enthusiasm but later, when I was running dry, it made me devilishly uneasy to see him poking around, searching for the pages that were supposed to trickle out of me like water from a tap. When there was nothing to show I felt exactly like some bitch whom he had harbored. He used to say about Jackie, I remembered—"it would have been all right if only she had slipped me a piece of ass once in a while." If I had been a woman I would have been only too glad to slip him a piece of ass: it would have been much easier than to feed him the pages which he expected.

Nevertheless, he tried to make me feel at ease. There was always plenty of food and wine, and now and then he would insist that I accompany him to a *dancing*. He was fond of going to a nigger joint on the Rue d'Odessa where there was a good-looking mulatto who used to come home with us occasionally. The one thing that bothered him was that he couldn't find a French girl who liked to drink. They were all too sober to satisfy him— He liked to bring a woman back to the studio and guzzle it with her before getting down to business. He also liked to have her think that he was an artist. As the man from whom he had rented the place was a painter, it was not difficult to create an impression; the canvases which we had found in the *armoire* were soon stuck about the place and one of the unfinished ones conspicuously mounted on the easel. Unfortunately they were all of a surrealistic quality and the impression they created was usually unfavorable. Between a whore, a concierge and a cabinet minister there is not much difference in taste where pictures are concerned. It was a matter of great relief to Fillmore when Mark Swift began to visit us regularly with the intention of doing my portrait. Fillmore had a great admiration for Swift. He was a genius, he said. And though there was something ferocious about everything he tackled nevertheless when he painted a man or an object you could recognize it for what it was.

At Swift's request I had begun to grow a beard. The shape of my skull, he said, required a beard. I had to sit by the window with the Eiffel Tower in back of me because he wanted the Eiffel Tower in the picture too. He also wanted the typewriter in the picture. Kruger got the habit of dropping in too about this time; he maintained that Swift knew nothing about painting. It exasperated him to see things out of proportion. He believed in Nature's laws, implicitly. Swift didn't give a fuck about Nature; he wanted to paint what was inside his head. Anyway, there was Swift's portrait of me stuck on the easel now, and though everything was out of proportion, even a cabinet minister could see that it was a human head, a man with a beard. The concierge, indeed, began to take a great interest in the picture; she thought the likeness was striking. And she liked the idea of showing the Eiffel Tower in the background.

Things rolled along this way peacefully for about a month or more. The neighborhood appealed to me, particularly at night when the full squalor and lugubrious-ness of it made itself felt. The little Place, so charming and tranquil at twilight, could assume the most dismal, sinister character when darkness came on. There was that long, high wall covering one side of the barracks against which there was always a couple embracing each other furtively—often in the rain. A depressing sight to see two lovers squeezed against a prison wall under a gloomy street light: as if they had been driven right to the last bounds. What went on inside the enclosure was also depressing. On a rainy day I used to stand by the window and look down on the activity below, quite as if it were something going on on another planet. It seemed incomprehensible to me. Everything done according to schedule, but a schedule that must have been devised by a lunatic. There they were, floundering around in the mud, the bugles blowing, the horses charging—all within four walls. A sham battle. A lot of tin soldiers who hadn't the least interest in learning how to kill or how to polish their boots or currycomb the horses. Utterly ridiculous the whole thing, but part of the scheme of things. When they had nothing to do they looked even more ridiculous; they scratched themselves, they walked about with their hands in their pockets, they looked up at the sky. And when an officer came along they clicked their heels and saluted. A madhouse, it seemed to me. Even the horses looked silly. And then sometimes the artillery was dragged out and they went clattering down the street on parade and people stood and gaped and admired the fine uniforms. To me they always looked like an army corps in retreat; something shabby, bedraggled, crestfallen about them, their uniforms too big for their bodies, all the alertness, which as individuals they possess to such a remarkable degree, gone now.

When the sun came out, however, things looked different. There was a ray of hope in their eyes, they walked more elastically, they showed a little enthusiasm. Then the color of things peeped out graciously and there was that fuss and bustle so characteristic of the French; at the *bistro* on the corner they chattered gaily over their drinks and the officers seemed more human, more French, I might say. When the sun comes out, any spot in Paris can look beautiful; and if there is a *bistro* with an awning rolled down, a few tables on the sidewalk and colored drinks in the glasses, then people look altogether human.

And they *are* human—the finest people in the world when the sun shines! So intelligent, so indolent, so carefree! It's a crime to herd such a people into barracks, to put them through exercises, to grade them into privates and sergeants and colonels and what not.

As I say, things were rolling along smoothly. Now and then Carl came along with a job for me, travel articles which he hated to do himself. They only paid fifty francs a piece, but they were easy to do because I had only to consult the back issues and revamp the old articles. People only read these things when they were sitting on a toilet or killing time in a waiting room. The principal thing was to keep the adjectives well furbished—the rest was a matter of dates and statistics. If it was an important article the head of the department signed it himself; he was a half-wit who couldn't speak any language well, but who knew how to find fault. If he found a paragraph that seemed to him well written he would say—"Now that's the way I want you to write! That's beautiful. You have my permission to use it in your book." These beautiful paragraphs we sometimes lifted from the encyclopaedia or an old guide book. Some of them Carl did put into his book—they had a surrealistic character.

Then one evening, after I had been out for a walk, I open the door and a woman springs out of the bedroom. So you're the writer!" she exclaims at once, and she looks at my beard as if to corroborate her impression. "What a horrid beard!" she says. "I think you people must be crazy around here." Fillmore is trailing after her with a blanket in his hand. "She's a princess," he says, smacking his lips as if he had just tasted some rare caviar. The two of them were dressed for the street; I couldn't understand what they were doing with the bedclothes. And then it occurred to me immediately that Fillmore must have dragged her into the bedroom to show her his laundry bag. He always did that with a new woman, especially if she was a *Francaise*. "No tickee, no shirtee!" that's what was stitched on the laundry bag, and somehow Fillmore had an obsession for explaining this motto to every female who arrived. But this dame was not a *Francaise*—he made that clear to me at once. She was Russian—and a princess, no less.

He was bubbling over with excitement, like a child that has just found a new toy. "She speaks five languages!" he said, obviously overwhelmed by such an accomplishment.

"Non, *four!*" she corrected promptly.

"Well, four then.... Anyway, she's a damned intelligent girl. You ought to hear her speak."

The princess was nervous—she kept scratching her thigh and rubbing her nose. "Why does he want to make his bed now?" she asked me abruptly. "Does he think he will get me that way? He's a big child. He behaves disgracefully. I took him to a Russian restaurant and he danced like a nigger." She wiggled her bottom to illustrate. "And he talks too much. Too loud. He talks nonsense." She swished about the room, examining the paintings and the books, keeping her chin well up all the time but scratching herself intermittently. Now and then she wheeled around like a battleship and delivered a broadside. Fillmore kept following her about with a bottle in one hand and a glass in the other. "Stop following me like that!" she exclaimed. "And haven't you anything to drink but this? Can't you get a bottle of champagne? I must have some champagne. My nerves! My nerves!"

Fillmore tries to whisper a few words in my ear. "An actress ... a movie star... some guy jilted her and she can't get over it.... I'm going to get her cockeyed...."

"I'll clear out then," I was saying, when the princess interrupted us with a shout. "Why do you whisper like that?" she cried, stamping her foot. "Don't you know that's not polite? And *you*, I thought you were going to take me out? I must get drunk tonight, I have told you that already."

"Yes, yes," said Fillmore, "we're going in a minute. I just want another drink."

"You're a pig!" she yelled. "But you're a nice boy too. Only you're loud. You have no manners." She turned to me. "Can I trust him to behave himself? I must get drunk tonight but I don't want him to disgrace me. Maybe I will come back here afterward. I would like to talk to you. You seem more intelligent."

As they were leaving the princess shook my hand cordially and promised to come for dinner some evening—"when I will be sober," she said.

"Fine!" I said. "Bring another princess along—or a countess, at least. We change the sheets every Saturday."

About three in the morning Fillmore staggers in... alone. Lit up like an ocean liner, and making a noise like a blind man with his cracked cane. Tap, tap, tap, down the weary lane.... "Going straight to bed," he says, as he marches past me. "Tell you all about it tomorrow." He goes inside to his room and throws back the covers. I hear him groaning—"what a woman! what a woman!" In a second he's out again, with his hat on and the cracked cane in his hand. "I knew something like that was going to happen. She's crazy!"

He rummages around in the kitchen a while and then comes back to the studio with a bottle of Anjou. I have to sit up and down a glass with him.

As far as I can piece the story together the whole thing started at the Rond-Point des Champs Elysees where he had dropped off for a drink on his way home. As usual at that hour the *terrasse* was crowded with buzzards. This one was sitting right on the aisle with a pile of saucers in front of her; she was getting drunk quietly all by herself when Fillmore happened along and caught her eye. "I'm drunk," she giggled, "won't you sit down?" And then, as though it were the most natural thing in the world to do, she began right off the bat with the yarn about her movie director, how he had given her the go-by and how she had thrown herself in the Seine and so forth and so on. She couldn't remember any more which bridge it was, only that there was a crowd around when they fished her out of the water. Besides, she didn't see what difference it made which bridge she threw herself from—why did he ask such questions? She was laughing hysterically about it, and then suddenly she had a desire to be off—she wanted to dance. Seeing him hesitate she opens her bag impulsively and pulls out a hundred franc note. The next moment, however, she decided that a hundred francs wouldn't go very far. "Haven't you any money at all?" she said. No, he hadn't very much in his pocket, but he had a checkbook at home. So they made a dash for the checkbook and then, of course, I had to happen in just as he was explaining to her the "No tickee, no shirtee" business.

On the way home they had stopped off at the Poisson d'Or for a little snack which she had washed down with a few vodkas. She was in her element there with everyone kissing her hand and murmuring *Princesse, Princesse.* Drunk as she was, she managed to collect her dignity. "Don't wiggle your behind like that!" she kept saying, as they danced.

It was Fillmore's idea, when he brought her back to the studio, to stay there. But, since she was such an intelligent girl and so erratic, he had decided to put up with her whims and postpone the grand event. He had even visualized the prospect of running across another princess and bringing the two of them back. When they started out for the evening, therefore, he was in a good humor and prepared, if necessary, to spend a few hundred francs on her. After all, one doesn't run across a princess every day.

This time she dragged him to another place, a place where she was still better known and where there would be no trouble in cashing a check, as she said. Everybody was in evening clothes and there was more spine-breaking, hand-kissing nonsense as the waiter escorted them to a table.

In the middle of a dance she suddenly walks off the floor, with tears in her eyes. "What's the matter?" he said, "what did I do this time?" And instinctively he put his hand to his backside, as though perhaps it might still be wiggling. "It's nothing," she said. "You didn't do anything. Come, you're a nice boy," and with that she drags him on to the floor again and begins to dance with abandon. "But what's the matter with you?" he murmured. "It's nothing," she repeated. "I saw somebody, that's all." And then, with a sudden spurt of anger—"why do you get me drunk? Don't you know it makes me crazy?"

"Have you got a check?" she says. "We must get out of here." She called the waiter over and whispered to him in Russian. "Is it a good check?" she asked, when the waiter had disappeared. And then, impulsively: "Wait for me downstairs in the cloakroom. I must telephone somebody."

After the waiter had brought the change Fillmore sauntered leisurely downstairs to the cloakroom to wait for her. He strode up and down, humming and whistling softly, and smacking his lips in anticipation of the caviar to come. Five minutes passed. Ten minutes. Still whistling softly. When twenty minutes had gone by and still no princess he at last grew suspicious. The cloakroom attendant said that she had left long ago. He dashed outside. There was a nigger in livery standing there with a big grin on his face. Did the nigger know where she had breezed to? Nigger grins. Nigger says: "Ah heerd Coupole, dassall sir!"

At the Coupole, downstairs, he finds her sitting in front of a cocktail with a dreamy, trancelike expression on her face. She smiles when she sees him.

"Was that a decent thing to do," he says, "to run away like that? You might have told me that you didn't like me...."

She flared up at this, got theatrical about it. And after a lot of gushing she commenced to whine and slobber. "I'm crazy," she blubbered. "And you're crazy too. You want me to sleep with you, and I don't want to sleep with you." And then she began to rave about her lover, the movie director whom she had seen on the dance floor. That's why she had to run away from the place. That's why she took drugs and got drunk every night. That's why she threw herself in the Seine. She babbled on this way about how crazy she was and then suddenly she had an idea. "Let's go to Bricktop's!" There was a man there whom she knew ... he had promised her a job once. She was certain he would help her.

"What's it going to cost?" asked Fillmore cautiously.

It would cost a lot, she let him know that immediately. "But listen, if you take me to Bricktop's, I promise to go home with you." She was honest enough to add that it might cost him five or six hundred francs. "But I'm worth it! You don't know what a woman I am. There isn't another women like me in all Paris...."

"That's what *you* think!" His Yankee blood was coming to the fore. "But I don't see it. I don't see that you're worth anything. You're just a poor crazy son-of-a-bitch. Frankly, I'd rather give fifty francs to some poor French girl; at least they give you something in return."

She hit the ceiling when he mentioned the French girls. "Don't talk to me about those women! I hate them! They're stupid... they're ugly ... they're mercenary. Stop it, I tell you!"

In a moment she had subsided again. She was on a new tack. "Darling," she murmured, "you don't know what I look like when I'm undressed. I'm *beautiful!*" And she held her breasts with her two hands.

But Fillmore remained unimpressed. "You're a bitch!" he said coldly. "I wouldn't mind spending a few hundred francs on you, but you're crazy. You haven't even washed your face. Your breath stinks. I don't give a damn whether you're a princess or not... I don't want any of your high-assed Russian variety. You ought to get out in the street and hustle for it. You're no better than any little French girl. You're not as good. I wouldn't piss away another sou on you. You ought to go to America—that's the place for a bloodsucking leech like you...."

She didn't seem to be at all put out by this speech. "I think you're just a little afraid of me," she said.

"Afraid of you? Of *you?*"

"You're just a little boy," she said. "You have no manners. When you know me better you will talk differently.... Why don't you try to be nice? If you don't want to go with me tonight, very well. I will be at the Rond-Point tomorrow between five and seven. I like you."

"I don't intend to be at the Rond-Point tomorrow, or any other night! I don't want to see you again... ever. I'm through with you. I'm going out and find myself a nice little French girl. You can go to hell!"

She looked at him and smiled wearily. "That's what you say now. But wait! Wait until you've slept with me. You don't know yet what a beautiful body I have. You think the French girls know how to make love ... wait! I will make you crazy about me. I like you. Only you're uncivilized. You're just a boy. You talk too much...."

"You're crazy," said Fillmore. "I wouldn't fall for you if you were the last woman on earth. Go home and wash your face." He walked off without paying for the drinks.

In a few days, however, the princess was installed. She's a genuine princess, of that we're pretty certain. But she has the clap. Anyway, life is far from dull here. Fillmore has bronchitis, the princess, as I was saying, has the clap, and I have the piles. Just exchanged six empty bottles at the Russian *epicene* across the way. Not a drop went down my gullet. No meat, no wine, no rich game, no women. Only fruit and paraffin oil, arnica drops and adrenalin ointment. And not a chair in the joint that's comfortable enough. Right now, looking at the princess, I'm propped up like a pasha. Pasha! That reminds me of her name: Macha. Doesn't sound so damned aristocratic to me. Reminds me of *The Living Corpse.*

At first I thought it was going to be embarrassing, a *menage a trois,* but not at all. I thought when I saw her move in that it was all up with me again, that I should have to find another place, but Fillmore soon gave me to understand that he was only putting her up until she got on her feet. With a woman like her I don't know what an expression like that means; as far as I can see she's been standing on her head all her life. She says the revolution drove her out of Russia, but I'm sure if it hadn't been the revolution it would have been something else. She's under the impression that she's a great actress; we never contradict her in anything she says because it's time wasted. Fillmore finds her amusing. When he leaves for the office in the morning he drops ten francs on her pillow and ten francs on mine; at night the three of us go to the Russian restaurant down below. The neighborhood is full of Russians and Macha has already found a place where she can run up a little credit. Naturally ten francs a day isn't anything for a princess; she wants caviar now and then and champagne, and she needs a complete new wardrobe in order to get a job in the movies again. She has nothing to do now except to kill time. She's putting on fat.

This morning I had quite a fright. After I had washed my face I grabbed her towel by mistake. We can't seem to train her to put her towel on the right hook. And when I bawled her out for it she answered smoothly: "My dear, if one can become blind from that I would have been blind years ago."

And then there's the toilet, which we all have to use. I try speaking to her in a fatherly way about the toilet seat. "Oh zut!" she says. "If you are so afraid I'll go to a cafe." But it's not necessary to do that, I explain. Just use ordinary precautions. "Tut tut!" she says, "I won't sit down then ... I'll stand up."

Everything is cockeyed with her around. First she wouldn't come across because she had the monthlies. For eight days that lasted. We were beginning to think she was faking it. But no, she wasn't faking. One day, when I was trying to put the place in order, I found some cotton batting under the bed and it was stained with blood. With her everything goes under the bed: orange peel, wadding, corks, empty bottles, scissors, used condoms, books, pillows.... She makes the bed only when it's time to retire. Most of the time she lies abed reading her Russian papers. "My dear," she says to me, "if it weren't for my papers I wouldn't get out of bed at all." That's it precisely! Nothing but Russian newspapers. Not a scratch of toilet paper around—nothing but Russian newspapers with which to wipe your ass.

Anyway, speaking of her idiosyncrasies, after the menstrual flow was over, after she had rested properly and put a nice layer of fat around her belt, still she wouldn't come across. Pretended that she only liked women. To take on a man she had to first be properly stimulated. Wanted us to take her to a bawdy house where they put on the dog and man act. Or better still, she said, would be Leda and the swan: the flapping of the wings excited her terribly.

One night, to test her out, we accompanied her to a place that she suggested. But before we had a chance to broach the subject to the madam, a drunken Englishman, who was sitting at the next table, fell into a conversation with us. He had already been upstairs twice but he wanted another try at it. He had only about twenty francs in his pocket, and not knowing any French, he asked us if we would help him to bargain with the girl he had his eye on. Happened she was a Negress, a powerful wench from Martinique, and beautiful as a panther. Had a lovely disposition too. In order to persuade her to accept the Englishman's remaining sous, Fillmore had to promise to go with her himself soon as she got through with the Englishman. The princess looked on, heard everything that was said, and then got on her high horse. She was insulted. "Well," said Fillmore, "you wanted some excitement—you can watch me do it!" She didn't want to watch him—she wanted to watch a drake. "Well, by Jesus," he said, "I'm as good as a drake any day... maybe a little better." Like that, one word led to another, and finally the only way we could appease her was to call one of the girls over and let them tickle each other... When Fillmore came back with the Negress her eyes were smoldering. I could see from the way Fillmore looked at her that she must have given an unusual performance and I began to feel lecherous myself. Fillmore must have sensed how I felt, and what an ordeal it was to sit and look on all night, for suddenly he pulled a hundred franc note out of his pocket and slapping it in front of me, he said: "Look here, you probably need a lay more than any of us. Take that and pick someone out for yourself." Somehow that gesture endeared him more to me than anything he had ever done for me, and he had done considerable. I accepted the money in the spirit it was given and promptly signaled to the Negress to get ready for another lay. That enraged the princess more than anything, it appeared. She wanted to know if there wasn't anyone in the place good enough for us except this Negress. I told her bluntly NO.

And it was so—the Negress was the queen of the harem. You had only to look at her to get an erection. Her eyes seemed to be swimming in sperm. She was drunk with all the demands made upon her. She couldn't walk straight any more—at least, it seemed that way to me. Going up the narrow winding stairs behind her I couldn't resist the temptation to slide my hand up her crotch; we continued up the stairs that way, she looking back at me with a cheerful smile and wiggling her ass a bit when it tickled her too much.

It was a good session all around. Everyone was happy. Vlacha seemed to be in a good mood too. And so the next evening, after she had had her ration of champagne and caviar, after she had given us another chapter out of the history of her life, Fillmore went to work on her. It seemed as though he was going to get his reward at last. She had ceased to put up a fight any more. She lay back with her legs apart and she let him fool around and fool around and then, just as he was climbing over her, just as he was going to slip it in, she informs him nonchalantly that she has a dose of clap. He rolled off her like a log. I heard him fumbling around in the kitchen for the black soap he used on special occasions, and in a few moments he was standing by my bed with a towel in his hands and saying—"can you beat that? that son-of-a-bitch of a princess has the clap!" He seemed pretty well scared about it. The princess meanwhile was munching an apple and calling for her Russian newspapers. It was quite a joke to her. "There are worse things than that," she said, lying there in her bed and talking to us through the open door. Finally Fillmore began to see it as a joke too and opening another bottle of Anjou he poured out a drink for himself and quaffed it down. It was only about one in the morning and so he sat there talking to me for a while. He wasn't going to be put off by a thing like that, he told me. Of course, he had to be careful... there was the old dose which had come on in Le Havre. He couldn't remember any more how that happened. Sometimes when he got drunk he forgot to wash himself. It wasn't anything very terrible, but you never knew what might develop later. He didn't want any one massaging his prostate gland. No, that he didn't relish. The first dose he ever got was at college. Didn't know whether the girl had given it to him or he to the girl; there was so much funny work going on about the campus you didn't know whom to believe. Nearly all the coeds had been knocked up some time or other. Too damned ignorant... even the profs were ignorant. One of the profs had himself castrated, so the rumor went....

Anyway, the next night he decided to risk it—with a condom. Not much risk in that, unless it breaks. He had bought himself some of the long fish skin variety—they were the most reliable, he assured me. But then, that didn't work either. She was too tight. "Jesus, there's nothing abnormal about me," he said. "How do you make that out? Somebody got inside her all right to give her that dose. He must have been abnormally small."

So, one thing after another failing, he just gave it up altogether. They he there now like brother and sister, with incestuous dreams. Says Macha, in her philosophic way: "In Russia it often happens that a man sleeps with a woman without touching her. They can go on that way for weeks and weeks and never think anything about it. Until paff! once he touches her... paff! paff! After that it's paff, paff, paff!"

All efforts are concentrated now on getting Macha into shape. Fillmore thinks if he cures her of the clap she may loosen up. A strange idea. So he's bought her a douche bag, a stock of permanganate, a whirling syringe and other little things which were recommended to him by a Hungarian doctor, a little quack of an abortionist over near the Place d'Aligre. It seems his boss had knocked up a sixteen-year-old girl once and she had introduced him to the Hungarian; and then after that the boss had a beautiful chancre and it was the Hungarian again. That's how one gets acquainted in Paris—genito-urinary friendships. Anyway, under our strict supervision, Macha is taking care of herself. The other night, though, we were in a quandary for a while. She stuck the suppository inside her and then she couldn't find the string attached to it. "My God!" she was yelling, "where is that string? My God! I can't find the string!"

"Did you look under the bed?" said Fillmore.

Finally she quieted down. But only for a few minutes. The next thing was: "My God! I'm bleeding again. I just had my period and now there are *gouttes* again. It must be that cheap champagne you buy. My God, do you want me to bleed to death?" She comes out with a kimono on and a towel stuck between her legs, trying to look dignified as usual. "My whole life is just like that," she says. "I'm a neurasthenic. The whole day running around and at night I'm drunk again. When I came to Paris I was still an innocent girl. I read only Villon and Baudelaire. But as I had then 300,000 Swiss francs in the bank I was crazy to enjoy myself, because in Russia they were always strict with me. And as I was even more beautiful then than I am now. I had all the men falling at my feet." Here she hitched up the slack which had accumulated around her belt. "You mustn't think I had a stomach like that when I came here ... that's from all the poison I was given to drink... those horrible *aperitifs* which the French are so crazy to drink.... So then I met my movie director and he wanted that I should play a part for him. He said I was the most gorgeous creature in the world and he was begging me to sleep with him every night. I was a foolish young virgin and so I permitted him to rape me one night. I wanted to be a great actress and I didn't know he was full of poison. So he gave me the clap ... and now I want that he should have it back again. It's his fault that I committed suicide in the Seine.... Why are you laughing? Don't you believe that I committed suicide? I can show you the newspapers... there is my picture in all the papers. I will show you the Russian papers some day... they wrote about me wonderfully.... But darling, you know that first I must have a new dress. I can't vamp this man with these dirty rags I am in. Besides, I still owe my dressmaker 12,000 francs...."

From here on it's a long story about the inheritance which she is trying to collect. She has a young lawyer, a Frenchman, who is rather timid, it seems, and he is trying to win back her fortune. From time to time he used to give her a hundred francs or so on account. "He's stingy, like all the French people," she says. "And I was so beautiful, too, that he couldn't keep his eyes off me. He kept begging me always to fuck him. I got so sick and tired of listening to him that one night I said yes, just to keep him quiet, and so as I wouldn't lose my hundred francs now and then." She paused a moment to laugh hysterically. "My dear," she continued, "it was too funny for words what happened to him. He calls me up on the phone one day and he says: "I must see you right away ... it's very important." And when I see him he shows me a paper from the doctor—and it's gonorrhea! My dear, I laughed in his face. How should I know that I still had the clap? "You wanted to fuck me and so I fucked you!" That made him quiet. That's how it goes in life ... you don't suspect anything, and then all of a sudden paff, paff, paff! He was such a fool that he fell in love with me all over again. Only he begged me to behave myself and not run around Montparnasse all night drinking and fucking. He said I was driving him crazy. He wanted to marry me and then his family heard about me and they persuaded him to go to Indo-China...."

From this Macha calmly switches to an affair she had with a Lesbian. "It was very funny, my dear, how she picked me up one night. I was at the "Fetiche" and I was drunk as usual. She took me from one place to the other and she made love to me under the table all night until I couldn't stand it any more. Then she took me to her apartment and for two hundred francs I let her suck me off. She wanted me to live with her but I didn't want to have her suck me off every night... it makes you too weak. Besides, I can tell you that I don't care so much for Lesbians as I used to. I would rather sleep with a man even though it hurts me. When I get terribly excited I can't hold myself back any more ... three, four, five times ... just like that! Paff, paff, paff! And then I bleed and that is very unhealthy for me because I am inclined to be anemic. So you see why once in a while I must let myself be sucked by a Lesbian...."

When the cold weather set in the princess disappeared. It was getting uncomfortable with just a little coal stove in the studio; the bedroom was like an icebox and the kitchen was hardly any better. There was just a little space around the stove where it was actually warm. So Macha had found herself a sculptor who was castrated. She told us about him before she left. After a few days she tried coming back to us, but Fillmore wouldn't hear of it. She complained that the sculptor kept her awake all night kissing her. And then there was no hot water for her douches. But finally she decided that it was just as well she didn't come back. "I won't have that candlestick next to me any more," she said. "Always that candlestick ... it made me nervous. If you had only been a fairy I would have stayed with you...."

With Macha gone our evenings took on a different character. Often we sat by the fire drinking hot toddies and discussing the life back there in the States. We talked about it as if we never expected to go back there again. Fillmore had a map of New York City which he had tacked on the wall; we used to spend whole evenings discussing the relative virtues of Paris and New York. And inevitably there always crept into our discussions the figure of Whitman, that one lone figure which America has produced in the course of her brief life. In Whitman the whole American scene comes to life, her past and her future, her birth and her death. Whatever there is of value in America Whitman has expressed, and there is nothing more to be said. The future belongs to the machine, to the robots. He was the Poet of the Body and the Soul, Whitman. The first and the last poet. He is almost undecipherable today, a monument covered with rude hieroglyphs for which there is no key. It seems strange almost to mention his name over here. There is no equivalent in the languages of Europe for the spirit which he immortalized. Europe is saturated with art and her soil is full of dead bones and her museums are bursting with plundered treasures, but what Europe has never had is a free, healthy spirit, what you might call a MAN. Goethe was the nearest approach, but Goethe was a stuffed shirt, by comparison. Goethe was a respectable citizen, a pedant, a bore, a universal spirit, but stamped with the German trade-mark, with the double eagle. The serenity of Goethe, the calm, Olympian attitude, is nothing more than the drowsy stupor of a German burgeois deity. Goethe is an end of something, Whitman is a beginning. After a discussion of this sort I would sometimes put on my things and go for a walk, bundled up in a sweater, a spring overcoat of Fillmore's and a cape over that. A foul, damp cold against which there is no protection except a strong spirit. They say America is a country of extremes, and it is true that the thermometer registers degrees of cold which are practically unheard of here; but the cold of a Paris winter is a cold unknown to America, it is psychological, an inner as well as an outer cold. If it never freezes here it never thaws either. Just as the people protect themselves against the invasion of their privacy, by their high walls, their bolts and shutters, their growling, evil-tongued, slatternly concierges, so they have learned to protect themselves against the cold and heat of a bracing, vigorous climate. They have fortified themselves: protection is the keyword. Protection and security. In order that they may rot in comfort. On a damp winter's night it is not necessary to look at the map to discover the latitude of Paris. It is a northern city, an outpost erected over a swamp filled in with skulls and bones. Along the boulevards there is a cold electrical imitation of heat. *Tout Va Bien* in ultraviolet rays that make the clients of the Dupont chain cafes look like gangrened cadavers. *Tout Va Bien!* That's the motto that nourishes the forlorn beggars who walk up and down all night under the drizzle of the violet rays. Wherever there are lights there is a little heat. One gets warm from watching the fat, secure bastards down their grogs, their steaming black coffees. Where the lights are there are people on the sidewalks, jostling one another, giving off a little animal heat through their dirty underwear and their foul, cursing breaths. Maybe for a stretch of eight or ten blocks there is a semblance of gaiety, and then it tumbles back into night, dismal, foul, black night like frozen fat in a soup tureen. Blocks and blocks of jagged tenements, every window closed tight, every shopfront barred and bolted. Miles and miles of stone prisons without the faintest glow of warmth; the dogs and the cats are all inside with the canary birds. The cockroaches and the bedbugs too are safely incarcerated. *Tout Va Bien.* If you haven't a sou why just take a few old newspapers and make yourself a bed on the steps of a cathedral. The doors are well bolted and there will be no draughts to disturb you. Better still is to sleep outside the Metro doors; there you will have company. Look at them on a rainy night, lying there stiff as mattresses—men, women, lice, all huddled together and protected by the newspapers against spittle and the vermin that walks without legs. Look at them under the bridges or under the market sheds. How vile they look in comparison with the clean, bright vegetables stacked up like jewels. Even the dead horses and the cows and sheep hanging from the greasy hooks look more inviting. At least we will eat these tomorrow and even the intestines will serve a purpose. But these filthy beggars lying in the rain, what purpose do they serve? What good can they do us? They make us bleed for five minutes, that's all.

Oh, well, these are night thoughts produced by walking in the rain after two thousand years of Christianity. At least now the birds are well provided for, and the cats and dogs. Every time I pass the concierge's window and catch the full icy impact of her glance I have an insane desire to throttle all the birds in creation. At the bottom of every frozen heart there is a drop or two of love—just enough to feed the birds.

Still I can't get it out of my mind what a discrepancy there is between ideas and living. A permanent dislocation, though we try to cover the two with a bright awning. And it won't go. Ideas have to be wedded to action; if there is no sex, no vitality in them, there is no action. Ideas cannot exist alone in the vacuum of the mind. Ideas are related to living: liver ideas, kidney ideas, interstitial ideas, etc. If it were only for the sake of an idea Copernicus would have smashed the existent macrocosm and Columbus would have foundered in the Sargasso Sea. The aesthetics of the idea breeds flowerpots and flowerpots you put on the window sill. But if there be no rain or sun of what use putting flow-erpots outside the window?

Fillmore is full of ideas about gold. The "mythos" of gold, he calls it. I like "mythos" and I like the idea of gold, but I am not obsessed by the subject and I don't see why we should make flowerpots, even of gold. He tells me that the French are hoarding their gold away in watertight compartments deep below the surface of the earth; he tells me that there is a little locomotive which runs around in these subterranean vaults and corridors. I like the idea enormously. A profound, uninterrupted silence in which the gold softly snoozes at a temperature of 17 54 degrees Centigrade. He says an army working 46 days and 3 7 hours would not be sufficient to count all the gold that is sunk beneath the Bank of France, and that there is a reserve supply of false teeth, bracelets, wedding rings, etc. Enough food also to last for eighty days and a lake on top of the gold pile to resist the shock of high explosives. Gold, he says, tends to become more and more invisible, a myth, and no more defalcations. Excellent! I am wondering what will happen to the world when we go off the gold standard in ideas, dress, morals, etc. *The gold standard of love!*

Up to the present, my idea in collaborating with myself has been to get off the gold standard of literature. My idea briefly has been to present a resurrection of the emotions, to depict the conduct of a human being in the stratosphere of ideas, that is, in the grip of delirium. To paint a pre-Socratic being, a creature part goat, part Titan. In short, to erect a world on the basis of the *omphalos,* not on an abstract idea nailed to a cross. Here and there you may have come across neglected statues, oases untapped, windmills overlooked by Cervantes, rivers that run uphill, women with five and six breasts ranged longitudinal-ly along the torso. (Writing to Gauguin, Strindberg said: *"J'ai vu des arbres que ne retrouverait aucun botaniste, des animaux que Cuvier n'a jamais soupconnes et des hommes que vous seul avez pu creer."*)

When Rembrandt hit par he went below with the gold ingots and the pemmican and the portable beds. Gold is a night word belonging to the chthonian mind: it has dream in it and mythos. We are reverting to alchemy, to that fake Alexandrian wisdom which pro-duced our inflated symbols. Real wisdom is being stored away in the sub-cellars by the misers of learning. The day is coming when they will be circling around in the middle air with magnetizers; to find a piece of ore you will have to go up ten thousand feet with a pair of instruments—in a cold latitude preferably—and establish telepathic communica-tion with the bowels of the earth and the shades of the dead. No more Klondikes. No more bonanzas. You will have to learn to sing and caper a bit, to read the zodiac and study your entrails. All the gold that is being tucked away in the pockets of the earth will have to be re-mined; all this symbolism will have to be dragged out again from the bowels of man. But first the instruments must be perfected. First it is necessary to invent better air-planes, to distinguish *where* the noise comes from and not go daffy just because you hear an explosion under your ass. And secondly it will be necessary to get adapted to the cold layers of the stratosphere, to become a cold-blooded fish of the air. No reverence. No piety. No longing. No regrets. No hysteria. Above all, as Philippe Datz says—"NO DISCOUR-AGEMENT!"

These are sunny thoughts inspired by a vermouth cassis at the Place de la Trinite. A Saturday afternoon and a "misfire" book in my hands. Everything swimming in a divine mucopus. The drink leaves a bitter herbish taste in my mouth, the lees of our Great Western civilization, rotting now like the toenails of the saints. Women are passing by—

regiments of them—all swinging their asses in front of me; the chimes are ringing and the buses are climbing the sidewalk and bussing one another. The *garcon* wipes the table with a dirty rag while the *patronne* tickles the cash register with fiendish glee. A look of vacuity on my face, blotto, vague in acuity, biting the asses that brush by me. In the belfry opposite the hunchback strikes with a golden mallet and the pigeons scream alarum. I open the book—the book which Nietzsche called "the best German book there is"—and it says:

"MEN WILL BECOME MORE CLEVER AND MORE ACUTE; BUT NOT BETTER, HAPPIER, AND STRONGER IN ACTION—OR, AT LEAST, ONLY AT EPOCHS. I FORESEE THE TIME WHEN GOD WILL HAVE NO MORE JOY IN THEM, BUT WILL BREAK UP EVERYTHING FOR A RENEWED CREATION. I AM CERTAIN THAT EVERYTHING IS PLANNED TO THIS END, AND THAT THE TIME AND HOUR IN THE DISTANT FUTURE FOR THE OCCURRENCE OF THIS RENOVATING EPOCH ARE ALREADY FIXED. BUT A LONG TIME WILL ELAPSE FIRST, AND WE MAY STILL FOR THOUSANDS AND THOUSANDS OF YEARS AMUSE OURSELVES ON THIS DEAR OLD SURFACE."

Excellent! At least a hundred years ago there was a man who had vision enough to see that the world was pooped out. *Our Western world!*—When I see the figures of men and women moving listlessly behind their prison walls, sheltered, secluded for a few brief hours, I am appalled by the potentialities for drama that are still contained in these feeble bodies. Behind the gray walls there are human sparks, and yet never a conflagration. Are these men and women, I ask myself, or are these shadows, shadows of puppets dangled by invisible strings? They move in freedom apparently, but they have nowhere to go. In one realm only are they free and there they may roam at will—but they have not yet learned how to take wing. So far there have been no dreams that have taken wing. Not one man has been born light enough, *gay* enough, to leave the earth! The eagles who flapped their mighty pinions for a while came crashing heavily to earth. They made us dizzy with the flap and whir of their wings. Stay on the earth, you eagles of the future! The heavens have been explored and they are empty. And what lies under the earth is empty too, filled with bones and shadows. Stay on the earth and swim another few hundred thousand years!

And now it is three o'clock in the morning and we have a couple of trollops here who are doing somersaults on the bare floor. Fillmore is walking around naked with a goblet in his hand, and that paunch of his is drumtight, hard as a fistula. All the Pernod and champagne and cognac and Anjou which he guzzled from three in the afternoon on, is gurgling in his trap like a sewer. The girls are putting their ears to his belly as if it were a music box. Open his mouth with a buttonhook and drop a slug in the slot. When the sewer gurgles I hear the bats flying out of the belfry and the dream slides into artifice.

The girls have undressed and we are examining the floor to make sure that they won't get any splinters in their ass. They are still wearing their high-heeled shoes. But the ass! The ass is worn down, scraped, sandpapered, smooth, hard, bright as a billiard ball or the skull of a leper. On the wall is Mona's picture: she is facing northeast on a line with Cracow written in green ink. To the left of her is the Dordogne, encircled with a red pencil. Suddenly I see a dark, hairy crack in front of me set in a bright, polished billiard ball; the legs are holding me like a pair of scissors. A glance at that dark, unstitched wound and a deep fissure in my brain opens up: all the images and memories that had been laboriously or absent-mindedly assorted, labeled, documented, filed, sealed and stamped break forth pell-mell like ants pouring out of a crack in the sidewalk; the world ceases to revolve, time stops, the very nexus of my dreams is broken and dissolved and my guts spill out in a grand schizophrenic rush, an evacuation that leaves me face to face with the Absolute. I see again the great sprawling mothers of Picasso, their breasts covered with spiders, their legend hidden deep in the labyrinth. And Molly Bloom lying on a dirty mattress for eternity. On the toilet door red chalk cocks and the madonna uttering the diapason of woe. I hear a wild, hysterical laugh, a room full of lockjaw, and the body that was black glows like phosphorus. Wild, wild, utterly uncontrollable laughter, and that crack laughing at me too, laughing through the mossy whiskers, a laugh that creases the bright, polished surface of the billiard ball. Great whore and mother of man with gin in her veins. Mother of all harlots, spider rolling us in your logarithmic grave, insatiable one, fiend whose laughter rives me! I look down into that sunken crater, world lost and without traces, and I hear the bells chiming, two nuns at the Palace Stanislas and the smell of rancid butter under their dresses, manifesto never printed because it was raining, war fought to further the cause of plastic surgery, the Prince of Wales flying around the world decorating the graves of unknown heroes. Every bat flying out of the belfry a lost cause, every whoopla a groan over the radio from the private trenches of the damned. Out of that dark, unstitched wound, that sink of abominations, that cradle of black-thronged cities where the music of ideas is drowned in cold fat, out of strangled Utopias is born a clown, a being divided between beauty and ugliness, between light and chaos, a clown who when he looks down and sidelong is Satan himself and when he looks upward sees a buttered angel, a snail with wings. When I look down into that crack I see an equation sign, the world at balance, a world reduced to zero and no trace of remainder. Not the zero on which Van Norden turned his flashlight, not the empty crack of the prematurely disillusioned man, but an Arabian zero rather, the sign from which spring endless mathematical worlds, the fulcrum which balances the stars and the light dreams and the machines lighter than air and the lightweight limbs and the explosives that produced them. Into that crack I would like to penetrate up to the eyes, make them waggle ferociously, dear, crazy, metallurgical eyes. When the eyes waggle then will I hear again Dostoevski's words, hear them rolling on page after page, with minutest observation, with maddest introspection, with all the undertones of misery now lightly, humorously touched, now swelling like an organ note until the heart bursts and there is nothing left but a blinding, scorching light, the radiant light that carries off the fecundating seeds of the stars. The story of art whose roots lie in massacre.

When I look down into this fucked-out cunt of a whore I feel the whole world beneath me, a world tottering and crumbling, a world used up and polished like a leper's skull. If there were a man who dared to say all that he thought of this world there would not be left him a square foot of ground to stand on. When a man appears the world bears down on him and breaks his back. There are always too many rotten pillars left standing, too much festering humanity for man to bloom. The superstructure is a lie and the foundation is a huge quaking fear. If at intervals of centuries there does appear a man with a desperate, hungry look in his eye, a man who would turn the world upside down in order to create a new race, the love that he brings to the world is turned to bile and he becomes a scourge. If now and then we encounter pages that explode, pages that wound and sear, that wring groans and tears and curses, know that they come from a man with his back up, a man whose only defenses left are his words and his words are always stronger than the lying, crushing weight of the world, stronger than all the racks and wheels which the cowardly invent to crush out the miracle of personality. If any man ever dared to translate all that is in his heart, to put down what is really his experience, what is truly his truth, I think then the world would go to smash, that it would be blown to smithereens and no god, no accident, no will could ever again assemble the pieces, the atoms, the indestructible elements that have gone to make up the world.

In the four hundred years since the last devouring soul appeared, the last man to know the meaning of ecstasy, there has been a constant and steady decline of man in art, in thought, in action. The world is pooped out: there isn't a dry fart left. Who that has a desperate, hungry eye can have the slightest regard for these existent governments, laws, codes, principles, ideals, ideas, totems, and taboos? If anyone knew what it meant to read the riddle of that thing which today is called a "crack" or a "hole," if any one had the least feeling of mystery about the phenomena which are labeled "obscene," this world would crack asunder. It is the obscene horror, the dry, fucked-out aspect of things which makes this crazy civilization look like a crater. It is this great yawning gulf of nothingness which the creative spirits and mothers of the race carry between their legs. When a hungry, desperate spirit appears and makes the guinea pigs squeal it is because he knows where to put the live wire of sex, because he knows that beneath the hard carapace of indifference there is concealed the ugly gash, the wound that never heals. And he puts the live wire right between the legs; he hits below the belt, scorches the very gizzards. It is no use putting on rubber gloves; all that can be coolly and intellectually handled belongs to the carapace and a man who is intent on creation always dives beneath, to the open wound, to the festering obscene horror. He hitches his dynamo to the tenderest parts; if only blood and pus gush forth, it is something. The dry, fucked-out crater is obscene. More obscene than anything is inertia. More blasphemous than the bloodiest oath is paralysis. If there is only a gaping wound left then it must gush forth though it produce nothing but toads and bats and homunculi.

Everything is packed into a second which is either consummated or not consummated. The earth is not an arid plateau of health and comfort, but a great sprawling female with velvet torso that swells and heaves with ocean billows; she squirms beneath a diadem of sweat and anguish. Naked and sexed she rolls among the clouds in the violet light of the stars. All of her, from her generous breasts to her gleaming thighs, blazes with furious ardor. She moves amongst the seasons and the years with a grand whoopla that seizes the torso with paroxysmal fury, that shakes the cobwebs out of the sky; she subsides on her pivotal orbits with volcanic tremors. She is like a doe at times, a doe that has fallen into a snare and lies waiting with beating heart for the cymbals to crash and the dogs to bark. Love and hate, despair, pity, rage, disgust—what are these amidst the fornications of the planets? What is war, disease, cruelty, terror, when night presents the ecstasy of myriad blazing suns? What is this chaff we chew in our sleep if it is not the remembrance of fang-whorl and star cluster.

She used to say to me, Mona, in her fits of exaltation, "you're a great human being," and though she left me here to perish, though she put beneath my feet a great howling pit of emptiness, the words that lie at the bottom of my soul leap forth and they light the shadows below me. I am one who was lost in the crowd, whom the fizzing lights made dizzy, a zero who saw everything about him reduced to mockery. Passed me men and women ignited with sulfur, porters in calcium livery opening the jaws of hell, fame walking on crutches, dwindled by the skyscrapers, chewed to a frazzle by the spiked mouth of the machines. I walked between the tall buildings toward the cool of the river and I saw the lights shoot up between the ribs of the skeletons like rockets. If I was truly a great human being, as she said, then what was the meaning of this slavering idiocy about me? I was a man with body and soul, I had a heart that was not protected by a steel vault. I had moments of ecstasy and I sang with burning sparks. I sang of the Equator, her red-feathered legs and the islands dropping out of sight. But nobody heard. A gun fired across the Pacific falls into space because the earth is round and pigeons fly upside down. I saw her looking at me across the table with eyes turned to grief; sorrow spreading inward flattened its nose against its spine; the marrow churned to pity had turned liquid. She was light as a corpse that floats in the Dead Sea. Her fingers bled with anguish and the blood turned to drool. With the wet dawn came the tolling of bells and along the fibers of my nerves the bells played ceaselessly and their tongues pounded in my heart and clanged with iron malice. Strange that the bells should toll so, but stranger still the body bursting, this woman turned to night and her maggot words gnawing through the mattress. I moved along under the Equator, heard the hideous laughter of the green-jawed hyena, saw the jackal with silken tail and the dick-dick and the spotted leopard, all left behind in the Garden of Eden. And then her sorrow widened, like the bow of a dreadnought and the weight of her sinking flooded my ears. Slime wash and sapphires slipping, sluicing through the gay neurons, and the spectrum spliced and the gunwales dipping. Soft as lion-pad I heard the gun carriages turn, saw them vomit and drool: the firmament sagged and all the stars turned black. Black ocean bleeding and the brooding stars breeding chunks of fresh-swollen flesh while overhead the birds wheeled and out of the hallucinated sky fell the balance with mortar and pestle and the bandaged eyes of justice. All that is here related moves with imaginary feet along the parallels of dead orbs; all that is seen with the empty sockets bursts like flowering grass. Out of nothingness arises the sign of infinity; beneath the ever-rising spirals slowly sinks the gaping hole. The land and the water make numbers joined, a poem written with flesh and stronger than steel or granite. Through endless night the earth whirls toward a creation unknown....

Today I awoke from a sound sleep with curses of joy on my lips, with gibberish on my tongue, repeating to myself like a litany—*"Fay ce que vouldras!... fay ce que vouldras!"* Do anything, but let it produce joy. Do anything, but let it yield ecstasy. So much crowds into my head when I say this to myself: images, gay ones, terrible ones, maddening ones, the wolf and the goat, the spider, the crab, syphilis with her wings outstretched and the door of the womb always on the latch, always open, ready like the tomb. Lust, crime, holiness: the fives of my adored ones, the failures of my adored ones, the words they left behind them, the words they left unfinished; the good they dragged after them and the evil, the sorrow, the discord, the rancor, the strife they created. But above all, *the ecstasy!*

Things, certain things about my old idols bring the tears to my eyes: the interruptions, the disorder, the violence, above all, the hatred they aroused. When I think of their deformities, of the monstrous styles they chose, of the flatulence and tediousness of their works, of all the chaos and confusion they wallowed in, of the obstacles they heaped up about them, I feel an exaltation. They were all mired in their own dung. All men who over-elaborated. So true is it that I am almost tempted to say: "Show me a man who over-elaborates and I will show you a great man!" What is called their "over-elaboration" is my meat: it is the sign of struggle, it is struggle itself with all the fibers clinging to it, the very aura and ambiance of the discordant spirit. And when you show me a man who express-es himself perfectly I will not say that he is not great, but I will say that I am unattracted ... I miss the cloying qualities. When I reflect that the task which the artist implicitly sets himself is to overthrow existing values, to make of the chaos about him an order which is his own, to sow strife and ferment so that by the emotional release those who are dead may be restored to life, then it is that I run with joy to the great and imperfect ones, their confusion nourishes me, their stuttering is like divine music to my ears. I see in the beau-tifully bloated pages that follow the interruptions the erasure of petty intrusions, of the dirty footprints, as it were, of cowards, liars, thieves, vandals, calumniators. I see in the swollen muscles of their lyric throats the staggering effort that must be made to turn the wheel over, to pick up the pace where one has left off. I see that behind the daily annoy-ances and intrusions, behind the cheap, glittering malice of the feeble and inert, there stands the symbol of life's frustrating power, and that he who would create order, he who would sow strife and discord, because he is imbued with will, such a man must go again and again to the stake and the gibbet. I see that behind the nobility of his gestures there lurks the specter of the ridiculousness of it all—that he is not only sublime, but absurd.

Once I thought that to be human was the highest aim a man could have, but I see now that it was meant to destroy me. Today I am proud to say that I am *inhuman,* that I belong not to men and governments, that I have nothing to do with creeds and principles. I have nothing to do with the creaking machinery of humanity—I belong to the earth! I say that lying on my pillow and I can feel the horns sprouting from my temples. I can see about me all those cracked forebears of mine dancing around the bed, consoling me, egging me on, lashing me with their serpent tongues, grinning and leering at me with their skulking skulls. *I am inhuman!* I say it with a mad, hallucinated grin, and I will keep on saying it though it rain crocodiles. Behind my words are all those grinning, leering, skulk-ing skulls, some dead and grinning a long time, some grinning as if they had lockjaw, some grinning with the grimace of a grin, the foretaste and aftermath of what is always going on. Clearer than all I see my own grinning skull, see the skeleton dancing in the wind, ser-pents issuing from the rotted tongue and the bloated pages of ecstasy slimed with excre-ment. And I join my slime, my excrement, my madness, my ecstasy to the great circuit which flows through the subterranean vaults of the flesh. All this unbidden, unwanted, drunken vomit will flow on endlessly through the minds of those to come in the inex-haustible vessel that contains the history of the race. Side by side with the human race there runs another race of beings, the inhuman ones, the race of artists who, goaded by unknown impulses, take the lifeless mass of humanity and by the fever and ferment with which they imbue it turn this soggy dough into bread and the bread into wine and the wine into song. Out of the dead compost and the inert slag they breed a song that con-taminates. I see this other race of individuals ransacking the universe, turning everything upside down, their feet always moving in blood and tears, their hands always empty, always clutching and grasping for the beyond, for the god out of reach: slaying everything with-in reach in order to quiet the monster that gnaws at their vitals. I see that when they tear their hair with the effort to comprehend, to seize this forever unattainable, I see that when they bellow like crazed beasts and rip and gore, I see that this is right, that there is no other path to pursue. A man who belongs to this race must stand up on the high place with gib-berish in his mouth and rip out his entrails. It is right and just, because he must! And any-thing that falls short of this frightening spectacle, anything less shuddering, less terrifying, less mad, less intoxicated, less contaminating, is not art. The rest is counterfeit. The rest is human. The rest belongs to life and lifelessness.

When I think of Stavrogin for example, I think of some divine monster standing on a high place and flinging to us his torn bowels. In *The Possessed* the earth quakes: it is not the catastrophe that befalls the imaginative individual, but a cataclysm in which a large portion of humanity is buried, wiped out forever. Stavrogin was Dostoevski and Dostoevski was the sum of all those contradictions which either paralyze a man or lead him to the heights. There was no world too low for him to enter, no place too high for him to fear to ascend. He went the whole gamut, from the abyss to the stars. It is a pity that we shall never again have the opportunity to see a man placed at the very core of mystery and, by his flashes, illuminating for us the depth and immensity of the darkness.

Today I am aware of my lineage. I have no need to consult my horoscope or my genealogical chart. What is written in the stars, or in my blood, I know nothing of. I know that I spring from the mythological founders of the race. The man who raises the holy bottle to his lips, the criminal who kneels in the marketplace, the innocent one who discovers that *all* corpses stink, the madman who dances with lightning in his hands, the friar who lifts his skirts to pee over the world, the fanatic who ransacks libraries in order to find the Word—all these are fused in me, all these make my confusion, my ecstasy. If I am inhuman it is because my world has slopped over its human bounds, because to be human seems like a poor, sorry, miserable affair, limited by the senses, restricted by moralities and codes, defined by platitudes and isms. I am pouring the juice of the grape down my gullet and I find wisdom in it, but my wisdom is not born of the grape, my intoxication owes nothing to wine....

I want to make a detour of those lofty arid mountain ranges where one dies of thirst and cold, that "extra-temporal" history, that absolute of time and space where there exists neither man, beast, nor vegetation, where one goes crazy with loneliness, with language that is mere words, where everything is unhooked, ungeared, out of joint with the times. I want a world of men and women, of trees that do not talk (because there is too much talk in the world as it is!) of rivers that carry you to places, not rivers that are legends, but rivers that put you in touch with other men and women, with architecture, religion, plants, animals—rivers that have boats on them and in which men drown, drown not in myth and legend and books and dust of the past, but in time and space and history. I want rivers that make oceans such as Shakespeare and Dante, rivers which do not dry up in the void of the past. Oceans, yes! Let us have more oceans, new oceans that blot out the past, oceans that create new geological formations, new topographical vistas and strange, terrifying continents, oceans that destroy and preserve at the same time, oceans that we can sail on, take off to new discoveries, new horizons. Let us have more oceans, more upheavals, more wars, more holocausts. Let us have a world of men and women with dynamos between their legs, a world of natural fury, of passion, action, drama, dreams, madness, a world that produces ecstasy and not dry farts. I believe that today more than ever a book should be sought after even if it has only *one* great page in it: we must search for fragments, splinters, toenails, anything that has ore in it, anything that is capable of resuscitating the body and soul.

It may be that we are doomed, that there is no hope for us, *any of us,* but if that is so then let us set up a last agonizing, bloodcurdling howl, a screech of defiance, a war whoop! Away with lamentation! Away with elegies and dirges! Away with biographies and histories, and libraries and museums! Let the dead eat the dead. Let us living ones dance about the rim of the crater, a last expiring dance. But a dance!

"I love everything that flows," said the great blind Milton of our times. I was thinking of him this morning when I awoke with a great bloody shout of joy: I was thinking of his rivers and trees and all that world of night which he is exploring. Yes, I said to myself, I too love everything that flows: rivers, sewers, lava, semen, blood, bile, words, sentences. I love the amniotic fluid when it spills out of the bag. I love the kidney with its painful gallstones, its gravel and what-not; I love the urine that pours out scalding and the clap that runs endlessly; I love the words of hysterics and the sentences that flow on like dysentery and mirror all the sick images of the soul; I love the great rivers like the Amazon and the Orinoco, where crazy men like Moravagine float on through dream and legend in an open boat and drown in the blind mouths of the river. I love everything that flows, even the menstrual flow that carries away the seed unfecund. I love scripts that flow, be they hieratic, esoteric, perverse, polymorph, or unilateral. I love everything that flows, everything that has time in it and becoming, that brings us back to the beginning where there is never end: the violence of the prophets, the obscenity that is ecstasy, the wisdom of the fanatic, the priest with his rubber litany, the foul words of the whore, the spittle that floats away in the gutter, the milk of the breast and the bitter honey that pours from the womb, all that is fluid, melting, dissolute and dissolvent, all the pus and dirt that in flowing is purified, that loses its sense of origin, that makes the great circuit toward death and dissolution. The great incestuous wish is to flow on, one with time, to merge the great image of the beyond with the here and now. A fatuous, suicidal wish that is constipated by words and paralyzed by thought.

It was close to dawn on Christmas Day when we came home from the Rue d'Odessa with a couple of Negresses from the telephone company. The fire was out and we were all so tired that we climbed into bed with our clothes on. The one I had, who had been like a bounding leopard all evening, fell sound asleep as I was climbing over her. For a while I worked over her as one works over a person who has been drowned or asphyxiated. Then I gave it up and fell sound asleep myself.

All during the holidays we had champagne morning, noon and night—the cheapest and the best champagne. With the turn of the year I was to leave for Dijon where I had been offered a trivial post as exchange professor of English, one of those Franco-American amity arrangements which is supposed to promote understanding and good will between sister republics. Fillmore was more elated than I by the prospect—he had good reason to be. For me it was just a transfer from one purgatory to another. There was no future ahead of me; there wasn't even a salary attached to the job. One was supposed to consider himself fortunate to enjoy the privilege of spreading the gospel of Franco-American amity. It was a job for a rich man's son.

The night before I left we had a good time. About dawn it began to snow: we walked about from one quarter to another taking a last look at Paris. Passing through the Rue St. Dominique we suddenly fell upon a little square and there was the Eglise Ste.-Clotilde. People were going to mass. Fillmore, whose head was still a little cloudy, was bent on going to mass too. "For the fun of it!" as he put it. I felt somewhat uneasy about it; in the first place I had never attended a mass, and in the second place I looked seedy and felt seedy. Fillmore, too, looked rather battered, even more disreputable than myself; his big slouch hat was on assways and his overcoat was still full of sawdust from the last joint we had been in. However, we marched in. The worst they could do would be to throw us out.

I was so astounded by the sight that greeted my eyes that I lost all uneasiness. It took me a little while to get adjusted to the dim light. I stumbled around behind Fillmore, holding his sleeve. A weird, unearthly noise assailed my ears, a sort of hollow drone that rose up out of the cold flagging. A huge, dismal tomb it was with mourners shuffling in and out. A sort of antechamber to the world below. Temperature about 55 or 60 Fahrenheit. No music except this undefinable dirge manufactured in the subcellar—like a million heads of cauliflower wailing in the dark. People in shrouds were chewing away with that hopeless, dejected look of beggars who hold out their hands in a trance and mumble an unintelligible appeal.

That this sort of thing existed I knew, but then one also knows that there are slaughterhouses and morgues and dissecting rooms. One instinctively avoids such places. In the street I had often passed a priest with a little prayer book in his hands laboriously memorizing his lines. *Idiot*, I would say to myself, and let it go at that. In the street one meets with all forms of dementia and the priest is by no means the most striking. Two thousand years of it has deadened us to the idiocy of it. However, when you are suddenly transported to the very midst of his realm, when you see the little world in which the priest functions like an alarm clock, you are apt to have entirely different sensations.

For a moment all this slaver and twitching of the lips almost began to have a meaning. Something was going on, some kind of dumb show which, not rendering me wholly stupefied, held me spellbound. All over the world, wherever there are these dim-lit tombs, you have this incredible spectacle—the same mean temperature, the same crepuscular glow, the same buzz and drone. All over Christendom, at certain stipulated hours, people in black are groveling before the altar where the priest stands up with a little book in one hand and a dinner bell or atomizer in the other and mumbles to them in a language which, even if it were comprehensible, no longer contains a shred of meaning. Blessing them, most likely. Blessing the country, blessing the ruler, blessing the firearms and the battleships and the ammunition and the hand grenades. Surrounding him on the altar are little boys dressed like angels of the Lord who sing alto and soprano. Innocent lambs. All in skirts, sexless, like the priest himself who is usually flat-footed and nearsighted to boot. A fine epicene caterwauling. Sex in a jockstrap, to the tune of J-mol.

I was taking it in as best I could in the dim light. Fascinating and stupefying at the same time. All over the civilized world, I thought to myself. All over the world. Marvelous. Rain or shine, hail, sleet, snow, thunder, lightning, war, famine, pestilence— makes not the slightest difference. Always the same mean temperature, the same mum-bo jumbo, the same high-laced shoes and the little angels of the Lord singing soprano and alto. Near the exit a little slot-box—to carry on the heavenly work. So that God's blessing may rain down upon king and country and battleships and high explosives and tanks and airplanes, so that the worker may have more strength in his arms, strength to slaughter horses and cows and sheep, strength to punch holes in iron girders, strength to sew buttons on other people's pants, strength to sell carrots and sewing machines and automobiles, strength to exterminate insects and clean stables and unload garbage cans and scrub lavatories, strength to write headlines and chop tickets in the subway. Strength... strength. All that lip chewing and hornswoggling just to furnish a little strength!

We were moving about from one spot to another, surveying the scene with that clear-headedness which comes after an all-night session. We must have made ourselves pretty conspicuous shuffling about that way with our coat collars turned up and never once cross-ing ourselves and never once moving our lips except to whisper some callous remark. Perhaps everything would have passed off without notice if Fillmore hadn't insisted on walking past the altar in the midst of the ceremony. He was looking for the exit, and he thought while he was at it, I suppose, that he would take a good squint at the holy of holies, get a close-up on it, as it were. We had gotten safely by and were marching toward a crack of light which must have been the way out when a priest suddenly stepped out of the gloom and blocked our path. Wanted to know where we were going and what we were doing. We told him politely enough that we were looking for the exit. We said "exit" because at the moment we were so flabbergasted that we couldn't think of the French for exit. Without a word of response he took us firmly by the arm and, opening the door, a side door it was, he gave us a push and out we tumbled into the blinding light of day. It happened so suddenly and unexpectedly that when we hit the sidewalk we were in a daze.

We walked a few paces, blinking our eyes, and then instinctively we both turned round; the priest was still standing on the steps, pale as a ghost and scowling like the devil himself. He must have been sore as hell. Later, thinking back on it, I couldn't blame him for it. But at that moment, seeing him with his long skirts and the little skull cap on his cranium, he looked so ridiculous that I burst out laughing. I looked at Fillmore and he began to laugh too. For a full minute we stood there laughing right in the poor bugger's face. He was so bewildered, I guess, that for a moment he didn't know what to do; sud-denly, however, he started down the steps on the run, shaking his fist at us as if he were in earnest. When he swung out of the enclosure he was on the gallop. By this time some pre-servative instinct warned me to get a move on. I grabbed Fillmore by the coat sleeve and started to run. He was saying, like an idiot: "No, no! I won't run!"—"Come on!" I yelled, "we'd better get out of here. That guy's mad clean through." And off we ran, beating it as fast as our legs would carry us.

On the way to Dijon, still laughing about the affair, my thoughts reverted to a ludi-crous incident, of a somewhat similar nature, which occurred during my brief sojourn in Florida. It was during the celebrated boom when, like thousands of others, I was caught with my pants down. Trying to extricate myself I got caught, along with a friend of mine, in the very neck of the bottle. Jacksonville, where we were marooned for about six weeks, was practically in a state of siege. Every bum on earth, and a lot of guys who had never been bums before, seemed to have drifted into Jacksonville. The YMCA, the Salvation Army, the firehouses and police stations, the hotels, the lodging houses, everything was full up. *Complet* absolutely, and signs everywhere to that effect.

The residents of Jacksonville had become so hardened that it seemed to me as if they were walking around in coats of mail. It was the old business of food again. Food and a place to flop. Food was coming up from below in trainloads—oranges and grapefruit and all sorts of juicy edibles. We used to pass by the freight sheds looking for rotten fruit—but even that was scarce.

One night, in desperation, I dragged my friend Joe to a synagogue, during the serv-ice. It was a Reformed congregation, and the rabbi impressed me rather favorably. The music got me too—that piercing lamentation of the Jews. As soon as the service was over I marched to the rabbi's study and requested an interview with him. He received me decently enough—until I made clear my mission. Then he grew absolutely frightened. I had only asked him for a handout on behalf of my friend Joe and myself. You would have thought, from the way he looked at me, that I had asked to rent the synagogue as a bowling alley. To cap it all, he suddenly asked me point-blank if I was a Jew or not. When I answered no, he seemed perfectly outraged. Why, pray, had I come to a Jewish pastor for aid? I told him naively that I had always had more faith in the Jews than in the Gentiles. I said it modestly, as if it were one of my peculiar defects. It was the truth too. But he wasn't a bit flattered. No, siree. He was horrified. To get rid of me he wrote out a note to the Salvation Army people. "That's the place for you to address yourself," he said, and brusquely turned away to tend his flock.

The Salvation Army, of course, had nothing to offer us. If we had had a quarter apiece we might have rented a mattress on the floor. But we hadn't a nickel between us. We went to the park and stretched ourselves out on a bench. It was raining and so we covered ourselves with newspapers. Weren't there more than a half hour, I imagine, when a cop came along and, without a word of warning, gave us such a sound fanning that we were up and on our feet in a jiffy, and dancing a bit too, though we weren't in any mood for dancing. I felt so goddamned sore and miserable, so dejected, so lousy, after being whacked over the ass by that half-witted bastard, that I could have blown up the City Hall.

The next morning, in order to get even with these hospitable sons of bitches, we presented ourselves bright and early at the door of a Catholic priest. This time I let Joe do the talking. He was Irish and he had a bit of a brogue. He had very soft, blue eyes, too, and he could make them water a bit when he wanted to. A sister in black opened the door for us; she didn't ask us inside, however. We were to wait in the vestibule until she went and called for the good father. In a few minutes he came, the good father, puffing like a locomotive. And what was it we wanted disturbing his likes at that hour of the morning? Something to eat and a place to flop, we answered innocently. And where did we hail from, the good father wanted to know at once. From New York. From New York, eh? Then ye'd better be gettin' back there as fast as ye kin, me lads, and without another word the big, bloated turnip-faced bastard shoved the door in our face.

About an hour later, drifting around helplessly like a couple of drunken schooners, we happened to pass by the rectory again. So help me God if the big, lecherous-looking turnip wasn't backing out of the alley in a limousine! As he swung past us he blew a cloud of smoke into our eyes. As though to say—"*That* for you!" A beautiful limousine it was, with a couple of spare tires in the back, and the good father sitting at the wheel with a big cigar in his mouth. Must have been a Corona Corona, so fat and luscious it was. Sitting pretty he was, and no two ways about it. I couldn't see whether he had skirts on or not. I could only see the gravy trickling from his lips—and the big cigar with that fifty-cent aroma.

All the way to Dijon I got to reminiscing about the past. I thought of all the things I might have said and done, which I hadn't said or done, in the bitter, humiliating moments when just to ask for a crust of bread is to make yourself less than a worm. Stone sober as I was, I was still smarting from those old insults and injuries. I could still feel that whack over the ass which the cop gave me in the park—though that was a mere bagatelle, a little dancing lesson, you might say. All over the States I wandered, and into Canada and Mexico. The same story everywhere. If you want bread you've got to get in harness, get in lock step. Over all the earth a gray desert, a carpet of steel and cement. Production! More nuts and bolts, more barbed wire, more dog biscuits, more lawn mowers, more ball bearings, more high explosives, more tanks, more poison gas, more soap, more toothpaste, more newspapers, more education, more churches, more libraries, more museums. *Forward!* Time presses. The embryo is pushing through the neck of the womb, and there's not even a gob of spit to ease the passage. A dry, strangulating birth. Not a wail, not a chirp. *Salut au monde!* Salute of twenty-one guns bombinating from the rectum. "I wear my hat as I please, indoors or out," said Walt. That was a time when you could still get a hat to fit your head. But time passes. To get a hat that fits now you have to walk to the electric chair. They give you a skull cap. A tight fit, what? But no matter! It fits.

You have to be in a strange country like France, walking the meridian that separates the hemispheres of life and death, to know what incalculable vistas yawn ahead. *The body electric! The democratic soul! Flood tide!* Holy-Mother of God, what does this crap mean? The earth is parched and cracked. Men and women come together like broods of vultures over a stinking carcass, to mate and fly apart again. Vultures who drop from the clouds like heavy stones. Talons and beak, that's what we are! A huge intestinal apparatus with a nose for dead meat. *Forward!* Forward without pity, without compassion, without love, without forgiveness. Ask no quarter and give none! More battleships, more poison gas, more high explosives! More gonococci! More streptococci! More bombing machines! More and more of it—until the whole fucking works is blown to smithereens, and the earth with it!

Stepping off the train I knew immediately that I had made a fatal mistake. The Lycee was a little distance from the station; I walked down the main street in the early dusk of winter, feeling my way toward my destination. A light snow was falling, the trees sparkled with frost. Passed a couple of huge, empty cafes that looked like dismal waiting rooms. Silent, empty gloom—that's how it impressed me. A hopeless, jerkwater town where mustard is turned out in carload lots, in vats and tuns and barrels and pots and cute-looking little jars.

The first glance at the Lycee sent a shudder through me. I felt so undecided that at the entrance I stopped to debate whether I would go in or not. But as I hadn't the price of a return ticket there wasn't much use debating the question. I thought for a moment of sending a wire to Fillmore, but then I was stumped to know what excuse to make. The only thing to do was to walk in with my eyes shut.

It happened that M. le Proviseur was out—his day off, so they said. A little hunchback came forward and offered to escort me to the office of M. le Censeur, second in charge. I walked a little behind him, fascinated by the grotesque way in which he hobbled along. He was a little monster, such as can be seen on the porch of any harassed cathedral in Europe.

The office of M. le Censeur was large and bare. I sat down in a stiff chair to wait while the hunchback darted off to search for him. I almost felt at home. The atmosphere of the place reminded me vividly of certain charity bureaus back in the States where I used to sit by the hour waiting for some mealy-mouthed bastard to come and cross-examine me.

Suddenly the door opened and, with a mincing step, M. le Censeur came prancing in. It was all I could do to suppress a titter. He had on just such a frock coat as Boris used to wear, and over his forehead there hung a bang, a sort of spitcurl such as Smerdyakov might have worn. Grave and brittle, with a lynxlike eye, he wasted no words of cheer on me. At once he brought forth the sheets on which were written the names of the students, the hours, the classes, etc., all in a meticulous hand. He told me how much coal and wood I was allowed and after that he promptly informed me that I was at liberty to do as I pleased in my spare time. This last was the first good thing I had heard him say. It sounded so reassuring that I quickly said a prayer for France—for the army and for the navy, the educational system, the *bistros,* the whole *goddamned works.*

This folderol completed, he rang a little bell, whereupon the hunchback promptly appeared to escort me to the office of M. l'Econome. Here the atmosphere was somewhat different. More like a freight station, with bills of lading and rubber stamps everywhere, and pasty-faced clerks scribbling away with broken pens in huge, cumbersome ledgers. My dole of coal and wood portioned out, off we marched, the hunchback and I, with a wheelbarrow, toward the dormitory. I was to have a room on the top floor, in the same wing as the *pions.* The situation was taking on a humorous aspect. I didn't know what the hell to expect next. Perhaps a spittoon. The whole thing smacked very much of preparation for a campaign; the only things missing were a knapsack and rifle—and a brass slug.

The room assigned me was rather large, with a small stove to which was attached a crooked pipe that made an elbow just over the iron cot. A big chest for the coal and wood stood near the door. The windows gave out on a row of forlorn little houses all made of stone in which lived the grocer, the baker, the shoemaker, the butcher, etc.—all imbecilic-looking clodhoppers. I glanced over the rooftops toward the bare hills where a train was clattering. The whistle of the locomotive screamed mournfully and hysterically.

After the hunchback had made the fire for me I inquired about the grub. It was not quite time for dinner. I flopped on the bed, with my overcoat on, and pulled the covers over me. Beside me was the eternal rickety night table in which the piss pot is hidden away. I stood the alarm on the table and watched the minutes ticking off. Into the well of the room a bluish light filtered in from the street. I listened to the trucks rattling by as I gazed vacantly at the stove pipe, at the elbow where it was held together with bits of wire. The coal chest intrigued me. Never in my life had I occupied a room with a coal chest. And never in my life had I built a fire or taught children. Nor, for that matter, never in my life had I worked without pay. I felt free and chained at the same time—like one feels just before election, when all the crooks have been nominated and you are beseeched to vote for the right man. I felt like a hired man, like a jack-of-all-trades, like a hunter, like a rover, like a galley slave, like a pedagogue, like a worm and a louse. I was free, but my limbs were shackled. A democratic soul with a free meal ticket, but no power of locomotion, no voice. I felt like a jellyfish nailed to a plank. Above all, I felt hungry. The hands were moving slowly. Still ten more minutes to kill before the fire alarm would go off. The shadows in the room deepened. It grew frightfully silent, a tense stillness that tautened my nerves. Little dabs of snow clung to the windowpanes. Far away a locomotive gave out a shrill scream. Then a dead silence again. The stove had commenced to glow, but there was no heat coming from it. I began to fear that I might doze off and miss the dinner. That would mean lying awake on an empty belly all night. I got panic-stricken.

Just a moment before the gong went off I jumped out of bed and, locking the door behind me, I bolted downstairs to the courtyard. There I got lost. One quadrangle after another, one staircase after another. I wandered in and out of the buildings searching frantically for the refectory. Passed a long line of youngsters marching in a column to God knows where; they moved along like a chain gang, with a slave driver at the head of the column. Finally I saw an energetic-looking individual, with a derby, heading toward me.

I stopped him to ask the way to the refectory. Happened I stopped the right man. It was M. le Proviseur, and he seemed delighted to have stumbled on me. Wanted to know right away if I were comfortably settled, if there was anything more he could do for me. I told him everything was O.K. Only it was a bit chilly, I ventured to add. He assured me that it was rather unusual, this weather. Now and then the fogs came on and a bit of snow, and then it became unpleasant for a while, and so on and so forth. All the while he had me by the arm, guiding me toward the refectory. He seemed like a very decent chap. A regular guy, I thought to myself. I even went so far as to imagine that I might get chummy with him later on, that he'd invite me to his room on a bitter cold night and make a hot grog for me. I imagined all sorts of friendly things in the few moments it required to reach the door of the refectory. Here, my mind racing on at a mile a minute, he suddenly shook hands with me and, doffing his hat, bade me good night. I was so bewildered that I tipped my hat also. It was the regular thing to do, I soon found out. Whenever you pass a prof, or even M. l'Econome, you doff the hat. Might pass the same guy a dozen times a day. Makes no difference. You've got to give the salute, even though your hat is worn out. It's the polite thing to do.

Anyway, I had found the refectory. Like an East Side clinic it was, with tiled walls, bare light, and marble-topped tables. And of course a big stove with an elbow pipe. The dinner wasn't served yet. A cripple was running in and out with dishes and knives and forks and bottles of wine. In a corner several young men conversing animatedly. I went up to them and introduced myself. They gave me a most cordial reception. Almost too cordial, in fact. I couldn't quite make it out. In a jiffy the room began to fill up; I was presented from one to the other quickly. Then they formed a circle about me and, filling the glasses, they began to sing....

L'autre soir l'idee m'est venue
Cre nom de Zeus d'enculer un pendu;
Le vent se leve sur la potence,
Voila mon pendu qui se balance,
J'ai du l'enculer en sautant,
Cre nom de Zeus, on est jamais content.

Baiser dans un con trop petit,
Cre nom de Zeus, on s'ecorche le vit;
Baiser dans un con trop large,
On ne sait pas ou l'on decharge;
Se branler etant bien emmerdant,
Cre nom de Zeus, on est jamais content.

With this, Quasimodo announced the dinner.

They were a cheerful group, *les surveillants.* There was Kroa who belched like a pig and always let off a loud fart when he sat down to table. He could fart thirteen times in succession, they informed me. He held the record. Then there was Monsieur le Prince, an athlete who was fond of wearing a tuxedo in the evening when he went to town; he had a beautiful complexion, just like a girl, and never touched the wine nor read anything that might tax his brain. Next to him sat Petit Paul, from the Midi, who thought of nothing but cunt all the time; he used to say every day—"*a partir de jeudi je ne parlerai plus de femmes.*" He and Monsieur le Prince were inseparable. Then there was Passeleau, a veritable young scallywag who was studying medicine and who borrowed right and left; he talked incessantly of Ronsard, Villon and Rabelais. Opposite me sat Mollesse, agitator and organizer of the *pions*, who insisted on weighing the meat to see if it wasn't short a few grams. He occupied a little room in the infirmary. His supreme enemy was Monsieur l'Econome, which was nothing particularly to his credit since everybody hated this individual. For companion Mollesse had one called Le Penible, a dour-looking chap with a hawklike profile who practiced the strictest economy and acted as moneylender. He was like an engraving by Albrecht Durer—a composite of all the dour, sour, morose, bitter, unfortunate, unlucky and introspective devils who compose the pantheon of Germany's medieval knights. A Jew, no doubt. At any rate, he was killed in an automobile accident shortly after my arrival, a circumstance which left me twenty-three francs to the good. With the exception of Renaud who sat beside me, the others have faded out of my memory; they belonged to that category of colorless individuals who make up the world of engineers, architects, dentists, pharmacists, teachers, etc. There was nothing to distinguish them from the clods whom they would later wipe their boots on. They were zeros in every sense of the word, ciphers who form the nucleus of a respectable and lamentable citizenry. They ate with their heads down and were always the first to clamor for a second helping. They slept soundly and never complained; they were neither gay nor miserable. The indifferent ones whom Dante consigned to the vestibule of Hell. The upper-crusters.

It was the custom after dinner to go immediately to town, unless one was on duty in the dormitories. In the center of town were the cafes—huge, dreary halls where the somnolent merchants of Dijon gathered to play cards and listen to the music. It was warm in the cafes, that is the best I can say for them. The seats were fairly comfortable, too. And there were always a few whores about who, for a glass of beer or a cup of coffee, would sit and chew the fat with you. The music, on the other hand, was atrocious. Such music! On a winter's night, in a dirty hole like Dijon, nothing can be more harassing, more nerve-racking, than the sound of a French orchestra. Particularly one of those lugubrious female orchestras with everything coming in squeaks and farts, with a dry, algebraic rhythm and the hygienic consistency of toothpaste. A wheezing and scraping performed at so many francs the hour—and the devil take the hindmost! The melancholy of it! As if old Euclid had stood up on his hind legs and swallowed prussic acid. The whole realm of Idea so thoroughly exploited by the reason that there is nothing left of which to make music except the empty slats of the accordion, through which the wind whistles and tears the ether to tatters. However, to speak of music in connection with this outpost is like dreaming of champagne when you are in the death cell. Music was the least of my worries. I didn't even think of cunt, so dismal, so chill, so barren, so gray was it all. On the way home the first night I noticed on the door of a cafe an inscription from the *Gargantua*. Inside the cafe it was like a morgue. However, *forward!*

I had plenty of time on my hands and not a sou to spend. Two or three hours of conversational lessons a day, and that was all. And what use was it, teaching these poor bastards English? I felt sorry as hell for them. All morning plugging away on *John Gilpin's Ride*, and in the afternoon coming to me to practice a dead language. I thought of the good time I had wasted reading Virgil or wading through such incomprehensible nonsense as *Hermann und Dorothea*. The insanity of it! Learning, the empty breadbasket! I thought of Carl who can recite *Faust* backwards, who never writes a book without praising the shit out of his immortal, incorruptible Goethe. And yet he hadn't sense enough to take on a rich cunt and get himself a change of underwear. There's something obscene in this love of the past which ends in breadlines and dugouts. Something obscene about this spiritual racket which permits an idiot to sprinkle holy water over Big Berthas and dreadnoughts and high explosives. Every man with a bellyful of the classics is an enemy to the human race.

Here was I, supposedly to spread the gospel of Franco-American amity—the emissary of a corpse who, after he had plundered right and left, after he had caused untold suffering and misery, dreamed of establishing universal peace. Pfui! What did they expect me to talk about, I wonder? About *Leaves of Grass,* about the tariff walls, about the Declaration of Independence, about the latest gang war? What? Just what, I'd like to know. Well, I'll tell you—I never mentioned these things. I started right off the bat with a lesson in the physiology of love. How the elephants make love—that was it! It caught like wildfire. After the first day there were no more empty benches. After that first lesson in English they were standing at the door waiting for me. We got along swell together. They asked all sorts of questions, as though they had never learned a damned thing. I let them fire away. I taught them to ask still more ticklish questions. *Ask anything!*—that was my motto. I'm here as a plenipotentiary from the realm of free spirits. I'm here to create a fever and a ferment. "In some ways," says an eminent astronomer, "the material universe appears to be passing away like a tale that is told, dissolving into nothingness like a vision." That seems to be the general feeling underlying the empty breadbasket of learning. Myself, I don't believe it. I don't believe a fucking thing these bastards try to shove down our throats.

Between sessions, if I had no book to read, I would go upstairs to the dormitory and chat with the *pions.* They were delightfully ignorant of all that was going on—especially in the world of art. Almost as ignorant as the students themselves. It was as if I had gotten into a private little madhouse with no exit signs. Sometimes I snooped around under the arcades, watching the kids marching along with huge hunks of bread stuck in their dirty mugs. I was always hungry myself, since it was impossible for me to go to breakfast which was handed out at some ungodly hour of the morning, just when the bed was getting toasty. Huge bowls of blue coffee with chunks of white bread and no butter to go with it. For lunch, beans or lentils with bits of meat thrown in to make it look appetizing. Food fit for a chain gang, for rock breakers. Even the wine was lousy. Things were either diluted or bloated. There were calories, but no cuisine. M. l'Econome was responsible for it all. So they said. I don't believe that, either. He was paid to keep our heads just above the water line. He didn't ask if we were suffering from piles or carbuncles; he didn't inquire if we had delicate palates or the intestines of wolves. Why should he? He was hired at so many grams the plate to produce so many kilowatts of energy. Everything in terms of horse power. It was all carefully reckoned in the fat ledgers which the pasty-faced clerks scribbled in morning, noon and night. Debit and credit, with a red line down the middle of the page.

Roaming around the quadrangle with an empty belly most of the time I got to feel slightly mad. Like Charles the Silly, poor devil—only I had no Odette Champ-divers with whom to play stinkfinger. Half the time I had to grub cigarettes from the students, and during the lessons sometimes I munched a bit of dry bread with them. As the fire was always going out on me I soon used up my allotment of wood. It was the devil's own time coaxing a little wood out of the ledger clerks. Finally I got so riled up about it that I would go out in the street and hunt for firewood, like an Arab. Astonishing how little firewood you could pick up in the streets of Dijon.

However, these little foraging expeditions brought me into strange precincts. Got to know the little street named after a M. Philibert Papillon—a dead musician, I Relieve—where there was a cluster of whorehouses. It was always more cheerful hereabouts; there was the smell of cooking, and wash hanging out to dry. Once in a while I caught a glimpse of the poor half-wits who lounged about inside. They were better off than the poor devils in the center of town whom I used to bump into whenever I walked through a department store. I did that frequently in order to get warm. They were doing it for the same reason, I suppose. Looking for someone to buy them a coffee. They looked a little crazy, with the cold and the loneliness. The whole town looked a bit crazy when the blue of evening settled over it. You could walk up and down the main drive any Thursday in the week 'til doomsday and never meet an expansive soul. Sixty or seventy thousand people— perhaps more—wrapped in woolen underwear and nowhere to go and nothing to do. Turning out mustard by the carload. Female orchestras grinding out *The Merry Widow*. Silver service in the big hotels. The ducal palace rotting away, stone by stone, limb by limb. The trees screeching with frost. A ceaseless clatter of wooden shoes. The University celebrating the death of Goethe, or the birth, I don't remember which. (Usually it's the deaths that are celebrated.) Idiotic affair, anyway. Everybody yawning and stretching.

Coming through the high driveway into the quadrangle a sense of abysmal futility always came over me. Outside bleak and empty; inside, bleak and empty. A scummy sterility hanging over the town, a fog of book-learning. Slag and cinders of the past. Around the interior courts were ranged the classrooms, little shacks such as you might see in the North woods, where the pedagogues back and forth with low moans, jumping out at you from the eaves, hanging like broken-necked criminals from the gargoyles. I kept looking back all the time, kept walking like a crab that you prong with a dirty fork. All those fat little monsters, those slablike effigies pasted on the facade of the Eglise St. Michel, they were following me down the crooked lanes and around corners. The whole facade of St. Michel seemed to open up like an album at night, leaving you face to face with the horrors of the printed page. When the lights went out and the characters faded away flat, dead as words, then it was quite magnificent, the facade; in every crevice of the old gnarled front there was the hollow chant of the nightwind and over the lacy rubble of cold stiff vestments there was a cloudy absinthe-like drool of fog and frost.

Here, where the church stood, everything seemed turned hind side front. The church itself must have been twisted off its base by centuries of progress in the rain and snow. It lay in the Place Edgar-Quinet, squat against the wind, like a dead mule. Through the Rue de la Monnaie the wind rushed like white hair streaming wild: it whirled around the white hitching posts which obstructed the free passage of omnibuses and twenty-mule teams. Swinging through this exit in the early morning hours I sometimes stumbled upon Monsieur Renaud who, wrapped in his cowl like a gluttonous monk, made overtures to me in the language of the sixteenth century. Falling in step with Monsieur Renaud, the moon busting through the greasy sky like a punctured balloon, I fell immediately into the realm of the transcendental. M. Renaud had a precise speech, dry as apricots, with a heavy Brandenburger base. Used to come at me full tilt from Goethe or Fichte, with deep base notes that rumbled in the windy corners of the Place like claps of last year's thunder. Men of Yucatan, men of Zanzibar, men of Tierra del Fuego, save me from this glaucous hog rind! The North piles up about me, the glacial fjords, the blue-tipped spines, the crazy lights, the obscene Christian chant that spread like an avalanche from Etna to the Aegean. Everything frozen tight as scum, the mind locked and rimed with frost, and through the melancholy bales of chitter-wit the choking gargle of louse-eaten saints. White I am and wrapped in wool, swaddled, fettered, hamstrung, but in this I have no part. White to the bone, but with a cold alkali base, with saffron-tipped fingers. White, aye, but no brother of learning, no Catholic heart. White and ruthless, as the men before me who sailed out of the Elbe. I look to the sea, to the sky, to what is unintelligible and distantly near.

The snow under foot scurries before the wind, blows, tickles, stings, lisps away, whirls aloft, showers, splinters, sprays down. No sun, no roar of surf, no breaker's surge. The cold north wind pointed with barbed shafts, icy, malevolent, greedy, blighting, paralyzing. The streets turn away on their crooked elbows; they break from the hurried sight, the stern glance. They hobble away down the drifting lattice work, wheeling the church hind side front, mowing down the statues, flattening the monuments, uprooting the trees, stiffening the grass, sucking the fragrance out of the earth. Leaves dull as cement: leaves no dew can bring to glisten again. No moon will ever silver their listless plight. The seasons are come to a stagnant stop, the trees blench and wither, the wagons roll m the mica ruts with slithering harplike thuds. In the hollow of the white-tipped hills, lurid and boneless Dijon slumbers. No man alive and walking through the night except the restless spirits moving southward toward the sapphire grids. Yet I am up and about, a walking ghost, a white man terrorized by the cold sanity of this slaughterhouse geometry. Who am I? What am I doing here? I fall between the cold walls of human malevolence, a white figure fluttering, sinking down through the cold lake, a mountain of skulls above me. I settle down to the cold latitudes, the chalk steps washed with indigo. The earth in its dark corridors knows my step, feels a foot abroad, a wing stirring, a gasp and a shudder. I hear the learning chaffed and chuzzled, the figures mounting upward, bat slime dripping aloft and clanging with pasteboard golden wings; I hear the trains collide, the chains rattle, the locomotive chugging, snorting, sniffing, steaming and pissing. All things come to me through the clear fog with the odor of repetition, with yellow hangovers and Gadzooks and whettikins. In the dead center, far below Dijon, far below the hyperborean regions, stands God Ajax, his shoulders strapped to the mill wheel, the olives crunching, the green marsh water alive with croaking frogs.

The fog and snow, the cold latitude, the heavy learning, the blue coffee, the unbuttered bread, the soup and lentils, the heavy pork-packer beans, the stale cheese, the soggy chow, the lousy wine have put the whole penitentiary into a state of constipation. And just when everyone has become shit-tight the toilet pipes freeze. The shit piles up like ant hills; one has to move down from the little pedestals and leave it on the floor. It lies there stiff and frozen, waiting for the thaw. On Thursdays the hunchback comes with his little wheelbarrow, shovels the cold, stiff turds with a broom and pan, and trundles off dragging his withered leg. The corridors are Uttered with toilet paper; it sticks to your feet like flypaper. When the weather moderates the odor gets ripe; you can smell it in Winchester forty miles away. Standing over that ripe dung in the morning, with a toothbrush, the stench is so powerful that it makes your head spin. We stand around in red flannel shirts, waiting to spit down the hole; it is like an aria from one of Verdi's great operas—an anvil chorus with pulleys and syringes. In the night, when I am taken short, I rush down to the private toilet of M. le Censeur, just off the driveway. My stool is always full of blood. His toilet doesn't flush either but at least there is the pleasure of sitting down. I leave my little bundle for him as a token of esteem.

Toward the end of the meal each evening the *veilleur de nuit* drops in for his bit of cheer. This is the only human being in the whole institution with whom I feel a kinship. He is a nobody. He carries a lantern and a bunch of keys. He makes the rounds through the night, stiff as an automaton. About the time the stale cheese is being passed around, in he pops for his glass of wine. He stands there, with paw outstretched, his hair stiff and wiry, like a mastiff's, his cheeks ruddy, his mustache gleaming with snow. He mumbles a word or two and Quasimodo brings him the bottle. Then, with feet solidly planted, he throws back his head and down it goes, slowly in one long draught. To me it's like he's pouring rubies down his gullet. Something about this gesture which seizes me by the hair. It's almost as if he were drinking down the dregs of human sympathy, as if all the love and compassion in the world could be tossed off like that, in one gulp—as if that were all that could be squeezed together day after day. A little less than a rabbit they have made him. In the scheme of things he's not worth the brine to pickle a herring. He's just a piece of live manure. And he knows it. When he looks around after his drink and smiles at us, the world seems to be falling to pieces. It's a smile thrown across an abyss. The whole stinking civilized world lies like a quagmire at the bottom of the pit, and over it, like a mirage, hovers this wavering smile.

It was the same smile which greeted me at night when I returned from my rambles, I remember one such night when, standing at the door waiting for the old fellow to finish his rounds, I had such a sense of well-being that I could have waited thus forever. I had to wait perhaps half an hour before he opened the door. I looked about me calmly and leisurely, drank everything in, the dead tree in front of the school with its twisted rope branches, the houses across the street which had changed color during the night, which curved now more noticeably, the sound of a train rolling through the Siberian wastes, the railings painted by Utrillo, the sky, the deep wagon ruts. Suddenly, out of nowhere, two lovers appeared; every few yards they stopped and embraced, and when I could no longer follow them with my eyes I followed the sound of their steps, heard the abrupt stop, and then the slow, meandering gait. I could feel the sag and slump of their bodies when they leaned against a rail, heard their shoes creak as the muscles tightened for the embrace. Through the town they wandered, through the crooked streets, toward the glassy canal where the water lay black as coal. There was something phenomenal about it. In all Dijon not two like them.

Meanwhile the old fellow was making the rounds; I could hear the jingle of his keys, the crunching of his boots, the steady, automatic tread. Finally I heard him coming through the driveway to open the big door, a monstrous, arched portal without a moat in front of it. I heard him fumbling at the lock, his hands stiff, his mind numbed. As the door swung open I saw over his head a brilliant constellation crowning the chapel. Every door was locked, every cell bolted. The books were closed.

The night hung close, dagger-pointed, drunk as a maniac. There it was, the infinitude of emptiness. Over the chapel, like a bishop's miter, hung the constellation, every night, during the winter months, it hung there low over the chapel. Low and bright, a handful of dagger points, a dazzle of pure emptiness. The old fellow followed me to the turn of the drive. The door closed silently. As I bade him good night I caught that desperate, hopeless smile again, like a meteoric flash over the rim of a lost world. And again I saw him standing in the refectory, his head thrown back and the rubies pouring down his gullet. The whole Mediterranean seemed to be buried inside him—the orange groves, the cypress trees, the winged statues, the wooden temples, the blue sea, the stiff masks, the mystic numbers, the mythological birds, the sapphire skies, the eaglets, the sunny coves, the blind bards, the bearded heroes. Gone all that. Sunk beneath the avalanche from the North. Buried, dead forever. A memory. A wild hope.

For just a moment I linger at the carriageway. The shroud, the pall, the unspeakable, clutching emptiness of it all. Then I walk quickly along the gravel path near the wall, past the arches and columns, the iron staircases, from one quadrangle to the other. Everything is locked tight. Locked for the winter. I find the arcade leading to the dormitory. A sickish light spills down over the stairs from the grimy, frosted windows. Everywhere the paint is peeling off. The stones are hollowed out, the banister creaks; a damp sweat oozes from the flagging and forms a pale, fuzzy aura pierced by the feeble red light at the head of the stairs. I mount the last flight, the turret, in a sweat and terror. In pitch darkness I grope my way through the deserted corridor, every room empty, locked, molding away. My hand slides along the wall seeking the keyhole. A panic comes over me as I grasp the doorknob. Always a hand at my collar ready to yank me back. Once inside the room I bolt the door. It's a miracle which I perform each night, the miracle of getting inside without being strangled, without being struck down by an ax. I can hear the rats scurrying through the corridor, gnawing away over my head between the thick rafters. The light glares like burning sulfur and there is the sweet, sickish stench of a room which is never ventilated. In the corner stands the coal box, just as I left it. The fire is out. A silence so intense that it sounds like Niagara Falls in my ears.

Alone, with a tremendous empty longing and dread. The whole room for my thoughts. Nothing but myself and what I think, what I fear. Could think the most fantastic thoughts, could dance, spit, grimace, curse, wail—nobody would ever know, nobody would ever hear. The thought of such absolute privacy is enough to drive me mad. It's like a clean birth. Everything cut away. Separate, naked, alone. Bliss and agony simultaneously. Time on your hands. Each second weighing on you like a mountain. You drown in it. Deserts, seas, lakes, oceans. Time beating away like a meat ax. Nothingness. The world. The me and the not-me. *Oomaharumooma.* Everything has to have a name. Everything has to be learned, tested, experienced. *Faites comme chez vous, cheri.*

The silence descends in volcanic chutes. Yonder, in the barren hills, rolling onward toward the great metallurgical regions, the locomotives are pulling their merchant products. Over steel and iron beds they roll, the ground sown with slag and cinders and purple ore. In the baggage car, kelps, fishplate, rolled iron, sleepers, wire rods, plates and sheets, laminated articles, hot rolled hoops, splints and mortar carriages, and Zores ore. The wheels U-80 millimeters or over. Pass splendid specimens of Anglo-Norman architecture, pass pedestrians and pederasts, open hearth furnaces, basic Bessemer mills, dynamos and transformers, pig iron castings and steel ingots. The public at large, pedestrians and pederasts, goldfish and spun-glass palm trees, donkeys sobbing, all circulating freely through quincuncial alleys. At the Place du Bresil a lavender eye.

Going back in a flash over the women I've known. It's like a chain which I've forged out of my own misery. Each one bound to the other. A fear of living separate, of staying born. The door of the womb always on the latch. Dread and longing. Deep in the blood the pull of paradise. The beyond. Always the beyond. It must have all started with the navel. They cut the umbilical cord, give you a slap on the ass, and presto! you're out in the world, adrift, a ship without a rudder. You look at the stars and then you look at your navel. You grow eyes everywhere—in the armpits, between the lips, in the roots of your hair, on the soles of your feet. What is distant becomes near, what is near becomes distant. Inner-outer, a constant flux, a shedding of skins, a turning inside out. You drift around like that for years and years, until you find yourself in the dead center, and there you slowly rot, slowly crumble to pieces, get dispersed again. Only your name remains.

It was spring before I managed to escape from the penitentiary, and then only by a stroke of fortune. A telegram from Carl informed me one day that there was a vacancy "upstairs"; he said he would send me the fare back if I decided to accept. I telegraphed back at once and as soon as the dough arrived I beat it to the station. Not a word to M. le Proviseur or anyone. French leave, as they say.

I went immediately to the hotel at 1 *bis,* where Carl was staying. He came to the door stark naked. It was his night off and there was a cunt in the bed as usual. "Don't mind her," he says, "she's asleep. If you need a lay you can take her on. She's not bad." He pulls the covers back to show me what she looks like. However, I wasn't thinking about a lay right away. I was too excited. I was like a man who has just escaped from jail. I just wanted to see and hear things. Coming from the station it was like a long dream. I felt as though I had been away for years.

It was not until I had sat down and taken a good look at the room that I realized I was back again in Paris. It was Carl's room and no mistake about it. Like a squirrel cage and shithouse combined. There was hardly room on the table for the portable machine he used. It was always like that, whether he had a cunt with him or not. Always a dictionary lying open on a gilt-edged volume of *Faust,* always a tobacco pouch, a beret, a bottle of *vin rouge,* letters, manuscripts, old newspapers, water colors, teapot, dirty socks, toothpicks, Kruschen Salts, condoms, etc. In the *bidet* were orange peels and the remnants of a ham sandwich.

"There's some food in the closet," he said. "Help yourself! I was just going to give myself an injection."

I found the sandwich he was talking about and a piece of cheese that he had nibbled at beside it. While he sat on the edge of the bed, dosing himself with his argyrol, I put away the sandwich and cheese with the aid of a little wine.

"I liked that letter you sent me about Goethe," he said, wiping his prick with a dirty pair of drawers.

"I'll show you the answer to it in a minute—I'm putting it in my book. The trouble with you is that you're not a German. You have to be German to understand Goethe. Shit, I'm not going to explain it to you now. I've put it all in the book.... By the way, I've got a new cunt now—not this one—this one's a half-wit. At least, I had her until a few days ago. I'm not sure whether she'll come back or not. She was living with me all the time you were away. The other day her parents came and took her away. They said she was only fifteen. Can you beat that? They scared the shit out of me too...."

I began to laugh. It was like Carl to get himself into a mess like that.

"What are you laughing for?" he said. "I may go to prison for it. Luckily, I didn't knock her up. And that's funny, too, because she never took care of herself properly. But do you know what saved me? So I think, at least. It was *Faust.* Yeah! Her old man happened to see it lying on the table. He asked me if I understood German. One thing led to another and before I knew it he was looking through my books. Fortunately I happened to have the Shakespeare open too. That impressed him like hell. He said I was evidently a very serious guy."

"What about the girl—what did *she* have to say?"

"She was frightened to death. You see, she had a little watch with her when she came; in the excitement we couldn't find the watch, and her mother insisted that the watch be found or she'd call the police. You see how things are here. I turned the whole place upside down—but I couldn't find the goddamned watch. The mother was furious. I liked her too, in spite of everything. She was even better-looking than the daughter. Here—I'll show you a letter I started to write her. I'm in love with her...."

"With the *mother?*"

"Sure. Why not? If I had seen the mother first I'd never have looked at the daughter. How did I know she was only fifteen? You don't ask a cunt how old she is before you lay her, do you?"

"Joe, there's something funny about this. You're not shitting me, are you?"

"Am I shitting you? Here—look at this!" And he shows me the water colors the girl had made—cute little things—a knife and a loaf of bread, the table and teapot, everything running uphill. "She was in love with me," he said. "She was just like a child. I had to tell her when to brush her teeth and how to put her hat on. Here—look at the lollypops! I used to buy her a few lollypops every day—she liked them."

"Well, what did she do when her parents came to take her away? Didn't she put up a row?"

"She cried a little, that's all. What *could* she do? She's under age.... I had to promise never to see her again, never to write her either. That's what I'm waiting to see now—whether she'll stay away or not. She was a virgin when she came here. The thing is, how long will she be able to go without a lay? She couldn't get enough of it when she was here. She almost wore me out."

By this time the one in bed had come to and was rubbing her eyes. She looked pretty young to me, too. Not bad looking, but dumb as hell. Wanted to know right away what we were talking about.

"She lives here in the hotel," said Carl. "On the third floor. Do you want to go to her room? I'll fix it up for you.

I didn't know whether I wanted to or not, but when I saw Carl mushing it up with her again I decided I did want to. I asked her first if she was too tired. Useless question. A whore is never too tired to open her legs. Some of them can fall asleep while you diddle them. Anyway, it was decided we would go down to her room. Like that I wouldn't have to pay the *patron* for the night.

In the morning I rented a room overlooking the little park down below where the sandwich-board men always came to eat their lunch. At noon I called for Carl to have breakfast with him. He and Van Norden had developed a new habit in my absence—they went to the Coupole for breakfast every day. "Why the Coupole?" I asked. "Why the Coupole?" says Carl. "Because the Coupole serves porridge at all hours and porridge makes you shit."—"I see," said I.

So it's just like it used to be again. The three of us walking back and forth to work. Petty dissensions, petty rivalries. Van Norden still bellyaching about his cunts and about washing the dirt out of his belly. Only now he's found a new diversion. He's found that it's less annoying to masturbate. I was amazed when he broke the news to me. I didn't think it possible for a guy like that to find any pleasure in jerking himself off. I was still more amazed when he explained to me how he goes about it. He had "invented" a new stunt, so he put it. "You take an apple," he says, "and you bore out the core. Then you rub some cold cream on the inside so as it doesn't melt too fast. Try it some time! It'll drive you crazy at first. Anyway, it's cheap and you don't have to waste much time."

"By the way," he says, switching the subject, "that friend of yours, Fillmore, he's in the hospital. I think he's nuts. Anyway, that's what his girl told me. He took on a French girl, you know, while you were away. They used to fight like hell. She's a big, healthy bitch—wild like. I wouldn't mind giving her a tumble, but I'm afraid she'd claw the eyes out of me. He was always going around with his face and hands scratched up. She looks bunged up too once in a while—or she used to. You know how these French cunts are—when they love they lose their minds."

Evidently things had happened while I was away. I was sorry to hear about Fillmore. He had been damned good to me. When I left Van Norden I jumped a bus and went straight to the hospital.

They hadn't decided yet whether he was completely off his base or not, I suppose, for I found him upstairs in a private room, enjoying all the liberties of the regular patients. He had just come from the bath when I arrived. When he caught sight of me he burst into tears. "It's all over," he says immediately. "They say I'm crazy—and I may have syphilis too. They say I have delusions of grandeur." He fell over onto the bed and wept quietly. After he had wept a while he lifted his head up and smiled—just like a bird coming out of a snooze. "Why do they put me in such an expensive room?" he said. "Why don't they put me in the ward—or in the bughouse? I can't afford to pay for this. I'm down to my last five hundred dollars."

"That's why they're keeping you here," I said. "They'll transfer you quickly enough when your money runs out. Don't worry."

My words must have impressed him, for I had no sooner finished than he handed me his watch and chain, his wallet, his fraternity pin, etc. "Hold on to them," he said. "These bastards'll rob me of everything I've got." And then suddenly he began to laugh, one of those weird, mirthless laughs which makes you believe a guy's goofy whether he is or not. "I know you'll think I'm crazy," he said, "but I want to atone for what I did. I want to get married. You see, I didn't know I had the clap. I gave her the clap and then I knocked her up. I told the doctor I don't care what happens to me, but I want him to let me get married first. He keeps telling me to wait until I get better—but I know I'm never going to get better. This is the end."

I couldn't help laughing myself, hearing him talk that way. I couldn't understand what had come over him. Anyway, I had to promise him to see the girl and explain things to her. He wanted me to stick by her, comfort her. Said he could trust me, etc. I said yes to everything in order to soothe him. He didn't seem exactly nuts to me—just caved-in like. Typical Anglo-Saxon crisis. An eruption of morals. I was rather curious to see the girl, to get the lowdown on the whole thing.

The next day I looked her up. She was living in the Latin Quarter. As soon as she realized who I was she became exceedingly cordial. Ginette she called herself. Rather big, rawboned, healthy, peasant type with a front tooth half eaten away. Full of vitality and a kind of crazy fire in her eyes. The first thing she did was to weep. Then, seeing that I was an old friend of her Jo-Jo—that was how she called him—she ran downstairs and brought back a couple of bottles of white wine. I was to stay and have dinner with her—she insisted on it. As she drank she became by turns gay and maudlin. I didn't have to ask her any questions—she went on like a self-winding machine. The thing that worried her principally was—would he get his job back when he was released from the hospital? She said her parents were well off, but they were displeased with her. They didn't approve of her wild ways. They didn't approve of him particularly—he had no manners, and he was an American. She begged me to assure her that he would get his job back, which I did without hesitancy. And then she begged me to know if she could believe what he said—that he was going to marry her. Because now, with a child under her belt, and a dose of clap besides, she was in no position to strike a match—with a Frenchman anyway. That was clear, wasn't it? Of course, I assured her. It was all clear as hell to me—except how in Christ's name Fillmore had ever fallen for her. However, one thing at a time. It was my duty now to comfort her, and so I just filled her up with a lot of baloney, told her everything would turn out all right and that I would stand godfather to the child, etc. Then suddenly it struck me as strange that she should have the child at all—especially as it was likely to be born blind. I told her that as tactfully as I could. "It doesn't make any difference," she said, "I want a child by him."

"Even if it's blind?" I asked.

"Mon Dieu, ne dites pas ca!" she groaned. *"Ne dites pas ca!"*

Just the same, I felt it was my duty to say it. She got hysterical and began to weep like a walrus, poured out more wine. In a few moments she was laughing boisterously. She was laughing to think how they used to fight when they got in bed. "He liked me to fight with him," she said. "He was a brute."

As we sat down to eat, a friend of hers walked in—a little tart who lived at the end of the hall. Ginette immediately sent me down to get some more wine. When I came back they had evidently had a good talk. Her friend, Yvette, worked in the police department. A sort of stool pigeon, as far as I could gather. At least that was what she was trying to make me believe. It was fairly obvious that she was just a little whore. But she had an obsession about the police and their doings. Throughout the meal they were urging me to accompany them to a *bal musette*. They wanted to have a gay time—it was so lonely for Ginette with Jo-Jo in the hospital. I told them I had to work, but that on my night off I'd come back and take them out. I made it clear too that I had no dough to spend on them. Ginette, who was really thunderstruck to hear this, pretended that that didn't matter in the least. In fact, just to show what a good sport she was, she insisted on driving me to work in a cab. She was doing it because I was a friend of Jo-Jo's. And therefore I was a friend of hers. "And also," thought I to myself, "if anything goes wrong with your Jo-Jo you'll come to me on the double-quick. Then you'll see what a friend I can be!" I was as nice as pie to her. In fact, when we got out of the cab in front of the office, I permitted them to persuade me into having a final Pernod together. Yvette wanted to know if she couldn't call for me after work. She had a lot of things to tell me in confidence, she said. But I managed to refuse without hurting her feelings. Unfortunately I did unbend sufficiently to give her my address.

Unfortunately, I say. As a matter of fact, I'm rather glad of it when I think back on it. Because the very next day things began to happen. The very next day, before I had even gotten out of bed, the two of them called on me. Jo-Jo had been removed from the hospital—they had incarcerated him in a little chateau in the country, just a few miles out of Paris. The *chateau,* they called it. A polite way of saying "the bughouse." They wanted me to get dressed immediately and go with them. They were in a panic.

Perhaps I might have gone alone—but I just couldn't make up my mind to go with these two. I asked them to wait for me downstairs while I got dressed, thinking that it would give me time to invent some excuse for not going. But they wouldn't leave the room. They sat there and watched me wash and dress, just as if it were an everyday affair. In the midst of it, Carl popped in. I gave him the situation briefly, in English, and then we hatched up an excuse that I had some important work to do. However, to smooth things over, we got some wine in and we began to amuse them by showing them a book of dirty drawings. Yvette had already lost all desire to go to the chateau. She and Carl were getting along famously. When it came time to go Carl decided to accompany them to the chateau. He thought it would be funny to see Fillmore walking around with a lot of nuts. He wanted to see what it was like in the nuthouse. So off they went, somewhat pickled, and in the best of humor.

All the time that Fillmore was at the chateau I never once went to see him. It wasn't necessary, because Ginette visited him regularly and gave me all the news. They had hopes of bringing him around in a few months, so she said. They thought it was alcoholic poisoning—nothing more. Of course, he had a dose—but that wasn't difficult to remedy. So far as they could see, he didn't have syphilis. That was something. So, to begin with, they used the stomach pump on him. They cleaned his system out thoroughly. He was so weak for a while that he couldn't get out of bed. He was depressed, too. He said he didn't want to be cured—he wanted to die. And he kept repeating this nonsense so insistently that finally they grew alarmed. I suppose it wouldn't have been a very good recommendation if he had committed suicide. Anyway, they began to give him mental treatment. And in between times they pulled out his teeth, more and more of them, until he didn't have a tooth left in his head. He was supposed to feel fine after that, yet strangely he didn't. He became more despondent than ever. And then his hair began to fall out. Finally he developed a paranoid streak—began to accuse them of all sorts of things, demanded to know by what right he was being detained, what he had done to warrant being locked up, etc. After a terrible fit of despondency he would suddenly become energetic and threaten to blow up the place if they didn't release him. And to make it worse, as far as Ginette was concerned, he had gotten all over his notion of marrying her. He told her straight up and down that he had no intention of marrying her, and that if she was crazy enough to go and have a child then she could support it herself. The doctors interpreted all this as a good sign. They said he was coming round. Ginette, of course, thought he was crazier than ever, but she was praying for him to be released so that she could take him to the country where it would be quiet and peaceful and where he would come to his right senses. Meanwhile her parents had come to Paris on a visit and had even gone so far as to visit the future son-in-law at the chateau. In their canny way they had probably figured it out that it would be better for their daughter to have a crazy husband than no husband at all. The father thought he could find something for Fillmore to do on the farm. He said that Fillmore wasn't such a bad chap at all. When he learned from Ginette that Fillmore's parents had money he became even more indulgent, more understanding.

The thing was working itself out nicely all around. Ginette returned to the provinces for a while with her parents. Yvette was coming regularly to the hotel to see Carl. She thought he was the editor of the paper. And little by little she became more confidential. When she got good and tight one day, she informed us that Ginette had never been anything but a whore, that Ginette was a bloodsucker, that Ginette never had been pregnant and was not pregnant now. About the other accusations we hadn't much doubt, Carl and I, but about not being pregnant, that we weren't so sure of.

"How did she get such a big stomach, then?" asked Carl.

Yvette laughed. "Maybe she uses a bicycle pump," she said. "No, seriously," she added, "the stomach comes from drink. She drinks like a fish, Ginette. When she comes back from the country, you will see, she will be blown up still more. Her father is a drunkard. Ginette is a drunkard. Maybe she had the clap, yes—but she is not pregnant."

"But why does she want to marry him? Is she really in love with him?"

"*Love?* Pfooh! She has no heart, Ginette. She wants someone to look after her. No Frenchman would ever marry her—she has a police record. No, she wants him because he's too stupid to find out about her. Her parents don't want her any more—she's a disgrace to them. But if she can get married to a rich American, then everything will be all right.... You think maybe she loves him a little, eh? You don't know her. When they were living together at the hotel, she had men coming to her room while he was at work. She said he didn't give her enough spending money He was stingy. That fur she wore-she told him her parents had given it to her, didn't she? Innocent fool! Why, I've seen her bring a man back to the hotel right while he was there. She brought the man to the floor below. I saw it with my own eyes. And what a man! An old derelict. He couldn't get an erection!"

If Fillmore, when he was released from the chateau, had returned to Paris, perhaps I might have tipped him off about his Ginette. While he was still under observation I didn't think it well to upset him by poisoning his mind with Yvette's slanders. As things turned out, he went directly from the chateau to the home of Ginette's parents. There, despite himself, he was inveigled into making public his engagement. The banns were published in the local papers and a reception was given to the friends of the family. Fillmore took advantage of the situation to indulge in all sorts of escapades. Though he knew quite well what he was doing he pretended to be still a little daffy. He would borrow his father-in-law's car, for example, and tear about the countryside all by himself; if he saw a town that he liked he would plank himself down and have a good time until Ginette came searching for him. Sometimes the father-in-law and he would go off together—on a fishing trip, presumably—and nothing would be heard of them for days. He became exasperatingly capricious and exacting. I suppose he figured he might as well get what he could out of it.

When he returned to Paris with Ginette he had a complete new wardrobe and a pocketful of dough. He looked cheerful and healthy, and had a fine coat of tan. He looked sound as a berry to me. But as soon as we had gotten away from Ginette he opened up. His job was gone and his money had all run out. In a month or so they were to be married. Meanwhile the parents were supplying the dough. "Once they've got me properly in their clutches," he said, "I'll be nothing but a slave to them. The father thinks he's going to open up a stationery store for me. Ginette will handle the customers, take in the money, etc., while I sit in the back of the store and write—or something. Can you picture me sitting in the back of a stationery store for the rest of my life? Ginette thinks it's an excellent idea. She likes to handle money. I'd rather go back to the chateau than submit to such a scheme."

For the time being, of course, he was pretending that everything was hunky-dory. I tried to persuade him to go back to America but he wouldn't hear of that. He said he wasn't going to be driven out of France by a lot of ignorant peasants. He had an idea that he would slip out of sight for a while and then take up quarters in some outlying section of the city where he'd not be likely to stumble upon her. But we soon decided that that was impossible: you can't hide away in France as you can in America.

"You could go to Belgium for a while," I suggested.

"But what'll I do for money?" he said promptly. "You can't get a job in these goddamned countries."

"Why don't you marry her and get a divorce, then?" I asked.

"And meanwhile she'll be dropping a kid. Who's going to take care of the kid, eh?"

"How do you know she's going to have a kid?" I said, determined now that the moment had come to spill the beans.

"How do I know?" he said. He didn't quite seem to know what I was insinuating.

I gave him an inkling of what Yvette had said. He listened to me in complete bewilderment. Finally he interrupted me. "It's no use going on with that," he said.

"I know she's going to have a kid, all right. I've felt it kicking around inside. Yvette's a dirty little slut. You see, I didn't want to tell you, but up until the time I went to the hospital I was shelling out for Yvette too. Then when the crash came I couldn't do any more for her. I figured out that I had done enough for the both of them.... I made up my mind to look after myself first. That made Yvette sore. She told Ginette that she was going to get even with me.... No, I wish it were true, what she said. Then I could get out of this thing more easily. Now I'm in a trap. I've promised to marry her and I'll have to go through with it. After that I don't know what'll happen to me. They've got me by the balls now."

Since he had taken a room in the same hotel with me I was obliged to see them frequently, whether I wanted to or not. Almost every evening I had dinner with them, preceded, of course, by a few Pernods. All through the meal they quarreled noisily. It was embarrassing because I had sometimes to take one side and sometimes the other. One Sunday afternoon, for example, after we had had lunch together, we repaired to a cafe on the corner of the Boulevard Edgar-Quinet. Things had gone unusually well this time. We were sitting inside at a little table, one alongside the other, our backs to a mirror. Ginette must have been passionate or something for she had suddenly gotten into a sentimental mood and was fondling him and kissing him in front of everybody, as the French do so naturally. They had just come out of a long embrace when Fillmore said something about her parents which she interpreted as an insult. Immediately her cheeks flushed with anger. We tried to mollify her by telling her that she had misunderstood the remark and then, under his breath, Fillmore said something to me in English—something about giving her a little soft soap. That was enough to set her completely off the handle. She said we were making fun of her. I said something sharp to her which angered her still more and then Fillmore tried to put in a word. "You're too quick-tempered," he said, and he tried to pat her on the cheek. But she, thinking that he had raised his hand to slap her face, she gave him a sound crack in the jaw with that big peasant hand of hers. For a moment he was stunned. He hadn't expected a wallop like that, and it stung. I saw his face go white and the next moment he raised himself from the bench and with the palm of his hand he gave her such a crack that she almost fell off her seat. "There! that'll teach you how to behave!" he said—in his broken French. For a moment there was a dead silence. Then, like a storm breaking, she picked up the cognac glass in front of her and hurled it at him with all her might. It smashed against the mirror behind us. Fillmore had already grabbed her by the arm, but with her free hand she grabbed the coffee glass and smashed it on the floor. She was squirming around like a maniac. It was all we could do to hold her. Meanwhile, of course, the *patron* had come running in and ordered us to beat it. "Loafers!" he called us. "Yes, loafers; that's it!" screamed Ginette. "Dirty foreigners! Thugs! Gangsters! Striking a pregnant woman!" We were getting black looks all around. A poor Frenchwoman with two American toughs. Gangsters. I was wondering how the hell we'd ever get out of the place without a fight. Fillmore, by this time, was as silent as a clam. Ginette was bolting it through the door, leaving us to face the music. As she sailed out she turned back with fist upraised and shouted; "I'll pay you back for this, you brute! You'll see! No foreigner can treat a decent Frenchwoman like that! Ah, no! Not like that!"

Hearing this the *patron,* who had now been paid for his drinks and his broken glasses, felt it incumbent to show his gallantry toward a splendid representative of French motherhood such as Ginette, and so, without more ado, he spat at our feet and shoved us out of the door. "Shit on you, you dirty loafers!" he said, or some such pleasantry.

Once in the street and nobody throwing things after us, I began to see the funny side of it. It would be an excellent idea, I thought to myself, if the whole thing were properly aired in court. *The whole thing!* With Yvette's little stories as a side dish. After all, the French have a sense of humor. Perhaps the judge, when he heard Fillmore's side of the story, would absolve him from marriage.

Meanwhile Ginette was standing across the street brandishing her fist and yelling at the top of her lungs. People were stopping to listen in, to take sides, as they do in street brawls. Fillmore didn't know what to do—whether to walk away from her, or to go over to her and try to pacify her. He was standing in the middle of the street with his arms outstretched, trying to get a word in edgewise. And Ginette still yelling: *"Gangster/ Brute/ Tu verras, salaud/"* and other complimentary things. Finally Fillmore made a move toward her and she, probably thinking that he was going to give her another good cuff, took it on a trot down the street. Fillmore came back to where I was standing and said: "Come on, let's follow her quietly." We started off with a thin crowd of stragglers behind us. Every once in a while she turned back toward us and brandished her fist. We made no attempt to catch up with her, just followed her leisurely down the street to see what she would do. Finally she slowed up her pace and we crossed over to the other side of the street, she was quiet now. We kept walking behind her, getting closer and closer. There were only about a dozen people behind us now—the others had lost interest. When we got near the corner she suddenly stopped and waited for us to approach. "Let me do the talking," said Fillmore, "I know how to handle her."

The tears were streaming down her face as we came up to her. Myself, I didn't know what to expect of her. I was somewhat surprised therefore when Fillmore walked up to her and said in an aggrieved voice: "Was that a nice thing to do? Why did you act that way?" Whereupon she threw her arms around his neck and began to weep like a child, calling him her little this and her little that. Then she turned to me imploringly. "You saw how he struck me," she said. "Is that the way to behave toward a woman?" I was on the point of saying yes when Fillmore took her by the arm and started leading her off. "No more of that," he said. "If you start again I'll crack you right here in the street."

I thought it was going to start up all over again. She had fire in her eyes. But evidently she was a bit cowed, too, for it subsided quickly. However, as she sat down at the cafe she said quietly and grimly that he needn't think it was going to be forgotten so quickly; he'd hear more about in later on ... perhaps tonight.

And sure enough she kept her word. When I met him the next day his face and hands were all scratched up. Seems she had waited until he got to bed and then, without a word, she had gone to the wardrobe and, dumping all his things out on the floor, she took them one by one and tore them to ribbons. As this had happened a number of times before, and as she had always sewn them up afterward, he hadn't protested very much. And that made her angrier than ever. What she wanted was to get her nails into him, and she did, to the best of her ability. Being pregnant she had a certain advantage over him.

Poor Fillmore! It was no laughing matter. She had him terrorized. If he threatened to run away she retorted by a threat to kill him. And she said it as if she meant it. "If you go to America," she said, "I'll follow you! You won't get away from me. A French girl always knows how to get vengeance." And the next moment she would be coaxing him to be "reasonable," to be *"sage,"* etc. Life would be so nice once they had the stationery store. He wouldn't have to do a stroke of work. She would do everything. He could stay in back of the store and write—or whatever he wanted to do.

It went on like this, back and forth, a seesaw, for a few weeks or so. I was avoiding them as much as possible, sick of the affair and disgusted with the both of them. Then one fine summer's day, just as I was passing the Credit Lyonnais, who comes marching down the steps but Fillmore. I greeted him warmly, feeling rather guilty because I had dodged him for so long. I asked him, with more than ordinary curiosity, how things were going. He answered me rather vaguely and with a note of despair in his voice.

"I've just gotten permission to go to the bank," he said, in a peculiar, broken, abject sort of way. "I've got about half an hour, no more. She keeps tabs on me." And he grasped my arm as if to hurry me away from the spot.

We were walking down toward the Rue de Rivoli. It was a beautiful day, warm, clear, sunny—one of those days when Paris is at its best. A mild pleasant breeze blowing, just enough to take that stagnant odor out of your nostrils. Fillmore was without a hat. Outwardly he looked the picture of health—like the average American tourist who slouches along with money jingling in his pockets.

"I don't know what to do any more," he said quietly. "You've got to do something for me. I'm helpless. I can't get a grip on myself. If I could only get away from her for a little while perhaps I'd come round all right. But she won't let me out of her sight. I just got permission to run to the bank—I had to draw some money. I'll walk around with you a bit and then I must hurry back—she'll have lunch waiting for me."

I listened to him quietly, thinking to myself that he certainly did need someone to pull him out of the hole he was in. He had completely caved in, there wasn't a speck of courage left in him. He was just like a child—like a child who is beaten every day and doesn't know any more how to behave, except to cower and cringe. As we turned under the colonnade of the Rue de Rivoli he burst into a long diatribe against France. He was fed up with the French. "I used to rave about them," he said, "but that was all literature. I know them now.... I know what they're really like. They're cruel and mercenary. At first it seems wonderful, because you have a feeling of being free. After a while it palls on you. Underneath it's all dead; there's no feeling, no sympathy, no friendship. They're selfish to the core. The most selfish people on earth! They think of nothing but money, money, money. And so goddamned respectable, so bourgeois! That's what drives me nuts. When I see her mending my shirts I could club her. Always mending, mending. Saving, saving. *Faut faire des economies!* That's all I hear her say all day long. You hear it everywhere. *Sois raisonnable, mon cheri! Sois raisonnable!* I don't want to be reasonable and logical. I hate it! I want to bust loose, I want to enjoy myself. I want to *do* something. I don't want to sit in a cafe and talk all day long. Jesus, we've got our faults—but we've got enthusiasm. It's better to make mistakes than not do anything. I'd rather be a bum in America than to be sitting pretty here. Maybe it's because I'm a Yankee. I was born in New England and I belong there, I guess. You can't become a European overnight. There's something in your blood that makes you different. It's the climate—and everything. We see things with different eyes. We can't make ourselves over, however much we admire the French. We're Americans and we've got to remain Americans. Sure, I hate those puritanical buggers back home—I hate 'em with all my guts. But I'm one of them myself. I don't belong here. I'm sick of it."

All along the arcade he went on like this. I wasn't saying a word. I let him spill it all out—it was good for him to get it off his chest. Just the same, I was thinking how strange it was that this same guy, had it been a year ago, would have been beating his chest like a gorilla and saying: "What a marvelous day! What a country! What a people!" And if an American had happened along and said one word against France Fillmore would have flattened his nose. He would have died for France—a year ago. I never saw a man who was so infatuated with a country, who was so happy under a foreign sky. It wasn't natural. When he said *France* it meant wine, women, money in the pocket, easy come, easy go. It meant being a bad boy, being on a holiday. And then, when he had had his fling, when the tent top blew off and he had a good look at the sky, he saw that it wasn't just a circus, but an arena, just like everywhere. And a damned grim one. I often used to think, when I heard him rave about glorious France, about liberty and all that crap, what it would have sounded like to a French workman, could he have understood Fillmore's words. No wonder they think we're all crazy. We *are* crazy to them. We're just a pack of children. Senile idiots. What we call life is a five-and-ten-cent store romance. That enthusiasm underneath—what is it? That cheap optimism which turns the stomach of any ordinary European? It's illusion. No, illusion's too good a word for it. Illusion means something. No, it's not that—it's *delusion*. It's sheer delusion, that's what. We're like a herd of wild horses with blinders over our eyes. On the rampage. Stampede. Over the precipice. Bango! Anything that nourishes violence and confusion. On! On! No matter where. And foaming at the lips all the while. Shouting Hallelujah! *Hallelujah!* Why? God knows. It's in the blood. It's the climate. It's a lot of things. It's the end, too. We're pulling the whole world down about our ears. We don't know why. It's our destiny. The rest is plain shit....

At the Palais Royal I suggested that we stop and have a drink. He hesitated a moment. I saw that he was worrying about her, about the lunch, about the bawling out he'd get.

"For Christ's sake," I said, "forget about her for a while. I'm going to order something to drink and I want you to drink it. Don't worry, I'm going to get you out of this fucking mess." I ordered two stiff whiskies.

When he saw the whiskies coming he smiled at me just like a child again.

"Down it!" I said, "and let's have another. This is going to do you good. I don't care what the doctor says—this time it'll be all right. Come on, down with it!"

He put it down all right and while the *garcon* disappeared to fetch another round he looked at me with brimming eyes, as though I were the last friend in the world. His lips were twitching a bit, too. There was something he wanted to say to me and he didn't quite know how to begin. I looked at him easily, as though ignoring the appeal and, shoving the saucers aside, I leaned over on my elbow and I said to him earnestly: "Look here, Fillmore, what is it you'd *really* like to do? Tell me!"

With that the tears gushed up and he blurted out: "I'd like to be home with my people. I'd like to hear English spoken." The tears were streaming down his face. He made no effort to brush them away. He just let everything gush forth. Jesus, I thought to myself, that's fine to have a release like that. Fine to be a complete coward at least once in your life. To let go that way. Great! Great! It did me so much good to see him break down that way that I felt as though I could solve any problem. I felt courageous and resolute. I had a thousand ideas in my head at once.

"Listen," I said, bending still closer to him, "if you mean what you said why don't you do it... why don't you go? Do you know what I would do, if I were in your shoes? I'd go today. Yes, by Jesus, I mean it... I'd go right away, without even saying good-bye to her. As a matter of fact that's the only way you can go—she'd never let you say good-bye. You know that."

The *garcon* came with the whiskies. I saw him reach forward with a desperate eagerness and raise the glass to his lips. I saw a glint of hope in his eyes—far-off, wild, desperate. He probably saw himself swimming across the Atlantic. To me it looked easy, simple as rolling off a log. The whole thing was working itself out rapidly in my mind. I knew just what each step would be. Clear as a bell, I was.

"Whose money is that in the bank?" I asked. "Is it her father's or is it yours?"

"It's mine!" he exclaimed. "My mother sent it to me. I don't want any of her goddamned money."

'That's swell!" I said. "Listen, suppose we hop a cab and go back there. Draw out every cent. Then we'll go to the British Consulate and get a visa. You're going to hop the train this afternoon for London. From London you'll take the first boat to America. I'm saying that because then you won't be worried about her trailing you. She'll never suspect that you went via London. If she goes searching for you she'll naturally go to Le Havre first, or Cherbourg.... And here's another thing—you're not going back to get your things. You're going to leave everything here. Let her keep them. With that French mind of hers she'll never dream that you scooted off without bag or baggage. It's incredible. A Frenchman would never dream of doing a thing like that... unless he was as cracked as you are."

"You're right!" he exclaimed. "I never thought of that. Besides, you might send them to me later on—if she'll surrender them! But that doesn't matter now. Jesus, though, I haven't even got a hat!"

"What do you need a hat for? When you get to London you can buy everything you need. All you need now is to hurry. We've got to find out when the train leaves."

"Listen," he said, reaching for his wallet, "I'm going to leave everything to you. Here, take this and do whatever's necessary. I'm too weak.... I'm dizzy."

I took the wallet and emptied it of the bills he had just drawn from the bank. A cab was standing at the curb. We hopped in. There was a train leaving the Gare du Nord at four o'clock, or thereabouts. I was figuring it out—the bank, the Consulate, the American Express, the station. Fine! Just about make it.

"Now buck up!" I said, "and keep your shirt on! Shit, in a few hours you'll be crossing the Channel. Tonight you'll be walking around in London and you'll get a good bellyful of English. Tomorrow you'll be on the open sea—and then, by Jesus, you're a free man and you needn't give a fuck what happens. By the time you get to New York this'll be nothing more than a bad dream."

This got him so excited that his feet were moving convulsively, as if he were trying to run inside the cab. At the bank his hand was trembling so that he could hardly sign his name. That was one thing I couldn't do for him—sign his name. But I think, had it been necessary, I could have sat him on the toilet and wiped his ass. I was determined to ship him off, even if I had to fold him up and put him in a valise.

It was lunch hour when we got to the British Consulate, and the place was closed. That meant waiting until two o'clock. I couldn't think of anything better to do, by way of killing time, than to eat. Fillmore, of course, wasn't hungry. He was for eating a sandwich. "Fuck that!" I said. "You're going to blow me to a good lunch. It's the last square meal you're going to have over here—maybe for a long while." I steered him to a cosy little restaurant and ordered a good spread. I ordered the best wine on the menu, regardless of price or taste. I had all his money in my pocket—oodles of it, it seemed to me. Certainly never before had I had so much in my fist at one time. It was a treat to break a thousand franc note. I held it up to the light first to look at the beautiful watermark. Beautiful money! One of the few things the French make on a grand scale. Artistically done, too, as if they cherished a deep affection even for the symbol.

The meal over, we went to a cafe. I ordered Chartreuse with the coffee. Why not? And I broke another bill—a five-hundred franc note this time. It was a clean, new, crisp bill. A pleasure to handle such money. The waiter handed me back a lot of dirty old bills that had been patched up with strips of gummed paper; I had a stack of five and ten franc notes and a bagful of chicken feed. Chinese money, with holes in it. I didn't know in which pocket to stuff the money any more. My trousers were bursting with coins and bills. It made me slightly uncomfortable also, hauling all that dough out in public. I was afraid we might be taken for a couple of crooks.

When we got to the American Express there wasn't a devil of a lot of time left. The British, in their usual fumbling farting way, had kept us on pins and needles. Here everybody was sliding around on castors. They were so speedy that everything had to be done twice. After all the checks were signed and clipped in a neat little holder, it was discovered that he had signed in the wrong place. Nothing to do but start all over again. I stood over him, with one eye on the clock, and watched every stroke of the pen. It hurt to hand over the dough. Not all of it, thank God—but a good part of it. I had roughly about 2,500 francs in my pocket. Roughly, I say. I wasn't counting by francs any more. A hundred, or two hundred, more or less—it didn't mean a goddamned thing to me. As for him, he was going through the whole transaction in a daze. He didn't know how much money he had. All he knew was that he had to keep something aside for Ginette. He wasn't certain yet how much—we were going to figure that out on the way to the station.

In the excitement we had forgotten to change all the money. We were already in the cab, however, and there wasn't any time to be lost. The thing was to find out how we stood. We emptied our pockets quickly and began to whack it up. Some of it was lying on the floor, some of it was on the seat. It was bewildering. There was French, American and English money. And all that chicken feed besides. I felt like picking up the coins and chucking them out of the window—just to simplify matters. Finally we sifted it all out; he held on to the English and American money, and I held on to the French money.

We had to decide quickly now what to do about Ginette—how much to give her, what to tell her, etc. He was trying to fix up a yarn for me to hand her—didn't want her to break her heart and so forth. I had to cut him short.

"Never mind what to tell her," I said. "Leave that to me. How much are you going to *give* her, that's the thing? Why give her anything?"

That was like setting a bomb under his ass. He burst into tears. Such tears! It was worse than before. I thought he was going to collapse on my hands. Without stopping to think, I said: "All right, let's give her all this French money. That ought to last her for a while."

"How much is it?" he asked feebly.

"I don't know—about 2,000 francs or so. More than she deserves anyway."

"Christ! Don't say that!" he begged. "After all, it's a rotten break I'm giving her. Her folks'll never take her back now. No, give it to her. Give her the whole damned business.... I don't care what it is."

He pulled a handkerchief out to wipe the tears away. "I can't help it," he said. "It's too much for me." I said nothing. Suddenly he sprawled himself out full length—I thought he was taking a fit or something—and he said: "Jesus, I think I ought to go. I ought to go back and face the music. If anything should happen to her I'd never forgive myself."

That was a rude jolt for me. "Christ!" I shouted, "you can't do that! Not now. It's too late. You're going to take the train and I'm going to tend to her myself. I'll go see her just as soon as I leave you. Why, you poor boob, if she ever thought you had tried to run away from her she'd murder you, don't you realize that? You can't go back any more. It's settled."

Anyway, what *could* go wrong? I asked myself. Kill herself? *Tantmieux.*

When we rolled up to the station we had still about twelve minutes to kill. I didn't dare to say good-bye to him yet. At the last minute, rattled as he was, I could see him jumping off the train and scooting back to her. Anything might swerve him. A straw. So I dragged him across the street to a bar and I said: "Now you're going to have a Pernod—your *last* Pernod and I'm going to pay for it... with *your* dough."

Something about this remark made him look at me uneasily. He took a big gulp of the Pernod and then, turning to me like an injured dog, he said: "I know I oughtn't to trust you with all that money, but... but.... Oh, well, do what you think best. I don't want her to kill herself, that's all."

"*Kill herself?*" I said. "Not her! You must think a hell of a lot of yourself if you can believe a thing like that. As for the money, though I hate to give it to her, I promise you I'll go straight to the post office and telegraph it to her. I wouldn't trust myself with it a minute longer than is necessary." As I said this I spied a bunch of post cards in a revolving rack. I grabbed one off— a picture of the Eiffel Tower it was—and made him write a few words. "Tell her you're sailing now. Tell her you love her and that you'll send for her as soon as you arrive.... I'll send it by *pneumatique* when I go to the post office. And tonight I'll see her. Everything'll be Jake, you'll see."

With that we walked across the street to the station. Only two minutes to go. I felt it was safe now. At the gate I gave him a slap on the back and pointed to the train. I didn't shake hands with him—he would have slobbered all over me. I just said: "Hurry! She's going in a minute." And with that I turned on my heel and marched off. I didn't even look round to see if he was boarding the train. I was afraid to.

I hadn't thought, all the while I was bundling him off, what I'd do once I was free of him. I had promised a lot of things—but that was only to keep him quiet. As for facing Ginette, I had about as little courage for it as he had. I was getting panicky myself. Everything had happened so quickly that it was impossible to grasp the nature of the situation in full. I walked away from the station in a kind of delicious stupor—with the post card in my hand. I stood against a lamppost and read it over. It sounded preposterous. I read it again, to make sure that I wasn't dreaming, and then I tore it up and threw it in the gutter.

I looked around uneasily, half expecting to see Ginette coming after me with a tomahawk. Nobody was following me. I started walking leisurely toward the Place Lafayette. It was a beautiful day, as I had observed earlier. Light, puffy clouds above, sailing with the wind. The awnings flapping. Paris had never looked so good to me; I almost felt sorry that I had shipped the poor bugger off. At the Place Lafayette I sat down facing the church and stared at the clock tower; it's not such a wonderful piece of architecture, but that blue in the dial face always fascinated me. It was bluer than ever today. I couldn't take my eyes off it.

Unless he were crazy enough to write her a letter, explaining everything, Ginette need never know what had happened. And even if she did learn that he had left her 2,500 francs or so she couldn't prove it. I could always say that he imagined it. A guy who was crazy enough to walk off without even a hat was crazy enough to invent the 2,500 francs, or whatever it was. How much was it, anyhow?, I wondered. My pockets were sagging with the weight of it. I hauled it all out and counted it carefully. There was exactly 2,875 francs and 35 centimes. More than I had thought. The 75 francs and 35 centimes had to be gotten rid of. I wanted an even sum—a clean 2,800 francs. Just then I saw a cab pulling up to the curb. A woman stepped out with a white poodle dog in her hands; the dog was peeing over her silk dress. The idea of taking a dog for a ride got me sore. I'm as good as her dog, I said to myself, and with that I gave the driver a sign and told him to drive me through the Bois. He wanted to know where exactly. "Anywhere," I said. "Go through the Bois, go all around it—and take your time, I'm in no hurry." I sank back and let the houses whizz by, the jagged roofs, the chimney pots, the colored walls, the urinals, the dizzy *carrefours*. Passing the Rond-Point I thought I'd go downstairs and take a leak. No telling what might happen down there. I told the driver to wait. It was the first time in my life I had let a cab wait while I took a leak. How much can you waste that way? Not very much. With what I had in my pocket I could afford to have two taxis waiting for me.

I took a good look around but I didn't see anything worth while. What I wanted was something fresh and unused—something from Alaska or the Virgin Islands. A clean fresh pelt with a natural fragrance to it. Needless to say, there wasn't anything like that walking about. I wasn't terribly disappointed. I didn't give a fuck whether I found anything or not. The thing is, never to be too anxious. Everything comes in due time.

We drove on past the Arc de Triomphe. A few sightseers were loitering around the remains of the Unknown Soldier. Going through the Bois I looked at all the rich cunts promenading in their limousines. They were whizzing by as if they had some destination. Do that, no doubt, to look important-to show the world how smooth run their Rolls Royces and their Hispano Suizas. Inside me things were running smoother than any Rolls Royce ever ran. It was just like velvet inside. Velvet cortex and velvet vertebrae. And velvet axle grease, what! It's a wonderful thing, for half an hour, to have money in your pocket and piss it away like a drunken sailor. You feel as though the world is yours. And the best part of it is, you don't know what to do with it. You can sit back and let the meter run wild, you can let the wind blow through your hair, you can stop and have a drink, you can give a big tip, and you can swagger off as though it were an everyday occurrence. But you can't create a revolution. You can't wash *all* the dirt out of your belly.

When we got to the Porte d'Auteuil I made him head for the Seine. At the Pont de Sevres I got out and started walking along the river, toward the Auteuil Viaduct. It's about the size of a creek along here and the trees come right down to the river's bank. The water was green and glassy, especially near the other side. Now and then a scow chugged by. Bathers in tights were standing in the grass sunning themselves. Everything was close and palpitant, and vibrant with the strong light.

Passing a beer garden I saw a group of cyclists sitting at a table. I took a seat nearby and ordered a *demi*. Hearing them jabber away I thought for a moment of Ginette. I saw her stamping up and down the room, tearing her hair, and sobbing and bleating, in that beastlike way of hers. I saw his hat on the rack. I wondered if his clothes would fit me. He had a raglan that I particularly liked. Well, by now he was on his way. In a little while the boat would be rocking under him. English! He wanted to hear English spoken. What an idea!

Suddenly it occurred to me that if I wanted I could go to America myself. It was the first time the opportunity had ever presented itself. I asked myself—"do you want to go?" There was no answer. My thoughts drifted out, toward the sea, toward the other side where, taking a last look back, I had seen the skyscrapers fading out in a flurry of snowflakes. I saw them looming up again, in that same ghostly way as when I left. Saw the lights creeping through their ribs. I saw the whole city spread out, from Harlem to the Battery, the streets choked with ants, the elevated rushing by, the theaters emptying. I wondered in a vague way what had ever happened to my wife.

After everything had quietly sifted through my head a great peace came over me. Here, where the river gently winds through the girdle of hills, lies a soil so saturated with the past that however far back the mind roams one can never detach it from its human background. Christ, before my eyes there shimmered such a golden peace that only a neurotic could dream of turning his head away. So quietly flows the Seine that one hardly notices its presence. It is always there, quiet and unobstrusive, like a great artery running through the human body. In the wonderful peace that fell over me it seemed as if I had climbed to the top of a high mountain; for a little while I would be able to look around me, to take in the meaning of the landscape.

Human beings make a strange fauna and flora. From a distance they appear negligible; close up they are apt to appear ugly and malicious. More than anything they need to be surrounded with sufficient space—space even more than time.

The sun is setting. I feel this river flowing through me—its past, its ancient soil, the changing climate. The hills gently girdle it about: its course is fixed.

TROPIC OF CAPRICORN

To Her

FOREWORD
to HISTORIA CALAMITATUM
(The story of my misfortunes)
Often the hearts of men and women are stirred, as likewise they are soothed in their sorrows, more by example than by words. And therefore, because I too have known some consolation from speech had with one who was a witness thereof, am I now minded to write of the sufferings which have sprung out of my misfortunes, for the eyes of one who, though absent, is of himself ever a consoler. This I do so that, in comparing your sorrows with mine, you may discover that yours are in truth nought, or at the most but of small account, and so shall you come to bear them more easily.
PETER ABELARD

On The Ovarian Trolley
Once you have given up the ghost, everything follows with dead certainty, even in the midst of chaos. From the beginning it was never anything but chaos: it was a fluid which enveloped me, which I breathed in through the gills. In the substrata, where the moon shone steady and opaque, it was smooth and fecundating; above it was a jangle and a discord. In everything I quickly saw the opposite, the contradiction, and between the real and the unreal the irony, the paradox. I was my own worst enemy. There was nothing I wished to do which I could just as well not do. Even as a child, when I lacked for nothing, I wanted to die: I wanted to surrender because I saw no sense in struggling. I felt that nothing would be proved, substantiated, added or subtracted by continuing an existence which I had not asked for. Everybody around me was a failure, or if not a failure, ridiculous. Especially the successful ones. The successful ones bored me to tears. I was sympathetic to a fault, but it was not sympathy that made me so. It was a purely negative quality, a weakness which blossomed at the mere sight of human misery. I never helped any one expecting that it would do any good; I helped because I was helpless to do otherwise. To want to change the condition of affairs seemed futile to me; nothing would be altered, I was convinced, except by a change of heart, and who could change the hearts of men? Now and then a friend was converted: it was something to make me puke. I had no more need of God than He had of me, and if there were one, I often said to myself, I would meet Him calmly and spit in His face.

What was most annoying was that at first blush people usually took me to be good, to be kind, generous, loyal, faithful. Perhaps I did possess these virtues but if so it was because I was indifferent: I could afford to be good, kind, generous, loyal, and so forth, since I was free of envy. Envy was the one thing I was never a victim of. I have never envied anybody or anything. On the contrary, I have only felt pity for everybody and everything.

From the very beginning I must have trained myself not to want anything too badly. From the very beginning I was independent, in a false way. I had need of nobody because I wanted to be free, free to do and to give only as my whims dictated. The moment anything was expected or demanded of me I balked. That was the form my independence took. I was corrupt, in other words, corrupt from the start. It's as though my mother fed me a poison, and though I was weaned young the poison never left my system. Even when she weaned me it seemed that I was completely indifferent; most children rebel, or make a pretense of rebelling, but I didn't give a damn. I was a philosopher when still in swaddling clothes. I was against life, on principle. What principle? The principle of futility. Everybody around me was struggling. I myself never made an effort. If I appeared to be making an effort it was only to please someone else; at bottom I didn't give a rap. And if you can tell me why this should have been so I will deny it, because I was born with a cussed streak in me and nothing can eliminate it. I heard later, when I had grown up, that they had a hell of a time bringing me out of the womb. I can understand that perfectly. Why budge? Why come out of a nice warm place, a cosy retreat in which everything is offered you gratis? The earliest remembrance I have is of the cold, the snow and ice in the gutter, the frost on the window panes, the chill of the sweaty green walls in the kitchen. Why do people live in outlandish climates in the *temperate* zones, as they are miscalled? Because people are naturally idiots, naturally sluggards, naturally cowards. Until I was about ten years old I never realized that there were "warm" countries, places where you didn't have to sweat for a living, nor shiver and pretend that it was tonic and exhilarating. Wherever there is cold there are people who work themselves to the bone and when they produce young they preach to the young the gospel of work—which is nothing, at bottom, but the doctrine of inertia. My people were entirely Nordic, which is to say *idiots*. Every wrong idea which has ever been expounded was theirs. Among them was the doctrine of cleanliness, to say nothing of righteousness. They were painfully clean. But inwardly they stank. Never once had they opened the door which leads to the soul; never once did they dream of taking a blind leap into the dark. After dinner the dishes were promptly washed and put in the closet; after the paper was read it was neatly folded and laid away on a shelf; after the clothes were washed they were ironed and folded and then tucked away in the drawers. Everything was for tomorrow, but tomorrow never came. The present was only a bridge and on this bridge they are still groaning, as the world groans, and not one idiot ever thinks of blowing up the bridge.

In my bitterness I often search for reasons to condemn them, the better to condemn myself. For I am like them too, in many ways. For a long while I thought I had escaped, but as time goes on I see that I am no better, that I am even a little worse, because I saw more clearly than they ever did and yet remained powerless to alter my life. As I look back on my life it seems to me that I never did anything of my own volition but always through the pressure of others. People often think of me as an adventurous fellow; nothing could be farther from the truth. My adventures were always adventitious, always thrust on me, always endured rather than undertaken. I am of the very essence of that proud, boastful Nordic people who have never had the least sense of adventure but who nevertheless have scoured the earth, turned it upside down, scattering relics and ruins everywhere. Restless spirits, but not adventurous ones. Agonizing spirits, incapable of living in the present. Disgraceful cowards, all of them, myself included. For there is only one great adventure and that is inward toward the self, and for that, time nor space nor even deeds matter.

Once every few years I was on the verge of making this discovery, but in characteristic fashion I always managed to dodge the issue. If I try to think of a good excuse I can think only of the environment, of the streets I knew and the people who inhabited them. I can think of no street in America, or of people inhabiting such a street, capable of leading one on toward the discovery of the self. I have walked the streets in many countries of the world but nowhere have I felt so degraded and humiliated as in America. I think of all the streets in America combined as forming a huge cesspool, a cesspool of the spirit in which everything is sucked down and drained away to everlasting shit. Over this cesspool the spirit of work weaves a magic wand; palaces and factories spring up side by side, and munition plants and chemical works and steel mills and sanatoriums and prisons and insane asylums. The whole continent is a nightmare producing the greatest misery of the greatest number. I was one, a single entity in the midst of the greatest jamboree of wealth and happiness (statistical wealth, statistical happiness) but I never met a man who was truly wealthy or truly happy. At least I knew that I was unhappy, unwealthy, out of whack and out of step. That was my only solace, my only joy. But it was hardly enough. It would have been better for my peace of mind, for my soul, if I had expressed my rebellion openly, if I had gone to jail for it, if I had rotted there and died. It would have been better if, like the mad Czolgosz, I had shot some good President McKinley, some gentle, insignificant soul like that who had never done anyone the least harm. Because in the bottom of my heart there was murder: I wanted to see America destroyed, razed from top to bottom. I wanted to see this happen purely out of vengeance, as atonement for the crimes that were committed against me and against others like me who have never been able to lift their voices and express their hatred, their rebellion, their legitimate blood lust.

I was the evil product of an evil soil. If the self were not imperishable, the "I" I write about would have been destroyed long ago. To some this may seem like an invention, but whatever I imagine to have happened did actually happen, *at least to me.* History may deny it, since I have played no part in the history of my people, but even if everything I say is wrong, is prejudiced, spiteful, malevolent, even if I am a liar and a poisoner, it is nevertheless the truth and it will have to be swallowed.

As to what happened...

Everything that happens, when it has significance, is in the nature of a contradiction. Until the one for whom this is written came along I imagined that somewhere outside, in life, as they say, lay the solution to all things. I thought, when I came upon her, that I was seizing hold of life, seizing hold of something which I could bite into. Instead I lost hold of life completely. I reached out for something to attach myself to—and I found nothing. But in reaching out, in the effort to grasp, to attach myself, left high and dry as I was, I nevertheless found something I had not looked for—*myself.* I found that what I had desired all my life was not to live—if what others are doing is called living—but to express myself. I realized that I had never the least interest in living, but only in this which I am doing now, something which is parallel to life, of it at the same time, and beyond it. What is true interests me scarcely at all, nor even what is real; only that interests me which I imagine to be, that which I had stifled every day in order to live. Whether I die today or tomorrow is of no importance to me, never has been, but that today even, after years of effort, I cannot say what I think and feel—that bothers me, that rankles. From childhood on I can see myself on the track of this specter, enjoying nothing, desiring nothing but this power, this ability. Everything else is a lie—everything I ever did or said which did not bear upon this. And that is pretty much the greater part of my life.

I was a contradiction in essence, as they say. People took me to be serious and high-minded, or to be gay and reckless, or to be sincere and earnest, or to be negligent and care-free. I was all these things at once—and beyond that I was something else, something which no one suspected, least of all myself. As a boy of six or seven I used to sit at my grandfather's workbench and read to him while he sewed. I remember him vividly in those moments when, pressing the hot iron against the seam of a coat, he would stand with one hand over the other and look out of the window dreamily. I remember the expression on his face, as he stood there dreaming, better than the contents of the books I read, better than the conversations we had or the games which I played in the street. I used to won-der what he was dreaming of, what it was that drew him out of himself. I hadn't learned yet how to dream wide-awake. I was always lucid, in the moment, and all of a piece. His daydreaming fascinated me. I knew that he had no connection with what he was doing, not the least thought for any of us, that he was alone and being alone he was free. I was never alone, least of all when I was by myself. Always, it seems to me, I was accompanied: I was like a little crumb of a big cheese, which was the world, I suppose, though I never stopped to think about it. But I know I never existed separately, never thought myself the big cheese, as it were. So that even when I had reason to be miserable, to complain, to weep, I had the illusion of participating in a common, a universal misery. When I wept the whole world was weeping—so I imagined. I wept very seldom. Mostly I was happy, I was laughing, I was having a good time. I had a good time because, as I said before, I real-ly didn't give a fuck about anything. If things were wrong with me they were wrong every-where, I was convinced of it. And things were wrong usually only when one cared too much. That impressed itself on me very early in life. For example, I remember the case of my young friend Jack Lawson. For a whole year he lay in bed, suffering the worst agonies. He was my best friend, so people said at any rate. Well, at first I was probably sorry for him and perhaps now and then I called at his house to inquire about him; but after a month or two had elapsed I grew quite callous about his suffering. I said to myself he ought to die and the sooner he dies the better it will be, and having thought thus I acted accordingly: that is to say, I promptly forgot about him, abandoned him to his fate. I was only about twelve years old at the time and I remember being proud of my decision. I remember the funeral too—what a disgraceful affair it was. There they were, friends and relatives all congregated about the bier and all of them bawling like sick monkeys. The mother especially gave me a pain in the ass. She was such a rare, spiritual creature, a Christian Scientist, I believe, and though she didn't believe in disease and didn't believe in death either, she raised such a stink that Christ himself would have risen from the grave. But not her beloved Jack! No, Jack lay there cold as ice and rigid and unbeckonable. He was dead and there were no two ways about it. I knew it and I was glad of it. I didn't waste any tears over it. I couldn't say that he was better off because after all the "he" had van-ished. *He* was gone and with him the sufferings he had endured and the suffering he had unwittingly inflicted on others. Amen!, I said to myself, and with that, being slightly hys-terical, I let a loud fart—right beside the coffin.

This caring too much—I remember that it only developed with me about the time I first fell in love. And even then I didn't care enough. If I had really cared I wouldn't be here now writing about it: I'd have died of a broken heart, or I'd have swung for it. It was a bad experience because it taught me how to live a lie. It taught me to smile when I did-n't want to smile, to work when I didn't believe in work, to live when I had no reason to go on living. Even when I had forgotten her I still retained the trick of doing what I didn't believe in.

It was all chaos from the beginning, as I have said. But sometimes I got so close to the center, to the very heart of the confusion, that it's a wonder things didn't explode around me.

It is customary to blame everything on the war. I say the war had nothing to do with me, with my life. At a time when others were getting themselves comfortable berths I was taking one miserable job after another, and never enough in it to keep body and soul together. Almost as quickly as I was hired I was fired. I had plenty of intelligence but I inspired distrust. Wherever I went I fomented discord—not because I was idealistic but because I was like a searchlight exposing the stupidity and futility of everything. Besides, I wasn't a good ass licker. That marked me, no doubt. People could tell at once when I asked for a job that I really didn't give a damn whether I got it or not. And of course I generally didn't get it. But after a time the mere looking for a job became an activity, a pastime, so to speak. I would go in and ask for most anything. It was a way of killing time— no worse, as far as I could see, than work itself. I was my own boss and I had my own hours, but unlike other bosses I entrained only my own ruin, my own bankruptcy. I was not a corporation or a trust or a state or a federation or a polity of nations—I was more like God, if anything.

This went on from about the middle of the war until... well, until one day I was trapped. Finally the day came when I did desperately want a job. I needed it. Not having another minute to lose, I decided that I would take the last job on earth, that of messenger boy. I walked into the employment bureau of the telegraph company—the Cosmodemonic Telegraph Company of North America—toward the close of the day, prepared to go through with it. I had just come from the public library and I had under my arm some fat books on economics and metaphysics. To my great amazement I was refused the job.

The guy who turned me down was a little runt who ran the switchboard. He seemed to take me for a college student, though it was clear enough from my application that I had long left school. I had even honored myself on the application with a Ph.D. degree from Columbia University. Apparently that passed unnoticed, or else was suspiciously regarded by this runt who had turned me down. I was furious, the more so because for once in my life I was in earnest. Not only that, but I had swallowed my pride, which in certain peculiar ways is rather large. My wife of course gave me the usual leer and sneer. I had done it as a gesture, she said. I went to bed thinking about it, still smarting, getting angrier and angrier as the night wore on. The fact that I had a wife and child to support didn't bother me so much; people didn't offer you jobs because you had a family to support, that much I understood only too well. No, what rankled was that they had rejected *me,* Henry V. Miller, a competent, superior individual who had asked for the lowest job in the world. That burned me up. I couldn't get over it. In the morning I was up bright and early, shaved, put on my best clothes and hotfooted it to the subway. I went immediately to the main offices of the telegraph company... up to the twenty-fifth floor or wherever it was that the president and the vice-presidents had their cubicles. I asked to see the president. Of course the president was either out of town or too busy to see me, but wouldn't I care to see the vice-president, or his secretary rather. I saw the vice-president's secretary, an intelligent, considerate sort of chap, and I gave him an earful. I did it adroitly, without too much heat, but letting him understand all the while that I wasn't to be put out of the way so easily.

When he picked up the telephone and demanded the general manager I thought it was just a gag, that they were going to pass me around like that from one to the other until I'd get fed up. But the moment I heard him talk I changed my opinion. When I got to the general manager's office, which was in another building uptown, they were waiting for me. I sat down in a comfortable leather chair and accepted one of the big cigars that were thrust forward. This individual seemed at once to be vitally concerned about the matter. He wanted me to tell him all about it, down to the last detail, his big hairy ears cocked to catch the least crumb of information which would justify something or other which was formulating itself inside his dome. I realized that by some accident I had really been instrumental in doing him a service. I let him wheedle it out of me to suit his fancy, observing all the time which way the wind was blowing. And as the talk progressed I noticed that he was warming up to me more and more. At last some one was showing a little confidence in me! That was all I required to get started on one of my favorite lines. For, after years of job hunting I had naturally become quite adept: I knew not only what *not* to say, but I knew also what to imply, what to insinuate. Soon the assistant general manager was called in and asked to listen to my story. By this time I knew what the story was. I understood that Hymie—"that little kike," as the general manager called him—had no business pretending that he was the employment manager. Hymie had usurped his prerogative, that much was clear. It was also clear that Hymie was a Jew and that Jews were not in good odor with the general manager, nor with Mr. Twilliger, the vice-president, who was a thorn in the general manager's side.

Perhaps it was Hymie, "the dirty little kike," who was responsible for the high percentage of Jews on the messenger force. Perhaps Hymie was really the one who was doing the hiring at the employment office—at Sunset Place, they called it. It was an excellent opportunity, I gathered, for Mr. Clancy, the general manager, to take down a certain Mr. Burns who, he informed me, had been the employment manager for some thirty years now and who was evidently getting lazy on the job.

The conference lasted several hours. Before it was terminated Mr. Clancy took me aside and informed me that he was going to make *me* the boss of the works. Before putting me into office, however, he was going to ask me as a special favor, and also as a sort of apprenticeship which would stand me in good stead, to work as a special messenger. I would receive the salary of employment manager, but it would be paid me out of a separate account. In short I was to float from office to office and observe the way affairs were conducted by all and sundry. I was to make a little report from time to time as to how things were going. And once in a while, so he suggested, I was to visit him at his home on the q.t. and have a little chat about the conditions in the hundred and one branches of the Cosmodemonic Telegraph Company in New York City. In other words I was to be a spy for a few months and after that I was to have the run of the joint. Maybe they'd make me a general manager too one day, or a vice-president. It was a tempting offer, even if it was wrapped up in a lot of horseshit. I said Yes.

In a few months I was sitting at Sunset Place hiring and firing like a demon. It was a slaughterhouse, so help me God. The thing was senseless from the bottom up. A waste of men, material and effort. A hideous farce against a backdrop of sweat and misery. But just as I had accepted the spying so I accepted the hiring and firing and all that went with it. I said Yes to everything. If the vice-president decreed that no cripples were to be hired I hired no cripples. If the vice-president said that all messengers over forty-five were to be fired without notice I fired them without notice. I did everything they instructed me to do, but in such a way that they had to pay for it. When there was a strike I folded my arms and waited for it to blow over. But I first saw to it that it cost them a good penny. The whole system was so rotten, so inhuman, so lousy, so hopelessly corrupt and complicated, that it would have taken a genius to put any sense or order into it, to say nothing of human kindness or consideration. I was up against the whole system of American labor, which is rotten at both ends. I was the fifth wheel on the wagon and neither side had any use for me, except to exploit me. In fact, everybody was being exploited—the president and his gang by the unseen powers, the employees by the officials, and so on and around, in and out and through the whole works. From my little perch at Sunset Place I had a bird's eye view of the whole American society. It was like a page out of the telephone book. Alphabetically, numerically, statistically, it made sense. But when you looked at it up close, when you examined the pages separately, or the parts separately, when you examined one lone individual and what constituted him, examined the air he breathed, the life he led, the chances he risked, you saw something so foul and degrading, so low, so miserable, so utterly hopeless and senseless, that it was worse than looking into a volcano. You could see the whole American life—economically, politically, morally, spiritually, artistically, statistically, pathologically. It looked like a grand chancre on a worn-out cock. It looked worse than that, really, because you couldn't even see anything resembling a cock any more. Maybe in the past this thing had life, did produce something, did at least give a moment's pleasure, a moment's thrill. But looking at it from where I sat it looked rottener than the wormiest cheese. The wonder was that the stench of it didn't carry 'em off.... I'm using the past tense all the time, but of course it's the same now, maybe even a bit worse. At least now we're getting it full stink.

By the time Valeska arrived on the scene I had hired several army corps of messengers. My office at Sunset Place was like an open sewer, and it stank like one. I had dug myself into the first-line trench and I was getting it from all directions at once. To begin with, the man I had ousted died of a broken heart a few weeks after my arrival. He held out just long enough to break me in and then he croaked. Things happened so fast that I didn't have a chance to feel guilty. From the moment I arrived at the office it was one long uninterrupted pandemonium. An hour before my arrival—I was always late—the place was already jammed with applicants. I had to elbow my way up the stairs and literally force my way in to get to my desk. Before I could take my hat off I had to answer a dozen telephone calls. There were three telephones on my desk and they all rang at once. They were bawling the piss out of me before I had even sat down to work. There wasn't even time to take a crap—until five or six in the afternoon. Hymie was worse off than I because he was tied to the switchboard. He sat there from eight in the morning until six, moving waybills around. A waybill was a messenger loaned by one office to another office for the day or a part of the day. None of the hundred and one offices ever had a full staff; Hymie had to play chess with the waybills while I worked like a madman to plug up the gaps. If by a miracle I succeeded of a day in filling all the vacancies, the next morning would find the situation exactly the same—or worse. Perhaps twenty per cent of the force was steady; the rest was driftwood. The steady ones drove the new ones away. The steady ones earned forty to fifty dollars a week, sometimes sixty or seventy-five, sometimes as much as a hundred dollars a week, which is to say that they earned far more than the clerks and often more than their own managers. As for the new ones, they found it difficult to earn ten dollars a week. Some of them worked an hour and quit, often throwing a batch of telegrams in the garbage can or down the sewer. And whenever they quit they wanted their pay immediately, which was impossible, because in the complicated bookkeeping which ruled no one could say what a messenger had earned until at least ten days later. In the beginning I invited the applicant to sit down beside me and I explained everything to him in detail. I did that until I lost my voice. Soon I learned to save my strength for the grilling that was necessary. In the first place, every other boy was a born liar, if not a crook to boot. Many of them had already been hired and fired a number of times. Some found it an excellent way to find another job, because their duty brought them to hundreds of offices which normally they would never have set foot in. Fortunately McGovern, the old trusty who guarded the door and handed out the application blanks, had a camera eye. And then there were the big ledgers behind me, in which there was a record of every applicant who had ever passed through the mill. The ledgers were very much like a police record; they were full of red ink marks, signifying this or that delinquency. To judge from the evidence I was in a tough spot. Every other name involved a theft, a fraud, a brawl, or dementia or perversion or idiocy. "Be careful—so-and-so is an epileptic!" "Don't hire this man—he's a nigger!" "Watch out—X has been in Dannemora—or else in Sing Sing.

If I had been a stickler for etiquette nobody would ever have been hired. I had to learn quickly, and not from the records or from those about me, but from experience. There were a thousand and one details by which to judge an applicant: I had to take them all in at once, and quickly, because in one short day, even if you are as fast as Jack Robinson, you can only hire so many and no more. And no matter how many I hired it was never enough. The next day it would begin all over again. Some I knew would last only a day, but I had to hire them just the same. The system was wrong from start to finish, but it was not my place to criticize the system. It was mine to hire and fire. I was in the center of a revolving disk which was whirling so fast that nothing could stay put. What was needed was a mechanic, but according to the logic of the higher-ups there was nothing wrong with the mechanism, everything was fine and dandy except that things were temporarily out of order. And things being temporarily out of order brought on epilepsy, theft, vandalism, perversion, niggers, Jews, whores and whatnot—sometimes strikes and lockouts. Whereupon, according to this logic, you took a big broom and you swept the stable clean, or you took clubs and guns and you beat sense into the poor idiots who were suffering from the illusion that things were fundamentally wrong. It was good now and then to talk of God, or to have a little community sing—maybe even a bonus was justifiable now and then, that is when things were getting too terribly bad for words. But on the whole, the important thing was to keep hiring and firing; as long as there were men and ammunition we were to advance, to keep mopping up the trenches. Meanwhile Hymie kept taking cathartic pills—enough to blow out his rear end if he had had a rear end, but he hadn't one any more, he only imagined he was taking a crap, he only imagined he was shitting on his can. Actually the poor bugger was in a trance. There were a hundred and one offices to look after and each one had a staff of messengers which was mythical, if not hypothetical, and whether the messengers were real or unreal, tangible or intangible, Hymie had to shuffle them about from morning to night while I plugged up the holes, which was also imaginary because who could say when a recruit had been dispatched to an office whether he would arrive there today or tomorrow or never. Some of them got lost in the subway or in the labyrinths under the skyscrapers; some rode around on the elevated line all day because with a uniform it was a free ride and perhaps they had never enjoyed riding around all day on the elevated lines. Some of them started for Staten Island and ended up in Canarsie, or else were brought back in a coma by a cop. Some forgot where they lived and disappeared completely. Some whom we hired for New York turned up in Philadelphia a month later, as though it were normal and according to Hoyle. Some would start for their destination and on the way decide that it was easier to sell newspapers and they would sell them, in the uniform we had given them, until they were picked up. Some went straight to the observation ward, moved by some strange preservative instinct.

When he arrived in the morning Hymie first sharpened his pencils; he did this religiously no matter how many calls were coming in, because, as he explained to me later, if he didn't sharpen the pencils first thing off the bat they would never get sharpened. The next thing was to take a glance out the window and see what the weather was like. Then, with a freshly sharpened pencil he made a little box at the head of the slate which he kept beside him and in it he gave the weather report. This, he also informed me, often turned out to be a useful alibi. If the snow were a foot thick or the ground covered with sleet, even the devil himself might be excused for not shuffling the waybills around more speedily, and the employment manager might also be excused for not filling up the holes on such days, no? But why he didn't take a crap first instead of plugging in on the switchboard soon as his pencils were sharpened was a mystery to me. That too he explained to me later. Anyway, the day always broke with confusion, complaints, constipation and vacancies. It also began with loud smelly farts, with bad breaths, with ragged nerves, with epilepsy, with meningitis, with low wages, with back pay that was overdue, with worn-out shoes, with corns and bunions, with fiat feet and broken arches, with pocketbooks missing and fountain pens lost or stolen, with telegrams floating in the sewer, with threats from the vice-president and advice from the managers, with wrangles and disputes, with cloudbursts and broken telegraph wires, with new methods of efficiency and old ones that had been discarded, with hope for better times and a prayer for the bonus which never came. The new messengers were going over the top and getting machine-gunned; the old ones were digging in deeper and deeper, like rats in a cheese. Nobody was satisfied, especially not the public. It took ten minutes to reach San Francisco over the wire, but it might take a year to get the message to the man whom it was intended for—or it might never reach him.

The Y. M. C. A., eager to improve the morale of working boys everywhere in America, was holding meetings at noon hour and wouldn't I like to send a few spruce-looking boys to hear William Carnegie Asterbilt Junior give a five-minute talk on service. Mr. Mallory of the Welfare League would like to know if I could spare a few minutes some time to tell me about the model prisoners who were on parole and who would be glad to serve in any capacity, even as messengers. Mrs. Guggenhoffer of the Jewish Charities would be very grateful if I would aid her in maintaining some broken-down homes which had broken down because everybody was either infirm, crippled or disabled in the family. Mr. Haggerty of the Runaway Home for Boys was sure he had just the right youngsters for me, if only I would give them a chance; all of them had been mistreated by their stepfathers or stepmothers. The Mayor of New York would appreciate it if I would give my personal attention to the bearer of said letter whom he could vouch for in every way—but why the hell he didn't give said bearer a job himself was a mystery. Man leaning over my shoulder hands me a slip of paper on which he has just written—"Me understand everything but me no hear the voices." Luther Winifred is standing beside him, his tattered coat fastened together with safety pins. Luther is two-sevenths pure Indian and five-sevenths German-American, so he explains. On the Indian side he is a Crow, one of the Crows from Montana. His last job was putting up window shades, but there is no ass in his pants and he is ashamed to climb a ladder in front of a lady. He got out of the hospital the other day and so he is still a little weak, but he is not too weak to carry messages, so he thinks.

And then there is Ferdinand Mish—how could I have forgotten him? He has been waiting in line all morning to get a word with me. I never answered the letters he sent me. Was that just? he asks me blandly. Of course not. I remember vaguely the last letter which he sent me from the Cat and Dog Hospital on the Grand Concourse, where he was an attendant. He said he repented that he had resigned his post "but it was on account of his father being too strict over him, not giving him any recreation or outside pleasure." "I'm twenty-five now," he wrote, "and I don't think I should ought to be sleeping no more with my father, do you? I know you are said to be a very fine gentleman and I am now self-dependent, so I hope..." McGovern, the old trusty, is standing by Ferdinand's side waiting for me to give him the sign. He wants to give Ferdinand the bum's rush—he remembers him from five years ago when Ferdinand lay down on the sidewalk in front of the main office in full uniform and threw an epileptic fit. No, shit, I can't do it! I'm going to give him a chance, the poor bastard. Maybe I'll send him to Chinatown where things are fairly quiet. Meanwhile, while Ferdinand is changing into a uniform in the back room, I'm getting an earful from an orphan boy who wants to "help make the company a success." He says that if I give him a chance he'll pray for me every Sunday when he goes to church, except the Sundays when he has to report to his parole officer. He didn't do nothing, it appears. He just pushed the fellow and the fellow fell on his head and got killed. *Next:* An ex-consul from Gibraltar. Writes a beautiful hand—too beautiful. I ask him to see me at the end of the day—something fishy about him. Meanwhile Ferdinand's thrown a fit in the dressing room. Lucky break! If it had happened in the subway, with a number on his hat and everything, I'd have been canned. *Next:* A guy with one arm and mad as hell because McGovern is showing him the door. "What the hell! I'm strong and healthy, ain't I?" he shouts, and to prove it he picks up a chair with his good arm and smashes it to bits. I get back to the desk and there's a telegram lying there for me. I open it. It's from George Blasini, ex-messenger No. 2459 of S.W. office. "I am sorry that I had to quit so soon, but the job was not fitted for my character idleness and I am a true lover of labor and frugality but many a time we be unable to control or subdue our personal pride." Shit!

In the beginning I was enthusiastic, despite the damper above and the clamps below. I had ideas and I executed them, whether it pleased the vice-president or not. Every ten days or so I was put on the carpet and lectured for having "too big a heart." I never had any money in my pocket but I used other people's money freely. As long as I was the boss I had credit. I gave money away right and left; I gave my clothes away and my linen, my books, everything that was superfluous. If I had had the power I would have given the company away to the poor buggers who pestered me. If I was asked for a dime I gave a half dollar, if I was asked for a dollar I gave five. I didn't give a fuck how much I gave away, because it was easier to borrow and give than to refuse the poor devils. I never saw such an aggregation of misery in my life, and I hope I'll never see it again. Men are poor everywhere—they always have been and they always will be. And beneath the terrible poverty there is a flame, usually so low that it is almost invisible. But it is there and if one has the courage to blow on it it can become a conflagration. I was constantly urged not to be too lenient, not to be too sentimental, not to be too charitable. Be firm! Be hard! they cautioned me. Fuck that! I said to myself, I'll be generous, pliant, forgiving, tolerant, tender. In the beginning I heard every man to the end; if I couldn't give him a job I gave him money, and if I had no money I gave him cigarettes or I gave him courage. But I gave! The effect was dizzying. Nobody can estimate the results of a good deed, of a kind word. I was swamped with gratitude, with good wishes, with invitations, with pathetic, tender little gifts. If I had had real power instead of being the fifth wheel on a wagon, God knows what I might not have accomplished. I could have used the Cosmodemonic Telegraph Company of North America as a base to bring all humanity to God; I could have transformed North and South America alike, and the Dominion of Canada too. I had the secret in my hand: it was to be generous, to be kind, to be patient. I did the work of five men. I hardly slept for three years. I didn't own a whole shirt and often I was so ashamed of borrowing from my wife, or robbing the kid's bank, that to get the carfare to go to work in the morning I would swindle the blind newspaperman at the subway station. I owed so much money all around that if I were to work for twenty years I would not have been able to pay it back. I took from those who had and I gave to those who needed, and it was the right thing to do, and I would do it all over again if I were in the same position.

I even accomplished the miracle of stopping the crazy turnover, something that nobody had dared to hope for. Instead of supporting my efforts they undermined me. According to the logic of the higher-ups the turnover had ceased because the wages were too high. So they cut the wages. It was like kicking the bottom out of a bucket. The whole edifice tumbled, collapsed on my hands. And, just as though nothing had happened they insisted that the gaps be plugged up immediately. To soften the blow a bit they intimated that I might even increase the percentage of Jews, I might take on a cripple now and then, if he were capable, I might do this and that, all of which they had informed me previously was against the code. I was so furious that I took on anything and everything; I would have taken on broncos and gorillas if I could have imbued them with the modicum of intelligence which was necessary to deliver messages. A few days previously there had been only five or six vacancies at closing time. Now there were three hundred, four hundred, five hundred—they were running out like sand. It was marvelous. I sat there and without asking a question I took them on in carload lots—niggers, Jews, paralytics, cripples, ex-convicts, whores, maniacs, perverts, idiots, any fucking bastard who could stand on two legs and hold a telegram in his hand. The managers of the hundred and one offices were frightened to death. I laughed. I laughed all day long thinking what a fine stinking mess I was making of it. Complaints were pouring in from all parts of the city. The service was crippled, constipated, strangulated. A mule could have gotten there faster than some of the idiots I put into harness.

The best thing about the new day was the introduction of female messengers. It changed the whole atmosphere of the joint. For Hymie especially it was a godsend. He moved his switchboard around so that he could watch me while juggling the waybills back and forth. Despite the added work he had a permanent erection. He came to work with a smile and he smiled all day long. He was in heaven. At the end of the day I always had a list of five or six who were worth trying out. The game was to keep them on the string, to promise them a job but to get a free fuck first. Usually it was only necessary to throw a feed into them in order to bring them back to the office at night and lay them out on the zinc-covered table in the dressing room. If they had a cosy apartment, as they sometimes did, we took them home and finished it in bed. If they liked to drink Hymie would bring a bottle along. If they were any good and really needed some dough Hymie would flash his roll and peel off a five spot or a ten spot, as the case might be. It makes my mouth water when I think of that roll he carried about with him. Where he got it from I never knew, because he was the lowest-paid man in the joint. But it was always there, and no matter what I asked for I got. And once it happened that we did get a bonus and I paid Hymie back to the last penny—which so amazed him that he took me out that night to Delmonico's and spent a fortune on me. Not only that, but the next day he insisted on buying me a hat and shirts and gloves. He even insinuated that I might come home and fuck his wife, if I liked, though he warned me that she was having a little trouble at present with her ovaries.

In addition to Hymie and McGovern I had as assistants a pair of beautiful blondes who often accompanied us to dinner in the evening. And there was O'Mara, an old friend of mine who had just returned from the Philippines and whom I made my chief assistant. There was also Steve Romero, a prize bull whom I kept around in case of trouble. And O'Rourke, the company detective, who reported to me at the close of day when he began his work. Finally I added another man to the staff—Kronski, a young medical student, who was diabolically interested in the pathological cases of which we had plenty. We were a merry crew, united in our desire to fuck the company at all costs. And while fucking the company we fucked everything in sight that we could get hold of, O'Rourke excepted, as he had a certain dignity to maintain, and besides he had trouble with his prostate and had lost all interest in fucking. But O'Rourke was a prince of a man, and generous beyond words. It was O'Rourke who often invited us to dinner in the evening and it was O'Rourke we went to when we were in trouble.

That was how it stood at Sunset Place after a couple of years had rolled by. I was saturated with humanity, with experiences of one kind and another. In my sober moments I made notes which I intended to make use of later if ever I should have a chance to record my experiences. I was waiting for a breathing spell. And then by chance one day, when I had been put on the carpet for some wanton piece of negligence, the vice-president let drop a phrase which stuck in my crop. He had said that he would like to see some one write a sort of Horatio Alger book about the messengers; he hinted that perhaps I might be the one to do such a job. I was furious to think what a ninny he was and delighted at the same time because secretly I was itching to get the thing off my chest. I thought to myself—you poor old futzer, you, just wait until I get it off my chest.... I'll give you an Horatio Alger book... just you wait! My head was in a whirl leaving his office. I saw the army of men, women and children that had passed through my hands, saw them weeping, begging, beseeching, imploring, cursing, spitting, fuming, threatening. I saw the tracks they left on the highways, the freight trains lying on the floor, the parents in rags, the coal box empty, the sink running over, the walls sweating and between the cold beads of sweat the cockroaches running like mad; I saw them hobbling along like twisted gnomes or falling backwards in the epileptic frenzy, the mouth twitching, the slaver pouring from the lips, the limbs writhing; I saw the walls giving way and the pest pouring out like a winged fluid, and the men higher up with their ironclad logic, waiting for it to blow over, waiting for everything to be patched up, waiting contentedly, smugly, with big cigars in their mouths and their feet on the desk, saying things were temporarily out of order. I saw the Horatio Alger hero, the dream of a sick America, mounting higher and higher, first messenger, operator, then manager, then chief, then superintendent, then vice-president, then president, then trust magnate, then beer baron, then Lord of all the Americas, the money god, the god of gods, the clay of clay, nullity on high, zero with ninety-seven thousand decimals fore and aft. You shits, I said to myself, I will give you the picture of twelve little men, zeros without decimals, ciphers, digits, the twelve uncrushable worms who are hollowing out the base of your rotten edifice. I will give you Horatio Alger as he looks the day after the Apocalypse, when all the stink has cleared away.

From all over the earth they had come to me to be succored. Except for the primitives there was scarcely a race which wasn't represented on the force. Except for the Ainus, the Maoris, the Papuans, the Veddas, the Lapps, the Zulus, the Patagonians, the Igorots, the Hottentots, the Tuaregs, except for the lost Tasmanians, the lost Grimaldi men, the lost Atlanteans, I had a representative of almost every species under the sun. I had two brothers who were still sun-worshipers, two Nestorians from the old Assyrian world; I had two Maltese twins from Malta and a descendant of the Mayas from Yucatan; I had a few of our little brown brothers from the Philippines and some Ethiopians from Abyssinia; I had men from the pampas of Argentina and stranded cowboys from Montana; I had Greeks, Letts, Poles, Croats, Slovenes, Ruthenians, Czechs, Spaniards, Welshmen, Finns, Swedes, Russians, Danes, Mexicans, Puerto Ricans, Cubans, Uruguayans, Brazilians, Australians, Persians, Japs, Chinese, Javanese, Egyptians, Africans from the Gold Coast and the Ivory Coast, Hindus, Armenians, Turks, Arabs, Germans, Irish, English, Canadians—and plenty of Italians and plenty of Jews. I had only one Frenchman that I can recall and he lasted about three hours. I had a few American Indians, Cherokees mostly, but no Tibetans, and no Eskimos: I saw names I could never have imagined and handwriting which ranged from cuneiform to the sophisticated and astoundingly beautiful calligraphy of the Chinese. I heard men beg for work who had been Egyptologists, botanists, surgeons, gold miners, professors of Oriental languages, musicians, engineers, physicians, astronomers, anthropologists, chemists, mathematicians, mayors of cities and governors of states, prison wardens, cowpunchers, lumberjacks, sailors, oyster pirates, stevedores, riveters, dentists, painters, sculptors, plumbers, architects, dope peddlers, abortionists, white slavers, sea divers, steeplejacks, farmers, cloak and suit salesmen, trappers, lighthouse keepers, pimps, aldermen, senators, every bloody thing under the sun, and all of them down and out, begging for work, for cigarettes, for carfare, *for a chance, Christ Almighty, just another chance!* I saw and got to know men who were saints, if there are saints in this world; I saw and spoke to savants, crapulous and uncrapulous ones; I listened to men who had the divine fire in their bowels, who could have convinced God Almighty that they were worthy of another chance, but not the vice-president of the Cosmococcic Telegraph Company. I sat riveted to my desk and I traveled around the world at lightning speed, and I learned that everywhere it is the same—hunger, humiliation, ignorance, vice, greed, extortion, chicanery, torture, despotism: the inhumanity of man to man: the fetters, the harness, the halter, the bridle, the whip, the spurs. The finer the caliber the worse off the man. Men were walking the streets of New York in that bloody, degrading outfit, the despised, the lowest of the low, walking around like auks, like penguins, like oxen, like

trained seals, like patient donkeys, like big jackasses, like crazy gorillas, like docile maniacs nibbling at the dangling bait, like waltzing mice, like guinea pigs, like squirrels, like
rabbits, and many and many a one was fit to govern the world, to write the greatest book
ever written. When I think of some of the Persians, the Hindus, the Arabs I knew, when
I think of the character they revealed, their grace, their tenderness, their intelligence, *their
holiness,* I spit on the white conquerors of the world, the degenerate British, the pigheaded Germans, the smug, self-satisfied French. The earth is one great sentient being, a planet saturated through and through with man, a live planet expressing itself falteringly and
stutteringly; it is not the home of the white race or the black race or the yellow race or the
lost blue race, but the home of *man* and all men are equal before God and will have their
chance, if not now then a million years hence. The little brown brothers of the Philippines
may bloom again one day and the murdered Indians of America north and south may also
come alive one day to ride the plains where now the cities stand belching fire and pestilence. Who has the last say? *Man!* The earth is his because he *is* the earth, its fire, its water,
its air, its mineral and vegetable matter, its spirit which is cosmic, which is imperishable,
which is the spirit of all the planets, which transforms itself through him, through endless
signs and symbols, through endless manifestations. Wait, you cosmococcic telegraphic
shits, you demons on high waiting for the plumbing to be repaired, wait, you dirty white
conquerors who have sullied the earth with your cloven hoofs, your instruments, your
weapons, your disease germs, wait, all you who are sitting in clover and counting your cop-
pers, it is not the end. The last man will have his say before it is finished. Down to the last
sentient molecule justice must be done—*and will be done!* Nobody is getting away with
anything, least of all the cosmococcic shits of North America.

When it came time for my vacation—I hadn't taken one for three years, I was so eager
to make the company a success!—I took three weeks instead of two and I wrote the book
about the twelve little men. I wrote it straight off, five, seven, sometimes eight thousand
words a day. I thought that a man, to be a writer, must do at least five thousand words a
day. I thought he must say everything all at once—in one book—and collapse afterwards.
I didn't know a thing about writing. I was scared shitless. But I was determined to wipe
Horatio Alger out of the North American consciousness. I suppose it was the worst book
any man has ever written. It was a colossal tome and faulty from start to finish. But it was
my first book and I was in love with it. If I had had the money, as Gide had, I would have
published it at my own expense. If I had had the courage that Whitman had, I would have
peddled it from door to door. Everybody I showed it to said it was terrible, I was urged to
give up the idea of writing. I had to learn, as Balzac did, that one must write volumes
before signing one's own name. I had to learn, as I soon did, that one must give up everything and not do anything else but write, that one must write and write and write, even if
everybody in the world advises you against it, even if nobody believes in you. Perhaps one
does it just because nobody believes; perhaps the real secret lies in making people believe.
That the book was inadequate, faulty, bad, *terrible,* as they said, was only natural. I was
attempting at the start what a man of genius would have undertaken only at the end. I
wanted to say the last word at the beginning. It was absurd and pathetic. It was a crushing defeat, but it put iron in my backbone and sulphur in my blood. I knew at least what
it was to fail. I knew what it was to attempt something big. Today, when I think of the circumstances under which I wrote that book, when I think of the overwhelming material
which I tried to put into form, when I think of what I hoped to encompass, I pat myself

on the back, I give myself a double A. I am proud of the fact that I made such a miserable failure of it; had I succeeded I would have been a monster. Sometimes, when I look over my notebooks, when I look at the names alone of those whom I thought to write about, I am seized with vertigo. Each man came to me with a world of his own; he came to me and unloaded it on my desk; he expected me to pick it up and put it on my shoulders. I had no time to make a world of my own: I had to stay fixed like Atlas, my feet on the elephant's back and the elephant on the tortoise's back. To inquire on what the tortoise stood would be to go mad.

I didn't dare to think of anything then except the "facts." To get beneath the facts I would have had to be an artist, and one doesn't become an artist overnight. First you have to be crushed, to have your conflicting points of view annihilated. You have to be wiped out as a human being in order to be born again an individual. You have to be carbonized and mineralized in order to work upwards from the least common denominator of the self. You have to get beyond pity in order to feel from the very roots of your being. One can't make a new heaven and earth with "facts." There are no "facts"—there is only *the fact* that man, every man everywhere in the world, is on his way to ordination. Some men take the long route and some take the short route. Every man is working out his destiny in his own way and nobody can be of help except by being kind, generous and patient. In my enthusiasm certain things were then inexplicable to me which now are clear. I think, for example, of Carnahan, one of the twelve little men I had chosen to write about. He was what is called a model messenger. He was a graduate of a prominent university, had a sound intelligence and was of exemplary character. He worked eighteen and twenty hours a day and earned more than any messenger on the force. The clients whom he served wrote letters about him, praising him to the skies; he was offered good positions which he refused for one reason or another. He lived frugally, sending the best part of his wages to his wife and children who lived in another city. He had two vices—drink and the desire to succeed. He could go for a year without drinking, but if he took one drop he was off. He had cleaned up twice in Wall Street and yet, before coming to me for a job, he had gotten no further than to be a sexton of a church in some little town. He had been fired from that job because he had broken into the sacramental wine and rung the bells all night long. He was truthful, sincere, earnest. I had implicit confidence in him and my confidence was proven by the record of his service which was without a blemish. Nevertheless he shot his wife and children in cold blood and then he shot himself. Fortunately none of them died; they all lay in the hospital together and they all recovered. I went to see his wife, after they had transferred him to jail, to get her help. She refused categorically. She said he was the meanest, crudest son of a bitch that ever walked on two legs—she wanted to see him hanged. I pleaded with her for two days, but she was adamant. I went to the jail and talked to him through the mesh. I found that he had already made himself popular with the authorities, had already been granted special privileges. He wasn't at all dejected. On the contrary, he was looking forward to making the best of his time in prison by "studying up" on salesmanship. He was going to be the best salesman in America after his release. I might almost say that he seemed happy. He said not to worry about him, he would get along all right. He said everybody was swell to him and that he had nothing to complain about. I left him somewhat in a daze. I went to a nearby beach and decided to take a swim. I saw everything with new eyes. I almost forgot to return home, so absorbed had I become in my speculations about this chap. Who could say that everything that happened to him had not happened for the best? Perhaps he might leave the prison a full-fledged evangelist instead of a salesman. Nobody could predict what he might do. And nobody could aid him because he was working out his destiny in his own private way.

There was another chap, a Hindu named Guptal. He was not only a model of good behavior—he was a saint. He had a passion for the flute which he played all by himself in his miserable little room. One day he was found naked, his throat slit from ear to ear, and beside him on the bed was his flute. At the funeral there were a dozen women who wept passionate tears, including the wife of the janitor who had murdered him. I could write a book about this young man who was the gentlest and the holiest man I ever met, who had never offended anybody and never taken anything from anybody, but who had made the cardinal mistake of coming to America to spread peace and love.

There was Dave Olinski, another faithful, industrious messenger who thought of nothing but work. He had one fatal weakness—he talked too much. When he came to me he had already been around the globe several times and what he hadn't done to make a living isn't worth telling about. He knew about twelve languages and he was rather proud of his linguistic ability. He was one of those men whose very willingness and enthusiasm is their undoing. He wanted to help everybody along, show everybody how to succeed. He wanted more work than we could give him—he was a glutton for work. Perhaps I should have warned him, when I sent him to his office on the East Side, that he was going to work in a tough neighborhood, but he pretended to know so much and he was so insistent on working in that locality (because of his linguistic ability) that I said nothing. I thought to myself—you'll find out quickly enough for yourself. And sure enough, he was only there a short time when he got into trouble. A tough Jewboy from the neighborhood walked in one day and asked for a blank. Dave, the messenger, was behind the desk. He didn't like the way the man asked for the blank. He told him he ought to be more polite. For that he got a box in the ears. That made him wag his tongue some more, whereupon he got such a wallop that his teeth flew down his throat and his jawbone was broken in three places. Still he didn't know enough to hold his trap. Like the damned fool that he was he goes to the police station and registers a complaint. A week later, while he's sitting on a bench snoozing, a gang of roughnecks break into the place and beat him to a pulp. His head was so battered that his brains looked like an omelette. For good measure they emptied the safe and turned it upside down. Dave died on the way to the hospital. They found five hundred dollars hidden away in the toe of his sock.... Then there was Clausen and his wife Lena. They came in together when he applied for the job. Lena had a baby in her arms and he had two little ones by the hand. They were sent to me by some relief agency. I put him on as a night messenger so that he'd have a fixed salary. In a few days I had a letter from him, a batty letter in which he asked me to excuse him for being absent as he had to report to his parole officer. Then another letter saying that his wife had refused to sleep with him because she didn't want any more babies and would I please come to see them and try to persuade her to sleep with him. I went to his home—a cellar in the Italian quarter. It looked like a bughouse. Lena was pregnant again, about seven months under way, and on the verge of idiocy. She had taken to sleeping on the roof because it was too hot in the cellar, also because she didn't want him to touch her any more. When I said it wouldn't make any difference now she just looked at me and grinned. Clausen had been in the war and maybe the gas had made him a bit goofy—at any rate he was foaming at the mouth. He said he would brain her if she didn't stay off that roof.

He insinuated that she was sleeping up there in order to carry on with the coal man who lived in the attic. At this Lena smiled again with that mirthless batrachian grin. Clausen lost his temper and gave her a swift kick in the ass. She went out in a huff taking the brats with her. He told her to stay out for good. Then he opened a drawer and pulled out a big Colt. He was keeping it in case he needed it some time, he said. He showed me a few knives, too, and a sort of blackjack which he had made himself. Then he began to weep. He said his wife was making a fool of him. He said he was sick of working for her because she was sleeping with everybody in the neighborhood. The kids weren't his because he couldn't make a kid any more even if he wanted to. The very next day, while Lena was out marketing, he took the kids up to the roof and with the blackjack he had shown me he beat their brains out. Then he jumped off the roof head first. When Lena came home and saw what happened she went off her nut. They had to put her in a strait jacket and call for the ambulance.... There was Schuldig, the rat who had spent twenty years in prison for a crime he had never committed. He had been beaten almost to death before he confessed; then solitary confinement, starvation, torture, perversion, dope. When they finally released him he was no longer a human being. He described to me one night his last thirty days in jail, the agony of waiting to be released. I have never heard anything like it; I didn't think a human being could survive such anguish. Freed, he was haunted by the fear that he might be obliged to commit a crime and be sent back to prison again. He complained of being followed, spied on, perpetually tracked. He said "they" were tempting him to do things he had no desire to do. "They" were the dicks who were on his trail, who were paid to bring him back again. At night, when he was asleep, they whispered in his ear. He was powerless against them because they mesmerized him first. Sometimes they placed dope under his pillow, and with it a revolver or a knife. They wanted him to kill some innocent person so that they would have a solid case against him this time. He got worse and worse. One night, after he had walked around for hours with a batch of telegrams in his pocket, he went up to a cop and asked to be locked up. He couldn't remember his name or address or even the office he was working for. He had completely lost his identity. He repeated over and over—"I'm innocent.... I'm innocent." Again they gave him the third degree. Suddenly he jumped up and shouted like a madman—"I'll confess... I'll confess"— and with that he began to reel off one crime after another. He kept it up for three hours. Suddenly, in the midst of a harrowing confession, he stopped short, gave a quick look about, like a man who has suddenly come to, and then, with the rapidity and the force which only a madman can summon he made a tremendous leap across the room and crashed his skull against the stone wall.... I relate these incidents briefly and hurriedly as they flash through my mind; my memory is packed with thousands of such details, with a myriad faces, gestures, tales, confessions all entwined and interlaced like the stupendous reeling facade of some Hindu temple made not of stone but of the experience of human flesh, a monstrous dream edifice built entirely of reality and yet not reality itself but merely the vessel in which the mystery of the human being is contained. My mind wanders to the clinic where in ignorance and good will I brought some of the younger ones to be cured. I can think of no more evocative image to convey the atmosphere of this place than the painting by Hieronymus Bosch in which the magician, after the manner of a dentist extracting a live nerve, is represented as the deliverer of insanity. All the trumpery and quackery of our scientific practitioners came to apotheosis in the person of the suave sadist who operated this clinic with the full concurrence and connivance of the law. He was a ringer for Caligari, except that he was minus the dunce cap. Pretending that he understood the secret regulations of the glands, invested with the power of a medieval monarch, oblivious of the pain he inflicted, ignorant of everything but his medical knowledge, he went to work on the human organism like a plumber sets to work on the underground drainpipes. In addition to the poisons he threw into the patient's system he had recourse to his fists or his knees as the case might be. Anything justified a "reaction." If the victim were lethargic he shouted at him, slapped him in the face, pinched his arm, cuffed him, kicked him. If on the contrary the victim were too energetic he employed the same methods, only with redoubled zest. The feelings of his subject were of no importance to him; whatever reaction he succeeded in obtaining was merely a demonstration or manifestation of the laws regulating the operation of the internal glands of secretion. The purpose of his treatment was to render the subject fit for society. But no matter how fast he worked, no matter whether he was successful or not successful, society was turning out more and more misfits. Some of them were so marvelously maladapted that when, in order to get the proverbial reaction, he slapped them vigorously on the cheek they responded with an uppercut or a kick in the balls. It's true, most of his subjects were exactly what he described them to be—incipient criminals. The whole continent was on the slide—is still on the slide—and not only the glands need regulating but the ball bearings, the armature, the skeletal structure, the cerebrum, the cerebellum, the coccyx, the larynx, the pancreas, the liver, the upper intestine and the lower intestine, the heart, the kidneys, the testicles, the womb, the Fallopian tubes, the whole goddamned works. The whole country is lawless, violent, explosive, demoniacal. It's in the air, in the climate, in the ultra-grandiose landscape, in the stone forests that are lying horizontal, in the torrential rivers that bite through the rocky canyons, in the supra-normal distances, the supernal arid wastes, the over-lush crops, the monstrous fruits, the mixture of quixotic bloods, the fatras of cults, sects, beliefs, the opposition of laws and languages, the contradictoriness of temperaments, principles, needs, requirements. The continent is full of buried violence, of the bones of antediluvian monsters and of lost races of man, of mysteries which are wrapped in doom. The atmosphere is at times so electrical that the soul is summoned out of its body and runs amok. Like the rain everything comes in bucketsful—or not at all. The whole continent is a huge volcano whose crater is temporarily concealed by a moving panorama which is partly dream, partly fear, partly despair. From Alaska to Yucatan it's the same story. Nature dominates. Nature wins out. Everywhere the same fundamental urge to slay, to ravage, to plunder. Outwardly they seem like a fine, upstanding people—healthy, optimistic, courageous. Inwardly they are filled, with worms. A tiny spark and they blow up.

Often it happens, as in Russia, that a man came in with a chip on his shoulder. He woke up that way, as if struck by a monsoon. Nine times out of ten he was a good fellow, a fellow whom everyone liked. But when the rage came on nothing could stop him. He was like a horse with the blind staggers and the best thing you could do for him was to shoot him on the spot. It always happens that way with peaceable people. One day they run amok. In America they're constantly running amok. What they need is an outlet for their energy, for their blood lust. Europe is bled regularly by war. America is pacifistic and cannibalistic. Outwardly it seems to be a beautiful honeycomb, with all the drones crawling over each other in a frenzy of work; inwardly it's a slaughterhouse, each man killing off his neighbor and sucking the juice from his bones. Superficially it looks like a bold, masculine world; actually it's a whorehouse run by women, with the native sons acting as pimps and the bloody foreigners selling their flesh. Nobody knows what it is to sit on his ass and be content. That happens only in the films where everything is faked, even the fires of hell. The whole continent is sound asleep and in that sleep a grand nightmare is taking place.

Nobody could have slept more soundly than I in the midst of this nightmare. The war, when it came along, made only a sort of faint rumble in my ears. Like my compatriots, I was pacifistic and cannibalistic. The millions who were put away in the carnage passed away in a cloud, much like the Aztecs passed away, and the Incas and the red Indians and the buffaloes. People pretended to be profoundly moved, but they weren't. They were simply tossing fitfully in their sleep. No one lost his appetite, no one got up and rang the fire alarm. The day I first realized that there had been a war was about six months or so after the armistice. It was in a street car on the 14th Street crosstown line. One of our heroes, a Texas lad with a string of medals across his chest, happened to see an officer passing on the sidewalk. The sight of the officer enraged him. He was a sergeant himself and he probably had good reason to be sore. Anyway, the sight of the officer enraged him so that he got up from his seat and began to bawl the shit out of the government, the army, the civilians, the passengers in the car, everybody and everything. He said if there was ever another war they couldn't drag him to it with a twenty-mule team. He said he'd see every son of a bitch killed before he'd go again himself; he said he didn't give a fuck about the medals they had decorated him with and to show that he meant it he ripped them off and threw them out the window; he said if he was ever in a trench with an officer again he'd shoot him in the back like a dirty dog, and that held good for General Pershing or any other general. He said a lot more, with some fancy cuss words that he'd picked up over there, and nobody opened his trap to gainsay him. And when he got through I felt for the first time that there had really been a war and that the man I was listening to had been in it and that despite his bravery the war had made him a coward and that if he did any more killing it would be wide-awake and in cold blood, and nobody would have the guts to send him to the electric chair because he had performed his duty toward his fellow men, which was to deny his own sacred instincts and so everything was just and fair because one crime washes away the other in the name of God, country and humanity, peace be with you all.

And the second time I experienced the reality of war was when ex-sergeant Griswold, one of our night messengers, flew off the handle one day and smashed the office to bits at one of the railway stations. They sent him to me to give him the gate, but I didn't have the heart to fire him. He had performed such a beautiful piece of destruction that I felt more like hugging and squeezing him; I was only hoping to Christ he would go up to the twenty-fifth floor, or wherever it was that the president and the vice-presidents had their offices, and mop up the whole bloody gang. But in the name of discipline, and to uphold the bloody farce it was, I had to do something to punish him or be punished for it myself, and so not knowing what less I could do I took him off the commission basis and put him back on a salary basis. He took it pretty badly, not realizing exactly where I stood, either for him or against him, and so I got a letter from him pronto, saying that he was going to pay me a visit in a day or two and that I'd better watch out because he was going to take it out of my hide. He said he'd come up after office hours and that if I was afraid I'd better have some strong-arm men around to look after me. I knew he meant every word he said and I felt pretty damned quaky when I put the letter down. I waited in for him alone, however, feeling that it would be even more cowardly to ask for protection. It was a strange experience. He must have realized the moment he laid eyes on me that I was a son of a bitch and a lying, stinking hypocrite, as he had called me in his letter. I was only that because he was what he was, which wasn't a hell of a lot better. He must have realized immediately that we were both in the same boat and that the bloody boat was leaking pretty badly. I could see something like that going on in him as he strode forward, outwardly still furious, still foaming at the mouth, but inwardly all spent, all soft and feathery. As for myself, what fear I had vanished the moment I saw him enter. Just being there quiet and alone, and being less strong, less *capable* of defending myself, gave me the drop on him. Not that I wanted to have the drop on him either. But it had turned out that way and I took advantage of it, naturally. The moment he sat down he went soft as putty. He wasn't a man any more, but just a big child. There must have been millions of them like him, big children with machine guns who could wipe out whole regiments without batting an eyelash; but back in the work trenches, without a weapon, without a clear, visible enemy, they were helpless as ants. Everything revolved about the question of food. The food and the rent—that was all there was to fight about—but there was no way, no clear, visible way, to fight for it. It was like seeing an army strong and well equipped, capable of licking anything in sight, and yet ordered to retreat every day, to retreat and retreat and retreat because that was the strategic thing to do, even though it meant losing ground, losing guns, losing ammunition, losing food, losing sleep, losing courage, losing life itself finally. Wherever there were men fighting for food and rent there was this retreat going on, in the fog, in the night, for no earthly reason except that it was the strategic thing to do. It was eating the heart out of him. To fight was easy, but to fight for food and rent was like fighting an army of ghosts. All you could do was to retreat, and while you retreated you watched your own brothers getting popped off, one after the other, silently, mysteriously, in the fog, in the dark, and not a thing to do about it. He was so damned confused, so perplexed, so hopelessly muddled and beaten, that he put his head in his arms and wept on my desk. And while he's sobbing like that suddenly the telephone rings and it's the vice-president's office—never the vice-president himself, but always *his office*—and they want this man Griswold fired immediately and I say Yes Sir! and I hang up. I don't say anything to Griswold about it but I walk home with him and I have dinner with him and his wife and kids. And when I leave him I say to myself that if I have to fire that guy somebody's going to pay for it—and anyway I want to know first where the order comes from and why. And hot and sullen I go right up to the vice-president's office in the morning and I ask to see the vice-president himself and did you give the order I ask—*and why?* And before he has a chance to deny it, or to explain his reason for it, I give him a little war stuff straight from the shoulder and where he don't like it and can't take it—and if you don't like it, Mr. Will Twilldilliger, you can take the job, my job and his job and you can shove them up your ass—and like that I walk out on him. I go back to the slaughterhouse and I go about my work as usual. I expect, of course, that I'll get the sack before the day's over. But nothing of the kind. No, to my amazement I get a telephone call from the general manager saying to take it easy, to just calm down a bit, yes, just go easy, don't do anything hasty, we'll look into it, etc. I guess they're still looking into it because Griswold went on working just as always—in fact, they even promoted him to a clerkship, which was a dirty deal, too, because as a clerk he earned less money than as a messenger, but it saved his pride and it also took a little more of the spunk out of him too, no doubt. But that's what happens to a guy when he's just a hero in his sleep. Unless the nightmare is strong enough to wake you up you go right on retreating, and either you end up on a bench or you end up as vice-president. It's all one and the same, a bloody fucking mess, a farce, a fiasco from start to finish. I know it as I was in it, because I woke up. And when I woke up I walked out on it. I walked out by the same door that I had walked in—without as much as a by-your-leave, sir!

Things take place instantaneously, but there's a long process to be gone through first. What you get when something happens is only the explosion, and the second before that the spark. But everything happens according to law—and with the full consent and collaboration of the whole cosmos. Before I could get up and explode the bomb had to be properly prepared, properly primed. After putting things in order for the bastards up above I had to be taken down from my high horse, had to be kicked around like a football, had to be stepped on, squelched, humiliated, fettered, manacled, made impotent as a jellyfish. All my life I have never wanted for friends, but at this particular period they seemed to spring up around me like mushrooms. I never had a moment to myself. If I went home of a night, hoping to take a rest, somebody would be there waiting to see me. Sometimes a gang of them would be there and it didn't seem to make much difference whether I came or not. Each set of friends I made despised the other set. Stanley, for example, despised the whole lot. Ulric too was rather scornful of the others. He had just come back from Europe after an absence of several years. We hadn't seen much of each other since boyhood and then one day, quite by accident, we met on the street. That day was an important day in my life because it opened up a new world to me, a world I had often dreamed about but never hoped to see. I remember vividly that we were standing on the corner of Sixth Avenue and 49th Street toward dusk. I remember it because it seemed utterly incongruous to be listening to a man talking about Mt. Aetna and Vesuvius and Capri and Pompeii and Morocco and Paris on the corner of Sixth Avenue and 49th Street, Manhattan. I remember the way he looked about as he talked, like a man who hadn't quite realized what he was in for but who vaguely sensed that he had made a horrible mistake in returning. His eyes seemed to be saying all the time—this has no value, no value whatever. He didn't say that, however, but just this over and over: "I'm sure you'd like it! I'm sure it's just the place for you." When he left me I was in a daze. I couldn't get hold of him again quickly enough. I wanted to hear it all over again, in minute detail. Nothing that I had read about Europe seemed to match this glowing account from my friend's own lips. It seemed all the more miraculous to me in that we had sprung out of the same environment. He had managed it because he had rich friends—and because he knew how to save his money. I had never known any one who was rich, who had traveled, who had money in the bank. All my friends were like myself, drifting from day to day, and never a thought for the future. O'Mara, yes, he had traveled a bit, almost all over the world—but as a bum, or else in the army, which was even worse than being a bum. My friend Ulric was the first fellow I had ever met who I could truly say had traveled. And he knew how to talk about his experiences.

As a result of that chance encounter on the street we met frequently thereafter, for a period of several months. He used to call for me in the evening after dinner and we would stroll through the park which was nearby. What a thirst I had! Every slightest detail about the other world fascinated me. Even now, years and years since, even now, when I know

Paris like a book, his picture of Paris is still before my eyes, still vivid, still real. Sometimes, after a rain, riding swiftly through the city in a taxi, I catch fleeting glimpses of this Paris he described; just momentary snatches, as in passing the Tuileries, perhaps, or a glimpse of Montmartre, of the Sacre Coeur, through the Rue Laffitte, in the last flush of twilight. *Just a Brooklyn boy!* That was an expression he used sometimes when he felt ashamed of his inability to express himself more adequately. And I was just a Brooklyn boy, too, which is to say one of the last and the least of men. But as I wander about, rubbing elbows with the world, seldom it happens that I meet any one who can describe so lovingly and faith- fully what he has seen and felt. Those nights in Prospect Park with my old friend Ulric are responsible, more than anything else, for my being here today. Most of the places he described for me I have still to see; some of them I shall perhaps never see. But they live inside me, warm and vivid, just as he created them in our rambles through the park.

Interwoven with this talk of the other world was the whole body and texture of Lawrence's work. Often, when the park had long been emptied, we were still sitting on a bench discussing the nature of Lawrence's ideas. Looking back on these discussions now I can see how confused I was, how pitifully ignorant of the true meaning of Lawrence's words. Had I really understood, my life could never have taken the course it did. Most of us live the greater part of our lives submerged. Certainly in my own case I can say that not until I left America did I emerge above the surface. Perhaps America had nothing to do with it, but the fact remains that I did not open my eyes wide and full and clear until I struck Paris. And perhaps that was only because I had renounced America, renounced my past.

My friend Kronski used to twit me about my "euphorias." It was a sly way he had of reminding me, when I was extraordinarily gay, that the morrow would find me depressed. It was true. I had nothing but ups and downs. Long stretches of gloom and melancholy followed by extravagant bursts of gaiety, of trancelike inspiration. Never a level in which I was myself. It sounds strange to say so, yet I was never myself. I was either anonymous or the person called Henry Miller raised to the nth degree. In the latter mood, for instance, I could spill out a whole book to Hymie while riding a trolley car. Hymie, who never sus- pected me of being anything but a good employment manager. I can see his eyes now as he looked at me one night when I was in one of my states of "euphoria." We had board- ed the trolley at the Brooklyn Bridge to go to some flat in Greenpoint where a couple of trollops were waiting to receive us. Hymie had started to talk to me in his usual way about his wife's ovaries. In the first place he didn't know precisely what ovaries meant and so I was explaining it to him in crude and simple fashion. In the midst of my explanation it suddenly seemed so profoundly tragic and ridiculous that Hymie shouldn't know what ovaries were that I became drunk, as drunk I mean as if I had had a quart of whisky under my belt. From the idea of diseased ovaries there germinated in one lightning-like flash a sort of tropical growth made up of the most heterogeneous assortment of odds and ends in the midst of which, securely lodged, tenaciously lodged, I might say, were Dante and Shakespeare. At the same instant I also suddenly recalled my whole private train of thought which had begun about the middle of the Brooklyn Bridge and which suddenly the word "ovaries" had broken. I realized that everything Hymie had said up till the word "ovaries" had sieved through me like sand. What I had begun, in the middle of the Brooklyn Bridge, was what I had begun time and time again in the past, usually when walking to my father's shop, a performance which was repeated day in and day out as if in a trance. What I had begun, in brief, was a book of the hours, of the tedium and monotony of my life in the midst of a ferocious activity. Not for years had I thought of this book which I used to write every day on my way from Delancey Street to Murray Hill. But going over the bridge, the sun setting, the skyscrapers gleaming like phosphorescent cadavers, the remembrance of the past set in... remembrance of going back and forth over the bridge, going to a job which was death, returning to a home which was a morgue, memorizing *Faust* looking down into the cemetery, spitting into the cemetery from the elevated train, the same guard on the platform every morning, an imbecile, the other imbeciles reading their newspapers, new skyscrapers going up, new tombs to work in and die in, the boats passing below, the Fall River Line, the Albany Day Line, why am I going to work, what will I do tonight, the warm cunt beside me and can I work my knuckles into her groin, run away and become a cowboy, try Alaska, the gold mines, get off and turn around, don't die yet, wait another day, a stroke of luck, river, end it, down, down, like a corkscrew, head and shoulders in the mud, legs free; fish will come and bite, tomorrow a new life, where, anywhere, why begin again, the same thing everywhere, death, death is the solution, but don't die yet, wait another day, a stroke of luck, a new face, a new friend, millions of chances, you're too young yet, you're melancholy, you don't die yet, wait another day, a stroke of luck, fuck anyway, and so on over the bridge into the glass shed, everybody glued together, worms, ants, crawling out of a dead tree and their thoughts crawling out the same way.... Maybe, being up high between the two shores, suspended above the traffic, above life and death, on each side the high tombs, tombs blazing with dying sunlight, the river flowing heedlessly, flowing on like time itself, maybe each time I passed up there, something was tugging away at me, urging me to take it in, to announce myself; anyway each time I passed on high I was truly alone and whenever that happened the book commenced to write itself, screaming the things which I never breathed, the thoughts I never uttered, the conversations I never held, the hopes, the dreams, the delusions I never admitted. If this then was the true self it was marvelous, and what's more it seemed never to change but always to pick up from the last stop, to continue in the same vein, a vein I had struck when I was a child and went down in the street for the first time alone and there frozen into the dirty ice of the gutter lay a dead cat, the first time I had looked at death and grasped it. From that moment I knew what it was to be isolated: every object, every living thing and every dead thing led its independent existence. My thoughts too led an independent existence. Suddenly, looking at Hymie and thinking of that strange word "ovaries," now stranger than any word in my whole vocabulary, this feeling of icy isolation came over me and Hymie sitting beside me was a bullfrog, absolutely a bullfrog and nothing more. I was jumping from the bridge head first, down into the primeval ooze, the legs clear and waiting for a bite; like that Satan had plunged through the heavens, through the solid core of the earth, head down and ramming through to the very hub of the earth, the darkest,' densest, hottest pit of hell. I was walking through the Mojave Desert and the man beside me was waiting for nightfall in order to fall on me and slay me. I was walking again in Dreamland and a man was walking above me on a tightrope and above him a man was sitting in an airplane spelling letters of smoke in the sky. The woman hanging on my arm was pregnant and in six or seven years the thing she was carrying inside her would be able to read the letters in the sky and he or she or it would know that it was a cigarette and later would smoke the cigarette, perhaps a package a day. In the womb nails formed on every finger, every toe; you could stop right there, at a toenail, the tiniest toenail imaginable, and you could break your head over it, trying to figure it out. On one side of the ledger are the books man has written, containing such a hodgepodge of wisdom and nonsense, of truth and falsehood, that if one lived to be as old as Methuselah one couldn't disentangle the mess; on the other side of the ledger things like toenails, hair, teeth, blood, *ovaries*, if you will, all incalculable and all written in another kind of ink, in another script, an incomprehensible, undecipherable script. The bullfrog eyes were trained on me like two collar buttons stuck in cold fat; they were stuck in the cold sweat of the primeval ooze. Each collar button was an ovary that had come unglued, an illustration out of the dictionary without benefit of lucubration; lackluster in the cold yellow fat of the eyeball each buttoned ovary produced a subterranean chill, the skating rink of hell where men stood upside down in the ice, the legs free and waiting for a bite. Here Dante walked unaccompanied, weighed down by his vision, and through endless circles gradually moving heavenward to be enthroned in his work. Here Shakespeare with smooth brow fell into the bottomless reverie of rage to emerge in elegant quartos and innuendoes. A glaucous frost of non-comprehension swept clear by gales of laughter. From the hub of the bullfrog's eye radiated clean white spokes of sheer lucidity not to be annotated or categorized, not to be numbered or defined, but revolving sightless in kaleidoscopic change. Hymie the bullfrog was an ovarian spud generated in the high passage between two shores: for him the skyscrapers had been built, the wilderness cleared, the Indians massacred, the buffaloes exterminated; for him the twin cities had been joined by the Brooklyn Bridge, the caissons sunk, the cables strung from tower to tower; for him men sat upside down in the sky writing words in fire and smoke; for him the anesthetic was invented and the high forceps and the Big Bertha which could destroy what the eye could not see; for him the molecule was broken down and the atom revealed to be without substance; for him each night the stars were swept with telescopes and worlds coming to birth photographed in the act of gestation; for him the barriers of time and space were set at nought and all movement, be it the flight of birds or the revolution of the planets, expounded irrefutably and incontestably by the high priests of the depossessed cosmos. Then, as in the middle of the bridge, in the middle of a walk, in the middle always, whether of a book, a conversation, or making love, it was borne in on me again that I had never done what I wanted and out of not doing what I wanted to do there grew up inside me this creation which was nothing but an obsessional plant, a sort of coral growth, which was expropriating everything, including life itself, until life itself became this which was denied but which constantly asserted itself, making life and killing life at the same time. I could see it going on after death, like hair growing on a corpse, people saying "death" but the hair still testifying to life, and finally no death but this life of hair and nails, the body gone, the spirit quenched, but in the death something still alive, expropriating space, causing time, creating endless movement. Through love this might happen, or sorrow, or being born with a club foot; the cause nothing, the event everything. *In the beginning was the Word....* Whatever this was, *the Word,* disease or creation, it was still running rampant; it would run on and on, outstrip time and space, outlast the angels, unseat God, unhook the universe. Any word contained all words—for him who had become detached through love or sorrow or whatever the cause. In every word the current ran back to the beginning which was lost and which would never be found again since there was neither beginning nor end but only that which expressed itself in beginning and end. So, on the ovarian trolley there was this voyage of man and bullfrog composed of identical stuff, neither better nor less than Dante but infi-

nitely different, the one not knowing precisely the meaning of anything, the other knowing too precisely the meaning of everything, hence both lost and confused through beginnings and endings, finally to be deposited at Java or India Street, Green-point, there to be
carried back into the current of life, so-called, by a couple of sawdust molls with twitching ovaries of the well-known gastropod variety.

What strikes me now as the most wonderful proof of my fitness, or unfitness, for the
times is the fact that nothing people were writing or talking about had any real interest for
me. Only the object haunted me, the separate, detached, insignificant *thing*. It might be
a part of the human body or a staircase in a vaudeville house; it might be a smokestack or
a button I had found in the gutter. Whatever it was it enabled me to open up, to surrender, to attach my signature. To the life about me, to the people who made up the world I
knew, I could not attach my signature. I was as definitely outside their world as a cannibal is outside the bounds of civilized society. I was filled with a perverse love of the thing-
in-itself—not a philosophic attachment, but a passionate, desperately passionate hunger,
as if in this discarded, worthless *thing* which everyone ignored there was contained the
secret of my own regeneration.

Living in the midst of a world where there was a plethora of the new I attached
myself to the old. In every object there was a minute particle which particularly claimed
my attention. I had a microscopic eye for the blemish, for the grain of ugliness which to
me constituted the sole beauty of the object. Whatever set the object apart, or made it
unserviceable, or gave it a date, attracted and endeared it to me. If this was perverse it was
also healthy, considering that I was not destined to belong to this world which was spring-
ing up about me. Soon I too would become like these objects which I venerated, a thing
apart, a non-useful member of society. I was definitely dated, that was certain. And yet I
was able to amuse, to instruct, to nourish. But never to be accepted, in a genuine way.
When I wished to, when I had the itch, I could single out any man, in any stratum of society, and make him listen to me. I could hold him spellbound, if I chose, but, like a magician, or a sorcerer, only as long as the spirit was in me. At bottom I sensed in others a distrust, an uneasiness, an antagonism which, because it was instinctive, was irremediable. I
should have been a clown; it would have afforded me the widest range of expression. But
I underestimated the profession. Had I become a clown, or even a vaudeville entertainer,
I would have been famous. People would have appreciated me precisely because they
would not have understood; but they would have understood that I was not to be understood. That would have been a relief, to say the least.

It was always a source of amazement to me how easily people could become riled just
listening to me talk. Perhaps my speech was somewhat extravagant, though often it happened when I was holding myself in with main force. The turn of a phrase, the choice of
an unfortunate adjective, the facility with which the words came to my lips, the allusions
to subjects which were taboo—everything conspired to set me off as an outlaw, as an
enemy of society. No matter how well things began sooner or later they smelled me out.
If I were modest and humble, for example, then I was too modest, too humble. If I were
gay and spontaneous, bold and reckless, then I was too free, too gay. I could never get
myself quite *au point* with the individual I happened to be talking to. If it were not a question of life and death—everything was life and death to me then—if it was merely a question of passing a pleasant evening at the home of some acquaintance, it was the same
thing. There were vibrations emanating from me, overtones and undertones, which

charged the atmosphere un-pleasantly. Perhaps the whole evening they had been amused by my stories, perhaps I had them in stitches, as it often happened, and everything seemed to augur well. But sure as fate something was bound to happen before the evening came to a close, some vibration set loose which made the chandelier ring or which reminded some sensitive soul of the pisspot under the bed. Even while the laughter was still dying off the venom was beginning to make itself felt. "Hope to see you again some time," they would say, but the wet, limp hand which was extended would belie the words.

Persona non grata! Jesus, how clear it seems to me now! No pick and choice possible: I had to take what was to hand and learn to like it. I had to learn to live with the scum, to swim like a sewer rat or be drowned. If you elect to join the herd you are immune. To be accepted and appreciated you must nullify yourself, make yourself indistinguishable from the herd. You may dream, if you dream alike. But if you dream something different you are not in America, of America American, but a Hottentot in Africa, or a Kalmuck, or a chimpanzee. The moment you have a "different" thought you cease to be an American. And the moment you become something different you find yourself in Alaska or Easter Island or Iceland.

Am I saying this with rancor, with envy, with malice? Perhaps. Perhaps I regret not having been able to become an American. *Perhaps.* In my zeal now, which is again *American,* I am about to give birth to a monstrous edifice, a skyscraper, which will last undoubtedly long after the other skyscrapers have vanished, but which will vanish too when that which produced it disappears. Everything American will disappear one day, more completely than that which was Greek, or Roman, or Egyptian. This is *one* of the ideas which pushed me outside the warm, comfortable bloodstream where, buffaloes all, we once grazed in peace. An idea that has caused me infinite sorrow, for not to belong to something enduring is the last agony. But I am not a buffalo and I have no desire to be one, I am not even a *spiritual* buffalo. I have slipped away to rejoin an older stream of consciousness, a race antecedent to the buffaloes, a race that will survive the buffalo.

All things, all objects animate or inanimate that are *different,* are veined with ineradicable traits. What is me is ineradicable, because it is different. This is a skyscraper, as I said, but it is *different* from the usual skyscraper a l'americaine. In this skyscraper there are no elevators, no seventy-third-story windows to jump from. If you get tired of climbing you are shit out of luck. There is no slot directory in the main lobby. If you are searching for somebody you will have to search. If you want a drink you will have to go out and get it; there are no soda fountains in this building, and no cigar stores, and no telephone booths. All the other skyscrapers have what you want! this one contains nothing but what I want, what I like. And somewhere in this skyscraper Valeska has her being, and we're going to get to her when the spirit moves me. For the time being she's all right, Valeska, seeing as how she's six feet under and by now perhaps picked clean by the worms. When she was in the flesh she was picked clean too, by the human worms who have no respect for anything which has a different tint, a different odor.

The sad thing about Valeska was the fact that she had nigger blood in her veins. It was depressing for everybody around her. She made you aware of it whether you wished to be or no. The nigger blood, as I say, and the fact that her mother was a trollop. The mother was white, of course. Who the father was nobody knew, not even Valeska herself.

Everything was going along smoothly until the day an officious little Jew from the vice-president's office happened to espy her. He was horrified, so he informed me confidentially, to think that I had employed a colored person as my secretary. He spoke as though she might contaminate the messengers. The next day I was put on the carpet. It was exactly as though I had committed sacrilege. Of course I pretended that I hadn't observed anything unusual about her, except that she was extremely intelligent and extremely capable. Finally the president himself stepped in. There was a short interview between him and Valeska during which he very diplomatically proposed to give her a better position in Havana. No talk of the blood taint. Simply that her services had been altogether remarkable and that they would like to promote her—to Havana. Valeska came back to the office in a rage. When she was angry she was magnificent. She said she wouldn't budge. Steve Romero and Hymie were there at the time and we all went out to dinner together. During the course of the evening we got a bit tight. Valeska's tongue was wagging. On the way home she told me that she was going to put up a fight; she wanted to know if it would endanger my job. I told her quietly that if she were fired I would quit too. She pretended not to believe it at first. I said I meant it, that I didn't care what happened. She seemed to be unduly impressed; she took me by the two hands and she held them very gently, the tears rolling down her cheeks.

That was the beginning of things. I think it was the very next day that I slipped her a note saying that I was crazy about her. She read the note sitting opposite me and when she was through she looked me square in the eye and said she didn't believe it. But we went to dinner again that night and we had more to drink and we danced and while we were dancing she pressed herself against me lasciviously. It was just the time, as luck would have it, that my wife was getting ready to have another abortion. I was telling Valeska about it as we danced. On the way home she suddenly said—"Why don't you let me lend you a hundred dollars?" The next night I brought her home to dinner and I let her hand the wife the hundred dollars. I was amazed how well the two of them got along. Before the evening was over it was agreed upon that Valeska would come to the house the day of the abortion and take care of the kid. The day came and I gave Valeska the afternoon off. About an hour after she had left I suddenly decided that I would take the afternoon off also. I started toward the burlesque on Fourteenth Street. When I was about a block from the theater I suddenly changed my mind. It was just the thought that if anything happened—if the wife were to kick off—I wouldn't feel so damned good having spent the afternoon at the burlesque. I walked around a bit, in and out of the penny arcades, and then I started homeward.

It's strange how things turn out. Trying to amuse the kid I suddenly remembered a trick my grandfather had shown me when I was a child. You take the dominoes and you make tall battleships out of them; then you gently pull the tablecloth on which the battleships are floating until they come to the edge of the table when suddenly you give a brisk tug and they fall onto the floor. We tried it over and over again, the three of us, until the kid got so sleepy that she toddled off to the next room and fell asleep. The dominoes were lying all over the floor and the tablecloth was on the floor too. Suddenly Valeska was leaning against the table, her tongue halfway down my throat, my hand between her legs. As I laid her back on the table she twined her legs around me. I could feel one of the dominoes under my feet—part of the fleet that we had destroyed a dozen times or more. I thought of my grandfather sitting on the bench, the way he had warned my mother one day that I was too young to be reading so much, the pensive look in his eyes as he pressed the hot iron against the wet seam of a coat; I thought of the attack on San Juan Hill which the Rough Riders had made, the picture of Teddy charging at the head of his volunteers in the big book which I used to read beside the workbench; I thought of the battleship "Maine" that floated over my bed in the little room with the iron-barred window, and of Admiral Dewey and of Schley and Sampson; I thought of the trip to the Navy Yard which I never made because on the way my father suddenly remembered that we had to call on the doctor that afternoon and when I left the doctor's office I didn't have any more tonsils nor any more faith in human beings.... We had hardly finished when the bell rang and it was my wife coming home from the slaughterhouse. I was still buttoning my fly as I went through the hall to open the gate. She was as white as flour. She looked as though she'd never be able to go through another one. We put her to bed and then we gathered up the dominoes and put the tablecloth back on the table. Just the other night in a *bistro,* as I was going to the toilet, I happened to pass two old fellows playing dominoes. I had to stop a moment and pick up a domino. The feeling of it immediately brought back the battleships, the clatter they made when they fell on the floor. And with the battleships my lost tonsils and my faith in human beings gone. So that every time I walked over the Brooklyn Bridge and looked down toward the Navy Yard I felt as though my guts were dropping out. Way up there, suspended between the two shores, I felt always as though I were hanging over a void; up there everything that had ever happened to me seemed unreal, and worse than unreal—*unnecessary.* Instead of joining me to life, to men, to the activity of men, the bridge seemed to break all connections. If I walked toward the one shore or the other it made no difference: either way was hell. Somehow I had managed to sever my connection with the world that human hands and human minds were creating. Perhaps my grandfather was right, perhaps I was spoiled in the bud by the books I read. But it is ages since books have claimed me. For a long time now I have practically ceased to read. But the taint is still there. Now people are books to me. I read them from cover to cover and toss them aside. I devour them, one after the other. And the more I read, the more insatiable I become. There is no limit to it. There could be no end, and there was none, until inside me a bridge began to form which united me again with the current of life from which as a child I had been separated.

A terrible sense of desolation. It hung over me for years. If I were to believe in the stars I should have to believe that I was completely under the reign of Saturn. Everything that happened to me happened too late to mean much to me. It was even so with my birth. Slated for Christmas I was born a half hour too late. It always seemed to me that I was meant to be the sort of individual that one is destined to be by virtue of being born on the 25th day of December. Admiral Dewey was born on that day and so was Jesus Christ... perhaps Krishnamurti too, for all I know. Anyway that's the sort of guy I was intended to be. But due to the fact that my mother had a clutching womb, that she held me in her grip like an octopus, I came out under another configuration—with a bad setup in other words. They say—the astrologers, I mean—that it will get better and better for me as I go on; the future, in fact, is supposed to be quite glorious. But what do I care about the future? It would have been better if my mother had tripped on the stairs the morning of the 25th of December and broken her neck: that would have given me a fair start! When I try to think, therefore, of where the break occurred I keep putting it back further and further, until there is no other way of accounting for it than by the retarded hour of birth. Even my mother, with her caustic tongue, seemed to understand it somewhat. "Always dragging behind, like a cow's tail"—that's how she characterized me. But is it my fault that she held me locked inside her until the hour had passed? Destiny had prepared me to be such and such a person; the stars were in the right conjunction and I was right with the stars and kicking to get out. But I had no choice about the mother who was to deliver me. Perhaps I was lucky not to have been born an idiot, considering all the circumstances. One thing seems clear, however—and this is a hangover from the 25th—that I was born with a crucifixion complex. That is, to be more precise, I was born a fanatic. *Fanatic!* I remember that word being hurled at me from early childhood on. By my parents especially. What is a fanatic? One who believes passionately and acts desperately upon what he believes. I was always believing in something and so getting into trouble. The more my hands were slapped the more firmly I believed. I *believed*—and the rest of the world did not! If it were only a question of enduring punishment one could go on believing till the end; but the way of the world is more insidious than that. Instead of being punished you are undermined, hollowed out, the ground taken from under your feet. It isn't even treachery, what I have in mind. Treachery is understandable and combatable. No, it is something worse, something *less* than treachery. It's a negativism that causes you to overreach yourself. You are perpetually spending your energy in the act of balancing yourself. You are seized with a sort of spiritual vertigo, you totter on the brink, your hair stands on end, you can't believe that beneath your feet lies an immeasurable abyss. It comes about through excess of enthusiasm, through a passionate desire to embrace people, to show them your love. The more you reach out toward the world the more the world retreats. Nobody wants real love, real hatred. Nobody wants you to put your hand in his sacred entrails—that's only for the priest in the hour of sacrifice. While you live, while the blood's still warm, you are to pretend that there is no such thing as blood and no such thing as a skeleton beneath the covering of flesh. *Keep off the grass!* That's the motto by which people live.

If you continue this balancing at the edge of the abyss long enough you become very very adept: no matter which way you are pushed you always right yourself. Being in constant trim you develop a ferocious gaiety, an unnatural gaiety, I might say. There are only two peoples in the world today who understand the meaning of such a statement—the Jews and the Chinese. If it happens that you are neither of these you find yourself in a strange predicament. You are always laughing at the wrong moment; you are considered cruel and heartless when in reality you are only tough and durable. But if you would laugh when others laugh and weep when they weep then you must be prepared to die as they die and live as they live. That means to be right and to get the worst of it at the same time. It means to be dead while you are alive and alive only when you are dead. In this company the world always wears a normal aspect, even under the most abnormal conditions. Nothing is right or wrong but thinking makes it so. You no longer believe in reality but in thinking. And when you are pushed off the dead end your thoughts go with you and they are of no use to you.

In a way, in a profound way, I mean, Christ was never pushed off the dead end. At the moment when he was tottering and swaying, as if by a great recoil, this negative backwash rolled up and stayed his death. The whole negative impulse of humanity seemed to coil up into a monstrous inert mass to create the human integer, the figure one, one and indivisible. There was a resurrection which is inexplicable unless we accept the fact that men have always been willing and ready to deny their own destiny. The earth rolls on, the stars roll on, but men, the great body of men which makes up the world, are caught in the image of the one and only one.

If one isn't crucified, like Christ, if one manages to survive, to go on living above and beyond the sense of desperation and futility, then another curious thing happens. It's as though one had actually died and actually been resurrected again; one lives a supernormal life, like the Chinese. That is to say, one is unnaturally gay, unnaturally healthy, unnaturally indifferent. The tragic sense is gone: one lives on like a flower, a rock, a tree, one with Nature and against Nature at the same time. If your best friend dies you don't even bother to go to the funeral; if a man is run down by a streetcar right before your eyes you keep on walking just as though nothing had happened; if a war breaks out you let your friends go to the front but you yourself take no interest in the slaughter. And so on and so on. Life becomes a spectacle and, if you happen to be an artist, you record the passing show. Loneliness is abolished, because all values, your own included, are destroyed. Sympathy alone flourishes, but it is not a human sympathy, a limited sympathy—it is something monstrous and evil. You care so little that you can afford to sacrifice yourself for anybody or anything. At the same time your interest, your curiosity, develops at an outrageous pace. This too is suspect, since it is capable of attaching you to a collar button just as well as to a cause. There is no fundamental, unalterable difference between things: all is flux, all is perishable. The surface of your being is constantly crumbling; within however you grow hard as a diamond. And perhaps it is this hard, magnetic core inside you which attracts others to you willy-nilly. One thing is certain, that when you die and are resurrected you belong to the earth and whatever is of the earth is yours inalienably. You become an anomaly of nature, a being without shadow; you will never die again but only pass away like the phenomena about you.

Nothing of this which I am now recording was known to me at the time that I was going through the great change. Everything I endured was in the nature of a preparation for that moment when, putting on my hat one evening, I walked out of the office, out of my hitherto private life, and sought the woman who was to liberate me from a living death. In the light of this I look back now upon my nocturnal rambles through the streets of New York, the white nights when I walked in my sleep and saw the city in which I was born as one sees things in a mirage. Often it was O'Rourke, the company detective, whom I accompanied through the silent streets. Often the snow was on the ground and the air chill and frosty. And O'Rourke talking interminably about thefts, about murders, about love, about human nature, about the Golden Age. He had a habit, when he was well launched upon a subject, of stopping suddenly in the middle of the street and planting his heavy foot between mine so that I couldn't budge. And then, seizing the lapel of my coat, he would bring his face to mine and talk into my eyes, each word boring in like the turn of a gimlet. I can see again the two of us standing in the middle of a street at four in the morning, the wind howling, the snow blowing down, and O'Rourke oblivious of everything but the story he had to get off his chest. Always as he talked I remember taking in the surroundings out of the corner of my eye, being aware not of what he was saying but of the two of us standing in Yorkville or on Allen Street or on Broadway. Always it seemed a little crazy to me, the earnestness with which he recounted his banal murder stories in the midst of the greatest muddle of architecture that man had ever created. While he was talking about fingerprints I might be taking stock of a coping or a cornice on a little red brick building just back of his black hat; I would get to thinking of the day the cornice had been installed, who might be the man who had designed it and why had he made it so ugly, so like every other lousy, rotten cornice which we had passed from the East Side up to Harlem and beyond Harlem, if we wanted to push on, beyond New York, beyond the Mississippi, beyond the Grand Canyon, beyond the Mojave Desert, everywhere in America where there are buildings for man and woman. It seemed absolutely crazy to me that each day of my life I had to sit and listen to other people's stories, the banal tragedies of poverty and distress, of love and death, of yearning and disillusionment. If, as it happened, there came to me each day at least fifty men, each pouring out his tale of woe, and with each one I had to be silent and "receive," it was only natural that at some point along the line I had to close my ears, had to harden my heart. The tiniest little morsel was sufficient for me; I could chew on it and digest it for days and weeks. Yet I was obliged to sit there and be inundated, to get out at night again and receive more, to sleep listening, to dream listening. They streamed in from all over the world, from every stratum of society, speaking a thousand different tongues, worshiping different gods, obeying different laws and customs. The tale of the poorest among them was a huge tome, and yet if each and every one were written out at length it might all be compressed to the size of the Ten Commandments, it might all be recorded on the back of a postage stamp, like the Lord's Prayer. Each day I was so stretched that my hide seemed to cover the whole world; and when I was alone, when I was no longer obliged to listen, I shrank to the size of a pinpoint. The greatest delight, and it was a rare one, was to walk the streets alone... to walk the streets at night when no one was abroad and to reflect on the silence that surrounded me. Millions lying on their backs, dead to the world, their mouths wide open and nothing but snores emanating from them. Walking amidst the craziest architecture ever invented, wondering why and to what end, if every day from these wretched hovels or magnificent palaces there had to stream forth an army of men itching to unravel their tale of misery. In a year, reckoning it modestly, I received twenty-five thousand tales; in two years fifty thousand; in four years it would be a hundred thousand; in ten years I would be stark mad. Already I knew enough people to populate a good-sized town. What a town it would be, if only they could be gathered together! Would they want skyscrapers? Would they want museums? Would they want libraries? Would they too build sewers and bridges and tracks and factories? Would they make the same little cornices of tin, one like another, on, on, ad infinitum, from Battery Park to the Golden Bay? I doubt it. Only the lash of hunger could stir them. The empty belly, the wild look in the eye, the fear, the fear of worse, driving them on. One after the other, all the same, all goaded to desperation, out of the goad and whip of hunger building the loftiest skyscrapers, the most redoubtable dreadnoughts, making the finest steel, the flimsiest lace, the most delicate glassware. Walking with O'Rourke and hearing nothing but theft, arson, rape, homicide was like listening to a little motif out of a grand symphony. And just as one can whistle an air of Bach and be thinking of a woman he wants to sleep with, so, listening to O'Rourke, I would be thinking of the moment when he would stop talking and say "what'll you have to eat?" In the midst of the most gruesome murder I could think of the pork tenderloin which we would be sure to get at a certain place farther up the line, and wonder too what sort of vegetables they would have on the side to go with it, and whether I would order pie afterwards or a custard pudding. It was the same when I slept with my wife now and then; while she was moaning and gibbering I might be wondering if she had emptied the grounds in the coffee pot, because she had the bad habit of letting things slide—the *important* things, I mean. Fresh coffee was important—and fresh bacon with the eggs. If she were knocked up again that would be bad, serious in a way, but more important than that was fresh coffee in the morning and the smell of bacon and eggs. I could put up with heartbreaks and abortions and busted romances, but I had to have something under my belt to carry on, and I wanted something nourishing, something appetizing. I felt exactly like Jesus Christ would have felt if he had been taken down from the cross and not permitted to die in the flesh. I am sure that the shock of crucifixion would have been so great that he would have suffered a complete amnesia as regards humanity. I am certain that after his wounds had healed he wouldn't have given a damn about the tribulations of mankind but would have fallen with the greatest relish upon a fresh cup of coffee and a slice of toast, assuming he could have had it.

Whoever, through too great love, which is monstrous after all, dies of his misery, is born again to know neither love nor hate, but to enjoy. And this joy of living, because it is unnaturally acquired, is a poison which eventually vitiates the whole world. Whatever is created beyond the normal limits of human suffering, acts as a boomerang and brings about destruction. At night the streets of New York reflect the crucifixion and death of Christ. When the snow is on the ground and there is the utmost silence there comes out of the hideous buildings of New York a music of such sullen despair and bankruptcy as to make the flesh shrivel. No stone was laid upon another with love or reverence; no street was laid for dance or joy. One thing has been added to another in a mad scramble to fill the belly, and the streets smell of empty bellies and full bellies and bellies half full. The streets smell of a hunger which has nothing to do with love; they smell of the belly which is insatiable and of the creations of the empty belly which are null and void.

In this null and void, in this zero whiteness, I learned to enjoy a sandwich, or a collar button. I could study a cornice or a coping with the greatest curiosity while pretending to listen to a tale of human woe. I can remember the dates on certain buildings and the names of the architects who designed them. I can remember the temperature and the velocity of the wind, standing at a certain corner; the tale that accompanied it is gone. I can remember that I was even then remembering something else, and I can tell you what it was that I was then remembering, but of what use? There was one man in me which had died and all that was left were his remembrances; there was another man who was alive, and that man was supposed to be me, myself, but he was alive only as a tree is alive, or a rock, or a beast of the field. Just as the city itself had become a huge tomb in which men struggled to earn a decent death so my own life came to resemble a tomb which I was constructing out of my own death. I was walking around in a stone forest the center of which was chaos; sometimes in the dead center, in the very heart of chaos, I danced or drank myself silly, or I made love, or I befriended some one, or I planned a new life, but it was all chaos, all stone, and all hopeless and bewildering. Until the time when I would encounter a force strong enough to whirl me out of this mad stone forest no life would be possible for me nor could one page be written which would have meaning. Perhaps in reading this, one has still the impression of chaos but this is written from a live center and what is chaotic is merely peripheral, the tangential shreds, as it were, of a world which no longer concerns me. Only a few months ago I was standing in the streets of New York looking about me as years ago I had looked about me; again I found myself studying the architecture, studying the minute details which only the dislocated eye takes in. But this time it was like coming down from Mars. What race of men is this, I asked myself. What does it mean? And there was no remembrance of suffering or of the life that was snuffed out in the gutter, only that I was looking upon a strange and incomprehensible world, a world so removed from me that I had the sensation of belonging to another planet. From the top of the Empire State Building I looked down one night upon the city which I knew from below: there they were, in true perspective, the human ants with whom I had crawled, the human lice with whom I had struggled. They were moving along at a snail's pace, each one doubtless fulfilling his microcosmic destiny. In their fruitless desperation they had reared this colossal edifice which was their pride and boast. And from the topmost ceiling of this colossal edifice they had suspended a string of cages in which the imprisoned canaries warbled their senseless warble. At the very summit of their ambition there were these little spots of beings warbling away for dear life. In a hundred years, I thought to myself, perhaps they would be caging live human beings, gay, demented ones, who would sing about the world to come. Perhaps they would breed a race of warblers who would warble while the others worked. Perhaps in every cage there would be a poet or a musician so that life below might flow on unimpeded, one with the stone, one with the forest, a rippling creaking chaos of null and void. In a thousand years they might all be demented, workers and poets alike, and everything fall back to ruin as has happened again and again. Another thousand years, or five thousand, or ten thousand, exactly where I am standing now to survey the scene, a little boy may open a book in a tongue as yet unheard of and about this life now passing, a life which the man who wrote the book never experienced, a life with deducted form and rhythm, with beginning and end, and the boy on closing the book will think to himself what a great race the Americans were, what a marvelous life there had once been on this continent which he is now inhabiting. But no race to come, except perhaps the race of blind poets, will ever be able to imagine the seething chaos out of which this future history was composed. Chaos! A howling chaos! No need to choose a particular day. Any day of my life—back there—would suit. Every day of my life, my tiny, microcosmic life, was a reflection of the outer chaos. Let me think back.... At seven-thirty the alarm went off. I didn't bounce out of bed. I lay there till eight-thirty, trying to gain a little more sleep. Sleep—how could I sleep? In the back of my mind was an image of the office where I was already due. I could see Hymie arriving at eight sharp, the switchboard already buzzing with demands for help, the applicants climbing up the wide wooden stairway, the strong smell of camphor from the dressing room. Why get up and repeat yesterday's song and dance? As fast as I hired them they dropped out. Working my balls off and not even a clean shirt to wear. Mondays I got my allowance from the wife— carfare and lunch money. I was always in debt to her and she was in debt to the grocer, the butcher, the landlord, and so on. I couldn't be bothered shaving—there wasn't time enough. I put on the torn shirt, gobble up the breakfast, and borrow a nickel for the subway. If she were in a bad mood I would swindle the money from the newsdealer at the subway. I get to the office out of breath, an hour behind time and a dozen calls to make before I even talk to an applicant. While I make one call there are three other calls waiting to be answered. I use two telephones at once. The switchboard is buzzing. Hymie is sharpening his pencils between calls. McGovern the doorman is standing at my elbow to give me a word of advice about one of the applicants, probably a crook, who is trying to sneak back under a false name. Behind me the cards and ledgers containing the name of every applicant who had ever passed through the machine. The bad ones are starred in red ink; some of them have six aliases after their names. Meanwhile the room is crawling like a hive. The room stinks with sweat, dirty feet, old uniforms, camphor, Lysol, bad breaths. Half of them will have to be turned away—not that we don't need them, but that even under the worst conditions they just won't do. The man in front of my desk, standing at the rail with palsied hands and bleary eyes, is an ex-mayor of New York City. He's seventy now and would be glad to take anything. He has wonderful letters of recommendation, but we can't take any one over forty-five years of age. Forty-five in New York is the deadline. The telephone rings and it's a smooth secretary from the Y.M.C.A. Wouldn't I make an exception for a boy who has just walked into his office—a boy who was in the reformatory for a year or so. *What did he do?* He tried to rape his sister. An Italian, of course. O'Mara, my assistant, is putting an applicant through the third degree. He suspects him of being an epileptic. Finally he succeeds and for good measure the boy throws a fit right there in the office. One of the women faints. A beautiful looking young woman with a handsome fur around her neck is trying to persuade me to take her on. She's a whore clean through and I know if I put her on there'll be hell to pay. She wants to work in a certain building uptown—because it is near home, she says. Nearing lunch time and a few cronies are beginning to drop in. They sit around watching me work, as if it were a vaudeville performance. Kronski, the medical student, arrives; he says one of the boys I've just hired has Parkinson's disease. I've been so busy I haven't had a chance to go to the toilet. All the telegraph operators, all the managers, suffer from hemorrhoids, so O'Rourke tells me. He's been having electrical massages for the last two years, but nothing works. Lunch time and there are six of us at the table. Some one will have to pay for me, as usual. We gulp it down and rush back. More calls to make, more applicants to interview. The vice-president is raising hell because we can't keep the force up to normal. Every paper in New York and for twenty miles outside New York carries long ads demanding help. All the schools have been canvassed for part-time messengers. All the charity bureaus and relief societies have been invoked. They drop out like flies. Some of them don't even last an hour.

It's a human flour mill. And the saddest thing about it is that it's totally unnecessary. But that's not my concern. Mine is to do or die, as Kipling says. I plug on, through one victim after another, the telephone ringing like mad, the place smelling more and more vile, the holes getting bigger and bigger. Each one is a human being asking for a crust of bread; I have his height, weight, color, religion, education, experience, etc. All the data will go into a ledger to be filed alphabetically and then chronologically. Names and dates. Fingerprints too, if we had the time for it. So that what? So that the American people may enjoy the fastest form of communication known to man, so that they may sell their wares more quickly, so that the moment you drop dead in the street your next of kin may be apprised immediately, that is to say, within an hour, unless the messenger to whom the telegram is entrusted decides to throw up the job and throw the whole batch of telegrams in the garbage can. Twenty million Christmas blanks, all wishing you a Merry Christmas and a Happy New Year, from the directors and president and vice-president of the Cosmodemonic Telegraph Company, and maybe the telegram reads "Mother dying, come at once," but the clerk is too busy to notice the message and if you sue for damages, spiritual damages, there is a legal department trained expressly to meet such emergencies and so you can be sure that your mother will die and you will have a Merry Christmas and Happy New Year just the same. The clerk, of course, will be fired and after a month or so he will come back for a messenger's job and he will be taken on and put on the night shift near the docks where nobody will recognize him, and his wife will come with the brats to thank the general manager, or perhaps the vice-president himself, for the kindness and consideration shown. And then one day everybody will be heartily surprised that said mes-

senger robbed the till and O'Rourke will be asked to take the night train for Cleveland or
Detroit and to track him down even if it costs ten thousand dollars. And then the vice-
president will issue an order that no more Jews are to be hired, but after three or four days
he will let up a bit because there are nothing but Jews coming for the job. And because it's
getting so very tough and the timber so damned scarce I'm on the point of hiring a midget
from the circus and I probably would have hired him if he hadn't broken down and confessed that he was a she. And to make it worse Valeska takes "it" under her wing, takes "it"
home that night and under pretense of sympathy gives "it" a thorough examination,
including a vaginal exploration with the index finger of the right hand. And the midget
becomes very amorous and finally very jealous. It's a trying day and on the way home I
bump into the sister of one of my friends and she insists on taking me to dinner. After
dinner we go to a movie and in the dark we begin to play with each other and finally it
gets to such a point that we leave the movie and go back to the office where I lay her out
on the zinc-covered table in the dressing room. And when I get home, a little after midnight, there's a telephone call from Valeska and she wants me to hop into the subway
immediately and come to her house, it's very urgent. It's an hour's ride and I'm dead weary,
but she said it was urgent and so I'm on the way. And when I get there I meet her cousin,
a rather attractive young woman, who, according to her own story, had just had an affair
with a strange man because she was tired of being a virgin. And what was all the fuss
about? Why this, that in her eagerness she had forgotten to take the usual precautions, and
maybe now she was pregnant and then what? They wanted to know what I thought should
be done and I said: *"Nothing."* And then Valeska takes me aside and she asks me if I
wouldn't care to sleep with her cousin, to break her in, as it were, so that there wouldn't be
a repetition of that sort of thing.

The whole thing was cockeyed and we were all laughing hysterically and then we
began to drink—the only thing they had in the house was kummel and it didn't take much
to put us under. And then it got more cockeyed because the two of them began to paw me
and neither one would let the other do anything. The result was I undressed them both
and put them to bed and they fell asleep in each other's arms. And when I walked out,
toward five a.m., I discovered I didn't have a cent in my pocket and I tried to bum a nickel from a taxi driver but nothing doing so finally I took off my fur-lined overcoat and I
gave it to him—for a nickel. When I got home my wife was awake and sore as hell because
I had stayed out so long. We had a hot discussion and finally I lost my temper and I clout-
ed her and she fell on the floor and began to weep and sob and then the kid woke up and
hearing the wife bawling she got frightened and began to scream at the top of her lungs.
The girl upstairs came running down to see what was the matter. She was in her kimono
and her hair was hanging down her back. In the excitement she got close to me and things
happened without either of us intending anything to happen. We put the wife to bed with
a wet towel around her forehead and while the girl upstairs was bending over her I stood
behind her and lifting her kimono I got it into her and she stood there a long time talking a lot of foolish, soothing nonsense. Finally I climbed into bed with the wife and to my
utter amazement she began to cuddle up to me and without saying a word we locked
horns and we stayed that way until dawn. I should have been worn out, but instead I was
wide-awake, and I lay there beside her planning to take the day off and look up the whore
with the beautiful fur whom I was talking to earlier in the day. After that I began to think
about another woman, the wife of one of my friends who always twitted me about my

indifference. And then I began to think about one after the other—all those whom I had passed up for one reason or another—until finally I fell sound asleep and in the midst of it I had a wet dream. At seven-thirty the alarm went off as usual and as usual I looked at my torn shirt hanging over the chair and I said to myself what's the use and I turned over. At eight o'clock the telephone rang and it was Hymie. Better get over quickly, he said, because there's a strike on. And that's how it went, day after day, and there was no reason for it, except that the whole country was cockeyed and what I relate was going on everywhere, either on a smaller scale or a larger scale, but the same thing everywhere, because it was all chaos and all meaningless.

It went on and on that way, day in and day out for almost five solid years. The continent itself perpetually wracked by cyclones, tornadoes, tidal waves, floods, droughts, blizzards, heat waves, pests, strikes, hold-ups, assassinations, suicides... a continuous fever and torment, an eruption, a whirlpool. I was like a man sitting in a lighthouse: below me the wild waves, the rocks, the reefs, the debris of shipwrecked fleets. I could give the danger signal but I was powerless to avert catastrophe. I *breathed* danger and catastrophe. At times the sensation of it was so strong that it belched like fire from my nostrils. I longed to be free of it all and yet I was irresistibly attracted. I was violent and phlegmatic at the same time. I was like the lighthouse itself—secure in the midst of the most turbulent sea. Beneath me was solid rock, the same shelf of rock on which the towering skyscrapers were reared. My foundations went deep into the earth and the armature of my body was made of steel riveted with hot bolts. Above all I was an eye, a huge searchlight which scoured far and wide, which revolved ceaselessly, pitilessly. This eye so wide-awake seemed to have made all my other faculties dormant; all my powers were used up in the effort to see, to take in the drama of the world.

If I longed for destruction it was merely that this eye might be extinguished. I longed for an earthquake, for some cataclysm of nature which would plunge the lighthouse into the sea. I wanted a metamorphosis, a change to fish, to leviathan, to destroyer. I wanted the earth to open up, to swallow everything in one engulfing yawn. I wanted to see the city buried fathoms deep in the bosom of the sea. I wanted to sit in a cave and read by candlelight. I wanted that eye extinguished so that I might have a chance to know my own body, my own desires. I wanted to be alone for a thousand years in order to reflect on what I had seen and heard—*and in order to forget*. I wanted something of the earth which was not of man's doing, something absolutely divorced from the human of which I was surfeited. I wanted something purely terrestrial and absolutely divested of idea. I wanted to feel the blood running back into my veins, even at the cost of annihilation. I wanted to shake the stone and the light out of my system. I wanted the dark fecundity of nature, the deep well of the womb, silence, or else the lapping of the black waters of death. I wanted to be that night which the remorseless eye illuminated, a night diapered with stars and trailing comets. To be of night so frighteningly silent, so utterly incomprehensible and eloquent at the same time. Never more to speak or to listen or to think. To be englobed and encompassed and to encompass and to englobe at the same time. No more pity, no more tenderness. To be human only terrestrially, like a plant or a worm or a brook. To be decomposed, divested of light and stone, variable as the molecule, durable as the atom, heartless as the earth itself.

***

It was just about a week before Valeska committed suicide that I ran into Mara. The week or two preceding that event was a veritable nightmare. A series of sudden deaths and strange encounters with women. First of all there was Pauline Janowski, a little Jewess of sixteen or seventeen who was without a home and without friends or relatives. She came to the office looking for a job. It was toward closing time and I didn't have the heart to turn her down cold. For some reason or other I took it into my head to bring her home for dinner and if possible try to persuade the wife to put her up for a while. What attracted me to her was her passion for Balzac. All the way home she was talking to me about *Lost Illusions*. The car was packed and we were jammed so tight together that it didn't make any difference what we were talking about because we were both thinking of only one thing. My wife of course was stupefied to see me standing at the door with a beautiful young girl. She was polite and courteous in her frigid way but I could see immediately that it was no use asking her to put the girl up. It was about all she could do to sit through the dinner with us. As soon as we had finished she excused herself and went to the movies. The girl started to weep. We were still sitting at the table, the dishes piled up in front of us. I went over to her and I put my arms around her. I felt genuinely sorry for her and I was perplexed as to what to do for her. Suddenly she threw her arms around my neck and she kissed me passionately. We stood there a long while embracing each other and then I thought to myself no, it's a crime, and besides maybe the wife didn't go to the movies at all, maybe she'll be ducking back any minute. I told the kid to pull herself together, that we'd take a trolley ride somewhere. I saw the child's bank lying on the mantelpiece and I took it to the toilet and emptied it silently. There was only about seventy-five cents in it. We got on a trolley and went to the beach. Finally we found a deserted spot and we lay down in the sand. She was hysterically passionate and there was nothing to do but to do it. I thought she would reproach me afterwards, but she didn't. We lay there a while and she began talking about Balzac again. It seems she had ambitions to be a writer herself. I asked her what she was going to do. She said she hadn't the least idea. When we got up to go she asked me to put her on the highway. Said she thought she would go to Cleveland or some place. It was after midnight when I left her standing in front of a gas station. She had about thirty-five cents in her pocketbook. As I started homeward I began cursing my wife for the mean bitch that she was. I wished to Christ it was she whom I had left standing on the highway with no place to go to. I knew that when I got back she wouldn't even mention the girl's name.

I got back and she was waiting up for me. I thought she was going to give me hell again. But no, she had waited up because there was an important message from O'Rourke. I was to telephone him soon as I got home. However, I decided not to telephone. I decided to get undressed and go to bed. Just when I had gotten comfortably seeded the telephone rang. It was O'Rourke. There was a telegram for me at the office—he wanted to know if he should open it and read it to me. I said of course. The telegram was signed Monica. It was from Buffalo. Said she was arriving at the Grand Central in the morning with her mother's body. I thanked him and went back to bed. No questions from the wife. I lay there wondering what to do. If I were to comply with the request that would mean starting things all over again. I had just been thanking my stars that I had gotten rid of Monica. And now she was coming back with her mother's corpse. Tears and reconciliation. No, I didn't like the prospect at all. Supposing I didn't show up? What then? There was always somebody around to take care of a corpse. Especially if the bereaved were an attractive young blonde with sparkling blue eyes. I wondered if she'd go back to her job in the restaurant. If she hadn't known Greek and Latin I would never have been mixed up with her. But my curiosity got the better of me. And then she was so goddamned poor, that too got me. Maybe it wouldn't have been so bad if her hands hadn't smelled greasy. That was the fly in the ointment—the greasy hands. I remember the first night I met her and we strolled through the park. She was ravishing to look at, and she was alert and intelligent. It was just the time when women were wearing short skirts and she wore them to advantage. I used to go to the restaurant night after night just to watch her moving around, watch her bending over to serve or stooping down to pick up a fork. And with the beautiful legs and the bewitching eyes a marvelous line about Homer, with the pork and sauerkraut a verse of Sappho's, the Latin conjugations, the odes of Pindar, with the dessert perhaps *The Rubaiyat* or *Cynara*. But the greasy hands and the frowsy bed in the boarding house opposite the marketplace—Whew! I couldn't stomach it. The more I shunned her the more clinging she became. Ten-page letters about love with footnotes on *Thus Spake Zarathustra*. And then suddenly silence and me congratulating myself heartily. No, I couldn't bring myself to go to the Grand Central Station in the morning. I rolled over and I fell sound asleep. In the morning I would get the wife to telephone the office and say I was ill. I hadn't been ill now for over a week—it was coming to me.

At noon I find Kronski waiting for me outside the office. He wants me to have lunch with him... there's an Egyptian girl he wants me to meet. The girls turns out to be a Jewess, but she came from Egypt and she looks like an Egyptian. She's hot stuff and the two of us are working on her at once. As I was supposed to be ill I decided not to return to the office but to take a stroll through the East Side. Kronski was going back to cover me up. We shook hands with the girl and we each went our separate ways. I headed toward the river where it was cool, having forgotten about the girl almost immediately. I sat on the edge of the pier with my legs dangling over the stringpiece. A scow passed with a load of red bricks. Suddenly Monica came to my mind. Monica arriving at the Grand Central Station with a corpse. A corpse f. o. b. New York! It seemed so incongruous and ridiculous that I burst out laughing. What had she done with it? Had she checked it or had she left it on a siding? No doubt she was cursing me out roundly. I wondered what she would really think if she could have imagined me sitting there at the dock with my legs dangling over the stringpiece. It was warm and sultry despite the breeze that was blowing off the river. I began to snooze. As I dozed off Pauline came to my mind. I imagined her walking along the highway with her hand up. She was a brave kid, no doubt about it. Funny that she didn't seem to worry about getting knocked up. Maybe she was so desperate she didn't care. And Balzac! That too was highly incongruous. Why Balzac? Well, that was her affair. Anyway she'd have enough to eat with, until she met another guy. But a kid like that thinking about becoming a writer! Well, why not? Everybody had illusions of one sort or another. Monica too wanted to be a writer. Everybody was becoming a writer. A writer! Jesus, how futile it seemed!

I dozed off... When I woke up I had an erection. The sun seemed to be burning right into my fly. I got up and I washed my face at the drinking fountain. It was still as hot and sultry as ever. The asphalt was soft as mush, the flies were biting, the garbage was rotting in the gutter. I walked about between the pushcarts and looked at things with an empty eye. I had a sort of lingering hard on all the while, but no definite object in mind. It was only when I got back to Second Avenue that I suddenly remembered the Egyptian Jewess from lunch time. I remembered her saying that she lived over the Russian restaurant near Twelfth Street. Still I hadn't any definite idea of what I was going to do. Just browsing about, killing time. My feet nevertheless were dragging me northward, toward Fourteenth Street. When I got abreast of the Russian restaurant I paused a moment and then I ran up the stairs three at a time. The hall door was open. I climbed up a couple of flights scanning the names on the doors. She was on the top floor and there was a man's name under hers. I knocked softly. No answer. I knocked again, a little harder. This time I heard some one moving about. Then a voice close to the door, asking who is it and at the same time the knob turning. I pushed the door open and stumbled into the darkened room. Stumbled right into her arms and felt her naked under the half-opened kimono. She must have come out of a sound sleep and only half realized who was holding her in his arms. When she realized it was me she tried to break away but I had her tight and I began kissing her passionately and at the same time backing her up toward the couch near the window. She mumbled something about the door being open but I wasn't taking any chance of letting her slip out of my arms. So I made a slight detour and little by little I edged her toward the door and made her shove it to with her ass. I locked it with my one free hand and then I moved her into the center of the room and with the free hand I unbuttoned my fly and got my pecker out and into position. She was so drugged with sleep that it was almost like working on an automaton. I could see too that she was enjoying the idea of being fucked half asleep. The only thing was that every time I made a lunge she grew more wide-awake. And as she grew more conscious she became more frightened. It was difficult to know how to put her to sleep again without losing a good fuck. I managed to tumble her on to the couch without losing ground and she was hot as hell now, twisting and squirming like an eel. From the time I had started to maul her I don't think she had opened her eyes once. I kept saying to myself—"an Egyptian fuck... an Egyptian fuck"— and so as not to shoot off immediately I deliberately began thinking about the corpse that Monica had dragged to the Grand Central Station and about the thirty-five cents that I had left with Pauline on the highway. Then bango! A loud knock on the door and with that she opens her eyes wide and looks at me in utmost terror. I started to pull away quickly but to my surprise she held me tight. "Don't move," she whispered in my ear. "Wait!" There was another loud knock and then I heard Kronski's voice saying "It's me, Thelma... it's me, *Izzy.*" At that I almost burst out laughing. We slumped back again into a natural position and as her eyes softly closed I moved it around inside her, gently, so as not to wake her up again. It was one of the most wonderful fucks I ever had in my life. I thought it was going to last forever. Whenever I felt in danger of going off I would stop moving and think—think for example of where I would like to spend my vacation, if I got one, or think of the shirts lying in the bureau drawer, or the patch in the bedroom carpet just at the foot of the bed. Kronski was still standing at the door—I could hear him changing about from one position to another. Every time I became aware of him standing there I jibbed her a little for good measure and in her half sleep she answered back, humorously, as though she understood what I meant by this put-and-take language. I didn't dare to think what she might be thinking or I'd have come immediately. Sometimes I skirted dangerously close to it, but the saving trick was always Monica and the corpse at the Grand Central Station.

The thought of that, the humorousness of it, I mean, acted like a cold douche.

When it was all over she opened her eyes wide and stared at me, as though she were taking me in for the first time. I hadn't a word to say to her; the only thought in my head was to get out as quickly as possible. As we were washing up I noticed a note on the floor near the door. It was from Kronski. His wife had just been taken to the hospital—he wanted her to meet him at the hospital. I felt relieved! It meant that I could break away without wasting any words.

The next day I had a telephone call from Kronski. His wife had died on the operating table. That evening I went home for dinner; we were still at the table when the bell rang. There was Kronski standing at the gate looking absolutely sunk. It was always difficult for me to offer words of condolence; with him it was absolutely impossible. I listened to my wife uttering her trite words of sympathy and I felt more than ever disgusted with her. "Let's get out of here," I said.

We walked along in absolute silence for a while. At the park we turned in and headed for the meadows. There was a heavy mist which made it impossible to see a yard ahead. Suddenly, as we were swimming along, he began to sob. I stopped and turned my head away. When I thought he had finished I looked around and there he was staring at me with a strange smile. "It's funny," he said, "how hard it is to accept death." I smiled too now and put my hand on his shoulder. "Go on," I said, "talk your head off. Get it off your chest." We started walking again, up and down over the meadows, as though we were walking under the sea. The mist had become so thick that I could just barely discern his features. He was talking quietly and madly. "I knew it would happen," he said. "It was too beautiful to last." The night before she was taken ill he had had a dream. He dreamt that he had lost his identity. "I was stumbling around in the dark calling my own name. I remember coming to a bridge, and looking down into the water I saw myself drowning. I jumped off the bridge head first and when I came up I saw Yetta floating under the bridge. She was dead." And then suddenly he added: "You were there yesterday when I knocked at the door, weren't you? I knew you were there and I couldn't go away. I knew too that Yetta was dying and I wanted to be with her, but I was afraid to go alone." I said nothing and he rambled on. "The first girl I ever loved died in the same way. I was only a kid and I couldn't get over it. Every night I used to go to the cemetery and sit by her grave. People thought I was out of my mind. I guess I was out of my mind. Yesterday, when I was standing at the door, it all came back to me. I was back in Trenton, at the grave, and the sister of the girl I loved was sitting beside me. She said it couldn't go on that way much longer, that I would go mad. I thought to myself that I really was mad and to prove it to myself I decided to do something mad and so I said to her it isn't *her* I love, it's *you*, and I pulled her over me and we lay there kissing each other and finally I screwed her, right beside the grave. And I think that cured me because I never went back there again and I never thought about her any more—until yesterday when I was standing at the door. If I could have gotten hold of you yesterday I would have strangled you. I don't know why I felt that way but it seemed to me that you had opened up a tomb, that you were violating the dead body of the girl I loved. That's crazy, isn't it? And why did I come to see you tonight? Maybe it's because you're absolutely indifferent to me... because you're not a Jew and I can talk to you... because you don't give a damn, and you're right.... Did you ever read *The Revolt of the Angels?*"

We had just arrived at the bicycle path which encircles the park. The lights of the boulevard were swimming in the mist. I took a good look at him and I saw that he was out of his head. I wondered if I could make him laugh. I was afraid, too, that if he once got started laughing he would never stop. So I began to talk at random, about Anatole France at first, and then about other writers, and finally, when I felt that I was losing him, I suddenly switched to General Ivolgin, and with that he began to laugh, not a laugh either, but a cackle, a hideous cackle, like a rooster with its head on the block. It got him so badly that he had to stop and hold his guts; the tears were streaming down his eyes and between the cackles he let out the most terrible, heartrending sobs. "I knew you would do me good," he blurted out, as the last outbreak died away. "I always said you were a crazy son of a bitch.... You're a Jew bastard yourself, only you don't know it.... Now tell me, you bastard, how was it yesterday? Did you get your end in? Didn't I tell you she was a good lay? And do you know who she's living with? Jesus, you were lucky you didn't get caught. She's living with a Russian poet—you know the guy, too. I introduced you to him once at the Cafe Royal. Better not let him get wind of it. He'll beat your brains out... and then he'll write a beautiful poem about it and send it to her with a bunch of roses. Sure, I knew him out in Stelton, in the anarchist colony. His old man was a Nihilist. The whole family's crazy. By the way, you'd better take care of yourself. I meant to tell you that the other day, but I didn't think you would act so quickly. You know she may have syphilis. I'm not trying to scare you. I'm just telling you for your own good...."

This outburst seemed to really assuage him. He was trying to tell me in his twisted Jewish way that he liked me. To do so he had to first destroy everything around me—the wife, the job, my friends, the "nigger wench," as he called Valeska, and so on. 'I think some day you're going to be a great writer," he said. *"But,"* he added maliciously, "first you'll have to suffer a bit. I mean *really* suffer, because you don't know what the word means yet. You only *think* you've suffered. You've got to fall in love first. That nigger wench now... you don't really suppose that you're in love with her, do you? Did you ever take a good look at her ass... how it's spreading, I mean? In five years she'll look like Aunt Jemima. You'll make a swell couple walking down the avenue with a string of pickaninnies trailing behind you. Jesus, I'd rather see you marry a Jewish girl. You wouldn't appreciate her, of course, but she'd be good for you. You need something to steady yourself. You're scattering your energies. Listen, why do you run around with all these dumb bastards you pick up? You seem to have a genius for picking up the wrong people. Why don't you throw yourself into something useful? You don't belong in that job—you could be a big guy somewhere. Maybe a labor leader... I don't know what exactly. But first you've got to get rid of that hatchet-faced wife of yours. Ugh! when I look at her I could spit in her face. I don't see how a guy like you could ever have married a bitch like that. What was it—just a pair of steaming ovaries? Listen, that's what's the matter with you—you've got nothing but sex on the brain.... No, I don't mean that either. You've got a mind and you've got passion and enthusiasm... but you don't seem to give a damn what you do or what happens to you. If you weren't such a romantic bastard I'd almost swear that you were a Jew. It's different with me—I never had anything to look forward to. But you've got something in you—only you're too damned lazy to bring it out. Listen, when I hear you talk sometimes I think to myself—if only that guy would put it down on paper! Why you could write a book that would make a guy like Dreiser hang his head. You're different from the Americans I know; somehow you don't belong, and it's a damned good thing you don't. You're a little cracked, too—I suppose you know that. But in a good way. Listen, a little while ago, if it had been anybody else who talked to me that way I'd have murdered him. I think I like you better because you didn't try to give me any sympathy. I know better than to expect sympathy from you. If you had said one false word tonight I'd have really gone mad. I know it. I was on the very edge. When you started in about General Ivolgin I thought for a minute it was all up with me. That's what makes me think you've got something in you... that was real cunning! And now let me tell *you* something... if you don't pull yourself together soon you're going to be screwy. You've got something inside you that's eating you up. I don't know what it is, but you can't put it over on me. I know you from the bottom up. I know there's something griping you—and it's not just your wife, nor your job, nor even that nigger wench whom you think you're in love with. Sometimes I think you were born in the wrong time. Listen, I don't want you to think I'm making an idol of you but there's something to what I say... if you had just a little more confidence in yourself you could be the biggest man in the world today. You wouldn't even have to be a writer. You might become another Jesus Christ for all I know. Don't laugh—I mean it. You haven't the slightest idea of your own possibilities... you're absolutely blind to everything except your own desires. You don't know what you want. You don't know because you never stop to think. You're letting people use you up. You're a damned fool, an idiot. If I had a tenth of what you've got I could turn the world upside down. You think that's crazy, eh? Well, listen to me... I was never more sane in my life. When I came to see you tonight I thought I was about ready to commit suicide. It doesn't make much difference whether I do it or not. But anyway, I don't see much point in doing it now. That won't bring her back to me. I was born unlucky. Wherever I go I seem to bring disaster. But I don't want to kick off yet... I want to do some good in the world first. That may sound silly to you, but it's true. I'd like to do something for others...."

He stopped abruptly and looked at me again with that strange wan smile. It was the look of a hopeless Jew in whom, as with all his race, the life instinct was so strong that, even though there was absolutely nothing to hope for, he was powerless to kill himself. That hopelessness was something quite alien to me. I thought to myself—if only we could change skins! Why, I could kill myself for a bagatelle! And what got me more than anything was the thought that he wouldn't even enjoy the funeral—his own wife's funeral! God knows, the funerals we had were sorry enough affairs, but there was always a bit of food and drink afterwards, and some good obscene jokes and some hearty belly laughs. Maybe I was too young to appreciate the sorrowful aspects, though I saw plainly enough how they howled and wept. But that never meant much to me because after the funeral, sitting in the beer garden next to the cemetery, there was always an atmosphere of good cheer despite the black garments and the crepes and the wreaths. It seemed to me, as a kid then, that they were really trying to establish some sort of communion with the dead person. Something almost Egyptianlike, when I think back on it. Once upon a time I thought they were just a bunch of hypocrites. But they weren't. They were just stupid, healthy Germans with a lust for life. Death was something outside their ken, strange to say, because if you went only by what they said you would imagine that it occupied a good deal of their thoughts. But they really didn't grasp it at all—not the way the Jew does, for example. They talked about the life hereafter but they never really believed in it. And if any one were so bereaved as to pine away they looked upon that person suspiciously, as you would look upon an insane person. There were limits to sorrow as there were limits to joy, that was the impression they gave me. And at the extreme limits there was always the stomach which had to be filled—with limburger sandwiches and beer and kummel and turkey legs if there were any about. They wept in their beer, like children. And the next minute they were laughing, laughing over some curious quirk in the dead person's character. Even the way they used the past tense had a curious effect upon me. An hour after he was shoveled under they were saying of the defunct—"he was always so good-natured"—as though the person in mind were dead a thousand years, a character in history, or a personage out of the *Nibelungenlied.* The thing was that he was dead, definitely dead for all time, and they, the living, were cut off from him now and forever, and today as well as tomorrow must be lived through, the clothes washed, the dinner prepared, and when the next one was struck down there would be a coffin to select and a squabble about the will, but it would be all in the daily routine and to take time off to grieve and sorrow was sinful because God, if there was a God, had ordained it that way and we on earth had nothing to say about it. To go beyond the ordained limits of joy or grief was wicked. To threaten madness was the high sin. They had a terrific animal sense of adjustment, marvelous to behold if it had been truly animal, horrible to witness when you realized that it was nothing more than dull German torpor, insensitivity. And yet, somehow, I preferred these animated stomachs to the hydra-headed sorrow of the Jew. At bottom I couldn't feel sorry for Kronski—I would have to feel sorry for his whole tribe. The death of his wife was only an item, a trifle, in the history of his calamities. As he himself had said, he was born unlucky. He was born to see things go wrong—because for five thousand years things had been going wrong in the blood of the race. They came into the world with that sunken, hopeless leer on their faces and they would go out of the world the same way. They left a bad smell behind them—a poison, a vomit of sorrow. The stink they were trying to take out of the world was the stink they themselves had brought into the world. I reflected on all this as I listened to him. I felt so well and clean inside that when we parted, after I had turned down a side street, I began to whistle and hum. And then a terrible thirst came upon me and I says to meself in me best Irish brogue—shure and it's a bit of a drink ye should be having now, me lad— and saying it I stumbled into a hole in the wall and I ordered a big foaming stein of beer and a thick hamburger sandwich with plenty of onions. I had another mug of beer and then a drop of brandy and I thought to myself in my callous way—if the poor bastard has- n't got brains enough to enjoy his own wife's funeral then I'll enjoy it for him. And the more I thought about it, the happier I grew, and if there was the least bit of grief or envy it was only for the fact that I couldn't change places with her, the poor dead Jewish soul, because death was something absolutely beyond the grip and comprehension of a dumb goy like myself and it was a pity to waste it on the likes of them as knew all about it and didn't need it anyway. I got so damned intoxicated with the idea of dying that in my drunken stupor I was mumbling to the God above to kill me this night, kill me, God, and let me know what it's all about. I tried my stinking best to imagine what it was like, giv- ing up the ghost, but it was no go. The best I could do was to imitate a death rattle, but on that I nearly choked, and then I got so damned frightened that I almost shit in my pants. That wasn't death, anyway. That was just choking. Death was more like what we went through in the park: two people walking side by side in the mist, rubbing against trees and bushes, and not a word between them. It was something emptier than the name itself and yet right and peaceful, dignified, if you like. It was not a continuation of life, but a leap in the dark and no possibility of ever coming back, not even as a grain of dust. And that was right and beautiful, I said to myself, because why would one want to come back. To taste it once is to taste it forever—life *or* death. Whichever way the coin flips is right, so long as you hold no stakes. Sure, it's tough to choke on your own spittle—it's disagreeable more than anything else. And besides, one doesn't always die choking to death. Sometimes one goes off in his sleep, peaceful and quiet as a lamb. The Lord comes and gathers you up into the fold, as they say. Anyway, you stop breathing. And why the hell should one want to go on breathing forever? Anything that would have to be done interminably would be torture. The poor human bastards that we are, we ought to be glad that somebody devised a way out. We don't quibble about going to sleep. A third of our lives we snore away like drunken rats. What about that? Is that tragic? Well then, say three-thirds of drunken radike sleep. Jesus, if we had any sense we'd be dancing with glee at the thought of it! We could all die in bed tomorrow, without pain, without suffering—if we had the sense to take advantage of our remedies. We don't want to die, that's the trouble with us. That's why God and the whole shooting match upstairs in our crazy dustbins. General Ivolgin! That got a cackle out of him... and a few dry sobs. I might as well have said limburger cheese. But General Ivolgin means something to him... something crazy. Limburger cheese would be too sober, too banal. It's all limburger cheese, however, including General Ivolgin, the poor drunken sap. General Ivolgin was evolved out of Dostoevski's limburger cheese, his own private brand. That means a certain flavor, a certain label. So people recognize it when they smell it, taste it. But what made this General Ivolgin limburger cheese? Why, whatever made limburger cheese, which is *x* and therefore unknowable. And so therefore? Therefore nothing... nothing at all. Full stop—or else a leap in the dark and no coming back.

As I was taking my pants off I suddenly remembered what the bastard had told me. I looked at my cock and it looked just as innocent as ever. "Don't tell me you've got the syph," I said, holding it in my hand and squeezing it a bit as though I might see a bit of pus squirting out. No, I didn't think there was much chance of having the syph. I wasn't born under that kind of star. The clap, yes, that was possible. Everybody had the clap sometime or other. But not syph! I knew he'd wish it on me if he could, just to make me realize what suffering was. But I couldn't be bothered obliging him. I was born a dumb but lucky goy. I yawned. It was all so much goddamned limburger cheese that syph or no syph, I thought to myself, if she's up to it I'll tear off another piece and call it a day. But evidently she wasn't up to it. She was for turning her ass on me. So I just lay there with a stiff prick up against her ass and I gave it to her by mental telepathy. And by Jesus, she must have gotten the message sound asleep though she was, because it wasn't any trouble going in by the stable door and besides I didn't have to look at her face which was one hell of a relief. I thought to myself, as I gave her the last hook and whistle—"me lad, it's limburger cheese and now you can turn over and snore...."

It seemed as if it would go on forever, the sex and death chant. The very next afternoon at the office I received a telephone call from my wife saying that her friend Arline had just been taken to the insane asylum. They were friends from the convent school in Canada where they had both studied music and the art of masturbation. I had met the whole flock of them little by little, including Sister Antolina who wore a truss and who apparently was the high priestess of the cult of onanism. They had all had a crush on Sister Antolina at one time or another. And Arline with the chocolate eclair mug wasn't the first of the little group to go to the insane asylum. I don't say it was masturbation that drove them there but certainly the atmosphere of the convent had something to do with it. They were all spoiled in the egg.

Before the afternoon was over my old friend MacGregor walked in. He arrived looking glum as usual and complaining about the advent of old age, though he was hardly past thirty. When I told him about Arline he seemed to liven up a bit. He said he always knew there was something wrong with her. Why? Because when he tried to force her one night she began to weep hysterically. It wasn't the weeping as much as what she said. She said she had sinned against the Holy Ghost and for that she would have to lead a life of continence. Recalling the incident he began to laugh in his mirthless way. "I said to her—well you don't need to do it if you don't want... just hold it in your hand. Jesus, when I said that I thought she'd go clean off her nut. She said I was trying to soil her innocence—that's the way she put it. And at the same time she took it in her hand and she squeezed it so hard I damned near fainted. Weeping all the while, too. And still harping on the Holy Ghost and her 'innocence,' I remembered what you told me once and so I gave her a sound slap in the jaw. It worked like magic. She quieted down after a bit, enough to let me slip it in, and then the real fun commenced. Listen, did you ever fuck a crazy woman? It's something to experience. From the instant I got it in she started talking a blue streak. I can't describe it to you exactly, but it was almost as though she didn't know I was fucking her. Listen, I don't know whether you've ever had a woman eat an apple while you were doing it... well, you can imagine how that affects you. This one was a thousand times worse. It got on my nerves so that I began to think I was a little queer myself.... And now here's something you'll hardly believe, but I'm telling you the truth. You know what she did when we got through? She put her arms around me and she thanked me.... Wait, that isn't all. Then she got out of bed and she knelt down and offered up a prayer for my soul. Jesus, I remember that so well. 'Please make Mac a better Christian,' she said. And me lying there with a limp cock listening to her. I didn't know whether I was dreaming or what. 'Please make Mac a better Christian!' Can you beat that?"

"What are you doing tonight?" he added cheerfully. Nothing special," I said.

"Then come along with me. I've got a gal I want you to meet.... *Paula*. I picked her up at the Roseland a few nights ago. She's not crazy—she's just a nymphomaniac. I want to see you dance with her. It'll be a treat... just to watch you. Listen, if you don't shoot off in your pants when she starts wiggling, well then I'm a son of a bitch. Come on, close the joint. What's the use of farting around in this place?"

There was a lot of time to kill before going to the Rose-land so we went to a little hole in the wall over near Seventh Avenue. Before the war it was a French joint; now it was a speakeasy run by a couple of wops. There was a tiny bar near the door and in the back a little room with a sawdust floor and a slot machine for music. The idea was that we were to have a couple of drinks and then eat. That was the *idea*. Knowing him as I did, however, I wasn't at all sure that we would be going to the Roseland together. If a woman should come along who pleased his fancy—and for that she didn't have to be either beautiful or sound of wind and limb—I knew he'd leave me in the lurch and beat it. The only thing that concerned me, when I was with him, was to make sure in advance that he had enough money to pay for the drinks we ordered. And, of course, never let him out of my sight until the drinks were paid for.

The first drink or two always plunged him into reminiscence. Reminiscences of cunt to be sure. His reminiscences were reminiscent of a story he had told me once and which made an indelible impression upon me. It was about a Scotchman on his deathbed. Just as he was about to pass away his wife, seeing him struggling to say something, bends over him tenderly and says—"What is it, Jock, what is it ye're trying to say?" And Jock, with a last effort, raises himself wearily and says: "Just cunt... cunt... cunt."

That was always the opening theme, and the ending theme, with MacGregor. It was his way of saying—*futility*. The leitmotif was disease, because between fucks, as it were, he worried his head off, or rather he worried the head off his cock. It was the most natural thing in the world, at the end of an evening, for him to say—"come on upstairs a minute, I want to show you my cock." From taking it out and looking at it and washing it and scrubbing it a dozen times a day naturally his cock was always swollen and inflamed. Every now and then he went to the doctor and he had it sounded. Or, just to relieve him, the doctor would give him a little box of salve and tell him not to drink so much. This would cause no end of debate, because as he would say to me, "if the salve is any good why do I have to stop drinking?" Or, "if I stopped drinking altogether do you think I would need to use the salve?" Of course, whatever I recommended went in one ear and out the other. He had to worry about something and the penis was certainly good food for worry. Sometimes he worried about his scalp. He had dandruff, as most everybody has, and when his cock was in good condition he forgot about that and he worried about his scalp. Or else his chest. The moment he thought about his chest he would start to cough. And such coughing! As though he were in the last stages of consumption. And when he was running after a woman he was as nervous and irritable as a cat. He couldn't get her quickly enough. The moment he had her he was worrying about how to get rid of her. They all had something wrong with them, some trivial little thing, usually, which took the edge off his appetite.

He was rehearsing all this as we sat in the gloom of the back room. After a couple of drinks he got up, as usual, to go to the toilet, and on his way he dropped a coin in the slot machine and the jiggers began to jiggle and with that he perked up and pointing to the glasses he said: "Order another round." He came back from the toilet looking extraordinarily complacent, whether because he had relieved his bladder or because he had run into a girl in the hallway, I don't know. Anyhow, as he sat down, he started in on another tack—very composed now and very serene, almost like a philosopher. You know, Henry, we're getting on in years. You and I oughtn't to be frittering our time away like this. If we're ever going to amount to anything it's high time we started in...." I had been hearing this line for years now and I knew what the upshot would be. This was just a little parenthesis while he calmly glanced about the room and decided which bimbo was the least sottish-looking. While he discoursed about the miserable failure of our lives his feet were dancing and his eyes were getting brighter and brighter. It would happen as it always happened that just as he was saying—"Now you take Woodruff, for instance. He'll never get ahead because he's just a natural mean scrunging son of a bitch..."—just at such a moment, as I say, it would happen that some drunken cow in passing the table would catch his eye and without the slightest pause he would interrupt his narrative to say "hello kid, why don't you sit down and have a drink with us?" And as a drunken bitch like that never travels alone, but always in pairs, why she'd respond with a "Certainly, can I bring my friend over?" And MacGregor, as though he were the most gallant chap in the world, would say "Why sure, why not? What's her name?" And then, tugging at my sleeve, he'd bend over and whisper: "Don't you beat it on me, do you hear? We'll give 'em one drink and get rid of them, see?"

And, as it always happened, one drink led to another and the bill was getting too high and he couldn't see why he should waste his money on a couple of bums so you go out first, Henry, and pretend you're buying some medicine and I'll follow in a few minutes... but wait for me, you son of a bitch, don't leave me in the lurch like you did the last time. And like I always did, when I got outside I walked away as fast as my legs would carry me, laughing to myself and thanking my lucky stars that I had gotten away from him as easily as I had. With all those drinks under my belt it didn't matter much where my feet were dragging me. Broadway lit up just as crazy as ever and the crowd thick as molasses. Just fling yourself into it like an ant and let yourself get pushed along. Everybody doing it, some for a good reason and some for no reason at all. All this push and movement representing action, success, get ahead. Stop and look at shoes or fancy shirts, the new fall overcoat, wedding rings at ninety-eight cents apiece. Every other joint a food emporium.

Every time I hit that runway toward dinner hour a fever of expectancy seized me. It's only a stretch of a few blocks, from Times Square to Fiftieth Street, and when one says Broadway that's all that's really meant and it's really nothing, just a chicken run and a lousy one at that, but at seven in the evening when everybody's rushing for a table there's a sort of electrical crackle in the air and your hair stands on end like antennae and if you're receptive you not only get every flash and flicker but you get the statistical itch, the *quid pro quo* of the interactive, interstitial, ectoplasmatic quantum of bodies jostling in space like the stars which compose the Milky Way, only this is the Gay White Way, the top of the world with no roof above and not even a crack or a hole under your feet to fall through and say it's a lie. The absolute impersonality of it brings you to a pitch of warm human delirium which makes you run forward like a blind nag and wag your delirious ears. Every one is so utterly, confoundedly not himself that you become automatically the personification of the whole human race, shaking hands with a thousand human hands, cackling with a thousand different human tongues, cursing, applauding, whistling, crooning, soliloquizing, orating, gesticulating, urinating, fecundating, wheedling, cajoling, whimpering, bartering, pimping, caterwauling, and so on and so forth. You are all the men who ever lived up to Moses, and beyond that you are a woman buying a hat, or a bird cage, or just a mouse trap. You can lie in wait in a show window, like a fourteen-carat gold ring, or you can climb the side of a building like a human fly, but nothing will stop the procession, not even umbrellas flying at lightning speed, nor double-decked walruses marching calmly to the oyster banks. Broadway, such as I see it now and have seen it for twenty-five years, is a ramp that was conceived by St. Thomas Aquinas while he was yet in the womb. It was meant originally to be used only by snakes and lizards, by the horned toad and the red heron, but when the great Spanish Armada was sunk the human kind wriggled out of the ketch and slopped over, creating by a sort of foul, ignominious squirm and wiggle the cuntlike cleft that runs from the Battery south to the golf links north through the dead and wormy center of Manhattan Island. From Times Square to Fiftieth Street all that St. Thomas Aquinas forgot to include in his *magnum opus* is here included, which is to say, among other things, hamburger sandwiches, collar buttons, poodle dogs, slot machines, gray bowlers, typewriter ribbons, orange sticks, free toilets, sanitary napkins, mint jujubes, billiard balls, chopped onions, crinkled doilies, manholes, chewing gum, sidecars and sourballs, cellophane, cord tires, magnetos, horse liniment, cough drops, feenamint, and that feline opacity of the hysterically endowed eunuch who marches to the soda fountain with a sawed-off shotgun between his legs. The before-dinner atmosphere, the blend of patchouli, warm pitchblende, iced electricity, sugared sweat and powdered urine drives one on to a fever of delirious expectancy. Christ will never more come down to earth nor will there be any lawgiver, nor will murder cease, nor theft, nor rape, and yet... and yet one expects something, something terrifyingly marvelous and absurd, perhaps a cold lobster with mayonnaise served gratis, perhaps an invention, like the electric light, like television, only more devastating, more soul-rending, an invention unthinkable that will bring a shattering calm and void, not the calm and void of death but of life such as the monks dreamed, such as is dreamed still in the Himalayas, in Tibet, in Lahore, in the Aleutian Islands, in Polynesia, in Easter Island, the dream of men before the flood, before the word was written, the dream of cave men and anthropophagists, of those with double sex and short tails, of those who are said to be crazy and have no way of defending themselves because they are outnumbered by those who are not crazy. Cold energy trapped by cunning brutes and then set free like explosive rockets, wheels intricately interwheeled to give the illusion of force and speed, some for light, some for power, some for motion, words wired by maniacs and mounted like false teeth, perfect, and repulsive as lepers, ingratiating, soft, slippery, nonsensical movement, vertical, horizontal, circular, between walls and through walls, for pleasure, for barter, for crime, for sex; all light, movement, power impersonally conceived, generated, and distributed throughout a choked, cuntlike cleft intended to dazzle and awe the savage, the yokel, the alien, but nobody dazzled or awed, this one hungry, that one lecherous, all one and the same and no different from the savage, the yokel, the alien, except for odds and ends, bric-a-brac, the soapsuds of thought, the sawdust of the mind. In the same cunty cleft, trapped and undazzled, millions have walked before me, among them one, Blaise Cendrars, who afterwards flew to the moon, thence back to earth and up the Orinoco impersonating a wild man but actually sound as a button, though no longer vulnerable, no longer mortal, a splendiferous hulk of a poem dedicated to the archipelago of insomnia. Of those with fever few hatched, among them myself still unhatched, but pervious and maculate, knowing with quiet ferocity the ennui of ceaseless drift and movement. Before dinner the slat and chink of sky light softly percolating through the bounded gray dome, the vagrant hemispheres spored with blue-egged nuclei coagulating, ramifying, in the one basket lobsters, in the other the germination of a world antiseptically personal and absolute. Out of the manholes, gray with the underground life, men of the future world saturated with shit, the iced electricity biting into them like rats, the day done in and darkness coming on like the cool, refreshing shadows of the sewers. Like a soft prick slipping out of an overheated cunt I, the still unhatched, making a few abortive wriggles, but either not dead and soft enough or else sperm-free and skating *ad astra,* for it is still not dinner and a peristaltic frenzy takes possession of the upper colon, the hypogastric region, the umbilical and the postpineal lobe. Boiled alive, the lobsters swim in ice, giving no quarter and asking no quarter, simply motionless and unmotivated in the ice-watered ennui of death, life drifting by the show window muffled in desolation, a sorrowful scurvy eaten away by ptomaine, the frozen glass of the window cutting like a jack-knife, clean and no remainder.

Life drifting by the show window... I too as much a part of life as the lobster, the fourteen-carat ring, the horse liniment, but very difficult to establish the fact, the fact being that life is merchandise with a bill of lading attached, what I choose to eat being more important than I the eater, each one eating the other and consequently eating, *the verb*, ruler of the roost. In the act of eating the host is violated and justice defeated temporarily. The plate and what's on it, through the predatory power of the intestinal apparatus, commands attention and unifies the spirit, first hypnotizing it, then slowly swallowing it, then masticating it, then absorbing it. The spiritual part of the being passes off like a scum, leaves absolutely no evidence or trace of its passage, vanishes, vanishes even more completely than a point in space after a mathematical discourse. The fever, which may return tomorrow, bears the same relation to life as the mercury in a thermometer bears to heat. Fever will not make life heat, which is what was to have been proved and thus consecrates the meat balls and spaghetti. To chew while thousands chew, each chew an act of murder, gives the necessary social cast from which you look out the window and see that even human kind can be slaughtered justly, or maimed, or starved, or tortured because, while chewing, the mere advantage of sitting in a chair with clothes on, wiping the mouth with a napkin, enables you to comprehend what the wisest men have never been able to comprehend, namely that there is no other way of life possible, said wise men often disdaining to use chair, clothes or napkin. Thus men scurrying through a cunty cleft of a street called Broadway every day at regular hours, in search of this or that, tend to establish this and that, which is exactly the method of mathematicians, logicians, physicists, astronomers and such like. The proof is the fact and the fact has no meaning except what is given to it by those who establish the facts.

The meat balls devoured, the paper napkin carefully thrown on the floor, belching a trifle and not knowing why or whither, I step out into the twenty-four-carat sparkle and fall in with the theater pack. This time I wander through the side streets following a blind man with an accordion. Now and then I sit on a stoop and listen to an aria. At the opera, the music makes no sense; here in the street it has just the right demented touch to give it poignancy. The woman who accompanies the blind man holds a tin cup in her hands; he is a part of life too, like the tin cup, like the music of Verdi, like the Metropolitan Opera House. Everybody and everything is a part of life, but when they have all been added together, still somehow it is not life. *When is it life*, I ask myself, *and why not now?* The blind man wanders on and I remain sitting on the stoop. The meat balls were rotten, the coffee was lousy, the butter was rancid. Everything I look at is rotten, lousy, rancid. The street is like a bad breath; the next street is the same, and the next and the next. At the corner the blind man stops again and plays "Home to Our Mountains." I find a piece of chewing gum in my pocket—I chew it. I chew for the sake of chewing. There is absolutely nothing better to do unless it were to make a decision, which is impossible. The stoop is comfortable and nobody is bothering me. I am part of the world, of life, as they say, and I belong and I don't belong.

I sit on the stoop for an hour or so, mooning. I come to the same conclusions I always come to when I have a minute to think for myself. Either I must go home immediately and start to write or I must run away and start a wholly new life. The thought of beginning a book terrifies me: there is so much to tell that I don't know where or how to begin. The thought of running away and beginning all over again is equally terrifying: it means working like a nigger to keep body and soul together. For a man of my temperament, the world being what it is, there is absolutely no hope, no solution. Even if I *could* write the book I want to write nobody would take it—I know my compatriots only too well. Even if I *could* begin again it would be no use, because fundamentally I have no desire to work and no desire to become a useful member of society. I sit there staring at the house across the way. It seems not only ugly and senseless, like all the other houses on the street, but from staring at it so intently, it has suddenly become absurd. The idea of constructing a place of shelter in that particular way strikes me as absolutely insane. The city itself strikes me as a piece of the highest insanity, everything about it, sewers, elevated lines, slot machines, newspapers, telephones, cops, doorknobs, flophouses, screens, toilet paper, everything. Everything could just as well not be and not only nothing lost but a whole universe gained. I look at the people brushing by me to see if by chance one of them might agree with me. Supposing I intercepted one of them and just asked him a simple question. Supposing I just said to him suddenly: *"Why do you go on living the way you do?"* He would probably call a cop. I ask myself—does any one ever talk to himself the way I do? I ask myself if there isn't something wrong with me. The only conclusion I can come to is *that I am different.* And that's a very grave matter, view it how you will. Henry, I say to myself, rising slowly from the stoop, stretching myself, brushing my trousers and spitting out the gum, Henry, I say to myself, you are young yet, you are just a spring chicken and if you let them get you by the balls you're an idiot because you're a better man than any of them only you need to get rid of your false notions about humanity. You have to realize, Henry me boy, that you're dealing with cutthroats, with cannibals, only they're dressed up, shaved, perfumed, but that's all they are—cutthroats, cannibals. The best thing for you to do now, Henry, is to go and get yourself a frosted chocolate and when you sit at the soda fountain keep your eyes peeled and forget about the destiny of man because you might still find yourself a nice lay and a good lay will clean your ballbearings out and leave a good taste in your mouth whereas this only brings on dyspepsia, dandruff, halitosis, encephalitis. And while I'm soothing myself thus a guy comes up to me to bum a dime and I hand him a quarter for good measure thinking to myself that if I had had a little more sense I'd have had a juicy pork chop with that instead of the lousy meat balls but what's the difference now it's all food and food makes energy and energy is what makes the world go round. Instead of the frosted chocolate I keep walking and soon I'm exactly where I intended to be all the time, which is in front of the ticket window of the Roseland. And now, Henry, says I to myself, if you're lucky your old pal MacGregor will be here and first he'll bawl the shit out of you for running away and then he'll lend you a five spot, and if you just hold your breath while climbing the stairs maybe you'll see the nymphomaniac too and you'll get a dry fuck. Enter very calmly, Henry, and keep your eyes peeled! And I enter as per instructions on velvet toes, checking my hat and urinating a little as a matter of course, then slowly redescending the stairs and sizing up the taxi girls all diaphanously gowned, powdered, perfumed, looking fresh and alert but probably bored as hell and leg weary. Into each and every one of them, as I shuffle about, I throw an imaginary fuck. The place is just plastered with cunt and fuck and that's why I'm reasonably sure to find my old friend MacGregor here. The way I no longer think about the condition of the world is marvelous.

I mention it because for a moment, just while I was studying a juicy ass, I had a relapse. I almost went into a trance again. I was thinking, Christ help me, that maybe I ought to beat it and go home and begin the book. A terrifying thought! Once I spent a whole evening sitting in a chair and saw nothing and heard nothing. I must have written a good-sized book before I woke up. Better not to sit down. Better to keep circulating. Henry, what you ought to do is to come here some time with a lot of dough and just see how far it'll take you. I mean a hundred or two hundred bucks, and spend it like water and say yes to everything. The haughty looking one with the statuesque figure, I bet she'd squirm like an eel if her palm were well greased. Supposing she said—*twenty bucks!* and you could say *Sure!* Supposing you could say—Listen, I've got a car downstairs... let's run down to Atlantic City for a few days. Henry, there ain't no car and there ain't no twenty bucks. *Don't sit down... keep moving.*

At the rail which fences off the floor I stand and watch them sailing around. This is no harmless recreation... this is serious business. At each end of the floor there is a sign reading "No Improper Dancing Allowed." Well and good. No harm in placing a sign at each end of the floor. In Pompeii they probably hung a phallus up. This is the American way. It means the same thing. I mustn't think about Pompeii or I'll be sitting down and writing a book again. *Keep moving, Henry. Keep your mind on the music.* I keep struggling to imagine what a lovely time I would have if I had the price of a string of tickets, but the more I struggle the more I slip back. Finally I'm standing knee deep in the lava beds and the gas is choking me. It wasn't the lava that killed the Pompeians, it was the poison gas that precipitated the eruption. That's how the lava caught them in such queer poses, with their pants down, as it were. If suddenly all New York were caught that way— what a museum it would make! My friend MacGregor standing at the sink scrubbing his cock... the abortionists on the East Side caught red-handed... the nuns lying in bed and masturbating one another... the auctioneer with an alarm clock in his hand... the telephone girls at the switchboard... J. P. Morganana sitting on the toilet bowl placidly wiping his ass... dicks with rubber hoses giving the third degree... strippers giving the last strip and tease....

Standing knee deep in the lava beds and my eyes choked with sperm: J. P. Morganana is placidly wiping his ass while the telephone girls plug the switchboards, while dicks with rubber hoses practice the third degree, while my old friend MacGregor scrubs the germs out of his cock and sweetens it and examines it under the microscope. Everybody caught with his pants down, including the strip teasers who wear no pants, no beards, no mustaches, just a little patch to cover their twinkling little cunts. Sister Antolina lying in the convent bed, her guts trussed up, her arms akimbo and waiting for the Resurrection, waiting, waiting for life without hernia, without intercourse, without sin, without evil, meanwhile nibbling a few animal crackers, a pimento, some fancy olives, a little headcheese. The Jewboys on the East Side, in Harlem, the Bronx, Canarsie, Brownsville, opening and closing the trapdoors, pulling out arms and legs, turning the sausage machine, clogging up the drains, working like fury for cash down and if you let a peep out of you out you go. With eleven hundred tickets in my pocket and a Rolls Royce waiting for me downstairs I could have the most excruciatingly marvelous time, throwing a fuck into each and every one respectively regardless of age, sex, race, religion, nationality, birth or breeding. There is no solution for a man like myself, I being what I am and the world being what it is. The world is divided into three parts of which two parts are meat balls and spaghetti and the other part a huge syphilitic chancre. The haughty one with the statuesque figure is probably a cold turkey fuck, a sort of *con anonyme* plastered with gold leaf in tin foil. Beyond despair and disillusionment there is always the absence of worse things and the emoluments of ennui. Nothing is lousier and emptier than the midst of bright gaiety clicked by the mechanical eye of the mechanical epoch, life maturing in a black box, a negative tickled with acid and yielding a momentaneous simulacrum of nothingness. At the outermost limit of this momentaneous nothingness my friend MacGregor arrives and is standing by my side and with him is the one he was talking about, the nymphomaniac called Paula. She has the loose, jaunty swing and perch of the double-barreled sex, all her movements radiating from the groin, always in equilibrium, always ready to flow, to wind and twist and clutch, the eyes going tic-toe, the toes twitching and twinkling, the flesh rippling like a lake furrowed by a breeze. This is the incarnation of the hallucination of sex, the sea nymph squirming in the maniac's arms. I watch the two of them as they move spasmodically inch by inch around the floor; they move like an octopus working up a rut. Between the dangling tentacles the music shimmers and flashes, now breaks in a cascade of sperm and rose water, forms again into an oily spout, a column standing erect without feet, collapses again like chalk, leaving the upper part of the leg phosphorescent, a zebra standing in a pool of golden marshmallow, one leg striped, the other molten. A golden marshmallow octopus with rubber hinges and molten hoofs, its sex undone and twisted into a knot. On the sea floor the oysters are doing the St. Vitus dance, some with lockjaw, some with double-jointed knees. The music is sprinkled with rat poison, with the rattlesnake's venom, with the fetid breath of the gardenia, the spittle of the sacred yak, the bolloxed sweat of the musk-rat, the leper's sugar-coated nostalgia. The music is a diarrhea, a lake of gasoline, stagnant with cockroaches and stale horse piss. The drooling notes are the foam and dribble of the epileptic, the night sweat of the fornicating nigger frigged by the Jew. All America is in the trombone's smear, that frazzled broken-down whinny of the gangrened sea cows stationed off Point Loma, Pawtucket, Cape Hatteras, Labrador, Canarsie and intermediate points. The octopus is dancing like a rubber dick—the rhumba of Spuyten Duyvil inedit. Laura the nympho is doing the rhumba, her sex exfoliated and twisted like a cow's tail. In the belly of the trombone lies the American soul farting its contented heart out. Nothing goes to waste—not the least spit of a fart. In the golden marsh-mallow dream of happiness, in the dance of the sodden piss and gasoline, the great soul of the American continent gallops like an octopus, all the sails unfurled, the hatches down, the engine whirring like a dynamo. The great dynamic soul caught in the click of the camera's eye, in the heat of rut, bloodless as a fish, slippery as mucus, the soul of the people miscegenating on the sea floor, popeyed with longing, harrowed with lust. The dance of Saturday night, of cantaloupes rotting in the garbage pail, of fresh green snot and slimy unguents for the tender parts. The dance of the slot machine and the monsters who invent them. The dance of the gat and the slugs who use them. The dance of the blackjack and the pricks who batter brains to a polypous pulp. The dance of the magneto world, the spark that unsparks, the soft purr of the perfect mechanism, the velocity race on a turntable, the dollar at par and the forests dead and mutilated. The Saturday night of the soul's hollow dance, each jumping jigger a functional unit in the St. Vitus dance of the ringworm's dream. Laura the nympho brandishing her cunt, her sweet rose-petal lips toothed with ballbearing clutches, her ass balled and socketed. Inch by inch, millimeter by millimeter they shove the copulating corpse around. And then crash! Like pulling a switch the music suddenly stops and with the stoppage the dancers come apart, arms and legs intact, like tea leaves dropping to the bottom of the cup. Now the air is blue with words, a slow sizzle as of fish on the griddle. The chaff of the empty soul rising like monkey chatter in the topmost branches of the trees. The air blue with words passing out through the ventilators, coming back again in sleep through corrugated funnels and smokestacks, winged like the antelope, striped like the zebra, now lying quiet as the mollusk, now spitting flame. Laura the nympho cold as a statue, her parts eaten away, her hair musically enraptured. On the brink of sleep Laura stands with muted lips, her words falling like pollen through a fog. The Laura of Petrarch seated in a taxi, each word ringing through the cash register, then sterilized, then cauterized. Laura the basilisk made entirely of asbestos, walking to the fiery stake with a mouth full of gum. Hunky-dory is the word on her lips. The heavy fluted lips of the sea shell, Laura's lips, the lips of lost Uranian love. All floating shadowward through the slanting fog. Last murmuring dregs of shell-like lips slipping off the Labrador coast, oozing eastward with the mud tides, easing starward in the iodine drift. Lost Laura, last of the Petrarchs, slowly fading on the brink of sleep. Not gray the world, but lackluster, the light bamboo sleep of spoon-backed innocence.

And this in the black frenzied nothingness of the hollow of absence leaves a gloomy feeling of saturated despondency not unlike the topmost tip of desperation which is only the gay juvenile maggot of death's exquisite rupture with life. From this inverted cone of ecstasy life will rise again into prosaic skyscraper eminence, dragging me by the hair and teeth, lousy with howling empty joy, the animated fetus of the unborn death maggot lying in wait for rot and putrefaction.

Sunday morning the telephone wakes me up. It's my friend Maxie Schnadig announcing the death of our friend Luke Ralston. Maxie has assumed a truly sorrowful tone of voice which rubs me the wrong way. He says Luke was such a swell guy. That too sounds the wrong note for me because while Luke was all right, he was only so-so, not precisely what you might call a swell guy. Luke was an ingrown fairy and finally, when I got to know him intimately, a big pain in the ass. I told Maxie that over the telephone; I could tell from the way he answered me that he didn't like it very much. He said Luke had always been a friend to me. It was true enough, but it wasn't enough. The truth was that I was really glad Luke had kicked off at the opportune moment: it meant that I could forget about the hundred and fifty dollars which I owed him. In fact, as I hung up the receiver I really felt joyous. It was a tremendous relief not to have to pay that debt. As for Luke's demise, that didn't disturb me in the least. On the contrary, it would enable me to pay a visit to his sister, Lottie, whom I always wanted to lay but never could for one reason or another. Now I could see myself going up there in the middle of the day and offering her my condolences. Her husband would be at the office and there would be nothing to interfere. I saw myself putting my arms around her and comforting her; nothing like tackling a woman when she is in sorrow. I could see her opening her eyes wide—she had beautiful, large gray eyes—as I moved her toward the couch. She was the sort of woman who would give you a fuck while pretending to be talking music or some such thing. She didn't like the naked reality, the bare facts, so to speak. At the same time she'd have enough presence of mind to slip a towel under her so as not to stain the couch. I knew her inside out. I knew that the best time to get her was now, now while she was running up a little fever of emotion over dear dead Luke—whom she didn't think much of, by the way. Unfortunately it was Sunday and the husband would be sure to be home. I went back to bed and I lay there thinking first about Luke and all that he had done for me and then about her, Lottie. Lottie Somers was her name—it always seemed a beautiful name to me. It matched her perfectly. Luke was stiff as a poker, with a sort of skull and bones face, and impeccable and just beyond words. She was just the opposite—soft, round, spoke with a drawl, caressed her words, moved languidly, used her eyes effectively. One would never take them for brother and sister. I got so worked up thinking about her that I tried to tackle the wife. But that poor bastard, with her Puritanical complex, pretended to be horrified. She liked Luke. She wouldn't say that he was a swell guy, because that wasn't like her, but she insisted that he was genuine, loyal, a true friend, etc. I had so many loyal, genuine, true friends that that was all horseshit to me. Finally we got into such an argument over Luke that she got an hysterical attack and began to weep and sob—in bed, mind you. That made me hungry. The idea of weeping before breakfast seemed monstrous to me. I went downstairs and I fixed myself a wonderful breakfast, and as I put it away I was laughing to myself, about Luke, about the hundred and fifty bucks that his sudden death had wiped off the slate, about Lottie and the way she would look at me when the moment came... and finally, the most absurd of all, I thought of Maxie, Maxie Schnadig, the faithful friend of Luke, standing at the grave with a big wreath and perhaps throwing a handful of earth on the coffin just as they were lowering it. Somehow that seemed just too stupid for words. I don't know why it should seem so ridiculous, but it did. Maxie was a simpleton. I tolerated him only because he was good for a touch now and then. And then too there was his sister Rita. I used to let him invite me to his home occasionally, pretending that I was interested in his brother who was deranged. It was always a good meal and the half-witted brother was real entertainment. He looked like a chimpanzee and he talked like one too. Maxie was too simple to suspect that I was merely enjoying myself; he thought I took a genuine interest in his brother. It was a beautiful Sunday and I had as usual about a quarter in my pocket. I walked along wondering where to go to make a touch. Not that it was difficult to scrape up a little dough, no, but the thing was to get the dough and beat it without being bored stiff. I could think of a dozen guys right in the neighborhood, guys who would fork it out without a murmur, but it would mean a long conversation afterwards—about art, religion, politics. Another thing I could do, which I had done over and over again in a pinch, was to visit the telegraph offices, pretending to pay a friendly visit of inspection and then, at the last minute, suggest that they rifle the till for a buck or so until the morrow. That would involve time and even worse conversation. Thinking it over coldly and calculatingly I decided that the best bet was my little friend Curley up in Harlem. If Curley didn't have the money he would filch it from his mother's purse. I knew I could rely on him. He would want to accompany me, of course, but I could always find a way of ditching him before the evening was over. He was only a kid and I didn't have to be too delicate with him.

What I liked about Curley was that, although only a kid of seventeen, he had absolutely no moral sense, no scruples, no shame. He had come to me as a boy of fourteen looking for a job as messenger. His parents, who were then in South America, had shipped him to New York in care of an aunt who seduced him almost immediately. He had never been to school because the parents were always traveling; they were carnival people who worked "the griffs and the grinds," as he put it. The father had been in prison several times. He was not his real father, by the way. Anyway, Curley came to me as a mere lad who was in need of help, in need of a friend more than anything. At first I thought I could do something for him. Everybody took a liking to him immediately, especially the women. He became the pet of the office. Before long, however, I realized that he was incorrigible, that at the best he had the makings of a clever criminal. I liked him, however, and I continued to do things for him, but I never trusted him out of my sight. I think I liked him particularly because he had absolutely no sense of honor. He would do anything in the world for me and at the same time betray me. I couldn't reproach him for it... it was amusing to me. The more so because he was frank about it. He just couldn't help it. His Aunt Sophie, for instance. He said she had seduced him. True enough, but the curious thing was that he let himself be seduced while they were reading the Bible together. Young as he was he seemed to realize that his Aunt Sophie had need of him in that way. So he let himself be seduced, as he said, and then, after I had known him a little while he offered to put me next to his Aunt Sophie. He even went so far as to blackmail her. When he needed money badly he would go to the aunt and wheedle it out of her—with sly threats of exposure. With an innocent face, to be sure. He looked amazingly like an angel, with big liquid eyes that seemed so frank and sincere. So ready to do things for you—almost like a faithful dog. And then cunning enough, once he had gained your favor, to make you humor his little whims. Withal extremely intelligent. The sly intelligence of a fox and—the utter heartlessness of a jackal.

It wasn't at all surprising to me, consequently, to learn that afternoon that he had been tinkering with Valeska. After Valeska he tackled the cousin who had already been deflowered and who was in need of some male whom she could rely upon. And from her finally to the midget who had made herself a pretty little nest at Valeska's. The midget interested him because she had a perfectly normal cunt. He hadn't intended to do anything with her because, as he said, she was a repulsive little Lesbian, but one day he happened to walk in on her as she was taking a bath, and that started things off. It was getting to be too much for him, he confessed, because the three of them were hot on his trail. He liked the cousin best because she had some dough and she wasn't reluctant to part with it. Valeska was too cagey, and besides she smelled a little too strong. In fact, he was getting sick of women. He said it was his Aunt Sophie's fault. She gave him a bad start. While relating this he busies himself going through the bureau drawers. The father is a mean son of a bitch who ought to be hanged, he says, not finding anything immediately. He shows me a revolver with a pearl handle... what would it fetch? A gun was too good to use on the old man... he'd like to dynamite him. Trying to find out *why* he hated the old man so, it developed that the kid was really stuck on his mother. He couldn't bear the thought of the old man going to bed with her. You don't mean to say that you're jealous of your old man, I ask. Yes, he's jealous. If I wanted to know the truth it's that he wouldn't mind sleeping with his mother. Why not? That's why he had permitted his Aunt Sophie to seduce him... he was thinking of his mother all the time. But don't you feel bad when you go through her pocketbook, I asked. He laughed. It's not *her* money, he said, it's *his*. And what have they done for me? They were always farming me out. The first thing they taught me was how to cheat people. That's a hell of a way to raise a kid....

There's not a red cent in the house. Curley's idea of a way out is to go with me to the office where he works and while I engage the manager in conversation go through the wardrobe and clean out all the loose change. Or, if I'm not afraid of taking a chance, he will go through the cash drawer. They'll never suspect *us*, he says. Had he ever done that before, I ask. Of course... a dozen or more times, right under the manager's nose. And wasn't there any stink about it? To be sure... they had fired a few clerks. Why don't you borrow something from your Aunt Sophie, I suggest. That's easy enough, only it means a quick diddle and he doesn't want to diddle her any more. She stinks, Aunt Sophie. What do you mean, *she stinks?* Just that... she doesn't wash herself regularly. Why, what's the matter with her? Nothing, just religious. And getting fat and greasy at the same time. But she likes to be diddled just the same? *Does she?* She's crazier than ever about it. It's disgusting. It's like going to bed with a sow. What does your mother think about her? Her? She's sore as hell at her. She thinks Sophie's trying to seduce the old man. Well, maybe she is! No, the old man's got something else. I caught him red-handed one night, in the movies, mushing it up with a young girl. She's a manicurist from the Astor Hotel. He's probably trying to squeeze a little dough out of her. That's the only reason he ever makes a woman. He's a dirty, mean son of a bitch and I'd like to see him get the chair some day! You'll get the chair yourself some day if you don't watch out. *Who, me?* Not *me!* I'm too clever. You're clever enough but you've got a loose tongue. I'd be a little more tight-lipped if I were you. You know, I added, to give him an extra jolt, O'Rourke is wise to you; if you ever fall out with O'Rourke it's all up with you.... Well, why doesn't he say something if he's so wise? I don't believe you. I explain to him at some length that O'Rourke is one of those people, and there are damned few in the world, who prefer *not* to make trouble for another person if they can help it. O'Rourke, I say, has the detective's instinct only in that he likes to *know* what's going on around him; people's characters are plotted out in his head, and filed there permanently, just as the enemy's terrain is fixed in the minds of army leaders. People think that O'Rourke goes around snooping and spying, that he derives a special pleasure in performing this dirty work for the company. Not so. O'Rourke is a born student of human nature. He picks things up without effort, due, to be sure, to his peculiar way of looking at the world. Now about you... I have no doubt that he knows everything about you. I never asked him, I admit, but I imagine so from the questions he poses now and then. Perhaps he's just giving you plenty of rope. Some night he'll run into you accidentally and perhaps he'll ask you to stop off somewhere and have a bite to eat with him. And out of a clear sky he'll suddenly say—you remember, Curley, when you were working up in SA office, the time that little Jewish clerk was fired for tapping the till? I think you were working overtime that night, weren't you? An interesting case, that. You know, they never discovered whether the clerk stole the money or not. They had to fire him, of course, for negligence, but we can't say for certain that he really stole the money. I've been thinking about that little affair now for quite some time. I have a hunch as to who took that money, but I'm not absolutely sure.... And then he'll probably give you a beady eye and abruptly change the conversation to something else. He'll probably tell you a little story about a crook he knew who thought he was very smart and getting away with it. He'll draw that story out for you until you feel as though you were sitting on hot coals. By that time you'll be wanting to beat it, but just when you're ready to go he'll suddenly be reminded of another very interesting little case and he'll ask you to wait just a little longer while he orders another dessert. And he'll go on like that for three or four hours at a stretch, never making the least overt insinuation, but studying you closely all the time, and finally, when you think you're free, just when you're shaking hands with him and breathing a sigh of relief, he'll step in front of you and, planting his big square feet between your legs, he'll grab you by the lapel and, looking straight through you, he'll say in a soft, winsome voice—wow *look here, my lad, don't you think you had better come clean?* And if you think he's only trying to browbeat you and that you can pretend innocence and walk away, you're mistaken. Because at that point, when he asks you to come clean, he means business and nothing on earth is going to stop him. When it gets to that point I'd recommend you to make a clean sweep of it, down to the last penny. He won't ask me to fire you and he won't threaten you with jail—he'll just quietly suggest that you put aside a little bit each week and turn it over to him. Nobody will be the wiser. He probably won't even tell me. No, he's very delicate about these things, you'll see.

"And supposing," says Curley suddenly, "that I tell him I stole the money in order to help you out? What then?" He began to laugh hysterically.

"I don't think O'Rourke would believe that," I said calmly. "You can try it, of course, if you think it will help you to clear your own skirts. But I rather think it will have a bad effect. O'Rourke knows me... he knows I wouldn't let you do a thing like that."

"But you did let me do it!"

"I didn't tell you to do it. You did it without my knowledge. That's quite different. Besides, can you prove that I accepted money from you? Won't it seem a little ridiculous to accuse me, the one who befriended you, of putting you up to a job like that? Who's going to believe you? Not O'Rourke. Besides, he hasn't trapped you yet. Why worry about it in advance? Maybe you could begin to return the money little by little before he gets after you. Do it anonymously."

By this time Curley was quite used up. There was a little schnapps in the cupboard which his old man kept in reserve and I suggested that we take a little to brace us up. As we were drinking the schnapps it suddenly occurred to me that Maxie had said he would be at Luke's house to pay his respects. It was just the moment to get Maxie. He would be full of slobbering sentiments and I could give him any old kind of cock-and-bull story. I could say that the reason I had assumed such a hard-boiled air on the phone was because I was harassed, because I didn't know where to turn for the ten dollars which I needed so badly. At the same time I might be able to make a date with Lottie. I began to smile thinking about it. If Luke could only see what a friend he had in me! The most difficult thing would be to go up to the bier and take a sorrowful look at Luke. *Not to laugh!*

I explained the idea to Curley. He laughed so heartily that the tears were rolling down his face. Which convinced me, by the way, that it would be safer to leave Curley downstairs while I made the touch. Anyway, it was decided on.

They were just sitting down to dinner when I walked in, looking as sad as I could possibly make myself look. Maxie was there and almost shocked by my sudden appearance. Lottie had gone already. That helped me to keep up the sad look. I asked to be alone with Luke a few minutes, but Maxie insisted on accompanying me. The others were relieved, I imagine, as they had been conducting the mourners to the bier all afternoon. And like the good Germans they were they didn't like having their dinner interrupted. As I was looking at Luke, still with that sorrowful expression I had mustered, I became aware of Maxie's eyes fixed on me inquisitively. I looked up and smiled at him in my usual way. He seemed absolutely nonplussed at this. "Listen, Maxie," I said, "are you sure they won't hear us?" He looked still more puzzled and grieved, but nodded reassuringly. "It's like this, Maxie... I came up here purposely to see you... to borrow a few bucks. I know it seems lousy but you can imagine how desperate I must be to do a thing like this." He was shaking his head solemnly as I spit this out, his mouth forming a big O as if he were trying to frighten the spirits away. "Listen, Maxie," I went on rapidly and trying to keep my voice down sad and low, "this is no time to give me a sermon. If you want to do something for me lend me ten bucks now, right away... slip it to me right here while I look at Luke. You know, I really liked Luke. I didn't mean all that over the telephone. You got me at a bad moment. The wife was tearing her hair out. We're in a mess, Maxie, and I'm counting on you to do something. Come out with me if you can and I'll tell you more about it...." Maxie, as I had expected, couldn't come out with me. He wouldn't think of deserting them at such a moment.... "Well, give it to me now," I said, almost savagely. "I'll explain the whole thing to you tomorrow. I'll have lunch with you downtown."

"Listen, Henry," says Maxie, fishing around in his pocket, embarrassed at the idea of being caught with a wad in his hand at that moment, "listen," he said, "I don't mind giving you the money, but couldn't you have found another way of reaching me? It isn't because of Luke... it's...." He began to hem and haw, not knowing really what he wanted to say.

"For Christ's sake," I muttered, bending over Luke more closely so that if anyone walked in on us they would never suspect what I was up to... "for Christ's sake, don't argue about it now... hand it over and be done with it.... I'm desperate, do you hear me?" Maxie was so confused and flustered that he couldn't disengage a bill without pulling the wad out of his pocket. Leaning over the coffin reverently I peeled off the topmost bill from the wad which was peeping out of his pocket. I couldn't tell whether it was a single or a ten spot. I didn't stop to examine it but tucked it away as rapidly as possible and straightened myself up. Then I took Maxie by the arm and returned to the kitchen where the family were eating solemnly but heartily. They wanted me to stay for a bite, and it was awkward to refuse, but I refused as best I could and beat it, my face twitching now with hysterical laughter.

At the corner, by the lamppost, Curley was waiting for me. By this time I couldn't restrain myself any longer. I grabbed Curley by the arm and rushing him down the street I began to laugh, to laugh as I have seldom laughed in my life. I thought it would never stop. Every time I opened my mouth to start explaining the incident I had an attack. Finally I got frightened. I thought maybe I might laugh myself to death. After I had managed to quiet down a bit, in the midst of a long silence, Curley suddenly says: *"Did you get it?"* That precipitated another attack, even more violent than before.

I had to lean against a rail and hold my guts. I had a terrific pain in the guts but a pleasurable pain.

What relieved me more than anything was the sight of the bill I had filched from Maxie's wad. It was a twenty-dollar bill! That sobered me up at once. And at the same time it enraged me a bit. It enraged me to think that in the pocket of that idiot, Maxie, there were still more bills, probably more twenties, more tens, more fives. If he had come out with me, as I suggested, and if I had taken a good look at that wad I would have felt no remorse in blackjacking him. I don't know why it should have made me feel so, but it enraged me. The most immediate thought was to get rid of Curley as quickly as possible—a five spot would fix him up—and then go on a little spree. What I particularly wanted was to meet some low-down, filthy cunt who hadn't a spark of decency in her. Where to meet one like that... *just like that?* Well, get rid of Curley first. Curley, of course, is hurt. He had expected to stick with me. He pretends not to want the five bucks, but when he sees that I'm willing to take it back, he quickly stows it away.

Again the night, the incalculably barren, cold, mechanical night of New York in which there is no peace, no refuge, no intimacy. The immense, frozen solitude of the million-footed mob, the cold, waste fire of the electrical display, the overwhelming meaninglessness of the perfection of the female who through perfection has crossed the frontier of sex and gone into the minus sign, gone into the red, like the electricity, like the neutral energy of the males, like planets without aspect, like peace programs, like love over the radio. To have money in the pocket in the midst of white, neutral energy, to walk meaningless and unfecundated through the bright glitter of the calcimined streets, to think aloud in full solitude on the edge of madness, to be of a city, a great city, to be of the last moment of time in the greatest city in the world and feel no part of it, is to become one-self a city, a world of dead stone, of waste light, of unintelligible motion, of imponderables and incalculables, of the secret perfection of all that is minus. To walk in money through the night crowd, protected by money, lulled by money, dulled by money, the crowd itself a money, the breath money, no least single object anywhere that is not money, money, money everywhere and still not enough, and then no money or a little money or less money or more money, but money, always money, and if you have money or you don't have money it is the money that counts and money makes money, *but what makes money make money?*

Again the dance hall, the money rhythm, the love that comes over the radio, the impersonal, wingless touch of the crowd. A despair that reaches down to the very soles of the boots, an ennui, a desperation. In the midst of the highest mechanical perfection to dance without joy, to be so desperately alone, to be almost inhuman because you are human. If there were life on the moon what more nearly perfect, joyless evidence of it could there be than this? If to travel away from the sun is to reach the chill idiocy of the moon, then we have arrived at our goal and life is but the cold, lunar incandescence of the sun. This is the dance of ice-cold life in the hollow of an atom, and the more we dance the colder it gets.

So we dance, to an ice-cold frenzied rhythm, to short waves and long waves, a dance on the inside of the cup of nothingness, each centimeter of lust running to dollars and cents. We taxi from one perfect female to another seeking the vulnerable defect, but they are flawless and impermeable in their impeccable lunar consistency. This is the icy white maidenhead of love's logic, the web of the ebbed tide, the fringe of absolute vacuity. And on this fringe of the virginal logic of perfection I am dancing the soul dance of white des-peration, the last white man pulling the trigger on the last emotion, the gorilla of despair beating his breast with immaculate gloved paws. I am the gorilla who feels his wings growing, a giddy gorilla in the center of a satin-like emptiness; the night too grows like an electrical plant, shooting white-hot buds into velvet black space. I am the black space of the night in which the buds break with anguish, a starfish swimming on the frozen dew of the moon. I am the germ of a new insanity, a freak dressed in intelligible language, a sob that is buried like a splinter in the quick of the soul. I am dancing the very sane and lovely dance of the angelic gorilla. These are my brothers and sisters who are insane and unangelic. We are dancing in the hollow of the cup of nothingness. We are of one flesh, but separated like stars.

In the moment all is clear to me, clear that in this logic there is no redemption, the city itself being the highest form of madness and each and every part, organic or inorgan-ic, an expression of this same madness. I feel absurdly and humbly great, not as megalo-maniac, but as human spore, as the dead sponge of life swollen to saturation. I no longer look into the eyes of the woman I hold in my arms but I swim through, head and arms and legs, and I see that behind the sockets of the eyes there is a region unexplored, the world of futurity, and here there is no logic whatever, just the still germination of events unbroken by night and day, by yesterday and tomorrow. The eye, accustomed to concen-tration on points in space, now concentrates on points in time; the eye sees forward and backward at will. The eye which was the I of the self no longer exists; this selfless eye neither reveals nor illuminates. It travels along the line of the horizon, a ceaseless, uninformed voyager. Trying to retain the lost body I grew in logic as the city, a point digit in the anatomy of perfection. I grew beyond my own death, spiritually bright and hard. I was divided into endless yesterdays, endless tomorrows, resting only on the cusp of the event, a wall with many windows, but the house gone. I must shatter the walls and windows, the last shell of the lost body, if I am to rejoin the present.

That is why I no longer look *into* the eyes or *through* the eyes, but by the legerdemain of will swim through the eyes, head and arms and legs, to explore the curve of vision. I see around myself as the mother who bore me once saw round the corners of time. I have broken the wall created by birth and the line of voyage is round and unbroken, even as the navel. No form, no image, no architecture, only concentric flights of sheer madness. I am the arrow of the dream's substantiality. I verify by flight. I nullify by dropping to earth.

Thus moments pass, veridic moments of time without space when I know all, and knowing all I collapse beneath the vault of the selfless dream.

Between these moments, in the interstices of the dream, life vainly tries to build up, but the scaffold of the city's mad logic is no support. As an individual, as flesh and blood, I am leveled down each day to make the fleshless, bloodless city whose perfection is the sum of all logic and death to the dream. I am struggling against an oceanic death in which my own death is but a drop of water evaporating. To raise my own individual life but a fraction of an inch above this sinking sea of death I must have a faith greater than Christ's, a wisdom deeper than that of the greatest seer. I must have the ability and the patience to formulate what is not contained in the language of our time, for what is now intelligible is meaningless. My eyes are useless, for they render back only the image of the known. My whole body must become a constant beam of light, moving with an ever greater rapidity, never arrested, never looking back, never dwindling. The city grows like a cancer; I must grow like a sun. The city eats deeper and deeper into the red; it is an insatiable white louse which must die eventually of inanition. I am going to starve the white louse which is eating me up. I am going to die as a city in order to become again a man. Therefore I close my ears, my eyes, my mouth.

Before I shall have become quite a man again I shall probably exist as a park, a sort of natural park in which people come to rest, to while away the time. What they say or do will be of little matter, for they will bring only their fatigue, their boredom, their hopelessness. I shall be a buffer between the white louse and the red corpuscle. I shall be a ventilator for removing the poisons accumulated through the effort to perfect that which is imperfectible. I shall be law and order as it exists in nature, as it is projected in dream. I shall be the wild park in the midst of the nightmare of perfection, the still, unshakable dream in the midst of frenzied activity, the random shot on the white billiard table of logic, I shall know neither how to weep nor protest, but I shall be there always in absolute silence to receive and to restore. I shall say nothing until the time comes again to be a man. I shall make no effort to preserve, no effort to destroy. I shall make no judgments, no criticisms. Those who have had enough will come to me for reflection and meditation; those who have not had enough will die as they lived, in disorder, in desperation, in ignorance of the truth of redemption. If one says to me, you must be religious, I shall make no answer. If one says to me, I have no time now, there's a cunt waiting for me, I shall make no answer. Or even if there be a revolution brewing, I shall make no answer. There will always be a cunt or a revolution around the corner, but the mother who bore me turned many a corner and made no answer, and finally she turned herself inside out *and I am the answer.*

Out of such a wild mania for perfection naturally no one would have expected an evolution to a wild park, not even I myself, but it is infinitely better, while attending death, to live in a state of grace and natural bewilderment. Infinitely better, as life moves toward a deathly perfection, to be just a bit of breathing space, a stretch of green, a little fresh air, a pool of water. Better also to receive men silently and to enfold them, for there is no answer to make while they are still frantically rushing to turn the corner.

I'm thinking now about the rock fight one summer's afternoon long long ago when I was staying with my Aunt Caroline up near Hell Gate. My cousin Gene and I had been corralled by a gang of boys while we were playing in the park. We didn't know which side we were fighting for but we were fighting in dead earnest amidst the rock pile by the river bank. We had to show even more courage than the other boys because we were suspected of being sissies. That's how it happened that we killed one of the rival gang. Just as they were charging us my cousin Gene let go at the ringleader and caught him in the guts with a handsome-sized rock. I let go almost at the same instant and my rock caught him in the temple and when he went down he lay there for good and not a peep out of him. A few minutes later the cops came and the boy was found dead. He was eight or nine years old, about the same age as us. What they would have done to us if they had caught us I don't know. Anyway, so as not to arouse any suspicion we hurried home; we had cleaned up a bit on the way and had combed our hair. We walked in looking almost as immaculate as when we had left the house. Aunt Caroline gave us our usual two big slices of sour rye with fresh butter and a little sugar over it and we sat there at the kitchen table listening to her with an angelic smile. It was an extremely hot day and she thought we had better stay in the house, in the big front room where the blinds had been pulled down, and play marbles with our little friend Joey Kasselbaum. Joey had the reputation of being a little backward and ordinarily we would have trimmed him, but that afternoon, by a sort of mute understanding, Gene and I allowed him to win everything we had. Joey was so happy that he took us down to his cellar later and made his sister pull up her dress and show us what was underneath. Weesie, they called her, and I remember that she was stuck on me instantly. I came from another part of the city, so far away it seemed to them, that it was almost like coming from another country. They even seemed to think that I talked differently from them. Whereas the other urchins used to pay to make Weesie lift her dress up, for us it was done with love. After a while we persuaded her not to do it any more for the other boys—we were in love with her and we wanted her to go straight.

When I left my cousin the end of the summer I didn't see him again for twenty years or more. When we did meet what deeply impressed me was the look of innocence he wore—the same expression as the day of the rock fight. When I spoke to him about the fight I was still more amazed to discover that he had forgotten that it was we who had killed the boy; he remembered the boy's death but he spoke of it as though neither he nor I had any part in it. When I mentioned Weesie's name he had difficulty in placing her. Don't you remember the cellar next door... *Joey Kasselbaum?* At this a faint smile passed over his face. He thought it extraordinary that I should remember such things. He was already married, a father, and working in a factory making fancy pipe cases. He considered it extraordinary to remember events that had happened so far back in the past.

On leaving him that evening I felt terribly despondent. It was as though he had attempted to eradicate a precious part of my life, and himself with it. He seemed more attached to the tropical fish which he was collecting than to the wonderful past. As for me I recollect everything, everything that happened that summer, and particularly the day of the rock fight. There are times, in fact, when the taste of that big slice of sour rye which his mother handed me that afternoon is stronger in my mouth than the food I am actually tasting. And the sight of Weesie's little bud almost stronger than the actual feel of what is in my hand. The way the boy lay there after we downed him, far far more impressive than the history of the World War. The whole long summer, in fact, seems like an idyll out of the Arthurian legends.

I often wonder what it was about this particular summer which makes it so vivid in my memory. I have only to close my eyes a moment in order to relive each day. The death of the boy certainly caused me no anguish—it was forgotten before a week had elapsed. The sight of Weesie standing in the gloom of the cellar with her dress lifted up, that too passed easily away. Strangely enough, the thick slice of rye bread which his mother handed me each day seems to possess more potency than any other image of that period. I wonder about it... wonder deeply. Perhaps it is that whenever she handed me the slice of bread it was with a tenderness and a sympathy that I had never known before. She was a very homely woman, my Aunt Caroline. Her face was marked by the pox, but it was a kind, winsome face which no disfigurement could mar. She was enormously stout and she had a very soft, a very caressing voice. When she addressed me she seemed to give me even more attention, more consideration, than her own son. I would like to have stayed with her always: I would have chosen her for my own mother had I been permitted. I remember distinctly how when my mother arrived on a visit she seemed peeved that I was so contented with my new life. She even remarked that I was ungrateful, a remark I never forgot, because then I realized for the first time that to be ungrateful was perhaps necessary and good for one. If I close my eyes now and I think about it, about the slice of bread, I think almost at once that in this house I never knew what it was to be scolded. I think if I had told my Aunt Caroline that I had killed a boy in the lot, told her just how it happened, she would have put her arms around me and forgiven me—instantly. That's why perhaps that summer is so precious to me. It was a summer of tacit and complete absolution. That's why I can't forget Weesie either. She was full of a natural goodness, a child who was in love with me and who made no reproaches. She was the first of the other sex to admire me for being *different*. After Weesie it was the other way round. I was loved, but I was hated too for being what I was. Weesie made an effort to understand. The very fact that I came from a strange country, that I spoke another language, drew her closer to me. The way her eyes shone when she presented me to her little friends is something I will never forget. Her eyes seemed to be bursting with love and admiration. Sometimes the three of us would walk to the riverside in the evening and sitting on the bank we would talk as children talk when they are out of sight of their elders. We talked then, I know it now so well, more sanely and more profoundly than our parents. To give us that thick slice of bread each day the parents had to pay a heavy penalty. The worst penalty was that they became estranged from us. For, with each slice they fed us we became not only more indifferent to them, but we became more and more superior to them. In our ungratefulness was our strength and our beauty. Not being devoted we were innocent of all crime. The boy whom I saw drop dead, who lay there motionless, without making the slightest sound or whimper, the killing of that boy seems almost like a clean, healthy performance. The struggle for food, on the other hand, seems foul and degrading and when we stood in the presence of our parents we sensed that they had come to us unclean and for that we could never forgive them. The thick slice of bread in the afternoons, precisely because it was not earned, tasted delicious to us. Never again will bread taste this way. Never again will it be given this way. The day of the murder it was even tastier than ever. It had a slight taste of terror in it which has been lacking ever since. And it was received with Aunt Caroline's tacit but complete absolution.

There is something about the rye bread which I am trying to fathom—something vaguely delicious, terrifying and liberating, something associated with first discoveries. I am thinking of another slice of sour rye which was connected with a still earlier period, when my little friend Stanley and I used to rifle the icebox. That was *stolen* bread and consequently even more marvelous to the palate than the bread which was given with love. But it was in the act of eating the rye bread, the walking around with it and talking at the same time, that something in the nature of revelation occurred. It was like a state of grace, a state of complete ignorance, of self-abnegation. Whatever was imparted to me in these moments I seem to have retained intact and there is no fear that I shall ever lose the knowledge that was gained. It was just the fact perhaps that it was not knowledge as we ordinarily think of it. It was almost like receiving a truth, though truth is almost too precise a word for it. The important thing about the sour rye discussions is that they always took place away from home, away from the eyes of our parents whom we feared but never respected. Left to ourselves there were no limits to what we might imagine. Facts had little importance for us; what we demanded of a subject was that it allow us opportunity to expand. What amazes me, when I look back on it, is how well we understood one another, how well we penetrated to the essential character of each and every one, young or old. At seven years of age we knew with dead certainty, for example, that such a fellow would end up in prison, that another would be a drudge, and another a good for nothing, and so on. We were absolutely correct in our diagnoses, much more correct, for example, than our parents, or our teachers, more correct, indeed, than the so-called psychologists. Alfie Betcha turned out to be an absolute bum; Johnny Gerhardt went to the penitentiary; Bob Kunst became a work horse. Infallible predictions. The learning we received only tended to obscure our vision. From the day we went to school we learned nothing; on the contrary, we were made obtuse, we were wrapped in a fog of words and abstractions.

With the sour rye the world was what it is essentially, a primitive world ruled by magic, a world in which fear plays the most important role. The boy who could inspire the most fear was the leader and he was respected as long as he could maintain his power. There were other boys who were rebels, and they were admired, but they never became the leader. The majority were clay in the hands of the fearless ones; a few could be depended on, but the most not. The air was full of tension—nothing could be predicted for the morrow. This loose, primitive nucleus of a society created sharp appetites, sharp emotions, sharp curiosity. Nothing was taken for granted; each day demanded a new test of power, a new sense of strength or of failure. And so, up until the age of nine or ten, we had a real taste of life—we were on our own. That is, those of us who were fortunate enough not to have been spoiled by our parents, those of us who were free to roam the streets at night and to discover things with our own eyes.

What I am thinking of, with a certain amount of regret and longing, is that this thoroughly restricted life of early boyhood seems like a limitless universe and the life which followed upon it, the life of the adult, a constantly diminishing realm. From the moment when one is put in school one is lost; one has the feeling of having a halter put around his neck. The taste goes out of the bread as it goes out of life. Getting the bread becomes more important than the eating of it. Everything is calculated and everything has a price upon it.

My cousin Gene became an absolute nonentity; Stanley became a first-rate failure. Besides these two boys, for whom I had the greatest affection, there was another, Joey, who has since become a letter carrier. I could weep when I think of what life has made them. As boys they were perfect, Stanley least of all because Stanley was more temperamental. Stanley went into violent rages now and then and there was no telling how you stood with him from day to day. But Joey and Gene were the essence of goodness; they were friends in the old meaning of the word. I think of Joey often when I go out into the country because he was what is called a country boy.

That meant, for one thing, that he was more loyal, more sincere, more tender, than the boys we knew. I can see Joey now coming to meet me; he was always running with arms wide open and ready to embrace me, always breathless with adventures that he was planning for my participation, always loaded with gifts which he had saved for my coming. Joey received me like the monarchs of old received their guests. Everything I looked at was mine. We had innumerable things to tell each other and nothing was dull or boring. The difference between our respective worlds was enormous. Though I was of the city too, still, when I visited my cousin Gene, I became aware of an even greater city, a city of New York proper in which my sophistication was negligible. Stanley knew no excursions from his own neighborhood, but Stanley had come from a strange land over the sea, Poland, and there was always between us the mark of the voyage. The fact that he spoke another tongue also increased our admiration for him. Each one was surrounded by a distinguishing aura, by a well-defined identity which was preserved inviolate. With the entrance into life these traits of difference fell away and we all became more or less alike and, of course, most unlike our own selves. And it is this loss of the peculiar self, of the perhaps unimportant individuality, which saddens me and makes the rye bread stand out glowingly. The wonderful sour rye went into the making of our individual selves; it was like the communion loaf in which all participate but from which each one receives only according to his peculiar state of grace. Now we are eating of the same bread, but without benefit of communion, without grace. We are eating to fill our bellies and our hearts are cold and empty. We are separate but not individual.

There was another thing about the sour rye and that was that we often ate a raw onion with it. I remember standing with Stanley in the late afternoons, a sandwich in hand, in front of the veterinary'? which was just opposite my home.

It always seemed to be late afternoon when Dr. McKinney elected to castrate a stallion, an operation which was done in public and which always gathered a small crowd. I remember the smell of the hot iron and the quivering of the horse's legs, Dr. McKinney's goatee, the taste of the raw onion and the smell of the sewer gas just behind us where they were laying in a new gas main. It was an olfactory performance through and through and, as Abelard so well describes it, practically painless. Not knowing the reason for the operation we used to hold long discussions afterwards which usually ended in a brawl. Nobody liked Dr. McKinney either; there was a smell of iodoform about him and of stale horse piss. Sometimes the gutter in front of his office was filled with blood and in the winter-time the blood froze into the ice and gave a strange look to his sidewalk. Now and then the big two-wheeled cart came, an open cart which smelled like the devil, and they whisked a dead horse into it. Rather it was hoisted in, the carcass, by a long chain which made a creaking noise like the dropping of an anchor. The smell of a bloated dead horse is a foul smell and our street was full of foul smells. On the corner was Paul Sauer's place where raw hides and trimmed hides were stacked up in the street; they stank frightfully too. And then the acrid odor coming from the tin factory behind the house—like the smell of modern progress. The smell of a dead horse, which is almost unbearable, is still a thousand times better than the smell of burning chemicals. And the sight of a dead horse with a bullet hole in the temple, his head lying in a pool of blood and his asshole burst-ing with the last spasmic evacuation, is still a better sight than that of a group of men in blue aprons coming out of the arched doorway of the tin factory with a hand truck loaded with bales of fresh-made tin. Fortunately for us there was a bakery opposite the tin facto-ry and from the back door of the bakery, which was only a grill, we could watch the bak-ers at work and get the sweet, irresistible odor of bread and cake. And if, as I say, the gas mains were being laid there was another strange medley of smells—the smell of earth just turned up, of rotted iron pipes, of sewer gas, and of the onion sandwiches which the Italian laborers ate whilst reclining against the mounds of upturned earth. There were other smells too, of course, but less striking; such, for instance, as the smell of Silverstein's tailor shop where there was always a great deal of pressing going on. This was a hot, fetid stench which can be best apprehended by imagining that Silverstein, who was a lean, smelly Jew himself, was cleaning out the farts which his customers had left behind in their pants. Next door was the candy and stationery shop owned by two daffy old maids who were reli-gious; here there was the almost sickeningly sweet smell of taffy, of Spanish peanuts, of jujubes and Sen-Sen and of Sweet Caporal cigarettes. The stationery store was like a beau-tiful cave, always cool, always full of intriguing objects; where the soda fountain was, which gave off another distinct odor, ran a thick marble slab which turned sour in the summertime and yet mingled pleasantly, the sourness, with the slightly ticklish, dry smell of the carbonated water when it was fizzed into the glass of ice cream.

With the refinements that come with maturity the smells faded out, to be replaced by only one other distinctly memorable, distinctly pleasurable smell—the odor of the cunt. More particularly the odor that lingers on the fingers after playing with a woman, for, if it has not been noticed before, this smell is even more enjoyable, perhaps because it already carries with it the perfume of the past tense, than the odor of the cunt itself. But this odor, which belongs to maturity, is but a faint odor compared with the odors attaching to child-hood. It is an odor which evaporates, almost as quickly in the mind's imagination, as in reality. One can remember many things about the woman one has loved but it is hard to remember the smell of her cunt—with anything like certitude. The smell of wet hair, on the other hand, a woman's wet hair, is much more powerful and lasting—why, I don't know. I can remember even now, after almost forty years, the smell of my Aunt Tillie's hair after she had taken a shampoo. This shampoo was performed in the kitchen which was always overheated. Usually it was a late Saturday afternoon, in preparation for a ball, which meant again another singular thing—that there would appear a cavalry sergeant with very beautiful yellow stripes, a singularly handsome sergeant who even to my eyes was far too gracious, manly and intelligent for an imbecile such as my Aunt Tillie. But anyway, there she sat on a little stool by the kitchen table drying her hair with a towel. Beside her was a little lamp with a smoked chimney and beside the lamp two curling irons the very sight of which filled me with an inexplicable loathing. Generally she had a little mirror propped up on the table; I can see her now making wry faces at herself as she squeezed the blackheads out of her nose. She was a stringy, ugly, imbecilic creature with two enormous buck teeth which gave her a horsey look whenever her lips drew back in a smile. She smelled sweaty, too, even after a bath. But the smell of her hair—that smell I can never forget, because somehow the smell is associated with my hatred and contempt for her. This smell, when the hair was just drying, was like the smell that comes up from the bottom of a marsh. There were two smells—one of the wet hair and another of the same hair when she threw it into the stove and it burst into flame. There were always curled knots of hair which came from her comb, and they were mixed with dandruff and the sweat of her scalp which was greasy and dirty. I used to stand by her side and watch her, wondering what the ball would be like and wondering how she would behave at the ball. When she was all primped up she would ask me if she didn't look beautiful and if I didn't love her, and of course I would tell her yes. But in the water closet later, which was in the hall just next to the kitchen, I would sit in the flickering light of the burning taper which was placed on the window ledge, and I would say to myself that she looked crazy. After she was gone I would pick up the curling irons and smell them and squeeze them. They were revolting and fascinating—like spiders. Everything about this kitchen was fascinating to me. Familiar as I was with it I never conquered it. It was at once so public and so intimate. Here I was given my bath, in the big tin tub, on Saturdays. Here the three sisters washed themselves and primped themselves. Here my grandfather stood at the sink and washed himself to the waist and later handed me his shoes to be shined. Here I stood at the window in the winter time and watched the snow fall, watched it dully, vacantly, as if I were in the womb and listening to the water running while my mother sat on the toilet. It was in the kitchen where the secret confabulations were held, frightening, odious sessions from which they always reappeared with long, grave faces or eyes red with weeping. Why they ran to the kitchen I don't know. But it was often while they stood thus in secret conference, haggling about a will or deciding how to dispense with some poor relative, that the door was suddenly opened and a visitor would arrive, whereupon the atmosphere immediately changed. Changed violently, I mean, as though they were relieved that some outside force had intervened to spare them the horrors of a protracted secret session. I remember now that, seeing that door open and the face of an unexpected visitor peering in, my heart would leap with joy. Soon I would be given a big glass pitcher and asked to run to the corner saloon where I would hand the pitcher in, through the little window at the family entrance, and wait until it was returned brimming with foamy suds. This little run to the corner for a pitcher of beer was an expedition of absolutely incalculable proportions. First of all there was the barber shop just below us, where Stanley's father practiced his profession. Time and again, just as I was dashing out for something, I would see the father giving Stanley a drubbing with the razor strop, a sight that made my blood boil. Stanley was my best friend and his father was nothing but a drunken Polack. One evening, however, as I was dashing out with the pitcher, I had the intense pleasure of seeing another Polack go for Stanley's old man with a razor. I saw his old man coming through the door backwards, the blood running down his neck, his face white as a sheet. He fell on the sidewalk in front of the shop, twitching and moaning, and I remember looking at him for a minute or two and walking on feeling absolutely contented and happy about it. Stanley had sneaked out during the scrimmage and was accompanying me to the saloon door. He was glad too, though he was a bit frightened. When we got back the ambulance was there in front of the door and they were lifting him in on the stretcher, his face and neck covered with a sheet. Sometimes it happened that Father Carroll's pet choirboy strolled by the house just as I was hitting the air. This was an event of primary importance. The boy was older than any of us and he was a sissy, a fairy in the making. His very walk used to enrage us. As soon as he was spotted the news went out in every direction and before he had reached the corner he was surrounded by a gang of boys all much smaller than himself who taunted him and mimicked him until he burst into tears. Then we would pounce on him, like a pack of wolves, pull him to the ground and tear the clothes off his back. It was a disgraceful performance but it made us feel good. Nobody knew yet what a fairy was, but whatever it was we were against it. In the same way we were against the Chinamen. There was one Chinaman, from the laundry up the street, who used to pass frequently and, like the sissy from Father Carroll's church, he too had to run the gantlet. He looked exactly like the picture of a coolie which one sees in the schoolbooks. He wore a sort of black alpaca coat with braided button holes, slippers without heels, and a pigtail. Usually he walked with his hands in his sleeves. It was his walk which I remember best, a sort of sly, mincing, feminine walk which was utterly foreign and menacing to us. We were in mortal dread of him and we hated him because he was absolutely indifferent to our gibes. We thought he was too ignorant to notice our insults. Then one day when we entered the laundry he gave us a little surprise. First he handed us the package of laundry; then he reached down below the counter and gathered a handful of lichee nuts from the big bag. He was smiling as he came from behind the counter to open the door. He was still smiling as he caught hold of Alfie Betcha and pulled his ears; he caught hold of each of us in turn and pulled our ears, still smiling. Then he made a ferocious grimace and, swift as a cat, he ran behind the counter and picked up a long, ugly-looking knife which he brandished at us. We fell over ourselves getting out of the place. When we got to the corner and looked around we saw him standing in the doorway with an iron in his hand looking very calm and peaceful. After this incident nobody would go to the laundry any more; we had to pay little Louis Pirossa a nickel each week to collect the laundry for us. Louis's father owned the fruit stand on the corner. He used to hand us the rotten bananas as a token of his affection. Stanley was especially fond of the rotten bananas as his aunt used to fry them for him. The fried bananas were considered a delicacy in Stanley's home. Once, on his birthday, there was a party given for Stanley and the whole neighborhood was invited. Everything went beautifully until it came to the fried bananas. Somehow nobody wanted to touch the bananas, as this was a dish known only to Polacks like Stanley's parents. It was considered disgusting to eat fried bananas. In the midst of the embarrassment some bright youngster suggested that crazy Willie Maine should be given the fried bananas. Willie Maine was older than any of us but unable to talk. He said nothing but *Bjork! Bjork!* He said this to everything. So when the bananas were passed to him he said *Bjork!* and he reached for them with two hands. But his brother George was there and George felt insulted that they should have palmed off the rotten bananas on his crazy brother. So George started a fight and Willie, seeing his brother attacked, began to fight also, screaming *Bjork! Bjork!* Not only did he strike out at the other boys but at the girls

too, which created a pandemonium. Finally Stanley's old man, hearing the noise, came up
from the barber shop with a strop in his hand. He took crazy Willie Maine by the scruff
of the neck and began to lambast him. Meanwhile his brother George had sneaked off to
call Mr. Maine senior. The latter, who was also a bit of a drunkard, arrived in his shirt
sleeves and seeing poor Willie being beaten by the drunken barber, he went for him with
two stout fists and beat him up unmercifully. Willie, who had gotten free meanwhile, was
on his hands and knees, gobbling up the fried bananas which had fallen on the floor. He
was stuffing them away like a billy goat, fast as he could find them. When the old man
saw him there chewing away like a goat he became furious and picking up the strop he
went after Willie with a vengeance. Now Willie began to howl—*Bjork! Bjork!*—and suddenly everybody began to laugh. That took the steam out of Mr. Maine and he relented.
Finally he sat down and Stanley's aunt brought him a glass of wine. Hearing the racket
some of the other neighbors came in and there was more wine and then beer and then
schnapps and soon everybody was happy and singing and whistling and even the kids got
drunk and then crazy Willie got drunk and again he got down on the floor like a billy goat
and he yelled *Bjork! Bjork!* and Alfie Betcha, who was very drunk though only eight years
old, bit crazy Willie Maine in the backside and then Willie bit him and then we all started biting each other and the parents stood by laughing and screaming with glee and it was
very very merry and there were more fried bananas and everybody ate them this time and
then there were speeches and more bumpers downed and crazy Willie Maine tried to sing
for us but could only sing *Bjork! Bjork!* It was a stupendous success, the birthday party,
and for a week or more no one talked of anything but the party and what good Polacks
Stanley's people were. The fried bananas, too, were a success and for a time it was hard to
get any rotten bananas from Louis Pirossa's old man because they were so much in
demand. And then an event occurred which cast a pall over the entire neighborhood—the
defeat of Joe Gerhardt at the hands of Joey Silverstein. The latter was the tailor's son; he
was a lad of fifteen or sixteen, rather quiet and studious looking, who was shunned by the
other older boys because he was a Jew. One day as he was delivering a pair of pants to
Fillmore Place he was accosted by Joey Gerhardt who was about the same age and who
considered himself a rather superior being. There was an exchange of words and then Joe
Gerhardt pulled the pants away from the Silverstein boy and threw them in the gutter.
Nobody had ever imagined that young Silverstein would reply to such an insult by
recourse to his fists and so when he struck out at Joe Gerhardt and cracked him square in
the jaw everybody was taken aback, most of all Joe Gerhardt himself. There was a fight
which lasted about twenty minutes and at the end Joe Gerhardt lay on the sidewalk unable
to get up. Whereupon the Silverstein boy gathered up the pair of pants and walked quietly and proudly back to his father's shop. Nobody said a word to him. The affair was
regarded as a calamity. Who had ever heard of a Jew beating up a Gentile? It was something inconceivable, and yet it had happened, right before everyone's eyes. Night after
night, sitting on the curb as we used to, the situation was discussed from every angle, but
without any solution until... well until Joe Gerhardt's younger brother, Johnny, became so
wrought up about it that he decided to settle the matter himself. Johnny, though younger
and smaller than his brother, was as tough and invincible as a young puma. He was typical of the shanty Irish who made up the neighborhood. His idea of getting even with
young Silverstein was to lie in wait for him one evening as the latter was stepping out of
the store and trip him up. When he tripped him up that evening he had provided himself

in advance with two little rocks which he concealed in his fists and when poor Silverstein went down he pounced on him and then with the two handsome little rocks he pounded poor Silverstein's temples. To his amazement Silverstein offered no resistance; even when he got up and gave him a chance to get to his feet Silverstein never so much as budged. Then Johnny got frightened and ran away. He must have been thoroughly frightened because he never came back again; the next that was heard of him was that he had been picked up out West somewhere and sent to a reformatory. His mother, who was a slatternly, jolly Irish bitch, said that it served him right and she hoped to God she'd never lay eyes on him again. When the boy Silverstein recovered he was not the same any more; people said the beating had affected his brain, that he was a little daffy. Joe Gerhardt, on the other hand, rose to prominence again. It seems that he had gone to see the Silverstein boy while he lay in bed and had made a deep apology to him. This again was something that had never been heard of before. It was something so strange, so unusual, that Joe Gerhardt was looked upon almost as a knight errant. Nobody had approved of the way Johnny behaved, and yet nobody would have thought of going to young Silverstein and apologizing to him. That was an act of such delicacy, such elegance, that Joe Gerhardt was looked upon as a real gentleman—the first and only gentleman in the neighborhood. It was a word that had never been used among us and now it was on everybody's lips and it was considered a distinction to be a gentleman. This sudden transformation of the defeated Joe Gerhardt into a gentleman I remember made a deep impression upon me. A few years later, when I moved into another neighborhood and encountered Claude de Lorraine, a French boy, I was prepared to understand and accept "a gentleman." This Claude was a boy such as I had never laid eyes on before. In the old neighborhood he would have been regarded as a sissy; for one thing he spoke too well, too correctly, too politely, and for another thing he was too considerate, too gentle, too gallant. And then, while playing with him, to hear him suddenly break into French as his mother or father came along, provided us with something like a shock. German we had heard and German was a permissible transgression, but French! why to talk French, or even to understand it, was to be thoroughly alien, thoroughly aristocratic, rotten, distingué. And yet Claude was one of us, as good as us in every way, even a little bit better, we had to admit secretly. But there was a blemish—his French! It antagonized us. He had no right to be living in our neighborhood, no right to be as capable and manly as he was. Often, when his mother called him in and we had said goodby to him, we got together in the lot and we discussed the Lorraine family backwards and forwards. We wondered what they ate, for example, because being French they must have different customs than ours. No one had ever set foot in Claude de Lorraine's home either—that was another suspicious and repugnant fact. Why? What were they concealing? Yet when they passed us in the street they were always very cordial, always smiled, always spoke in English and a most excellent English it was. They used to make us feel rather ashamed of ourselves—they were superior, that's what it was. And there was still another baffling thing—with the other boys a direct question brought a direct answer, but with Claude de Lorraine there was never any direct answer. He always smiled very charmingly before replying and he was very cool, collected, employing an irony and a mockery which was beyond us. He was a thorn in our side, Claude de Lorraine, and when finally he moved out of the neighborhood we all breathed a sigh of relief. As for myself, it was only maybe ten or fifteen years later that I thought about this boy and his strange, elegant behavior. And it was then that I felt I had made a bad blunder. For suddenly one day it occurred to me that Claude de Lorraine had come up to me on a certain occasion obviously to win my friendship and I had treated him rather cavalierly. At the time I thought of this incident it suddenly dawned on me that Claude de Lorraine must have seen something different in me and that he had meant to honor me by extending the hand of friendship. But back in those days I had a code of honor, such as it was, and that was to run with the herd. Had I become a bosom friend of Claude de Lorraine I would have been betraying the other boys. No matter what advantages lay in the wake of such a friendship they were not for me; I was one of the gang and it was my duty to remain aloof from such as Claude de Lorraine. I remembered this incident once again, I must say, after a still greater interval—after I had been in France a few months and the word *raisonnable* had come to acquire a wholly new significance for me. Suddenly one day, overhearing it, I thought of Claude de Lorraine's overtures on the street in front of his house. I recalled vividly that he had used the word *reasonable*. He had probably asked me to be *reasonable,* a word which then would never have crossed my lips as there was no need for it in my vocabulary. It was a word, like gentleman, which was rarely brought out and then only with great discretion and circumspection. It was a word which might cause others to laugh at you. There were lots of words like that—*really,* for example. No one I knew had ever used the word *really*—until Jack Lawson came along. He used it because his parents were English and, though we made fun of him, we forgave him for it. *Really* was a word which reminded me immediately of little Carl Ragner from the old neighborhood. Carl Ragner was the only son of a politician who lived on the rather distinguished little street called Fillmore Place. He lived near the end of the street in a little red brick house which was always beautifully kept. I remember the house because passing it on my way to school I used to remark how beautifully the brass knobs on the door were polished. In fact, nobody else had brass knobs on their doors. Anyway, little Carl Ragner was one of those boys who was not allowed to associate with other boys. He was rarely seen, as a matter of fact. Usually it was a Sunday that we caught a glimpse of him walking with his father. Had his father not been a powerful figure in the neighborhood Carl would have been stoned to death. He was really impossible, in his Sunday garb. Not only did he wear long pants and patent leather shoes, but he sported a derby and a cane. At six years of age a boy who would allow himself to be dressed up in this fashion must be a ninny—that was the consensus of opinion. Some said he was sickly, as though that were an excuse for his eccentric dress. The strange thing is that I never once heard him speak. He was so elegant, so refined, that perhaps he had imagined it was bad manners to speak in public. At any rate, I used to lie in wait for him Sunday mornings just to see him pass with his old man. I watched him with the same avid curiosity that I would watch the firemen cleaning the engines in the firehouse. Sometimes on the way home he would be carrying a little box of ice cream, the smallest size they had, probably just enough for him, for his dessert. Dessert was another word which had somehow become familiar to us and which we used derogatorily when referring to the likes of little Carl Ragner and his family. We could spend hours wondering what these people ate for *dessert,* our pleasure consisting principally in bandying about this new-found word, *dessert,* which had probably been smuggled out of the Ragner household. It must also have been about this time that Santos Dumont came into fame. For us there was something grotesque about the name Santos Dumont. About his exploits we were not much concerned—just the name. For most of us it smelled of sugar, of Cuban plantations, of the strange Cuban flag which had a star in the corner and which was always highly regarded by those who saved the little cards which were given away with Sweet Caporal cigarettes and on which there were represented either the flags of the different nations or the leading soubrettes of the stage or the famous pugilists. Santos Dumont, then, was something delightfully foreign, in contradistinction to the usual foreign person or object, such as the Chinese laundry, or Claude de Lorraine's haughty French family. Santos Dumont was a magical word which suggested a beautiful flowing mustache, a sombrero, spurs, something airy, delicate, humorous, quixotic. Sometimes it brought up the aroma of coffee beans and of straw mats, or, because it was so thoroughly outlandish and quixotic, it would entail a digression concerning the life of the Hottentots. For there were among us, older boys who were beginning to read and who would entertain us by the hour with fantastic tales which they had gleaned from books such as *Ayesha* or Ouida's *Under Two Flags*. The real flavor of knowledge is most definitely associated in my mind with the vacant lot at the corner of the new neighborhood where I was transplanted at about the age of ten. Here, when the fall days came on and we stood about the bonfire roasting chippies and raw potatoes in the little cans which we carried, there ensued a new type of discussion which differed from the old discussions I had known in that the origins were always bookish. Some one had just read a book of adventure, or a book of science, and forthwith the whole street became animated by the introduction of a hitherto unknown subject. It might be that one of these boys had just discovered that there was such a thing as the Japanese current and he would try to explain to us how the Japanese current came into existence and what the purpose of it was. This was the only way we learned things— against the fence, as it were, while roasting chippies and raw potatoes. These bits of knowledge sunk deep—so deep, in fact, that later, confronted with a more accurate knowledge it was often difficult to dislodge the older knowledge. In this way it was explained to us one day by an older boy that the Egyptians had known about the circulation of the blood, something which seemed so natural to us that it was hard later to swallow the story of the discovery of the circulation of the blood by an Englishman named Harvey. Nor does it seem strange to me now that in those days most of our conversation was about remote places, such as China, Peru, Egypt, Africa, Iceland, Greenland. We talked about ghosts, about God, about the transmigration of souls, about Hell, about astronomy, about strange birds and fish, about the formation of precious stones, about rubber plantations, about methods of torture, about the Aztecs and the Incas, about marine life, about volcanoes and earthquakes, about burial rites and wedding ceremonies in various parts of the earth, about languages, about the origin of the American Indian, about the buffaloes dying out, about strange diseases, about cannibalism, about wizardry, about trips to the moon and what it was like there, about murderers and highwaymen, about the miracles in the Bible, about the manufacture of pottery, about a thousand and one subjects which were never mentioned at home or in school and which were vital to us because we were starved and the world was full of wonder and mystery and it was only when we stood shivering in the vacant lot that we got to talking seriously and felt a need for communication which was at once pleasurable and terrifying. The wonder and the mystery of life—which is throttled in us as we become responsible members of society! Until we were pushed out to work the world was very small and we were living on the fringe of it, on the frontier, as it were, of the unknown. A small Greek world which was nevertheless deep enough to provide all manner of variation, all manner of adventure and speculation. Not so very small either, since it held in reserve the most boundless potentialities. I have gained nothing by the enlargement of my world; on the contrary, I have lost. I want to become more and more childish and to pass beyond childhood in the opposite direction. I want to go exactly contrary to the normal line of development, pass into a superinfantile realm of being which will be absolutely crazy and chaotic but not crazy and chaotic as the world about me. I have been an adult and a father and a responsible member of society. I have earned my daily bread. I have adapted myself to a world which never was mine. I want to break through this enlarged world and stand again on the frontier of an unknown world which will throw this pale, unilateral world into shadow. I want to pass beyond the responsibility of fatherhood to the irresponsibility of the anarchic man who cannot be coerced nor wheedled nor cajoled nor bribed nor traduced. I want to take as my guide Oberon the nightrider who, under the spread of his black wings, eliminates both the beauty and the horror of the past; I want to flee toward a perpetual dawn with a swiftness and relentlessness that leaves no room for remorse, regret, or repentance. I want to outstrip the inventive man who is a curse to the earth in order to stand once again before an impassable deep which not even the strongest wings will enable me to traverse. Even if I must become a wild and natural park inhabited only by idle dreamers I must not stop to rest here in the ordered fatuity of responsible, adult life. I must do this in remembrance of a life beyond all comparison with the life which was promised me, in remembrance of the life of a child who was strangled and stifled by the mutual consent of those who had surrendered. Everything which the fathers and the mothers created I disown. I am going back to a world even smaller than the old Hellenic world, going back to a world which I can always touch with outstretched arms, the world of what I know and see and recognize from moment to moment. Any other world is meaningless to me, and alien and hostile. In retraversing the first bright world which I knew as a child I wish not to rest there but to muscle back to a still brighter world from which I must have escaped. What this world is like I do not know, nor am I even sure that I will find it, but it is my world and nothing else intrigues me.

The first glimpse, the first realization, of the bright new world came through my meeting Roy Hamilton. I was in my twenty-first year, probably the worst year of my whole life. I was in such a state of despair that I had decided to leave home. I thought and spoke only of California where I had planned to go to start a new life. So violently did I dream of this new promised land that later, when I had returned from California, I scarcely remembered the California I had seen but thought and spoke only of the California which I had known in my dreams. It was just prior to my leave-taking that I met Hamilton. He was a dubious half brother to my old friend MacGregor; they had only recently made each other's acquaintance, as Roy, who had lived most of his life in California, had been under the impression all along that his real father was Mr. Hamilton and not Mr. MacGregor. As a matter of fact it was in order to disentangle the mystery surrounding his parentage that he had come East. Living with the MacGregors had apparently brought him no nearer to a solution of the mystery. Indeed he seemed to be more perplexed than ever after getting acquainted with the man who he had concluded must be his legitimate father. He was perplexed, as he later admitted to me, because in neither man could he find any resemblance to the man he considered himself to be. It was probably this harassing problem of deciding whom to take for a father which had stimulated the development of his own character. I say this, because immediately upon being introduced to him, I felt that I was in the presence of a being such as I had never known before. I had been prepared, through

MacGregor's description of him, to meet a rather "strange" individual, "strange" in MacGregor's mouth meaning slightly cracked. He was indeed strange, but so sharply sane that I at once felt exalted. For the first time I was talking to a man who got behind the meaning of words and went to the very essence of things. I felt that I was talking to a philosopher, not a philosopher such as I had encountered through books, but a man who philosophized constantly—and *who lived this philosophy which he expounded.* That is to say, he had no theory at all, except to penetrate to the very essence of things and, in the light of each fresh revelation to so live his life that there would be a minimum of discord between the truths which were revealed to him and the exemplification of these truths in action. Naturally his behavior was strange to those about him. It had not, however, been strange to those who knew him out on the Coast where, as he said, he was in his own element. There apparently he was regarded as a superior being and was listened to with the utmost respect, even with awe.

I came upon him in the midst of a struggle which I only appreciated many years later. At the time I couldn't see the importance which he attached to finding his real father; in fact, I used to joke about it because the role of the father meant little to me, or the role of the mother, for that matter. In Roy Hamilton I saw the ironic struggle of a man who had already emancipated himself and yet was seeking to establish a solid biological link for which he had absolutely no need. This conflict over the real father had, paradoxically, made him a superfather. He was a teacher and an exemplar; he had only to open his mouth for me to realize that I was listening to a wisdom which was utterly different from anything which I had heretofore associated with that word. It would be easy to dismiss him as a mystic, for a mystic he undoubtedly was, but he was the first mystic I had ever encountered who also knew how to keep his feet on the ground.

He was a mystic who knew how to invent practical things, among them a drill such as was badly needed for the oil industry and from which he later made a fortune. Because of his strange metaphysical talk, however, nobody at the time gave much heed to his very practical invention. It was regarded as another one of his cracked ideas.

He was continually talking about himself and his relation to the world about, a quality which created the unfortunate impression that he was simply a blatant egotist. It was even said, which was true enough as far as it went, that he seemed more concerned about the truth of Mr. MacGregor's fatherhood than about Mr. MacGregor, the father. The implication was that he had no real love for his new-found father but was simply deriving a strong personal gratification from the truth of the discovery, that he was exploiting his discovery in his usual self-aggrandizing way. It was deeply true, of course, because Mr. MacGregor in the flesh was infinitely less than Mr. MacGregor as symbol of the lost father. But the MacGregors knew nothing about symbols and would never have understood even had it been explained to them. They were making a contradictory effort to at once embrace the long lost son and at the same time reduce him to an understandable level on which they could seize him not as the "long lost" but simply as the son. Whereas it was obvious to any one with the least intelligence that this son was not a son at all but a sort of spiritual father, a sort of Christ, I might say, who was making a most valiant effort to accept as blood and flesh what he had already all too clearly freed himself from.

I was surprised and flattered, therefore, that this strange individual whom I looked upon with the warmest admiration should elect to make me his confidant. By comparison I was very bookish, intellectual, and worldly in a wrong way. But almost immediately I discarded this side of my nature and allowed myself to bask in the warm, immediate light which his profound and natural intuition of things created. To come into his presence gave me the sensation of being undressed, or rather peeled, for it was much more than mere nakedness which he demanded of the person he was talking to. In talking to me he addressed himself to a me whose existence I had only dimly suspected, the me, for example, which emerged when, suddenly, reading a book, I realized that I had been dreaming. Few books had this faculty of putting me into a trance, this trance of utter lucidity in which, unknown to oneself, one makes the deepest resolutions. Roy Hamilton's conversation partook of this quality. It made me more than ever alert, preternaturally alert, without at the same time crumbling the fabric of dream. He was appealing in other words, to the germ of the self, to the being who would eventually outgrow the naked personality, the synthetic individuality, and leave me truly alone and solitary in order to work out my own proper destiny.

Our talk was like a secret language in the midst of which the others went to sleep or faded away like ghosts. For my friend MacGregor it was baffling and irritating; he knew me more intimately than any of the other fellows but he had never found anything in me to correspond to the character which I now presented him with. He spoke of Roy Hamilton as a bad influence, which again was deeply true since this unexpected meeting with his half brother served more than anything else to alienate us. Hamilton opened my eyes and gave me new values, and though later I was to lose the vision which he had bequeathed me, nevertheless I could never again see the world, or my friends, as I had seen them prior to his coming. Hamilton altered me profoundly, as only a rare book, a rare personality, a rare experience, can alter one. For the first time in my life I understood what it was to experience a vital friendship and yet not to feel enslaved or attached because of the experience. Never, after we parted, did I feel the need of his actual presence; he had given himself completely and I possessed him without being possessed.

It was the first clean, whole experience of friendship, and it was never duplicated by any other friend. Hamilton was friendship itself, rather than a friend. He was the symbol personified and consequently entirely satisfactory, hence no longer necessary to me. He himself understood this thoroughly. Perhaps it was the fact of having no father that pushed him along the road toward the discovery of the self, which is the final process of identification with the world and the realization consequently of the uselessness of ties. Certainly, as he stood then, in the full plenitude of self-realization, no one was necessary to him, least of all the father of flesh and blood whom he vainly sought in Mr. MacGregor. It must have been in the nature of a last test for him, his coming East and seeking out his real father, for when he said good-by, when he renounced Mr. MacGregor and Mr. Hamilton also, he was like a man who had purified himself of all dross. Never have I seen a man look so single, so utterly alone and alive and confident of the future as Roy Hamilton looked when he said good-by. And never have I seen such confusion and misunderstanding as he left behind with the MacGregor family. It was as though he had died in their midst, had been resurrected, and was taking leave of them as an utterly new, unknown individual. I can see them now standing in the areaway, their hands sort of foolishly, helplessly empty, weeping they knew not why, unless it was because they were bereft of something they had never possessed. I like to think of it in just this way. They were bewildered and bereft, and vaguely, so very vaguely aware that somehow a great opportunity had been offered them which they had not the strength or the imagination to seize.

It was this which the foolish, empty fluttering of the hands indicated to me; it was a gesture more painful to witness than anything I can imagine. It gave me the feeling of the horrible inadequacy of the world when brought face to face with truth. It gave me the feeling of the stupidity of the blood tie and of the love which is not spiritually imbued.

I look back rapidly and I see myself again in California. I am alone and I am working like a slave in the orange grove at Chula Vista. Am I coming into my own? I think not. I am a very wretched, forlorn, miserable person. I seem to have lost everything. In fact, I am hardly a person—I am more nearly an animal. All day long I am standing or walking behind the two jackasses which are hitched to my sledge. I have no thoughts, no dreams, no desires. I am thoroughly healthy and empty. I am a nonentity. I am so thoroughly alive and healthy that I am like the luscious deceptive fruit which hangs on the Californian trees. One more ray of sun and I will be rotten. *"Pourri avant d'etre muri!"*

Is it really *me* that is rotting in this bright California sunshine? Is there nothing left of me, of all that I was up to this moment? Let me think a bit.... There was Arizona. I remember now that it was already night when I first set foot on Arizona soil. Just light enough to catch the last glimpse of a fading mesa. I am walking through the main street of a little town whose name is lost. What am I doing here on this street, in this town? Why, I am in love with Arizona, an Arizona of the mind which I search for in vain with my two good eyes. In the train there was still with me the Arizona which I had brought from New York—even after we had crossed the state line. Was there not a bridge over a canyon which had startled me out of my reverie? A bridge such as I had never seen before, a natural bridge created by a cataclysmic eruption thousands of years ago? And over this bridge I had seen a man crossing, a man who looked like an Indian, and he was riding a horse and there was a long saddlebag hanging beside the stirrup. A natural millenary bridge which in the dying sun with air so clear looked like the youngest, newest bridge imaginable. And over that bridge so strong, so durable, there passed, praise be to God, just a man and a horse, nothing more. This then was Arizona, and Arizona was *not* a figment of the imagination but the imagination itself dressed as a horse and rider. And this was even more than the imagination itself because there was no aura of ambiguity but only sharp and dead isolate the thing itself which was the dream and the dreamer himself seated on horseback. And as the train stops I put my foot down and my foot has put a deep hole in the dream; I am in the Arizona town which is listed in the timetable and it is only the geographical Arizona which anybody can visit who has the money. I am walking along the main street with a valise and I see hamburger sandwiches and real estate offices. I feel so terribly deceived that I begin to weep. It is dark now and I stand at the end of a street, where the desert begins, and I weep like a fool. Which me is this weeping? Why it is the new little me which had begun to germinate back in Brooklyn and which is now in the midst of a vast desert and doomed to perish. *Now, Roy Hamilton, I need you!* I need you for one moment, just one little moment, while I am falling apart. I need you because I was not quite ready to do what I have done. And do I not remember your telling me that it was unnecessary to make the trip, but to do it if I must? Why didn't you persuade me not to go? Ah, to persuade was never his way. And to ask advice was never my way. So here I am, bankrupt in the desert, and the bridge which was real is behind me and what is unreal is before me and Christ only knows I am so puzzled and bewildered that if I could sink into the earth and disappear I would do so. I look back rapidly and I see another man who was left to perish quietly in the bosom of his family—*my father*. I understand better what happened to him if I go back very, very far and think of such streets as Maujer, Conselyea, Humboldt... Humboldt particularly. These streets belonged to a neighborhood which was not far removed from our neighborhood but which was different, more glamorous, more mysterious. I had been on Humboldt Street only once as a child and I no longer remember the reason for that excursion unless it was to visit some sick relative languishing in a German hospital. But the street itself made a most lasting impression upon me; why I have not the faintest idea. It remains in my memory as the most mysterious and the most promising street that ever I have seen. Perhaps when we were making ready to go my mother had, as usual, promised something spectacular as a reward for accompanying her. I was always being promised things which never materialized. Perhaps then, when I got to Humboldt Street and looked upon this new world with astonishment, perhaps I forgot completely what had been promised me and the street itself became the reward. I remember that it was very wide and that there were high stoops, such as I had never seen before, on either side of the street. I remember too that in a dressmaker's shop on the first floor of one of these strange houses there was a bust in the window with a tape measure slung around the neck and I know that I was greatly moved by this sight. There was snow on the ground but the sun was out strong and I recall vividly how about the bottoms of the ash barrels which had been frozen into the ice there was then a little pool of water left by the melting snow. The whole street seemed to be melting in the radiant winter's sun. On the bannisters of the high stoops the mounds of snow which had formed such beautiful white pads were now beginning to slide, to disintegrate, leaving dark patches of the brownstone which was then much in vogue. The little glass signs of the dentists and physicians, tucked away in the corners of the windows, gleamed brilliantly in the noonday sun and gave me the feeling for the first time that these offices were perhaps not the torture chambers which I knew them to be. I imagined, in my childish way, that here in this neighborhood, in this street particularly, people were more friendly, more expansive, and of course infinitely more wealthy. I must have expanded greatly myself though only a tot, because for the first time I was looking upon a street which seemed devoid of terror. It was the sort of street, ample, luxurious, gleaming, melting which later, when I began reading Dostoevski, I associated with the thaws of St. Petersburg. Even the churches here were of a different style of architecture; there was something semi-Oriental about them, something grandiose and warm at the same time, which both frightened me and intrigued me. On this broad, spacious street I saw that the houses were set well back from the sidewalk, reposing in quiet and dignity, and unmarred by the intercalation of shops and factories and veterinary stables. I saw a street composed of nothing but residences and I was filled with awe and admiration. All this I remember and no doubt it influenced me greatly, yet none of this is sufficient to account for the strange power and attraction which the very mention of Humboldt Street still evokes in me. Some years later I went back in the night to look at this street again, and I was even more stirred than when I had looked upon it for the first time. The aspect of the street of course had changed, but it was night and the night is always less cruel than the day. Again I experienced the strange delight of spaciousness, of that luxuriousness which was now somewhat faded but still redolent, still assertive in a patchy way as once the brown-stone bannisters had asserted themselves through the melting snow. Most distinct of all, however, was the almost voluptuous sensation of being on the verge of a discovery. Again I was strongly aware of my mother's presence, of the big puffy sleeves of her fur coat, of the cruel swiftness with which she had whisked me through the street years ago and of the stubborn tenacity with which I had feasted my eyes on all that was new and strange. On the occasion of this second visit I seemed to dimly recall another character out of my childhood, the old housekeeper whom they called by the outlandish name of Mrs. Kicking. I could not recall her being taken ill but I did seem to recall the fact that we were paying her a visit at the hospital where she was dying and that this hospital must have been near Humboldt Street which was not dying but which was radiant in the melting snow of a winter's noon. What then had my mother promised me that I have never since been able to recall? Capable as she was of promising anything, perhaps that day, in a fit of abstraction, she had promised something so preposterous that even I with all my childish credulity could not quite swallow it. And yet, if she had promised me the moon, though I knew it was out of the question, I would have struggled to invest her promise with a crumb of faith. I wanted desperately everything that was promised me, and if, upon reflection I realized that it was clearly impossible, I nevertheless tried in my own way to grope for a means of making these promises realizable. That people could make promises without ever having the least intention of fulfilling them was something unimaginable to me. Even when I was most cruelly deceived I still believed; I believed that something extraordinary and quite beyond the other person's power had intervened to make the promise null and void.

This question of belief, this old promise that was never fulfilled, is what makes me think of my father who was deserted at the moment of his greatest need. Up to the time of his illness neither my father nor my mother had ever shown any religious inclinations. Though always upholding the church to others, they themselves never set foot in a church from the time that they were married. Those who attended church too regularly they looked upon as being a bit daffy. The very way they said—"so and so is religious"—was enough to convey the scorn and contempt, or else the pity, which they felt for such individuals. If now and then, because of us children, the pastor called at the house unexpectedly, he was treated as one to whom they were obliged to defer out of ordinary politeness but whom they had nothing in common with, whom they were a little suspicious of, in fact, as representative of a species midway between a fool and a charlatan. To us, for example, they would say "a lovely man," but when their cronies came round and the gossip began to fly, then one would hear an entirely different brand of comment, accompanied usually by peals of scornful laughter and sly mimicry.

My father fell mortally ill as a result of swearing off too abruptly. All his life he had been a jolly hail fellow well met: he had put on a rather becoming paunch, his cheeks were well filled out and red as a beet, his manners were easy and indolent, and he seemed destined to live on into a ripe old age, sound and healthy as a nut. But beneath this smooth and jolly exterior things were not at all well. His affairs were in bad shape, the debts were piling up, and already some of his older friends were beginning to drop him. My mother's attitude was what worried him most. She saw things in a black light and she took no trouble to conceal it. Now and then she became hysterical and went at him hammer and tongs, swearing at him in the vilest language and smashing the dishes and threatening to run away for good. The upshot of it was that he arose one morning determined never to touch another drop. Nobody believed that he meant it seriously; there had been others in the family who swore off, who went on the water wagon, as they used to say, but who quickly tumbled off again. No one in the family, and they had all tried at different times, had ever become a successful teetotaler. But my old man was different. Where or how he got the strength to maintain his resolution, God only knows. It seems incredible to me, because had I been in his boots myself I would have drunk myself to death. Not the old man, however. This was the first time in his life he had ever shown any resolution about anything. My mother was so astounded that, idiot that she was, she began to make fun of him, to quip him about his strength of will which had heretofore been so lamentably weak. Still he stuck to his guns. His drinking pals faded away rather quickly. In short, he soon found himself almost completely isolated. That must have cut him to the quick, for before very many weeks had passed, he became deathly ill and a consultation was held. He recovered a bit, enough to get out of bed and walk about, but still a very sick man. He was supposed to be suffering from ulcers of the stomach, though nobody was quite sure exactly what ailed him. Everybody understood, however, that he had made a mistake in swearing off so abruptly. It was too late, however, to return to a temperate mode of living. His stomach was so weak that it wouldn't even hold a plate of soup. In a couple of months he was almost a skeleton. And old. He looked like Lazarus raised from the grave.

One day my mother took me aside and with tears in her eyes begged me to go visit the family doctor and learn the truth about my father's condition. Dr. Rausch had been the family physician for years. He was a typical "Dutchman" of the old school, rather weary and crochety now after years of practicing and yet unable to tear himself completely away from his patients. In his stupid Teutonic way he tried to scare the less serious patients away, tried to argue them into health, as it were. When you walked into his office he didn't even bother to look up at you, but kept on writing or whatever it might be that he was doing while firing random questions at you in a perfunctory and insulting manner. He behaved so rudely, so suspiciously, that ridiculous as it may sound, it almost appeared as though he expected his patients to bring with them not only their ailments, but the *proof* of their ailments. He made one feel that there was not only something wrong physically but that there was also something wrong mentally. "You only imagine it" was his favorite phrase, which he flung out with a nasty, leering gibe. Knowing him as I did, and detesting him heartily, I came prepared, that is, with the laboratory analysis of my father's stool. I had also an analysis of his urine in my overcoat pocket, should he demand further proofs.

When I was a boy Dr. Rausch had shown some affection for me, but ever since the day I went to him with a dose of clap he had lost confidence in me and always showed a sour puss when I stuck my head through the door. Like father like son was his motto, and I was therefore not at all surprised when, instead of giving me the information which I demanded, he began to lecture me and the old man at the same time for our way of living. "You can't go against Nature," he said with a wry, solemn face, not looking at me as he uttered the words but making some useless notation in his big ledger. I walked quietly up to his desk, stood beside him a moment without making a sound, and then, when he looked up with his usual aggrieved, irritated expression, I said—"I didn't come here for moral instruction... I want to know what's the matter with my father." At this he jumped up and turning to me with his most severe look, he said, like the stupid, brutal Dutchman that he was: "Your father hasn't a chance of recovering; he'll be dead in less than six months." I said "Thank you, that's all I wanted to know," and I made for the door. Then, as though he felt that he had committed a blunder, he strode after me heavily and, putting his hand on my shoulder, he tried to modify the statement by hemming and hawing and saying I don't mean that it is absolutely certain he will die, etc., which I cut short by opening the door and yelling at him, at the top of my lungs, so that his patients in the anteroom would hear it—"I think you're a goddamned old fart and I hope you croak, good night!"

When I got home I modified the doctor's report somewhat by saying that my father's condition was very serious but that if he took good care of himself he would pull through all right. This seemed to cheer the old man up considerably. Of his own accord he took to a diet of milk and zwieback which, whether it was the best thing or not, certainly did him no harm. He remained a sort of semi-invalid for about a year, becoming more and more calm inwardly as time went on and apparently determined to let nothing disturb his peace of mind, nothing, no matter if everything went to hell. As he grew stronger he took to making a daily promenade to the cemetery which was nearby. There he would sit on a bench in the sun and watch the old people potter around the graves. The proximity to the grave, instead of rendering him morbid, seemed to cheer him up. He seemed, if anything, to have become reconciled to the idea of eventual death, a fact which no doubt he had heretofore refused to look in the face. Often he came home with flowers which he had picked in the cemetery, his face beaming with a quiet, serene joy, and seating himself in the armchair he would recount the conversation which he had had that morning with one of the other valetudinarians who frequented the cemetery. It was obvious after a time that he was really enjoying his sequestration, or rather not just enjoying it, but profiting deeply from the experience in a way that was beyond my mother's intelligence to fathom. He was getting lazy, was the way she expressed it. Sometimes she put it even more extremely, tapping her head with her forefinger as she spoke, but not saying anything overtly because of my sister who was without question a little wrong in the head.

And then one day, through the courtesy of an old widow who used to visit her son's grave every day and was, as my mother would say, "religious," he made the acquaintance of a minister belonging to one of the neighboring churches. This was a momentous event in the old man's life. Suddenly he blossomed forth and that little sponge of a soul which had almost atrophied through lack of nourishment took on such astounding proportions that he was almost unrecognizable. The man who was responsible for this extraordinary change in the old man was in no way unusual himself; he was a Congregationalist minister attached to a modest little parish which adjoined our neighborhood. His one virtue was that he kept his religion in the background. The old man quickly fell into a sort of boyish idolatry; he talked of nothing but this minister whom he considered his friend. As he had never looked at the Bible in his life, nor any other book for that matter, it was rather startling, to say the least, to hear him say a little prayer before eating. He performed this little ceremony in a strange way, much the way one takes a tonic, for example. If he recommended me to read a certain chapter of the Bible he would add very seriously—"it will do you good." It was a new medicine which he had discovered, a sort of quack remedy which was guaranteed to cure all ills and which one might take even if he had no ills, because in any case it could certainly do no harm. He attended all the services, all the functions which were held at the church, and between times, when out for a stroll, for example, he would stop off at the minister's home and have a little chat with him. If the minister said that the president was a good soul and should be re-elected the old man would repeat to every one exactly what the minister had said and urge them to vote for the president's re-election. Whatever the minister said was right and just and nobody could gainsay him. There's no doubt that it was an education for the old man. If the minister had mentioned the pyramids in the course of his sermon the old man immediately began to inform himself about the pyramids. He would talk about the pyramids as though every one owed it to himself to become acquainted with the subject. The minister had said that the pyramids were one of the crowning glories of man, ergo not to know about the pyramids was to be disgracefully ignorant, almost sinful. Fortunately the minister didn't dwell much on the subject of sin; he was of the modern type of preacher who prevailed on his flock more by arousing their curiosity than by appealing to their conscience. His sermons were more like a night-school extension course and for such as the old man, therefore, highly entertaining and stimulating. Every now and then the male members of the congregation were invited to a little blowout which was intended to demonstrate that the good pastor was just an ordinary man like themselves and could, on occasion, enjoy a hearty meal and even a glass of beer. Moreover it was observed that he even sang—not religious hymns, but jolly little songs of the popular variety. Putting two and two together one might even infer from such jolly behavior that now and then he enjoyed getting a little piece of tail—always in moderation, to be sure. That was the word that was balsam to the old man's lacerated soul— "moderation." It was like discovering a new sign in the zodiac. And though he was still too ill to attempt a return to even a moderate way of living, nevertheless it did his soul good. And so, when Uncle Ned, who was continually going on the water wagon and continually falling off it again, came round to the house one evening the old man delivered him a little lecture on the virtue of moderation. Uncle Ned was, at that moment, *on* the water wagon and so, when the old man, moved by his own words, suddenly went to the sideboard to fetch a decanter of wine every one was shocked. No one had ever dared invite Uncle Ned to drink when he had sworn off; to venture such a thing constituted a serious breach of loyalty. But the old man did it with such conviction that no one could take offense, and the result was that Uncle Ned took a small glass of wine and went home that evening without stopping off at a saloon to quench his thirst. It was an extraordinary happening and there was much talk about it for days after. In fact, Uncle Ned began to act a bit queer from that day on. It seems that he went the next day to the wine store and bought a bottle of sherry which he emptied into the decanter. He placed the decanter on the sideboard, just as he had seen the old man do, and, instead of polishing it off in one swoop, he contented himself with a glassful at a time—"just a thimbleful," as he put it. His behavior was so remarkable that my aunt, who was unable to quite believe her eyes, came one day to the house and held a long conversation with the old man. She asked him, among other things, to invite the minister to the house some evening so that Uncle Ned might have the opportunity of falling under his beneficent influence. The long and short of it was that Ned was soon taken into the fold and, like the old man, seemed to be thriving under the experience. Things went fine until the day of the picnic. That day, unfortunately, was an unusually warm day and, what with the games, the excitement, the hilarity, Uncle Ned developed an extraordinary thirst. It was not until he was three sheets to the wind that some one observed the regularity and the frequency with which he was running to the beer keg. It was then too late. Once in that condition he was unmanageable. Even the minister could do nothing with him. Ned broke away from the picnic quietly and went on a little rampage which lasted for three days and nights. Perhaps it would have lasted longer had he not gotten into a fist fight down at the waterfront where he was found lying unconscious by the night watchman. He was taken to the hospital with a concussion of the brain from which he never recovered. Returning from the funeral the old man said with a dry eye—"Ned didn't know what it was to be temperate. It was his own fault. Anyway, he's better off now...."

And as though to prove to the minister that he was not made of the same stuff as Uncle Ned he became even more assiduous in his churchly duties. He had gotten himself promoted to the position of "elder," an office of which he was extremely proud and by grace of which he was permitted during the Sunday services to aid in taking up the collection. To think of my old man marching up the aisle of a Congregational church with a collection box in his hand; to think of him standing reverently before the altar with this collection box while the minister blessed the offering, seems to me now something so incredible that I scarcely know what to say of it. I like to think, by contrast, of the man he was when I was just a kid and I would meet him at the ferry house of a Saturday noon. Surrounding the entrance to the ferry house there were then three saloons which of a Saturday noon were filled with men who had stopped off for a little bite at the free lunch counter and a schooner of beer. I can see the old man, as he stood in his thirtieth year, a healthy, genial soul with a smile for every one and a pleasant quip to pass the time of day, see him with his arm resting on the bar, his straw hat tipped on the back of his head, his left hand raised to down the foaming suds. My eye was then on about a level with his heavy gold chain which was spread crosswise over his vest; I remember the shepherd plaid suit which he wore in midsummer and the distinction it gave him among the other men at the bar who were not lucky enough to have been born tailors. I remember the way he would dip his hand into the big glass bowl on the free lunch counter and hand me a few pretzels, saying at the same time that I ought to go and have a look at the scoreboard in the window of the *Brooklyn Times* nearby. And perhaps, as I ran out of the saloon to see who was winning, a string of cyclists would pass close to the curb, holding to the little strip of asphalt which had been laid down expressly for them. Perhaps the ferry boat was just coming into the dock and I would stop a moment to watch the men in uniform as they pulled away at the big wooden wheels to which the chains were attached. As the gates were thrown open and the planks laid down a mob would rush through the shed and make for the saloons which adorned the nearest corners. Those were the days when the old man knew the meaning of "moderation," when he drank because he was truly thirsty, and to down a schooner of beer by the ferry house was a man's prerogative. Then it was as Melville has so well said: "Feed all things with food convenient for them—that is, if the food be procurable. The food of thy soul is light and space; feed it then on light and space. But the food of the body is champagne and oysters; feed it then on champagne and oysters; and so shall it merit a joyful resurrection, if there is any to be." Yes, then it seems to me that the old man's soul had not yet shrivelled up, that it was endlessly bounded by light and space and that his body, heedless of the resurrection, was feeding on all that was convenient and procurable—if not champagne and oysters, at least good lager beer and pretzels. Then his body had not been condemned, nor his way of living, nor his absence of faith. Nor was he yet surrounded by vultures, but only by good comrades, ordinary mortals like himself who looked neither high nor low but straight ahead, the eye always fixed on the horizon and content with the sight thereof.

And now, as a battered wreck, he has made himself into an elder of the church and he stands before the altar, gray and bent and withered, while the minister gives his blessing to the measly collection which will go to make a new bowling alley. Perhaps it was necessary for him to experience the birth of the soul, to feed this spongelike growth with that light and space which the Congregational church offered. But what a poor substitute for a man who had known the joys of that food which the body craved and which, without the pangs of conscience, had flooded even his spongelike soul with a light and space that was ungodly but radiant and terrestrial. I think again of his seemly little "corporation" over which the thick gold chain was strung and I think that with that death of his paunch there was left to survive only the sponge of a soul, a sort of appendix to his own bodily death. I think of the minister who had swallowed him up as a sort of inhuman sponge eater, the keeper of a wigwam hung with spiritual scalps. I think of what subsequently ensued as a kind of tragedy in sponges, for though he promised light and space, no sooner had he passed out of my father's life than the whole airy edifice came tumbling down.

It all came about in the most ordinary lifelike way. One evening, after the customary men's meeting, the old man came home with a sorrowful countenance. They had been informed that evening that the minister was taking leave of them. He had been offered a more advantageous position in the township of New Rochelle and, despite his great reluctance to desert his flock, he had decided to accept the offer. He had of course accepted it only after much meditation—as a duty, in other words. It would mean a better income, to be sure, but that was nothing compared to the grave responsibilities which he was about to assume. They had need of him in New Rochelle and he was obeying the voice of his conscience. All this the old man related with the same unctuousness that the minister had given to his words. But it was immediately apparent that the old man was hurt. He couldn't see why New Rochelle could not find another minister. He said it wasn't fair to tempt the minister with a bigger salary. *We need him here,* he said ruefully, with such sadness that I almost felt like weeping. He added that he was going to have a heart-to-heart talk with the minister, that if anybody could persuade him to remain it was he. In the days that followed he certainly did his best, no doubt much to the minister's discomfiture. It was distressing to see the blank look on his face when he returned from these conferences. He had the expression of a man who was trying to grasp at a straw to keep from drowning. Naturally the minister remained adamant. Even when the old man broke down and wept before him he could not be moved to change his mind. That was the turning point. From that moment on the old man underwent a radical change. He seemed to grow bitter and querulous. He not only forgot to say grace at the table but he abstained from going to church. He resumed his old habit of going to the cemetery and basking on a bench. He became morose, then melancholy, and finally there grew into his face an expression of permanent sadness, a sadness encrusted with disillusionment, with despair, with futility. He never again mentioned the man's name, nor the church, nor any of the elders with whom he had once associated. If he happened to pass them in the street he bade them the time of day without stopping to shake hands. He read the newspapers diligently, from back to front, without comment. Even the ads he read, every one, as though trying to block up a huge hole which was constantly before his eyes. I never heard him laugh again. At the most he would give us a sort of weary, hopeless smile, a smile which faded instantly and left us with the spectacle of a life extinct. He was dead as a crater, dead beyond all hope of resurrection. And not even had he been given a new stomach, or a tough new intestinal tract, would it have been possible to restore him to life again. He had passed beyond the lure of champagne and oysters, beyond the need of light and space. He was like the dodo which buries its head in the sand and whistles out of its asshole. When he went to sleep in the Morris chair his lower jaw dropped like a hinge that has become unloosened; he had always been a good snorer but now he snored louder than ever, like a man who was in truth dead to the world. His snores, in fact, were very much like the death rattle, except that they were punctuated by an intermittent long drawn out whistling of the peanut stand variety. He seemed, when he snored, to be chopping the whole universe to bits so that we who succeeded him would have enough kindling wood to last a lifetime. It was the most horrible and fascinating snoring that I have ever listened to: it was stertorous and stentorian, morbid and grotesque; at times it was like an accordion collapsing, at other times like a frog croaking in the swamps; after a prolonged whistle there sometimes followed a frightful wheeze as if he were giving up the ghost, then it would settle back again into a regular rise and fall, a steady hollow chopping as though he stood stripped to the waist, with ax in hand, before the accumulated madness of all the bric-a-brac of this world. What gave these performances a slightly crazy quality was the mummy-like expression of the face in which the big blubber lips alone came to life; they were like the gills of a shark snoozing on the surface of the still ocean. Blissfully he snored away on the bosom of the deep, never disturbed by a dream or a draught, never fitful, never plagued by an unsatisfied desire; when he closed his eyes and collapsed, the light of the world went out and he was alone as before birth, a cosmos gnashing itself to bits. He sat there in his Morris chair as Jonah must have sat in the body of the whale, secure in the last refuge of a black hole, expecting nothing, desiring nothing, not dead but buried alive, swallowed whole and unscathed, the big blubber lips gently flapping with the flux and reflux of the white breath of emptiness. He was in the land of Nod searching for Cain and Abel but encountering no living soul, no word, no sign. He drove with the whale and scraped the icy black bottom; he covered furlongs at top speed, guided only by the fleecy manes of undersea beasts. He was the smoke that curled out of the chimney tops, the heavy layers of cloud that obscured the moon, the thick slime that made the slippery linoleum floor of the ocean depths. He was deader than dead because alive and empty, beyond all hope of resurrection in that he had traveled beyond the limits of light and space and securely nestled himself in the black hole of nothingness. He was more to be envied than pitied, for his sleep was not a lull or an interval but sleep itself which is the deep and hence sleeping ever deepening, deeper and deeper in sleep sleeping, the sleep of the deep in deepest sleep, at the nethermost depth full slept, the deepest and sleepest sleep of sleep's sweet sleep. He was asleep. He *is* asleep. He *will* be asleep. Sleep. Sleep. *Father, sleep, I beg you, for we who are awake are boiling in horror....*

With the world fluttering away on the last wings of a hollow snore I see the door opening to admit Grover Watrous. "Christ be with you!" he says, dragging his clubfoot along. He is quite a young man now and he has found God. There is only one God and Grover Watrous has found Him and so there is nothing more to say except that everything has to be said over again in Grover Watrous' new God-language. This bright new language which God invented especially for Grover Watrous intrigues me enormously, first because I had always considered Grover to be a hopeless dunce, second because I notice that there are no longer any tobacco stains on his agile fingers. When we were boys Grover lived next door to us. He would visit me from time to time in order to practice a duet with me. Though he was only fourteen or fifteen he smoked like a trooper. His mother could do nothing against it because Grover was a genius and a genius had to have a little liberty, particularly when he was also unfortunate enough to have been born with a clubfoot. Grover was the kind of genius who thrives on dirt. He not only had nicotine stains on his fingers but he had filthy black nails which would break under hours of practicing, imposing upon young Grover the ravishing obligation of tearing them off with his teeth. Grover used to spit out broken nails along with the bits of tobacco which got caught in his teeth. It was delightful and stimulating. The cigarettes burned holes into the piano and, as my mother critically observed, also *tarnished* the keys. When Grover took leave the parlor stank like the backroom of an undertaker's establishment. It stank of dead cigarettes, sweat, dirty linen, Graver's oaths and the dry heat left by the dying notes of Weber, Berlioz, Liszt and Co. It stank too of Graver's running ear and of his decaying teeth. It stank of his mother's pampering and whimpering. His own home was a stable divinely suited to his genius, but the parlor of our home was like the waiting room of a mortician's office and Grover was a lout who didn't even know enough to wipe his feet. In the wintertime his nose ran like a sewer and, Grover being too engrossed in his music to bother wiping his nose, his cold snot was left to trickle down until it reached his lips where it was sucked in by a very long white tongue. To the flatulent music of Weber, Berlioz, Liszt and Co. it added a piquant sauce which made those empty devils palatable. Every other word from Grover's lips was an oath, his favorite expression being—"I can't get the fucking thing right!" Sometimes he grew so annoyed that he would take his fists and pound the piano like a madman. It was his genius coming out the wrong way. His mother, in fact, used to attach a great deal of importance to these fits of anger; they convinced her that he had something in him. Other people simply said that Grover was impossible. Much was forgiven, however, because of his clubfoot. Grover was sly enough to exploit this bad foot; whenever he wanted anything badly he developed pains in the foot. Only the piano seemed to have no respect for this maimed member. The piano therefore was an object to be cursed and kicked and pounded to bits. If he were in good form, on the other hand, Grover would remain at the piano for hours on end; in fact, you couldn't drag him away. On such occasions his mother would go stand in the grass plot in front of the house and waylay the neighbors in order to squeeze a few words of praise out of them. She would be so carried away by her son's "divine" playing that she would forget to cook the evening meal. The old man, who worked in the sewers, usually came home grumpy and famished. Sometimes he would march directly upstairs to the parlor and yank Grover off the piano stool. He had a rather foul vocabulary himself and when he let loose on his genius of a son there wasn't much left for Grover to say. In the old man's opinion Grover was just a lazy son of a bitch who could make a lot of noise. Now and then he threatened to chuck the fucking piano out of the window—and Grover with it. If the mother were rash enough to interfere during these scenes he would give her a clout and tell her to go piss up the end of a rope. He had his moments of weakness too, of course, and in such a mood he might ask Grover what the hell he was rattling away at, and if the latter said, for example, "why the Sonata *Pathetique*," the old buzzard would say—"What the hell does that mean? Why in Christ's name don't they put it down in plain English?" The old man's ignorance was even harder for Grover to bear than his brutality. He was heartily ashamed of his old man and when the latter was out of sight he would ridicule him unmercifully. When he got a little older he used to insinuate that he wouldn't have been born with a clubfoot if the old man hadn't been such a mean bastard. He said that the old man must have kicked his mother in the belly when she was pregnant. This alleged kick in the belly must have affected Grover in diverse ways, for when he had grown up to be quite a young man, as I was saying, he suddenly took to God with such a passion that there was no blowing your nose before him without first asking God's permission.

Graver's conversion followed right upon the old man's deflation, which is why I am reminded of it. Nobody had seen the Watrouses for a number of years and then, right in the midst of a bloody snore, you might say, in pranced Grover scattering benedictions and calling upon God as his witness as he rolled up his sleeves to deliver us from evil. What I noted first in him was the change in his personal appearance; he had been washed clean in the blood of the Lamb. He was so immaculate, indeed, that there was almost a perfume emanating from him. His speech too had been cleaned up; instead of wild oaths there were now nothing but blessings and invocations. It was not a conversation which he held with us but a monologue in which, if there were any questions, he answered them himself. As he took the chair which was offered him he said with the nimbleness of a jack rabbit that God had given his only beloved Son in order that we might enjoy life everlasting. Did we really want this life everlasting—or were we simply going to wallow in the joys of the flesh and die without knowing salvation? The incongruity of mentioning the "joys of the flesh" to an aged couple, one of whom was sound asleep and snoring, never struck him, to be sure. He was so alive and jubilant in the first flush of God's merciful grace that he must have forgotten that my sister was dippy, for, without even inquiring how she had been, he began to harangue her in this newfound spiritual palaver to which she was entirely impervious because, as I say, she was minus so many buttons that if he had been talking about chopped spinach it would have been just as meaningful to her. A phrase like "the pleasures of the flesh" meant to her something like a beautiful day with a red parasol. I could see by the way she sat on the edge of her chair and bobbed her head that she was only waiting for him to catch his breath in order to inform him that the pastor—*her* pastor, who was an Episcopalian—had just returned from Europe and that they were going to have a fair in the basement of the church where she would have a little booth fitted up with doilies from the five-and-ten-cent store. In fact, no sooner had he paused a moment than she let loose—about the canals of Venice, the snow in the Alps, the dog carts in Brussels, the beautiful liverwurst in Munich. She was not only religious, my sister, but she was clean daffy. Grover had just slipped in something about having seen a new heaven and a new earth... *for the first heaven and the first earth were passed away,* he said, mumbling the words in a sort of hysterical glissando in order to unburden himself of an oracular message about the New Jerusalem which God had established on earth and in which he, Grover Watrous, once foul of speech and marred by a twisted foot, had found the peace and the calm of the righteous. *"There shall he no more death..."* he started to shout when my sister leaned forward and asked him very innocently if he liked to bowl because the pastor had just installed a beautiful new bowling alley in the basement of the church and she knew he would be pleased to see Grover because he was a lovely man and he was kind to the poor. Grover said that it was a sin to bowl and that he belonged to no church because the churches were godless; he had even given up playing the piano because God needed him for higher things. *"He that overcometh shall inherit all things,"* he added, *"and I will he his God, and he shall he my son."* He paused again to blow his nose in a beautiful white handkerchief, whereupon my sister took the occasion to remind him that in the old days he always had a running nose but that he never wiped it. Grover listened to her very solemnly and then remarked that he had been cured of many evil ways. At this point the old man woke up and, seeing Grover sitting beside him large as life, he was quite startled and for a moment or two he was not sure, it seemed, whether Grover was a morbid phenomenon of dream or an hallucination, but the sight of the clean handkerchief brought him quickly to his wits. "Oh, it's you!" he exclaimed. "The Watrous boy, what? Well, what in the name of all that's holy are you doing here?"

"I came in the name of the Holy of Holies," said Grover unabashed. "I have been purified by the death of Calvary and I am here in Christ's sweet name that ye may be redeemed and walk in light and power and glory."

The old man looked dazed. "Well, what's come over you?" he said, giving Grover a feeble, consolatory smile. My mother had just come in from the kitchen and had taken a stand behind Graver's chair. By making a wry grimace with her mouth she was trying to convey to the old man that Grover was cracked. Even my sister seemed to realize that there was something wrong with him, especially when he had refused to visit the new bowling alley which her lovely pastor had expressly installed for young men such as Grover and his likes.

What was the matter with Grover? Nothing, except that his feet were solidly planted on the fifth foundation of the great wall of the Holy City of Jerusalem, the fifth foundation made entirely of sardonyx, whence he commanded a view of a pure river of the water of life issuing from the throne of God. And the sight of this river of life was to Graver like the bite of a thousand fleas in his lower colon. Not until he had run at least seven times around the earth would he be able to sit quietly on his ass and observe the blindness and the indifference of men with something like equanimity. He was alive and purged, and though to the eyes of the sluggish, sluttish spirits who are sane he was "cracked," to me he seemed infinitely better off this way than before. He was a pest who could do you no harm. If you listened to him long enough you became somewhat purged yourself, though perhaps unconvinced. Graver's bright new language always caught me in the midriff and through inordinate laughter cleansed me of the dross accumulated by the sluggish sanity about me. He was alive as Ponce de Leon had hoped to be alive; alive as only a few men have ever been. And being unnaturally alive he didn't mind in the least if you laughed in his face, nor would he have minded if you had stolen the few possessions which were his. He was alive and empty, which is so close to Godhood that it is crazy.

With his feet solidly planted on the great wall of the New Jerusalem Graver knew a joy which is incommensurable. Perhaps if he had not been born with a clubfoot he would not have known this incredible joy. Perhaps it was well that his father had kicked the mother in the belly while Graver was still in the womb. Perhaps it was that kick in the belly which had sent Graver soaring, which made him so thoroughly alive and awake that even in his sleep he was delivering God's messages. The harder he labored the less he was fatigued. He had no more worries, no regrets, no clawing memories. He recognized no duties, no obligations, except to God. And what did God expect of him? Nothing, nothing... except to sing His praises. God only asked of Grover Watrous that he reveal himself alive in the flesh. He only asked of him to be more and more alive. And when fully alive Grover was a voice and this voice was a flood which made all dead things into chaos and this chaos in turn became the mouth of the world in the very center of which was the verb *to be. In the beginning there was the Word, and the Word was with God, and the word was God.* So God was this strange little infinitive which is all there is—and is it not enough? For Grover it was more than enough: it was everything. Starting from this Verb what difference did it make which road he traveled? To leave the Verb was to travel away from the center, to erect a Babel. Perhaps God had deliberately maimed Grover Watrous in order to hold him to the center, to the Verb. By an invisible cord God held Grover Watrous to his stake which ran through the heart of the world and Grover became the fat goose which laid a golden egg every day....

Why do I write of Grover Watrous? Because I have met thousands of people and none of them were alive in the way that Grover was. Most of them were more intelligent, many of them were brilliant, some of them were even famous, but none were alive and empty as Grover was. Grover was inexhaustible. He was like a bit of radium which, even if buried under a mountain does not lose its power to give off energy. I had seen plenty of so-called *energetic* people before—is not America filled with them?—but never in the shape of a human being, a reservoir of energy. And what created this inexhaustible reservoir of energy? An illumination. Yes, it happened in the twinkling of an eye, which is the only way that anything important ever does happen. Overnight all Grover's preconceived values were thrown overboard. Suddenly, just like that, he ceased moving as other people move. He put the brakes on and he kept the motor running. If once, like other people, he had thought it was necessary to get somewhere now he knew that somewhere was anywhere and therefore right here and so why move? Why not park the car and keep the motor running? Meanwhile the earth itself is turning and Grover knew it was turning and knew that he was turning with it. Is the earth getting anywhere? Grover must undoubtedly have asked himself this question and must undoubtedly have satisfied himself that it was *not* getting anywhere. Who, then, had said that we must get somewhere? Grover would inquire of this one and that where they were heading for and the strange thing was that although they were all heading for their individual destinations none of them ever stopped to reflect that the one inevitable destination for all alike was the grave. This puzzled Grover because nobody could convince him that death was not a certainty, whereas anybody could convince anybody else that any other destination was an uncertainty. Convinced of the dead certainty of death Grover suddenly became tremendously and overwhelmingly alive. For the first time in his life he began to live, and at the same time the clubfoot dropped completely out of his consciousness. This is a strange thing, too, when you come to think of it, because the clubfoot, just like death, was another ineluctable fact. Yet the clubfoot dropped out of mind, or, what is more important, all that had been attached to the clubfoot. In the same way, having accepted death, death too dropped out of Grover's mind. Having seized on the single certainty of death all the uncertainties vanished. The rest of the world was now limping along with clubfooted uncertainties and Grover Watrous alone was free and unimpeded. Grover Watrous was the personification of certainty. He may have been wrong, but he was certain. *And what good does it do to be right if one has to limp along with a clubfoot?* Only a few men have ever realized the truth of this and their names have become very great names. Grover Watrous will probably never be known, but he is very great just the same. This is probably the reason why I write about him—just the fact that I had enough sense to realize that Grover had achieved greatness even though nobody else will admit it. At the time I simply thought that Grover was a harmless fanatic, yes, a little "cracked," as my mother insinuated. But every man who has caught the truth of certitude was a little cracked and it is only these men who have accomplished anything for the world. Other men, other *great* men, have destroyed a little here and there, but these few whom I speak of, and among whom I include Grover Watrous, were capable of destroying everything in order that the truth might live. Usually these men were born with an impediment, with a clubfoot, so to speak, and by a strange irony it is only the clubfoot which men remember. If a man like Grover becomes dispossessed of his clubfoot, the world says that he has become "possessed." This is the logic of incertitude and its fruit is misery. Grover was the only truly joyous being I ever met in my life and this, therefore, is a little monument which I am erecting in his memory, in the memory of his joyous certitude. It is a pity that he had to use Christ for a crutch, but then what does it matter how one comes by the truth so long as one pounces upon it and lives by it?

AN INTERLUDE

Confusion is a word we have invented for an order which is not understood. I like to dwell on this period when things were taking shape because the order, if it were understood, must have been dazzling. In the first place there was Hymie, Hymie the bullfrog, and there were also his wife's ovaries which had been rotting away for a considerable time. Hymie was completely wrapped up in his wife's rotting ovaries. It was the daily topic of conversation; it took precedence now over the cathartic pills and the coated tongue. Hymie dealt in "sexual proverbs," as he called them. Everything he said began from or led up to the ovaries. Despite everything he was still nicking it off with the wife—prolonged snakelike copulations in which he would smoke a cigarette or two before uncunting. He would endeavor to explain to me how the pus from the rotting ovaries put her in heat. She had always been a good fuck, but now she was better than ever. Once the ovaries were ripped out there'd be no telling how she'd take it. She seemed to realize that too. Ergo, fuck away! Every night, after the dishes were cleared away, they'd strip down in their little birdlike apartment and lie together like a couple of snakes. He tried to describe it to me on a number of occasions—the way she fucked. It was like an oyster inside, an oyster with soft teeth that nibbled away at him. Sometimes it felt as though he were right inside her womb, so soft and fluffy it was, and those soft teeth biting away at his pecker and making him delirious. They used to lie scissors-fashion and look up at the ceiling. To keep from coming he would think about the office, about the little worries which plagued him and kept his bowels tied up in a knot. In between orgasms he would let his mind dwell on someone else, so that when she'd start working on him again he might imagine he was having a brand new fuck with a brand new cunt. He used to arrange it so that he could look out the window while it was going on. He was getting so adept at it that he could undress a woman on the boulevard there under his window and transport her to the bed; not only that, but he could actually make her change places with his wife, all without uncunting. Sometimes he'd fuck away like that for a couple of hours and never even bother to shoot off. Why waste it! he would say.

Steve Romero, on the other hand, had a hell of a time holding it in. Steve was built like a bull and he scattered his seed freely. We used to compare notes sometimes sitting in the chop suey joint around the corner from the office. It *was* a strange atmosphere. Maybe it was because there was no wine. Maybe it was the funny little black mushrooms they served us. Anyway it wasn't difficult to get started on the subject. By the time Steve met us he would already have had his workout, a shower and a rubdown. He was clean inside and out. Almost a perfect specimen of a man. Not very bright, to be sure, but a good egg, a companion. Hymie, on the other hand, was like a toad. He seemed to come to the table direct from the swamps where he had passed a mucky day. Filth rolled off his lips like honey. In fact, you couldn't call it filth, in his case, because there wasn't any other ingredient with which you might compare it. It was all one fluid, a slimy, sticky substance made entirely of sex. When he looked at his food he saw it as potential sperm; if the weather were warm he would say it was good for the balls; if he took a trolley ride he knew in advance that the rhythmic movement of the trolley would stimulate his appetite, would give him a slow, "personal" hard on, as he put it. Why "personal" I never found out, but that was his expression. He liked to go out with us because we were always reasonably sure of picking up something decent. Left to himself he didn't always fare so well. With us he got a change of meat-Gentile cunt, as he put it. He liked Gentile cunt. Smelled sweeter, he said. Laughed easier too.... Sometimes in the very midst of things. The one thing he couldn't tolerate was dark meat. It amazed and disgusted him to see me traveling around with Valeska. Once he asked me if she didn't smell kind of extra strong like. I told him I liked it that way—strong and smelly, with lots of gravy around it. He almost blushed at that. Amazing how delicate he could be about some things. Food for example. Very finicky about his food. Perhaps a racial trait. Immaculate about his person, too. Couldn't stand the sight of a spot on his clean cuffs. Constantly brushing himself off, constantly taking his pocket mirror out to see if there was any food between his teeth. If he found a crumb he would hide his face behind the napkin and extract it with his pearl-handled toothpick. The ovaries of course he couldn't see. Nor could he smell them either, because his wife too was an immaculate bitch. Douching herself all day long in preparation for the evening nuptials. It was tragic, the importance she gave to her ovaries.

Up until the day she was taken to the hospital she was a regular fucking block. The thought of never being able to fuck again frightened the wits out of her. Hymie of course told her it wouldn't make any difference to him one way or the other. Glued to her like a snake, a cigarette in his mouth, the girls passing below on the boulevard, it was hard for him to imagine a woman not being able to fuck any more. He was sure the operation would be successful. *Successful!* That's to say that she'd fuck even better than before. He used to tell her that, lying on his back looking up at the ceiling. "You know I'll always love you," he would say. "Move over just a little bit, will you.... there, like that.... that's it. What was I saying? Oh yes... why sure, why should you worry about things like that? Of course I'll be true to you. Listen, pull away just a little bit... yeah, that's it.... that's fine." He used to tell us about it in the chop suey joint. Steve would laugh like hell. Steve couldn't do a thing like that. He was too honest—especially with women. That's why he never had any luck—little Curley, for example—Steve hated Curley—would always get what he wanted.... He was a born liar, a born deceiver. Hymie didn't like Curley much either. He said he was dishonest, meaning of course dishonest in money matters. About such things Hymie was scrupulous. What he disliked especially was the way Curley talked about his aunt. It was bad enough, in Hymie's opinion, that he should be screwing the sister of his own mother, but to make her out to be nothing but a piece of stale cheese, that was too much for Hymie. One ought to have a bit of respect for a woman, provided she's not a whore. If she's a whore that's different. Whores are not women. Whores are whores. That was how Hymie looked at things.

The real reason for this dislike, however, was that whenever they went out together Curley always got the best choice. And not only that, but it was usually with Hymie's money that Curley managed it. Even the way Curley asked for money irritated Hymie—it was like extortion, he said. He thought it was partly my fault, that I was too lenient with the kid. "He's got no moral character," Hymie would say. "And what about *you,* your moral character?" I would ask. "Oh *me!* Shit, I'm too old to have any moral character. But Curley's only a kid."

"You're jealous, that's what," Steve would say.

"Me? Me jealous of *him?"* And he'd try to smother the idea with a scornful little laugh. It made him wince, a jab like that. "Listen," he would say, turning to me, "did I ever act jealous toward you? Didn't I always turn a girl over to you if you asked me? What about that red-haired girl in SU office... you remember... the one with the big teats? Wasn't that a nice piece of ass to turn over to a friend? But I did it, didn't I? I did it because you said you liked big teats. But I wouldn't do it for Curley. He's a little crook. Let him do his own digging."

As a matter of fact, Curley was digging away very industriously. He must have had five or six on the string at one time, from what I could gather. There was Valeska, for example—he had made himself pretty solid with her. She was so damned pleased to have some one fuck her without blushing that when it came to sharing him with her cousin and then with the midget she didn't put up the least objection. What she liked best was to get in the tub and let him fuck her under water. It was fine until the midget got wise to it. Then there was a nice rumpus which was finally ironed out on the parlor floor. To listen to Curley talk he did everything but climb the chandeliers. And always plenty of pocket money to boot. Valeska was generous, but the cousin was a softy. If she came within a foot of a stiff prick she was like putty. An unbuttoned fly was enough to put her in a trance. It was almost shameful the things Curley made her do. He took pleasure in degrading her. I could scarcely blame him for it, she was such a prim, priggish bitch in her street clothes. You'd almost swear she didn't own a cunt, the way she carried herself in the street. Naturally, when he got her alone he made her pay for her highfalutin' ways. He went at it cold-bloodedly. "Fish it out!" he'd say, opening his fly a little. "Fish it out with your tongue!" (He had it in for the whole bunch because, as he put it, they were sucking one another off behind his back.) Anyway, once she got the taste of it in her mouth you could do anything with her. Sometimes he'd stand her on her hands and push her around the room that way, like a wheelbarrow. Or else he'd do it dog fashion, and while she groaned and squirmed he'd nonchalantly light a cigarette and blow the smoke between her legs. Once he played her a dirty trick doing it that way. He had worked her up to such a state that she was beside herself. Anyway, after he had almost polished the ass off her with his back-scuttling he pulled out for a second, as though to cool his cock off, and then very slowly and gently he shoved a big long carrot up her twat. "That, Miss Abercrombie," he said, "is a sort of Doppelganger to my regular cock," and with that he unhitches himself and yanks up his pants. Cousin Abercrombie was so bewildered by it all that she let a tremendous fart and out tumbled the carrot. At least, that's how Curley related it to me. He was an outrageous liar, to be sure, and there may not be a grain of truth in the yarn, but there's no denying that he had a flair for such tricks. As for Miss Abercrombie and her high-tone Narragansett ways, well, with a cunt like that one can always imagine the worst. By comparison Hymie was a purist. Somehow Hymie and his fat circumcised dick were two different things. When he got a personal hard on, as he said, he really meant that he was irresponsible. He meant that Nature was asserting itself—through his, Hymie

Laubscher's, fat circumcised dick. It was the same with his wife's cunt. It was something she wore between her legs, like an ornament. It was a part of Mrs. Laubscher but it wasn't Mrs. Laubscher personally, if you get what I mean.

Well, all this is simply by way of leading up to the general sexual confusion which prevailed at this time. It was like taking a flat in the Land of Fuck. The girl upstairs, for instance... she used to come down now and then, when the wife was giving a recital, to look after the kid. She was so obviously a simpleton that I didn't give her any notice at first. But like all the others she had a cunt too, a sort of impersonal personal cunt which she was unconsciously conscious of. The oftener she came down the more conscious she got, in her unconscious way. One night, when she was in the bathroom, after she had been in there a suspiciously long while, she got me to thinking of things. I decided to take a peep through the keyhole and see for myself what was what. Lo and behold, if she isn't standing in front of the mirror stroking and petting her little pussy. Almost talking to it, she was. I was so excited I didn't know what to do first. I went back into the big room, turned out the lights, and lay there on the couch waiting for her to come out. As I lay there I could still see that bushy cunt of hers and the fingers strumming it like. I opened my fly to let my pecker twitch about in the cool of the dark. I tried to mesmerize her from the couch, or at least I tried letting my pecker mesmerize her. "Come here, you bitch," I kept saying to myself, "come in here and spread that cunt over me." She must have caught the message immediately, for in a jiffy she had opened the door and was groping about in the dark to find the couch. I didn't say a word, I didn't make a move. I just kept my mind riveted on her cunt moving quietly in the dark like a crab. Finally she was standing beside the couch. She didn't say a word either. She just stood there quietly and as I slid my hand up her legs she moved one foot a little to open her crotch a bit more. I don't think I ever put my hand into such a juicy crotch in all my life. It was like paste running down her legs, and if there had been any billboards handy I could have plastered up a dozen or more. After a few moments, just as naturally as a cow lowering its head to graze, she bent over and put it in her mouth. I had my whole four fingers inside her, whipping it up to a froth. Her mouth was stuffed full and the juice pouring down her legs. Not a word out of us, as I say. Just a couple of quiet maniacs working away in the dark like gravediggers. It was a fucking Paradise and I knew it, and I was ready and willing to fuck my brains away if necessary. She was probably the best fuck I ever had. She never once opened her trap—not that night, nor the next night, nor any night. She'd steal down like that in the dark, soon as she smelled me there alone, and plaster her cunt all over me. It was an enormous cunt, too, when I think back on it. A dark, subterranean labyrinth fitted up with divans and cosy corners and rubber teeth and syringes and soft nestles and eiderdown and mulberry leaves. I used to nose in like the solitary worm and bury myself in a little cranny where it was absolutely silent, and so soft and restful that I lay like a dolphin on the oyster banks. A slight twitch and I'd be "in the Pullman reading a newspaper or else up an impasse where there were mossy round cobblestones and little wicker gates which opened and shut automatically. Sometimes it was like riding the shoot-the-shoots, a steep plunge and then a spray of tingling sea crabs, the bulrushes swaying feverishly and the gills of tiny fishes lapping against me like harmonica stops. In the immense black grotto there was a silk-and-soap organ playing a predaceous black music. When she pitched herself high, when she turned the juice on full, it made a violaceous purple, a deep mulberry stain like twilight, a ventriloqual twilight such as dwarfs and cretins enjoy when they menstruate. It made me think of cannibals chewing flowers, of Bantus running amuck, of wild unicorns rutting in rhododendron beds. Everything was anonymous and unformulated, John Doe and his wife Emmy Doe; above us the gas tanks and below the marine life. Above the belt, as I say, she was batty. Yes, absolutely cuckoo, though still abroad and afloat. Perhaps that was what made her cunt so marvelously impersonal. It was one cunt out of a million, a regular Pearl of the Antilles, such as Dick Osborn discovered when reading Joseph Conrad. In the broad Pacific of sex she lay, a gleaming silver reef surrounded with human anemones, human starfish, human madrepores. Only an Osborn could have discovered her, given the proper latitude and longitude of cunt. Meeting her in the daytime, watching her slowly going daft, it was like trapping a weasel when night came on. All I had to do was to lie down in the dark with my fly open and wait. She was like Ophelia suddenly resurrected among the Kaffirs. Not a word of any language could she remember, especially not English. She was a deaf-mute who had lost her memory, and with the loss of memory she had lost her frigidaire, her curling irons, her tweezers and handbag. She was even more naked than a fish, except for the tuft of hair between her legs. And she was even slipperier than a fish because after all a fish has scales and she had none. It was dubious at times whether I was in her or she in me. It was open warfare, the newfangled Pancrace, with each one biting his own ass. Love among the newts and the cutout wide open. Love without gender and without lysol. Incubational love, such as the wolverines practice above the tree line. On the one side the Arctic Ocean, on the other the Gulf of Mexico. And though we never referred to it openly there was always with us King Kong, King Kong asleep in the wrecked hull of the Titanic among the phosphorescent bones of millionaires and lampreys. No logic could drive King Kong away. He was the giant truss that supports the soul's fleeting anguish. He was the wedding cake with hairy legs and arms a mile long. He was the revolving screen on which the news passes away. He was the muzzle of the revolver that never went off, the leper armed with sawed-off gonococci.

It was here in the void of hernia that I did all my quiet thinking via the penis. There was first of all the binomial theorem, a phrase which had always puzzled me: I put it under the magnifying glass and studied it from X to Z. There was Logos, which somehow I had always identified with breath: I found that on the contrary it was a sort of obsessional stasis, a machine which went on grinding corn long after the granaries had been filled and the Jews driven out of Egypt. There was Bucephalus, more fascinating to me perhaps than any word in my whole vocabulary: I would trot it out whenever I was in a quandary, and with it of course Alexander and his entire purple retinue. What a horse! Sired in the Indian Ocean, the last of the line, and never once mated, except to the Queen of the Amazons during the Mesopotamian adventure. There was the Scotch Gambit! An amazing expression which had nothing to do with chess. It came to me always in the shape of a man on stilts, page 2,498 of Funk and Wagnall's Unabridged Dictionary. A gambit was a sort of leap in the dark with mechanical legs. A leap for no purpose—*hence gambit!* Clear as a bell and perfectly simple, once you grasped it. Then there was Andromeda, and the Gorgon Medusa, and Castor and Pollux of heavenly origin, mythological twins, eternally fixed in the ephemeral Stardust. There was lucubration, a word distinctly sexual and yet suggesting such cerebral connotations as to make me uneasy. Always "midnight lucubrations," the midnight being ominously significant. And then arras. Somebody some time or other had been stabbed "behind the arras." I saw an altar cloth made of asbestos and in it was a grievous rent such as Caesar himself might have made.

It was very quiet thinking, as I say, the kind that the men of the Old Stone Age must have indulged in. Things were neither absurd nor explicable. It was a jigsaw puzzle which, when you grew tired, you could push away with two feet. Anything could be put aside with ease, even the Himalaya mountains. It was just the opposite kind of thinking from Mahomet's. It led absolutely nowhere and was hence enjoyable. The grand edifice which you might construct throughout the course of a long fuck could be toppled over in the twinkling of an eye. It was the fuck that counted and not the construction work. It was like living in the Ark during the Flood, everything provided for down to a screwdriver. What need to commit murder, rape or incest when all that was demanded of you was to kill time? Rain, rain, rain, but inside the Ark everything dry and toasty, a pair of every kind and in the larder fine Westphalian hams, fresh eggs, olives, pickled onions, Worcestershire sauce and other delicacies. God had chosen me, Noah, to establish a new heaven and a new earth. He had given me a stout boat with all seams caulked and properly dried. He had given me also the knowledge to sail the stormy seas. Maybe when it stopped raining there would be other kinds of knowledge to acquire, but for the present a nautical knowledge sufficed. The rest was chess in the Cafe Royal, Second Avenue, except that I had to imagine a partner, a clever Jewish mind that would make the game last until the rains ceased. But, as I said before, I had no time to be bored; there were my old friends, Logos, Bucephalus, arras, lucubration and so on. Why play chess?

Locked up like that for days and nights on end I began to realize that thinking, when it is not masturbative, is lenitive, healing, pleasurable. The thinking that gets you nowhere takes you everywhere; all other thinking is done on tracks and no matter how long the stretch, in the end there is always the depot or the roundhouse. In the end there is always a red lantern which says STOP! But when the penis gets to thinking there is no stop or let: it is a perpetual holiday, the bait fresh and the fish always nibbling at the line. Which reminds me of another cunt, Veronica something or other, who always got me thinking the wrong way. With Veronica it was always a tussle in the vestibule. On the dance floor you'd think she was going to make you a permanent present of her ovaries, but as soon as she hit the air she'd start thinking, thinking of her hat, of her purse, of her aunt who was waiting up for her, of the letter she forgot to mail, of the job she was going to lose—all kinds of crazy, irrelevant thoughts which had nothing to do with the thing in hand. It was like she had suddenly switched her brain to her cunt—the most alert and canny cunt imaginable. It was almost a metaphysical cunt, so to speak. It was a cunt which thought out problems, and not only that, but a special kind of thinking it was, with a metronome going. For this species of displaced rhythmic lucubration a peculiar dim light was essential. It had to be just about dark enough for a bat and yet light enough to find a button if one happened to come undone, and roll on the floor of the vestibule. You can see what I mean. A vague yet meticulous precision, a steely awareness that simulated absent-mindedness. And fluttery and fluky at the same time, so that you could never determine whether it was fish or fowl. *What is this I hold in my hand? Vine or superfine?* The answer was always duck soup. If you grabbed her by the boobies she would squawk like a parrot: if you got under her dress she would wriggle like an eel; if you held her too tight she would bite like a ferret. She lingered and lingered and lingered. Why? What was she after? Would she give in after an hour or two? Not a chance in a million. She was like a pigeon trying to fly with its legs caught in a steel trap. She pretended she had no legs. But if you made a move to set her free she would threaten to moult on you.

Because she had such a marvelous ass and because it was also so damned inaccessible
I used to think of her as the Pons Asinorum. Every schoolboy knows that the Pons
Asinorum is not to be crossed except by two white donkeys led by a blind man. I don't
know why it is so, but that's the rule as it was laid down by old Euclid. He was so full of
knowledge, the old buzzard, that one day—I suppose purely to amuse himself—he built a
bridge which no living mortal could ever cross. He called it the Pons Asinorum because
he was the owner of a pair of beautiful white donkeys, and so attached was he to these
donkeys that he would let nobody take possession of them. And so he conjured a dream
in which he, the blind man, would one day lead the donkeys over the bridge and into the
happy hunting grounds for donkeys. Well, Veronica was very much in the same boat. She
thought so much of her beautiful white ass that she wouldn't part with it for anything. She
wanted to take it with her to Paradise when the time came. As for her cunt—which by the
way she never referred to at all—as for her cunt, I say, well that was just an accessory to
be brought along. In the dim light of the vestibule, without ever referring overtly to her
two problems, she somehow made you uncomfortably aware of them. That is, she made
you aware in the manner of a prestidigitator. You were to take a look or a feel only to be
finally deceived, only to be shown that you had not seen and had not felt. It was a very
subtle sexual algebra, the midnight lucubration which would earn you an A or a B next
day, but nothing more. You passed your examinations, you got your diploma, and then you
were turned loose. In the meantime you used your ass to sit down and your cunt to make
water with. Between the textbook and the lavatory there was an intermediate zone which
you were never to enter because it was labeled fuck. You might diddle and piddle, but you
might not fuck. The light was never completely shut off, the sun never streamed in.
Always just light or dark enough to distinguish a bat. And just that little eerie flicker of
light was what kept the mind alert, on the lookout, as it were, for bags, pencils, buttons,
keys, et cetera. You couldn't really think because your mind was already engaged. The mind
was kept in readiness, like a vacant seat at the theater on which the owner has left his opera
hat.

Veronica, as I say, had a talking cunt, which was bad because its sole function seemed
to be to talk one out of a fuck. Evelyn, on the other hand, had a laughing cunt. She lived
upstairs too, only in another house. She was always trotting in at mealtimes to tell us a
new joke. A comedienne of the first water, the only really funny woman I ever met in my
life. Everything was a joke, fuck included. She could even make a stiff prick laugh, which
is saying a good deal. They say a stiff prick has no conscience, but a stiff prick that laughs
too is phenomenal. The only way I can describe it is to say that when she got hot and
bothered, Evelyn, she put on a ventriloqual act with her cunt. You'd be ready to slip it in
when suddenly the dummy between her legs would let out a guffaw. At the same time it
would reach out for you and give you a playful little tug and squeeze. It could sing too, this
dummy of a cunt. In fact it behaved just like a trained seal.

Nothing is more difficult than to make love in a circus. Putting on the trained seal act
all the time made her more inaccessible than if she had been trussed up with iron thongs.
She could break down the most "personal" hard on in the world. Break it down with
laughter. At the same time it wasn't quite as humiliating as one might be inclined to imagine. There was something sympathetic about this vaginal laughter. The whole world
seemed to unroll like a pornographic film whose tragic theme is impotence. You could
visualize yourself as a dog, or a weasel, or a white rabbit. Love was something on the side,

a dish of caviar, say, or a wax heliotrope. You could see the ventriloquist in you talking about caviar or heliotropes, but the real person was always a weasel or a white rabbit. Evelyn was always lying in the cabbage patch with legs spread open offering a bright green leaf to the first comer. But if you made a move to nibble it the whole cabbage patch would explode with laughter, a bright, dewy, vaginal laughter such as Jesus H. Christ and Immanuel Pussyfoot Kant never dreamed of, because if they had the world would not be what it is today and besides there would have been no Kant and no Christ Almighty. The female seldom laughs, but when she does it's volcanic. When the female laughs the male had better scoot to the cyclone cellar. Nothing will stand up under that vaginating chortle, not even ferroconcrete. The female, when her risibility is once aroused, can laugh down the hyena or the jackal or the wildcat. Now and then one hears it at a lynching bee, for example. It means that the lid is off, that everything goes. It means that she will forage for herself—and watch out that you don't get your balls cut off! It means that if the pest is coming SHE is coming first, and with huge spiked thongs that will flay the living hide off you. It means that she will lay not only with Tom, Dick and Harry, but with Cholera, Meningitis, Leprosy; it means that she will lay herself down on the altar like a mare in rut and take on all comers, including the Holy Ghost. It means that what it took the poor male, with his logarithmic cunning, five thousand, ten thousand, twenty thousand years to build, she will pull down in a night. She will pull it down and pee on it, and nobody will stop her once she starts laughing in earnest. And when I said about Veronica that her laugh would break down the most "personal" hard on imaginable I meant it: she would break down the *personal* erection and hand you back an impersonal one that was like a red-hot ramrod. You might not get very far with Veronica herself, but with what she had to give you could travel far and no mistake about it. Once you came within earshot of her it was like you had gotten an overdose of Spanish fly. Nothing on earth could bring it down again, unless you put it under a sledge-hammer.

It was going on this way all the time, even though every word I say is a lie. It was a personal tour in the impersonal world, a man with a tiny trowel in his hand digging a tunnel through the earth to get to the other side. The idea was to tunnel through and find at last the Culebra Cut, the *ne plus ultra,* of the honeymoon of flesh. And of course there was no end to the digging. The best I might hope for was to get stuck in the dead center of the earth, where the pressure was strongest and most even all around, and stay stuck there forever. That would give me the feeling of Ixion on the wheel, which is one sort of salvation and not entirely to be sneezed at. On the other hand I was a metaphysician of the instinctivist sort: it was impossible for me to stay stuck anywhere, even in the dead center of the earth. It was most imperative to find and to enjoy the metaphysical fuck, and for that I would be obliged to come out on to a wholly new tableland, a mesa of sweet alfalfa and polished monoliths, where the eagles and the vultures flew at random.

Sometimes sitting in the park of an evening, especially a park littered with papers and bits of food, I would see one pass by, one that seemed to be going toward Tibet, and I would follow her with the round eye, hoping that suddenly she would begin to fly, for if she did that, if she would begin to fly, I knew I would be able to fly also, and that would mean an end to the digging and the wallowing. Sometimes, probably because of twilight or other disturbances, it seemed as though she actually did fly on rounding a corner. That is, she would suddenly be lifted from the ground for the space of a few feet, like a plane too heavily loaded; but just that sudden involuntary life, whether real or imaginary it did-n't matter, gave me hope, gave me courage to keep the still round eye riveted on the spot.

There were megaphones inside which yelled "Go on, keep going, stick it out," and all that nonsense. But why? To what end? Whither? Whence? I would set the alarm clock in order to be up and about at a certain hour, *but why up and about?*

Why get up at all? With that little trowel in my hand I was working like a galley slave and not the slightest hope of reward involved. Were I to continue straight on I would dig the deepest hole any man had ever dug. On the other hand, if I had truly wanted to get to the other side of the earth, wouldn't it have been much simpler to throw away the trow-el and just board an airplane for China? But the body follows *after* the mind. The simplest thing for the body is not always easy for the mind. And when it gets particularly difficult and embarrassing is that moment when the two start going in opposite directions.

Laboring with the trowel was bliss: it left the mind completely free and yet there was never the slightest danger of the two being separated. If the she-animal suddenly began groaning with pleasure, if the she-animal suddenly began to throw a pleasurable connip-tion fit, the jaws moving like old shoelaces, the chest wheezing and the ribs creaking, if the she-bugger suddenly started to fall apart on the floor, to the collapse of joy and over-exasperation, just at the moment, not a second this side or that, the promised tableland would heave in sight like a ship coming up out of a fog and there would be nothing to do but plant the stars and stripes on it and claim it in the name of Uncle Sam and all that's holy. These misadventures happened so frequently that it was impossible not to believe in the reality of a realm which was called Fuck, because that was the only name which might be given to it, and yet it was more than fuck and by fucking one only began to approach it. Everybody had at one time or another planted the flag in this territory, and yet nobody was able to lay claim to it permanently. It disappeared overnight—sometimes in the twin-kling of an eye. It was No Man's Land and it stank with the litter of invisible deaths. If a truce were declared you met in this terrain and shook hands or swapped tobacco. But the truces never lasted very long. The only thing that seemed to have permanency was the "zone between" idea. Here the bullets flew and the corpses piled up; then it would rain and finally there would be nothing left but a stench.

This is all a figurative way of speaking about what is unmentionable. What is unmen-tionable is pure fuck and pure cunt: it must be mentioned only in deluxe editions, other-wise the world will fall apart. What holds the world together, as I have learned from bit-ter experience, is sexual intercourse. But *fuck,* the real thing, *cunt,* the real thing, seems to contain some unidentified element which is far more dangerous than nitroglycerin. To get an idea of the real thing you must consult a Sears Roebuck catalogue endorsed by the Anglican Church. On page twenty-three you will find a picture of Priapus juggling a corkscrew on the end of his weeny; he is standing in the shadow of the Parthenon by mis-take; he is naked except for a perforated jock-strap which was loaned for the occasion by the Holy Rollers of Oregon and Saskatchewan. Long distance is on the wire demanding to know if they should sell short or long. He says *go fuck yourself* and hangs up the receiv-er. In the background Rembrandt is studying the anatomy of our Lord Jesus Christ who, if you remember, was crucified by the Jews and then taken to Abyssinia to be pounded with quoits and other objects. The weather seems to be fair and warmer, as usual, except for a slight mist rising up out of the Ionian; this is the sweat of Neptune's balls which were castrated by the early monks, or perhaps it was by the Manicheans in the time of the

Pentecostal plague. Long strips of horsemeat are hanging out to dry and the flies are everywhere, just as Homer describes it in ancient times. Hard by is a McCormick threshing machine, a reaper and binder with a thirty-six horsepower engine and no cutout. The harvest is in and the workers are counting their wages in the distant fields. This is the flush of dawn on the first day of sexual intercourse in the old Hellenistic world, now faithfully reproduced for us in color thanks to the Zeiss Brothers and other patient zealots of industry. But this is not the way it looked to the men of Homer's time who were on the spot. Nobody knows how the god Priapus looked when he was reduced to the ignominy of balancing a corkscrew on the end of his weeny. Standing that way in the shadow of the Parthenon he undoubtedly fell a-dreaming of far-off cunt; he must have lost consciousness of the corkscrew and the threshing and reaping machine; he must have grown very silent within himself and finally he must have lost even the desire to dream. It is my idea, and of course I am willing to be corrected if I am wrong, that standing thus in the rising mist he suddenly heard the Angelus peal and lo and behold there appeared before his very eyes a gorgeous green marshland in which the Choctaws were making merry with the Navajos; in the air above were the white condors, their ruffs festooned with marigolds. He saw also a huge slate on which was written the body of Christ, the body of Absalom and the evil which is lust. He saw the sponge soaked with frogs' blood, the eyes which Augustine had sewn into his skin, the vest which was not big enough to cover our iniquities. He saw these things in the whilomst moment when the Navajos were making merry with the Choctaws and he was so taken by surprise that suddenly a voice issued from between his legs, from the long thinking reed which he had lost in dreaming, and it was the most inspired, the most shrill and piercing, the most jubilant and ferocious cachinnating sort of voice that had ever wongled up from the depths. He began to sing through that long cock of his with such divine grace and elegance that the white condors came down out of the sky and shat huge purple eggs all over the green marshland. Our Lord Christ got up from his stone bed and, marked by the quoit though he was, he danced like a mountain goat. The fellaheen came out of Egypt in their chains, followed by the warlike Igorots and the snail-eating men of Zanzibar.

This is how things stood on the first day of sexual intercourse in the old Hellenistic world. Since then things have changed a great deal. It is no longer polite to sing through your weeny, nor is it permitted even to condors to shit purple eggs all over the place. All this is scatological, eschatological and ecumenical. It is forbidden. *Verboten.* And so the Land of Fuck becomes ever more receding: it becomes mythological. Therefore am I constrained to speak mythologically. I speak with extreme unction, and with precious unguents too. I put away the clashing cymbals, the tubas, the white marigolds, the oleanders and the rhododendrons. Up with the thorns and the manacles! Christ is dead and mangled with quoits. The fellaheen are bleaching in the sands of Egypt, their wrists loosely shackled. The vultures have eaten away every decomposing crumb of flesh. All is quiet, a million golden mice nibbling at the unseen cheese. The moon is up and the Nile ruminates on her riparian ravages. The earth belches silently, the stars twitch and bleat, the rivers slip their banks. It's like this.... There are cunts which laugh and cunts which talk; there are crazy, hysterical cunts shaped like ocarinas and there are planturous, seismographic cunts which register the rise and fall of sap; there are cannibalistic cunts which open wide like the jaws of the whale and swallow alive; there are also masochistic cunts which close up like the oyster and have hard shells and perhaps a pearl or two inside; there are dithyrambic cunts which dance at the very approach of the penis and go wet all over in ecstasy; there are the porcupine cunts which unleash their quills and wave little flags at Christmas time; there are telegraphic cunts which practice the Morse code and leave the mind full of dots and dashes; there are the political cunts which are saturated with ideology and which deny even the menopause; there are vegetative cunts which make no response unless you pull them up by the roots; there are the religious cunts which smell like Seventh Day Adventists and are full of beads, worms, clamshells, sheep droppings and now and then dried bread crumbs; there are the mammalian cunts which are lined with otter skin and hibernate during the long winter; there are cruising cunts fitted out like yachts, which are good for solitaries and epileptics; there are glacial cunts in which you can drop shooting stars without causing a flicker; there are miscellaneous cunts which defy category or description, which you stumble on once in a lifetime and which leave you seared and branded; there are cunts made of pure joy which have neither name nor antecedent and these are the best of all, but whither have they flown?

And then there is the one cunt which is all, and this we shall call the super-cunt, since it is not of this land at all but of that bright country to which we were long ago invited to fly. Here the dew is ever sparkling and the tall reeds bend with the wind. It is here that the great father of fornication dwells, Father Apis, the mantic bull who gored his way to heaven and dethroned the gelded deities of right and wrong. From Apis sprang the race of unicorns, that ridiculous beast of ancient writ whose learned brow lengthened into a gleaming phallus, and from the unicorn by gradual stages was derived the late-city man of which Oswald Spengler speaks. And from the dead cock of this sad specimen arose the giant skyscraper with its express elevators and observation towers. We are the last decimal point of sexual calculation; the world turns like a rotten egg in its crate of straw. Now for the aluminum wings with which to fly to that far-off place, the bright country where Apis, the father of fornication, dwells. Everything goes forward like oiled clocks; for each minute of the dial there are a million noiseless clocks which tick off the rinds of time. We are traveling faster than the lightning calculator, faster than starlight, faster than the magician can think. Each second is a universe of time. And each universe of time is but a wink of sleep in the cosmogony of speed. When speed comes to its end we shall be there, punctual as always and blissfully undenominated. We shall shed our wings, our clocks and our mantelpieces to lean on. We will rise up feathery and jubilant, like a column of blood, and there will be no memory to drag us down again. This time I call the realm of the super-cunt, for it defies speed, calculation or imagery. Nor has the penis itself a known size or weight. There is only the sustained feel of fuck, the fugitive in full flight, the nightmare smoking his quiet cigar, little Nemo walks around with a seven-day hard on and a wonderful pair of blue balls bequeathed by Lady Bountiful. It is Sunday morning around the corner from Evergreen Cemetery.

It is Sunday morning and I am lying blissfully dead to the world on my bed of ferroconcrete. Around the corner is the cemetery, which is to say—the *world of sexual intercourse*. My balls ache with the fucking that is going on, but it is all going on beneath my window, on the boulevard where Hymie keeps his copulating nest. I am thinking of one woman and the rest is blotto. I say I am thinking of her, but the truth is I am dying a stellar death. I am lying there like a sick star waiting for the light to go out. Years ago I lay on this same bed and I waited and waited to be born. Nothing happened. Except that my mother, in her Lutheran rage, threw a bucket of water over me. My mother, poor imbecile that she was, thought I was lazy. She didn't know that I had gotten caught in the stellar drift, that I was being pulverized to a black extinction out there on the farthest rim of the universe. She thought it was sheer laziness that kept me riveted to the bed. She threw the bucket of water over me: I squirmed and shivered a bit, but I continued to lie there on my ferroconcrete bed. I was immovable. I was a burned-out meteor adrift somewhere in the neighborhood of Vega.

And now I'm on the same bed and the light that's in me refuses to be extinguished. The world of men and women are making merry in the cemetery grounds. They are having sexual intercourse, God bless them, and I am alone in the Land of Fuck. It seems to me that I hear the clanking of a great machine, the linotype bracelets passing through the wringer of sex. Hymie and his nymphomaniac of a wife are lying on the same level with me, only they are across the river. The river is called Death and it has a bitter taste. I have waded through it many times, up to the hips, but somehow I have neither been petrified nor immortalized. I am still burning brightly inside, though outwardly dead as a planet. From this bed I have gotten up to dance, not once but hundreds, thousands of times. Each time I came away I had the conviction that I had danced the skeleton dance on a *terrain vague.* Perhaps I had wasted too much of my substance on suffering; perhaps I had the crazy idea that I would be the first metallurgical bloom of the human species; perhaps I was imbued with the notion that I was both a sub-gorilla and a super-god. On this bed of ferroconcrete I remember everything and everything is in rock crystal. There are never any animals, only thousands and thousands of human beings all talking at once, and for each word they utter I have an answer immediately, sometimes before the word is out of their mouths. There is plenty of killing, but no blood. The murders are perpetrated with cleanliness, and always in silence. But even if everyone were killed there would still be conversation, and the conversation would be at once intricate and easy to follow. Because it is I who create it! I know it, and that is why it never drives me mad. I have conversations which may take place only twenty years hence, when I meet the right person, the one whom I shall create, let us say, when the proper time comes. All these talks take place in a vacant lot which is attached to my bed like a mattress. Once I gave it a name, this *terrain vague:* I called it Ubiguchi, but somehow Ubiguchi never satisfied me, it was too intelligible, too full of meaning. It would be better to keep it just *terrain vague,* which is what I intend to do. People think that vacuity is nothingness, but it is not so. Vacuity is a discordant fullness, a crowded ghostly world in which the soul goes reconnoitering. As a boy I remember standing in the vacant lot as if I were a very lively soul standing naked in a pair of shoes. The body had been stolen from me because I had no particular need of it. I could exist with or without a body then. If I killed a little bird and roasted it over the fire and ate it, it was not because I was hungry but because I wanted to know about Timbuktu or Tierra del Fuego. I had to stand in the vacant lot and eat dead birds in order to create a desire for that bright land which later I would inhabit alone and people with nostalgia. I expected ultimate things of this place, but I was deplorably deceived. I went as far as one could go in a state of complete deadness, and then by a law, which must be the law of creation, I suppose, I suddenly flared up and began to live inexhaustibly, like a star whose light is unquenchable. Here began the real cannibalistic excursions which have meant so much to me: no more dead chippies picked from the bonfire, but live human meat, tender, succulent human flesh, secrets like fresh bloody livers, confidences like swollen tumors that have been kept on ice. I learned not to wait for my victim to die, but to eat into him while he was talking to me. Often when I walked away from an unfinished meal I discovered that it was nothing more than an old friend minus an arm or a leg. I sometimes left him standing there—a trunk full of stinking intestines.

Being of the city, of the only city in the world and no place like Broadway anywhere, I used to walk up and down staring at the floodlit hams and other delicacies. I was a schizerino from the sole of my boots to the tips of my hair. I lived exclusively in the gerundive, which I understood only in Latin. Long before I had read of her in the *Black Book* I was cohabiting with Hilda, the giant cauliflower of my dreams. We traversed all the morganatic diseases together and a few which were *ex cathedra*. We dwelt in the carcass of the instincts and were nourished by ganglionic memories. There was never *a* universe, but millions and billions of universes, all of them put together no bigger than a pinhead. It was a vegetal sleep in the wilderness of the mind. It was the past, which alone comprises eternity. Amidst the fauna and flora of my dreams I would hear long distance calling. Messages were dropped on my table by the deformed and the epileptic. Hans Castorp would call sometimes and together we would commit innocent crimes. Or, if it were a bright freezing day, I would do a turn in the velodrome with my Presto bike from Chemnitz, Bohemia.

Best of all was the skeleton dance. I would first wash all my parts at the sink, change my linen, shave, powder, comb my hair, don my dancing pumps. Feeling abnormally light inside and out I would wind in and out of the crowd for a time to get the proper human rhythm, the weight and substance of flesh. Then I would make a beeline for the dance floor, grab a hunk of giddy flesh and begin the autumnal pirouette. It was like that I walked into the hairy Greek's place one night and ran smack into her. She seemed blue-black, white as chalk, ageless. There was not just the flow to and from, but the endless chute, the voluptuousness of intrinsic restlessness. She was mercurial and at the same time of a savory weight. She had the marmoreal stare of a faun embedded in lava. The time has come, I thought, to wander back from the periphery. I made a move toward the center, only to find the ground shifting from under my feet. The earth slid rapidly beneath my bewildered feet. I moved again out of the earth belt and behold, my hands were full of meteoric flowers. I reached for her with two flaming hands but she was more elusive than sand. I thought of my favorite nightmares, but she was unlike anything which had made me sweat and gibber. In my delirium I began to prance and neigh. I bought frogs and mated them with toads. I thought of the easiest thing to do, which is to die, but I did nothing. I stood still and began to petrify at the extremities. That was so wonderful, so healing, so eminently sensible, that I began to laugh way down inside the viscera, like a hyena crazed with rut. Maybe I would turn into a rosetta stone! I just stood still and waited. Spring came, and fall, and then winter. I renewed my insurance policy automatically. I ate grass and the roots of deciduous trees. I sat for days on end looking at the same film. Now and then I brushed my teeth. If you fired an automatic at me the bullets glanced off and made a queer tat-a-tat ricocheting against the walls. Once up a dark street, felled by a thug, I felt a knife go clean through me. It felt like a spritz bath. Strange to say, the knife left no holes in my skin. The experience was so novel that I went home and stuck knives into all parts of my body. More needle baths. I sat down, pulled all the knives out, and again I marveled that there was no trace of blood, no holes, no pain. I was just about to bite into my arm when the telephone rang. It was long distance calling. I never knew who put in the calls because no one ever came to the phone. However, the skeleton dance....

Life is drifting by the show window. I lie there like a floodlit ham waiting for the ax to fall. As a matter of fact, there is nothing to fear, because everything is cut neatly into fine little slices and wrapped in cellophane. Suddenly all the lights of the city are extinguished and the sirens sound their warning. The city is enveloped in poison gas, bombs are bursting, mangled bodies flying through the air. There is electricity everywhere, and blood and splinters and loudspeakers. The men in the air are full of glee; those below are screaming and bellowing. When the gas and the flames have eaten all the flesh away the skeleton dance begins. I watch from the show window which is now dark. It is better than the sack of Rome because there is more to destroy.

Why do the skeletons dance so ecstatically, I wonder. Is it the fall of the world? Is it the dance of death which has been so often heralded? To see millions of skeletons dancing in the snow while the city founders is an awesome sight. Will anything ever grow again? Will babes come out of the womb? Will there be food and wine? There are men in the air, to be sure. They will come down to plunder. There will be cholera and dysentery and those who were above and triumphant will perish like the rest. I have the sure feeling that I will be the last man on earth. I will emerge from the show window when it is all over and walk calmly amidst the ruins. I will have the whole earth to myself.

Long distance calling! To inform me that I am not utterly alone. Then the destruction was not complete? It's discouraging. Man is not even able to destroy himself; he can only destroy others. I am disgusted. What a malicious cripple! What cruel delusions! So there are more of the species about and they will tidy up the mess and begin again. God will come down again in flesh and blood and take up the burden of guilt. They will make music and build things in stone and write it all down in little books. Pfui! What blind tenacity, what clumsy ambitions!

I am on the bed again. The old Greek world, the dawn of sexual intercourse—and Hymie! Hymie Laubscher always on the same level, looking down on the boulevard across the river. There is a lull in the nuptial feast and the clam fritters are brought in. *Move over just a little,* he says. *There, like that, that's it!* I hear frogs croaking in the swamp outside my window. Big cemetery frogs nourished by the dead. They are all huddled together in sexual intercourse; they are croaking with sexual glee.

I realize now how Hymie was conceived and brought into being. Hymie the bullfrog! His mother was at the bottom of the pack and Hymie, then an embryo, was hidden away in her sac. It was in the early days of sexual intercourse and there were no Marquis of Queensbury rules to hinder. It was fuck and be fucked—and the devil take the hindmost.

It has been that way ever since the Greeks—a blind fuck in the mud and then a quick spawn and then death. People are fucking on different levels but it's always in a swamp and the litter is always destined for the same end. When the house is torn down the bed is left standing: the cosmosexual altar.

I was polluting the bed with dreams. Stretched out taut on the ferroconcrete my soul would leave its body and roam from place to place on a little trolley such as is used in department stores for making change. I made ideological changes and excursions; I was a vagabond in the country of the brain. Everything was absolutely clear to me because done in rock crystal; at every egress there was written in big letters ANNIHILATION. The fright of extinction solidified me; the body became itself a piece of ferroconcrete. It was ornamented by a permanent erection in the best taste. I had achieved that state of vacuity so earnestly desired by certain devout members of esoteric cults. I was no more. *I was not even a personal hard on.*

It was about this time, adopting the pseudonym Samson Lackawanna, that I began my depredations. The criminal instinct in me had gotten the upper hand. Whereas heretofore I had been only an errant soul, a sort of Gentile Dybbuk, now I became a flesh-filled ghost. I had taken the name which pleased me and I had only to act instinctively. In Hong Kong, for instance, I made my entry as a book agent. I carried a leather purse filled with Mexican dollars and I visited religiously all those Chinese who were in need of further education. At the hotel I rang for women like you would ring for whisky and soda. Mornings I studied Tibetan in order to prepare for the journey to Lhasa. I already spoke Yiddish fluently, and Hebrew too. I could count two rows of figures at once. It was so easy to swindle the Chinese that I went back to Manila in disgust. There I took a Mr. Rico in hand and taught him the art of selling books with no handling charges. All the profit came from ocean freight rates, but it was sufficient to keep me in luxury while it lasted.

The breath had become as much a trick as breathing. Things were not dual merely, but multiple. I had become a cage of mirrors reflecting vacuity. But vacuity once stoutly posited I was at home and what is called creation was merely a job of filling up holes. The trolley conveniently carried me about from place to place and in each little side pocket of the great vacuum I dropped a ton of poems to wipe out the idea of annihilation. I had ever before me boundless vistas. I began to live in the vista, like a microscopic speck on the lens of a giant telescope. There was no night in which to rest. It was perpetual starlight on the arid surface of dead planets. Now and then a lake black as marble in which I saw myself walking amidst brilliant orbs of light. So low hung the stars and so dazzling was the light they shed, that it seemed as if the universe were only about to be born. What rendered the impression stronger was that I was alone; not only were there no animals, no trees, no other beings, but there was not even a blade of grass, not even a dead root. In that violet incandescent light without even the suggestion of a shadow, motion itself seemed to be absent. It was like a blaze of pure consciousness, thought become God. And God, for the first time in my knowledge, was clean-shaven. I was also clean-shaven, flawless, deadly accurate. I saw my image in the marble black lakes and it was diapered with stars. Stars, stars... like a clout between the eyes and all remembrance fast run out. I was Samson and I was Lackawanna and I was dying as one being in the ecstasy of full consciousness.

And now here I am, sailing down the river in my little canoe. Anything you would like to have me do I will do for you—gratis. This is the Land of Fuck, in which there are no animals, no trees, no stars, no problems. Here the spermatozoon reigns supreme. Nothing is determined in advance, the future is absolutely uncertain, the past is non-existent. For every million born 999,999 are doomed to die and never again be born. But the one that makes a home run is assured of life eternal. Life is squeezed into a seed, which is a soul. Everything has soul, including minerals, plants, lakes, mountains, rocks. Everything is sentient, even at the lowest stage of consciousness.

Once this fact is grasped there can be no more despair. At the very bottom of the ladder, *chez* the spermatozoa, there is the same condition of bliss as at the top, *chez* God. God is the summation of all the spermatozoa come to full consciousness. Between the bottom and the top there is no stop, no halfway station. The river starts somewhere in the mountains and flows on into the sea. On this river that leads to God the canoe is as serviceable as the dreadnought. From the very start the journey is homeward.

Sailing down the river.... Slow as the hookworm, but tiny enough to make every bend. And slippery as an eel withal. What is your name? shouts someone. *My name? Why just call me God—God the embryo.* I go sailing on. Somebody would like to buy me a hat. What size do you wear, imbecile! he shouts. *What size? Why size X!* (And why do they always shout at me? Am I supposed to be deaf?) The hat is lost at the next cataract. *Tant pis*—for the hat. Does God need a hat? God needs only to become God, more and more God. All this voyaging, all these pitfalls, the time that passes, the scenery, and against the scenery *man,* trillions and trillions of things called man, like mustard seeds. Even in embryo God has no memory. The backdrop of consciousness is made up of infinitesimally minute ganglia, a coat of hair soft as wool. The mountain goat stands alone amidst the Himalayas; he doesn't question how he got to the summit. He grazes quietly amidst the *decor;* when the time comes he will travel down again. He keeps his muzzle to the ground, grubbing for the sparse nourishment which the mountain peaks afford. In this strange Capricornian condition of embryosis God the he-goat ruminates in stolid bliss among the mountain peaks. The high altitudes nourish the germ of separation which will one day estrange him completely from the soul of man, which will make him a desolate, rocklike father dwelling forever apart in a void which is unthinkable. But first come the morganatic diseases, of which we must now speak....

There is a condition of misery which is irremediable—because its origin is lost in obscurity. Bloomingdale's, for example, can bring about this condition. All department stores are symbols of sickness and emptiness, but Bloomingdale's is my special sickness, my incurable obscure malady. In the chaos of Bloomingdale's there is an order, but this order is absolutely crazy to me: it is the order which I would find on the head of a pin if I were to put it under the microscope. It is the order of an accidental series of accidents accidentally conceived. This order has, above all, an odor—and it is the odor of Bloomingdale's which strikes terror into my heart. In Bloomingdale's I fall apart completely: I dribble onto the floor, a helpless mess of guts and bones and cartilage. There is the smell, not of decomposition, but of misalliance. Man, the miserable alchemist, has welded together, in a million forms and shapes, substances and essences which have nothing in common. Because in his mind there is a tumor which is eating him away insatiably; he has left the little canoe which was taking him blissfully down the river in order to construct a bigger, safer boat in which there may be room for everyone. His labors take him so far afield that he has lost all remembrance of why he left the little canoe. The ark is so full of bric-a-brac that it has become a stationary building above a subway in which the smell of linoleum prevails and predominates. Gather together all the significance hidden away in the interstitial miscellany of Bloomingdale's and put it on the head of a pin and you will have left a universe in which the grand constellations move without the slightest danger of collision. It is this microscopic chaos which brings on my morganatic ailments. In the street I began to stab horses at random, or I lift a skirt here and there looking for a letter box, or I put a postage stamp across a mouth, an eye, a vagina. Or I suddenly decide to climb a tall building, like a fly, and once having reached the roof I do fly with real wings and I fly and fly and fly, covering towns like Weehawken, Hoboken, Hackensack, Canarsie, Bergen Beach in the twinkling of an eye. Once you become a real schizerino flying is the easiest thing in the world; the trick is to fly with the etheric body, to leave behind in Bloomingdale's your sack of bones, guts, blood and cartilage; to fly only with your immutable self which, if you stop a moment to reflect, is always equipped with wings.

Flying this way, in full daylight, has advantages over the ordinary night-flying which everybody indulges in. You can leave off from moment to moment, as quick and decisive as stepping on a brake; there is no difficulty in finding your other self, because the moment you leave off you *are* your other self, which is to say, the so-called whole self. Only, as the Bloomingdale experience goes to prove, this whole self, about which so much boasting has been done, falls apart very easily. The smell of linoleum, for some strange reason, will always make me fall apart and collapse on the floor. It is the smell of all the unnatural things which were glued together in me, which were assembled, so to say, by negative consent.

It is only after the third meal that the morning gifts, bequeathed by the phony alliance of the ancestors, begin to drop away and the true rock of the self, the happy rock sheers up out of the muck of the soul. With nightfall the pin-head universe begins to expand. It expands organically, from an infinitesimal nuclear speck, in the way that minerals or star clusters form. It eats into the surrounding chaos like a rat boring through store cheese. All chaos could be gathered together on a pinhead, but the self, microscopical at the start, works up to a universe from any point in space. This is not the self about which books are written, but the ageless self which has been farmed out through millenary ages to men with names and dates, the self which begins and ends as a worm, which *is* the worm in the cheese called the world. Just as the slightest breeze can set a vast forest in motion so, by some unfathomable impulse from within, the rocklike self can begin to grow, and in this growth nothing can prevail against it. It's like Jack Frost at work, and the whole world a windowpane. No hint of labor, no sound, no struggle, no rest; relentless, remorseless, unremitting, the growth of the self goes on. Only two items on the bill of fare: the self and the not-self. And an eternity in which to work it out. In this eternity, which has nothing to do with time or space, there are interludes in which something like a thaw sets in. The form of the self breaks down, but the self, like climate, remains. In the night the amorphous matter of the self assumes the most fugitive forms; error seeps in through the portholes and the wanderer is unlatched from his door. This door which the body wears, if opened out onto the world, leads to annihilation. It is the door in every fable out of which the magician steps; nobody has ever read of him returning home through the selfsame door. If opened inward there are infinite doors, all resembling trapdoors: no horizons are visible, no airlines, no rivers, no maps, no tickets. Each *couche* is a halt for the night only, be it five minutes or ten thousand years. The doors have no handles and they never wear out. Most important to note—there is no end in sight. All these halts for the night, so to speak, are like abortive explorations of a myth. One can feel his way about, take bearings, observe passing phenomena; one can even feel at home. But there is no taking root. Just at the moment when one begins to feel "established" the whole terrain founders, the soil underfoot is afloat, the constellations are shaken loose from their moorings, the whole known universe, including the imperishable self, starts moving silently, ominously, shudderingly serene and unconcerned, toward an unknown, unseen destination. All the doors seem to be opening at once; the pressure is so great that an implosion occurs and in the swift plunge the skeleton bursts asunder. It was some such gigantic collapse which Dante must have experienced when he situated himself in Hell; it was not a bottom which he touched, but a core, a dead center from which time itself is reckoned. Here the comedy begins, from here it is seen to be divine.

All this by way of saying that in going through the revolving door of the Amarillo Dance Hall one night, some twelve or fourteen years ago, the great event took place. The interlude which I think of as the Land of Fuck, a realm of time more than of space, is for me the equivalent of that Purgatory which Dante has described in nice detail. As I put my hand on the brass rail of the revolving door to leave the Amarillo Dance Hall, all that I had previously been, was, and about to be foundered. There was nothing unreal about it; the very time in which I was born passed away, carried off by a mightier stream. Just as I had previously been bundled out of the womb, so now I was shunted back to some timeless vector where the process of growth is kept in abeyance. I passed into the world of effects. There was no fear, only a feeling of fatality. My spine was socketed to the node; I was up against the coccyx of an implacable new world. In the plunge the skeleton blew apart, leaving the immutable ego as helpless as a squashed louse.

If from this point I do not begin, it is because there is no beginning. If I do not fly at once to the bright land it is because wings are of no avail. It is zero hour and the moon is at nadir....

Why I think of Maxie Schnadig I don't know, unless it is because of Dostoevski. The night I sat down to read Dostoevski for the first time was a most important event in my life, even more important than my first love. It was the first deliberate, conscious act which had significance for me; it changed the whole face of the world. Whether it is true that the clock stopped that moment when I looked up after the first deep gulp I don't know any more. But the world stopped dead for a moment, that I know. It was my first glimpse into the soul of a man, or shall I say simply that Dostoevski was the first man to reveal his soul to me? Maybe I had been a bit queer before that, without realizing it, but from the moment that I dipped into Dostoevski I was definitely, irrevocably, contentedly queer. The ordinary, waking, workaday world was finished for me. Any ambition or desire I had to write was also killed—for a long time to come. I was like those men who have been too long in the trenches, too long under fire. Ordinary human suffering, ordinary human jealousy, ordinary human ambitions—it was just so much shit to me.

I can visualize best my condition when I think of my relations with Maxie and his sister Rita. At the time Maxie and I used to go swimming together a great deal, that I remember well. Often we passed the whole day and night at the beach. I had only met Maxie's sister once or twice; whenever I brought up her name Maxie would rather frantically begin to talk about something else. That annoyed me because I was really bored to death with Maxie's company, tolerating him only because he loaned me money readily and bought me things which I needed. Every time we started for the beach I was in hopes his sister would turn up unexpectedly. But no, he always managed to keep her out of reach. Well, one day as we were undressing in the bathhouse and he was showing me what a fine tight scrotum he had, I said to him right out of the blue—"Listen, Maxie, that's all right about your nuts, they're fine and dandy, and there's nothing to worry about but where in hell is Rita all the time, why don't you bring her along some time and let me take a good look at her quim... yes, *quim,* you know what I mean." Maxie, being a Jew from Odessa, had never heard the word quim before. He was deeply shocked by my words and yet at the same time intrigued by this new word. In a sort of daze he said to me—"Jesus, Henry, you oughtn't to say a thing like that to me!" "Why not?" I answered. "She's got a cunt, your sister, hasn't she?" I was about to add something else when he broke into a terrific fit of laughter. That saved the situation, for the time being. But Maxie didn't like the idea at all deep down. All day long it bothered him, though he never referred to our conversation again. No, he was very silent that day. The only form of revenge he could think of was to urge me to swim far beyond the safety zone in the hope of tiring me out and letting me drown. I could see so clearly what was in his mind that I was possessed with the strength of ten men. Damned if I would go drown myself just because his sister like all other women happened to have a cunt.

It was at Far Rockaway where this took place. After we had dressed and eaten a meal I suddenly decided that I wanted to be alone and so, very abruptly, at the corner of a street, I shook hands and said good-by. And there I was! Almost instantaneously I felt alone in the world, alone as one feels only in moments of extreme anguish. I think I was picking my teeth absentmindedly when this wave of loneliness hit me full on, like a tornado. I stood there on the street corner and sort of felt myself all over to see if I had been hit by something. It was inexplicable, and at the same time it was very wonderful, very exhilarating, like a double tonic, I might say. When I say that I was at Far Rockaway I mean that I was standing at the end of the earth, at a place called Xanthos, if there be such a place, and surely there ought to be a word like this to express no place at all. If Rita had come along then I don't think I would have recognized her. I had become an absolute stranger standing in the very midst of my own people. They looked crazy to me, my people, with their newly sunburned faces and their flannel trousers and their clockwork stockings. They had been bathing like myself because it was a pleasant, healthy recreation and now like myself they were full of sun and food and a little heavy with fatigue. Up until this loneliness hit me I too was a bit weary, but suddenly, standing there completely shut off from the world, I woke up with a start. I became so electrified that I didn't dare move for fear I would charge like a bull or start to climb the wall of a building or else dance and scream. Suddenly I realized that all this was because I was really a brother to Dostoevski, that perhaps I was the only man in all America who knew what he meant in writing those books. Not only that, but I felt all the books I would one day write myself germinating inside me: they were bursting inside like ripe cocoons. And since up to this time I had written nothing but fiendishly long letters about everything and nothing, it was difficult for me to realize that there must come a time when I should begin, when I should put down the first word, *the first real word*. And this time was now! That was what dawned on me.

I used the word Xanthos a moment ago. I don't know whether there is a Xanthos or not, and I really don't care one way or another, but there must be a place in the world, perhaps in the Grecian islands, where you come to the end of the known world and you are thoroughly alone and yet you are not frightened of it but rejoice, because at this dropping off place you can feel the old ancestral world which is eternally young and new and fecundating. You stand there, wherever the place is, like a newly hatched chick beside its eggshell. This place is Xanthos, or as it happened in my case, Far Rockaway.

There I was! It grew dark, a wind came up, the streets became deserted, and finally it began to pour cats and dogs. Jesus, that finished me! When the rain came down, and I got it smack in the face staring at the sky, I suddenly began to bellow with joy. I laughed and laughed and laughed, exactly like an insane man. Nor did I know what I was laughing about. I wasn't thinking of a thing. I was just overwhelmed with joy, just crazy with delight in finding myself absolutely alone. If then and there a nice juicy quim had been handed me on a platter, if all the quims in the world had been offered me for to make my choice,

I wouldn't have batted an eyelash. I had what no quim could give me. And just about at that point, thoroughly drenched but still exultant, I thought of the most irrelevant thing in the world—*carfare!* Jesus, the bastard Maxie had walked off without leaving me a sou. There I was with my fine budding antique world and not a penny in my jeans. Herr Dostoevski Junior had now to begin to walk here and there peering into friendly and unfriendly faces to see if he could pry loose a dime. He walked from one end of Far Rockaway to the other but nobody seemed to give a fuck about handing out carfare in the rain. Walking about in that heavy animal stupor which comes with begging I got to thinking of Maxie the window trimmer and how the first time I spied him he was standing in the show window dressing a mannikin. And from that in a few minutes to Dostoevski, then the world stopped dead, and then, like a great rosebush opening in the night, his sister Rita's warm, velvety flesh.

Now this is what is rather strange.... A few minutes after I thought of Rita, her private and extraordinary quim, I was in the train, bound for New York and dozing off with a marvelous languid erection. And stranger still, when I got out of the train, whom should I bump into rounding a corner but Rita herself. And as though she had been informed telepathically of what was going on in my brain, Rita too was hot under the whiskers. Soon we were sitting in a chop suey joint, seated side by side in a little booth, behaving exactly like a pair of rabbits in rut. On the dance floor we hardly moved. We were wedged in tightly and we stayed that way, letting them jog and jostle us about as they might. I could have taken her home to my place, as I was alone at the time, but no, I had a notion to bring her back to her own home, stand her up in the vestibule and give her a fuck right under Maxie's nose—which I did. In the midst of it I thought again of the mannikin in the show window and of the way he had laughed that afternoon when I let drop the word quim. I was on the point of laughing aloud when suddenly I felt that she was coming, one of those long drawn out orgasms such as you get now and then in a Jewish cunt. I had my hands under her buttocks, the tips of my fingers just inside her cunt, in the lining, as it were; as she began to shudder I lifted her from the ground and raised her gently up and down on the end of my cock. I thought she would go off her nut completely, the way she began to carry on. She must have had four or five orgasms like that in the air, before I put her feet down on the ground. I took it out without spilling a drop and made her lie down in the vestibule. Her hat had rolled off into a corner and her handbag had spilled open and a few coins had tumbled out. I note this because just before I gave it to her good and proper I made a mental note to pocket a few coins for my carfare home. Anyway, it was only a few hours since I had said to Maxie in the bathhouse that I would like to take a look at his sister's quim, and here it was now smack up against me, sopping wet and throwing out one squirt after another. If she had been fucked before she had never been fucked properly, that's a cinch. And I myself was never in such a fine cool collected scientific frame of mind as now lying on the floor of the vestibule right under Maxie's nose, pumping it into the private, sacred, and extraordinary quim of his sister Rita. I could have held it in indefinitely—it was incredible how detached I was and yet thoroughly aware of every quiver and jolt she made. But somebody had to pay for making me walk around in the rain grubbing a dime. Somebody had to pay for the ecstasy produced by the germination of all those unwritten books inside me. Somebody had to verify the authenticity of this private, concealed cunt which had been plaguing me for weeks and months. Who better qualified than I? I thought so hard and fast between orgasms that my cock must have grown another inch or two. Finally I decided to make an end of it by turning her over and back-scuttling her. She balked a bit at first, but when she felt the thing slipping out of her she nearly went crazy. "Oh yes, oh yes, do it, do it!" she gibbered, and with that I really got excited, I had hardly slipped it into her when I felt it coming, one of those long agonizing spurts from the tip of the spinal column. I shoved it in so deep that I felt as if something had given way. We fell over, exhausted, the both of us, and panted like dogs. At the same time, however, I had the presence of mind to feel around for a few coins. Not that it was necessary, because she had already loaned me a few dollars, but to make up for the carfare which I was lacking in Far Rockaway. Even then, by Jesus, it wasn't finished. Soon I felt her mouth. I had still a sort of semi hard on. She got it into her mouth and she began to caress it with her tongue. I saw stars. The next thing I knew her feet were around my neck and my tongue up her twat. And then I had to get over her again and shove it in, up to the hilt. She squirmed around like an eel, so help me God. And then she began to come again, long, drawn out, agonizing orgasms, with a whimpering and gibbering that was hallucinating. Finally I had to pull it out and tell her to stop. What a quim! And I had only asked to take a look at it!

Maxie with his talk of Odessa revived something which I had lost as a child. Though I had never a very clear picture of Odessa the aura of it was like the little neighborhood in Brooklyn which meant so much to me and from which I had been torn away too soon. I get a very definite feeling of it every time I see an Italian painting without perspective; if it is a picture of a funeral procession, for example, it is exactly the sort of experience which I knew as a child, one of intense immediacy. If it is a picture of the open street, the women sitting in the windows are sitting *on* the street and not above it and away from it. Everything that happens is known immediately by everybody, just as among primitive people. Murder is in the air, chance rules.

Just as in the Italian primitives this perspective is lacking, so in the little old neighborhood from which I was uprooted as a child there were these parallel vertical planes on which everything took place and through which, from layer to layer, everything was communicated, as if by osmosis. The frontiers were sharp, clearly defined, but they were not impassable. I lived then, as a boy, close to the boundary between the north and the south side. I was just a little bit over on the north side, just a few steps from a broad thoroughfare called North Second Street, which was for me the real boundary line between the north and the south side. The actual boundary was Grand Street, which led to Broadway Ferry, but this street meant nothing to me, except that it was already beginning to be filled with Jews. No, North Second Street was the mystery street, the frontier between two worlds. I was living, therefore, between two boundaries, the one real, the other imaginary—as I have lived all my life. There was a little street, just a block long, which lay between Grand Street and North Second Street, called Fillmore Place. This little street was obliquely opposite the house my grandfather owned and in which we lived. It was the most enchanting street I have ever seen in all my life. It was the ideal street—for a boy, a lover, a maniac, a drunkard, a crook, a lecher, a thug, an astronomer, a musician, a poet, a tailor, a shoemaker, a politician. In fact this was just the sort of street it was, containing just such representatives of the human race, each one a world unto himself and all living together harmoniously and inharmoniously, *but together,* a solid corporation, a close knit human spore which could not disintegrate unless the street itself disintegrated.

So it seemed, at least. Until the Williamsburg Bridge was opened, whereupon there followed the invasion of the Jews from Delancey Street, New York. This brought about the disintegration of our little world, of the little street called Fillmore Place, which like the name itself was a street of value, of dignity, of light, of surprises. The Jews came, as I say, and like moths they began to eat into the fabric of our lives until there was nothing left but this mothlike presence which they brought with them everywhere. Soon the street began to smell bad, soon the real people moved away, soon the houses began to deteriorate and even the stoops fell away, like the paint. Soon the street looked like a dirty mouth with all the prominent teeth missing, with ugly charred stumps gaping here and there, the lips rotting, the palate gone. Soon the garbage was knee deep in the gutter and the fire escapes filled with bloated bedding, with cockroaches, with dried blood. Soon the kosher sign appeared on the shop windows and there was poultry everywhere and lox and sour pickles and enormous loaves of bread. Soon there were baby carriages in every areaway and on the stoops and in the little yards and before the shop fronts. And with the change the English language also disappeared; one heard nothing but Yiddish, nothing but this sputtering, choking, hissing tongue in which God and rotten vegetables sound alike and mean alike.

We were among the first families to move away, following the invasion. Two or three times a year I came back to the old neighborhood, for a birthday or for Christmas or Thanksgiving. With each visit I marked the loss of something I had loved and cherished. It was like a bad dream. It got worse and worse. The house in which my relatives still lived was like an old fortress going to ruin; they were stranded in one of the wings of the fortress, maintaining a forlorn, island life, beginning themselves to look sheepish, hunted, degraded. They even began to make distinctions between their Jewish neighbors, finding some of them quite human, quite decent, clean, kind, sympathetic, charitable, etc. etc. To me it was heartrending. I could have taken a machine gun and mowed the whole neighborhood down, Jew and Gentile together.

It was about the time of the invasion that the authorities decided to change the name of North Second Street to Metropolitan Avenue. This highway, which to the Gentiles had been the road to the cemeteries, now became what is called an artery of traffic, a link between two ghettos. On the New York side the river front was rapidly being transformed owing to the erection of the skyscrapers. On our side, the Brooklyn side, the warehouses were piling up and the approaches to the various new bridges created plazas, comfort stations, poolrooms, stationery shops, ice-cream parlors, restaurants, clothing stores, hock shops, etc. In short everything was becoming *metropolitan,* in the odious sense of the word.

As long as we lived in the old neighborhood we never referred to Metropolitan Avenue: it was always North Second Street, despite the official change of name. Perhaps it was eight or ten years later, when I stood one winter's day at the corner of the street facing the river and noticed for the first time the great tower of the Metropolitan Life Insurance Building, that I realized that North Second Street was no more. The imaginary boundary of my world had changed. My glance traveled now far beyond the cemeteries, far beyond the rivers, far beyond the city of New York or the State of New York, beyond the whole United States indeed. At Point Loma, California, I had looked out upon the broad Pacific and I had felt something there which kept my face permanently screwed in another direction. I came back to the old neighborhood, I remember, one night with my old friend Stanley who had just come out of the army, and we walked the streets sadly and wistfully. A European can scarcely know what this feeling is like. Even when a town becomes modernized, in Europe, there are still vestiges of the old. In America, though there are vestiges, they are effaced, wiped out of the consciousness, trampled upon, obliterated, nullified by the new. The new is, from day to day, a moth which eats into the fabric of life, leaving nothing finally but a great hole. Stanley and I, we were walking through this terrifying hole. Even a war does not bring this kind of desolation and destruction. Through war a town may be reduced to ashes and the entire population wiped out, but what springs up again resembles the old. Death is fecundating, for the soil as well as for the spirit. In America the destruction is complete, annihilating. There is no rebirth, only a cancerous growth, layer upon layer of new, poisonous tissue, each one uglier than the previous one.

We were walking through this enormous hole, as I say, and it was a winter's night, clear, frosty, sparkling, and as we came through the south side toward the boundary line we saluted all the old relics or the spots where things had once stood and where there had been once something of ourselves. And as we approached North Second Street, between Fillmore Place and North Second Street—a distance of only a few yards and yet such a rich, full area of the globe—before Mrs. O'Melio's shanty I stopped and looked up at the house where I had known what it was to really have a being. Everything had shrunk now to diminutive proportions, including the world which lay beyond the boundary line, the world which had been so mysterious to me and so terrifyingly grand, so delimited. Standing there in a trance I suddenly recalled a dream which I have had over and over, which I still dream now and then, and which I hope to dream as long as I live. It was the dream of passing the boundary line. As in all dreams the remarkable thing is the vividness of the reality, the fact that *one is in reality* and not dreaming. Across the line I am unknown and absolutely alone. Even the language has changed. In fact, I am always regarded as a stranger, a foreigner. I have unlimited time on my hands and I am absolutely content in sauntering through the streets. There is only *one* street, I must say—the continuation of the street on which I lived. I come finally to an iron bridge over the railroad yards. It is always nightfall when I reach the bridge, though it is only a short distance from the boundary line. Here I look down upon the webbed tracks, the freight stations, the tenders, the storage sheds, and as I gaze down upon this cluster of strange moving substances a process of metamorphosis takes place, *just as in a dream*. With the transformation and deformation I become aware that this is the old dream which I have dreamed so often. I have a wild fear that I shall wake up, and indeed I know that I will wake up shortly, just at the moment when in the midst of a great open space I am about to walk into the house which contains something of the greatest importance for me. Just as I go toward this house the lot on which I am standing begins to grow vague at the edges, to dissolve, to vanish. Space rolls in on me like a carpet and swallows me up, and with it of course the house which I never succeed in entering.

There is absolutely no transition from this, the most pleasurable dream I know, to the heart of a book called *Creative Evolution*. In this book by Henri Bergson, which I came to as naturally as to the dream of the land beyond the boundary, I am again quite alone, again a foreigner, again a man of indeterminate age standing on an iron bridge observing a peculiar metamorphosis without and within. If this book had not fallen into my hands at the precise moment it did, perhaps I would have gone mad. It came at a moment when another huge world was crumbling on my hands. If I had never understood a thing which was written in this book, if I have preserved only the memory of one word, *creative*, it is quite sufficient. This word was my talisman. With it I was able to defy the whole world, and especially my friends.

There are times when one must break with one's friends in order to understand the meaning of friendship. It may seem strange to say so, but the discovery of this book was equivalent to the discovery of a weapon, an implement, wherewith I might lop off all the friends who surrounded me and who no longer meant anything to me. This book became my friend because it taught me that I had no need of friends. It gave me the courage to stand alone, and it enabled me to appreciate loneliness. I have never understood the book; at times I thought I was on the point of understanding, but I never really did understand. It was more important for me not to understand. With this book in my hands, reading aloud to my friends, questioning them, explaining to them, I was made clearly to understand that I had no friends, that I was alone in the world. Because in not understanding the meaning of the words, neither I nor my friends, one thing became very clear and that was that there were ways of not understanding and that the difference between the non-understanding of one individual and the non-understanding of another created a world of terra firma even more solid than differences of understanding. Everything which once I thought I had understood crumbled, and I was left with a clean slate. My friends, on the other hand, entrenched themselves more solidly in the little ditch of understanding which they had dug for themselves. They died comfortably in their little bed of understanding, to become useful citizens of the world. I pitied them, and in short order I deserted them one by one, without the slightest regret.

What was there then in this book which could mean so much to me and yet remain obscure? I come back to the word *creative*. I am sure that the whole mystery lies in the realization of the meaning of this word. When I think of the book now, and the way I approached it, I think of a man going through the rites of initiation. The disorientation and reorientation which comes with the initiation into any mystery is the most wonderful experience which it is possible to have.

Everything which the brain has labored for a lifetime to assimilate, categorize and synthesize has to be taken apart and reordered. Moving day for the soul! And of course it's not for a day, but for weeks and months that this goes on. You meet a friend on the street by chance, one whom you haven't seen for several weeks, and he has become an absolute stranger to you. You give him a few signals from your new perch and if he doesn't cotton you pass him up—*for good*. It's exactly like mopping up a battlefield: all those who are hopelessly disabled and agonizing you dispatch with one swift blow of your club. You move on, to new fields of battle, to new triumphs or defeats. But you move! And as you move the world moves with you, with terrifying exactitude. You seek out new fields of operation, new specimens of the human race whom you patiently instruct and equip with the new symbols. You choose sometimes those whom you would never have looked at before. You try everybody and everything within range, provided they are ignorant of the revelation. It was in this fashion that I found myself sitting in the busheling room of my father's establishment, reading aloud to the Jews who were working there. Reading to them from this new Bible in the way that Paul must have talked to the disciples. With the added disadvantage, to be sure, that these poor Jew bastards could not read the English language. Primarily I was directing myself toward Bunchek the cutter, who had a rabbinical mind. Opening the book I would pick a passage at random and read it to them in a transposed English almost as primitive as pidgin English. Then I would attempt to explain, choosing for example and analogy the things they were familiar with. It was amazing to me how well they understood, how much better they understood, let me say, than a college professor or a literary man or any educated man. Naturally what they understood had nothing to do finally with Bergson's book, as a book, but was not that the purpose of such a book as this? My understanding of the meaning of a book is that the book itself disappears from sight, that it is chewed alive, digested and incorporated into the system as flesh and blood which in turn creates new spirit and reshapes the world. It was a great communion feast which we shared in the reading of this book and the outstanding feature of it was the chapter on Disorder which, having penetrated me through and through, has endowed me with such a marvelous sense of order that if a comet suddenly struck the earth and jarred everything out of place, stood everything upside down, turned everything inside out, I could orient myself to the new order in the twinkling of an eye. I have no fear or illusions about disorder any more than I have of death. The labyrinth is my happy hunting ground and the deeper I burrow into the maze the more oriented I become.

With *Creative Evolution* under my arm I board the elevated line at the Brooklyn Bridge after work and I commence the journey homeward toward the cemetery. Sometimes I get on at Delancey Street, the very heart of the ghetto, after a long walk through the crowded streets. I enter the elevated line below the ground, like a worm being pushed through the intestines. I know each time I take my place in the crowd which mills about the platform that I am the most unique individual down there. I look upon everything which is happening about me like a spectator from another planet. My language, my world, is under my arm. I am the guardian of a great secret; if I were to open my mouth and talk I would tie up traffic. What I have to say, and what I am holding in every night of my life on this journey to and from the office, is absolute dynamite. I am not ready yet to throw my stick of dynamite. I nibble at it meditatively, ruminatively, cogently. Five more years, ten more years perhaps, and I will wipe these people out utterly. If the train in making a curve gives a violent lurch I say to myself *fine! jump the track, annihilate them!* I never think of myself as being endangered should the train jump the track. We're wedged in like sardines and all the hot flesh pressed against me diverts my thoughts. I become conscious of a pair of legs wrapped around mine. I look down at the girl sitting in front of me, I look her right in the eye, and I press my knees still further into her crotch. She grows uneasy, fidgets about in her seat, and finally she turns to the girl next to her and complains that I am molesting her. The people about look at me hostilely. I look out of the window blandly and pretend I have heard nothing. Even if I wished to I can't remove my legs, little by little though, the girl, by a violent pushing and squiggling, manages to unwrap her legs from mine. I find myself almost in the same situation with the girl next to her, the one she was addressing her complaints to. Almost at once I feel a sympathetic touch and then, to my surprise, I hear her tell the other girl that one can't help these things, that it is really not the man's fault but the fault of the company for packing us in like sheep. And again I feel the quiver of her legs against mine, a warm, human pressure, like squeezing one's hand. With my one free hand I manage to open my book. My object is twofold: first I want her to see the kind of book I read, second, I want to be able to carry on the leg language without attracting attention. It works beautifully. By the time the train empties a bit

I am able to take a seat beside her and converse with her—about the book, naturally. She's a voluptuous Jewess with enormous liquid eyes and the frankness which comes from sensuality. When it comes time to get off we walk arm in arm through the streets, toward her home. I am almost on the confines of the old neighborhood. Everything is familiar to me and yet repulsively strange. I have not walked these streets for years and now I am walking with a Jew girl from the ghetto, a beautiful girl with a strong Jewish accent. I look incongruous walking beside her. I can sense that people are staring at us behind our backs. I am the intruder, the goy who has come down into the neighborhood to pick off a nice ripe cunt. She on the other hand seems to be proud of her conquest; she's showing me off to her friends. This is what I picked up in the train, an educated goy, a refined goy! I can almost hear her think it. Walking slowly I'm getting the lay of the land, all the practical details which will decide whether I call for her after dinner or not. There's no thought of asking her to dinner. It's a question of what time and where to meet and how will we go about it, because, as she lets drop just before we reach the door, she's got a husband who's a traveling salesman and she's got to be careful. I agree to come back and to meet her at the corner in front of the candy store at a certain hour. If I want to bring a friend along she'll bring her girl friend. No, I decide to see her alone. It's agreed. She squeezes my hand and darts off into a dirty hallway. I beat it quickly back to the elevated station and hasten home to gulp down the meal.

It's a summer's night and everything flung wide open. Riding back to meet her the whole past rushes up kaleidoscopically. This time I've left the book at home. It's cunt I'm out for now and no thought of the book is in my head. I am back again this side of the boundary line, each station whizzing past making my world grow more diminutive. I am almost a child by the time I reach the destination. I am a child who is horrified by the metamorphosis which has taken place. What has happened to me, a man of the Fourteenth Ward, to be jumping off at this station in search of a Jewish cunt? Supposing I do give her a fuck, what then? What have I got to say to a girl like that? What's a fuck when what I want is love? Yes, suddenly it comes over me like a tornado.... Una, the girl I loved, the girl who lived here in this neighborhood, Una with big blue eyes and flaxen hair, Una who made me tremble just to look at her, Una whom I was afraid to kiss or even to touch her hand. *Where is Una?* Yes, suddenly, that's the burning question: *where is Una?* In two seconds I am completely unnerved, completely lost, desolate, in the most horrible anguish and despair. How did I ever let her go? Why? What happened? *When* did it happen? I thought of her like a maniac night and day, year in and year out, and then, without even noticing it, she drops out of my mind, like that, like a penny falling through a hole in your pocket. Incredible, monstrous, mad. Why all I had to do was to ask her to marry me, ask her hand—that's all. If I had done that she would have said yes immediately. She loved me, she loved me desperately. Why yes, I remember now, I remember how she looked at me the last time we met. I was saying good-by because I was leaving that night for California, leaving everybody to begin a new life. And I never had any intention of leading a new life. I intended to ask her to marry me, but the story I had framed like a dope came out of my lips so naturally that I believed it myself, and so I said good-by and I walked off, and she stood there looking after me and I felt her eyes pierce me through and through, I heard her howling inside, but like an automaton I kept on walking and finally I turned the corner and that was the end of it. Good-by! Like that. Like in a coma. And I meant to say *come to me! Come to me because I can't live any more without you!*

I am so weak, so rocky, that I can scarcely climb down the El steps. Now I know what's happened—I've crossed the boundary line! This Bible that I've been carrying around with me is to instruct me, initiate me into a new way of life. The world I knew is no more, it is dead, finished, cleaned up. And everything that I was is cleaned up with it. I am a carcass getting an injection of new life. I am bright and glittery, rabid with new discoveries, but in the center it is still leaden, still slag. I begin to weep—right there on the El stairs. I sob aloud, like a child. Now it dawns on me with full clarity: *you are alone in the world!* You are alone... alone... alone. It is bitter to be alone... bitter, bitter, bitter, bitter. There is no end to it, it is unfathomable, and it is the lot of every man on earth, but especially mine... especially mine. Again the metamorphosis. Again everything totters and careens. I am in the dream again, the painful, delirious, pleasurable, maddening dream of beyond the boundary. I am standing in the center of the vacant lot, but my home I do not see. I have no home. The dream was a mirage. There never was a house in the midst of the vacant lot. That's why I was never able to enter it. My home is not in this world, nor in the next. I am a man without a home, without a friend, without a wife. I am a monster who belongs to a reality which does not exist yet. Ah, but it does exist, it will exist, I am sure of it. I walk now rapidly, head down, muttering to myself. I've forgotten about my rendezvous so completely that I never even noticed whether I walked past her or not. Probably I did. Probably I looked right at her and didn't recognize her. Probably she didn't recognize me either. I am mad, mad with pain, mad with anguish. I am desperate. But I am not lost. No, there *is* a reality to which I belong. It's far away, very far away. I may walk from now till doomsday with head down and never find it. But it is there, I am sure of it. I look at people murderously. If I could throw a bomb and blow the whole neighborhood to smithereens I would do it. I would be happy seeing them fly in the air, mangled, shrieking, torn apart, annihilated. I want to annihilate the whole earth. I am not a part of it. It's mad from start to finish. The whole shooting match. It's a huge piece of stale cheese with maggots festering inside it. Fuck it! Blow it to hell! Kill, kill, kill: Kill them all, Jews and Gentiles, young and old, good and bad....

I grow light, light as a feather, and my pace becomes more steady, more calm, more even. What a beautiful night it is! The stars shining so brightly, so serenely, so remotely. Not mocking me precisely, but reminding me of the futility of it all. Who are you, young man, to be talking of the earth, of blowing things to smithereens? Young man, we have been hanging here for millions and billions of years. We have seen it all, everything, and still we shine peacefully every night, we light the way, we still the heart. Look around you, young man, see how still and beautiful everything is. Do you see, even the garbage lying in the gutter looks beautiful in this light. Pick up the little cabbage leaf, hold it gently in your hand. I bend down and pick up the cabbage leaf lying in the gutter. It looks absolutely new to me, a whole universe in itself. I break a little piece off and examine that. Still a universe. Still unspeakably beautiful and mysterious. I am almost ashamed to throw it back in the gutter. I bend down and deposit it gently with the other refuse. I become very thoughtful, very, very calm. I love everybody in the world. I know that somewhere at this very moment there is a woman waiting for me and if only I proceed very calmly, very gently, very slowly, I will come to her. She will be standing on a corner perhaps and when I come in sight she will recognize me—immediately. I believe this, so help me God! I believe that everything is just and ordained. My home? Why it is the world—the whole world! I am at home everywhere, only I did not know it before. But I know now. There is no boundary line any more. There never was a boundary line: it was I who made it. I walk slowly and blissfully through the streets. The beloved streets. Where everybody walks and everybody suffers without showing it. When I stand and lean against a lamppost to light my cigarette even the lamppost feels friendly. It is not a thing of iron—it is a creation of the human mind, shaped a certain way, twisted and formed by human hands, blown on with human breath, placed by human hands and feet. I turn round and rub my hand over the iron surface. It almost seems to speak to me. It is a human lamppost. It *belongs*, like the cabbage leaf, like the torn socks, like the mattress, like the kitchen sink. Everything stands in a certain way in a certain place, as our mind stands in relation to God. The world, in its visible, tangible substance, is a map of our love. Not God but *life* is love. Love, love, love. And in the midmost midst of it walks this young man, myself, who is none other than Gottlieb Leberecht Muller.

Gottlieb Leberecht Muller! This is the name of a man who lost his identity. Nobody could tell him who he was, where he came from or what had happened to him. In the movies, where I first made the acquaintance of this individual, it was assumed that he had met with an accident in the war. But when I recognized myself on the screen, knowing that I had never been to the war, I realized that the author had invented this little piece of fiction in order not to expose me. Often I forget which is the real me. Often in my dreams I take the draught of forgetfulness, as it is called, and I wander forlorn and desperate, seeking the body and the name which is mine. And sometimes between the dream and reality there is only the thinnest line. Sometimes while a person is talking to me I step out of my shoes and, like a plant drifting with the current, I begin the voyage of my rootless self. In this condition I am quite capable of fulfilling the ordinary demands of life— of finding a wife, of becoming a father, of supporting the household, of entertaining friends, of reading books, of paying taxes, of performing military service, and so on and so forth. In this condition I am capable, if needs be, of killing in cold blood, for the sake of my family or to protect my country, or whatever it may be. I am the ordinary, routine citizen who answers to a name and who is given a number in his passport. I am thoroughly irresponsible for my fate.

Then one day, without the slightest warning, I wake up and looking about me I understand absolutely nothing of what is going on about me, neither my own behavior nor that of my neighbors, nor do I understand why the governments are at war or at peace, whichever the case may be. At such moments I am born anew, born and baptized by my right name: Gottlieb Leberecht Muller! Everything I do in my right name is looked upon as crazy. People make furtive signs behind my back, sometimes to my face even. I am forced to break with friends and family and loved ones. I am obliged to break camp. And so, just as naturally as in dream, I find myself once again drifting with the current, usually walking along a highway, my face set toward the sinking sun. Now all my faculties become alert. I am the most suave, silky, cunning animal—and I am at the same time what might be called a holy man. I know how to fend for myself. I know how to avoid work, how to avoid entangling relationships, how to avoid pity, sympathy, bravery, and all the other pitfalls. I stay in place or with a person just long enough to obtain what I need, and then I'm off again. I have no goal: the aimless wandering is sufficient unto itself. I am free as a bird, sure as an equilibrist. Manna falls from the sky; I have only to hold out my hands and receive. And everywhere I leave the most pleasant feeling behind me, as though, in accepting the gifts that are showered upon me, I am doing a real favor to others. Even my dirty linen is taken care of by loving hands. Because everybody loves a right-living man! Gottlieb! What a beautiful name it is! Gottlieb! I say it to myself over and over. Gottlieb Leberecht Muller!

In this condition I have always fallen in with thieves and rogues and murderers, and how kind and gentle they have been with me! As though they were my brothers. And are they not, indeed? Have I not been guilty of every crime, and suffered for it? And is it not just because of my crimes that I am united so closely to my fellowman? Always, when I see a light of recognition in the other person's eyes, I am aware of this secret bond. It is only the just whose eyes never light up. It is the just who have never known the secret of human fellowship. It is the just who are committing the crimes against man, the just who are the real monsters. It is the just who demand our fingerprints, who prove to us that we have died even when we stand before them in the flesh. It is the just who impose upon us arbitrary names, false names, who put false dates in the register and bury us alive. I prefer the thieves, the rogues, the murderers, unless I can find a man of my own stature, my own quality.

I have never found such a man! I have never found a man as generous as myself, as forgiving, as tolerant, as carefree, as reckless, as clean at heart. I forgive myself for every crime I have committed. I do it in the name of humanity. I know what it means to be human, the weakness and the strength of it. I suffer from this knowledge and I revel in it also. If I had the chance to be God I would reject it. If I had the chance to be a star I would reject it. The most wonderful opportunity which life offers is to be human. It embraces the whole universe. It includes the knowledge of death, which not even God enjoys.

At the point from which this book is written I am the man who baptized himself anew. It is many years since this happened and so much has come in between that it is difficult to get back to that moment and retrace the journey of Gottlieb Leberecht Muller. However, perhaps I can give the clue if I say that the man which I now am was born out of a wound. That wound went to the heart. By all man-made logic I should have been dead. I was in fact given up for dead by all who once knew me; I walked about like a ghost in their midst. They used the past tense in referring to me, they pitied me, they shoveled me under deeper and deeper. Yet I remember how I used to laugh then, as always, how I made love to other women, how I enjoyed my food and drink, and the soft bed which I clung to like a fiend. Something had killed me, and yet I was alive. But I was alive without a memory, without a name; I was cut off from hope as well as from remorse or regret. I had no past and I would probably have no future; I was buried alive in a void which was the wound that had been dealt me. I *was the wound itself.*

I have a friend who talks to me from time to time about the Miracle of Golgotha of which I understand nothing. But I do know something about the miraculous wound which I received, the wound which killed me in the eyes of the world and out of which I was born anew and rebaptized. I know something of the miracle of this wound which I lived and which healed with my death. I tell it as of something long past, but it is with me always. Everything is long past and seemingly invisible, like a constellation which has sunk forever beneath the horizon.

What fascinates me is that anything so dead and buried as I was could be resuscitated, and not just once, but innumerable times. And not only that, but each time I faded out

I plunged deeper than ever into the void, so that with each resuscitation the miracle becomes greater. And never any stigmata! The man who is reborn is always the same man, more and more himself with each rebirth. He is only shedding his skin each time, and with his skin his sins. The man whom God loves is truly a right-living man. The man whom God loves is the onion with a million skins. To shed the first layer is painful beyond words; the next layer is less painful, the next still less, until finally the pain becomes pleasurable, more and more pleasurable, a delight, an ecstasy. And then there is neither pleasure nor pain, but simply darkness yielding before the light. And as the darkness falls away the wound comes out of its hiding place: the wound which is man, man's love, is bathed in light. The identity which was lost is recovered. Man walks forth from his open wound, from the grave which he had carried about with him so long.

In the tomb which is my memory I see her buried now, the one I loved better than all else, better than the world, better than God, better than my own flesh and blood. I see her festering there in that bloody wound of love, so close to me that I could not distinguish her from the wound itself. I see her struggling to free herself, to make herself clean of love's pain, and with each struggle sinking back again into the wound, mired, suffocated, writhing in blood. I see the terrible look in her eyes, the mute piteous agony, the look of the beast that is trapped. I see her opening her legs for deliverance and each orgasm a groan of anguish. I hear the walls falling, the walls caving in on us and the house going up in flames. I hear them calling us from the street, the summons to work, the summons to arms, but we are nailed to the floor and the rats are biting into us. The grave and womb of love entombing us, the night filling our bowels and the stars shimmering over the black bottomless lake. I lose the memory of words, of her name even which I pronounce like a monomaniac. I forgot what she looked like, what she felt like, what she smelt like, what she fucked like, piercing deeper and deeper into the night of the fathomless cavern. I followed her to the deepest hole of her being, to the charnel house of her soul, to the breath which had not yet expired from her lips. I sought relentlessly for her whose name was not written anywhere, I penetrated to the very altar and found—nothing. I wrapped myself around this hollow shell of nothingness like a serpent with fiery coils; I lay still for six centuries without breathing as world events sieved through to the bottom forming a slimy bed of mucus. I saw the constellations wheeling about the huge hole in the ceiling of the universe; I saw the outer planets and the black star which was to deliver me. I saw the Dragon shaking itself free of dharma and karma, saw the new race of man stewing in the yolk of futurity. I saw through to the last sign and symbol, *hut I could not read her face.* I could see only the eyes shining through, huge, fleshy-like luminous breasts, as though I were swimming behind them in the electric effluvia of her incandescent vision. How had she come to expand thus beyond all grip of consciousness? By what monstrous law had she spread herself thus over the face of the world, revealing everything and yet concealing herself? She was hidden in the face of the sun, like the moon in eclipse; she was a mirror which had lost its quicksilver, the mirror which yields both the image and the horror. Looking into the backs of her eyes, into the pulpy translucent flesh, I saw the brain structure of all formations, all relations, all evanescence. I saw the brain within the brain, the endless machine endlessly turning, the word Hope revolving on a spit, roasting, dripping with fat, revolving ceaselessly in the cavity of the third eye. I heard her dreams mumbled in lost tongues, the stifled screams reverberating in minute crevices, the gasps, the groans, the pleasurable sighs, the swish of lashing whips. I heard her call my own name which I had not yet uttered, I heard her curse and shriek with rage. I heard everything magnified a thousand times, like a homunculus imprisoned in the belly of an organ. I caught the muffled breathing of the world, as if fixed in the very crossroads of sound.

Thus we walked and slept and ate together, the Siamese twins whom Love had joined and whom Death alone could separate.

We walked upside down, hand in hand, at the neck of the bottle. She dressed in black almost exclusively, except for patches of purple now and then. She wore no underclothes, just a simple sheath of black velvet saturated with a diabolical perfume. We went to bed at dawn and got up just as it was darkling. We lived in black holes with drawn curtains, we ate from black plates, we read from black books. We looked out of the black hole of our life into the black hole of the world. The sun was permanently blacked out, as though to aid us in our continuous internecine strife. For sun we had Mars, for moon Saturn; we lived permanently in the zenith of the underworld. The earth had ceased to revolve and through the hole in the sky above us there hung the black star which never twinkled. Now and then we had fits of laughter, crazy, batrachian laughter which made the neighbors shudder. Now and then we sang, delirious, off key, full tremolo. We were locked in throughout the long dark night of the soul, a period of incommensurable time which began and ended in the manner of an eclipse. We revolved about our own egos, like phantom satellites. We were drunk with our own image which we saw when we looked into each other's eyes. How then did we look to others? As the beast looks to the plant, as the stars look to the beast. Or as God would look to man if the devil had given him wings. And with it all, in the fixed, close intimacy of a night without end she was radiant, jubilant, an ultra-black jubilation streaming from her like a steady flow of sperm from the Mithraic Bull. She was double barreled, like a shotgun, a female bull with an acetylene torch in her womb. In heat she focused on the grand cosmocrator, her eyes rolled back to the whites, her lips a-slaver. In the blind hole of sex she waltzed like a trained mouse, her jaws unhinged like a snake's, her skin horripilating in barbed plumes. She had the insatiable lust of a unicorn, the itch that laid the Egyptians low. Even the hole in the sky through which the lackluster star shone down was swallowed up in her fury.

We lived glued to the ceiling, the hot rancid fumes of the everyday life steaming up and suffocating us. We lived at marble heat, the ascending glow of human flesh warming the snakelike coils in which we were locked. We lived riveted to the nethermost depths, our skins smoked to the color of a gray cigar by the fumes of worldly passion. Like two heads carried on the pikes of our executioners we circled slowly and fixedly over the heads and shoulders of the world below. What was life on the solid earth to us who were decapitated and forever joined at the genitals? We were the twin snakes of Paradise, lucid in heat and cool as chaos itself. Life was a perpetual black fuck about a fixed pole of insomnia. Life was Scorpio conjunction Mars, conjunction Mercury, conjunction Venus, conjunction Saturn, conjunction Pluto, conjunction Uranus, conjunction quicksilver, laudanum, radium, bismuth. The grand conjunction was every Saturday night, Leo fornicating with Draco in the house of brother and sister. The great *malheur* was a ray of sunlight stealing through the curtains. The great curse was Jupiter, king of the fishes, that he might flash a benevolent eye.

The reason why it is difficult to tell it is because I remember too much. I remember everything, but like a dummy sitting on the lap of a ventriloquist. It seems to me that throughout the long, uninterrupted connubial solstice I sat on her lap (even when she was standing) and spoke the lines she had taught me. It seems to me that she must have commanded God's chief plumber to keep the black star shining through the hole in the ceiling, must have bid him to rain down perpetual night and with it all the crawling torments that move noiselessly about in the dark so that the mind becomes a twirling awl burrowing frantically into black nothingness. Did I only imagine that she talked incessantly, or had I become such a marvelously trained dummy that I intercepted the thought before it reached the lips? The lips were finely parted, smoothed down with a thick paste of dark blood; I watched them open and close with the utmost fascination, whether they hissed a viper's hate or cooed like a turtle dove. They were always close up, as in the movie stills, so that I knew every crevice, every pore, and when the hysterical slavering began I watched the spittle fume and foam as though I were sitting in a rocking chair under Niagara Falls. I learned what to do just as though I were a part of her organism; I was better than a ventriloquist's dummy because I could act without being violently jerked by strings. Now and then I did things impromptu like, which sometimes pleased her enormously; she would pretend, of course, not to notice these irruptions, but I could always tell when she was pleased by the way she preened herself. She had the gift for transformation; almost as quick and subtle she was as the devil himself. Next to the panther and the jaguar she did the bird stuff best: the wild heron, the ibis, the flamingo, the swan in rut. She had a way of swooping suddenly, as if she had spotted a ripe carcass, diving right into the bowels, pouncing immediately on the tidbits—the heart, the liver, or the ovaries—and making off again in the twinkling of an eye. Did someone spot her, she would lie stone quiet at the base of a tree, her eyes not quite closed but immovable in that fixed stare of the basilisk. Prod her a bit and she would become a rose, a deep black rose with the most velvety petals and of a fragrance that was overpowering. It was amazing how marvelously I learned to take my cue; no matter how swift the metamorphosis I was always there in her lap, bird lap, beast lap, snake lap, rose lap, what matter: the lap of laps, the lip of lips, tip to tip, feather to feather, the yoke in the egg, the pearl in the oyster, a cancer clutch, a tincture of sperm and cantharides. Life was Scorpio conjunction Mars, conjunction Venus, Saturn, Uranus, et cetera; love was conjunctivitis of the mandibles, clutch this, clutch that, clutch, clutch, the mandibular clutch-clutch of the mandala wheel of lust. Come food time I could already hear her peeling the eggs, and inside the egg *cheep-cheep*, blessed omen of the next meal to come. I ate like a monomaniac: the prolonged dreamlit voracity of the man who is thrice breaking his fast. And as I ate she purred, the rhythmic predatory wheeze of the succubus devouring her young. What a blissful night of love! Saliva, sperm, succubation, sphincteritis all in one: the conjugal orgy in the Black Hole of Calcutta.

Out there where the black star hung, a Pan-Islamic silence, as in the cavern world where even the wind is stilled. Out there, did I dare to brood on it, the spectral quietude of insanity, the world of men lulled, exhausted by centuries of incessant slaughter. Out there one gory encompassing membrane within which all activity took place, the hero-world of lunatics and maniacs who had quenched the light of the heavens with blood. How peaceful our little dove-and-vulture life in the dark! Flesh to bury in with teeth or penis, abundant odorous flesh with no mark of knife or scissors, no scar of exploded shrapnel, no mustard burns, no scalded lungs. Save for the hallucinating hole in the ceiling, an almost perfect womb life. But the hole was there—like a fissure in the bladder—and no wadding could plug it permanently, no urination could pass off with a smile. Piss large and freely, aye, but how forget the rent in the belfry, the silence unnatural, the imminence, the terror, the doom of the "other" world? Eat a bellyful, aye, and tomorrow another bellyful, and tomorrow and tomorrow and tomorrow—but *finally,* what then? *Finally!* What was *finally?* A change of ventriloquist, a change of lap, a shift in the axis, another rift in the vault... *what? what?* I'll tell you—sitting in her lap, petrified by the still, pronged beams of the black star, horned, snaffled, hitched and trepanned by the telepathic acuity of our interacting agitation, I thought of nothing at all, nothing that was outside the cell we inhabited, not even the thought of a crumb on a white tablecloth. I thought purely within the walls of our amoebic life, the pure thought such as Immanuel Pussyfoot Kant gave us and which only a ventriloquist's dummy could reproduce. I thought out every theory of science, every theory of art, every grain of truth in every cockeyed system of salvation. I calculated everything out to a pinpoint with gnostic decimals to boot, like *primes* which a drunk hands out at the finish of a six-day race. But everything was calculated for another life which somebody else would live some day— *perhaps.* We were at the very neck of the bottle, *her and I,* as they say, but the neck of the bottle had been broken off and the bottle was only a fiction.

I remember how the second time I met her she told me that she had never expected to see me again, and the next time I saw her she said she thought I was a dope fiend, and the next time she called me a god, and after that she tried to commit suicide and then I tried and then she tried again, and nothing worked except to bring us closer together, so close indeed that we interpenetrated, exchanged personalities, name, identity, religion, father, mother, brother. Even her body went through a radical change, not once but several times. At first she was big and velvety, like the jaguar, with that silky, deceptive strength of the feline species, the crouch, the spring, the pounce; then she grew emaciated, fragile, delicate, almost like a cornflower, and with each change thereafter she went through the subtlest modulations—of skin, muscle, color, posture, odor, gait, gesture, et cetera. She changed like a chameleon. Nobody could say what she really was like because with each one she was an entirely different person. After a time she didn't even know herself what she was like. She had begun this process of metamorphosis before I met her, as I later discovered. Like so many women who think themselves ugly she had willed to make herself beautiful, dazzlingly beautiful. To do this she first of all renounced her name, then her family, her friends, everything which might attach her to the past. With all her wits and faculties she devoted herself to the cultivation of her beauty, of her charm, which she already possessed to a high degree but which she had been made to believe were nonexistent. She lived constantly before the mirror, studying every movement, every gesture, every slightest grimace. She changed her whole manner of speech, her diction, her intonation, her accent, her phraseology. She conducted herself so skilfully that it was impossible even to broach the subject of origins. She was constantly on her guard, even in her sleep. And, like a good general, she discovered quickly enough that the best defense is attack. She never left a single position unoccupied; her outposts, her scouts, her sentinels were stationed everywhere. Her mind was a revolving searchlight which was never dimmed.

Blind to her own beauty, her own charm, her own personality, to say nothing of her identity, she launched her full powers toward the fabrication of a mythical creature, a Helen, a Juno, whose charms neither man nor woman would be able to resist. Automatically, without the slightest knowledge of legend, she began to create little by little the ontological background, the mythic sequence of events preceding the conscious birth. She had no need to remember her lies, her fictions—she had only to bear in mind her role. There was no lie too monstrous for her to utter, for in her adopted role she was absolutely faithful to herself. She did not have to *invent* a past: she *remembered* the past which belonged to her. She was never outflanked by a direct question since she never presented herself to an adversary except obliquely. She presented only the angles of the ever-turning facets, the blinding prisms of light which she kept constantly revolving. She was never a being, such as might finally be caught in repose, but the mechanism itself, relentlessly operating the myriad mirrors which would reflect the myth she had created. She had no poise whatsoever; she was eternally poised above her multiple identities in the vacuum of the self. She had not intended to make herself a legendary figure, she had merely wanted her beauty to be recognized. But in the pursuit of beauty, she soon forgot her quest entirely, became the victim of her own creation. She became so stunningly beautiful that at times she was frightening, at times positively uglier than the ugliest woman in the world. She could inspire horror and dread, especially when her charm was at its height. It was as though the will, blind and uncontrollable, shone through the creation, exposing the monster which it is.

In the dark, locked away in the black hole with no world looking on, no adversary, no rivals, the blinding dynamism of the will slowed down a bit, gave her a molten copperish glow, the words coming out of her mouth like lava, her flesh clutching ravenously for a hold, a perch on something solid and substantial, something in which to reintegrate and repose for a few moments. It was like a frantic long-distance message, an S O S from a sinking ship. At first I mistook it for passion, for the ecstasy produced by flesh rubbing against flesh. I thought I had found a living volcano, a female Vesuvius. I never thought of a human ship going down in an ocean of despair, in a Sargasso of impotence. Now I think of that black star gleaming through the hole in the ceiling, that fixed star which hung above our conjugal cell, more fixed, more remote than the Absolute, and I know it was her, emptied of all that was properly herself: a dead black sun without aspect. I know that we were conjugating the verb love like two maniacs trying to fuck through an iron grate. I said that in the frantic grappling in the dark I sometimes forgot her name, what she looked like, who she was. It's true. I overreached myself in the dark. I slid off the flesh rails into the endless space of sex, into the channel-orbits established by this one and that one: Georgiana, for instance, of only a brief afternoon, Thelma, the Egyptian whore, Carlotta, Alannah, Una, Mona, Magda, girls of six or seven; waifs, will-o'-the-wisps, faces, bodies, thighs, a subway brush, a dream, a memory, a desire, a longing. I could start with Georgiana of a Sunday afternoon near the railroad tracks, her dotted Swiss dress, her swaying haunch, her Southern drawl, her lascivious mouth, her molten breasts; I could start with Georgiana, the myriad branched candelabra of sex, and work outwards and upwards through the ramification of cunt into the nth dimension of sex, world without end. Georgiana was like the membrane of the tiny little ear of an unfinished monster called sex. She was transparently alive and breathing in the light of the memory of a brief afternoon on the avenue, the first tangible odor and substance of the world of fuck which is in itself a being limitless and undefinable, like our world the world. The whole world of fuck like unto the ever-increasing membrane of the animal we call sex, which is like another being growing into our own being and gradually displacing it, so that in time the human world will be only a dim memory of this new, all-inclusive, all-procreative being which is giving birth to itself.

It was precisely this snakelike copulation in the dark, this double-jointed, double-barreled hookup, which put me in the strait jacket of doubt, jealousy, fear, loneliness. If I began my hemstitching with Georgiana and the myriad-branched candelabra of sex I was certain that she too was at work building membrane, making ears, eyes, toes, scalp and whatnot of sex. She would begin with the monster who had raped her, assuming there was truth in the story; in any case she too began somewhere on a parallel track, working upwards and outwards through this multiform, uncreated being through whose body we were both striving desperately to meet. Knowing only a fraction of her life, possessing only a bag of lies, of inventions, of imaginings, of obsessions and delusions, putting together tag ends, coke dreams, reveries, unfinished sentences, jumbled dream talk, hysterical ravings, ill-disguised fantasies, morbid desires, meeting now and then a name become flesh, overhearing stray bits of conversation, observing smuggled glances, half-arrested gestures, I could well credit her with a pantheon of her own private fucking gods, of only too vivid flesh and blood creatures, men of perhaps that very afternoon, of perhaps only an hour ago, her cunt perhaps still choked with the sperm of the last fuck. The more submissive she was, the more passionately she behaved, the more abandoned she looked, the more uncertain I became. There was no beginning, no personal, individual starting point; we met like experienced swordsmen on the field of honor now crowded with the ghosts of victory and defeat. We were alert and responsive to the least thrust, as only the practiced can be.

We came together under cover of dark with our armies and from opposite sides we forced the gates of the citadel. There was no resisting our bloody work; we asked for no quarter and we gave none. We came together swimming in blood, a gory, glaucous reunion in the night with all the stars extinguished save the fixed black star hanging like a scalp above the hole in the ceiling. If she were properly coked she would vomit it forth like an oracle, everything that had happened to her during the day, yesterday, the day before, the year before last, *everything*, down to the day she was born. And not a word of it was true, not a single detail. Not a moment did she stop, for if she had, the vacuum she created in her flight would have brought about an explosion fit to sunder the world. She was the world's lying machine in microcosm, geared to the same unending, devastating fear which enables men to throw all their energies into creation of the death apparatus. To look at her one would think her fearless, one would think her the personification of courage and she *was,* so long as she was not obliged to turn in her traces. Behind her lay the calm fact of reality, a colossus which dogged her every step. Every day this colossal reality took on new proportions, every day it became more terrifying, more paralyzing. Every day she had to grow swifter wings, sharper jaws, more piercing, hypnotic eyes. It was a race to the outermost limits of the world, a race lost from the start, and no one to stop it. At the edge of the vacuum stood Truth, ready in one lightning-like sweep to recover the stolen ground. It was so simple and obvious that it drove her frantic. Marshal a thousand personalities, commandeer the biggest guns, deceive the greatest minds, make the longest detour—still the end would be defeat. In the final meeting everything was destined to fall apart—the cunning, the skill, the power, everything. She would be a grain of sand on the shore of the biggest ocean, and, worse than anything, she would resemble each and every other grain of sand on that ocean's shore. She would be condemned to recognize her unique self everywhere until the end of time. What a fate she had chosen for herself! That her uniqueness should be engulfed in the universal! That her power should be reduced to the utmost node of passivity! It was maddening, hallucinating. It could not be! It *must* not be! Onward! Like the black legions. Onward! Through every degree of the ever-widening circle. Onward and away from the self, until the last substantial particle of the soul be stretched to infinity. In her panic-stricken flight she seemed to bear the whole world in her womb. We were being driven out of the confines of the universe toward a nebula which no instrument could visualize. We were being rushed to a pause so still, so prolonged, that death by comparison seems a mad witches' revel.

In the morning, gazing at the bloodless crater of her face. Not a line in it, not a wrinkle, not a single blemish! The look of an angel in the arms of the Creator. *Who killed Cock Robin? Who massacred the Iroquois?* Not I, my lovely angel could say, and by God, who, gazing at that pure, blameless face, could deny her? Who could see in that sleep of innocence that one half of the face belonged to God and the other half to Satan? The mask was smooth as death, cool, lovely to the touch, waxen, like a petal open to the faintest breeze. So alluringly still and guileless was it that one could drown in it, one could go down into it, body and all, like a diver, and nevermore return. Until the eyes opened upon the world she would lie like that, thoroughly extinguished and gleaming with a reflected light, like the moon itself. In her deathlike trance of innocence she fascinated even more; her crimes dissolved, exuded through the pores, she lay coiled like a sleeping serpent riveted to the earth. The body, strong, lithe, muscular, seemed possessed of a weight unnatural; she had a more than human gravity, the gravity, one might almost say, of a warm corpse. She was like one might imagine the beautiful Nefertiti to have been after the first thousand years of mummification, a marvel of mortuary perfection, a dream of flesh preserved from mortal decay. She lay coiled at the base of a hollow pyramid, enshrined in the vacuum of her own creation like a sacred relic of the past. Even her breathing seemed stopped, so profound was her slumber. She had dropped below the human sphere, below the animal sphere, below the vegetative sphere even: she had sunk down to the level of the mineral world where animation is just a notch above death. She had so mastered the art of deception that even the dream was powerless to betray her. She had learned how not to dream: when she coiled up in sleep she automatically switched off the current. If one could have caught her thus and opened up the skull one would have found it absolutely void. She kept no disturbing secrets; everything was killed off which could be humanly killed. She might live on endlessly, like the moon, like any dead planet, radiating an hypnotic effulgence, creating tides of passion, engulfing the world in madness, discoloring all earthly substances with her magnetic, metallic rays. Sowing her own death she brought everyone about her to fever pitch. In the heinous stillness of her sleep she renewed her own magnetic death by union with the cold magma of the lifeless planetary worlds. She was magically intact. Her gaze fell upon one with a transpiercing fixity: it was the moon-gaze through which the dead dragon of life gave off a cold fire. The one eye was a warm brown, the color of an autumn leaf; the other washazel, the magnetic eye which flickered like a compass needle. Even in sleep this eye continued to flicker under the shutter of the lid; it was the only apparent sign of life in her.

The moment she opened her eyes she was wide awake. She awoke with a violent start, as if the sight of the world and its human paraphernalia were a shock. Instantly she was in full activity, lashing about like a great python. What annoyed her was the light! She awoke cursing the sun, cursing the glare of reality. The room had to be darkened, the candles lit, the windows tightly shut to prevent the noise of the street from penetrating the room. She moved about naked with a cigarette dangling from the corner of her mouth. Her toilet was an affair of great preoccupation; a thousand trifling details had to be attended to before she could so much as don a bathrobe. She was like an athlete preparing for the great event of the day. From the roots of her hair, which she studied with keen attention, to the shape and length of her toenails, every part of her anatomy was thoroughly inspected before sitting down to breakfast. Like an athlete I said she was, but in fact she was more like a mechanic overhauling a fast plane for a test flight. Once she slipped on her dress she was launched for the day, for the flight which might end perhaps in Irkutsk or Teheran. She would take on enough fuel at breakfast to last the entire trip. The breakfast was a prolonged affair: it was the one ceremony of the day over which she dawdled and lingered. It was exasperatingly prolonged, indeed. One wondered if she would ever take off, one wondered if she had forgotten the grand mission which she had sworn to accomplish each day. Perhaps she was dreaming of her itinerary, or perhaps she was not dreaming at all but simply allowing time for the functional processes of her marvelous machine so that once embarked there would be no turning back. She was very calm and self-possessed at this hour of the day; she was like a great bird of the air perched on a mountain crag, dreamily surveying the terrain below. It was not from the breakfast table that she would suddenly swoop and dive to pounce upon her prey. No, from the early morning perch she would take off slowly and majestically, synchronizing her every movement with the pulse of the motor. All space lay before her, her direction dictated only by caprice. She was almost the image of freedom, were it not for the Saturnian weight of her body and the abnormal span of her wings. However poised she seemed, especially at the take-off, one sensed the terror which motivated the daily flight. She was at once obedient to her destiny and at the same time frantically eager to overcome it. Each morning she soared aloft from her perch, as from some Himalayan peak; she seemed always to direct her flight toward some uncharted region into which, if all went well, she would disappear forever. Each morning she seemed to carry aloft with her this desperate, last-minute hope; she took leave with calm, grave dignity, like one about to go down into the grave. Never once did she circle about the flying field; never once did she cast a glance backward toward those whom she was abandoning. Nor did she leave the slightest crumb of personality behind her; she took to the air with all her belongings, with every slightest scrap of evidence which might testify to the fact of her existence. She didn't even leave the breath of a sigh behind, not even a toenail. A clean exit, such as the Devil himself might make for reasons of his own. One was left with a great void on his hands. One was deserted, and not only deserted, but betrayed, inhumanly betrayed. One had no desire to detain her nor to call her back; one was left with a curse on his lips, with a black hatred which darkened the whole day. Later, moving about the city, moving slowly in pedestrian fashion, crawling like the worm, one gathered rumors of her spectacular flight; she had been seen rounding a certain point, she had dipped here or there for what reason no one knew, she had done a tailspin elsewhere, she had passed like a comet, she had written letters of smoke in the sky, and so on and so forth. Everything she had done was enigmatic and exasperating, done apparently without purpose. It was like a symbolic and ironic commentary on human life, on the behavior of the antlike creature man, viewed from another dimension.

Between the time she took off and the time she returned I lived the life of a full-blooded schizerino. It was not an eternity which elapsed, because somehow eternity has to do with peace and with victory, it is something man made, something earned: no, I expe-

rienced an entr'acte in which every hair turns white to the roots, in which every millimeter of skin itches and burns until the whole body becomes a running sore. I see myself sitting before a table in the dark, my hands and feet growing enormous, as though elephan-
tiasis were overtaking me at a gallop. I hear the blood rushing up to the brain and pounding at the eardrums like Himalayan devils with sledge-hammers; I hear her flapping her
huge wings, even in Irkutsk, and I know she is pushing on and on, ever further away, ever
further beyond reach. It is so quiet in the room and so frightfully empty that I shriek and
howl just to make a little noise, a little human sound. I try to lift myself from the table but
my feet are too heavy and my hands have become like the shapeless feet of the rhinocer-
os. The heavier my body becomes the lighter the atmosphere of the room; I am going to
spread and spread until I fill the room with one solid mass of stiff jelly. I shall fill up even
the cracks in the wall; I shall grow through the wall like a parasitic plant, spreading and
spreading until the whole house is an indescribable mass of flesh and hair and nails. I
know that this is death, but I am powerless to kill the knowledge of it, or the knower.
Some tiny particle of me is alive, some speck of consciousness persists, and, as the inert
carcass expands, this flicker of life becomes sharper and sharper and gleams inside me like
the cold fire of a gem. It lights up the whole gluey mass of pulp so that I am like a diver
with a torch in the body of a dead marine monster. By some slender hidden filament I am
still connected with the life above the surface of the deep, but it is so far away, the upper
world, and the weight of the corpse so great that, even if it were possible, it would take
years to reach the surface. I move around in my own dead body, exploring every nook and
cranny of its huge, shapeless mass. It is an endless exploration, for with the ceaseless
growth the whole topography changes, slipping and drifting like the hot magma of the
earth. Never for a minute is there terra firma, never for a minute does anything remain still
and recognizable: it is a growth without landmarks, a voyage in which the destination
changes with every least move or shudder. It is this interminable filling of space which kills
all sense of space or time; the more the body expands the tinier becomes the world, until
at last I feel that everything is concentrated on the head of a pin. Despite the floundering
of this enormous dead mass which I have become, I feel that what sustains it, the world
out of which it grows, is no bigger than a pinhead. In the midst of pollution, in the very
heart and gizzard of death, as it were, I sense the seed, the miraculous, infinitesimal lever
which balances the world. I have overspread the world like a syrup and the emptiness of
it is terrifying, but there is no dislodging the seed; the seed has become a little knot of cold
fire which roars like a sun in the vast hollow of the dead carcass.

When the great plunder-bird returns exhausted from her flight she will find me here
in the midst of my nothingness, I, the imperishable schizerino, a blazing seed hidden in
the heart of death. Every day she thinks to find another means of sustenance, but there is
no other, only this eternal seed of light which by dying each day I rediscover for her. Fly,
O devouring bird, fly to the limits of the universe! Here is your nourishment glowing in
the sickening emptiness you have created! You will come back to perish once more in the
black hole; you will come back again and again, for you have not the wings to carry you
out of the world. This is the only world you can inhabit, this tomb of the snake where
darkness reigns.

And suddenly for no reason at all, when I think of her returning to her nest, I remember Sunday mornings in the little old house near the cemetery. I remember sitting at the
piano in my nightshirt, working away at the pedals with bare feet, and the folks lying in

bed toasting themselves in the next room. The rooms opened one on the other, telescope fashion, as in the good old American railroad flats. Sunday mornings one lay in bed until one was ready to screech with well-being. Toward eleven or so the folks used to rap on the wall of my room for me to come and play for them. I would dance into the room like the Fratellini Brothers, so full of flame and feathers that I could hoist myself like a derrick to the topmost limb of the tree of heaven. I could do anything and everything single-hand-ed, being double-jointed at the same time. The old man called me "Sunny Jim," because I was full of "Force," full of vim and vigor. First I would do a few handsprings for them on the carpet before the bed; then I would sing falsetto, trying to imitate a ventriloquist's dummy; then I would dance a few light fantastic steps to show which way the wind lay, and zoom! like a breeze I was on the piano stool and doing a velocity exercise. I always began with Czerny, in order to limber up for the performance. The old man hated Czerny, and so did I, but Czerny was the *plat du jour* on the bill of fare then, and so Czerny it was until my joints were rubber. In some vague way Czerny reminds me of the great empti-ness which came upon me later. What a velocity I would work up, riveted to the piano stool! It was like swallowing a bottle of tonic at one gulp and then having someone strap you to the bed. After I had played about ninety-eight exercises I was ready to do a little improvising. I used to take a fistful of chords and crash the piano from one end to the other, then sullenly modulate into "The Burning of Rome" or the "Ben Hur Chariot Race" which everybody liked because it was intelligible noise. Long before I read Wittgenstein's *Tractatus Logico-Philosophicus* I was composing the music to it, in the key of sassafras. I was learned then in science and philosophy, in the history of religions, in inductive and deductive logic, in liver mantic, in the shape and weight of skulls, in pharmacopoeia and metallurgy, in all the useless branches of learning which give you indigestion and melan-cholia before your time. This vomit of learned truck was stewing in my guts the whole week long, waiting for it to come Sunday to be set to music. In between "The Midnight Fire Alarm" and "Marche Militaire" I would get my inspiration, which was to destroy all the existent forms of harmony and create my own cacophony. Imagine Uranus well aspect-ed to Mars, to Mercury, to the Moon, to Jupiter, to Venus. It's hard to imagine because Uranus functions best when it is badly aspected, when it is "afflicted," so to speak. Yet that music which I gave off Sunday mornings, a music of well-being and of well-nourished desperation, was born of an illogically well-aspected Uranus firmly anchored in the Seventh House. I didn't know it then, I didn't know that Uranus existed, and lucky it was that I was ignorant. But I can see it now, because it was a fluky joy, a phony well-being, a destructive sort of fiery creation. The greater my euphoria the more tranquil the folks became. Even my sister who was dippy became calm and composed. The neighbors used to stand outside the window and listen, and now and then I would hear a burst of applause, and then bang, zip! like a rocket I was off again—Velocity Exercise No. 947%- If I happened to espy a cockroach crawling up the wall I was in bliss: that would lead me without the slightest modulation to Opus Izzit of my sadly corrugated clavichord. One Sunday, just like that, I composed one of the loveliest scherzos imaginable—to a louse. It was spring and we were all getting the sulphur treatment; I had been poring all week over Dante's *Inferno* in English. Sunday came like a thaw, the birds driven so crazy by the sud-den heat that they flew in and out of the window, immune to the music. One of the German relatives had just arrived from Hamburg, or Bremen, a maiden aunt who looked like a bull-dyker. Just to be near her was sufficient to throw me into a fit of rage. She used to pat me on the head and tell me I would be another Mozart. I hated Mozart, and I hate him still, and so to get even with her I would play badly, play all the sour notes I knew. And then came the little louse, as I was saying, a real louse which had gotten buried in my winter underwear. I got him out and I put him tenderly on the tip of a black key. Then I began to do a little gigue around him with my right hand; the noise had probably deafened him. He was hypnotized, it seemed, by my nimble pyrotechnic. This trancelike immobility finally got on my nerves. I decided to introduce a chromatic scale, coming down on him full force with my third finger. I caught him fair and square, but with such force that he was glued to my fingertip. That put the St. Vitus Dance in me. From then on the scherzo commenced. It was a potpourri of forgotten melodies spiced with aloes and the juice of porcupines, played sometimes in three keys at once and pivoting always like a waltzing mouse around the immaculate conception. Later, when I went to hear Prokofiev, I understood what was happening to him; I understood Whitehead and Russell and Jeans and Eddington and Rudolf Eucken and Frobenius and Link Gillespie; I understood why, if there had never been a binomial theorem, man would have invented it; I understood why electricity and compressed air, to say nothing of Sprudel baths and fango packs. I understood very clearly, I must say, that man has a dead louse in his blood, and that when you're handed a symphony or a fresco or a high explosive you're really getting an ipecac reaction which was not included in the predestined bill of fare. I understood too why I had failed to become the musician I was. All the compositions I had created in my head, all these private and artistic auditions which were permitted me, thanks to St. Hildegarde or St. Bridget, or John of the Cross, or God knows whom, were written for an age to come, an age with less instruments and stronger antennae, stronger eardrums too. A different kind of suffering has to be experienced before such music can be appreciated. Beethoven staked out the new territory—one is aware of its presence when he erupts, when he breaks down in the very core of his stillness. It is a realm of new vibrations—to us only a misty nebula, for we have yet to pass beyond our own conception of suffering. We have yet to ingest this nebulous world, its travail, its orientation. I was permitted to hear an incredible music lying prone and indifferent to the sorrow about me. I heard the gestation of the new world, the sound of torrential rivers taking their course, the sound of stars grinding and chafing, of fountains clotted with blazing gems. All music is still governed by the old astronomy, is the product of the hothouse, a panacea for *Weltschmerz*. Music is still the antidote for the nameless, but this is not yet *music*. Music is planetary fire, an irreducible which is all sufficient; it is the slate-writing of the gods, the abracadabra which the learned and the ignorant alike muff because the axle has been unhooked. Look to the bowels, to the unconsolable and ineluctable! Nothing is determined, nothing is settled or solved. All this that is going on, all music, all architecture, all law, all government, all invention, all discovery—all this is velocity exercises in the dark, Czerny with a capital Zed riding a crazy white horse in a bottle of mucilage. One of the reasons why I never got anywhere with the bloody music is that it was always mixed up with sex. As soon as I was able to play a song the cunts were around me like flies. To begin with, it was largely Lola's fault. Lola was my first piano teacher. Lola Niessen. It was a ridiculous name and typical of the neighborhood we were living in then. It sounded like a stinking bloater, or a wormy cunt. To tell the truth, Lola was not exactly a beauty. She looked somewhat like a Kalmuck or a Chinook, with sallow complexion and bilious-looking eyes. She had a few warts and wens, not to speak of the mustache. What excited me, however, was her hairiness; she had wonderful long fine black hair which she arranged in ascending and descending buns on her Mongolian skull. At the nape of the neck she curled it up in a serpentine knot. She was always late in coming, being a conscientious idiot, and by the time she arrived I was always a bit enervated from masturbating. As soon as she took the stool beside me, however, I became excited again, what with the stinking perfume she soused her armpits with. In the summer she wore loose sleeves and I could see the tufts of hair under her arms. The sight of it drove me wild. I imagined her as having hair all over, even in her navel. And what I wanted to do was to roll in it, bury my teeth in it. I could have eaten Lola's hair as a delicacy, if there had been a bit of flesh attached to it. Anyway she was hairy, that's what I want to say, and being hairy as a gorilla she got my mind off the music and on to her cunt. I was so damned eager to see that cunt of hers that finally one day I bribed her little brother to let me have a peep at her while she was in the bath. It was even more wonderful than I had imagined: she had a shag that reached from the navel to the crotch, an enormous thick tuft, a sporran, rich as a hand-woven rug. When she went over it with the powder puff I thought I would faint. The next time she came for the lesson I left a couple of buttons open on my fly. She didn't seem to notice anything amiss. The following time I left my whole fly open. This time she caught on. She said, "I think you've forgotten something, Henry." I looked at her, red as a beet, and I asked her blandly *what?* She pretended to look away while pointing to it with her left hand. Her hand came so close that I couldn't resist grabbing it and pushing it in my fly. She got up quickly, looking pale and frightened. By this time my prick was out of my fly and quivering with delight. I closed in on her and I reached up under her dress to get at that hand-woven rug I had seen through the keyhole. Suddenly I got a sound box on the ears, and then another and then she took me by the ear and leading me to a corner of the room she turned my face to the wall and said, "Now button up your fly, you silly boy!" We went back to the piano in a few moments—back to Czerny and the velocity exercises. I couldn't see a sharp from a flat any more, but I continued to play because I was afraid she might tell my mother of the incident. Fortunately it was not an easy thing to tell one's mother.

The incident, embarrassing as it was, marked a decided change in our relations. I thought that the next time she came she would be severe with me, but on the contrary, she seemed to have dolled herself up, to have sprinkled more perfume over herself, and she was even a bit gay, which was unusual for Lola because she was a morose, withdrawn type. I didn't dare to open my fly again, but I would get an erection and hold it throughout the lesson, which she must have enjoyed because she was always stealing sidelong glances in that direction. I was only fifteen at the time, and she was easily twenty-five or twenty-eight. It was difficult for me to know what to do, unless it was to deliberately knock her down one day while my mother was out. For a time I actually shadowed her at night, when she went out alone. She had a habit of going out for long walks alone in the evening. I used to dog her steps; hoping she would get to some deserted spot near the cemetery where I might try some rough tactics. I had a feeling sometimes that she knew I was following her and that she enjoyed it. I think she was waiting for me to waylay her—I think that was what she wanted. Anyway, one night I was lying in the grass near the railroad tracks; it was a sweltering summer's night and people were lying about anywhere and everywhere, like panting dogs. I wasn't thinking of Lola at all—I was just mooning there, too hot to think about anything. Suddenly I see a woman coming along the narrow cinderpath. I'm lying sprawled out on the embankment and nobody around that I can notice.

The woman is coming along slowly, head down, as though she were dreaming. As she gets close I recognize her. "Lola!" I call. "Lola!" She seems to be really astonished to see me there. "Why, what are you doing here?" she says, and with that she sits down beside me on the embankment. I didn't bother to answer her, I didn't say a word—I just crawled over her and flattened her. "Not here, please," she begged, but I paid no attention. I got my hand between her legs, all tangled up in that thick sporran of hers, and she was sopping wet, like a horse slavering. It was my first fuck, by Jesus, and it had to be that a train would come along and shower hot sparks over us. Lola was terrified. It was her first fuck too, I guess, and she probably needed it more than I, but when she felt the sparks she wanted to tear loose. It was like trying to hold down a wild mare. I couldn't keep her down, no matter how I wrestled with her. She got up, shook her clothes down, and adjusted the bun at the nape of her neck. "You must go home," she says. "I'm not going home," I said, and with that I took her by the arm and started walking. We walked along in dead silence for quite a distance. Neither of us seemed to be noticing where we were going. Finally we were out on the highway and up above us were the reservoirs and near the reservoirs was a pond. Instinctively I headed toward the pond. We had to pass under some low-hanging trees as we neared the pond. I was helping Lola to stoop down when suddenly she slipped, dragging me with her. She made no effort to get up; instead she caught hold of me and pressed me to her, and to my complete amazement I also felt her slip her hand in my fly. She caressed me so wonderfully that in a jiffy I came in her hand. Then she took my hand and put it between her legs. She lay back completely relaxed and opened her legs wide. I bent over and kissed every hair on her cunt; I put my tongue in her navel and licked it clean. Then I lay with my head between her legs and lapped up the drool that was pouring from her. She was moaning now and clutching wildly with her hands; her hair had come completely undone and was lying over her bare abdomen. To make it short, I got it in again, and I held it a long time, for which she must have been damned grateful because she came I don't know how many times—it was like a pack of firecrackers going off, and with it all she sunk her teeth into me, bruised my lips, clawed me, ripped my shirt and what the hell not. I was branded like a steer when I got home and took a look at myself in the mirror.

It was wonderful while it lasted, but it didn't last long. A month later the Niessens moved to another city, and I never saw Lola again. But I hung her sporran over the bed and I prayed to it every night. And whenever I began the Czerny stuff I would get an erection, thinking of Lola lying in the grass, thinking of her long black hair, the bun at the nape of her neck, the groans she vented and the juice that poured out of her. Playing the piano was just one long vicarious fuck for me. I had to wait another two years before I would get my end in again, as they say, and then it wasn't so good because I got a beautiful dose with it, and besides it wasn't in the grass and it wasn't summer, and there was no heat in it but just a cold mechanical fuck for a buck in a dirty little hotel room, the bastard trying to pretend she was coming and not coming any more than Christmas was coming. And maybe it wasn't her that gave me the clap, but her pal in the next room who was laying up with my friend Simmons. It was like this—I had finished so quick with my mechanical fuck that I thought I'd go in and see how it was going with my friend Simmons. Lo and behold, they were still at it, and they were going strong. She was a Czech, his girl, and a bit sappy; she hadn't been at it very long, apparently, and she used to forget herself and enjoy the act. Watching her hand it out, I decided to wait and have a go at her myself. And so I did. And before the week was out I had a discharge, and after that I figured it would be blueballs or rocks in the groin.

Another year or so and I was giving lessons myself, and as luck would have it, the mother of the girl I'm teaching is a slut, a tramp and a trollop if ever there was one. She was living with a nigger, as I later found out. Seems she couldn't get a prick big enough to satisfy her. Anyway, every time I started to go home she'd hold me up at the door and rub it up against me. I was afraid of starting in with her because rumor had it that she was full of syph, but what the hell are you going to do when a hot bitch like that plasters her cunt up against you and slips her tongue halfway down your throat. I used to fuck her standing up in the vestibule, which wasn't so difficult because she was light and I could hold her in my hands like a doll. And like that I'm holding her one night when suddenly I hear a key being fitted into the lock, and she hears it too and she's frightened stiff. There's nowhere to go. Fortunately there's a portiere hanging at the doorway and I hide behind that. Then I hear her black buck kissing her and saying *how are yer, honey?* and she's saying how she had been waiting up for him and better come right upstairs because she can't wait and so on. And when the stairs stop squeaking I gently open the door and sally out, and then by God I have a real fright because if that black buck ever finds out I'll have my throat slit and no mistake about it. And so I stop giving lessons at that joint, but soon the daughter is after me—just turning sixteen—and won't I come and give her lessons at a friend's house? We begin the Czerny exercises all over again, sparks and everything. It's the first smell of fresh cunt I've had, and it's wonderful, like newmown hay. We fuck our way through one lesson after another and in between lessons we do a little extra fucking. And then one day it's the sad story—she's knocked up and what to do about it? I have to get a Jewboy to help me out, and he wants twenty-five bucks for the job and I've never seen twenty-five bucks in my life. Besides, she's under age. Besides, she might have blood poisoning. I give him five bucks on account and beat it to the Adirondacks for a couple of weeks. In the Adirondacks I meet a schoolteacher who's dying to take lessons. More velocity exercises, more condoms and conundrums. Every time I touched the piano I seemed to shake a cunt loose. If there was a party I had to bring the fucking music roll along; to me it was just like wrapping my penis in a handkerchief and slinging it under my arm. In vacation time, at a farmhouse or an inn, where there was always a surplus of cunt, the music had an extraordinary effect. Vacation time was a period I looked forward to the whole year, not because of the cunts so much as because it meant no work. Once out of harness I became a clown. I was so chock-full of energy that I wanted to jump out of my skin. I remember one summer in the Catskills meeting a girl named Francie. She was beautiful and lascivious, with strong Scotch teats and a row of white even teeth that was dazzling. It began in the river where we were swimming. We were holding on to the boat and one of her boobies had slipped out of bounds. I slipped the other one out for her and then I undid the shoulder straps. She ducked under the boat coyly and I followed and as she was coming up for air I wiggled the bloody bathing suit off her and there she was floating like a mermaid with her big strong teats bobbing up and down like bloated corks. I wriggled out of my tights and we began playing like dolphins under the side of the boat. In a little while her girl friend came along in a canoe. She was a rather hefty girl, a sort of strawberry blonde with agate-colored eyes and full of freckles. She was rather shocked to find us in the raw, but we soon tumbled her out of the canoe and stripped her. And then the three of us began to play tag under the water, but it was hard to get anywhere with them because they were slippery as eels. After we had had enough of it we ran to a little bathhouse which was standing in the field like an abandoned sentry box. We had brought our clothes along and we were going to get dressed, the three of us, in this little box. It was frightfully hot and sultry and the clouds were gathering for a storm. Agnes—that was Francie's friend—was in a hurry to get dressed. She was beginning to be ashamed of herself standing there naked in front of us. Francie, on the other hand, seemed to be perfectly at ease. She was sitting on the bench with her legs crossed and smoking a cigarette. Anyway, just as Agnes was pulling on her chemise there came a flash of lightning and a terrifying clap of thunder right on the heels of it. Agnes screamed and dropped her chemise. There came another flash in a few seconds and again a peal of thunder, dangerously close. The air got blue all around us and the flies began to bite and we felt nervous and itchy and a bit panicky too. Especially Agnes who was afraid of the lightning and even more afraid of being found dead and the three of us stark naked. She wanted to get her things on and run for the house, she said. And just as she got that off her chest the rain came down, in bucketsful. We thought it would stop in a few minutes and so we stood there naked looking out at the steaming river through the partly opened door. It seemed to be raining rocks and the lightning kept playing around us incessantly. We were all thoroughly frightened now and in a quandary as to what to do. Agnes was wringing her hands and praying out loud; she looked like a George Grosz idiot, one of those lopsided bitches with a rosary around the neck and yellow jaundice to boot. I thought she was going to faint on us or something. Suddenly I got the bright idea of doing a war dance in the rain— to distract them. Just as I jump out to commence my shindig a streak of lightning flashes and splits open a tree not far off. I'm so damned scared that I lose my wits. Always when I'm frightened I laugh. So I laughed, a wild, bloodcurdling laugh which made the girls scream. When I heard them scream, I don't know why, but I thought of the velocity exercises, and with that I felt that I was standing in the void and it was blue all around and the rain was beating a hot-and-cold tattoo on my tender flesh. All my sensations had gathered on the surface of the skin and underneath the outermost layer of skin I was empty, light as a feather, lighter than air or smoke or talcum or magnesium or any goddamned thing you want. Suddenly I was a Chippewa and it was the key of sassafras again and I didn't give a fuck whether the girls were screaming or fainting or shitting in their pants, which they were minus anyway. Looking at crazy Agnes with the rosary around her neck and her big breadbasket blue with fright I got the notion to do a sacrilegious dance, with one hand cupping my balls and the other hand thumbing my nose at the thunder and lightning. The rain was hot and cold and the grass seemed full of dragonflies. I hopped about like a kangaroo and I yelled at the top of my lungs—"O Father, you wormy old son of a bitch, pull in that fucking lightning or Agnes won't believe in you any more! Do you hear me, you old prick up there, stop the shenanigans... you're driving Agnes nutty. Hey you, are you deaf, you old futzer?" And with a continuous rattle of this defiant nonsense on my lips I danced around the bathhouse, leaping and bounding like a gazelle and using the most frightful oaths I could summon. When the lightning cracked I jumped higher and when the thunder clapped I roared like a lion and then I did a handspring and then I rolled in the grass like a cub and I chewed the grass and spit it out for them and I pounded my chest like a gorilla and all the time I could see the Czerny exercises resting on the piano, the white page full of sharps and flats, and the fucking idiot, think I to myself, imagining that that's the way to learn how to manipulate the well-tempered clavichord.

And suddenly I thought that Czerny might be in heaven by now and looking down on me and so I spat up at him high as I could spit and when the thunder rolled again I yelled with all my might—"You bastard, Czerny, *you* up there, may the lightning twist your balls off... may you swallow your own crooked tail and strangle yourself... do you hear me, you crazy prick?"

But in spite of all my good efforts Agnes was getting more delirious. She was a dumb Irish Catholic and she had never heard God spoken to that way before. Suddenly, while I was dancing about in the rear of the bathhouse she bolted for the river. I heard Francie scream—"Bring her back, she'll drown herself! Bring her back!" I started after her, the rain still coming down like pitchforks, and yelling to her to come back, but she ran on blindly as though possessed of the devil, and when she got to the water's edge she dove straight in and made for the boat. I swam after her and as we got to the side of the boat, which I was afraid she would capsize, I got hold of her round the waist with my one hand and I started to talk to her calmly and soothingly, as though I was talking to a child. "Go away from me," she said, "you're an atheist!" Jesus, you could have knocked me over with a feather, so astonished I was to hear that. So that was it? All that hysteria because I was insulting the Lord Almighty. I felt like batting her one in the eye to bring her to her senses. But we were out over our heads and I had a fear that she would do some mad thing like pulling the boat over our heads if I didn't handle her right. So I pretended that I was terribly sorry and I said I didn't mean a word of it, that I had been scared to death, and so on and so forth, and as I talked to her gently, soothingly, I slipped my hand down from her waist and I gently stroked her ass. That was what she wanted all right. She was talking to me blubberingly about what a good Catholic she was and how she had tried not to sin, and maybe she was so wrapped up in what she was saying she didn't know what I was doing, but just the same when I got my hand in her crotch and said all the beautiful things I could think of, about God, about love, about going to church and confessing and all that crap, she must have felt something because I had a good three fingers inside her and working them around like drunken bobbins. "Put your arms around me, Agnes," I said softly, slipping my hand out and pulling her to me so that I could get my legs between hers.... "There, that's a girl... take it easy now... it'll stop soon." And still talking about the church, the confessional, God, love, and the whole bloody mess I managed to get it inside of her. "You're very good to me," she said, just as though she didn't know my prick was in her, "and I'm sorry I acted like a fool." "I know, Agnes," I said, "it's all right... listen, grab me tighter... yeah, that's it." "I'm afraid the boat's going to tip over," she says, trying her best to keep her ass in position by paddling with her right hand. "Yes, let's get back to the shore," I said, and I start to pull away from her. "Oh don't leave me," she says, clutching me tighter. "Don't leave me, I'll drown." Just then Francie comes running down to the water. "Hurry," says Agnes, "hurry... I'll drown."

Francie was a good sort, I must say. She certainly wasn't a Catholic and if she had any morals they were of the reptilian order. She was one of those girls who are born to fuck. She had no aims, no great desires, showed no jealousy, held no grievances, was constantly cheerful and not at all unintelligent. At nights when we were sitting on the porch in the dark talking to the guests she would come over and sit on my lap with nothing on underneath her dress and I would slip it into her as she laughed and talked to the others. I think she would have brazened it out before the Pope if she had been given a chance. Back in the city, when I called on her at her home, she pulled the same stunt off in front of her mother whose sight, fortunately, was growing dim. If we went dancing and she got too hot in the pants she would drag me to a telephone booth and, queer girl that she was, she'd actually talk to some one, some one like Agnes, for example while pulling off the trick. She seemed to get a special pleasure out of doing it under people's noses; she said there was more fun in it if you didn't think about it too hard. In the crowded subway, coming home from the beach, say, she'd slip her dress around so that the slit was in the middle and take my hand and put it right on her cunt. If the train was tightly packed and we were safely wedged in a corner she'd take my cock out of my fly and hold it in her two hands, as though it were a bird. Sometimes she'd get playful and hang her bag on it, as though to prove that there wasn't the least danger. Another thing about her was that she didn't pretend that I was the only guy she had on the string. Whether she told me everything I don't know, but she certainly told me plenty. She told me about her affairs laughingly, while she was climbing over me or when I had it in her, or just when I was about to come. She would tell me how they went about it, how big they were or how small, what they said when they got excited and so on and so forth, giving me every possible detail, just as though I were going to write a textbook on the subject. She didn't seem to have the least feeling of sacredness about her own body or her feelings or anything connected with herself. "Francie, you bloody fucker," I used to say, "you've got the morals of a clam." "But you like me, don't you?" she'd answer. "Men like to fuck, and so do women. It doesn't harm anybody and it doesn't mean you have to love everyone you fuck, does it? I wouldn't want to be in love; it must be terrible to have to fuck the same man all the time, don't you think? Listen, if you didn't fuck anybody but me all the time you'd get tired of me quick, wouldn't you? Sometimes it's nice to be fucked by some one you don't know at all. Yes, I think that's the best of all," she added—"there's no complications, no telephone numbers, no love letters, no scraps, what? Listen, do you think this is very bad? Once I tried to get my brother to fuck me; you know what a sissy he is—he gives everybody a pain. I don't remember exactly how it was any more, but anyway we were in the house alone and I was passionate that day. He came into my bedroom to ask me for something. I was lying there with my dress up, thinking about it and wanting it terribly, and when he came in I didn't give a damn about his being my brother, I just thought of him as a man, and so I lay there with my skirt up and I told him I wasn't feeling well, that I had a pain in my stomach. He wanted to run right out and get something for me but I told him no, just to rub my stomach a bit, that would do it good. I opened my waist and made him rub my bare skin. He was trying to keep his eyes on the wall, the big idiot, and rubbing me as though I were a piece of wood. 'It's not there, you chump,' I said, 'it's lower down... what are you afraid of?' And I pretended that I was in agony. Finally he touched me accidentally. 'There! that's it!' I shouted. 'Oh do rub it, it feels so good!' Do you know, the big sap actually massaged me for five minutes without realizing that it was all a game? I was so exasperated that I told him to get the hell out and leave me alone. 'You're a eunuch,' I said, but he was such a sap I don't think he knew what the word meant." She laughed, thinking what a ninny her brother was. She said he probably still had his maiden. What did I think about it—was it so terribly bad? Of course she knew I wouldn't think anything of the kind. "Listen, Francie," I said, "did you ever tell that story to the cop you're going with?" She guessed she hadn't. "I guess so too," I said. "He'd beat the piss out of you if he ever heard that yarn." "He's socked me already," she answered promptly. "*What?*" I said, "you let him beat you up?" "I don't ask him to," she said, "but you know how quick-tempered he is. I don't let anybody else sock me but somehow coming from him I don't mind it so much. Sometimes it makes me feel good inside.... I don't know, maybe a woman ought to get beaten up once in a while. It doesn't hurt so much, if you really like a guy. And afterwards he's so damned gentle—I almost feel ashamed of myself...."

It isn't often you get a cunt who'll admit such things—I mean a regular cunt and not a moron. There was Trix Miranda, for example, and her sister, Mrs. Costello. A fine pair of birds they were. Trix, who was going with my friend MacGregor, tried to pretend to her own sister, with whom she was living, that she had no sexual relations with MacGregor. And the sister was pretending to all and sundry that she was frigid, that she couldn't have any relations with a man even if she wanted to, because she was "built too small." And meanwhile my friend MacGregor was fucking them silly, both of them, and they both knew about each other but still they lied like that to each other. Why? I couldn't make it out. The Costello bitch was hysterical; whenever she felt that she wasn't getting a fair percentage of the lays that MacGregor was handing out she'd throw a pseudo-epileptic fit. That meant throwing towels over her, patting her wrists, opening her bosom, chafing her legs and finally hoisting her upstairs to bed where my friend MacGregor would look after her as soon as he had put the other one to sleep. Sometimes the two sisters would lie down together to take a nap of an afternoon; if MacGregor were around he would go upstairs and lie between them. As he explained it to me laughingly, the trick was for him to pretend to go to sleep. He would lie there breathing heavily, opening now one eye, now the other, to see which one was really dozing off. As soon as he was convinced that one of them was asleep he'd tackle the other. On such occasions he seemed to prefer the hysterical sister, Mrs. Costello, whose husband visited her about once every six months. The more risk he ran, the more thrill he got out of it, he said. If it were with the other sister, Trix, whom he was supposed to be courting, he had to pretend that it would be terrible if the other one were to catch them like that, and at the same time, he admitted to me, he was always hoping that the other one would wake up and catch them. But the married sister, the one who was "built too small," as she used to say, was a wily bitch and besides she felt guilty toward her sister and if her sister had ever caught her in the act she'd probably have pretended that she was having a fit and didn't know what she was doing. Nothing on earth could make her admit that she was actually permitting herself the pleasure of being fucked by a man.

I knew her quite well because I was giving her lessons for a time, and I used to do my damnedest to make her admit that she had a normal cunt and that she'd enjoy a good fuck if she could get it now and then. I used to tell her wild stories, which were really thinly disguised accounts of her own doings, and yet she remained adamant. I had even gotten her to the point one day—and this beats everything—where she let me put my finger inside her. I thought sure it was settled.

It's true she was dry and a bit tight, but I put that down to her hysteria. But imagine getting that far with a cunt and then having her say to your face, as she yanks her dress down violently—"you see, I told you I wasn't built right!" "I don't see anything of the kind," I said angrily. "What do you expect me to do—use a microscope on you?"

"I like that," she said, pretending to get on her high horse. "What a way of talking to me!"

"You know damned well you're lying," I continued. "Why do you lie like that? Don't you think it's human to have a cunt and to use it once in a while? Do you want it to dry up on you?"

"Such language!" she said, biting her underlip and reddening like a beet. "I always thought you were a gentleman."

"Well, you're no lady," I retorted, "because even a lady admits to a fuck now and then, and besides ladies don't ask gentlemen to stick their fingers up inside them and see how small they're built."

"I never asked you to touch me," she said. "I wouldn't think of asking you to put your hand on me, on my private parts anyway."

"Maybe you thought I was going to swab your ear for you, is that it?"

"I thought of you like a doctor at that moment, that's all I can say," she said stiffly, trying to freeze me out.

"Listen," I said, taking a wild chance, "let's pretend that it was all a mistake, that nothing happened, nothing at all. I know you too well to think of insulting you like that. I wouldn't think of doing a thing like that to you—no, damned if I would. I was just wondering if maybe you weren't right in what you said, if maybe you aren't built rather small. You know, it all went so quick I couldn't tell what I felt... I don't think I even put my finger inside you. I must have just touched the outside—that's about all. Listen, sit down here on the couch... let's be friends again." I pulled her down beside me—she was melting visibly—and I put my arm around her waist, as though to console her more tenderly. "Has it always been like that?" I asked innocently, and I almost laughed the next moment, realizing what an idiotic question it was. She hung her head coyly, as though we were touching on an unmentionable tragedy. "Listen, maybe if you sat on my lap..." and I hoisted her gently on to my lap, at the same time delicately putting my hand under her dress and resting it lightly on her knee... "maybe if you sat a moment like this, you'd feel better... there, that's it, just snuggle back in my arms... are you feeling better?" She didn't answer, but she didn't resist either; she just lay back limply and closed her eyes. Gradually and very gently and smoothly I moved my hand up her leg, talking to her in a low, soothing voice all the time. When I got my fingers into her crotch and parted the little lips she was as moist as a dishrag. I massaged it gently, opening it up more and more, and still handing out a telepathic line about women sometimes being mistaken about themselves and how sometimes they think they're very small when really they're quite normal, and the longer I kept it up the juicier she got and the more she opened up. I had four fingers inside her and there was room inside for more if I had had more to put in. She had an enormous cunt and it had been well reamed out, I could feel. I looked at her to see if she was still keeping her eyes shut. Her mouth was open and she was gasping but her eyes were tight shut, as though she were pretending to herself that it was all a dream. I could move her about roughly now—no danger of the slightest protest. And maliciously perhaps, I jostled her about unnecessarily, just to see if she would come to. She was as limp as a feather pillow and even when her head struck the arm of the sofa she showed no sign of irritation. It was as though she had anesthetized herself for a gratuitous fuck. I pulled all her clothes off and threw them on the floor, and after I had given her a bit of a workout on the sofa I slipped it out and laid her on the floor, on her clothes; and then I slipped it in again and she held it tight with that suction valve she used so skillfully, despite the outward appearance of coma.

It seems strange to me that the music always passed off into sex. Nights, if I went out alone for a walk, I was sure to pick up someone—a nurse, a girl coming out of a dance hall, a salesgirl, anything with a skirt on. If I went out with my friend MacGregor in his car— just a little spin to the beach, he would say—I would find myself by midnight sitting in some strange parlor in some queer neighborhood with a girl on my lap, usually one I didn't give a damn about because MacGregor was even less selective than I. Often, stepping in his car I'd say to him—"listen, no cunts tonight, what?" And he'd say—"Jesus, no, I'm fed up... just a little drive somewhere... maybe to Sheepshead Bay, what do you say?" We wouldn't have gone more than a mile when suddenly he'd pull the car up to the curb and nudge me. "Get a look at that," he'd say, pointing to a girl strolling along the sidewalk. "Jesus, what a leg!" Or else—"Listen, what do you say we ask her to come along? Maybe she can dig up a friend." And before I could say another word he'd be hailing her and handing out his usual patter, which was the same for everyone. And nine times out of ten the girl came along. And before we'd gone very far, feeling her up with his free hand, he'd ask her if she didn't have a friend she could dig up to keep us company. And if she put up a fuss, if she didn't like being pawed over that way too quickly, he'd say—"All right, get the hell out then... we can't waste any time on the likes of you!" And with that he'd slow up and shove her out. "We can't be bothered with cunts like that, can we Henry?" he'd say, chuckling softly. "You wait, I promise you something good before the night's over." And if I reminded him that we were going to lay off for one night he'd answer:

"Well, just as you like.... I was only thinking it might make it more pleasant for you." And then suddenly the brakes would pull us up and he'd be saying to some silky silhouette looming out of the dark—"hello sister, what yer doing—taking a little stroll?" And maybe this time it would be something exciting, a dithery little bitch with nothing else to do but pull up her skirt and hand it to you. Maybe we wouldn't even have to buy her a drink, just haul up somewhere on a side road and go at it, one after the other, in the car. And if she was an empty-headed bimbo, as they usually were, he wouldn't even bother to drive her home. "We're not going that way," he'd say, the bastard that he was. "You'd better jump out here," and with that he'd open the door and out with her. His next thought was, of course, was she clean? That would occupy his mind all the way back. "Jesus, we ought to be more careful," he'd say. "You don't know what you're getting yourself into picking them up like that. Ever since that last one—you remember, the one we picked up on the Drive—I've been itchy as hell. Maybe it's just nervousness... I think about it too much. Why can't a guy stick to one cunt, tell me that, Henry. You take Trix, now, she's a good kid, you know that. And I like her too, in a way, but... shit, what's the use of talking about it? You know me—I'm a glutton. You know, I'm getting so bad that sometimes when I'm on my way to a date—mind you, with a girl I want to fuck, and everything fixed too—as I say, sometimes I'm rolling along and maybe out of the corner of my eye I catch a flash of a leg crossing the street and before I know it I've got her in the car and the hell with the other girl. I must be cunt-struck, I guess... what do you think? Don't tell me," he would add quickly. "I know you, you bugger... you'll be sure to tell me the worst." And then, after a pause—"you're a funny guy, do you know that? I never notice you refusing anything, but somehow you don't seem to be worrying about it all the time. Sometimes you strike me as though you didn't give a damn one way or the other. And you're a steady bastard too—

almost a monogamist, I'd say. How you can keep it up so long with one woman beats me. Don't you get bored with them? Jesus, I know so well what they're going to say. Sometimes I feel like saying... you know, just breeze in on 'em and say: 'Listen, kid, don't say a word... just fish it out and open your legs wide.'" He laughed heartily. "Can you imagine the expression on Trix's face if I pulled a line like that on her? I'll tell you, once I came pretty near doing it. I kept my hat and coat on. *Was she sore!* She didn't mind my keeping my coat on so much, but the hat! I told her I was afraid of a draught... of course there wasn't any draught. The truth is, I was so damned impatient to get away that I thought if I kept my hat on I'd be off quicker. Instead I was there all night with her. She put up such a row that I couldn't get her quiet.... But listen, that's nothing. Once I had a drunken Irish bitch and this one had some queer ideas. In the first place, she never wanted it in bed... always on the table. You know, that's all right once in a while, but if you do it often it wears you out. So one night—I was a little tight, I guess—I says to her, no, nothing doing, you drunken bastard... you're gonna go to bed with me tonight. I want a real fuck—*in bed.* You know, I had to argue with that bitch for an hour almost before I could persuade her to go to bed with me, and then only on the agreement that I was to keep my hat on. Listen, can you picture me getting over that stupid bitch with my hat on? And stark naked to boot! I asked her... I said, 'why do you want me to keep my hat on?' You know what she said? She said it seemed more genteel. Can you imagine what a mind that cunt had? I used to hate myself for going with that bitch. I never went to her sober, that's one thing. I'd have to be tanked up first and kind of blind and batty—you know how I get sometimes...." I knew very well what he meant. He was one of my oldest friends and one of the most cantankerous bastards I ever knew. Stubborn wasn't the word for it. He was like a mule—a pigheaded Scotchman. And his old man was even worse. When the two of them got into a rage it was a pretty sight. The old man used to dance, positively *dance* with rage. If the old lady got between she'd get a sock in the eye. They used to put him out of the house regularly. Out he'd go, with all his belongings, including the furniture, including the piano too. In a month or so he'd be back again—because they always gave him credit at home. And then he'd come home drunk some night with a woman he'd picked up somewhere and the rumpus would start all over again. It seems they didn't mind so much his coming home with a girl and keeping her all night, but what they did object to was the cheek of him asking his mother to serve them breakfast in bed. If his mother tried to bawl him out he'd shut her up by saying—"What are you trying to tell me? You wouldn't have been married yet if you hadn't been knocked up." The old lady would wring her hands and say—'What a son! What a son! God help me, what have I done to deserve this?" To which he'd remark, "Aw forget it! You're just an old prune!" Often as not his sister would come up to try and smooth matters out. "Jesus, Wallie," she'd say, "it's none of my business what you do, but can't you talk to your mother more respectfully?" Whereupon MacGregor would make his sister sit on the bed and start coaxing her to bring up the breakfast. Usually he'd have to ask his bedmate what her name was in order to present her to his sister. "She's not a bad kid," he'd say, referring to his sister. "She's the only decent one in the family.... Now listen, Sis, bring up some grub, will yer? Some nice bacon and eggs, eh, what do you say? Listen, is the old man around? What's his mood today? I'd like to borrow a couple of bucks. You try and worm it out of him, will you? I'll get you something nice for Christmas." Then, as though everything were settled, he'd pull back the covers to expose the wench beside him. "Look at her, Sis, ain't she beautiful? Look at that leg! Listen, you ought to get yourself a man... you're too skinny. Patsy here, I bet she doesn't go begging for it, eh Patsy?" and with that a sound slap on the rump for Patsy. "Now scram, Sis, I want some coffee... and don't forget, make the bacon crisp! Don't get any of that lousy store bacon... get something extra. And be quick about it!"

What I liked about him were his weaknesses; like all men who practice will power he was absolutely flabby inside. There wasn't a thing he wouldn't do—out of weakness. He was always very busy and he was never really doing anything. And always boning up on something, always trying to improve his mind. For example, he would take the unabridged dictionary and, tearing out a page each day, would read it through religiously on his way back and forth from the office. He was full of facts, and the more absurd and incongruous the facts, the more pleasure he derived from them. He seemed to be bent on proving to all and sundry that life was a farce, that it wasn't worth the game, that one thing canceled out another, and so on. He was brought up on the North Side, not very far from the neighborhood in which I had spent my childhood. He was very much a product of the North Side, too, and that was one of the reasons why I liked him. The way he talked, out of the corner of his mouth, for instance, the tough air he put on when talking to a cop, the way he spat in disgust, the peculiar curse words he used, the sentimentality, the limited horizon, the passion for playing pool or shooting craps, the staying up all night swapping yarns, the contempt for the rich, the hobnobbing with politicians, the curiosity about worthless things, the respect for learning, the fascination of the dance hall, the saloon, the burlesque, talking about seeing the world and never budging out of the city, idolizing no matter whom so long as the person showed "spunk," a thousand and one little traits or peculiarities of this sort endeared him to me because it was precisely such idiosyncrasies which marked the fellows I had known as a child. The neighborhood was composed of nothing, it seemed, but lovable failures. The grownups behaved like children and the children were incorrigible. Nobody could rise very far above his neighbor or he'd be lynched. It was amazing that any one ever became a doctor or a lawyer. Even so, he had to be a good fellow, had to pretend to talk like everyone else, and he had to vote the Democratic ticket. To hear MacGregor talk about Plato or Nietzsche, for instance, to his buddies was something to remember. In the first place, to even get permission to talk about such things as Plato or Nietzsche to his companions, he had to pretend that it was only by accident that he had run across their names; or perhaps he'd say that he had met an interesting drunk one night in the back room of a saloon and this drunk had started talking about these guys Nietzsche and Plato. He would even pretend he didn't quite know how the names were pronounced. Plato wasn't such a dumb bastard, he would say apologetically. Plato had an idea or two in his bean, yes sir, yes siree. He'd like to see one of those dumb politicians at Washington trying to lock horns with a guy like Plato. And he'd go on, in this roundabout, matter of fact fashion to explain to his crapshooting friends just what kind of a bright bird Plato was in his time and how he measured up against other men in other times. Of course, he was probably a eunuch, he would add, by way of throwing a little cold water on all this erudition. In those days, as he nimbly explained, the big guys, the philosophers, often had their nuts cut off—a fact!—so as to be out of all temptation. The other guy, Nietzsche, he was a real case, a case for the bughouse. He was supposed to be in love with his sister. Hypersensitive like. Had to live in a special climate—in Nice, he thought it was. As a rule he didn't care much for the Germans, but this guy Nietzsche was different. As a matter of fact, he hated the Germans, this Nietzsche. He claimed he was a

Pole or something like that. He had them dead right, too. He said they were stupid and swinish, and by God, he knew what he was talking about. Anyway, he showed them up. He said they were full of shit, to make it brief, and by God, wasn't he right though? Did you see the way those bastards turned tail when they got a dose of their own medicine? "Listen, I know a guy who cleaned out a nestful of them in the Argonne region—he said they were so goddamned low he wouldn't shit on them. He said he wouldn't even waste a bullet on them—he just bashed their brains in with a club. I forget this guy's name now, but anyway he told me he saw aplenty in the few months he was there. He said the best fun he got out of the whole fucking business was to pop off his own major. Not that he had any special grievance against him—he just didn't like his mug. He didn't like the way the guy gave orders. Most of the officers that were killed got it in the back, he said. Served them right, too, the pricks! He was just a lad from the North Side. I think he runs a pool-room now down near Wallabout Market. A quiet fellow, minds his own business. But if you start talking to him about the war he goes off the handle. He says he'd assassinate the President of the United States if they ever tried to start another war. Yeah, and he'd do it too, I'm telling you.... But shit, what was that I wanted to tell you about Plato? Oh yeah...."

When the others were gone he'd suddenly shift gears. "You don't believe in talking like that, do you?," he'd begin. I had to admit I didn't. "You're wrong," he'd continue. "You've got to keep in with people, you don't know when you may need one of these guys. You act on the assumption that you're free, independent! You act as though you were superior to these people. Well, that's where you make a big mistake. How do you know where you'll be five years from now, or even six months from now? You might be blind, you might be run over by a truck, you might be put in the bughouse; you can't tell what's going to happen to you. Nobody can. You might be as helpless as a baby...."

"So what?" I would say.

"Well, don't you think it would be good to have a friend when you need one? You might be so goddamned helpless you'd be glad to have some one help you across the street. You think these guys are worthless; you think I'm wasting my time with them. Listen, you never know what a man might do for you some day. Nobody gets anywhere alone...."

He was touchy about my independence, what he called my indifference. If I was obliged to ask him for a little dough he was delighted. That gave him a chance to deliver a little sermon on friendship. "So you have to have money, too?" he'd say, with a big satisfied grin spreading all over his face. "So the poet has to eat too? Well, well.... It's lucky you came to me, Henry me boy, because I'm easy with you, I know you, you heartless son of a bitch. Sure, what do you want? I haven't got very much, but I'll split it with you. That's fair enough, isn't it? Or do you think, you bastard, that maybe I ought to give you it all and go out and borrow something for myself? I suppose you want a *good* meal, eh? Ham and eggs wouldn't be good enough, would it? I suppose you'd like me to drive you to the restaurant too, eh? Listen, get up from that chair a minute—I want to put a cushion under your ass. Well, well, so you're broke! Jesus, you're always broke—I never remember seeing you with money in your pocket. Listen, don't you ever feel ashamed of yourself? You talk about those bums I hang out with... well listen, mister, those guys never come and bum me for a dime like you do. They've got more pride—they'd rather steal it than come and grub it off me. But *you*, shit, you're full of highfalutin' ideas, you want to reform the world and all that crap—you don't want to work for money, no, not you... you expect somebody to hand it to you on a silver platter. Huh! Lucky there's guys like me around that understand you. You need to get wise to yourself, Henry. You're dreaming. Everybody wants to eat, don't you know that? Most people are willing to work for it—they don't lie in bed all day like you and then suddenly pull on their pants and run to the first friend at hand. Supposing I wasn't here, what would you have done? Don't answer... I know what you're going to say. But listen, you can't go on all your life like that. Sure, you talk fine—it's a pleasure to listen to you. You're the only guy I know that I really enjoy talking to, but where's it going to get you? One of these days they'll lock you up for vagrancy. You're just a bum, don't you know that? You're not even as good as those other bums you preach about. Where are you when I'm in a jam? You can't be found. You don't answer my letters, you don't answer the telephone, you even hide sometimes when I come to see you. Listen, I know—you don't have to explain to me. I know you don't want to hear my stories all the time. But shit, sometimes I really have to talk to you. A fucking lot you care though. So long as you're out of the rain and putting another meal under your belt you're happy. You don't think about your friends—until you're desperate. That's no way to behave, *is it?* Say no and I'll give you a buck. Goddamn it, Henry, you're the only real friend I've got, but you're a son of a bitch of a mucker if I know what I'm talking about. You're just a born good for nothing son of a bitch. You'd rather starve than turn your hand to something useful...."

Naturally I'd laugh and hold my hand out for the buck he had promised me. That would irritate him afresh. "You're ready to say anything, aren't you, if only I give you the buck I promised you? What a guy! Talk about morals—Jesus, you've got the ethics of a rattlesnake. *No,* I'm not giving it to you yet, by Christ. I'm going to torture you a little more first. I'm going to make you *earn* this money, if I can. Listen, what about shining my shoes—do that for me, will you? They'll never get shined if you don't do it now." I pick up the shoes and ask him for the brush. I don't mind shining his shoes, not in the least. But that too seems to incense him. "You're going to shine them, are you? Well, by Jesus, that beats all hell. Listen, where's your pride—didn't you ever have any? And you're the guy that knows everything. It's amazing. You know so goddamned much that you have to shine your friend's shoes to worm a meal out of him. A fine pickle! Here, you bastard, here's the brush! Shine the other pair too while you're at it.

A pause. He's washing himself at the sink and humming a bit. Suddenly, in a bright, cheerful tone—"How is it out today, Henry? Is it sunny? Listen, I've got just the place for you. What do you say to scallops and bacon with a little tartar sauce on the side? It's a little joint down near the inlet. A day like today is just the day for scallops and bacon, eh what, Henry? Don't tell me you've got something to do... if I haul you down there you've got to spend a little time with me, you know that, don't you? Jesus, I wish I had your disposition. You just drift along, from minute to minute. Sometimes I think you're a damned sight better off than any of us, even if you are a stinking son of a bitch and a traitor and a thief. When I'm with you the day seems to pass like a dream. Listen, don't you see what I mean when I say I've got to see you sometimes? I go nuts being all by myself all the time. Why do I go chasing around after cunt so much? Why do I play cards all night? Why do I hang out with those bums from the Point? I need to talk to someone, that's what."

A little later at the bay, sitting out over the water, with a shot of rye in him and waiting for the sea food to be served up.... "Life's not so bad if you can do what you want, eh Henry? If I make a little dough I'm going to take a trip around the world—and you're coming along with me. Yes, though you don't deserve it, I'm going to spend some real money on you one day. I want to see how you'd act if I gave you plenty of rope. I'm going to *give* you the money, *see....* I won't pretend to lend it to you. We'll see what'll happen to your fine ideas when you have some dough in your pocket. Listen, when I was talking about Plato the other day I meant to ask you something: I meant to ask you if you ever read that yam of his about Atlantis. Did you? *You did?* Well, what do you think of it? Do you think it was just a yarn, or do you think there might have been a place like that once?"

I didn't dare to tell him that I suspected there were hundreds and thousands of continents whose existence past or future we hadn't even begun to dream about, so I simply said I thought it quite possible indeed that such a place as Atlantis might once have been.

"Well, it doesn't matter much one way or the other, I suppose," he went on, "but I'll tell you what I think. I think there must have been a time like that once, a time when men were different. I can't believe that they always were the pigs they are now and have been for the last few thousand years. I think it's just possible that there was a time when men knew how to live, when they knew how to take it easy and to enjoy life. Do you know what drives me crazy? It's looking at my old man. Ever since he's retired he sits in front of the fire all day long and mopes. To sit there like a broken-down gorilla, that's what he slaved for all his life. Well shit, if I thought that was going to happen to me I'd blow my brains out now. Look around you... look at the people we know.... do you know one that's worth while? What's all the fuss about, I'd like to know? *We've got to live, they say. Why?* that's what I want to know. They'd all be a damned sight better off dead. They're all just so much manure. When the war broke out and I saw them go off to the trenches I said to myself *good,* maybe they'll come back with a little sense! A lot of them didn't come back, of course. But the others!—listen, do you suppose they got more *human,* more considerate? Not at all! They're all butchers at heart, and when they're up against it they squeal. They make me sick, the whole fucking lot of 'em. I see what they're like, bailing them out every day. I see it from both sides of the fence. On the other side it stinks even worse. Why, if I told you some of the things I knew about the judges who condemn these poor bastards you'd want to slug them. All you have to do is look at their faces. Yes sir, Henry, I'd like to think there was once a time when things were different. We haven't seen any real life— and we're not going to see any. This thing is going to last another few thousand years, if I know anything about it. You think I'm mercenary. You think I'm cuckoo to want to earn a lot of money, don't you? Well I'll tell you, I want to earn a little pile so that I can get my feet out of this muck. I'd go off and live with a nigger wench if I could get away from this atmosphere. I've worked my balls off trying to get where I am, which isn't very far. I don't believe in work any more than you do—I was trained that way, that's all. If I could put over a deal, if I could swindle a pile out of one of these dirty bastards I'm dealing with, I'd do it with a clear conscience. I know a little too much about the law, that's the trouble. But I'll fool them yet, you'll see. And when I put it over I'll put it over big...."

Another shot of rye as the sea food's coming along and he starts in again. 'I meant that about taking you on a trip with me. I'm thinking about it seriously. I suppose you'll tell me you've a wife and a kid to look after. Listen when are you going to break off with that battle-ax of yours? Don't you know that you've got to ditch her?" He begins to laugh softly. "Ho! Ho! To think that I was the one who picked her out for you! Did I ever think you'd be chump enough to get hitched up to her? I thought I was recommending you a nice piece of tail and you, you poor slob, you marry her. Ho ho! Listen to me, Henry, while you've got a little sense left: don't let that sour-balled puss muck up your life for you,

do you get me? I don't care what you do or where you go. I'd hate to see you leave town....
I'd miss you, I'm telling you that frankly, but Jesus, if you have to go to Africa, beat it, get
out of her clutches, she's no good for you. Sometimes when I get hold of a good cunt I
think to myself now there's something nice for Henry—and I have in mind to introduce
her to you, and then of course I forget. But Jesus, man, there's thousands of cunts in the
world you can get along with. To think that you had to pick on a mean bitch like that....
Do *you* want more bacon? You'd better eat what you want now, you know, there won't be
any dough later. *Have another drink, eh?* Listen, if you try to run away from me today I
swear I'll never lend you a cent.... What was I saying? Oh yeah, about that screwy bitch
you married. Listen, are you going to do it or not? Every time I see you you tell me you're
going to run away, but you never do it. You don't think you're supporting her, I hope? She
don't *need* you, you sap, don't you see that? She just wants to torture you. As for the kid....
well, shit, if I were in your boots I'd drown it. That sounds kind of mean, doesn't it, but
you know what I mean. You're not a father. I don't know what the hell you are... I just
know you're too goddamned good a fellow to be wasting your life on them. Listen, why
don't you try to make something of yourself? You're young yet and you make a good
appearance. Go off somewhere, way the hell off, and start all over again. If you need a little money I'll raise it for you. It's like throwing it down a sewer, I know, but I'll do it for
you just the same. The truth is, Henry, I like you a hell of a lot. I've taken more from you
than I would from anybody in the world. I guess we have a lot in common, coming from
the old neighborhood. Funny I didn't know you in those days. Shit, I'm getting sentimental...."

The day wore on like that, with lots to eat and drink, the sun out strong, a car to tote
us around, cigars in between, dozing a little on the beach, studying the cunts passing by,
talking, laughing, singing a bit too—one of many, many days I spent like that with
MacGregor. Days like that really seemed to make the wheel stop. On the surface it was
jolly and happy-go-lucky; time passing like a sticky dream. But underneath it was fatalis-
tic, premonitory, leaving me the next day morbid and restless. I knew very well I'd have to
make a break some day; I knew very well I was pissing my time away. But I knew also that
there was nothing I could do about it—*yet*. Something had to happen, something big,
something that would sweep me off my feet. All I needed was a push, but it had to be
some force outside my world that could give me the right push, that I was certain of. I
couldn't eat my heart out, because it wasn't in my nature. All my life things had worked
out all right—*in the end*. It wasn't in the cards for me to exert myself. Something had to
be left to Providence—in my case a whole lot. Despite all the outward manifestations of
misfortune or mismanagement I knew that I was born with a silver spoon in my mouth.
And with a double crown, too. The external situation was bad, admitted—but what bothered me more was the internal situation. I was really afraid of myself, of my appetite, my
curiosity, my flexibility, my permeability, my malleability, my geniality, my powers of adaptation. No situation in itself could frighten me: I somehow always saw myself sitting pretty, sitting inside a buttercup, as it were, and sipping the honey. Even if I were flung in jail
I had a hunch I'd enjoy it. It was because I knew how not to resist, I suppose. Other people wore themselves out tugging and straining and pulling; my strategy was to float with
the tide. What people did to me didn't bother me nearly so much as what they were doing
to others or to themselves. I was really so damned well off inside that I had to take on the
problems of the world. And that's why I was in a mess all the time. I wasn't synchronized

with my own destiny, so to speak. I was trying to live out the world destiny. If I got home of an evening, for instance, and there was no food in the house, not even for the kid, I would turn right around and go looking for the food. But what I noticed about myself, and that was what puzzled me, was that no sooner outside and hustling for the grub than I was back at the *Weltanschauung* again. I didn't think of food for *us* exclusively, I thought of food in general, food in all its stages, everywhere in the world at that hour, and how it was gotten and how it was prepared and what people did if they didn't have it and how maybe there was a way to fix it so that everybody would have it when they wanted it and no more time wasted on such an idiotically simple problem. I felt sorry for the wife and kid, sure, but I also felt sorry for the Hottentots and the Australian bushmen, not to mention the starving Belgians and the Turks and the Armenians. I felt sorry for the human race, for the stupidity of man and his lack of imagination. Missing a meal wasn't so terrible—it was the ghastly emptiness of the street that disturbed me profoundly. All those bloody houses, one like another, and all so empty and cheerless looking. Fine paving stones under foot and asphalt in the middle of the street and beautifully-hideously-elegant brownstone stoops to walk up, and yet a guy could walk about all day and all night on this expensive material and be looking for a crust of bread. That's what got me. The incongruousness of it. If one could only dash out with a dinner bell and yell "Listen, listen, people, I'm a guy what's hungry. Who wants shoes shined? Who wants the garbage brought out? Who wants the drainpipes cleaned out?" If you could only go out in the street and put it to them clear like that. But no, you don't dare to open your trap. If you tell a guy in the street you're hungry you scare the shit out of him, he runs like hell. That's something I never understood. I don't understand it yet. The whole thing is so simple—you just say Yes when some one comes up to you. And if you can't say Yes you can take him by the arm and ask some other bird to help you out. Why you have to don a uniform and kill men you don't know, just to get that crust of bread, is a mystery to me. That's what I think about, more than about whose trap it's going down or how much it costs. Why should I give a fuck about what anything costs? I'm here to live, not to calculate. And that's just what the bastards don't want you to do—*to live!* They want you to spend your whole life adding up figures. That makes sense to them. That's reasonable. That's intelligent. If I were running the boat things wouldn't be so orderly perhaps, but it would be gayer, by Jesus! You wouldn't have to shit in your pants over trifles. Maybe there wouldn't be macadamized roads and streamlined cars and loudspeakers and gadgets of a million billion varieties, maybe there wouldn't even be glass in the windows, maybe you'd have to sleep on the ground, maybe there wouldn't be French cooking and Italian cooking and Chinese cooking, maybe people would kill each other when their patience was exhausted and maybe nobody would stop them because there wouldn't be any jails or any cops or judges, and there certainly wouldn't be any cabinet ministers or legislatures because there wouldn't be any goddamned laws to obey or disobey, and maybe it would take months and years to trek from place to place, but you wouldn't need a visa or a passport or a *carte d'identite* because you wouldn't be registered anywhere and you wouldn't bear a number and if you wanted to change your name every week you could do it because it wouldn't make any difference since you wouldn't own anything except what you could carry around with you and why would you want to own anything when everything would be free?

During this period when I was drifting from door to door, job to job, friend to friend, meal to meal, I did try nevertheless to rope off a little space for myself which might be an anchorage; it was more like a life buoy in the midst of a swift channel. To get within a mile of me was to hear a huge dolorous bell tolling. Nobody could see the anchorage—it was buried deep in the bottom of the channel. One saw me bobbing up and down on the surface, rocking gently sometimes or else swinging backwards and forwards agitatedly. What held me down safely was the big pigeonholed desk which I put in the parlor. This was the desk which had been in the old man's tailoring establishment for the last fifty years, which had given birth to many bills and many groans, which had housed strange souvenirs in its compartments, and which finally I had filched from him when he was ill and away from the establishment; and now it stood in the middle of the floor in our lugubrious parlor on the third floor of a respectable brownstone house in the dead center of the most respectable neighborhood in Brooklyn. I had to fight a tough battle to install it there, but I insisted that it be there in the midmost midst of the shebang. It was like putting a mastodon in the center of a dentist's office. But since the wife had no friends to visit her and since my friends didn't give a fuck if it were suspended from the chandelier, I kept it in the parlor and I put all the extra chairs we had around it in a big circle and then I sat down comfortably and I put my feet up on the desk and dreamed of what I would write if I could write. I had a spittoon alongside of the desk, a big brass one from the same establishment, and I would spit in it now and then to remind myself that it was there. All the pigeonholes were empty and all the drawers were empty; there wasn't a thing on the desk or in it except a sheet of white paper on which I found it impossible to put so much as a pothook.

When I think of the titanic efforts I made to canalize the hot lava which was bubbling inside me, the efforts I repeated thousands of times to bring the funnel into place and capture a word, a phrase, I think inevitably of the men of the old stone age. A hundred thousand, two hundred thousand years, three hundred thousand years to arrive at the idea of the paleolith. A phantom struggle, because they weren't dreaming of such a thing as the paleolith. It came without effort, born of a second, a miracle you might say, except that everything which happens is miraculous. Things happen or they don't happen, that's all. Nothing is accomplished by sweat and struggle. Nearly everything which we call life is just insomnia, an agony because we've lost the habit of falling asleep. We don't know how to let go. We're like a Jack-in-the-box perched on top of a spring and the more we struggle the harder it is to get back in the box.

I think if I had been crazy I couldn't have hit upon a better scheme to consolidate my anchorage than to install this Neanderthal object in the middle of the parlor. With my feet on the desk, picking up the current, and my spinal column snugly socketed in a thick leather cushion, I was in an ideal relation to the flotsam and jetsam which was whirling about me, and which, because they were crazy and part of the flux, my friends were trying to convince me was life. I remember vividly the first contact with reality that I got through my feet, so to speak. The million words or so which I had written, mind you, well ordered, well connected, were as nothing to me—crude ciphers from the old stone age—because the contact was through the head and the head is a useless appendage unless you're anchored in midchannel deep in the mud. Everything I had written before was museum stuff, and most writing is still museum stuff and that's why it doesn't catch fire, doesn't inflame the world. I was only a mouthpiece for the ancestral race which was talking through me; even my dreams were not authentic, not bona fide Henry Miller dreams. To sit still and think one thought which would come up out of me, out of the life buoy, was a Herculean task. I didn't lack thoughts nor words nor the power of expression—I lacked something much more important: the lever which would shut off the juice. The bloody machine wouldn't stop, that was the difficulty. I was not only in the middle of the current but the current was running through me and I had no control over it whatever.

I remember the day I brought the machine to a dead stop and how the other mechanism, the one that was signed with my own initials and which I had made with my own hands and my own blood slowly began to function. I had gone to the theater nearby to see a vaudeville show; it was the matinee and I had a ticket for the balcony. Standing on line in the lobby, I already experienced a strange feeling of consistency. It was as though I were coagulating, becoming a recognizable consistent mass of jelly. It was like the ultimate stage in the healing of a wound. I was at the height of normality, which is a very abnormal condition. Cholera might come and blow its foul breath in my mouth—it wouldn't matter. I might bend over and kiss the ulcers of a leprous hand, and no harm could possibly come to me. There was not just a balance in this constant warfare between health and disease, which is all that most of us may hope for, but there was a plus integer in the blood which meant that, for a few moments at least, disease was completely routed. If one had the wisdom to take root in such a moment, one would never again be ill or unhappy or even die. But to leap to this conclusion is to make a jump which would take one back further than the old stone age. At that moment I wasn't even dreaming of taking root; I was experiencing for the first time in my life the meaning of the miraculous. I was so amazed when I heard my own cogs meshing that I was willing to die then and there for the privilege of the experience.

What happened was this.... As I passed the doorman holding the torn stub in my hand the lights were dimmed and the curtain went up. I stood a moment slightly dazed by the sudden darkness. As the curtain slowly rose I had the feeling that throughout the ages man had always been mysteriously stilled by this brief moment which preludes the spectacle. I could feel the curtain rising *in man.* And immediately I also realized that this was a symbol which was being presented to him endlessly in his sleep and that if he had been awake the players would never have taken the stage but he, Man, would have mounted the boards. I didn't think this thought—it was a realization, as I say, and so simple and overwhelmingly clear was it that the machine stopped dead instantly and I was standing in my own presence bathed in a luminous reality. I turned my eyes away from the stage and beheld the marble staircase which I should take to go to my seat in the balcony. I saw a man slowly mounting the steps, his hand laid across the balustrade. The man could have been myself, the old self which had been sleepwalking ever since I was born. My eye didn't take in the entire staircase, just the few steps which the man had climbed or was climbing in the moment that I took it all in. The man never reached the top of the stairs and his hand was never removed from the marble balustrade. I felt the curtain descend, and for another few moments I was behind the scenes moving amidst the sets, like the property man suddenly roused from his sleep and not sure whether he is still dreaming or looking at a dream which is being enacted on the stage. It was as fresh and green, as strangely new as the bread and cheese lands which the Biddenden maidens saw every day of their long life joined at the hips. I saw only that which was alive! the rest faded out in a penumbra. And it was in order to keep the world alive that I rushed home without waiting to see the performance and sat down to describe the little patch of staircase which is imperishable.

It was just about this time that the Dadaists were in full swing, to be followed shortly by the surrealists. I never heard of either group until some ten years later; I never read
a French book and I never had a French idea. I was perhaps the unique Dadaist in
America, and I didn't know it. I might just as well have been living in the jungles of the
Amazon for all the contact I had with the outside world. Nobody understood what I was
writing about or why I wrote that way. I was so lucid that they said I was daffy. I was
describing the New World—unfortunately a little too soon because it had not yet been
discovered and nobody could be persuaded that it existed. It was an ovarian world, still
hidden away in the Fallopian tubes. Naturally nothing was clearly formulated: there was
only the faint suggestion of a backbone visible, and certainly no arms or legs, no hair, no
nails, no teeth. Sex was the last thing to be dreamed of; it was the world of Chronos and
his ovicular progeny. It was the world of the iota, each iota being indispensable, frighteningly logical, and absolutely unpredictable. There was no such thing as a *thing*, because
the concept "thing" was missing.

I say it was a New World I was describing, but like the New World which Columbus
discovered it turned out to be a far older world than any we have known. I saw beneath
the superficial physiognomy of skin and bone the indestructible world which man has
always carried within him; it was neither old nor new, really, but the eternally true world
which changes from moment to moment. Everything I looked at was palimpsest and there
was no layer of writing too strange for me to decipher. When my companions left me of
an evening I would often sit down and write to my friends the Australian bushmen or the
Mound Builders of the Mississippi Valley or to the Igorots in the Philippines. I had to
write English, naturally, because it was the only language I spoke, but between my language and the telegraphic code employed by my bosom friends there was a world of difference. Any primitive man would have understood me, any man of archaic epochs would
have understood me: only those about me, that is to say, a continent of a hundred million
people, failed to understand my language. To write intelligibly for them I would have been
obliged first of all to kill something, secondly, to arrest time. I had just made the realization that life is indestructible and that there is no such thing as time, only the present. Did
they expect me to deny a truth which it had taken me all my life to catch a glimpse of?
They most certainly did. The one thing they did not want to hear about was that life is
indestructible. Was not their precious new world reared on the destruction of the innocent, on rape and plunder and torture and devastation? Both continents had been violated; both continents had been stripped and plundered of all that was precious—in *things*.
No greater humiliation, it seems to me, was meted out to any man than to Montezuma;
no race was ever more ruthlessly wiped out than the American Indian; no land was ever
raped in the foul and bloody way that California was raped by the gold diggers. I blush to
think of our origins—our hands are steeped in blood and crime. And there is no letup to
the slaughter and the pillage, as I discovered at first hand traveling throughout the length
and breadth of the land. Down to the closest friend every man is a potential murderer.
Often it wasn't necessary to bring out the gun or the lasso or the branding iron—they had
found subtler and more devilish ways of torturing and killing their own. For me the most
excruciating agony was to have the word annihilated before it had even left my mouth. I
learned, by bitter experience, to hold my tongue; I learned to sit in silence, and even smile,
when actually I was foaming at the mouth. I learned to shake hands and say how do you

do to all these innocent-looking fiends who were only waiting for me to sit down in order to suck my blood.

How was it possible, when I sat down in the parlor at my prehistoric desk, to use this code language of rape and murder? I was alone in this great hemisphere of violence, but I was not alone as far as the human race was concerned. I was lonely amidst a world of *things* lit up by phosphorescent flashes of cruelty. I was delirious with an energy which could not be unleashed except in the service of death and futility. I could not begin with a full statement—it would have meant the strait jacket or the electric chair. I was like a man who had been too long incarcerated in a dungeon—I had to feel my way slowly, falteringly, lest I stumble and be run over. I had to accustom myself gradually to the penalties which freedom involves. I had to grow a new epidermis which would protect me from this burning light in the sky.

The ovarian world is the product of a life rhythm. The moment a child is born it becomes part of a world in which there is not only the life rhythm but the death rhythm. The frantic desire to live, to live at any cost, is not a result of the life rhythm in us, but of the death rhythm. There is not only no need to keep alive at any price, but, if life is undesirable, it is absolutely wrong. This keeping oneself alive, out of a blind urge to defeat death, is in itself a means of sowing death. Every one who has not fully accepted life, who is not incrementing life, is helping to fill the world with death. To make the simplest gesture with the hand can convey the utmost sense of life; a word spoken with the whole being can give life. Activity in itself means nothing: it is often a sign of death. By simple external pressure, by force of surroundings and example, by the very climate which activity engenders, one can become part of a monstrous death machine, such as America, for example. What does a dynamo know of life, of peace, of reality? What does any individual American dynamo know of the wisdom and energy, of the life abundant and eternal possessed by a ragged beggar sitting under a tree in the act of meditation? What is *energy?* What is *life?* One has only to read the stupid twaddle of the scientific and philosophic textbooks to realize how less than nothing is the wisdom of these energetic Americans. Listen, they had me on the run, these crazy horsepower fiends; in order to break their insane rhythm, their death rhythm, I had to resort to a wave length which, until I found the proper sustenance in my own bowels, would at least nullify the rhythm they had set up. Certainly I did not need this grotesque, cumbersome, antediluvian desk which I had installed in the parlor; certainly I didn't need twelve empty chairs placed around it in a semicircle; I needed only elbow room in which to write and a thirteenth chair which would take me out of the zodiac they were using and put me in a heaven beyond heaven. But when you drive a man almost crazy and when, to his own surprise perhaps, he finds that he still has some resistance, some powers of his own, then you are apt to find such a man acting very much like a primitive being. Such a man is apt not only to become stubborn and dogged, but superstitious, a believer in magic and a practicer of magic. Such a man is beyond religion—it is his religiousness he is suffering from. Such a man becomes a monomaniac, bent on doing one thing only and that is to break the evil spell which has been put upon him. Such a man is beyond throwing bombs, beyond revolt; he wants to stop reacting, whether inertly or ferociously. This man, of all men on earth, wants the act to be a manifestation of life. If, in the realization of his terrible need, he begins to act regressively, to become unsocial, to stammer and stutter, to prove so utterly unadapted as to be incapable of earning a living, know that this man has found his way back to the womb and source of life and that tomorrow, instead of the contemptible object of ridicule which you have made of him, he will stand forth as a *man* in his own right and all the powers of the world will be of no avail against him.

Out of the crude cipher with which he communicates from his prehistoric desk with the archaic men of the world a new language builds up which cuts through the death language of the day like wireless through a storm. There is no magic in this wave length any more than there is magic in the womb. Men are lonely and out of communication with one another because all their inventions speak only of death. Death is the automaton which rules the world of activity. Death is silent, because it has no mouth. Death has never *expressed* anything. Death is wonderful too—*after life.* Only one like myself who has opened his mouth and spoken, only one who has said Yes, Yes, Yes, and again Yes! can open wide his arms to death and know no fear. Death as a reward, yes! Death as a result of fulfillment, yes! Death as a crown and shield, yes! But not death from the roots, isolating men, making them bitter and fearful and lonely, giving them fruitless energy, filling them with a will which can only say No! The first word any man writes when he has found himself, his own rhythm, which is the life rhythm, is Yes! Everything he writes thereafter is Yes, Yes, Yes—Yes in a thousand million ways. No dynamo, no matter how huge—not even a dynamo of a hundred million dead souls—can combat one man saying Yes!

The war was on and men were being slaughtered, one million, two million, five million, ten million, twenty million, finally a hundred million, then a billion, everybody, man, woman and child, down to the last one. *"No!"* they were shouting, *"No! they shall not pass!"* And yet everybody passed; everybody got a free pass, whether he shouted Yes or No. In the midst of this triumphant demonstration of spiritually destructive osmosis I sat with my feet planted on the big desk trying to communicate with Zeus the Father of Atlantis and with his lost progeny, ignorant of the fact that Apollinaire was to die the day before the Armistice in a military hospital, ignorant of the fact that in his "new writing" he had penned these indelible lines:

> Be forbearing when you compare us
> With those who were the perfection of order.
> We who everywhere seek adventure,
> We are not your enemies.
> We would give you vast and strange domains
> Where flowering mystery waits for him would pluck it.

Ignorant that in this same poem he had also written:

> Have compassion on us who are always fighting on the frontiers
> Of the boundless future,
> Compassion for our errors, compassion for our sins.

I was ignorant of the fact that there were men then living who went by the outlandish names of Blaise Cendrars, Jacques Vache, Louis Aragon, Tristan Tzara, Rene Crevel, Henri de Montherlant, Andre Breton, Max Ernst, Georges Grosz; ignorant of the fact that on July 14, 1916, at the Saal Waag, in Zurich, the first Dada Manifesto had been proclaimed—"manifesto by Monsieur Antipyrine"—that in this strange document it was stated: "Dada is life without slippers or parallel... severe necessity without discipline or morality and we spit on humanity." Ignorant of the fact that the Dada Manifesto of 1918 contained these lines: "I am writing a manifesto and I want nothing, yet I say certain things, and I am against manifestoes as a matter of principle, as I am also against principles.... I write this manifesto to show that one may perform opposed actions together, in a single fresh respiration; I am against action; for continual contradiction, for affirmation also, I am neither for nor against and I do not explain for I hate good sense.... There is a literature which does not reach the voracious mass. The work of creators, sprung from a real necessity on the part of the author, and for himself. Consciousness of a supreme egotism where the stars waste away.... Each page must explode, either with the profoundly serious and heavy, the whirlwind, dizziness, the new, the eternal, with the overwhelming hoax, with an enthusiasm for principles or with the mode of typography. On the one hand a staggering fleeing world, affianced to the jinglebells of the infernal gamut, on the other hand: *new beings....* "

Thirty-two years later and I am still saying Yes! Yes, Monsieur Antipyrine! Yes, Monsieur Tristan Bustanoby Tzara! Yes, Monsieur Max Ernst Geburt! Yes! Monsieur Rene Crevel, now that you are dead by suicide, yes, the world is crazy, you were right. Yes, Monsieur Blaise Cendrars, you were right to kill. Was it the day of the Armistice that you brought out your little book—*J'ai tue?* Yes, "keep on my lads, humanity...." Yes, Jacques Vache, quite right—"Art ought to be something funny and a trifle boring." Yes, my dear dead Vache, how right you were and how funny and how boring and touching and tender and true: "It is of the essence of symbols to be symbolic." Say it again, from the other world! Have you a megaphone up there? Have you found all the arms and legs that were blown off during the melee? Can you put them together again? Do you remember the meeting at Nantes in 1916 with Andre" Breton? Did you celebrate the birth of hysteria together? Had he told you, Breton, that there was only the marvelous and nothing but the marvelous and that the marvelous is always marvelous—and isn't it marvelous to hear it again, even though your ears are stopped? I want to include here, before passing on, a little portrait of you by Emile Bouvier for the benefit of my Brooklyn friends who may not have recognized me then but who will now, I am sure....

"... he was not all crazy, and could explain his conduct when occasion required. His actions, none the less, were as disconcerting as Jarry's worst eccentricities. For example, he was barely out of hospital when he hired himself out as a stevedore, and he thereafter passed his afternoons in unloading coal on the quays along the Loire. In the evening, on the other hand, he would make the rounds of the cafes and cinemas, dressed in the height of fashion and with many variations of costume. What was more, in time of war, he would strut forth sometimes in the uniform of a lieutenant of hussars, sometimes in that of an English officer, of an aviator or of a surgeon. In civil life, he was quite as free and easy, thinking nothing of introducing Breton under the name of Andre Salmon, while he took unto himself, but quite without vanity, the most wonderful tides and adventures. He never said good morning nor good evening nor good-by, and never took any notice of letters, except those from his mother, when he had to ask for money. He did not recognize his best friends from one day to another...."

Do you recognize me, lads? Just a Brooklyn boy communicating with the red-haired albinos of the Zuni region. Making ready, with feet on the desk, to write "strong works, works forever incomprehensible," as my dead comrades were promising. These "strong works"—would you recognize them if you saw them? Do you know that of the millions who were killed not one death was necessary to produce "the strong work?" *New beings,* yes! We have need of new beings still. We can do without the telephone, without the automobile, without the high-class bombers—but we can't do without new beings. If Atlantis was submerged beneath the sea, if the Sphinx and the Pyramids remain an eternal riddle, it is because there were no more new beings being born. Stop the machine a moment! Flash back! Flash back to 1914, to the Kaiser sitting on his horse. Keep him sitting there a moment with his withered arm clutching the bridle rein. Look at his mustache! Look at his haughty air of pride and arrogance! Look at his cannon fodder lined up in strictest discipline, all ready to obey the word, to get shot, to get disemboweled, to be burned in quicklime. Hold it a moment, now, and look at the other side: the defenders of our great and glorious civilization, the men who will war to end war. Change their clothes, change their uniforms, change horses, change flags, change terrain. My, is that the Kaiser I see on a white horse? Are those the terrible Huns? And where is Big Bertha? Oh, I see—I thought it was pointing toward Notre-Dame? Humanity, me lads, humanity always marching in the van.... And the strong works we were speaking of? Where are the strong works? Call up the Western Union and dispatch a messenger fleet of foot—not a cripple or an octogenarian, but a young one! Ask him to find the great work and bring it back. We need it. We have a brand-new museum ready waiting to house it—and cellophane and the Dewey decimal system to file it. All we need is the name of the author. Even if he has no name, even if it is an anonymous work, we won't kick. Even if it has a little mustard gas in it we won't mind. Bring it back dead or alive—there's a twenty-five thousand dollar reward for the man who fetches it.

And if they tell you that these things had to be, that things could not have happened otherwise, that France did her best and Germany her best and that little Liberia and little Ecuador and all the other allies also did their best, and that since the war everybody has been doing his best to patch things up or to forget, tell them that their best is not good enough, that we don't want to hear any more this logic of "doing the best one can," tell them we don't want the best of a bad bargain, we don't believe in bargains good or bad, nor in war memorials. We don't want to hear about the logic of events—or any kind of logic. *"Je ne parte pas logique"* said Montherlant, *"je parte generosite."* I don't think you heard it very well, since it was in French. I'll repeat it for you, in the Queen's own language: "I'm not talking logic, I'm talking generosity." That's bad English, as the Queen herself might speak it, but it's clear. *Generosity*—do you hear? You never practice it, any of you, either in peace or in war. You don't know the meaning of the word. You think to supply guns and ammunition to the winning side is generosity; you think sending Red Cross nurses to the front, or the Salvation Army, is generosity. You think a bonus twenty years too late is generosity; you think a little pension and a wheel chair is generosity; you think if you give a man his old job back it's generosity. You don't know what the fucking word means, you bastards! To be generous is to say Yes before the man even opens his mouth. To say Yes you have to be first a surrealist or a Dadaist, because you have understood what it means to say No. You can even say Yes and No at the same time, provided you do more than is expected of you. Be a stevedore in the daytime and a Beau Brummel in the nighttime. Wear any uniform so long as it's not yours. When you write your mother ask her to cough up a little dough so that you may have a clean rag to wipe your ass with. Don't be disturbed if you see your neighbor going after his wife with a knife: he probably has good reason to go after her, and if he kills her you may be sure he had the satisfaction of knowing *why* he did it. If you're trying to improve your mind, stop it! There's no improving the mind. Look to your heart and gizzard—the brain is in the heart.

Ah yes, if I had known then that these birds existed—Cendrars, Vache, Grosz, Ernst, Apollinaire—if I had known that then, if I had known that in their own way they were thinking exactly the same things as I was, I think I'd have blown up. Yes, I think I'd have gone off like a bomb. But I was ignorant. Ignorant of the fact that almost fifty years previously a crazy Jew in South America had given birth to such startlingly marvelous phrases as "doubt's duck with the vermouth lips" or "I have seen a fig eat an onager"—that about the same time a Frenchman, who was only a boy, was saying: "Find flowers that are chairs"... "my hunger is the black air's bits"... "his heart, amber and spunk." Maybe at the same time, or thereabouts, while Jarry was saying "in eating the sound of moths," and Apollinaire repeating after him "near a gentleman swallowing himself," and Breton murmuring softly "night's pedals move uninterruptedly," perhaps "in the air beautiful and black" which the lone Jew had found under the Southern Cross another man, also lonely and exiled and of Spanish origin, was preparing to put down on paper these memorable words: 'I seek, all in all, to console myself for my exile, for my exile from eternity, for that *unearthing (destierro)* which I am fond of referring to as my unheavening.... At present, I think that the best way to write this novel is to tell how it should be written. It is the novel of the novel, the creation of creation. Or God of God, *Deus de Deo."* Had I known he was going to add this, this which follows, I would surely have gone off like a bomb.... "By being crazy is understood losing one's reason. Reason, but not the truth, for there are madmen who speak truths while others keep silent...." Speaking of these things, speaking of the war and the war dead, I cannot refrain from mentioning that some twenty years later I ran across this in French by a Frenchman. O miracles of miracles! *"Il faut le dire, il y a des cadavres que je ne respecte qu'a moitie."* Yes, yes, and again yes! O, let us do some rash thing—for the sheer pleasure of it! Let us do something live and magnificent, even if destructive! Said the mad cobbler: "All things are generated out of the grand mystery, and proceed out of one degree into another. Whatever goes forward in its degree, the same receives no abominate."

Everywhere in all times the same ovarian world announcing itself. Yet also, parallel with these announcements, these prophecies, these gynecological manifestoes, parallel and contemporaneous with them new totem poles, new taboos, new war dances. While into the air so black and beautiful the brothers of man, the poets, the diggers of the future, were spitting their magic lines, in this same time, O profound and perplexing riddle, other men were saying: "Won't you please come and take a job in our ammunition factory. We promise you the highest wages, the most sanitary and hygienic conditions. The work is so easy that even a child could do it." And if you had a sister, a wife, a mother, an aunt, as long as she could manipulate her hands, as long as she could prove that she had no bad habits, you were invited to bring her or them along to the ammunition works. If you were shy of soiling your hands they would explain to you very gently and intelligently just how these delicate mechanisms operated, what they did when they exploded, and why you must not waste even your garbage because... *et ipso facto e pluribus unum.* The thing that impressed me, going the rounds in search of work, was not so much that they made me vomit every day (assuming I had been lucky enough to put something into my guts), but that they always demanded to know if you were of good habits, if you were steady, if you were sober, if you were industrious, if you had ever worked before and if not why not. Even the garbage, which I had gotten the job of collecting for the municipality, was precious to them, the killers. Standing knee deep in the muck, the lowest of the low, a coolie, an outcast, still I was part of the death racket. I tried reading the *Inferno* at night, but it was in English and English is no language for a Catholic work. "Whatever enters in itself into its selfhood, viz., into its own lubet...." *Lubet!* If I had had a word like that to conjure with then, how peacefully I might have gone about my garbage collecting! How sweet, in the night, when Dante is out of reach and the hands smell of muck and slime, to take unto oneself this word which in the Dutch means "lust" and in Latin "lubitum" or the divine *beneplacitum.* Standing knee deep in the garbage I said one day what Meister Eckhart is reported to have said long ago: "I truly have need of God, but God has need of me too." There was a job waiting for me in the slaughterhouse, a nice little job of sorting entrails, but I couldn't raise the fare to get to Chicago. I remained in Brooklyn, in my own palace of entrails, and turned round and round on the plinth of the labyrinth. I remained at home seeking the "germinal vesicle," "the dragon castle on the floor of the sea," "the Heavenly Heart," "the field of the square inch," "the house of the square foot," "the dark pass," "the space of former Heaven." I remained locked in, a prisoner of Forculus, god of the door, of Cardea, god of the hinge, and of Limentius, god of the threshold. I spoke only with their sisters, the three goddesses called Fear, Pallor and Fever. I saw no "Asian luxury," as had St. Augustine, or as he imagined he had. Nor did I see "the two twins born, so near together, that the second held the first by the heel." But I saw a street called Myrtle Avenue, which runs from Borough Hall to Fresh Pond Road, and down this street no saint ever walked (else it would have crumbled), down this street no miracle ever passed, nor any poet, nor any species of human genius, nor did any flower ever grow there, nor did the sun strike it squarely, nor did the rain ever wash it. For the genuine Inferno which I had to postpone for twenty years I give you Myrtle Avenue, one of the innumerable bridlepaths ridden by iron monsters which lead to the heart of America's emptiness. If you have only seen Essen or Manchester or Chicago or Levallois-Perret or Glasgow or Hoboken or Canarsie or Bayonne you have seen nothing of the magnificent emptiness of progress and enlightenment. Dear reader, you must see Myrtle Avenue before you die, if only to realize how far into the future Dante saw. You must believe me that on this street, neither in the houses which line it, nor the cobblestones which pave it, nor the elevated structure which cuts it atwain, neither in any creature that bears a name and lives thereon, neither in any animal, bird or insect passing through it to slaughter or already slaughtered, is there hope of "lubet," "sublimate" or "abominate." It is a street not of sorrow, for sorrow would be human and recognizable, but of sheer emptiness: it is emptier than the most extinct volcano, emptier than a vacuum, emptier than the word God in the mouth of an unbeliever.

I said I did not know a word of French then, and it is true, but I was just on the brink of making a great discovery, a discovery which would compensate for the emptiness of Myrtle Avenue and the whole American continent. I had almost reached the shore of that great French ocean which goes by the name of Elie Faure, an ocean which the French themselves had hardly navigated and which they had mistaken, it seems, for an inland sea. Reading him even in such a withered language as English has become I could see that this man who had described the glory of the human race on his cuff was Father Zeus of Atlantis whom I had been searching for. An ocean I called him, but he was also a world symphony. He was the first musician the French have produced; he was exalted and controlled, an anomaly, a Gallic Beethoven, a great physician of the soul, a giant lightning rod. He was also a sunflower turning with the sun, always drinking in the light, always radiant and blazing with vitality. He was neither an optimist nor a pessimist, any more than one can say that the ocean is beneficent or malevolent. He was a believer in the human race. He added a cubit to the race, by giving it back its dignity, its strength, its need of creation. He saw everything as creation, as solar joy. He didn't record it in orderly fashion, he recorded it musically. He was indifferent to the fact that the French have a tin ear—he was orchestrating for the whole world simultaneously. What was my amazement then, when some years later I arrived in France, to find that there were no monuments erected to him, no streets named after him. Worse, during eight whole years I never once heard a Frenchman mention his name. He had to die in order to be put in the pantheon of French deities—and how sickly must they look, his deific contemporaries, in the presence of this radiant sun! If he had not been a physician, and thus permitted to earn a livelihood, what might not have happened to him! Perhaps another able hand for the garbage trucks! The man who made the Egyptian frescoes come alive in all their flaming colors, this man could just as well have starved to death for all the public cared. But he was an ocean and the critics drowned in this ocean, and the editors and the publishers and the public too. It will take aeons for him to dry up, to evaporate. It will take about as long as for the French to acquire a musical ear.

If there had been no music I would have gone to the madhouse like Nijinsky. (It was just about this time that they discovered that Nijinsky was mad. He had been found giving his money away to the poor—always a bad sign!) My mind was filled with wonderful treasures, my taste was sharp and exigent, my muscles were in excellent condition, my appetite was strong, my wind sound. I had nothing to do except to improve myself, and I was going crazy with the improvements I made every day. Even if there were a job for me to fill I couldn't accept it, because what I needed was not work but a life more abundant. I couldn't waste time being a teacher, a lawyer, a physician, a politician or anything else that society had to offer. It was easier to accept menial jobs because it left my mind free. After I was fired from the garbage trucks I remember taking up with an Evangelist who seemed to have great confidence in me. I was a sort of usher, collector and private secretary. He brought to my attention the whole world of Indian philosophy. Evenings when I was free I would meet with my friends at the home of Ed Bauries who lived in an aristocratic section of Brooklyn. Ed Bauries was an eccentric pianist who couldn't read a note. He had a bosom pal called George Neumiller with whom he often played duets. Of the dozen or so who congregated at Ed Bauries' home nearly every one of us could play the piano. We were all between twenty-one and twenty-five at the time; we never brought any women along and we hardly ever mentioned the subject of woman during these sessions. We had plenty of beer to drink and a whole big house at our disposal, for it was in the summertime, when his folks were away, that we held our gatherings. Though there were a dozen other homes like this which I could speak of, I mention Ed Bauries' place because it was typical of something I have never encountered elsewhere in the world. Neither Ed Bauries himself nor any of his friends suspected the sort of books I was reading then nor the things which were occupying my mind. When I blew in I was greeted enthusiastically—as a clown. It was expected of me to start things going. There were about four pianos scattered throughout the big house, to say nothing of the celesta, the organ, guitars, mandolins, fiddles and what not. Ed Bauries was a nut, a very affable, sympathetic and gener-

ous one too. The sandwiches were always of the best, the beer plentiful, and if you wanted to stay the night he could fix you up on a divan just as pretty as you liked. Coming
down the street—a big, wide street, somnolent, luxurious, a street altogether out of the
world—I could hear the tinkle of the piano in the big parlor on the first floor. The windows were wide open and as I got into range I could see Al Burger or Connie Grimm
sprawling in their big easy chairs, their feet on the window sill, and big beer mugs in their
hands. Probably George Neumiller was at the piano, improvising, his shirt peeled off and
a big cigar in his mouth. They were talking and laughing while George fooled around,
searching for an opening. Soon as he hit a theme he would call for Ed and Ed would sit
beside him, studying it out in his unprofessional way, then suddenly pouncing on the keys
and giving tit for tat. Maybe when I'd walk in somebody would be trying to stand on his
hands in the next room—there were three big rooms on the first floor which opened one
on to the other and back of them was a garden, an enormous garden, with flowers, fruit
trees, grape vines, statues, fountains and everything. Sometimes when it was too hot they
brought the celesta or the little organ into the garden (and a keg of beer, naturally) and
we'd sit around in the dark laughing and singing—until the neighbors forced us to stop.
Sometimes the music was going on all through the house at once, on every floor. It was
really crazy then, intoxicating, and if there had been women around it would have spoiled
it. Sometimes it was like watching an endurance contest—Ed Bauries and George
Neumiller at the grand piano, each trying to wear the other out, changing places without
stopping, crossing hands, sometimes falling away to plain chopsticks, sometimes going
like a Wurlitzer. And always something to laugh about all the time. Nobody asked what
you did, what you thought about, and so forth. When you arrived at Ed Bauries' place you
checked your identification marks. Nobody gave a fuck what size hat you wore or how
much you paid for it. It was entertainment from the word go—and the sandwiches and
the drinks were on the house. And when things got going, three or four pianos at once,
the celesta, the organ, the mandolins, the guitars, beer running through the halls, the mantelpieces full of sandwiches and cigars, a breeze coming through from the garden, George
Neumiller stripped to the waist and modulating like a fiend, it was better than any show
I've ever seen put on and it didn't cost a cent. In fact, with the dressing and undressing
that went on, I always came away with a little extra change and a pocketful of good cigars.
I never saw any of them between times—only Monday nights throughout the summer,
when Ed held open house.

   Standing in the garden listening to the din I could scarcely believe that it was the
same city. And if I had ever opened my trap and exposed my guts it would have been all
over. Not one of these bozos amounted to anything, as the world reckons. They were just
good eggs, children, fellows who liked music and who liked a good time. They liked it so
much that sometimes we had to call the ambulance. Like the night Al Burger twisted his
knee while showing us one of his stunts. Everybody so happy, so full of music, so lit up,
that it took him an hour to persuade us he was really hurt. We try to carry him to a hospital but it's too far away and besides, it's such a good joke, that we drop him now and then
and that makes him yell like a maniac. So finally we telephone for help from a police box,
and the ambulance comes and the patrol wagon too. They take Al to the hospital and the
rest of us to the hoosegow. And on the way we sing at the top of our lungs. And after we're
bailed out we're still feeling good and the cops are feeling good too, and so we all adjourn
to the basement where there's a cracked piano and we go on singing and playing. All this

is like some period B.C. in history which ends not because there's a war but because even a joint like Ed Bauries' is not immune to the poison seeping in from the periphery. Because every street is becoming a Myrtle Avenue, because emptiness is filling the whole continent from the Atlantic to the Pacific. Because, after a certain time, you can't enter a single house throughout the length and breadth of the land and find a man standing on his hands singing. It just ain't done any more. And there ain't two pianos going at once anywhere, nor are there two men anywhere willing to play all night just for the fun of it. Two men who can play like Ed Bauries and George Neumiller are hired by the radio or the movies and only a thimbleful of their talent is used and the rest is thrown into the garbage can. Nobody knows, judging from public spectacles, what talent is disposable in the great American continent. Later on, and that's why I used to sit around on doorsteps in Tin Pan Alley, I would while away the afternoons listening to the professionals mugging it out. That was good too, but it was different. There was no fun in it, it was a perpetual rehearsal to bring in dollars and cents. Any man in America who had an ounce of humor in him was saving it up to put himself across. There were some wonderful nuts among them too, men I'll never forget, men who left no name behind them, and they were the best we produced. I remember an anonymous performer on the Keith circuit who was probably the craziest man in America, and perhaps he got fifty dollars a week for it. Three times a day, every day in the week, he came out and held the audience spellbound. He didn't have an act—he just improvised. He never repeated his jokes or his stunts. He gave himself prodigally, and I don't think he was a hop fiend either. He was one of those guys who are born in the corn crakes and the energy and the joy in him was so fierce that nothing could contain it. He could play any instrument and dance any step and he could invent a story on the spot and string it out till the bell rang. He was not only satisfied to do his own act but he would help the others out. He would stand in the wings and wait for the right moment to break into the other guy's act. He was the whole show and it was a show that contained more therapy than the whole arsenal of modern science. They ought to have paid a man like this the wages which the President of the United States receives. They ought to sack the President of the United States and the whole Supreme Court and set up a man like this as ruler. This man could cure any disease on the calendar. He was the kind of guy, moreover, as would do it for nothing, if you asked him to. This is the type of man which empties the insane asylums. He doesn't propose a cure—he makes everybody crazy. Between this solution and a perpetual state of war, which is civilization, there is only one other way out—and that is the road we will all take eventually because everything else is doomed to failure. The type that represents this one and only way bears a head with six faces and eight eyes; the head is a revolving lighthouse, and instead of a triple crown at the top, as there might well be, there is a hole which ventilates what few brains there are. There is very little brain, as I say, because there is very little baggage to carry about, because living in full consciousness, the gray matter passes off into light. This is the only type of man one can place above the comedian; he neither laughs nor weeps, he is beyond suffering. We don't recognize him yet because he is too close to us, right under the skin, as a matter of fact. When the comedian catches us in the guts this man, whose name might be God, I suppose, if he had to use a name, speaks up. When the whole human race is rocking with laughter, laughing so hard that it hurts, I mean, everybody then has his foot on the path. In that moment everybody can just as well be God as anything else. In that moment you have the annihilation of dual, triple, quadruple and multiple consciousness, which is what makes the gray matter coil up in dead folds at the top of the skull. At that moment you can really feel the hole in the top of the head; you know that you once had an eye there and that this eye was capable of taking in everything at once. The eye is gone now, but when you laugh until the tears flow and your belly aches, you are really opening the skylight and ventilating the brains. Nobody can persuade you at that moment to fake a gun and kill your enemy; neither can anybody persuade you to open a fat tome containing the metaphysical truths of the world and read it. If you know what freedom means, absolute freedom and not a relative freedom, then you must recognize that this is the nearest to it you will ever get. If I am against the condition of the world it is not because I am a moralist—it is because I want to laugh more. I don't say that God is one grand laugh: I say that you've got to laugh hard before you can get anywhere near God. My whole aim in life is to get near to God, that is, to get nearer to myself. That's why it doesn't matter to me what road I take. But music is very important. Music is a tonic for the pineal gland. Music isn't Bach or Beethoven; music is the can opener of the soul. It makes you terribly quiet inside, makes you aware that there's a roof to your being.

The stabbing horror of life is not contained in calamities and disasters, because these things wake one up and one gets very familiar and intimate with them and finally they become tame again... no, it is more like being in a hotel room in Hoboken, let us say, and just enough money in one's pocket for another meal. You are in a city that you never expect to be in again and you have only to pass the night in your hotel room, but it takes all the courage and pluck you possess to stay in that room. There must be a good reason why certain cities, certain places, inspire such loathing and dread. There must be some kind of perpetual murder going on in these places. The people are of the same race as you, they go about their business as people do anywhere, they build the same sort of house, no better, no worse, they have the same system of education, the same currency, the same newspapers—and yet they are absolutely different from the other people you know, and the whole atmosphere is different, and the rhythm is different and the tension is different. It's almost like looking at yourself in another incarnation. You know, with a most disturbing certitude, that what governs life is not money, not politics, not religion, not training, not race, not language, not customs, but something else, something you're trying to throttle all the time and which is really throttling you, because otherwise you wouldn't be terrified all of a sudden and wonder how you were going to escape. Some cities you don't even have to pass a night in—just an hour or two is enough to unnerve you. I think of Bayonne that way. I came on it in the night with a few addresses that had been given me. I had a brief case under my arm with a prospectus of the *Encyclopaedia Britannica*. I was supposed to go under cover of dark and sell the bloody encyclopedia to some poor devils who wanted to improve themselves. If I had been dropped off at Helsingfors I couldn't have felt more ill at ease than walking the streets of Bayonne. It wasn't an American city to me. It wasn't a city at all, but a huge octopus wriggling in the dark. The first door I came to looked so forbidding I didn't even bother to knock; I went like that to several addresses before I could summon the courage to knock. The first face I took a look at frightened the shit out of me. I don't mean timidity or embarrassment—I mean fear. It was the face of a hod carrier, an ignorant mick who would as like fell you with an ax as spit in your eye. I pretended I had the wrong name and hurried on to the next address. Each time the door opened I saw another monster. And then I came at last to a poor simp who really wanted to improve himself and that broke me down. I felt truly ashamed of myself, of my country,

my race, my epoch. I had a devil of a time persuading him not to buy the damned encyclopedia. He asked me innocently what then had brought me to his home—and without
a minute's hesitation I told him an astounding lie, a lie which was later to prove a great
truth. I told him I was only pretending to sell the encyclopedia in order to meet people
and write about them. That interested him enormously, even more than the encyclopedia.
He wanted to know what I would write about him, if I could say. It's taken me twenty
years to answer that question, but here it is. If you would still like to know, John Doe of
the City of Bayonne, this is it.... I owe you a great deal because after that lie I told you I
left your house and I tore up the prospectus furnished me by the *Encyclopaedia Britannica*
and I threw it in the gutter. I said to myself I will never again go to people under false pre-
tenses even if it is to give them the Holy Bible. I will never again sell anything, even if I
have to starve. I am going home now and I will sit down and really write about people.
And if anybody knocks at my door to sell me something I will invite him in and say "why
are you doing this?" And if he says it is because he has to make a living I will offer him
what money I have and beg him once again to think what he is doing. I want to prevent
as many men as possible from pretending that they have to do this or that because they
must earn a living. *It is not true.* One can starve to death—it is much better. Every man
who voluntarily starves to death jams another cog in the automatic process. I would rather
see a man take a gun and kill his neighbor, in order to get the food he needs, than keep
up the automatic process by pretending that he has to earn a living. That's what I want to
say, Mr. John Doe.

I pass on. Not the stabbing horror of disaster and calamity, I say, but the automatic
throwback, the stark panorama of the soul's atavistic struggle. A bridge in North Carolina,
near the Tennessee border. Coming out of lush tobacco fields, low cabins everywhere and
the smell of fresh wood burning. The day passed in a thick lake of waving green. Hardly
a soul in sight. Then suddenly a clearing and I'm over a big gulch spanned by a rickety
wooden bridge. This is the end of the world! How in God's name I got here and why I'm
here I don't know. *How am I going to eat?* And if I ate the biggest meal imaginable I
would still be sad, frightfully sad. I don't know where to go from here. This bridge is the
end, the end of me, the end of my known world. This bridge is insanity: there is no reason why it should stand there and no reason why people should cross it. I refuse to budge
another step, I balk at crossing that crazy bridge. Nearby is a low wall which I lie against
trying to think what to do and where to go. I realize quietly what a terribly civilized person I am—the need I have for people, conversation, books, theater, music, cafes, drinks,
and so forth. It's terrible to be civilized, because when you come to the end of the world
you have nothing to support the terror of loneliness. To be civilized is to have complicated needs. And a man, when he is full blown, shouldn't need a thing. All day I had been
moving through tobacco fields, and growing more and more uneasy. What have I to do
with all this tobacco? What am I heading into? People everywhere are producing crops
and goods for other people—and I am like a ghost sliding between all this unintelligible
activity. I want to find some kind of work, but I don't want to be a part of this thing, this
infernal automatic process. I pass through a town and I look at the newspaper telling what
is happening in that town and its environs. It seems to me that *nothing* is happening, that
the clock has stopped but that these poor devils are unaware of it. I have a strong intuition, moreover, that there is murder in the air. I can smell it. A few days back I passed the
imaginary line which divides the North from the South. I wasn't aware of it until a darky

came along driving a team; when he gets alongside of me he stands up in his seat and doffs his hat most respectfully. He had snow-white hair and a face of great dignity. That made me feel horrible: it made me realize that there are still slaves. This man had to tip his hat to me—because I was of the white race. Whereas I should have tipped my hat to him! I should have saluted him as a survivor of all the vile tortures the white men have inflicted on the black. I should have tipped my hat first, to let him know that I am not a part of this system, that I am begging forgiveness for all my white brethren who are too ignorant and cruel to make an honest overt gesture. Today I feel their eyes on me all the time; they watch from behind doors, from behind trees. All very quiet, very peaceful, seemingly. Nigger never say nuthin'. Nigger he hum all time. White man think nigger learn his place. Nigger learn nuthin'. Nigger wait. Nigger watch everything white man do. Nigger no say nuthin', no sir, no siree. But just the same the nigger is killing the white man off! Every time the nigger looks at a white man he's putting a dagger through him. It's not the heat, it's not the hookworm, it's not the bad crops that's killing the South off—it's the nigger! The nigger is giving off a poison, whether he means to or not. The South is coked and doped with nigger poison.

Pass on.... Sitting outside a barber shop by the James River. I'll be here just ten minutes, while I take a load off my feet. There's a hotel and a few stores opposite me; it all tails off quickly, ends like it began—for no reason. From the bottom of my soul I pity the poor devils who are born and die here. There is no earthly reason why this place should exist. There is no reason why anybody should cross the street and get himself a shave and haircut, or even a sirloin steak. Men, buy yourselves a gun and kill each other off! Wipe this street out of my mind forever—it hasn't an ounce of meaning in it.

The same day, after nightfall. Still plugging on, digging deeper and deeper into the South. I'm coming away from a little town by a short road leading to the highway. Suddenly I hear footsteps behind me and soon a young man passes me on the trot, breathing heavily and cursing with all his might. I stand there a moment, wondering what it's all about. I hear another man coming on the trot; he's an older man and he's carrying a gun. He breathes fairly easy, and not a word out of his trap. Just as he comes in view the moon breaks through the clouds and I catch a good look at his face. He's a man-hunter. I stand back as the others come up behind him. I'm trembling with fear. It's the sheriff, I hear a man say, and he's going to get him. Horrible. I move on toward the highway waiting to hear the shot that will end it all. I hear nothing—just this heavy breathing of the young man and the quick, eager steps of the mob following behind the sheriff. Just as I get near the main road a man steps out of the darkness and comes over to me very quietly. "Where yer goin', son?" he says, quiet like and almost tenderly. I stammer out something about the next town. "Better stay right here, son," he says. I didn't say another word. I let him take me back into town and hand me over like a thief. I lay on the floor with about fifty other blokes. I had a marvelous sexual dream which ended with the guillotine.

I plug on.... It's just as hard to go back as to go forward. I don't have the feeling of being an American citizen any more. The part of America I came from, where I had some rights, where I felt free, is so far behind me that it's beginning to get fuzzy in my memory. I feel as though someone's got a gun against my back all the time. Keep moving, is all I seem to hear. If a man talks to me I try not to seem too intelligent. I try to pretend that I am vitally interested in the crops, in the weather, in the elections. If I stand and stop they look at me, whites and blacks—they look me through and through as though I were juicy and edible. I've got to walk another thousand miles or so as though I had a deep purpose, as though I were really going somewhere. I've got to look sort of grateful, too, that nobody has yet taken a fancy to plug me. It's depressing and exhilarating at the same time. You're a marked man—and yet nobody pulls the trigger. They let you walk unmolested right into the Gulf of Mexico where you can drown yourself.

Yes sir, I reached the Gulf of Mexico and I walked right into it and drowned myself. I did it gratis. When they fished the corpse out they found it was marked F.O.B. Myrtle Avenue, Brooklyn; it was returned C.O.D. When I was asked later why I had killed myself I could only think to say—*because I wanted to electrify the cosmos!* I meant by that a very simple thing—The Delaware, Lackawanna and Western had been electrified, the Seaboard Air Line had been electrified, but the soul of man was still in the covered wagon stage. I was born in the midst of civilization and I accepted it very naturally—what else was there to do? But the joke was that nobody else was taking it seriously. I was the only man in the community who was truly civilized. There was no place for me—as yet. And yet the books I read, the music I heard assured me that there were other men in the world like myself. I had to go and drown myself in the Gulf of Mexico in order to have an excuse for continuing this pseudo-civilized existence. I had to delouse myself of my spiritual body, as it were.

When I woke up to the fact that as far as the scheme of things goes I was less than dirt I really became quite happy. I quickly lost all sense of responsibility. And if it weren't for the fact that my friends got tired of lending me money I might have gone on indefinitely pissing the time away. The world was like a museum to me; I saw nothing to do but eat into this marvelous chocolate layer cake which the men of the past had dumped on our hands. It annoyed everybody to see the way I enjoyed myself. Their logic was that art was very beautiful, oh yes, indeed, but you must work for a living and then you will find that you are too tired to think about art. But it was when I threatened to add a layer or two on my own account to this marvelous chocolate layer cake that they blew up on me. That was the finishing touch. That meant I was definitely crazy. First I was considered to be a useless member of society; then for a time I was found to be a reckless, happy-go-lucky corpse with a tremendous appetite; now I had become crazy. (*Listen, you bastard, you find yourself a job... we're through with you!*) In a way it was refreshing, this change of front. I could feel the wind blowing through the corridors. At least "we" were no longer becalmed. It was war, and as a corpse I was just fresh enough to have a little fight left in me. War is revivifying. War stirs the blood. It was in the midst of the world war, which I had forgotten about, that this change of heart took place. I got myself married overnight, to demonstrate to all and sundry that I didn't give a fuck one way or the other. Getting married was O.K. in their minds. I remember that, on the strength of the announcement, I raised five bucks immediately. My friend MacGregor paid for the license and even paid for the shave and haircut which he insisted I go through with in order to get married. They said you couldn't go without being shaved; I didn't see any reason why you couldn't get hitched up without a shave and haircut, but since it didn't cost me anything I submitted to it. It was interesting to see how everybody was eager to contribute something to our maintenance. All of a sudden, just because I had shown a bit of sense, they came flocking around us— and couldn't they do this and couldn't they do that for us? Of course the assumption was that now I would surely be going to work, now I would see that life is serious business. It never occurred to them that I might let my wife work for me. I was really very decent to her in the beginning. I wasn't a slave driver. All I asked for was carfare—to hunt for the mythical job—and a little pin money for cigarettes, movies, et cetera. The important things, such as books, music albums, gramophones, porterhouse steaks and such like I found we could get on credit, now that we were married. The installment plan had been invented expressly for guys like me. The down payment was easy—the rest I left to Providence. One has to live, they were always saying. Now, by God, that's what I said to myself—*One has to live! Live first and pay afterwards.* If I saw an overcoat I liked I went in and bought it. I would buy it a little in advance of the season too, to show that I was a serious-minded chap. Shit, I was a married man and soon I would probably be a father—I was entitled to a winter overcoat at least, no? And when I had the overcoat I thought of stout shoes to go with it—a pair of thick cordovans such as I had wanted all my life but never could afford. And when it grew bitter cold and I was out looking for the job I used to get terribly hungry sometimes—it's really healthy going out like that day after day prowling about the city in rain and snow and wind and hail—and so now and then I'd drop in to a cosy tavern and order myself a juicy porterhouse steak with onions and french fried potatoes. I took out life insurance and accident insurance too—it's important, when you're married, to do things like that, so they told me. Supposing I should drop dead one day—what *then?* I remember the guy telling me that, in order to clinch his argument. I had already told him I would sign up, but he must have forgotten it. I had said, yes, immediately, out of force of habit, but as I say, he had evidently overlooked it—or else it was against the code to sign a man up until you had delivered the full sales talk. Anyway, I was just getting ready to ask him how long it would take before you could make a loan on the policy when he popped the hypothetical question: *Supposing you should drop dead one day—what then?* I guess he thought I was a little off my nut the way I laughed at that. I laughed until the tears rolled down my face. Finally he said—"I don't see that I said anything so funny." "Well," I said, getting serious for a moment, "take a good look at me. Now tell me, do you think I'm the sort of fellow who gives a fuck what happens once he's dead?" He was quite taken aback by this, apparently, because the next thing he said was: "I don't think that's a very ethical attitude, Mr. Miller. I'm sure you wouldn't want your wife to..." "Listen," I said, "supposing I told you I don't give a fuck what happens to my wife when I die—what then?" And since this seemed to injure his ethical susceptibilities still more I added for good measure—"As far as I'm concerned you don't have to pay the insurance when I croak—I'm only doing this to make you feel good. I'm trying to help the world along, don't you see? You've got to live, haven't you? Well, I'm just putting a little food in your mouth, that's all. If you have anything else to sell, trot it out. I buy anything that sounds good. I'm a buyer not a seller. I like to see people looking happy—that's why I buy things. Now listen, how much did you say that would come to per week? Fifty-seven cents? Fine. What's fifty-seven cents? You see that piano—that comes to about thirty-nine cents a week, I think. Look around you... everything you see costs so much a week. You say, *if I should die, what then?* Do you suppose I'm going to die on all these people? That would be a hell of a joke. No, I'd rather have them come and take the things away—if I can't pay for them, I mean...." He was fidgeting about and there was a rather glassy stare in his eye, I thought. "Excuse me," I said, interrupting myself, "but wouldn't you like to have a little drink—to wet the policy?" He said he thought not, but I insisted, and besides, I hadn't signed the papers yet and my urine would have to be examined and approved of and all sorts of stamps and seals would have to be affixed—I knew all that crap by heart—

so I thought we might have a little snifter first and in that way protract the serious business, because honestly, buying insurance or buying anything was a real pleasure to me and gave me the feeling that I was just like every other citizen, *a man, what!* and not a monkey. So I got out a bottle of sherry (which is all that was allowed me) and I poured out a generous glassful for him, thinking to myself that it was fine to see the sherry going because maybe the next time they'd buy something better for me. "I used to sell insurance too once upon a time," I said, raising the glass to my lips. "Sure, I can sell anything. The only thing is—I'm lazy. Take a day like today—isn't it nicer to be indoors, reading a book or listening to the phonograph? Why should I go out and hustle for an insurance company? If I had been working today you wouldn't have caught me in—isn't that so? No, I think it's better to take it easy and help people out when they come along... like with you, for instance. It's much nicer to buy things than to sell them, don't you think? *If you have the money,* of course! In this house we don't need much money. As I was saying, the piano comes to about thirty-nine cents a week, or forty-two maybe, and the...."

"Excuse me, Mr. Miller," he interrupted, "but don't you think we ought to get down to signing these papers?"

"Why, of course." I said cheerfully. "Did you bring them all with you? Which one do you think we ought to sign first? By the way, you haven't got a fountain pen you'd like to sell me, have you?"

"Just sign right here," he said, pretending to ignore my remarks. "And here, that's it. Now then, Mr. Miller, I think I'll say good day—and you'll be hearing from the company in a few days."

"Better make it sooner," I remarked, leading him to the door, "because I might change my mind and commit suicide."

"Why, of course, why yes, Mr. Miller, certainly we will. Good day now, good day!"

Of course the installment plan breaks down eventually, even if you're an assiduous buyer such as I was. I certainly did my best to keep the manufacturers and the advertising men of America busy, but they were disappointed in me it seems. Everybody was disappointed in me. But there was one man in particular who was more disappointed in me than anyone and that was a man who had really made an effort to befriend me and whom I had let down. I think of him and the way he took me on as his assistant—so readily and graciously—because later, when I was hiring and firing like a forty-two horse caliber revolver, I was betrayed right and left myself, but by that time I had become so inoculated that it didn't matter a damn. But this man had gone out of his way to show me that he believed in me. He was the editor of a catalogue for a great mail order house. It was an enormous compendium of horseshit which was put out once a year and which took the whole year to make ready. I hadn't the slightest idea what it was all about and why I dropped into his office that day I don't know, unless it was because I wanted to get warm, as I had been knocking about the docks all day trying to get a job as a checker or some damned thing. It was cosy in his office and I made him a long speech so as to get thawed out. I didn't know what job to ask for—just a job, I said. He was a sensitive man and very kindhearted. He seemed to guess that I was a writer, or wanted to be a writer, because soon he was asking me what I liked to read and what was my opinion of this writer and that writer. It just happened that I had a list of books in my pocket—books I was searching for at the public library—and so I brought it out and showed it to him. "Great Scott!" he exclaimed, "do you really read these books?" I modestly shook my head in the affirmative, and then as often happened to me when I was touched off by some silly remark like that, I began to talk about Hamsun's *Mysteries* which I had just been reading. From then on the man was like putty in my hands. When he asked me if I would like to be his assistant he apologized for offering me such a lowly position; he said I could take my time learning the ins and outs of the job, he was sure it would be a cinch for me. And then he asked me if he couldn't lend me some money, out of his own pocket, until I got paid. Before I could say yes or no he had fished out a twenty-dollar bill and thrust it in my hand. Naturally I was touched. I was ready to work like a son of a bitch for him. Assistant editor—it sounded quite good, especially to the creditors in the neighborhood. And for a while I was so happy to be eating roast beef and chicken and tenderloins of pork that I pretended I liked the job. Actually it was difficult for me to keep awake. What I had to learn I had learned in a week's time. And after that? After that I saw myself doing penal servitude for life. In order to make the best of it I whiled away the time writing stories and essays and long letters to my friends. Perhaps they thought I was writing up new ideas for the company, because for quite a while nobody paid any attention to me. I thought it was a wonderful job. I had almost the whole day to myself, for my writing, having learned to dispose of the company's work in about an hour's time. I was so enthusiastic about my own private work that I gave orders to my underlings not to disturb me except at stipulated moments. I was sailing along like a breeze, the company paying me regularly and the slave drivers doing the work I had mapped out for them, when one day, just when I am in the midst of an important essay on *The Anti-Christ,* a man whom I had never seen before walks up to my desk, bends over my shoulder, and in a sarcastic tone of voice begins to read aloud what I had just written. I didn't need to inquire who he was or what he was up to—the only thought in my head was, and that I repeated to myself frantically—*Will I get an extra week's pay?* When it came time to bid good-by to my benefactor I felt a little ashamed of myself, particularly when he said, right off the bat like—"I tried to get you an extra week's pay but they wouldn't hear of it. I wish there was something I could do for you—you're only standing in your own way, you know. To tell you the truth, I still have the greatest faith in you—but I'm afraid you're going to have a hard time of it, for a while. You don't fit in anywhere. Some day you'll make a great writer, I feel sure of it. Well, excuse me," he added, shaking hands with me warmly, "I've got to see the boss. Good luck to you!"

I felt a bit cut up about the incident. I wished it had been possible to prove to him then and there that his faith was justified. I wished I could have justified myself before the whole world at that moment: I would have jumped off the Brooklyn Bridge if it would have convinced people that I wasn't a heartless son of a bitch. I had a heart as big as a whale, as I was soon to prove, but nobody was examining into my heart. Everybody was being let down hard—not only the installment companies, but the landlord, the butcher, the baker, the gas, water and electricity devils, *everybody*. If only I could get to believe in this business of work! To save my life I couldn't see it. I could only see that people were working their balls off because they didn't know any better. I thought of the speech I had made which won me the job. In some ways I was very much like Herr Nagel myself. No telling from minute to minute what I would do. No knowing whether I was a monster or a saint. Like so many wonderful men of our time, Herr Nagel was a desperate man—and it was this very desperation which made him such a likable chap. Hamsun didn't know what to make of this character himself: he knew he existed, and he knew that there was something more to him than a mere buffoon and a mystifier. I think he loved Herr Nagel more than any other character he created. And why? Because Herr Nagel was the unacknowledged saint which every artist is—the man who is ridiculed because his solutions, which are truly profound, seem too simple for the world. No man *wants* to be an artist— he is driven to it because the world refuses to recognize his proper leadership. Work meant nothing to me, because the real work to be done was being evaded. People regarded me as lazy and shiftless, but on the contrary I was an exceedingly active individual. Even if it was just hunting for a piece of tail, that was something, and well worth while, especially if compared to other forms of activity—such as making buttons or turning screws, or even removing appendixes. And why did people listen to me so readily when I applied for a job? Why did they find me entertaining? For the reason, no doubt, that I had always spent my time profitably. I brought them gifts—from my hours at the public library, from my idle ramblings through the streets, from my intimate experiences with women, from my afternoons at the burlesque, from my visits to the museum and the art galleries. Had I been a dud, just a poor honest bugger who wanted to work his balls off for so much a week, they wouldn't have offered me the jobs they did, nor would they have handed me cigars or taken me to lunch or lent me money, as they frequently did. I must have had something to offer which perhaps unknowingly they prized beyond horsepower or technical ability. I didn't know myself what it was, because I had neither pride, nor vanity, nor envy. About the big issues I was clear, but confronted by the petty details of life I was bewildered. I had to witness this same bewilderment on a colossal scale before I could grasp what it was all about. Ordinary men are often quicker in sizing up the practical situation: their ego is commensurate with the demands made upon it: the world is not very different from what they imagine it to be. But a man who is completely out of step with the rest of the world is either suffering from a colossal inflation of his ego or else the ego is so submerged as to be practically non-existent. Herr Nagel had to dive off the deep end in search of his true ego; his existence was a mystery, to himself and to everyone else. I couldn't afford to leave things hanging in suspense that way—the mystery was too intriguing. Even if I had to rub myself like a cat against every human being I encountered, I was going to get to the bottom of it. Rub long enough and hard enough and the spark will come!

The hibernation of animals, the suspension of life practiced by certain low forms of life, the marvelous vitality of the bedbug which lies in wait endlessly behind the wallpaper, the trance of the Yogi, the catalepsy of the pathologic individual, the mystic's union with the cosmos, the immortality of cellular life, all these things the artist learns in order to awaken the world at the propitious moment. The artist belongs to the X root race of man; he is the spiritual microbe, as it were, which carries over from one root race to another. He is not crushed by misfortune, because he is not a part of the physical, racial scheme of things. His appearance is always synchronous with catastrophe and dissolution; he is the cyclical being which lives in the epicycle. The experience which he acquires is never used for personal ends; it serves the larger purpose to which he is geared. Nothing is lost on him, however trifling. If he is interrupted for twenty-five years in the reading of a book he can go on from the page where he left off as though nothing had happened in between. Everything that happens in between, which is "life" to most people, is merely an interruption in his forward round. The eternality of his work, when he expresses himself, is merely the reflection of the automatism of life in which he is obliged to lie dormant, a sleeper on the back of sleep, waiting for the signal which will announce the moment of birth. This is the big issue, and this was always clear to me, even when I denied it. The dissatisfaction which drives one on from one word to another, one creation to another, is simply a protest against the futility of postponement. The more awake one becomes, as artistic microbe, the less desire one has to do anything. Fully awake, everything is just and there is no need to come out of the trance. Action, as expressed in creating a work of art, is a concession to the automatic principle of death. Drowning myself in the Gulf of Mexico I was able to partake of an active life which would permit the real self to hibernate until I was ripe to be born. I understood it perfectly, though I acted blindly and confusedly. I swam back into the stream of human activity until I got to the source of all action and there I muscled in, calling myself personnel director of a telegraph company, and allowed the tide of humanity to wash over me like great white-capped breakers. All this active life, preceding the final act of desperation, led me from doubt to doubt, blinding me more and more to the real self which, like a continent choked with the evidences of a great and thriving civilization, had already sunk beneath the surface of the sea. The colossal ego was submerged, and what people observed moving frantically above the surface was the periscope of the soul searching for its target. Everything that came within range had to be destroyed, if I were ever to rise again and ride the waves. This monster which rose now and then to fix its target with deadly aim, which dove again and roved and plundered ceaselessly would, when the time came, rise for the last time to reveal itself as an ark, would gather unto itself a pair of each kind and at last, when the floods abated, would settle down on the summit of a lofty mountain peak thence to open wide its doors and return to the world what had been preserved from the catastrophe.

If I shudder now and then, when I think of my active life, if I have nightmares, possibly it is because I think of all the men I robbed and murdered in my day sleep. I did everything which my nature bade me to do. Nature is eternally whispering in one's ear—"if you would survive you must kill!" Being human, you kill not like the animal but automatically, and the killing is disguised and its ramifications are endless, so that you kill without even thinking about it, you kill without need. The men who are the most honored are the greatest killers. They believe that they are serving their fellowmen, and they are sincere in believing so, but they are heartless murderers and at moments, when they come awake, they realize their crimes and perform frantic, quixotic acts of goodness in order to expiate their guilt. The goodness of man stinks more than the evil which is in him, for the goodness is not yet acknowledged, not an affirmation of the conscious self. Being pushed over the precipice, it is easy at the last moment to surrender all one's possessions, to turn and extend a last embrace to all who are left behind. How are we to stop the blind rush? How are we to stop the automatic process, each one pushing the other over the precipice?

As I sat at my desk, over which I had put up a sign reading "Do not abandon all hope ye who enter here!"—as I sat there saying Yes, No, Yes, No, I realized, with a despair that was turning to white frenzy, that I was a puppet in whose hands society had placed a Gatling gun. If I performed a good deed it was no different, ultimately, than if I had performed a bad deed. I was like an equals sign through which the algebraic swarm of humanity was passing. I was a rather important, active equals sign, like a general in time of war, but no matter how competent I were to become I could never change into a plus or a minus sign. Nor could anyone else, as far as I could determine. Our whole life was built up on this principle of equation. The integers had become symbols which were shuffled about in the interests of death. Pity, despair, passion, hope, courage—these were the temporal refractions caused by looking at equations from varying angles. To stop the endless juggling by turning one's back on it, or by facing it squarely and writing about it, would be no help either. In a hall of mirrors there is no way to turn your back on yourself. *I will not do this. I will do some other thing!* Very good. But can you do nothing at all? Can you stop thinking about not doing anything? Can you stop dead, and without thinking, radiate the truth which you know? That was the idea which lodged in the back of my head and which burned and burned, and perhaps when I was most expansive, most radiant with energy, most sympathetic, most willing, helpful, sincere, good, it was this fixed idea which was shining through, and automatically I was saying—"why, don't mention it.... nothing at all, I assure you.... no, please don't thank me, it's nothing," etc. etc. From firing the gun so many hundreds of times a day perhaps I didn't even notice the detonations any more; perhaps I thought I was opening pigeon traps and filling the sky with milky white fowl. Did you ever see a synthetic monster on the screen, a Frankenstein realized in flesh and blood? Can you imagine how he might be trained to pull a trigger and see pigeons flying at the same time? Frankenstein is not a myth: Frankenstein is a very real creation born of the personal experience of a sensitive human being. The monster is always more real when it does not assume the proportions of flesh and blood. The monster of the screen is nothing compared to the monster of the imagination; even the existent pathologic monsters who find their way into the police station are but feeble demonstrations of the monstrous reality which the pathologist lives with. But to be the monster and the pathologist at the same time—that is reserved for certain species of men who, disguised as artists, are supremely aware that sleep is an even greater danger than insomnia. In order not to fall asleep, in order not to become victims of that insomnia which is called "living," they resort to the drug of putting words together endlessly. This is *not* an automatic process, they say, because there is always present the illusion that they can stop it at will. But they cannot stop; they have only succeeded in creating an illusion, which is perhaps a feeble something, but it is far from being wide awake and neither active nor inactive. *I wanted to he wide awake without talking or writing about it, in order to accept life absolutely.* I mentioned the archaic men in the remote places of the world with whom I was communicating frequently. Why did I think these "savages" more capable of understanding me than the men and women who surrounded me? Was I crazy to believe such a thing? I don't think so in the least. These "savages" are the degenerate remnants of earlier races of man who, I believe, must have had a greater hold on reality. The immortality of the race is constantly before our eyes in these specimens of the past who linger on in withered splendor. Whether the human race is immortal or not is not my concern, but the vitality of the race does mean something to me, and that it should be active or dormant means even more. As the vitality of the new race banks down the vitality of the old races manifests itself to the waking mind with greater and greater significance. The vitality of the old races lingers on even in death, but the vitality of the new race which is about to die seems already nonexistent. *If a man were taking a swarming hive of bees to the river to drown them....* That was the image I carried about in me. If only I were the man, and not the bee! In some vague, inexplicable way I knew that I *was* the man, that I would not be drowned in the hive, like the others. Always, when we came forward in a group, I was signaled to stand apart; from birth I was favored that way, and, no matter what tribulations I went through, I knew they were not fatal or lasting. Also, another strange thing took place in me whenever I was called to stand forth. I knew that I was superior to the man who was summoning me! The tremendous humility which I practiced was not hypocritical but a condition provoked by the realization of the fateful character of the situation. The intelligence which I possessed, even as a stripling, frightened me; it was the intelligence of a "savage," which is always superior to that of civilized men in that it is more adequate to the exigencies of circumstance. It is a *life* intelligence, even though life has seemingly passed them by. I felt almost as if I had been shot forward into a round of existence which for the rest of mankind had not yet attained its full rhythm. I was obliged to mark time if I were to remain with them and not be shunted off to another sphere of existence. On the other hand, I was in many ways lower than the human beings about me. It was as though I had come out of the fires of hell not entirely purged. I had still a tail and a pair of horns, and when my passions were aroused I breathed a sulphurous poison which was annihilating. I was always called a "lucky devil." The good that happened to me was called "luck," and the evil was always regarded as a result of my shortcomings. Rather, as the fruit of my blindness. Rarely did anyone ever spot the evil in me! I was as adroit, in this respect, as the devil himself. But that I was frequently blind, everybody could see that. And at such times I was left alone, shunned, like the devil himself. Then I left the world, returned to the fires of hell—voluntarily. These comings and goings are as real to me, more real, in fact, than anything that happened in between. The friends who think they know me know nothing about me for the reason that the real me changed hands countless times. Neither the men who thanked me, nor the men who cursed me, knew with whom they were dealing. Nobody ever got on to a solid footing with me, because I was constantly liquidating my personality. I was keeping what is called the "personality" in abeyance for the moment when, leaving it to coagulate, it would adopt a proper human rhythm. I was hiding my face until the moment when I would find myself in step with the world. All this was, of course, a mistake. Even the role of artist is worth adopting, while marking time. Action is important, even if it entails futile activity. One should not say Yes, No, Yes, No, even seated in the highest place. One should not be drowned in the human tidal wave, even for the sake of becoming a Master. One must beat with his own rhythm—at any price. I accumulated thousands of years of experience in a few short years, but the experience was wasted because I had no need of it. I had already been crucified and marked by the cross; I had been born free of the need to suffer—and yet I knew no other way to struggle forward than to repeat the drama. All my intelligence was against it. Suffering is futile, my intelligence told me over and over, but I went on suffering *voluntarily*. Suffering has never taught me a thing; for others it may still be necessary, but for me it is nothing more than an algebraic demonstration of spiritual inadaptability. The whole drama which the man of today is acting out through suffering does not exist for me: it never did, actually. All my Calvaries were rosy crucifixions, pseudo-tragedies to keep the fires of hell burning brightly for the real sinners who are in danger of being forgotten.

Another thing... the mystery which enveloped my behavior grew deeper the nearer I came to the circle of uterine relatives. The mother from whose loins I sprang was a complete stranger to me. To begin with, after giving birth to me she gave birth to my sister, whom I usually refer to as my brother. My sister was a sort of harmless monster, an angel who had been given the body of an idiot. It gave me a strange feeling, as a boy, to be growing up and developing side by side with this being who was doomed to remain all her life a mental dwarf. It was impossible to be a brother to her because it was impossible to regard this atavistic hulk of a body as a "sister." She would have functioned perfectly, I imagine, among the Australian primitives. She might even have been raised to power and eminence among them, for, as I said, she was the essence of goodness, she knew no evil. But so far as living the civilized life goes she was helpless; she not only had no desire to kill but she had no desire to thrive at the expense of others. She was incapacitated for work, because even if they had been able to train her to make caps for high explosives, for example, she might absent-mindedly throw her wages in the river on the way home or she might give them to a beggar in the street. Often in my presence she was whipped like a dog for having performed some beautiful act of grace in her absent-mindedness, as they called it. Nothing was worse, I learned as a child, than to do a good deed without reason. I had received the same punishment as my sister, in the beginning, because I too had a habit of giving things away, especially new things which had just been given me. I had even received a beating once, at the age of five, for having advised my mother to cut a wart off her finger. She had asked me what to do about it one day and, with my limited knowledge of medicine, I told her to cut it off with the scissors, which she did, like an idiot. A few days later she got blood poisoning and then she got hold of me and she said—"you told me to cut it off, didn't you?" and she gave me a sound thrashing. From that day on I knew that I was born in the wrong household. From that day on I learned like lightning. Talk about adaptation! By the time I was ten I had lived out the whole theory of evolution. And there I was, evolving through all the phases of animal life and yet chained to this creature called my "sister" who was evidently a primitive being and who would never, even at the age of ninety, arrive at a comprehension of the alphabet. Instead of growing up like a stalwart tree I began to lean to one side, in complete defiance of the law of gravity. Instead of shooting out limbs and leaves I grew windows and turrets. The whole being, as it grew, was turning into stone, and the higher I shot up the more I defied the law of gravity. I was a phenomenon in the midst of the landscape, but one which attracted people and elicited praise. If the mother who bore us had only made another effort perhaps a marvelous white buffalo might have been born and the three of us might have been permanently installed in a museum and protected for life. The conversations which took place between the leaning tower of Pisa, the whipping post, the snoring machine and the pterodactyl in human flesh were, to say the least, a bit queer. Anything might be the subject of conversation—a bread crumb which the "sister" had overlooked in brushing the tablecloth or Joseph's coat of many colors which, in the old man's tailoring brain, might have been either double-breasted or cutaway or frock. If I came from the ice pond, where I had been skating all afternoon, the important thing was not the ozone which I had breathed free of charge, nor the geometric convolutions which were strengthening my muscles, but the little spot of rust under the clamps which, if not rubbed off immediately, might deteriorate the whole skate and bring about the dissolution of some pragmatic value which was incomprehensible to my prodigal turn of thought. This little rust spot, to take a trifling example, might entrain the most hallucinating results. Perhaps the "sister," in searching for the kerosene can, might overturn the jar of prunes which were being stewed and thus endanger all our lives by robbing us of the required calories in the morrow's meal. A severe beating would have to be given, not in anger, because that would disturb the digestive apparatus, but silently and efficiently, as a chemist would beat up the white of an egg in preparation for a minor analysis. But the "sister," not understanding the prophylactic nature of the punishment, would give vent to the most bloodcurdling screams and this would so affect the old man that he would go out for a walk and return two or three hours later blind drunk and, what was worse, scratching a little paint off the rolling doors in his blind staggers. The little piece of paint that had been chipped off would bring on a battle royal which was very bad for my dream life, because in my dream life I frequently changed places with my sister, accepting the tortures inflicted upon her and nourishing them with my supersensitive brain. It was in these dreams, always accompanied by the sound of glass breaking, of shrieks, curses, groans and sobs, that I gathered an unformulated knowledge of the ancient mysteries, of the rites of initiation, of the transmigration of souls and so on. It might begin with a scene from real life—the sister standing by the blackboard in the kitchen, the mother towering over her with a ruler, saying two and two makes how much? and the sister screaming *jive*. Bang! *no, seven,* Bang! *no, thirteen, eighteen, twenty!* I would be sitting at the table, doing my lessons, just as in real life during these scenes, when by a slight twist or squirm, perhaps as I saw the ruler come down on the sister's face, suddenly I would be in another realm where glass was unknown, as it was unknown to the Kickapoos or the Lenni-Lenape. The faces of those about me were familiar—they were my uterine relatives who, for some mysterious reason, failed to recognize me in this new *ambiance*. They were garbed in black and the color of their skin was ash gray, like that of the Tibetan devils. They were all fitted out with knives and other instruments of torture: they belonged to the caste of sacrificial butchers. I seemed to have absolute liberty and the authority of a god, and yet by some capricious turn of events the end would be that I'd be lying on the sacrificial block and one of my charming uterine relatives would be bending over me with a gleaming knife to cut out my heart. In sweat and terror I would begin to recite "my lessons" in a high, screaming voice, faster and faster, as I felt the knife searching for my heart. Two and two is four, five and five is ten, earth, air, fire, water, Monday, Tuesday, Wednesday, hydrogen, oxygen, nitrogen, Meocene, Pleocene, Eocene, the Father, the Son, the Holy Ghost, Asia, Africa, Europe, Australia, red, blue, yellow, the sorrel, the persimmon, the pawpaw, the catalpa... *faster and faster...* Odin, Wotan, Parsifal, King Alfred, Frederick the Great, the Hanseatic League, the Battle of Hastings, Thermopylae, 1492, 1776, 1812, Admiral Farragut, Pickett's charge, The Light Brigade, we are gathered here today, the Lord is my shepherd, I shall not, one and indivisible, no, 16, no, 27, help! murder! police!—and yelling louder and louder and going faster and faster I go completely off my nut and there is no more pain, no more terror, even though they are piercing me everywhere with knives. Suddenly I am absolutely calm and the body which is lying on the block, which they are still gouging with glee and ecstasy, feels nothing because I, the owner of it, have escaped. I have become a tower of stone which leans over the scene and watches with scientific interest. I have only to succumb to the law of gravity and I will fall on them and obliterate them. But I do not succumb to the law of gravity because I am too fascinated by the horror of it all. I am so fascinated, in fact, that I grow more and more windows. And as the light penetrates the stone interior of my being I can feel that my roots, which are in the earth, are alive and that I shall one day be able to remove myself at will from this trance in which I am fixed.

So much for the dream, in which I am helplessly rooted. But in actuality, when the dear uterine relatives come, I am as free as a bird and darting to and fro like a magnetic needle. If they ask me a question I give them five answers, each of which is better than the other; if they ask me to play a waltz I play a double-breasted sonata for the left hand; if they ask me to help myself to another leg of chicken I clean up the plate, dressing and all;

if they urge me to go out and play in the street I go out and in my enthusiasm I cut my cousin's head open with a tin can; if they threaten to give me a thrashing I say go to it, I don't mind! If they pat me on the head for my good progress at school I spit on the floor to show that I have still something to learn. I do everything they wish me to do *plus*. If they wish me to be quiet and say nothing I become as quiet as a rock: I don't hear when they speak to me, I don't move when I'm touched, I don't cry when I'm pinched, I don't budge when I'm pushed. If they complain that I'm stubborn I become as pliant and yielding as rubber. If they wish me to get fatigued so that I will not display too much energy I let them give me all kinds of work to do and I do the jobs so thoroughly that I collapse on the floor finally like a sack of wheat. If they wish me to be reasonable I become ultra-reasonable, which drives them crazy. If they wish me to obey I obey to the letter, which causes endless confusion. And all this because the molecular life of brother-and-sister is incompatible with the atomic weights which have been allotted us. Because she doesn't grow at all I grow like a mushroom; because she has no personality I become a colossus; because she is free of evil I become a thirty-two-branched candelabra of evil; because she demands nothing of anyone I demand everything; because she inspires ridicule everywhere I inspire fear and respect; because she is humiliated and tortured I wreak vengeance upon everyone, friend and foe alike; because she is helpless I make myself all-powerful. The gigantism from which I suffered was simply the result of an effort to wipe out the little stain of rust which had attached itself to the family skate, so to speak. That little stain of rust under the clamps made me a champion skater. It made me skate so fast and furiously that even when the ice had melted I was still skating, skating through mud, through asphalt, through brooks and rivers and melon patches and theories of economics and so forth. I could skate through hell, I was that fast and nimble.

But all this fancy skating was of no use—Father Coxcox, the Pan-American Noah, was always calling me back to the Ark. Every time I stopped skating there was a cataclysm—the earth opened up and swallowed me. I was a brother to every man and at the same time a traitor to myself. I made the most astounding sacrifices, only to find that they were of no value. Of what use was it to prove that I could be what was expected of me when I did not want to be any of these things? Every time you come to the limit of what is demanded of you, you are faced with the same problem—to be yourself! And with the first step you make in this direction you realize that there is neither plus nor minus; you throw the skates away and swim. There is no suffering any more because there is nothing which can threaten your security. And there is no desire to be of help to others even, because why rob them of a privilege which must be earned? Life stretches out from moment to moment in stupendous infinitude. Nothing can be more real than what you suppose it to be. Whatever you think the cosmos to be it is and it could not possibly be anything else as long as you are you and I am I. You live in the fruits of your action and your action is the harvest of your thought. Thought and action are one, because swimming you are in it and of it, and *it* is everything you desire it to be, no more, no less. Every stroke counts for eternity. The heating and cooling system is one system, and Cancer is separated from Capricorn only by an imaginary line. You don't become ecstatic and you are not plunged into violent grief; you don't pray for rain, neither do you dance a jig. You live like a happy rock in the midst of the ocean: you are fixed while everything about you is in turbulent motion. You are fixed in a reality which permits the thought that nothing is fixed, that even the happiest and mightiest rock will one day be utterly dissolved and fluid as the ocean from which it was born.

This is the musical life which I was approaching by first skating like a maniac through all the vestibules and corridors which lead from the outer to the inner. My struggles never brought me near it, nor did my furious activity, nor my rubbing elbows with humanity. All that was simply a movement from vector to vector in a circle which, however the perimeter expanded, remained withal parallel to the realm I speak of. The wheel of destiny can be transcended at any moment because at every point of its surface it touches the real world and only a spark of illumination is necessary to bring about the miraculous, to transform the skater to a swimmer and the swimmer to a rock. The rock is merely an image of the act which stops the futile rotation of the wheel and plunges the being into full consciousness. And full consciousness is indeed like an inexhaustible ocean which gives itself to sun and moon and also *includes* the sun and moon. Everything which is is born out of the limitless ocean of light—even the night.

Sometimes, in the ceaseless revolutions of the wheel, I caught a glimpse of the nature of the jump which it was necessary to make. To jump clear of the clockwork—that was the liberating thought. To be something more, something *different,* than the most brilliant maniac of the earth! The story of man on earth bored me. Conquest, even the conquest of evil, bored me. To radiate goodness is marvelous, because it is tonic, invigorating, vitalizing. But just *to be* is still more marvelous, because it is endless and requires no demonstration. To be is music, which is a profanation of silence in the interest of silence, and therefore beyond good and evil. Music is the manifestation of action without activity. It is the pure act of creation swimming on its own bosom. Music neither goads nor defends, neither seeks nor explains. Music is the noiseless sound made by the swimmer in the ocean of consciousness. It is a reward which can only be given by oneself. It is the gift of the god which one is because he has ceased thinking about God. It is an augur of the god which every one will become in due time, when all that *is* will *be* beyond imagination.

CODA

Not long ago I was walking the streets of New York. Dear old Broadway. It was night and the sky was an Oriental blue, as blue as the gold in the ceiling of the *Pagode,* rue de Babylone, when the machine starts clicking. I was passing exactly below the place where we first met. I stood there a moment looking up at the red lights in the windows. The music sounded as it always sounded—light, peppery, enchanting. I was alone and there were millions of people around me. It came over me, as I stood there, that I wasn't thinking of her any more; I was thinking of this book which I am writing, and the book had become more important to me than her, than all that had happened to us. Will this book be the truth, the whole truth, and nothing but the truth, so help me God? Plunging into the crowd again I wrestled with this question of "truth." For years I have been trying to tell this story and always the question of truth has weighed upon me like a nightmare. Time and again I have related to others the circumstances of our life, and I have always told the truth. But the truth can also be a lie. The truth is not enough. Truth is only the core of a totality which is inexhaustible.

I remember that the first time we were ever separated this idea of totality seized me by the hair. She pretended, when she left me, or maybe she believed it herself, that it was necessary for our welfare. I knew in my heart that she was trying to be free of me, but I was too cowardly to admit it to myself. But when I realized that she could do without me, even for a limited time, the truth which I had tried to shut out began to grow with alarming rapidity. It was more painful than anything I had ever experienced before, but it was also healing. When I was completely emptied, when the loneliness had reached such a point that it could not be sharpened any further, I suddenly felt that, to go on living, this intolerable truth had to be incorporated into something greater than the frame of personal misfortune. I felt that I had made an imperceptible switch into another realm, a realm of tougher, more elastic fiber, which the most horrible truth was powerless to destroy. I sat down to write her a letter telling her that I was so miserable over the thought of losing her that I had decided to begin a book about her, a book which would immortalize her. It would be a book, I said, such as no one had ever seen before. I rambled on ecstatically, and in the midst of it I suddenly broke off to ask myself why I was so happy.

Passing beneath the dance hall, thinking again of this book, I realized suddenly that our life had come to an end: I realized that the book I was planning was nothing more than a tomb in which to bury her—and the me which had belonged to her. That was some time ago, and ever since I have been trying to write it. Why is it so difficult? Why? Because the idea of an "end" is intolerable to me.

Truth lies in this knowledge of the end which is ruthless and remorseless. We can know the truth and accept it, or we can refuse the knowledge of it and neither die nor be born again. In this manner it is possible to live forever, a negative life as solid and complete, or as dispersed and fragmentary, as the atom. And if we pursue this road far enough, even this atomic eternity can yield to nothingness and the universe itself fall apart.

For years now I have been trying to tell this story; each time I have started out I have chosen a different route. I am like an explorer who, wishing to circumnavigate the globe, deems it unnecessary to carry even a compass. Moreover, from dreaming over it so long, the story itself has come to resemble a vast, fortified city, and I who dream it over and over, am outside the city, a wanderer, arriving before one gate after another too exhausted to enter. And as with the wanderer, this city in which my story is situated eludes me perpetually. Always in sight it nevertheless remains unattainable, a sort of ghostly citadel floating in the clouds. From the soaring, crenellated battlements flocks of huge white geese swoop down in steady, wedge-shaped formation. With the tips of their blue-white wings they brush the dreams that dazzle my vision. My feet move confusedly; no sooner do I gain a foothold than I am lost again. I wander aimlessly, trying to gain a solid, unshakable foothold whence I can command a view of my life, but behind me there lies only a welter of crisscrossed tracks, a groping, confused, encircling, the spasmodic gambit of the chicken whose head has just been lopped off.

Whenever I try to explain to myself the peculiar pattern which my life has taken, when I reach back to the first cause, as it were, I think inevitably of the girl I first loved. It seems to me that everything dates from that aborted affair. A strange, masochistic affair it was, ridiculous and tragic at the same time. Perhaps I had the pleasure of kissing her two or three times, the sort of kiss one reserves for a goddess. Perhaps I saw her alone several times. Certainly she could never have dreamed that for over a year I walked past her home every night hoping to catch a glimpse of her at the window. Every night after dinner I would get up from the table and take the long route which led to her home. She was never at the window when I passed and I never had the courage to stand in front of the house and wait. Back and forth I passed, back and forth, but never hide nor hair of her. Why didn't I write her? Why didn't I call her up? Once I remember summoning enough pluck to invite her to the theater. I arrived at her home with a bunch of violets, the first and only time I ever bought flowers for a woman. As we were leaving the theater the violets dropped from her corsage, and in my confusion I stepped on them. I begged her to leave them there, but she insisted on gathering them up. I was thinking how awkward I was—it was only long afterwards that I recalled the smile she had given me as she stooped down to pick up the violets.

It was a complete fiasco. In the end I ran away. Actually I was running away from another woman, but the day before leaving town I decided to see her once again. It was mid-afternoon and she came out to talk to me in the street, in the little areaway which was fenced off. She was already engaged to another man; she pretended to be happy about it but I could see, blind as I was, that she wasn't as happy as she pretended to be. If I had only said the word I am sure she would have dropped the other fellow; perhaps she would even have gone away with me. I preferred to punish myself. I said good-by nonchalantly and I went down the street like a dead man. The next morning I was bound for the Coast, determined to start a new life.

The new life was also a fiasco. I ended up on a ranch in Chula Vista, the most miserable man that ever walked the earth. There was this girl I loved and there was the other woman, for whom I felt only a profound pity. I had been living with her for two years, this other woman, but it seemed like a lifetime. I was twenty-one and she admitted to be thirty-six. Every time I looked at her I said to myself—when I am thirty she will be forty-five, when I am forty she will be fifty-five, when I am fifty she will be sixty-five. She had fine wrinkles under the eyes, laughing wrinkles, but wrinkles just the same. When I kissed her they were magnified a dozen times. She laughed easily, but her eyes were sad, terribly sad. They were Armenian eyes. Her hair, which had been red once, was now a peroxide blonde. Otherwise she was adorable—a Venusian body, a Venusian soul, loyal, lovable, grateful, everything a woman should be, *except that she was fifteen years older*. The fifteen years' difference drove me crazy. When I went out with her I thought only—how will it be ten years hence? Or else, what age does she seem to have now? Do I look old enough for her? Once we got back to the house it was all right. Climbing the stairs I would run my finger up her crotch, which used to make her whinny like a horse. If her son, who was almost my age, were in bed we would close the doors and lock ourselves in the kitchen. She'd lie on the narrow kitchen table and I'd slough it into her. It was marvelous. And what made it more marvelous was that with each performance I would say to myself—*This is the last time... tomorrow I will beat it!* And then, since she was the janitress, I would go down to the cellar and roll the ash barrels out for her. In the morning, when the son had left for work, I would climb up to the roof and air the bedding. Both she and the son had T.B.... Sometimes there were no table bouts. Sometimes the hopelessness of it all got me by the throat and I would put on my things and go for a walk. Now and then I forgot to return. And when I did that I was more miserable than ever, because I knew that she would be waiting for me with those large sorrowful eyes. I'd go back to her like a man who had a sacred duty to perform. I'd lie down on the bed and let her caress me; I'd study the wrinkles under her eyes and the roots of her hair which were turning red. Lying there like that, I would often think about the other one, the one I loved, would wonder if she were lying down for it too, or... Those long walks I took three hundred and sixty-five days of the year!—I would go over them in my mind lying beside the other woman. How many times since have I relived these walks! The dreariest, bleakest, ugliest streets man ever created. In anguish I relive these walks, these streets, these first smashed hopes. The window is there, but no Melisande; the garden too is there, but no sheen of gold. Pass and repass, the window always vacant. The evening star hangs low; Tristan appears, then Fidelio, and then Oberon. The hydra-headed dog barks with all his mouths and though there are no swamps I hear the frogs croaking everywhere. Same houses, same car lines, same everything. She is hiding behind the curtain, she is waiting for me to pass, she is doing this or doing that.... *but she is not there, never, never, never.* Is it a grand opera or is it a hurdy-gurdy playing? It is Amato bursting his golden lung; it is the *Rubaiyat,* it is Mount Everest, it is a moonless night, it is a sob at dawn, it is a boy making believe, it is Puss in the Boot, it is Mauna Loa, it is fox or astrakhan, it is of no stuff and no time, it is endless and it begins over and over, under the heart, in the back of the throat, in the soles of the feet, and why not just once, just once, for the love of Christ, just a shadow or a rustle of the curtain, or a breath on the windowpane, something once, if only a lie, something to stop the pain, to stop this walking up and down, up and down.... Walking homeward. Same houses, same lampposts, same everything. I walk past my own home, past the cemetery, past the gas tanks, past the car barns, past the reservoir, out into the open country. I sit beside the road with my head in my hands and sob. Poor bugger that I am, I can't contract my heart enough to burst the veins. I would like to suffocate with grief but instead I give birth to a rock.

Meanwhile the other one is waiting. I can see her again as she sat on the low stoop waiting for me, her eyes large and dolorous, her face pale and trembling with eagerness. *Pity* I always thought it was brought me back, but now as I walk toward her and see the look in her eyes I don't know any more what it is, only that we will go inside and lie together and she will get up half weeping, half laughing, and she will grow very silent and watch me, study me as I move about, and never ask me what is torturing me, never, never, because that is the one thing she fears, the one thing she dreads to know. *I don't love you!* Can't she hear me screaming it? *I don't love you!* Over and over I yell it, with lips tight, with hatred in my heart, with despair, with hopeless rage. But the words never leave my lips. I look at her and I am tongue-tied. I can't do it.... Time, time, endless time on our hands and nothing to fill it but lies.

Well, I don't want to rehearse the whole of my life leading up to the fatal moment—it is too long and too painful. Besides, did my life really lead up to this culminating moment? I doubt it. I think there were innumerable moments when I had the chance to make a beginning, but I lacked the strength and the faith. On the evening in question I deliberately walked out on myself: I walked right out of the old life and into the new. There wasn't the slightest effort involved. I was thirty then. I had a wife and child and what is called a "responsible" position. These are the facts and facts mean nothing. The truth is my desire was so great it became a reality. At such a moment what a man *does* is of no great importance, it's what he *is* that counts. It's at such a moment that a man becomes an angel. That is precisely what happened to me: *I became an angel.* It is not the purity of an angel which is so valuable, as the fact it can fly. An angel can break the pattern anywhere at any moment and find its heaven; it has the power to descend into the lowest matter and to extricate itself at will. The night in question I understood it perfectly. I was pure and inhuman, I was detached, I had wings. I was depossessed of the past and I had no concern about the future. I was beyond ecstasy. When I left the office I folded my wings and hid them beneath my coat.

The dance hall was just opposite the side entrance of the theater where I used to sit in the afternoons instead of looking for work. It was a street of theaters and I used to sit there for hours at a time dreaming the most violent dreams. The whole theatrical life of New York was concentrated in that one street, so it seemed. It was Broadway, it was success, fame, glitter, paint, the asbestos curtain and the hole in the curtain. Sitting on the steps of the theater I used to stare at the dance hall opposite, at the string of red lanterns which even in the summer afternoons were lit up. In every window there was a spinning ventilator which seemed to waft the music into the street, where it was broken by the jangled din of traffic. Opposite the other side of the dance hall was a comfort station and here too I used to sit now and then, hoping either to make a woman or make a touch. Above the comfort station, on the street level, was a kiosk with foreign papers and magazines; the very sight of these papers, of the strange languages in which they were printed, was sufficient to dislocate me for the day.

Without the slightest premeditation I climbed the stairs to the dance hall, went directly to the little window of the booth where Nick, the Greek, sat with a roll of tickets in front of him. Like the urinal below and the steps of the theater, this hand of the Greek now seems to me a separate and detached thing—the enormous hairy hand of an ogre borrowed from some horrible Scandinavian fairy tale. It was the hand which spoke to me always, the hand which said "Miss Mara will not be here tonight," or "Yes, Miss Mara is coming late tonight." It was this hand which I dreamt of as a child when I slept in the bedroom with the barred window. In my fevered sleep suddenly this window would light up, to reveal the ogre clutching at the bars. Night after night the hairy monster visited me, clutching at the bars and gnashing its teeth. I would awake in a cold sweat, the house dark, the room absolutely silent.

Standing at the edge of the dance floor I notice her coming toward me; she is coming with sails spread, the large full face beautifully balanced on the long, columnar neck. I see a woman perhaps eighteen, perhaps thirty, with blue-black hair and a large white face, a full white face in which the eyes shine brilliantly. She has on a tailored blue suit of duveteen. I remember distinctly now the fullness of her body, and that her hair was fine and straight, parted on the side, like a man's. I remember the smile she gave me—knowing, mysterious, fugitive—a smile that sprang up suddenly, like a puff of wind.

The whole being was concentrated in the face. I could have taken just the head and walked home with it; I could have put it beside me at night, on a pillow, and made love to it. The mouth and the eyes, when they opened up, the whole being glowed from them. There was an illumination which came from some unknown source, from a center hidden deep in the earth. I could think of nothing but the face, the strange, womblike quality of the smile, the engulfing immediacy of it. The smile was so painfully swift and fleeting that it was like the flash of a knife. This smile, this face, was borne aloft on a long white neck, the sturdy, swanlike neck of the medium—and of the lost and the damned.

I stand on the corner under the red lights, waiting for her to come down. It is about two in the morning and she is signing off. I am standing on Broadway with a flower in my buttonhole, feeling absolutely clean and alone. Almost the whole evening we have been talking about Strindberg, about a character of his named Henriette. I listened with such

tense alertness that I fell into a trance. It was as if, with the opening phrase, we had started on a race—in opposite directions. Henriette! Almost immediately the name was mentioned she began to talk about herself, without ever quite losing hold of Henriette.
Henriette was attached to her by a long, invisible string which she manipulated imperceptibly with one finger, like the street hawker who stands a little removed from the black
cloth on the sidewalk, apparently indifferent to the little mechanism which is jiggling on
the cloth, but betraying himself by the spasmodic movement of the little finger to which
the black thread is attached. Henriette is me, my real self, she seemed to be saying. She
wanted me to believe that Henriette was really the incarnation of evil. She said it so naturally, so innocently, with an almost subhuman candor—how was I to believe that she
meant it? I could only smile as though to show her I was convinced.

Suddenly I feel her coming. I turn my head. Yes, there she is coming full on, the sails
spread, the eyes glowing. For the first time I see now what a carriage she has. She comes
forward like a bird, a human bird wrapped in a soft fur. The engine is going full steam: I
want to shout, to give a blast that will make the whole world cock its ears. What a walk!
It's not a walk, it's a glide. Tall, stately, full-bodied, self-possessed, she cuts the smoke and
jazz and red-light glow like the queen mother of all the slippery Babylonian whores. On
the corner of Broadway just opposite the comfort station, this is happening. Broadway—
it's her realm. This is Broadway, this is New York, this is America. She's America on foot,
winged and sexed. She is the lubet, the abominate and the sublimate—with a dash of
hydrochloric acid, nitroglycerin, laudanum and powdered onyx. Opulence she has, and
magnificence; it's America right or wrong, and the ocean on either side. For the first time
in my life the whole continent hits me full force, hits me between the eyes. This is
America, buffaloes or no buffaloes, America the emery wheel of hope and disillusionment.
Whatever made America made her, bone, blood, muscle, eyeball, gait, rhythm, poise, confidence, brass and hollow gut. She's almost on top of me, the full face gleaming like calcium. The big soft fur is slipping from her shoulder. She doesn't notice it. She doesn't seem
to care if her clothes should drop off. She doesn't give a fuck about anything. It's America
moving like a streak of lightning toward the glass warehouse of red-blooded hysteria.
Amurrica, fur or no fur, shoes or no shoes. Amurrica C.O.D. *And scram, you bastards,
before we plug you!* It's got me in the guts, I'm quaking. Something's coming to me and
there's no dodging it. She's coming head on, through the plate glass window. If she would
only stop a second, if she would only let me be for just one moment. But no, not a single
moment does she grant me. Swift, ruthless, imperious, like Fate itself she is on me, a sword
cutting me through and through....

She has me by the hand, she holds it tight. I walk beside her without fear. Inside me
the stars are twinkling; inside me a great blue vault where a moment ago the engines were
pounding furiously.

One can wait a whole lifetime for a moment like this. The woman whom you never
hoped to meet now sits before you, and she talks and looks exactly like the person you
dreamed about. But strangest of all is that you never realized before that you had dreamed
about her. Your whole past is like a long sleep which would have been forgotten had there
been no dream. And the dream too might have been forgotten had there been no memory, but remembrance is there in the blood and the blood is like an ocean in which everything is washed away but that which is new and more substantial even than life: reality.

We are seated in a little booth in the Chinese restaurant across the way. Out of the corner of my eye I catch the flicker of the illuminated letters running up and down the sky. She is still talking about Henriette, or maybe it is about herself. Her little black bonnet, her bag and fur are lying beside her on the bench. Every few minutes she lights a fresh cigarette which burns away as she talks. There is no beginning nor end; it spurts out of her like a flame and consumes everything within reach. No knowing how or where she began. Suddenly she is in the midst of a long narrative, a fresh one, but it is always the same. Her talk is as formless as dream: there are no grooves, no walls, no exits, no stops. I have the feeling of being drowned in a deep mesh of words, of crawling painfully back to the top of the net, of looking into her eyes and trying to find there some reflection of the significance of her words—but I can find nothing, nothing except my own image wavering in a bottomless well. Though she speaks of nothing but herself I am unable to form the slightest image of her being. She leans forward, with elbows on the table, and her words inundate me; wave after wave rolling over me and yet nothing builds up inside me, nothing that I can seize with my mind. She's telling me about her father, about the strange life they led at the edge of Sherwood Forest where she was born, or at least she *was* telling me about this, but now it's about Henriette again, or is it Dostoevski?—I'm not sure—but anyway, suddenly I realize that she's not talking about any of these any more but about a man who took her home one night and as they stood on the stoop saying good-night he suddenly reached down and pulled up her dress. She pauses a moment as though to reassure me that this is what she means to talk about. I look at her bewilderedly. I can't imagine by what route we got to this point. *What man?* What had he been saying to her? I let her continue, thinking that she will probably come back to it, but no, she's ahead of me again and now it seems the man, *this* man, is already dead, a suicide, and she is trying to make me understand that it was an awful blow to her, but what she really seems to convey is that she is proud of the fact that she drove a man to suicide. I can't picture the man as dead; I can only think of him as he stood on her stoop lifting her dress, a man without a name but alive and perpetually fixed in the act of bending down to lift up her dress. There is another man who was her father and I see him with a string of race horses, or sometimes in a little inn just outside Vienna; rather I see him on the roof of the inn flying kites to while the time away. And between this man who was her father and the man with whom she was madly in love I can make no separation. He is someone in her life about whom she would rather not talk, but just the same she comes back to him all the time, and though I'm not sure that it was *not* the man who lifted up her dress neither am I sure that it wasn't the man who committed suicide. Perhaps it's the man whom she started to talk about when we sat down to eat. Just as we were sitting down I remember now that she began to talk rather hectically about a man whom she had just seen entering the cafeteria. She even mentioned his name, but I forgot it immediately. But I remember her saying that she had lived with him and that he had done something which she didn't like—she didn't say what—and so she had walked out on him, left him flat, without a word of explanation. And then, just as we were entering the chop suey joint, they ran into each other and she was still trembling over it as we sat down in the little booth.... For one long moment I have the most uneasy sensation. Maybe every word she uttered was a lie! Not an ordinary lie, no, something worse, something indescribable. Only sometimes the truth comes out like that too, especially if you think you're never going to see the person again. Sometimes you can tell a perfect stranger what you would never dare reveal to your most intimate friend. It's like going to sleep in the midst of a party; you become so interested in yourself that you go to sleep. And when you're sound asleep you begin to talk to someone, someone who was in the same room with you all the time and therefore understands everything even though you begin in the middle of a sentence. And perhaps this other person goes to sleep also, or was always asleep, and that's why it was so easy to encounter him, and if he doesn't say anything to disturb you then you know that what you are saying is real and true and that you are wide-awake and there is no other reality except this being wide-awake asleep. Never before have I been so wide-awake and so sound asleep at the same time. If the ogre in my dreams had really pushed the bars aside and taken me by the hand I would have been frightened to death and consequently now dead, that is, forever asleep and therefore always at large, and nothing would be strange any more, nor untrue, even if what happened did not happen. What happened must have happened long ago, in the night undoubtedly. And what is now happening is also happening long ago, in the night, and this is no more true than the dream of the ogre and the bars which would not give, except that now the bars are broken and she whom I feared has me by the hand and there is no difference between that which I feared and what is, because I was asleep and now I am wide-awake asleep and there is nothing more to fear, nor to expect, nor to hope for, but just this which is and which knows no end.

She wants to go. To go.... Again her haunch, that slippery glide as when she came down from the dance hall and moved into me. Again her words... "suddenly for no reason at all, he bent down and lifted up my dress." She's slipping the fur around her neck; the little black bonnet sets her face off like a cameo. The round, full face, with Slavic cheekbones. How could I dream this, never having seen it? How could I know that she would rise like this, close and full, the face full white and blooming like a magnolia? I tremble as the fullness of her thigh brushes me. She seems even a little taller than I, though she is not. It's the way she holds her chin. She doesn't notice where she's walking. She walks *over* things, on, on, with eyes wide open and staring into space. No past, no future. Even the present seems dubious. The self seems to have left her, and the body rushes forward, the neck full and taut, white as the face, full like the face. The talk goes on, in that low, throaty voice. No beginning, no end. I'm aware not of time nor the passing of time, but of timelessness. She's got the little womb in the throat hooked up to the big womb in the pelvis. The cab is at the curb and she is still chewing the cosmological chaff of the outer ego. I pick up the speaking tube and connect with the double uterus. Hello, hello, are you there? Let's go! Let's get on with it—cabs, boats, trains, naphtha launches; beaches, bedbugs, highways, byways, ruins; relics, old world, new world, pier, jetty; the high forceps, the swinging trapeze, the ditch, the delta, the alligators, the crocodiles, talk, talk, and more talk; then roads again and more dust in the eyes, more rainbows, more cloudbursts, more breakfast foods, more creams, more lotions. And when all the roads have been traversed and there is left only the dust of our frantic feet there will still remain the memory of your large full face so white, and the wide mouth with fresh lips parted, the teeth chalk white and each one perfect, and in this remembrance nothing can possibly change because this, like your teeth, is perfect....

It is Sunday, the first Sunday of my new life, and I am wearing the dog collar you fastened around my neck. A new life stretches before me. It begins with the day of rest. I lie back on a broad green leaf and I watch the sun bursting in your womb. What a clabber and clatter it makes! All this expressly for me, what? If only you had a million suns in you! If only I could lie here forever enjoying the celestial fireworks!

I lie suspended over the surface of the moon. The world is in a womblike trance: the inner and the outer ego are in equilibrium. You promised me so much that if I never come out of this it will make no difference. It seems to me that it is exactly 25,960 years since I have been asleep in the black womb of sex. It seems to me that I slept perhaps 365 years too many. But at any rate I am now in the right house, among the sixes, and what lies behind me is well and what lies ahead is well. You come to me disguised as Venus, but you are Lilith, and I know it. My whole life is in the balance; I will enjoy the luxury of this for one day. Tomorrow I shall tip the scales. Tomorrow the equilibrium will be finished; if I ever find it again it will be in the blood and not in the stars. It is well that you promise me so much. I need to be promised nearly everything, for I have lived in the shadow of the sun too long. I want light and chastity—and a solar fire in the guts. I want to be deceived and disillusioned so that I may complete the upper triangle and not be continually flying off the planet into space. I believe everything you tell me, but I know also that it will all turn out differently. I take you as a star and a trap, as a stone to tip the scales, as a judge that is blindfolded, as a hole to fall into, as a path to walk, as a cross and an arrow. Up to the present I traveled the opposite way of the sun; henceforth I travel two ways, as sun and as moon. Henceforth I take on two sexes, two hemispheres, two skies, two sets of everything. Henceforth I shall be double-jointed and double-sexed. Everything that happens will happen twice. I shall be as a visitor to this earth, partaking of its blessings and carrying off its gifts. I shall neither serve nor be served. I shall seek the end in myself.

I look out again at the sun—my first full gaze. It is blood-red and men are walking about on the rooftops. Everything above the horizon is clear to me. It is like Easter Sunday. Death is behind me and birth too. I am going to live now among the life maladies. I am going to live the spiritual life of the pygmy, the secret life of the little man in the wilderness of the bush. Inner and outer have changed places. Equilibrium is no longer the goal—the scales must be destroyed. Let me hear you promise again all those sunny things you carry inside you. Let me try to believe for one day, while I rest in the open, that the sun brings good tidings. Let me rot in splendor while the sun bursts in your womb. I believe all your lies implicitly. I take you as the personification of evil, as the destroyer of the soul, as the maharanee of the night. Tack your womb up on my wall, so that I may remember you. We must get going. Tomorrow, tomorrow....

September, 1938
Villa Seurat, Paris

BLACK SPRING

For Anais Nin

Can I be as I believe myself or as others believe me to be? Here is where these lines become a confession in the presence of my unknown and unknowable me, unknown and unknowable for myself. Here is where I create the legend wherein I must bury myself.
Miguel De Unamuno

1. The Fourteenth Ward

What is not in the open street is false, derived, that is to say, *literature.*

I am a patriot—of the Fourteenth Ward, Brooklyn, where I was raised. The rest of the United States doesn't exist for me, except as idea, or history, or literature. At ten years of age I was uprooted from my native soil and removed to a cemetery, a *Lutheran* cemetery, where the tombstones were always in order and the wreaths never faded.

But I was born in the street and raised in the street. «The post-mechanical open street where the most beautiful and hallucinating iron vegetation,» etc.... Born under the sign of Aries which gives a fiery, active, energetic and somewhat restless body. *With Mars in the ninth house!*

To be born in the street means to wander all your life, to be free. It means accident and incident, drama, movement. It means above all dream. A harmony of irrelevant facts which gives to your wandering a metaphysical certitude. In the street you learn what human beings really are; otherwise, or afterwards, you invent them. What is not in the open street is false, derived, that is to say, *literature.* Nothing of what is called «adventure» ever approaches the flavor of the street. It doesn't matter whether you fly to the Pole, whether you sit on the floor of the ocean with a pad in your hand, whether you pull up nine cities one after the other, or whether, like Kurtz, you sail up the river and go mad. No matter how exciting, how intolerable the situation, there are always exits, always ameliorations, comforts, compensations, newspapers, religions. But once there was none of this. Once you were free, wild, murderous—

The boys you worshiped when you first came down into the street remain with you all your life. They are the only real heroes. Napoleon, Lenin, Capone—all fiction. Napoleon is nothing to me in comparison with Eddie Carney, who gave me my first black eye. No man I have ever met seems as princely, as regal, as noble, as Lester Reardon who, by the mere act of walking down the street, inspired fear and admiration. Jules Verne never led me to the places that Stanley Borowski had up his sleeve when it came dark. Robinson Crusoe lacked imagination in comparison with Johnny Paul. All these boys of the Fourteenth Ward have a flavor about them still. They were not invented or imagined: they were real. Their names ring out like gold coins— Tom Fowler, Jim Buckley, Matt Owen, Rob Ramsay, Harry Martin, Johnny Dunne, to say nothing of Eddie Carney or the great Lester Reardon. Why, even now when I say Johnny Paul the names of the saints leave a bad taste in my mouth. Johnny Paul was the living Odyssey of the Fourteenth Ward; that he later became a truck driver is an irrelevant fact.

Before the great change no one seemed to notice that the streets were ugly or dirty. If the sewer mains were opened you held your nose. If you blew your nose you found snot in your handkerchief and not your nose. There was more of inward peace and contentment. There was the saloon, the race track, bicycles, fast women and trot horses. Life was still moving along leisurely. In the Fourteenth Ward, at least. Sunday mornings no one was dressed. If Mrs. Gorman came down in her wrapper with dirt in her eyes to bow to the priest—"Good morning, Father!» «Good morning, Mrs. Gorman!»—the street was purged of all sin. Pat McCarren carried his handkerchief in the tailflap of his frock coat; it was nice and handy there, like the shamrock in his buttonhole. The foam was on the lager and people stopped to chat with one another.

In my dreams I come back to the Fourteenth Ward as a paranoiac returns to his obsessions. When I think of those steel-gray battleships in the Navy Yard I see them lying there in some astrologic dimension in which I am the gunnersmith, the chemist, the dealer in high explosives, the undertaker, the coroner, the cuckold, the sadist, the lawyer and contender, the scholar, the restless one, the jolt-head, and the brazen-faced.

Where others remember of their youth a beautiful garden, a fond mother, a sojourn at the seashore, I remember, with a vividness as if it were etched in acid, the grim, soot-covered walls and chimneys of the tin factory opposite us and the bright, circular pieces of tin that were strewn in the street, some bright and gleaming, others rusted, dull, copperish, leaving a stain on the fingers; I remember the ironworks where the red furnace glowed and men walked toward the glowing pit with huge shovels in their hands, while outside were the shallow wooden forms like coffins with rods through them on which you scraped your shins or broke your neck. I remember the black hands of the ironmolders, the grit that had sunk so deep into the skin that nothing could remove it, not soap, nor elbow grease, nor money, nor love, nor death. Like a black mark on them! Walking into the furnace like devils with black hands—and later, with flowers over them, cool and rigid in their Sunday suits, not even the rain can wash away the grit. All these beautiful gorillas going up to God with swollen muscles and lumbago and black hands....

For me the whole world was embraced in the confines of the Fourteenth Ward. If anything happened outside it either didn't happen or it was unimportant. If my father went outside that world to fish it was of no interest to me. I remember only his boozy breath when he came home in the evening and opening the big green basket spilled the squirming, goggle-eyed monsters on the floor. If a man went off to the war I remember only that he came back of a Sunday afternoon and standing in front of the minister's house puked up his guts and then wiped it up with his vest. Such was Rob Ramsay, the minister's son. I remember that everybody liked Rob Ramsay—he was the black sheep of the family. They liked him because he was a good-for-nothing and he made no bones about it. Sundays or Wednesdays made no difference to him: you could see him coming down the street under the drooping awnings with his coat over his arm and the sweat rolling down his face; his legs wobbly, with that long, steady roll of a sailor coming ashore after a long cruise; the tobacco juice dribbling from his lips, together with warm, silent curses and some loud and foul ones too. The utter indolence, the insouciance of the man, the obscenities, the sacrilege. Not a man of God, like his father. No, a man who inspired love! His frailties were human frailties and he wore them jauntily, tauntingly, flauntingly, like banderillas. He would come down the warm open street with the gas mains bursting and the air full of sun and shit and oaths and maybe his fly would be open and his suspenders undone, or maybe his vest bright with vomit. Sometimes he came charging down the street, like a bull skidding on all fours, and then the street cleared magically, as if the manholes had opened up and swallowed their offal. Crazy Willy Maine would be standing on the shed over the paint shop, with his pants down, jerking away for dear life. There they stood in the dry electrical crackle of the open street with the gas mains bursting. A tandem that broke the minister's heart.

That was how he was then, Rob Ramsay. A man on a perpetual spree. He came back from the war with medals, and with fire in his guts. He puked up in front of his own door and he wiped up his puke with his own vest. He could clear the street quicker than a machine gun. *Faugh a balla!* That was his way. And a little later, in his warm-heartedness, in that fine, careless way he had, he walked off the end of a pier and drowned himself.

I remember him so well and the house he lived in. Because it was on the doorstep of Rob Ramsay's house that we used to congregate in the warm summer evenings and watch the goings-on over the saloon across the street. A coming and going all night long and nobody bothered to pull down the shades. Just a stone's throw away from the little burlesque house called The Bum. All around The Bum were the saloons, and Saturday nights there was a long line outside, milling and pushing and squirming to get at the ticket window. Saturday nights, when the Girl in Blue was in her glory, some wild tar from the Navy Yard would be sure to jump out of his seat and grab off one of Millie de Leon's garters. And a little later that night they'd be sure to come strolling down the street and turn in at the family entrance. And soon they'd be standing in the bedroom over the saloon, pulling off their tight pants and the women yanking off their corsets and scratching themselves like monkeys, while down below they were scuttling the suds and biting each other's ears off, and such a wild, shrill laughter all bottled up inside there, like dynamite evaporating. All this from Rob Ramsay's doorstep, the old man upstairs saying his prayers over a kerosene lamp, praying like an obscene nanny goat for an end to come, or when he got tired of praying coming down in his nightshirt, like an old leprechaun, and belaying us with a broomstick.

From Saturday afternoon on until Monday morning it was a period without end, one thing melting into another. Saturday morning already—how it happened God only knows—you could *feel* the war vessels lying at anchor in the big basin. Saturday mornings my heart was in my mouth. I could see the decks being scrubbed down and the guns polished and the weight of those big sea monsters resting on the dirty glass lake of the basin was a luxurious weight on me. I was already dreaming of running away, of going to far places. But I got only as far as the other side of the river, about as far north as Second Avenue and Twenty-eighth Street, via the Belt Line. There I played the Orange Blossom Waltz and in the entr'actes I washed my eyes at the iron sink. The piano stood in the rear of the saloon. The keys were very yellow and my feet wouldn't reach to the pedals. I wore a velvet suit because velvet was the order of the day.

Everything that passed on the other side of the river was sheer lunacy: the sanded floor, the argand lamps, the mica pictures in which the snow never melted, the crazy Dutchmen with steins in their hands, the iron sink that had grown such a mossy coat of slime, the woman from Hamburg whose ass always hung over the back of the chair, the courtyard choked with sauerkraut.... Everything in three-quarter time that goes on forever. I walk between my parents, with one hand in my mother's muff and the other in my father's sleeve. My eyes are shut tight, tight as clams which draw back their lids only to weep.

All the changing tides and weather that passed over the river are in my blood. I can still feel the slipperiness of the big handrail which I leaned against in fog and rain, which sent through my cool forehead the shrill blasts of the ferryboat as she slid out of the slip. I can still see the mossy planks of the ferry slip buckling as the big round prow grazed her sides and the green, juicy water sloshed through the heaving, groaning planks of the slip. And overhead the sea gulls wheeling and diving, making a dirty noise with their dirty beaks, a hoarse, preying sound of inhuman feasting, of mouths fastened down on refuse, of scabby legs skimming the green-churned water.

One passes imperceptibly from one scene, one age, one life to another. Suddenly, walking down a street, be it real or be it a dream, one realizes for the first time that the years have flown, that all this has passed forever and will live on only in memory; and then the memory turns inward with a strange, clutching brilliance and one goes over these scenes and incidents perpetually, in dream and reverie, while walking a street, while lying with a woman, while reading a book, while talking to a stranger ... suddenly, but always with terrific insistence and always with terrific accuracy, these memories intrude, rise up like ghosts and permeate every fiber of one's being. Henceforward everything moves on shifting levels—our thoughts, our dreams, our actions, our whole life. A parallelogram in which we drop from one platform of our scaffold to another. Henceforward we walk split into myriad fragments, like an insect with a hundred feet, a centipede with soft-stirring feet that drinks in the atmosphere; we walk with sensitive filaments that drink avidly of past and future, and all things melt into music and sorrow; we walk against a united world, asserting our dividedness. All things, as we walk, splitting with us into a myriad iridescent fragments. The great fragmentation of maturity. The great change. In youth we were whole and the terror and pain of the world penetrated us through and through. There was no sharp separation between joy and sorrow: they fused into one, as our waking life fuses with dream and sleep. We rose one being in the morning and at night we went down into an ocean, drowned out completely, clutching the stars and the fever of the day.

And then comes a time when suddenly all seems to be reversed. We live in the mind, in ideas, in fragments. We no longer drink in the wild outer music of the streets—we *remember* only. Like a monomaniac we relive the drama of youth. Like a spider that picks up the thread over and over and spews it out according to some obsessive, logarithmic pattern. If we are stirred by a fat bust it is the fat bust of a whore who bent over on a rainy night and showed us for the first time the wonder of the great milky globes; if we are stirred by the reflections on a wet pavement it is because at the age of seven we were suddenly speared by a premonition of the life to come as we stared unthinkingly into that bright, liquid mirror of the street. If the sight of a swinging door intrigues us it is the memory of a summer's evening when all the doors were swinging softly and where the light bent down to caress the shadow there were golden calves and lace and glittering parasols and through the chinks in the swinging door, like fine sand sifting through a bed of rubies, there drifted the music and the incense of gorgeous unknown bodies. Perhaps when that door parted to give us a choking glimpse of the world, perhaps then we had the first intimation of the great impact of sin, the first intimation that here over little round tables spinning in the light, our feet idly scraping the sawdust, our hands touching the cold stem of a glass, that here over these little round tables which later we are to look at with such yearning and reverence, that here, I say, we are to feel in the years to come the first iron of love, the first stains of rust, the first black, clawing hands of the pit, the bright circular pieces of tin in the streets, the gaunt soot-colored chimneys, the bare elm tree that lashes out in the summer's lightning and screams and shrieks as the rain beats down, while out of the hot earth the snails scoot away miraculously and all the air turns blue and sulphurous. Here over these tables, at the first call, the first touch of a hand, there is to come the bitter, gnawing pain that gripes at the bowels; the wine turns sour in our bellies and a pain rises from the soles of the feet and the round tabletops whirl with the anguish and the fever in our bones at the soft, burning touch of a hand. Here there is buried legend after legend of youth and melancholy, of savage nights and mysterious bosoms dancing on the wet mirror of the pavement, of women chuckling softly as they scratch themselves, of wild sailors' shouts, of long queues standing in front of the lobby, of boats brushing each other in the fog and tugs snorting furiously against the rush of tide while up on the Brooklyn Bridge a man is standing in agony, wait-to jump, or waiting to write a poem, or waiting for the blood to leave his vessels because if he advances another foot the pain of his love will kill him.

The plasm of the dream is the pain of separation. The dream lives on after the body is buried. We walk the streets with a thousand legs and eyes, with furry antennae picking up the slightest clue and memory of the past. In the aimless to and fro we pause now and then, like long, sticky plants, and we swallow whole the live morsels of the past. We open up soft and yielding to drink in the night and the oceans of blood which drowned the sleep of our youth. We drink and drink with an insatiable thirst. We are never whole again, but living in fragments, and all our parts separated by thinnest membrane. Thus when the fleet maneuvers in the Pacific it is the whole saga of youth flashing before your eyes, the dream of the open street and the sound of gulls wheeling and diving with garbage in their beaks; or it's the sound of the trumpet and flags flying and all the unknown parts of the earth sailing before your eyes without dates or meaning, wheeling like the tabletop in an iridescent sheen of power and glory. Day comes when you stand on the Brooklyn Bridge looking down into black funnels belching smoke and the gun barrels gleam and the buttons gleam and the water divides miraculously under the sharp, cutting prow, and like ice and lace, like a breaking and a smoking, the water churns green and blue with a cold incandescence, with the chill of champagne and burnt gills. And the prow cleaves the waters in an unending metaphor: the heavy body of the vessel moves on, with the prow ever dividing, and the weight of her is the unweighable weight of the world, the sinking down into unknown barometric pressures, into unknown geologic fissures and caverns where the waters roll melodiously and the stars turn over and die and hands reach up and grasp and clutch and never seize nor close but clutch and grasp while the stars die out one by one, myriads of them, myriads and myriads of worlds sinking down into cold incandescence, into fuliginous night of green and blue with broken ice and the burn of champagne and the hoarse cry of gulls, their beaks swollen with barnacles, their foul garbaged mouths stuffed forever under the silent keel of the ship.

One looks down from the Brooklyn Bridge on a spot of foam or a little lake of gasoline or a broken splinter or an empty scow; the world goes by upside down with pain and light devouring the innards, the sides of flesh bursting, the spears pressing in against the cartilage, the very armature of the body floating off into nothingness. Passes through you crazy words from the ancient world, signs and portents, the writing on the wall, the chinks of the saloon door, the cardplayers with their clay pipes, the gaunt tree against the tin factory, the black hands stained even in death. One walks the street at night with the bridge against the sky like a harp and the festered eyes of sleep burn into the shanties, deflower the walls; the stairs collapse in a smudge and the rats scamper across the ceiling; a voice is nailed against the door and long creepy things with furry antennae and thousand legs drop from the pipes like beads of sweat. Glad, murderous ghosts with the shriek of night-wind and the curses of warm-legged men; low, shallow coffins with rods through the body; grief-spit drooling down into the cold, waxen flesh, searing the dead eyes, the hard, chipped lids of dead clams. One walks around in a circular cage on shifting levels, stars and clouds under the escalator, and the of the cage revolve and there are no men and women without tails or claws, while over all things are written the letters of the alphabet in iron and permanganate. One walks round and round in a circular cage to the roll of drum-fire; the theater burns and the actors go on mouthing their lines; the bladder bursts, the teeth fall out, but the wailing of the clown is like the noise of dandruff falling. One walks around on moonless nights in the valley of craters, valley of dead fires and whitened skulls, of birds without wings. Round and round one walks, seeking the hub and nodality, but the fires are burned to ash and the sex of things is hidden in the finger of a glove.

And then one day, as if suddenly the flesh came undone and the blood beneath the flesh had coalesced with the air, suddenly the whole world roars again and the very skeleton of the body melts like wax. Such a day it may be when first you encounter Dostoievsky. You remember the smell of the tablecloth on which the book rests; you look at the clock and it is only five minutes from eternity; you count the objects on the mantelpiece because the sound of numbers is a totally new sound in your mouth, because everything new and old, or touched and forgotten, is a fire and a mesmerism. Now every door of the cage is open and whichever way you walk is a straight line toward infinity, a straight, mad line over which the breakers roar and great rocs of marble and indigo swoop to lower their fevered eggs. Out of the waves beating phosphorescent step proud and prancing the enameled horses that marched with Alexander, their tight-proud bellies glowing with calcium, their nostrils dipped in laudanum. Now it is all snow and lice, with the great band of Orion slung around the ocean's crotch.

It was-exactly five minutes past seven, at the corner of Broadway and Kosciusko Street, when Dostoievsky first flashed across my horizon. Two men and a woman were dressing a shop window. From the middle of the upper legs down the mannikins were all wire. Empty shoe boxes lay banked against the window like last year's snow....

That is how Dostoievsky's name came in. Unostentatiously. Like an old shoe box. The Jew who pronounced his name for me had thick lips; he could not say Vladivostok, for instance, nor Carpathians—but he could say Dostoievsky divinely. Even now, when I say Dostoievsky, I see again his big, blubbery lips and the thin thread of spittle stretching like a rubber band as he pronounced the word. Between his two front teeth there was a more than usual space; it was exactly in the middle of this cavity that the word Dostoievsky quivered and stretched, a thin, iridescent film of sputum in which all the gold of twilight had collected—for the sun was just going down over Kosciusko Street and the traffic overhead was breaking into a spring thaw, a chewing and grinding noise as if the mannikins in their wire legs were chewing each other alive. A little later, when I came to the land of the Houyhnhnms, I heard the same chewing and grinding overhead and again the spittle in a man's mouth quivered and stretched and shone iridescent in a dying sun. This time it is at the Dragon's Gorge: a man standing over me with a rattan stick and banging away with a wild Arabian smile. Again, as if my brain were a uterus, the walls of the world gave Henry. The name Swift was like a clear, hard pissing aghast the tin-plate lid of the world. Overhead the green fire-eater, his delicate intestines wrapped in tarpaulin; two enormous milk-white teeth champing down over a belt of black-greased cogs connecting with the shooting gallery and the Turkish Baths; the belt of cogs slipping over a frame of bleached bones. The green dragon of Swift moves over the cogs with an endless pissing sound, grinding down fine and foreshortened the human-sized midgets that are sucked in like macaroni. In and out of the esophagus, up and down and around the scapular bones and the mastoid delta, falling through the bottomless pit of the viscera, gurgitating and exgurgitating, the crotch spreading and slipping, the cogs moving on relentlessly, chewing alive all the fine, foreshortened macaroni hanging by the whiskers from the dragon's red gulch. I look into the milk-white smile of the barker, that fanatical Arabian smile which came out of the Dreamland fire, and then I step quietly into the open belly of the dragon. Between the crazy slats of the skeleton that holds the revolving cogs the land of the Houyhnhnms spreads out before me; that hissing, pissing noise in my ears as if the language of men were made of seltzer water. Up and down over the greasy black belt, over the Turkish baths, through the house of the winds, over the sky-blue waters, between the clay pipes and the silver balls dancing on liquid jets: the infra-human world of fedoras and banjos, of bandannas and black cigars; butterscotch stretching from peg to Winnipeg, beer bottles bursting, spun-glass molasses and hot tamales, surf-roar and griddle sizzle, foam and eucalyptus, dirt, chalk, confetti, a woman's white thigh, a broken oar; the razzle-dazzle of wooden slats, the meccano puzzle, the smile that never comes off, the wild Arabian smile with spits of fire, the red gulch and the green intestines....

O world, strangled and collapsed, where are the Strong white teeth? O world, sinking with the silver balls and the corks and the life-preservers, where are the rosy scalps? O glab and glairy, O glabrous world now chewed to a frazzle, under what dead moon do you lie cold and gleaming?

2. Third or Fourth Day of Spring

To piss warm and drink cold, as Trimalchio says, because our mother the earth is in the middle, made round like an egg, and has all good things in herself, like a honeycomb.

The house wherein I passed the most important years of my life had only three rooms. One was the room in which my grandfather died. At the funeral my mother's grief was so violent that she almost yanked my grandfather out of the coffin. He looked ridiculous, my dead grandfather, weeping with his daughter's tears. As if he were weeping over his own funeral.

In another room my aunt gave birth to twins. When I heard *twins,* she being so thin and barren, I said to myself—why twins? why not triplets? why not quadruplets? why stop? So thin and scraggly she was, and the room so small—with green walls and a dirty iron sink in the corner. Yet it was the only room in the house which could produce twins—or triplets, or jackasses.

The third room was an alcove where I contracted the measles, chicken pox, scarlet fever, diphtheria, et cetera: all the lovely diseases of childhood which make time stretch out in everlasting bliss and agony, especially when Providence has provided a window over the bed with bars and ogres to claw at them and sweat as thick as carbuncles, rapid as a river and sprouting, sprouting as if it were always spring and tropics, with thick tenderloin steaks for hands and feet heavier than lead or light as snow, feet and hands separated by oceans of time or incalculable latitudes of light, the little knob of the brain hidden away like a grain of sand and the toenails rotting blissfully under the ruins of Athens. In this room I heard nothing but inanities. With each fresh, lovely disease my parents became more addlepated. («Just think, when you were a little baby I took you to the sink and I said baby you don't want to drink from the bottle any more do you and you said No and I smashed the bottle in the sink.») Into this room softly treading («treading softly,» said General Smerdiakov) came Miss Sonowska, spinster of dubious age with a green-black dress. And with her came the smell of old cheese—her sex had turned rancid under the dress. But Miss Sonowska also brought with her the sack of Jerusalem and the nails that so pierced the hands of Jesus that the holes have never disappeared. After the Crusades the Black Death; after Columbus syphilis; after Miss Sonowska schizophrenia.

Schizophrenia! Nobody thinks any more how marvelous it is that the whole world is diseased. No point of reference, no frame of health. God might just as well be typhoid fever. No absolutes. Only light years of deferred progress. When I think of those centuries in which all Europe grappled with the Black Death I realize how radiant life can be if only we are bitten in the right place! The dance and fever in the midst of that corruption! Europe may never again dance so ecstatically. And syphilis! The advent of syphilis! There it was, like a morning star hanging over the rim of the world.

In 1927 I sat in the Bronx listening to a man reading from the diary of a drug addict. The man could scarcely read, he was laughing so hard. Two phenomena utterly disparate: a man lying in luminol, so taut that his feet stretch beyond the window, leaving the upper half of his body in ecstasy; the other man, who is the same man, sitting in the Bronx and laughing his guts out because he doesn't understand.

Aye, the great sun of syphilis is setting. *Low visibility:* forecast for the Bronx, for America, for the whole modern world. Low visibility accompanied by great gales of laughter. No new stars on the horizon. *Catastrophes ... only catastrophes!*

I am thinking of that age to come when God is born again, when men will fight and kill for God as now and for a long time to come men are going to fight for food. I am thinking of that age when work will be forgotten and books assume their true place in life, when perhaps there will be no more books, just one great big book—a Bible. For me the book is the man and my book is the man I am, the confused man, the negligent man, the reckless man, the lusty, obscene, boisterous, thoughtful, scrupulous, lying, diabolically truthful man that I am. I am thinking that in that age to come I shall not be overlooked. Then my history will become important and the scar which I leave upon the face of the world will have significance. I can not forget that I am making history, a history on the side which, like a chancre, will eat away the other meaningless history. I regard myself not as a book, a record, a document, but as a history of our time—a history of *all* time.

If I was unhappy in America, if I craved more room, more adventure, more freedom of expression, it was because I needed these things. I am grateful to America for having made me realize my needs. I served my sentence there. At present I have no needs. I am a man without a past and without a future. *I am*—that is all. I am not concerned with your likes and dislikes; it doesn't matter to me whether you are convinced that what I say is so or not. It is all the same to me if you drop me here and now. I am not an atomizer from which you can squeeze a thin spray of hope. I see America spreading disaster. I see America as a black curse upon the world. I see a long night settling in and that mushroom which has poisoned the world withering at the roots.

And so it is with a premonition of the end—be it tomorrow or three hundred years hence—that I feverishly write this book. So it is too that my thoughts sputter out now and then, that I am obliged to rekindle the flame again and again, not with courage alone, but with desperation—for there is no one I can trust to say these things for me. My faltering and groping, my search for any and every means of expression, is a sort of divine stuttering. *I am dazzled by the glorious collapse of the world!*

Every evening, after dinner, I take the garbage down to the courtyard. Coming up I stand with empty pail at the staircase window gazing at the Sacre Coeur high up on the hill of Montmartre. Every evening, when I take the garbage down, I think of myself standing out on a high hill in resplendent whiteness. It is no sacred heart that inspires me, no Christ I am thinking of. Something better than a Christ, something bigger than a heart, something beyond God Almighty I think of—myself. *I am a man.* That seems to me sufficient.

I am a man of God and a man of the Devil. To each his due. Nothing eternal, nothing absolute. Before me always the image of the body, our triune god of penis and testicles. On the right, God the Father; on the left and hanging a little lower, God the Son; and between and above them the Holy Ghost. I can never forget that this holy trinity is man-made, that it will undergo infinite changes—but as long as we come out of wombs with arms and legs, as long as there are stars above us to drive us mad and grass under our feet to cushion the wonder in us, just so long will this body serve for all the tunes that we may whistle.

Today it is the third or fourth day of spring and I am sitting at the Place Clichy in full sunshine. Today, sitting here in the sun, I tell you it doesn't matter a damn whether the world is going to the dogs or not; it doesn't matter whether the world is right or wrong, good or bad. *It is*—and that suffices. The world is what it is and I am what I am. I say it not like a squatting Buddha with legs crossed, but out of a gay, hard wisdom, out of an inner security. This out there and this in me, all this, *everything,* the resultant of inexplicable forces. A chaos whose order is beyond comprehension. Beyond *human* comprehension.

As a human being walking around at twilight, at dawn, at strange hours, unearthly hours, the sense of being alone and unique fortifies me to such a degree that when I walk with the multitude and seem no longer to be a human being but a mere speck, a gob of spit, I begin to think of myself alone in space, a single being surrounded by the most magnificent empty streets, a human biped walking between the skyscrapers when all the inhabitants have fled and I am alone walking, singing, commanding the earth. I do not have to look in my vest pocket to find my soul; it is there all the time, bumping against my ribs, swelling, inflated with song. If I just left a gathering where it was agreed that all is dead, now as I walk the streets, alone and identical with God, I know that this is a lie. The evidence of death is before my eyes constantly; but this death of the world, a death constantly going on, does not move from the periphery in, to engulf me, this death is at my very feet, moving from me outward, my own death a step in advance of me always. The world is the mirror of myself dying, the world not dying any more than I die, I more alive a thousand years from now than this moment and this world in which I am now dying also more alive then than now though dead a thousand years. When each thing is lived through to the end there is no death and no regrets, neither is there a false springtime; each moment lived pushes open a greater, wider horizon from which there is no escape save living.

The dreamers dream from the neck up, their bodies securely strapped to the electric chair. To imagine a new world is to live it daily, each thought, each glance, each step, each gesture killing and recreating, death always a step in advance. To spit on the past is not enough. To proclaim the future is not enough. One must act *as if* the past were dead and the future unrealizable. One must act *as if* the next step were the last, which it is. Each step forward is the last, and with it a world dies, one's self included. We are here of the earth never to end, the past never ceasing, the future never beginning, the present never ending. The never-never world which we hold in our hands and see and yet is not ourselves. We are that which is never concluded, never shaped to be recognized, all there is and yet not the whole, the parts so much greater than the whole that only God the mathematician can figure it out.

Laughter! counseled Rabelais. For all your ilk *laughter!* Jesus but it's hard to take his sane, gay wisdom after all the quack medicines we've poured down our throats. How can one laugh when the lining is worn off his stomach? How can one laugh after all the misery they've poisoned us with, the whey-faced, lantern-jawed, sad, suffering, solemn, serious, seraphic spirits? I understand the treachery that inspired them. I forgive them their genius. But it's hard to free oneself from all the sorrow they've created.

When I think of all the fanatics who were crucified, and those who were not fanatics, but simple idiots, all slaughtered for the sake of ideas, I begin to draw a smile. Bottle up every avenue of escape, I say. Bring the lid down hard on the New Jerusalem! Let's feel each other belly to belly, *without hope!* Washed and unwashed, murderer and evangelist, the whey-faced guys and the three-quarter moons, the weather vanes and the bullet-heads—let them only get closer together, let them stew for a few centuries in this cul-de-sac!

Either the world is too slack or I am not taut enough. If I became unintelligible I would be understood immediately. The difference between understanding and non-understanding is as fine as a hair, *finer,* the difference of a millimeter, a thread of space between China and Neptune. No matter how far out of whack I get, the ratio remains the same; it has nothing to do with clarity, precision, et cetera. (The et cetera is important!) The mind blunders because it is too precise an instrument; the threads break against the mahogany knots, against the cedar and ebony of alien matter. We talk about reality as if it were something commensurable, a piano exercise, or a lesson in physics. The Black Death came with the return of the Crusaders. Syphilis came with the return of Columbus. *Reality will come too! Reality prime,* says my friend Kronstadt. From a poem written on the ocean floor....

To prognosticate this reality is to be off either by a millimeter or by a million light years. The difference is a quantum formed by the intersection of streets. A quantum is a functional disorder created by trying to squeeze oneself into a frame of reference. A reference is a discharge from an old employer, that is to say, a mucopus from an old disease.

These are thoughts born of the street, *genus epileptoid.* You walk out with the guitar and the strings snap —because the idea is not embedded morphologically. To recall the dream one must keep the eyes closed and not budge. The slightest stir and the whole fabric falls apart. In the street I expose myself to the destructive, disintegrating elements that surround me. I let everything wreak its own havoc with me. I bend over to spy on the secret processes, *to obey* rather than to command.

There are huge blocks of my life which are gone forever. Huge blocks gone, scattered, wasted in talk, action, reminiscence, dream. There was never any time when I was living *one* life, the life of a husband, a lover, a friend. Wherever I was, whatever I was engaged in, I was leading multiple lives. Thus, whatever it is that I choose to regard as *my* story is lost, drowned, indissolubly fused with the lives, the drama, the stories of others.

I am a man of the old world, a seed that was transplanted by the wind, a seed which failed to blossom in the mushroom oasis of America. I belong on the heavy tree of the past. My allegiance, physical and spiritual, is with the men of Europe, those who were once Franks, Gauls, Vikings, Huns, Tatars, what not. The climate for my body and soul is here where there is quickness and corruption. I am proud *not* to belong to this century.

For those stargazers who are unable to follow the act of revelation I append herewith a few horoscopic brushstrokes in the margin of my *Universe of Death*....

I am Chancre, the crab, which moves sideways and backwards and forwards at will. I move in strange tropics and deal in high explosives, embalming fluid, jasper, myrrh, smaragd, fluted snot, and porcupines' toes. Because of Uranus which crosses my longitudinal I am inordinately fond of cunt, hot chitterlings, and water bottles. Neptune dominates my ascendant. That means I am composed of a watery fluid, that I am volatile, quixotic, unreliable, independent, and evanescent. Also quarrelsome. With a hot pad under my ass I can play the braggart or the buffoon as good as any man, no matter what sign he be born under. This is a self-portrait which yields only the missing parts—an anchor, a dinner bell, the remains of a beard, the hind part of a cow. In short, I am an idle fellow who pisses his time away. I have absolutely nothing to show for my labors except my genius. But there comes a time, even in the life of an idle genius, when he has to go to the window and vomit up the excess baggage. If you are a genius you have to do that— if for no other reason than to build a little comprehensible world of your own which will not run down like an eight-day clock! And the more ballast you throw overboard the easier you rise above the esteem of your neighbors. Until you find yourself all alone in the stratosphere. Then you tie a stone around your neck and you jump feet first. That brings about the complete destruction of anagogic dream interpretation together with mercurial stomatitis brought about by inunctions. You have the dream for nighttime and the horse laugh for daytime.

And so, when I stand at the bar of Little Tom Thumb and see these men with three-quarter faces coming up through the trapdoors of hell with pulleys and braces, dragging locomotives and pianos and cuspidors, I say to myself: «Grand! Grand! All this bric-a-brac, all this machinery coming to me on a silver platter! It's grand! It's marvelous! It's a poem created while I was asleep.»

What little I have learned about writing amounts to this: *it is not what people think it is.* It is an absolutely new thing each time with each individual. Valparaiso, for example. Valparaiso, when I say it, means something totally different from anything it ever meant before. It may mean an English cunt with all her front teeth gone and the bartender standing in the middle of the street searching for customers. It may mean an angel in a silk shirt running his lacy fingers over a black harp. It may mean an odalisque with a mosquito netting around her ass. It may mean any of these things, or none, but whatever it may mean you can be sure it will be something different, something new. Valparaiso is always five minutes before the end, a little this side of Peru, or maybe three inches nearer. It's the accidental square inch that you do with fever because you've got a hot pad under your ass and the Holy Ghost in your bowels—orthopedic mistakes included. It means «to piss warm and drink cold,» as Trimalchio says, «because our mother the earth is in the middle, made round like an egg, and has all good things in herself, like a honeycomb.»

And now, ladies and gentlemen, with this little universal can opener which I hold in my hands I am about to open a can of sardines. With this little can opener which I hold in my hands it's all the same—whether you want to open a box of sardines or a drugstore. It's the third or fourth day of spring, as I've told you several times already, and even though it's a poor, shabby, reminiscent spring, the thermometer is driving me crazy as a bedbug. You thought I was sitting at the Place Clichy all the time, drinking an *aperitif* perhaps. As a matter of fact I *was* sitting at the Place Clichy, but that was two or three years ago. And I *did* stand at the bar of Little Tom Thumb, but that was a long time ago and since then a crab has been gnawing at my vitals. All this began in the Metro (first-class) with the phrase —*«l'homme que j'etais, je ne le suis plus.»*

Walking past the railroad yards I was plagued by two fears—one, that if I lifted my eyes a little higher they would dart out of my head; two, that my bunghole was dropping out. A tension so strong that all ideation became instantly rhombohedral. Imagined the whole world declaring a holiday to think about static. On that day so many suicides that there would not be wagons enough to collect the dead. Passing the railroad yards at the Porte I catch the sickening stench from the cattle trains. It's like this: all day today and all day yesterday —three or four years ago, of course—they have been standing there body to body in fear and sweat. Their bodies are saturated with doom. Passing them my mind is terribly lucid, my thoughts crystal clear. I'm in such a hurry to spill out my thoughts that I am running past them in the dark. I too am in great fear. I too am sweating and panting, thirsty, saturated with doom. I'm going by them like a letter through the post. Or not I, but certain ideas of which I am the harbinger. And these ideas are already labeled and docketed, already sealed, stamped and watermarked. They run in series, my ideas, like electric coils. To live *beyond* illusion or *with* it? that's the question. Inside me a terrifying gem which will not wear away, a gem which scratches the windowpanes as I flee through the night. The cattle are lowing and bleating. They stand there in the warm stench of their own dung. I hear again now the music of the A Minor Quartet, the agonized flurries of the strings. There's a madman inside me and he's hacking away, hacking and hacking until he strikes the final discord. *Pure annihilation,* as distinguished from lesser, muddier annihilations. Nothing to be mopped up afterwards. A wheel of light rolling up to the precipice— and over into the bottomless pit. I, Beethoven, I created it! I, Beethoven, I destroy it!

From now on, ladies and gentlemen, you are entering Mexico. From now on everything will be wonderful and beautiful, marvelously beautiful, marvelously wonderful. Increasingly marvelously beautiful and wonderful. From now on no more washlines, no suspenders, no flannel underwear. Always summer and everything true to pattern. If it's a horse it's a horse for all time. If it's apoplexy it's apoplexy, and not St. Vitus's Dance. No early morning whores, no gardenias. No dead cats in the gutter, no sweat and perspiration. If it be a lip it must be a lip that trembles eternally. For in Mexico, ladies and gentlemen, it's always high noon and what glows is fuchsia and what's dead is dead and no feather dusters. You lie on a cement bed and you sleep like an acetylene torch. When you strike it rich it's a bonanza. When you don't strike it rich it's misery, *worse than misery.* No arpeggios, no grace notes, no cadenzas. Either you hold the clue or you don't hold the clue. Either you start with pure melody or you start with listerine. But no Purgatory and no elixir. It's Fourth Eclogue or Thirteenth Arrondissement!

3. A Saturday Afternoon

This is better than reading Vergil.

It is a Saturday afternoon and this Saturday afternoon is distinct from all other Saturday afternoons, but in no wise like a Monday afternoon or a Thursday afternoon. On this day, as I ride toward the Neuilly Bridge past the little island of Robinson with its temple at the far end and in the temple the little statue like a cotyledon in the mouth of a bell, I have such a sense of being at home that it seems incredible that I was born in America. The stillness of the water, the fishing boats, the iron stakes that mark the channel, the low lying tugs with sluggish curves, the black scows and bright stanchions, the sky never changing, the river bending and twisting, the hills spreading out and ever girdling the valley, the perpetual change of panorama and yet the constancy of it, the variety and movement of life under the fixed sign of the tricolor, all this is the history of the Seine which is in my blood and will go down into the blood of those who come after me when they move along these shores of a Saturday afternoon.

As I cross the bridge at Boulogne, along the road that leads to Meudon, I turn round and roll down the hill into Sevres. Passing through a deserted street I see a little restaurant in a garden; the sun is beating through the leaves and spangling the tables. I dismount.

What is better than reading Vergil or memorizing Goethe *(alles Vergangliche ist nur em Gleichnis,* etc.)?

Why, eating outdoors under an awning for eight francs at Issy-les-Moulineaux. *Pourtant je suis a Sevres.* No matter. I have been thinking lately of writing a *Journal d'un Fou* which I imagine to have found at Issy-les-Moulineaux. And since that *fou* is largely myself I am not eating at Sevres, but at Issy-les-Moulineaux. And what does the *fou* say when the waitress comes with the big canette of beer? *Don't worry about errors when you're writing. The biographers will explain all errors.* I am thinking of my friend Carl who has spent the last four days getting started on a description of the woman he's writing about. «I can't do it! I can't do it!» he says. Very well, says the *fou,* let *me* do it for you. *Begin!* That's the principal thing. Supposing her nose is not aquiline? Supposing it's a celestial nose? What difference? When a portrait commences badly it's because you're not describing the woman you have in mind: you are thinking more about those who are going to look at the portrait than about the woman who is sitting for you. Take Van Norden— he's another case. He has been trying for two months to get started with his novel. Each time I meet him he has a new opening for his book. It never gets beyond the opening. Yesterday he said: «You see what my problem's like. It isn't just a question of how to begin: the first line decides the cast of the whole book. Now here's a start I made the other day: Dante wrote a poem about a place called H——. H-dash, because I don't want any trouble with the censors.»

Think of a book opening with H-dash! A little private hell which mustn't offend the censors! I notice that when Whitman starts a poem he writes: «I, Walt, in my 37th year and in perfect health! ... I am afoot with my vision.... I dote on myself.... Walt Whitman, a kosmos, of Manhattan the son, turbulent, fleshy, sensual, eating, drinking and breeding.... Unscrew the locks from the doors! Unscrew the doors themselves from their jambs.... Here or henceforward it is all the same to me.... I exist as I am, that is enough....»

With Walt it is always Saturday afternoon. If the woman be hard to describe he admits it and stops at the third line. Next Saturday, the weather permitting, he may add a missing tooth, or an ankle. Everything can wait, can bide its time. «*I accept Time absolutely.*» Whereas my friend Carl, who has the vitality of a bedbug, is pissing in his pants because four days have elapsed and he has only a negative in his hand. «I don't see any reason,» says he, «why I should ever die—barring an untoward accident.» And then he rubs his hands and closets himself in his room to live out his immortality. He lives on like a bedbug hidden in the wallpaper.

The hot sun is beating through the awning. I am delirious because I am dying so fast. Every second counts. I do not hear the second that has just ticked off—I am clinging like a madman to this second which has not yet announced itself.... What is better than reading Vergil? *This!* This expanding moment which has not defined itself in ticks or beats, this eternal moment which destroys all values, degrees, differences. This gushing upward and outward from a hidden source. No truths to utter, no wisdom that can be imparted. A gush and a babble, a speaking to all men at once, everywhere, and in all languages. Now is the thinnest veil between madness and sanity. Now is everything so simple that it mocks one. From this peak of drunkenness one rolls down into the plateau of good health where one reads Vergil and Dante and Montaigne and all the others who spoke only of the moment, the expanding moment that is heard forever.... Talking to all men at once. A gush and a babble. This is the moment when I raise the glass to my lips, observing as I do so the fly that has settled on my pinkie; and the fly is as important to this moment as my hand or the glass it holds or the beer that is in the glass or the thoughts that are born of the beer and die with the beer. This is the moment when I know that a sign reading «To Versailles,» or a sign reading «To Suresnes,» any and all signs pointing to this or that place, should be ignored, that one should always go toward the place for which there is no sign. This is the moment when the deserted street on which I have chosen to sit is throbbing with people and all the crowded streets are empty. This is the moment when any restaurant is the right restaurant so long as it was not indicated to you by somebody. This is the best food, though it is the worst I have ever tasted. This is the food which no one but genius will touch—always within reach, easily digested, and leaving an appetite for more. «The roquefort, was it good?» asks the waitress. *Divine!* The stalest, the wormiest, the lousiest roquefort that was ever fabricated, saturated with the worms of Dante, of Vergil, Homer, Boccaccio, Rabelais, Goethe, all the worms that ever were and have passed on into cheese. To eat this cheese one must have genius. This is the cheese wherein I bury myself, I, Miguel Feodor Francois Wolfgang Valentine Miller.

The approach to the bridge is paved with cobblestones. I ride so slowly that each cobble sends a separate and distinct message to my spinal column and on up through the vertebrae to that crazy cage in which the medulla oblongata flashes its semaphores. And as I cross the bridge at Sevres, looking to the right of me and left, crossing any bridge, whether it be over the Seine, the Marne, the Ourcq, the Aude, the Loire, the Lot, the River Shannon or the Liffey, the East River or the Hudson, the Mississippi, the Colorado, the Amazon, the Orinoco, the Jordan, the Tigris, the Iriwaddy, crossing any and every bridge and I have crossed them all, including the Nile, the Danube, the Volga, the Euphrates, crossing the bridge at Sevres I yell, like that maniac St. Paul—«O death, where is thy sting?» In back of me Sevres, before me Boulogne, but this that passes under me, this Seine that started up somewhere in a myriad simultaneous trickles, this still jet rushing on from out of a million billion roots, this still mirror bearing the clouds along and stifling the past, rushing on and on and on while between the mirror and the clouds moving transversally I, a complete corporate entity, a universe bringing countless centuries to a conclusion, I and this that passes beneath me and this that floats above me and all that surges through me, I and this, I and that joined up in one continuous movement, this Seine and every Seine that is spanned by a bridge is the miracle of a man crossing it on a bicycle.

This is better than reading Vergil....

Heading back toward St. Cloud, the wheel rolling very slowly, the speedometer in the crazy gray cage clicking like a newsreel. I am a man whose manometer is intact; I am a man on a machine and the machine is in control; I am riding downhill with the brakes on; I could ride just as contentedly on a treadmill and let the mirror pass over me and history under me, or vice versa. I am riding in full sunlight, a man impervious to all except the phenomena of light. The hill of St. Cloud rises up before me on the left, the trees are bending over me to shadow me, the way is smooth and never-ending, the little statue rests in the bell of the temple like a cotyledon. Every Middle Age is good, whether in man or history. It is full sunlight and the roads extend in every direction, and all the roads are downhill. I would not level the road nor remove any of the bumps. Each jolt sends a fresh message to the signal tower. I have marked all the spots in passing: to retrace my thoughts I have only to retrace my journey, re-feel these bumps.

At the St. Cloud bridge I come to a full stop. I am in no hurry—I have the whole day to piss away. I put my bicycle in the rack under the tree and go to the urinal to take a leak. It is all gravy, even the urinal. As I stand there looking up at the house fronts a demure young woman leans out of a window to watch me. How many times have I stood thus in this smiling, gracious world, the sun splashing over me and the birds twittering crazily, and found a woman looking down at me from an open window, her smile crumbling into soft little bits which the birds gather in their beaks and deposit sometimes at the base of a urinal where the water gurgles melodiously and a man comes along with his fly open and pours the steaming contents of his bladder over the dissolving crumbs. Standing thus, with heart and fly and bladder open, I seem to recall every urinal I ever stepped into—all the most pleasant sensations, all the most luxurious memories, as if my brain were a huge divan smothered with cushions and my life one long snooze on a hot, drowsy afternoon. I do not find it so strange that America placed a urinal in the center of the Paris exhibit at Chicago. I think it belongs there and I think it a tribute which the French should appreciate. True, there was no need to fly the tricolor above it. *Un peau trop fort, ca!* And yet, how is a Frenchman to know that one of the first things which strikes the eye of the American visitor, which thrills him, warms him to the very gizzard, is this ubiquitous urinal? How is a Frenchman to know that what impresses the American in looking at a *pissotiere,* or a *vespasienne,* or whatever you choose to call it, is the fact that he is in the midst of a people who admit to the necessity of peeing now and then and who know also that to piss one has to use a pisser and that if it is not done publicly it will be done privately and that it is no more incongruous to piss in the street than underground where some old derelict can watch you to see that you commit no nuisance.

I am a man who pisses largely and frequently, which they say is a sign of great mental activity. However it be, I know that I am in distress when I walk the streets of New York. Wondering constantly where the next stop will be and if I can hold out that long. And while in winter, when you are broke and hungry, it is fine to stop off for a few minutes in a warm underground comfort station, when spring comes it is quite a different matter. One likes to piss in sunlight, among human beings who watch and smile down at you. And while the female squatting down to empty her bladder in a china bowl may not be a sight to relish, no man with any feeling can deny that the sight of the male standing behind a tin strip and looking out on the throng with that contented, easy, vacant smile, that long, reminiscent, pleasurable look in his eye, is a good thing. To relieve a full bladder is one of the great human joys.

There are certain urinals I go out of my way to make —such as the battered rattletrap outside the deaf and dumb asylum, corner of the Rue St. Jacques and the Rue de l'Abbe-de-l'Epee, or the Pneu Hutchinson one by the Luxembourg Gardens, corner Rue d'Assas and Rue Guynemer. Here, on a balmy night in spring, through what concatenation of events I do not know or care, I rediscovered my old friend Robinson Crusoe. The whole night passed in reminiscence, in pain and terror, *joyous* pain, *joyous* terror.

«The wonders of this man's life»—so reads the preface to the original edition—«exceed all that is to be found extant; the life of one man being scarce capable of a greater variety.» The island now known as Tobago, at the mouth of the mighty Orinoco, thirty miles northwest of Trinidad. Where the man Crusoe lived in solitude for eight and twenty years. The footprints in the sand, so beautifully embossed on the cover. The man Friday. The umbrella.... Why had this simple tale so fascinated the men of the eighteenth century? *Voici* Larousse:

«... le recit des aventures d'un homme qui, jete dans une ile deserte, trouve les moyens de se suffire et meme de se creer un bonheur relatif, que complete l'arrivee d'un autre etre humain, d'un sauvage, Vendredi, que Robinson a arrache des mains de ses ennemis.... L'interet du roman n'est pas dans la verite psychologique, mais dans l'abondance des details minutieux qui donnent une impression saisissante de realite.»

So Robinson Crusoe not only found a way of getting along, but even established for himself a relative happiness! Bravo! One man who was satisfied with a *relative* happiness. So un-Anglo-Saxon! So pre-Christian! Bringing the story up to date, Larousse to the contrary, we have here then the account of an artist who wanted to build himself a world, a story of perhaps the first genuine neurotic, a man who had himself shipwrecked in order to live outside his time in a world of his own which he could share with another human being, *meme un sauvage*. The remarkable thing to note is that, acting out his neurotic impulse, he did find a relative happiness even though alone on a desert island, with nothing more perhaps than an old shot-gun and a pair of torn breeches. A clean slate, with twenty-five thousand years of post-Magdalenian «progress» buried in his neurones. An eighteenth-century conception of relative happiness! And when Friday comes along, though Friday, or *Vendredi,* is only a savage and does not speak the language of Crusoe, the circle is complete. I should like to read the book again—and I will some rainy day. A remarkable book, coming at the culmination of our marvelous Faustian culture. Men like Rousseau, Beethoven, Napoleon, Goethe on the horizon. The whole civilized world staying up nights to read it in ninety-seven different tongues. A picture of reality in the eighteenth century. Henceforward no more desert isles. Henceforward wherever one happens to be born is a desert isle. Every man his own civilized desert, the island of self on which he is shipwrecked: happiness, relative or absolute, is out of the question. Henceforward everyone is running away from himself to find an imaginary desert isle, to live out this dream of Robinson Crusoe. Follow the classic flights, of Melville, Rimbaud, Gauguin, Jack London, Henry James, D. H. Lawrence ... thousands of them. None of them found happiness. Rimbaud found cancer. Gauguin found syphilis. Lawrence found the white plague. The plague— that's it! Be it cancer, syphilis, tuberculosis, or what not. *The plague!* The plague of modern progress: colonization, trade, free Bibles, war, disease, artificial limbs, factories, slaves, insanity, neuroses, psychoses, cancer, syphilis, tuberculosis, anemia, strikes, lockouts, starvation, nullity, vacuity, restlessness, striving, despair, ennui, suicide, bankruptcy, arterio-sclerosis, megalomania, schizophrenia, hernia, cocaine, prussic acid, stink bombs, tear gas, mad dogs, auto-suggestion, auto-intoxication, psychotherapy, hydrotherapy, electric massages, vacuum cleaners, pemmican, grape nuts, hemorrhoids, gangrene. No desert isles. No Paradise. Not even *relative* happiness. Men running away from themselves so frantically that they look for salvation under the ice floes or in tropical swamps, or else they climb the Himalayas or asphyxiate themselves in the stratosphere....

What fascinated the men of the eighteenth century was the vision of the end. They had enough. They wanted to retrace their steps, climb back into the womb again.

THIS IS AN ADDENDA FOR LAROUSSE....

What impressed me, in the urinal by the Luxembourg, was how little it mattered what the book contained; it was the moment of reading it that counted, the moment that contained the book, the moment that definitely and for all time placed the book in the living ambiance of a room with its sunbeams, its atmosphere of convalescence, its homely chairs, its rag carpet, its odor of cooking and washing, its mother image bulking large and totemlike, its windows giving out on the street and throwing into the retina the jumbled issues of idle, sprawling figures, of gnarled trees, trolley wires, cats on the roof, tattered nightmares dancing from the clotheslines, saloon doors swinging, parasols unfurled, snow clotting, horses slipping, engines racing, the panes frosted, the trees sprouting. The story of Robinson Crusoe owes its appeal—for me, at least—to the moment in which I discovered it. It lives on in an ever-increasing phantasmagoria, a living part of a life filled with phantasmagoria. For me Robinson Crusoe belongs in the same category as certain parts of Vergil—or, *what time is it?* For, whenever I think of Vergil, I think automatically—*what time is it?* Vergil to me is a bald-headed guy with spectacles tilting back in his chair and leaving a grease mark on the blackboard; a bald-headed guy opening wide his mouth in a delirium which he simulated five days a week for four successive years; a big mouth with false teeth producing this strange oracular nonsense: *rari nantes in gurgite vasto*. Vividly I recall the unholy joy with which he pronounced this phrase. A *great* phrase, according to this bald-pated, goggle-eyed son of a bitch. We scanned it and we parsed it, we repeated it after him, we swallowed it like cod liver oil, we chewed it like dyspepsia tablets, we opened wide our mouths as he did and we reproduced the miracle day after day five days in the week, year in and year out, like worn-out records, until Vergil was done for and out of our lives for good and all.

But every time this goggle-eyed bastard opened wide his mouth and the glorious phrase rolled out I heard what was most important for me to hear at that moment—*what time is it?* Soon time to go to Math. Soon time for recess. Soon time to wash up.... I am one individual who is going to be honest about Vergil and his fucking *rari nantes in gurgite vasto*. I say without blushing or stammering, without the least confusion, regret or remorse that recess in the toilet was worth a thousand Vergils, always was and always will be. At recess we came alive. At recess we who were Gentile and had no better sense grew delirious: in and out of the cabinets we ran, slamming the doors and breaking the locks. We seemed to have been taken with delirium tremens. As we pelted each other with food and shouted and cursed and tripped each other up, we muttered now and then—*rari nantes in gurgite vasto*. The din we created was so great, and the damage so vast, that whenever we Gentiles went to the toilet the Latin teacher went with us, or if he were eating out that day then the History teacher followed us in. And a wry face they could make, standing in the toilet with delicate, buttered sandwich in hand listening to the pooping and squawking of us brats. The moment they left the toilet to get a breath of fresh air we raised our voices in song, which was not considered reprehensible, but which no doubt was a condition greatly envied by the bespectacled professors who had to use the toilet now and then themselves, learned as they were.

O the wonderful recesses in the toilet! To them I owe my knowledge of Boccaccio, of Rabelais, of Petronius, of *The Golden Ass.* All my good reading, you might say, was done in the toilet. At the worst, *Ulysses,* or a detective story. There are passages in *Ulysses* which can be read only in the toilet—if one wants to extract the full flavor of their content. And this is not to denigrate the talent of the author. This is simply to move him a little closer to the good company of Abelard, Petrarch, Rabelais, Villon, Boccaccio—all the fine, lusty genuine spirits who recognized dung for dung and angels for angels. Fine company, and no *rari nantes in gurgite vasto.* And the more ramshackle the toilet, the more dilapidated it be, the better. (Same for urinals.) To enjoy Rabelais, for example— such a passage as «How to Rebuild the Walls of Paris»—I recommend a plain, country toilet, a little outhouse in the corn patch, with a crescent sliver of light coming through the door. No buttons to push, no chain to pull, no pink toilet paper. Just a rough-carved seat big enough to frame your behind, and two other holes of dimensions suitable for other behinds. If you can bring a friend along and have him sit beside you, excellent! A good book is always more enjoyable in good company. A beautiful half-hour you can while away sitting in the outhouse with a friend—a half-hour which will remain with you all your life, and the book it contained, and the odor thereof.

No harm, I say, can ever be done a great book by taking it with you to the toilet. Only the little books suffer thereby. Only the little books make ass wipers. Such a one is *Little Caesar,* now translated into French and forming one of the *Passions* series. Turning the pages over it seems to me that I am back home again reading the headlines, listening to the goddamned radios, riding tin buggies, drinking cheap gin, buggering virgin harlots with a corn cob, stringing up niggers and burning them alive. Something to give one diarrhoea. And the same goes for the *Atlantic Monthly,* or any other monthly, for Aldous Huxley, Gertrude Stein, Sinclair Lewis, Hemingway, Dos Passes, Dreiser, etc., etc....

I hear no bell ringing inside me when I bring these birds to the water closet. I pull the chain and down the sewer they go. Down the Seine and into the Atlantic Ocean. Maybe a year hence they will bob up again—on the shores of Coney Island, or Midland Beach, or Miami, along with dead jelly fish, snails, clams, used condoms, pink toilet paper, yesterday's news, tomorrow's suicides—

No more peeping through keyholes! No more masturbating in the dark! No more public confessions! *Unscrew the doors from their jambs!* I want a world where the vagina is represented by a crude, honest slit, a world that has feeling for bone and contour, for raw, primary colors, a world that has fear and respect for its animal origins. I'm sick of looking at cunts all tickled up, disguised, deformed, idealized. Cunts with nerve ends exposed. I don't want to watch young virgins masturbating in the privacy of their boudoirs or biting their nails or tearing their hair or lying on a bed full of bread crumbs for a whole chapter. I want Madagascan funeral poles, with animal upon animal and at the top Adam and Eve, and Eve with a crude, honest slit between the legs. I want hermaphrodites who are real hermaphrodites, and not make-believes walking around with an atrophied penis or a dried-up cunt. I want a classic purity, where dung is dung and angels are angels. The Bible a la King James, for example. Not the Bible of Wycliffe, not the Vulgate, not the Greek, not the Hebrew, but the glorious, death-dealing Bible that was created when the English language was in flower, when a vocabulary of twenty thousand words sufficed to build a monument for all time. A Bible written in Svenska or Tegalic, a Bible for the Hottentots or the Chinese, a Bible that has to meander through the trickling sands of French is no Bible—it is a counterfeit and a fraud. The King James Version was created by a race of bone-crushers. It revives the primitive mysteries, revives rape, murder, incest, revives epilepsy, sadism, megalomania, revives demons, angels, dragons, leviathans, revives magic, exorcism, contagion, incantation, revives fratricide, regicide, patricide, suicide, revives hypnotism, anarchism, somnambulism, revives the song, the dance, the act, revives the mantic, the chthonian, the arcane, the mysterious, revives the power, the evil, and the glory that is God. All brought into the open on a colossal scale, and so salted and spiced that it will last until the next Ice Age.

A classic purity, then—and to hell with the Post Office authorities! For what is it enables the classics to live at all, if indeed they be living on and not dying as we and all about us are dying? What preserves them against the ravages of time if it be not the salt that is in them? When I read Petronius or Apuleius or Rabelais, how close they seem! That salty tang! That odor of the menagerie! The smell of horse piss and lion's dung, of tiger's breath and elephant's hide. Obscenity, lust, cruelty, boredom, wit. Real eunuchs. Real hermaphrodites. Real pricks. Real cunts. *Real banquets!* Rabelais rebuilds the walls of Paris with human cunts. Trimalchio tickles his own throat, pukes up his own guts, wallows in his own swill. In the amphitheater, where a big, sleepy pervert of a Caesar lolls dejectedly, the lions and the jackals, the hyenas, the tigers, the spotted leopards are crunching real human bones— whilst the coming men, the martyrs and imbeciles, are walking up the golden stairs shouting *Hallelujah!*

When I touch the subject of toilets I relive some of my best moments. Standing in the urinal at Boulogne, with the hill of St. Cloud to the right of me and the woman in the window above me, and the sun beating down on the still river water, I see the strange American I am passing on this quiet knowledge to other Americans who will follow me, who will stand in full sunlight in some charming corner of France and ease their full bladders. And I wish them all well and no gravel in the kidneys.

In passing I recommend certain other urinals which I know well, where perhaps there may be no woman to smile down at you, but where there is a broken wall, an old belfry, the facade of a palace, a square covered with colored awnings, a horse trough, a fountain, a covey of doves, a bookstall, a vegetable market.... Nearly always the French have chosen the right spot for their urinals. Off hand I think of one in Carcassonne which, if I chose the hour well, afforded me an incomparable view of the citadel; so well is it placed that, unless one be burdened and distraught, there must rise up again the same surging pride, the same wonder and awe, the same fierce attachment for this scene as was felt by the weary knight or monk when, pausing at the foot of the hill where now runs the stream that washed away the epidemic, he glanced up to rest his eyes on the grim, battle-stained turrets flung against a wind-swept sky.

And immediately I think of another—just outside the Palais des Papes, in Avignon. A mere stone's throw away from the charming little square which, on a night in spring, seems strewn with velvets and laces, with masks and confetti; so still flows the time that one can hear little horns blowing faint, the past gliding by like a ghost, and then drowned in the deep hammerstroked gongs that smash the voiceless music of the night. Just a stone's throw away from the obscure little quarter where the red lights blaze. There, toward the cool of the evening, you will find the crooked little streets humming with activity, the women, clad in bathing suit or chemise, lounging on the doorsteps, cigarette in mouth, calling to the passers-by. As night falls the walls seem to grow together and from all the little lanes that trickle into the gulch there spills a crowd of curious hungry men who choke the narrow streets, who mill around, dart aimlessly here and there like tailed sperm seeking the ovum, and finally are sucked in by the open maws of the brothels.

Nowadays, as one stands in the urinal beside the Palace, one is hardly aware of this other life. The Palace stands abrupt, cold, tomblike, before a bleak open square. Facing it is a ridiculous-looking building called Institute of Music. There they stand, facing each other across an empty lot. Gone the Popes. Gone the music. Gone all the color and speech of a glorious epoch. Were it not for the little quarter behind the Institute who could imagine what once was that life within the Palace walls? When this tomb was alive I believe that there was no separation between the Palace and the twisted lanes below; I believe that the dirty little hovels, with their rubbled roofs, ran right up to the door of the Palace. I believe that when a Pope stepped out of his gorgeous hive into the glitter of sunlight he communicated instantaneously with the life about him. Some traces of that life the frescoes still retain: the life of outdoors, of hunting, fishing, gaming, of falcons and dogs and women and flashing fish. A large, Catholic life, with intense blues and luminous greens, the life of sin and grace and repentance, a life of high yellows and golden browns, of winestained robes and salmon-colored streams. In that marvelous cubicle in a corner of the Palace, whence one overlooks the unforgettable roofs of Avignon and the broken bridge across the Rhone, in this cubicle where they say the Popes penned their bulls, the frescoes are still so fresh, so natural, so life-breathing, that even this tomb which is the Palace today seems more alive than the world outdoors. One can well imagine a great father of the Church sitting there at his writing table, with a Papal bull before him and a huge tankard at his elbow. And one can also easily imagine a fine, fat wench sitting on his knees, while down below, in the huge kitchen, whole animals are being roasted on the spit, and the lesser dignitaries of the Church, good trenchermen that they were, drinking and carousing to their hearts' content behind the comfort and security of the great walls. No schisms, no hairsplitting, no schizophrenia. When disease came it swept through hovel and castle, through the rich joints of the fathers and the tough joints of the peasants. When the spirit of God descended upon Avignon, it did not stop at the Musical Institute across the way; it penetrated the walls, the flesh, the hierarchies of rank and caste. It flourished as mightily in the red light district as up above on the hill. The Pope could not lift up his skirts and pass untouched. Inside the walls and outside the walls it was one life: faith, fornication, bloodshed. Primary colors. Primary passions. The frescoes tell the story. How they lived each day and the whole day long speaks louder than the books. What the Popes mumbled in their beards is one thing—what they commanded to be painted on their walls is another. Words are dead.

4. The Angel Is My Watermark!

The object of these pages is to relate the genesis of a masterpiece. The masterpiece is hanging on the wall in front of me; it is dry now. I am putting this down to remember the process, because I shall probably never do another like it.

We must go back a bit.... For two whole days I am wrestling with something. If I were to describe it in a word I should say that I have been like a cartridge that's jammed. This is almost deadly accurate, for when I came out of a dream this morning the only image that persisted was that of my big trunk crumpled up like an old hat.

The first day the struggle is undefinable. It is strong enough, however, to paralyze. I put on my hat and go to the Renoir Exhibition and from Renoir I go to the Louvre and from the Louvre I go to the Rue de Rivoli —where it no longer resembles the Rue de Rivoli. There I sit over a beer for three hours, fascinated by the monsters passing me.

The next morning I get up with the conviction that I will do something. There is that fine light tension which augurs well. My notebook lies beside me. I pick it up and riffle the pages absent-mindedly. I riffle them again—this time more attentively. The notes are arranged in cryptic lines: a simple phrase may record a year's struggle. Some of the lines I cannot decipher any more myself—my biographers will take care of them.

I am still obsessed by the idea that I am going to write today. I am merely flipping the pages of my notebook as a warming up exercise. So I imagine. But cursorily and swiftly as I sweep over these notes something fatal is happening to me.

What happens is that I have touched Tante Melia. And now my whole life rushes up in one gush, like a geyser that has just broken through the earth. I am walking home with Tante Melia and suddenly I realize that she is crazy. She is asking me for the moon. «Up there!» she shrieks. «*Up there!*»

It is about ten in the morning when this line shrieks at me. From this moment on— up until four o'clock this morning—I am in the hands of unseen powers. I put the type- writer away and I commence to record what is being dictated to me. Pages and pages of notes, and for each incident I am reminded of where to find the context. All the folders in which my manuscripts are assorted have been emptied on the floor. I am lying on the floor with a pencil, feverishly annotating my work. This continues and continues. I am exultant, and at the same time I am worried. If it continues at this rate I may have a hem- orrhage.

About three o'clock I decide to obey no longer. I will go out and eat. Perhaps it will blow over after lunch. I go on my bicycle in order to draw the blood from my head. I carry no notebook with me—purposely. If the dictation starts again, *tant pis*. I'm out for lunch!

At three o'clock you can get only a cold snack. I order cold chicken with mayonnaise. It costs a little more than I usually spend, but that's exactly why I order it. And after a lit- tle debate I order a heavy Burgundy instead of the usual *vin ordinaire*. I am hoping that all this will distract me. The wine ought to make me a little drowsy.

I'm on the second bottle and the tablecloth is covered with notes. My head is extraor- dinarily light. I order cheese and grapes and pastry. Amazing what an appetite I have! And yet, somehow, it doesn't seem to be going down *my* stomach; seems as if some one else were eating all this for me. Well, at least, *I* shall have to pay for it! That's standing on solid ground.... I pay and off I go again on the wheel. Stop at a cafe for a black coffee. Can't manage to get both feet on solid ground. Some one is dictating to me constantly—and with no regard for my health.

I tell you, the whole day passes this way. I've surrendered long ago. O. K., I say to myself. If it's *ideas* today, then it's ideas. *Princesse, a vos ordres.* And I slave away, as though it were exactly what I wanted to do myself.

After dinner I am quite worn out. The ideas are still inundating me, but I am so exhausted that I can lie back now and let them play over me like an electric massage. Finally I am weak enough to be able to pick up a book and rest. It's an old issue of a magazine. Here I will find peace. To my amazement the page falls open on these words: «Goethe and his Demon.» The pencil is in my hand again, the margin crammed with notes.

It is midnight. I am exhilarated. The dictation has ceased. A free man again. I'm so damned happy that I'm wondering if I shouldn't take a little spin before sitting down to write. The bike is in my room. It's dirty. The bike, I mean. I get a rag and begin cleaning it. I clean every spoke, I oil it thoroughly, I polish the mudguards. She's spick and span. I'll go through the Bois de Boulogne—

As I'm washing my hands I suddenly get a gnawing pain in the stomach. I'm hungry, that's what's the matter. Well, now that the dictation has ceased I'm free to do as I like. I uncork a bottle, cut off a big chunk of bread, bite into a sausage. The sausage is full of garlic. Fine. In the Bois de Boulogne a garlic breath goes unnoticed. A little more wine. Another hunk of bread. This time it's me who's eating and no mistake about it. The other meals were wasted. The wine and the garlic mingle odorously. I'm belching a little.

I sit down for a moment to smoke a cigarette. There's a pamphlet at my elbow, about three inches square. It's called *Art and Madness*. The ride is off. It's getting too late to write anyway. It's coming over me that what I really want to do is to paint a picture. In 1927 or '8 I was on the way to becoming a painter. Now and then, in fits and starts, I do a water color. It comes over you like that: you feel like a water color and you do one. In the insane asylum they paint their fool heads off. They paint the chairs, the walls, the tables, the bedsteads ... an amazing productivity. If we rolled up our sleeves and went to work the way these idiots do what might we not accomplish in a lifetime!

The illustration in front of me, done by an inmate of Charenton, has a very fine quality about it. I see a boy and girl kneeling close together and in their hands they are holding a huge lock. Instead of a penis and vagina the artist has endowed them with keys, very big keys which interpenetrate. There is also a big key in the lock. They look happy and a little absent-minded.... On page 85 there is a landscape. It looks exactly like one of Hilaire Hiler's paintings. In fact, it is better than any of Hiler's. The only peculiar feature of it is that in the foreground there are three miniature men who are deformed. Not badly deformed either—they simply look as if they were too heavy for their legs. The rest of the canvas is so good that one would have to be squeamish indeed to be annoyed at this. Besides, is the world so perfect that there are not three men anywhere who are too heavy for their legs? It seems to me that the insane have a right to their vision as well as we.

I'm very eager to start in. Just the same, I'm at a loss for ideas. The dictation has ceased. I have half a mind to copy one of these illustrations. But then I'm a little ashamed of myself—to copy the work of a lunatic is the worst form of plagiarism.

Well, begin! That's the thing. Begin with a horse! I have vaguely in mind the Etruscan horses I saw in the Louvre. (Note: in all the great periods of art the horse was very close to man!) I begin to draw. I begin naturally with the easiest part of the animal—the horse's ass. A little opening for the tail which can be stuck in afterwards. Hardly have I begun to do the trunk when I notice at once that it is too elongated. Remember, you are drawing a horse—not a liverwurst! Vaguely, vaguely it seems to me that some of those Ionian horses I saw on the black vases had elongated trunks; and the legs began inside the body, delineated by a fine stenciled line which you could look at or not look at according to your anatomical instincts. With this in mind I decide on an Ionian horse. But now fresh difficulties ensue. It's the legs. The shape of a horse's leg is baffling when you have only your memory to rely on. I can recall only about as much as from the fetlock down, which is to say, *the hoof.* To put meat on the hoof is a delicate task, extremely delicate. And to make the legs join the body naturally, not as if they were stuck on with glue. My horse already has five legs: the easiest thing to do is to transform one of them into a phallus erectus. No sooner said than done. And now he's standing just like a terra cotta figure of the sixth century b.c. The tail isn't in yet, but I've left an opening just above the asshole. The tail can be put in any time. The main thing is to get him into action, to make him prance like. So I twist the front legs up. Part of him is in motion, the rest is standing stock still. With the proper kind of tail I could turn him into a fine kangaroo.

During the leg experiments the stomach has become dilapidated. I patch it up as best I can—until it looks like a hammock. Let it go at that. If it doesn't look like a horse when I'm through I can always turn it into a hammock. (Weren't there people sleeping in a horse's stomach on one of the vases I saw?)

Nobody who has not examined the horse's skull attentively can ever imagine how difficult it is to draw. To make it a skull and not a feedbag. To put the eyes in without making the horse laugh. To keep the expression horsey, and not let it grow human. At this point, I admit frankly, I am completely disgusted with my prowess. I have a mind to erase and begin all over again. But I detest the eraser. I would rather convert the horse into a dynamo or a grand piano than erase my work completely.

I close my eyes and try very calmly to picture a horse in my mind's eye. I rub my hands over the mane and the shoulders and the flanks. Seems to me I remember very distinctly how a horse feels, especially that way he has of shuddering when a fly is bothering him. And that warm, squirmy feel of the veins. (In Chula Vista I used to currycomb the jackasses before going to the fields. Thinks I—if only I could make a jackass of him, that would be something!)

So I start all over again—with the mane this time. Now the mane of a horse is something entirely different from a pigtail, or the tresses of a mermaid. Chirico puts wonderful manes on his horses. And so does Valentine Prax. The mane is something, I tell you—it's not just a marcel wave. It has to have the ocean in it, and a lot of mythology. What makes hair and teeth and fingernails does not make a horse's mane. It's something apart.... However, when I get into a predicament of this sort I know that I can extricate myself later when it comes time to apply the color. The drawing is simply the excuse for color. The color is the toccata: drawing belongs to the realm of idea. (Michelangelo was right in despising Da Vinci. Is there anything more ghastly, more sickishly ideational than the «Last Supper»? Is there anything more pretentious than the «Mona Lisa»?

As I say, a little color will put life into the mane. The stomach is still a little out of order, I see. Very well. Where it is convex I make it concave and vice versa. Now suddenly my horse is galloping, his nostrils are snorting fire. But with two eyes he looks still a bit silly, a bit too human. Ergo, rub out an eye. Fine. He's getting more and more horsey. He's gotten kind of cute-looking too—like Charley Chase of the movies....

To keep him well within the genus he represents I finally decide to give him stripes. The idea is that if he won't lose his playfulness I can turn him into a zebra. So I put in the stripes. Now, damn it all, he seems to be made of cardboard. The stripes have flattened him out, glued him to the paper. Well, if I close my eyes again I ought to be able to recall the Cinzano horse—he has stripes too, and beautiful ones. Maybe I ought to go down for an *aperitif* and look at a Cinzano. It's getting late for *aperitifs*. Maybe I'll do a little plagiarizing after all. If a lunatic can draw a man on a bicycle he can draw a horse too.

It's remarkable—I find gods and goddesses, devils, bats, sewing machines, flowerpots, rivers, bridges, locks and keys, epileptics, coffins, skeletons—but not a damned horse! If the lunatic who compiled this brochure had wanted to draw a truly profound observation he would have had something to remark about this curious omission. When the horse is missing there is something radically amiss! Human art goes hand in hand with the horse. It's not enough to hint that the symbolists and the imagists are, or were, a little *detraques*. We want to know, in a study of insanity, what has become of the horse!

Once more I turn to the landscape on page 85. It's an excellent composition despite the geometrical stiffness. (The insane have a terrific obsession for logic and order, as have the French.) I have something to work from now: mountains, bridges, terraces, trees.... One of the great merits of insane art is that a bridge is always a bridge and a house a house. The three little men who are balancing themselves on their canes in the foreground are not absolutely necessary to the composition, especially since I already have the Ionian horse which occupies considerable space. I am searching for a setting in which to place the horse and there is something very wistful and very intriguing about this landscape with its crenelated parapets and its sugar-loaf escarpments and the houses with so many windows, as if the inmates were deathly afraid of suffocating. It's very reminiscent of the beginnings of landscape painting— and yet it's completely outside all definitive periods. I should say roughly that it lies in a zone between Giotto and Santos Dumont—with just a faint intimation of the post-mechanical street which is to come. And now, with this as a guide before me, I pick up courage. *Allons-y!*

Right under the horse's ass, where his croup begins and ends, and where Salvador Dali would most likely put a Louis Quinze chair or a watch spring, I begin to draw with free and easy strokes a straw hat, a melon. Beneath the hat I put a face—carelessly, because my ideas are large and sweeping. Wherever the hand falls I do something, following the insinuating deviations of the line. In this manner I take the huge phallus erectus, which was once a fifth leg, and bend it into a man's arm—so! Now I have a man in a big straw hat tickling the horse in the rumps. Fine! Fine and dandy! Should it seem a little grotesque, a little out of keeping with the pseudo-medieval character of the original composition, I can always attribute it to the aberration of the *fou* who inspired me. (Here, for the first time, a suspicion enters my head that I may not be altogether there myself! But on page 366 it says: «*Enfin, pour Matisse, le sentiment de l'objet peut s'exprimer avec toute licence, sans direction intellectuelle ou exactitude visuelle: c'est forigine de rexpression.*» To go on.... After a slight difficulty with the man's feet I solve the problem by putting the lower half of his body behind the parapet. He is leaning over the parapet, dreaming most likely, and at the same time he is ^tickling the horse's ribs. (Along the rivers of France you will often stumble across men leaning over a parapet and dreaming—particularly after they have voided a bagful of urine.)

To shorten my labors, and also to see how much space will be left, I put in a quantity of bold diagonal stripes or planks, for the bridge flooring. This kills at least a third of the picture, as far as composition goes. Now come the terraces, the escarpments, the three trees, the snow-topped mountains, the houses and all the windows that go with them. It's like a jigsaw puzzle. Wherever a cliff refuses to finish properly I make it the side of a house, or the roof of another house which is hidden. Gradually I work my way up toward the top of the picture where the frame happily cuts things short. It remains to put in the trees—and the mountains.

Now trees again are very ticklish propositions. To make a tree, and not a bouquet! Even though I put forked lightning inside the foliage, to lend a hint of structure, it's no go. A few airy clouds, then, to do away with some of the superfluous foliage. (Always a good dodge to simplify your problem by removing it.) But the clouds look like pieces of tissue paper that had blown off the wedding bouquets. A cloud is so light, so less than nothing, and yet it's not tissue paper. Everything that has form has invisible substance. Michelangelo sought it all his life—in marble, in verse, in love, in architecture, in crime, in God.... (Page 390: «Si l'artiste poursuit la creation authentique, son souci est ailleurs que sur l'objet, qui pent etre sacrifie et soumis mix necessites de l'invention.»)

I come to the mountain—like Mahomet. By now I am beginning to realize the meaning of liberation. A mountain! What's a mountain? It's a pile of dirt which never wears away, at least, not in historical time. A mountain's too easy. I want a volcano. I want a reason for my horse to be snorting and prancing. Logic, logic! «Le fou montre un souci constant de logique!» (Les Francais aussi.) Well, I'm not a fou, especially not a French fou: I can take a few liberties, particularly with the work of an imbecile. So I draw the crater first and work down toward the foot of the mountain to join up with the bridgework and the roofs of the houses below. Out of the errors I make cracks in the mountainside—to represent the damage done by the volcano. This is an active volcano and its sides are bursting.

When I'm all through I have a shirt on my hands. A shirt, precisely! I can recognize the collar band and the sleeves. All it needs is a Rogers Peet label and size 16 or what have you.... One thing, however, stands out unmistakably clear and clean, and that is the bridge. It's strange, but if you can draw an arch the rest of the bridge follows naturally. Only an engineer can ruin a bridge.

It's almost finished, as far as the drawing goes. All the loose ends at the bottom I join up to make cemetery gates. And in the upper left-hand corner, where there is a hole left by the volcano, I draw an angel. It is an object of an original nature, a purely gratuitous invention, and highly symbolic. It is a sad angel with a fallen stomach, and the wings are supported by umbrella ribs. It seems to come down from beyond the cadre of my ideas and hover mystically above the wild Ionian horse that is now lost to man.

Have you ever sat in a railway station and watched people killing time? Do they not sit a little like crestfallen angels—with their broken arches and their fallen stomachs? Those eternal few minutes in which they are condemned to be alone with themselves—does it not put umbrella ribs in their wings?

All the angels in religious art are false. If you want to see angels you must go to the Grand Central Depot, or the Gare St. Lazare. Especially the Gare St. Lazare— Salle des Pas Perdus.

My theory of painting is to get the drawing done with as quickly as possible and slap in the color. After all, I'm a colorist, not a draught horse. *Alors,* out with the tubes!

I start painting the side of a house, in raw umber. Not very effective. I put a liberal dash of crimson alizarin in the wall next to it. A little too pretty, too Italian. All in all, I'm not starting out so well with my colors. There's a rainy day atmosphere somewhat reminiscent of Utrillo. I don't like Utrillo's quiet imbecility, nor his rainy days, nor his suburban streets. I don't like the way his women stick their behinds out at you either.... I get the bread knife out. May as well try a loaded impasto. In the act of squeezing out a generous assortment of colors the impulse seizes me to add a gondola to the composition. Directly below the bridge I insert it, which automatically launches it.

And now suddenly I know the reason for the gondola. Among the Renoirs the other day there was a Venetian scene, and the inevitable gondola of course. Now what intrigued me, weakly enough, was that the man who sat in the gondola was so distinctly a man, though he was only a speck of black, hardly separable from all the other specks which made up the sunlight, the choppy sea, the crumbling palaces, the sailboats, etc. He was just a speck in that fiery combination of colors—and yet he was distinctly a man. You could even tell that he was a Frenchman and that he was of the 1870's or thereabouts....

This isn't the end of the gondola. Two days before I left for America—1927 or '8—we held a big session at the house. It was at the height of my water-color career.

It began in a peculiar way, this water-color mania.

Through hunger, I might say. That and the extreme cold. For weeks I had been hanging out with my friend Joe in poolrooms and comfort stations, wherever there was animal heat and no expense. On our way back to the morgue one evening we noticed a reproduction of Turner's in the window of a department store. That's exactly the way in which it all began. One of the most active, one of the most enjoyable periods of my barren life. When I say that we littered the floor with paintings I am not exaggerating. As fast as they dried we hung them up—and the next day we took them down and hung up another collection. We painted on the backs of old ones, we washed them off, we scraped them with the knife, and in the course of these experiments we discovered, by accident, some astonishing things. We discovered how to get interesting results with coffee grounds and bread crumbs, with coal and arnica; we laid the paintings in the bathtub and let them soak for hours, and then with a loaded brush we approached these dripping omelettes and we let fly at them. Turner started all this—and the severe winter of *1927-28.*

Two nights before my departure, as I was saying, a number of painters come to the house to inspect our work. They are all good eggs and not above taking an interest in the work of amateurs. The water colors are lying about on the floor, as usual, drying. As a last experiment we walk over them, spilling a little wine as we go. Astonishing what effects a dirty heel will produce, or a drop of wine falling from a height of three feet with the best of intentions. The enthusiasm mounts. Two of my friends are working on the walls with chunks of coal. Another is boiling coffee in order to get some nice fresh grounds. The rest of us are drinking.

In the midst of the festivities—about three a.m.—my wife walks in. She seems a little depressed. Taking me aside she shows me a steamship ticket. I look at it. «What's that for?» I said. «You've got to go away,» she answers. «But I don't want to go away,» I said. «I'm quite happy here.» «So I see,» she says, rather sardonically.

Anyway I go. And when we're pulling up the Thames the only thought in my mind is to see the Turner collection at the Tate Gallery. Finally I get there and I see the famous Turners. And as luck would have it one of the half-wits there takes a fancy to me. I find that he's a magnificent water-colorist himself. Works entirely by lamplight. I really hated to leave London, he made it so agreeable for me. Anyway, pulling out of Southampton I thought to myself—«the circle is complete now: from the department store window to here.»

However, to get on.... This gondola is going to be the *piece de resistance!* But first I must clean up the walls. Taking the bread knife and dipping it into the *laque* carmine I apply a liberal dose to the windows of the houses. Holy Jesus! Immediately the houses are in flames! If I were really mad, and riot simulating the madness of a madman, I'd be putting firemen into the picture and I'd make ladders out of the bold diagonal planks of the bridge flooring. But my insanity takes the form of building a conflagration. I set all the houses on fire—first with carmine, then with vermilion, and finally with a bloody concoction of all three. This part of the picture is clear and decisive: it's a holocaust.

The result of my incendiarism is that I've singed the horse's back. Now he's neither a horse nor a zebra. He's become a fire-eating dragon. And where the missing tail belonged there is now a bunch of fire-crackers, and with a bunch of fire-crackers up his ass not even an Ionian horse can preserve his dignity. I could, of course, go on to make a real dragon; but this conversion and patching-up is getting on my nerves. If you start with a horse you ought to keep it a horse—or eliminate it entirely. Once you begin to tamper with an animal's anatomy you can go through the whole phylogenetic process.

With a solid opaque green and indigo I blot the horse out. In my mind, to be sure, he's still there. People may look at this opaque object and think—how strange! how curious! But *I* know that at bottom it's a horse. At the bottom of everything there's some animal: that's our deepest obsession. When I see human beings squirming up toward the light like wilted sunflowers, I say to myself: «Squirm, you bastards, and pretend all you like, but at bottom you're a turtle or a guinea-pig.» Greece was mad about horses and if they had had the wisdom to remain half horse instead of playing the Titan—well, we might have been spared a great many mythological pains.

When you're an *instinctive* water-colorist everything happens according to God's will. Thus, if you are bidden to paint the cemetery gates a clear gamboge, you do it and you don't grumble about it. Never mind if they are too vivid for such somber portals. Perhaps there is an unknown justification. And truly, when I paint in this bright liquid yellow, this yellow which is to me the finest of all yellows (even yellower than the mouth of the Yangtsze Kiang), I am radiant, radiant. Something dreary, cloying, oppressive has been washed away forever. I would not be surprised if it were the Cypress Hills Cemetery which I passed in disgust and mortification for so many years, which I looked down on from the bend in the elevated line, which I spat into from the platform of the train. Or St. John's Cemetery, with its crazy leaden angels, where I worked as a grave-digger. Or the Montparnasse Cemetery which in winter looks as if it had been shellshocked. Cemeteries, cemeteries.... By God, I refuse to be buried in a cemetery! I won't have any imbeciles standing over me with a sprinkler and looking mournful. I won't have it!

While these thoughts have been passing through my head I have been inadvertently smearing the trees and the terraces with a dry brush. The trees gleam now like a coat of mail, the boughs are studded with silver and turquoise links. If I had a crucifixion on hand

I could cover the bodies of the martyrs with jeweled pock-marks. On the wall opposite me is a scene from the wilds of Ethiopia. The body of Christ crucified lies on the floor covered with smallpox; the bloodthirsty Jews —black, Ethiopian Jews—are pounding him with iron quoits. They have a most ferociously gleeful expression. I bought the picture because of the pockmarks, *why* I didn't know at the time. It's only now that I've discovered the reason. Only now that I recall a certain picture over a cellar on the Bowery, entitled «Death on Bugs.» Happened I was just coming away from a lunatic, a professional visit which had not been altogether unpleasant. It's broad afternoon and the dirty throat of the Bowery is choked with clots of phlegm. Just below Cooper Square three bums are stretched out flat beside a lamppost, *A la* Breughel. A penny arcade is going full blast. A weird, unearthly chant rises up from the streets, like a man with a cleaver fighting his way through delirium tremens. And there, over the slanting cellar door, is this painting called «Death on Bugs.» A naked woman with long flaxen hair lies on the bed scratching herself. The bed is floating in the middle air and about it dances a man with a squirt gun. He has that same imbecilic air about him as these Jews with the iron quoits. The picture is stippled with pockmarks —to represent that cosmopolitan bloodsucking wingless depressed bug of reddish-brown color and vile odor which infests houses and beds and goes by the formidable name of *Cimex lectularius.*

And here I am now with a dry brush applying the stigmata to the three trees. The clouds are covered with bedbugs, the volcano is belching bedbugs; the bedbugs are scrambling down the steep chalk cliffs and drowning themselves in the river. I am like that young immigrant on the second floor of a poem by some Ivanovich or other who tosses about on the bedsprings haunted by the misery of his starved, wasted life, despairing of all the beauty beyond his grasp. My whole life seems to be wrapped up in that dirty handkerchief, the Bowery, which I walked through day after day, year in and year out—a dose of smallpox whose scars never disappear. If I had a name then it was Cimex Lectularius. If I had a home it was a slide trombone. If I had a passion it was to wash myself clean.

In a fury now I take the brush and dipping it in all the colors successively I commence to smudge the cemetery gates. I smudge and smudge until the lower half of the picture is as thick as chocolate, until the picture actually smells of pigment. And when it is completely ruined I sit there with a vacant enjoyment and twiddle my thumbs.

And then suddenly I get a real inspiration. I take it to the sink and after soaking it well I scrub it with the nail brush. I scrub and scrub and then I hold the picture upside down, letting the colors coagulate. Then gingerly, very gingerly, I flatten it out on my desk. It's a masterpiece, I tell you! I've been studying it for the last three hours....

You may say it's just an accident, this masterpiece, and so it is! But then, so is the Twenty-third Psalm. Every birth is miraculous—and inspired. What appears now before my eyes is the result of innumerable mistakes, withdrawals, erasures, hesitations; it is also the result of certitude. You would like to give the nail brush credit, and the water credit. Do so—by all means. Give everybody and everything credit. Credit Dante, credit Spinoza, credit Hieronymus Bosch. Credit Cash and debit Societe Anonyme. Put in the Day Book: *Tante Melia.* So. Draw a balance. Out by a penny, eh? If you could take a penny from your pocket and balance the books you would do so. But you are no longer dealing with actual pennies. There is no machine clever enough to devise, to counterfeit, this penny which does not exist. The world of real and counterfeit is behind us. Out of the tangible we have invented the intangible.

When you can draw up a clean balance you will no longer have a picture. Now you have an intangible, an accident, and you sit up all night with the open ledger cracking your skull over it. You have a minus sign on your hands. All live, interesting data is labeled minus. When you find the plus equivalent you have—*nothing.* You have that imaginary, momentary something called «a balance.» A balance never *is.* It's a fraud, like stopping the clock, or like calling a truce. You strike a balance in order to add a hypothetical weight, in order to create a reason for your existence.

I have never been able to draw a balance. I am always *minus* something. I have a reason therefore to go on. I am putting my whole life into the balance in order that it may produce nothing. To get to nothing you have to lay out an infinitude of figures. That's just it: in the living equation the sign for myself is infinity. To get nowhere you must traverse every known universe: you must be everywhere in order to be nowhere. To have disorder you must destroy *every* form of order. To go mad you must have a terrific accumulation of sanities. All the madmen whose works have inspired me were touched by a cold sanity. They have taught me nothing—because the balance sheets which they bequeathed to us have been falsified. Their calculations are meaningless to me—because the figures have been altered. The marvelous gilt-edged ledgers which they handed down have the hideous beauty of plants which are forced in the night.

My masterpiece! It's like a splinter under the nail. I ask you, now that you are looking at it, do you see in it the lakes beyond the Urals? do you see the mad Kotchei balancing himself with a paper parasol? do you see the arch of Trajan breaking through the smoke of Asia? do you see the penguins thawing in the Himalayas? do you see the Creeks and the Seminoles gliding through the cemetery gates? do you see the fresco from the Upper Nile, with its flying geese, its bats and aviaries? do you see the marvelous pommels of the Crusaders and the saliva that washed them down? do you see the wigwams belching fire? do you see the alkali sinks and the mule bones and the gleaming borax? do you see the tomb of Belshazzar, or the ghoul who is rifling it? do you see the new mouths which the Colorado will open up? do you see the starfish lying on their backs and the molecules supporting them? do you see the bursting eyes of Alexander, or the grief that inspired it? do you see the ink on which the squibs are feeding?

No, I'm afraid you don't! You see only the bleak blue angel frozen by the glaciers. You do not even see the umbrella ribs, because you are not trained to look for umbrella ribs. But you see an angel, and you see a horse's ass. And you may keep them: *they are for you!* There are no pockmarks on the angel now—only a cold blue spotlight which throws into relief his fallen stomach and his broken arches. The angel is there to lead you to Heaven, where it is all plus and no minus. The angel is there like a watermark, a guarantee of your faultless vision. The angel has no goiter; it is the artist who has the goiter. The angel is there to drop sprigs of parsley in your omelette, to put a shamrock in your buttonhole. I could scrub the mythology out of the horse's mane; I could scrub the yellow out of the Yangtsze Kiang; I could scrub the date out of the man in the gondola; I could scrub out the clouds and the tissue paper in which were wrapped the bouquets with forked lightning.... *But the angel I can't scrub out. The angel is my watermark.*

5. The Tailor Shop

I've got a motter: always merry and bright!

The day used to start like this: «Ask so-and-so for a little something on account, *but don't insult him!*» They were ticklish bastards, all these old farts we catered to. It was enough to drive any man to drink. There we were, just opposite the Olcott, Fifth Avenue tailors even though we weren't on the Avenue. A joint corporation of father and son, with mother holding the boodle.

Mornings, eight a.m. or thereabouts, a brisk intellectual walk from Delancey Street and the Bowery to just below the Waldorf. No matter how fast I walked old man Bendix was sure to be there ahead of me, raising hell with the cutter because neither of the bosses was on the job. How was it we could never get there ahead of that old buzzard Bendix? He had nothing to do, Bendix, but run from the tailor to the shirtmaker and from the shirtmaker to the jeweler's; his rings were either too loose or too tight, his watch was either twenty-five seconds slow or thirty-three seconds fast. He raised hell with everybody, including the family doctor, because the latter couldn't keep his kidneys clear of gravel. If we made him a sack coat in August by October it was too large for him, or too small. When he could find nothing to complain about he would dress on the right side so as to have the pleasure of bawling the pants maker out because he was strangling his, H. W. Bendix's, balls. A difficult guy. Touchy, whimsical, mean, crotchety, miserly, capricious, malevolent. When I look back on it all now, see the old man sitting down to table with his boozy breath and saying *shit why don't someone smile, why do you all look so glum,* I feel sorry for him and for all merchant tailors who have to kiss rich people's asses. If it hadn't been for the Olcott bar across the way and the sots he picked up there God knows what would have become of the old man. He certainly got no sympathy at home. My mother hadn't the least idea what it meant to be kissing rich people's backsides. All she knew how to do was to groan and lament all day, and with her groaning and lamenting she brought on the boozy breath and the potato dumplings grown cold. She got us so damned jumpy with her anxiety that we would choke on our own spittle, my brother and I. My brother was a halfwit and he got on the old man's nerves even more than H. W. Bendix with his «Pastor So-and-so's going to Europe.... Pastor So-and-so's going to open a bowling alley,» etc. «Pastor So-and-so's an ass,» the old man would say, «and why aren't the dumplings hot?»

There were three Bendixes—H. W., the grumpy one, A. F., whom the old man referred to in the ledger as Albert, and R.N., who never visited the shop because his legs were cut off, a circumstance, however, which did not prevent him from wearing out his trousers in due season. R. N. I never saw in the flesh. He was an item in the ledger which Bunchek the cutter spoke of glowingly because there was always a little schnapps about when it came time to try on the new trousers. The three brothers were eternal enemies; they never referred to one another in our presence. If Albert, who was a little cracked and had a penchant for dotted vests, happened to see a cutaway hanging on the rack with the words H. W. Bendix written in green ink on the try-on notice, he would give a feeble little grunt and say—«feels like spring today, eh?» There was not supposed to be a man by the name of H. W. Bendix in existence, though it was obvious to all and sundry that we were not making clothes for ghosts.

Of the three brothers I liked Albert the best. He had arrived at that ripe age when the bones become as brittle as glass. His spine had the natural curvature of old age, as though he were preparing to fold up and return to the womb. You could always tell when Albert was arriving because of the commotion in the elevator —a great cussing and whining followed by a handsome tip which accompanied the process of bringing the floor of the elevator to a dead level with the floor of our tailor shop. If it could not be brought to within a quarter of an inch exactitude there was no tip and Albert with his brittle bones and his bent spine would have a devil of a time choosing the right buttons to go with his dotted vest, his *latest* dotted vest. (When Albert died I inherited all his vests—they lasted me right through the war.) If it happened, as was sometimes the case, that the old man was across the street taking a little nip when Albert arrived, then somehow the whole day became disorganized. I remember periods when Albert grew so vexed with the old man that sometimes we did not see him for three days; meanwhile the vest buttons were lying around on little cards and there was talk of nothing but vest buttons, vest buttons, as if the vest itself didn't matter, only the buttons. Later, when Albert had grown accustomed to the old man's careless ways—they had been growing accustomed to each other for twenty-seven years—he would give us a ring to notify us that he was on the way. And just before hanging up he would add: «I suppose it's all right my coming in at eleven o'clock ... it won't inconvenience you?» The purport of this little query was twofold. It meant—«I suppose you'll have the decency to be on hand when I arrive and not make me fiddle around for a half-hour while you swill it down with your cronies across the street.» *And,* it also meant—«At eleven o'clock I suppose there is little danger of bumping into a certain individual bearing the initials H. W.?» In the twenty-seven years during which we made perhaps 1,578 garments for the three Bendix brothers it so happened that they never met, not in our presence at least. When Albert died R. N. and H. W. both had mourning bands put on their sleeves, on all the left sleeves of their sack coats and overcoats—that is, those which were not black coats—but nothing was said of the deceased, nor even *who* he was. R. N., of course, had a good excuse for not going to the funeral—his legs were gone. H. W. was too mean and too proud to even bother offering an excuse.

About ten o'clock was the time the old man usually chose to go down for his first nip. I used to stand at the window facing the hotel and watch George Sandusky hoisting the big trunks on to the taxis. When there were no trunks to be hoisted George used to stand there with his hands clasped behind his back and bow and scrape to the clients as they swung in and out of the revolving doors. George Sandusky had been scraping and bowing and hoisting and opening doors for about twelve years when I first came to the tailor shop and took up my post at the front window. He was a charming, soft-spoken man with beautiful white hair, and strong as an ox. He had raised this ass-kissing business to an art. I was amazed one day when he came up the elevator and ordered a suit from us. In his off hours he was a gentleman, George Sandusky. He had quiet tastes—always a blue serge or an Oxford gray. A man who knew how to conduct himself at a funeral or a wedding.

After we got to know each other he gave me to understand that he had found Jesus. With the smooth tongue he had, and the brawn, and the active help of said Jesus he had managed to lay aside a nest egg, a little something to ward off the horrors of old age. He was the only man I ever met in that period who had not taken out life insurance. He maintained that God would look after those who were left behind just as He had looked after him, George Sandusky. He had no fear of the world collapsing upon his decease. God had taken care of everybody and everything up to date— no reason to suppose He would fall down on the job after George Sandusky's death. When one day George retired it was difficult to find a man to replace him. There was no one oily or unctuous enough to fill the bill. No one who could bow and scrape like George. The old man always had a great affection for George. He used to try to persuade him to take a drink now and then, but George always refused with that habitual and stubborn politeness which had endeared him to the Olcott guests.

The old man often had moods when he would ask anybody to take a drink with him, even such as George Sandusky. Usually late in the afternoon on a day when things were going wrong, when nothing but bills were coming in. Sometimes a week would pass without a customer showing up, or if one did show up it was only to complain, to ask for an alteration, to bawl the piss out of the coat maker, or to demand a reduction in the price. Things like this would make the old man so blue that all he could do was to put on his hat and go for a drink. Instead of going across the street as usual he would wander off base a bit, duck into the Breslin or the Broztell, sometimes getting as far off the path as the Ansonia where his idol, Julian Legree, kept a suite of rooms.

Julian, who was then a matinee idol, wore nothing but gray suits, every shade of gray imaginable, but only grays. He had that depressingly cheerful demeanor of the beefy-faced English actor who lounges about here and there swapping stories with woolen salesmen, liquor dealers, and others of no account. His accent alone was enough to make men swarm about him; it was English in the traditional stage sense, warm, soapy, glutinous English which gives to even the most insignificant thought an appearance of importance. Julian never said anything that was worth recording but that voice of his worked magic on his admirers. Now and then, when he and the old man were doing the rounds, they would pick up a derelict such as Corse Payton who belonged across the river in the ten-twenty-thirties. Corse Payton was the idol of Brooklyn! Corse Payton was to art what Pat McCarren was to politics.

What the old man had to say during these discussions was always a source of mystery to me. The old man had never read a book in his life, nor had he ever been to a play since the days when the Bowery gave way to Broadway. I can see him standing there at the free lunch counter—Julian was very fond of the caviar and the sturgeon that was served at the Olcott—sponging it up like a thirsty dog. The two matinee idols discussing Shakespeare—whether *Hamlet* or *Lear* was the greatest play ever written. Or else arguing the merits of Bob Ingersoll.

Behind the bar at that time were three doughty Irishmen, three low-down micks such as made the bars of that day the congenial haunts they were. They were so highly thought of, these three, that it was considered a privilege to have such as Patsy O'Dowd, for example, call you a goddamned degenerate cocksucking son of a bitch who hadn't sense enough to button up his fly. And if, in return for the compliment, you asked him if he wouldn't have a little something himself, said Patsy O'Dowd would coldly and sneeringly reply that only such as yourself were fit to pour such rotgut down your throat, and so saying he would scornfully lift your glass by the stem and wipe the mahogany because that was part of his job and he was paid to do it but be damned to you if you thought you could entice such as him to poison his intestines with the vile stuff. The more vicious his insults the more he was esteemed; financiers who were accustomed to having their asses wiped with silk handkerchiefs would drive all the way uptown, after the ticker closed down, in order to have this foulmouthed bastard of an Irish mick call them goddamned degenerate cock-sucking sons of bitches. It was the end of a perfect day for them.

The boss of this jaunty emporium was a portly little mart with aristocratic shanks and the head of a lion. He always marched with his stomach thrown forward, a little wine cask hidden under his vest. He usually gave a stiff, supercilious nod to the sots at the bar, unless they happened to be guests of the hotel, in which case he would pause a moment, extend three fat little fingers with blue veins and then, with a swirl of his mustache and a gingerly, creaky pirouette, he would whisk away. He was the only enemy the old man had. The old man simply couldn't stomach him. He had a feeling that Tom Moffatt looked down upon him. And so when Tom Moffatt came round to order his clothes the old man would tack on ten or fifteen per cent to cover the rents in his pride. But Tom Moffatt was a genuine aristocrat: he never questioned the price and he never paid his bills. If we dunned him he would get his accountant to find a discrepancy in our statements. And when it came time to order another pair of flannel trousers, or a cutaway, or a dinner jacket, he would sail in with his usual portly dignity, his stomach well forward, his mustache waxed, his shoes brightly polished and squeaky as always, and with an air of weary indifference, of aloof disdain, he would greet the old man as follows: «Well, have you straightened out that error yet?» Upon which the old man would fly into a rage and palm off a remnant or a piece of American goods on his enemy Tom Moffatt. A long correspondence ensued over the «little error» in our statements. The old man was beside himself. He hired an expert accountant who drew up statements three feet long—but to no avail. Finally the old man hit upon an idea.

Toward noon one day, after he had had his usual portion, after he had stood treat to all the woolen salesmen and the trimmings salesmen who were gathered at the bar, he quietly picked up the bar stubs and taking a little silver pencil which was attached to his watch chain he signed his name to the checks and sliding them across to Patsy O'Dowd he said: «Tell Moffatt to charge them up to my account.» Then he quietly moved off and, inviting a few of his select cronies, he took a table in the dining room and commanded a spread. And when Adrian the frog presented the bill he calmly said: «Give me a pencil. There ... them's my demi-quivers. Charge it up to my account.» Since it was more pleasant to eat in the company of others he would always invite his cronies to lunch with him, saying to all and sundry—«if that bastard Moffatt won't pay for his clothes then we'll eat them.» And so saying he would commandeer a juicy squab, or a lobster a la Newburg, and wash it down with a fine Moselle or any other vintage that Adrian the frog might happen to recommend.

To all this Moffatt, surprisingly enough, pretended to pay no heed. He continued to order his usual allotment of clothes for winter, spring, fall and summer, and he also continued to squabble about the bill which had become easier to do now since it was complicated with bar checks, telephone calls, squabs, lobsters, champagne, fresh strawberries, Benedictines, etc., etc. In fact, the old man was eating into that bill so fast that spindleshanks Moffatt couldn't wear his clothes out quickly enough. If he came in to order a pair of flannel trousers the old man had already eaten it the next day.

Finally Moffatt evinced an earnest desire to have the account straightened out. The correspondence ceased. Patting me on the back one day as I happened to be standing in the lobby he put on his most cordial manner and invited me upstairs to his private office. He said he had always regarded me as a very sensible young man and that we could probably straighten the matter out between ourselves, without bothering the old man. I looked over the accounts and I saw that the old man had eaten way into the minus side. I had probably eaten up a few raglans and shooting jackets myself. There was only one thing to do if we were to keep Tom Moffatt's despised patronage and that was to find an error in the account. I took a bundle of bills under my arm and promised the old geezer that I would look into the matter thoroughly.

The old man was delighted when he saw how things stood. We kept looking into the matter for years. Whenever Tom Moffatt came round to order a suit the old man would greet him cheerily and say: «Have you straightened out that little error yet? Now here's a fine Barathea weave that I laid aside for you....» And Moffatt would frown and grimace and strut back and forth like a turkey cock, his comb bristling, his thin little legs blue with malice. A half hour later the old man would be standing at the bar swilling it down. «Just sold Moffatt another dinner jacket,» he would say. «By the way, Julian, what would you like to order for lunch today?»

It was toward noon, as I say, that the old man usually went down for an appetizer; lunch lasted anywhere from noon till four or five in the afternoon. It was marvelous the companionship the old man enjoyed in those days. After lunch the troupe would stagger out of the elevator, spitting and guffawing, their cheeks aflame, and lodge themselves in the big leather chairs beside the cuspidors. There was Ferd Pattee who sold silk linings and trimmings such as skeins of thread, buttons, chest padding, canvas, etc. A great hulk of a man, like a liner that's been battered by a typhoon, and always walking about in a somnambulistic state; so tired he was that he could scarcely move his lips, yet that slight movement of the lips kept everybody about him in stitches. Always muttering to himself—about cheeses particularly. He was passionate about cheese, about schmierkase and limburger especially—the moldier the better. In between the cheeses he told stories about Heine and Schubert, or he would ask for a match just as he was about to break wind and hold it under his seat so that we could tell him the color of the flame. He never said goodby or see you tomorrow; he commenced talking where he had left off the day before, as though there had been no interruption of time. No matter whether it was nine in the morning or six in the evening he walked with the same exasperating slow shambling gait, muttering in his vici-kids, his head down, his linings and trimmings under his arm, his breath foul, his nose purple and translucent. Into the thickest traffic he would walk with head down, schmierkase in one pocket and limburger in the other. Stepping out of the elevator he would say in that weary monotonous voice of his that he had some new linings and the cheese was fine last night were you thinking of returning the book he had loaned you and better pay up soon if you want more goods like to see some dirty pictures please scratch my back there a little higher that's it excuse me I'm going to fart now have you the time I can't waste all day here better tell the old man to put on his hat it's time to go for a drink. Still mumbling and grumbling he turns on his big scows and presses the elevator button while the old man with a straw hat on the back of his head is making a slide for the home plate from the back of the store, his face lit up with love and gratitude and saying: «Well, Ferd, how are you this morning? It's good to see you.» And Ferd's big heavy mask of a face relaxes for a moment into a broad amiable grin. Just a second he holds it and then, lifting his voice he bellows at the top of his lungs—so that even Tom Moffatt across the way can hear it—«BETTER PAY UP SOON WHAT THE HELL DO YOU THINK I'M SELLING THESE THINGS FOR?»

And as soon as the elevator has started down out conies little Rubin from the busheling room and with a wild look in his eye he says to me: «Would you like me to sing for you?» He knows damned well that I would. So, going back to the bench, he picks up the coat that he's stitching and with a wild Cossack shout he lets loose.

If you were to pass him in the street, little Rubin, you would say «dirty little kike,» and perhaps he was a dirty little kike but he knew how to sing and when you were broke he knew how to put his hand in his pocket and when you were sad he was sadder still and if you tried to step on him he spat on your shoe and if you were repentant he wiped it off and he brushed you down and put a crease in your trousers like Jesus H. Christ himself couldn't do.

They were all midgets in the busheling room— Rubin, Rapp, and Chaimowitz. At noon they brought out big round loaves of Jewish bread which they smeared with sweet butter and slivers of lox. While the old man was ordering squabs and Rhine wine Bunchek the cutter and the three little bushelmen sat on the big bench among the goose irons and the legs and sleeves and talked earnestly and solemnly about things like the rent or the ulcers that Mrs. Chaimowitz had in her womb. Bunchek was an ardent member of the Zionist party. He believed that the Jews had a happy future ahead of them. But despite it all he could never properly pronounce a word like «screw.» He always said: «He *scruled* her.» Besides his passion for Zionism Bunchek had another obsession and that was to make a coat one day that would hug the neck. Nearly all the customers were round-shouldered and potbellied, especially the old bastards who had nothing to do all day but run from the shirtmaker to the tailor and from the tailor to the jeweler's and from the jeweler's to the dentist and from the dentist to the druggist. There were so many alterations to be made that by the time the clothes were ready to be worn the season had passed and they had to be put away until next year, and by next year the old bastards had either gained twenty pounds or lost twenty pounds and what with sugar in their urine and water in the blood it was hell to please them even when the clothes did fit.

Then there was Paul Dexter, a $10,000-a-year man but always out of work. Once he almost had a job, but it was $9,000 a year and his pride wouldn't permit him to accept it. And since it was important to be well groomed, in the pursuit of this mythical job, Paul felt it incumbent upon him to patronize a good tailor such as the old man. Once he landed the job everything would be settled in full. There was never any question about that in Paul's mind. He was thoroughly honest. But he was a dreamer. He came from Indiana. And like all dreamers from Indiana he had such a lovable disposition, such a smooth, mellow, honeyed way that if he had committed incest the world would have forgiven him. When he had on the right tie, when he had chosen the proper cane and gloves, when the lapels were softly rolled and the shoes didn't squeak, when he had a quart of rye under his belt and the weather wasn't too damp or dismal then there flowed from his personality such a warm current of love and understanding that even the trimmings salesmen, hardened as they were to soft language, melted in their boots. Paul, when all circumstances were favorably conjoined, could walk up to a man, any man on God's green earth and, taking him by the lapel of his coat, drown him in love. Never did I see a man with such powers of persuasion, such magnetism. When the flood began to rise in him he was invincible.

Paul used to say: «Start with Marcus Aurelius, or Epictetus, and the rest will follow.» He didn't recommend studying Chinese or learning Provencal: he began with the fall of the Roman Empire. It was my great ambition in those days to win Paul's approbation, but Paul was difficult to please. He frowned when I showed him *Thus Spake Zarathustra*. He frowned when he saw me sitting on the bench with the midgets trying to expound the meaning of *Creative Evolution*. Above all, he loathed the Jews. When Bunchek the cutter appeared, with a piece of chalk and a tape measure slung around his neck, Paul became excessively polite and condescending. He knew that Bunchek despised him, but because Bunchek was the old man's right hand man he rubbed him down with oil, he larded him with compliments. So that eventually even Bunchek had to admit that there was something to Paul, some strange mark of personality which, despite his shortcomings, endeared him to every one.

Outwardly Paul was all cheerfulness. But at bottom he was morose. Every now and then Cora, his wife, would sail in with eyes brimming with tears and implore the old man to take Paul in hand. They used to stand at the round table near the window conversing in a low voice. She was a beautiful woman, his wife, tall, statuesque, with a deep contralto voice that seemed to quiver with anguish whenever she mentioned Paul's name. I could see the old man putting his hand on her shoulder, soothing her, and promising her all sorts of things no doubt. She liked the old man, I could see that. She used to stand very close to him and look into his eyes in a way that was irresistible. Sometimes the old man would put his hat on and the two of them would go down the elevator together, arm in arm, as if they were going to a funeral. Off looking for Paul again. Nobody knew where to find him when he had a drinking fever on. For days on end he would disappear from sight. And then one day he would turn up, crestfallen, repentant, humiliated, and beg everybody's forgiveness. At the same time he would hand in his suit to be dry cleaned, to have the vomit stains removed, and a bit of expert repairing done at the knees.

It was after a bout that Paul talked most eloquently. He used to sit back in one of the deep leather chairs, the gloves in one hand, the cane between his legs, and discourse about Marcus Aurelius. He talked even better when he came back from the hospital, after he had had the fistula repaired. The way he lowered himself into the big leather chair made me think then that he came expressly to the tailor shop because nowhere else could he find such a comfortable seat. It was a painful operation either to sit down or to get up. But once accomplished Paul seemed to be in bliss and the words rolled off his tongue like liquid velvet. The old man could listen to Paul all day long. He used to say that Paul had the gift of gab, but that was only his inarticulate way of saying that Paul was the most lovable creature on God's earth and that he had a fire in his bowels. And when Paul was too conscience-stricken to order another suit the old man would coax him into it, saying to Paul all the while, «Nothing's too good for you, Paul... nothing!»

Paul must have recognized something of a kindred nature in the old man too. Never have I seen two men look at each other with such a warm glow of admiration. Sometimes they would stand there looking into each other's eyes adoringly until the tears came. In fact, neither of them was ashamed of showing his tears, something which seems to have gone out of the world now. I can see Paul's homely freckled face and his rather thick, blubbery lips twitching as the old man told him for the thousandth time what a great guy he was. Paul never spoke to the old man about things he wouldn't understand. But into the simple, everyday things which he discoursed about so earnestly he put such a wealth of tenderness that the old man's soul seemed to leave his body and when Paul was gone he was like a man bereaved. He would go then into the little cubbyhole of an office and he would sit there quietly all by himself staring ecstatically at the row of pigeon coops which were filled with letters unanswered and bills unpaid. It used to affect me so, to see him in one of these moods, that I would sneak quietly down the stairs and start to walk home, down the Avenue to the Bowery and along the Bowery to the Brooklyn Bridge, and then over the bridge past the string of cheap flops that extended from City Hall to Fulton Ferry. And if it were a summer's evening, and the entranceways crowded with loungers, I would look among these wasted figures searchingly, wondering how many Pauls there were among them and what it is about life that makes these obvious failures so endearing to men. The others, the successful ones, I had seen with their pants off; I had seen their crooked spines, their brittle bones, their varicose veins, their tumors, their sunken chests, their big breadbaskets which had grown shapeless with years of swilling it. Yes, all the silk-lined duffers I knew well— we had the best families in America on our roster. And what a pus and filth when they opened their dirty traps!

It seemed as though when they had undressed before their tailor they felt compelled to unload the garbage which had accumulated in the plugged-up sinks which they had made of their minds. All the beautiful diseases of boredom and riches. Talked about them-selves *ad nauseam*. Always «I,» «I.» I and my kidneys. I and my gout. I and my liverworts. When I think of Paul's dreadful hemorrhoids, of the marvelous fistula they repaired, of all the love and learning that issued from his grievous wounds, then I think that Paul was not of this age at all but sib brother to Moses Maimonides, he who under the Moors gave us those astounding learned treatises on «hemorrhoids, warts, carbuncles,» etc.

In the case of all these men whom the old man so cherished death came quickly and unexpectedly. In Paul's case it happened while he was at the seashore. He was drowned in a foot of water. Heart failure, they said. And so, one fine day Cora came up the elevator, clad in her beautiful mourning garb, and wept all over the place. Never had she looked more beautiful to me, more svelte, more statuesque. Her ass particularly—I remember how caressingly the velvet clung to her figure. Again they stood near the round table at the front window, and this time she wept copiously. And again the old man put on his hat and down the elevator they went, arm in arm.

A short time later the old man, moved by some strange whim, urged me to call on Paul's wife and offer my condolences. When I rang the bell at her apartment I was trem-bling. I almost expected her to come out stark naked, with perhaps a mourning band around her breasts. I was infatuated with her beauty, with her years, with that somnolent, plantlike quality she had brought from Indiana and the perfume which she bathed in. She greeted me in a low-cut mourning gown, a beautiful clinging gown of black velvet. It was the first rime I had ever had a tete-a-tete with a woman bereft, a woman whose breasts seemed to sob out loud. I didn't know what to say to her, especially about Paul. I stam-mered and blushed, and when she asked me to sit beside her on the couch I almost fell over her in my embarrassment.

Sitting there on the low sofa, the place flooded with soft lights, her big heaving loins rubbing against me, the Malaga pounding my temples and all this crazy talk about Paul and how good he was, I finally bent over and without saying a word I raised her dress and slipped it into her. And as I got it into her and began to work it around she took to moan-ing like, a sort of delirious, sorrowful guilt punctuated with gasps and little shrieks of joy and anguish, saying over and over again—«I never thought you would do this ... I never thought you would do this!» And when it was all over she ripped off the velvet dress, the beautiful low-cut mourning gown, and she put my head down on her and she told me to kiss it and with her two strong arms she squeezed me almost in half and moaned and sobbed. And then she got up and she walked around the room naked for a while. And then finally she got down on her knees beside the sofa where I was stretched out and she said in a low tearful voice—«You promise me you'll love me always, won't you? You promise me?» And I said Yes with one hand working around in her crotch. Yes I said and I thought to myself what a sap you've been to wait so long. She was so wet and juicy down there, and so childlike, so trustful, why anybody could have come along and had what's what. She was a pushover.

Always merry and bright! Regularly, every season, there were a few deaths. Sometimes it was a good egg like Paul, or Julian Legree, sometimes a bartender who had picked his nose with a rusty nail—hail and hearty one day, dead the next—but regularly, like the movement of the seasons themselves, the old buzzards dropped off, one by one. *Alors,* nothing to do but draw a red line slantwise down the right-hand side of the ledger and mark «dead.» Each death brought a little business —a new black suit or else mourning bands on the left sleeve of every coat. Those who ordered mourning bands were cheapskates, according to the old man. And so they were.

As the old 'uns died off they were replaced by young blood. *Young blood!* That was the war cry all along the Avenue, wherever there were silk-lined suits for sale. A fine bloody crew they were, the young bloods. Gamblers, racetrack touts, stockbrokers, ham actors, prize fighters, etc. Rich one day, poor the next. No honor, no loyalty, no sense of responsibility. A fine bunch of gangrened syphilitics they were, most of 'em. Came back from Paris or Monte Carlo with dirty postcards and a string of big blue rocks in their groin. Some of them with balls as big as a lamb's fry.

One of them was the Baron Carola von Eschenbach. He had earned a little money in Hollywood posing as the Crown Prince. It was the period when it was considered riotously funny to see the Crown Prince plastered with rotten eggs. It must be said for the Baron that he was a good double for the Crown Prince. A death's head with arrogant nose, a waspish stride, a corseted waist, lean and ravished as Martin Luther, dour, glum, fanatical, with that brassy, fatuous glare of the Junker class. Before going to Hollywood he was just a nobody, the son of a German brewer in Frankfort. He wasn't even a baron. But afterwards, when he had been knocked about like a medicine ball, when his front teeth had been pushed down his throat and the neck of a broken bottle had traced a deep scar down his left cheek, afterwards when he had been taught to flaunt a red necktie, twirl a cane, clip his mustache short, like Chaplin, then he became somebody. Then he stuck a monocle in his eye and named himself Baron Carola von Eschenbach. And all might have gone beautifully for him had he not fallen for a redhaired walk-on who was rotting away with syphilis. That finished him.

Up the elevator he came one day in a cutaway and spats, a bright red rose in his buttonhole and the monocle stuck in his eye. Blithe and dapper he looked, and the card he took out of his wallet was handsomely engraved. It bore a coat of arms which had been in the family, so he said, for nine hundred years. «The family skeleton,» he called it. The old man was highly pleased to have a baron among his clients, especially if he paid cash, as this one promised to do. And then too it was exhilarating to see the baron come sailing in with a pair of soubrettes on his arm—each time a different pair. Even more exhilarating when he invited them into the dressing room and asked them to help him off with his trousers. It was a European custom, he explained.

Gradually he got acquainted with all the old cronies who hung out in the front of the shop. He showed them how the Crown Prince walked, how he sat down, how he smiled. One day he brought a flute with him and he played the Lorelei on it. Another day he came in with a finger of his pigskin glove sticking out of his fly. Each day he had a new trick up his sleeve. He was gay, witty, amusing. He knew a thousand jokes, some that had never been told before. He was a riot.

And then one day he took me aside and asked me if I could lend him a dime—for carfare. He said he couldn't pay for the clothes he had ordered but he expected a job soon in a little movie house on Ninth Avenue, playing the piano. And then, before I knew it, he began to weep. We were standing in the dressing room and the curtains were drawn, fortunately. I had to lend him a handkerchief to wipe his eyes. He said he was tired of playing the clown, that he dropped in to our place every day because it was warm there and because we had comfortable seats. He asked me if I couldn't take him to lunch—he had had nothing but coffee and buns for the last three days.

I took him to a little German restaurant on Third Avenue, a bakery and restaurant combined. The atmosphere of the place broke him down completely. He could talk of nothing but the old days, the old days, the days before the war. He had intended to be a painter, and then the war came. I listened attentively and when he got through I proposed that he come to my home for dinner that evening—perhaps I could put him up with us. He was overwhelmed with gratitude. Sure, he would come—at seven o'clock *punkt*. Fine!

At the dinner table my wife was amused by his stories. I hadn't said anything about his being broke. Just that he was a baron—the Baron von Eschenbach, a friend of Charlie Chaplin's. My wife—one of my first ones—was highly flattered to sit at the same table with a baron. And puritanical bastard that she was, she never so much as blushed when he told a few of his risque stories. She thought they were delightful— *so European*. Finally, however, it came time to spill the beans. I tried to break the news gently, but how can you be gentle about a subject like syphilis? I didn't call it syphilis at first—I said «venereal disease.» *Maladie intime, quoi!* But just that little word «venereal» sent a shudder through my wife. She looked at the cup he was holding to his lips and then she looked at me imploringly, as though to say—«how could you ask a man like that to sit at the same table with us?» I saw that it was necessary to bring the matter to a head at once. «The baron here is going to stay with us for a while,» I said quietly. «He's broke and he needs a place to flop.» My word, I never saw a woman's expression change so quickly. «*You!*» she said, «*you* ask *me* to do that? And what about the baby? You want us all to have syphilis, is that it? It's not enough that *he* has it—you want the baby to have it too!»

The baron of course was frightfully embarrassed by this outburst. He wanted to leave at once. But I told him to keep his shirt on. I was used to these scenes. Anyway, he got so wrought up that he began to choke over his coffee. I thumped him on the back until he was blue in the face. The rose fell out of his buttonhole on to the plate. It looked strange there, as though he had coughed it up out of his own blood. It made me feel so goddamned ashamed of my wife that I could have strangled her on the spot. He was still choking and sputtering as I led him to the bathroom. I told him to wash his face in cold water. My wife followed us in and watched in murderous silence as he performed his ablutions. When he had wiped his face she snatched the towel from his hands and, flinging the bathroom window open, flung it out. That made me furious. I told her to get the hell out of the bathroom and mind her own business. But the baron stepped between us and flung himself at my wife supplicatingly. «You'll see, my good woman, and you, Henry, you won't have to worry about a thing. I'll bring all my syringes and ointments and I'll put them in a little valise—there, under the sink. You mustn't turn me away, I have nowhere to go. I'm a desperate man. I'm alone in the world. You were so good to me before—why must you be cruel now? Is it my fault that I have the syph? Anybody can get the syph. It's human. You'll see, I'll pay you back a thousand times. I'll do anything for you. I'll make the beds, I'll wash the dishes... I'll cook for you....» He went on and on like that, never stopping to take a breath for fear that she would say No. And after he had gotten all through with his promises, after he had begged her forgiveness a hundred times, after he had knelt down and tried to kiss her hand which she drew away abruptly, he sat down on the toilet seat, in his cutaway and spats, and he began to sob, to sob like a child. It was ghastly, the sterile, white-enameled bathroom and the splintering light as if a thousand mirrors had been shattered under a magnifying glass, and then this wreck of a baron, in his cutaway and spats, his spine filled with mercury, his sobs coming like the short puffs of a locomotive getting under way. I didn't know what the hell to do. A man sitting on the toilet like that and sobbing—it got under my skin. Later I became inured to it. I got hard-boiled. I feel quite certain now that had it not been for the two hundred and fifty bed patients whom he was obliged to visit twice a day at the hospital in Lyons, Rabelais would never have been so boisterously gay. I'm sure of it.

Anyhow, apropos the sobs.... A little later, when another kid was on the way and no means of getting rid of it, though still hoping, still hoping that something would happen, a miracle perhaps, and her stomach blown up like a ripe watermelon, about the sixth or seventh month, as I say, she used to succumb to fits of melancholy and, lying on the bed with that watermelon staring her in the eye, she would commence to sob fit to break your heart. Maybe I'd be in the other room, stretched out on the couch, with a big, fat book in my hands, and those sobs of hers would make me think of the Baron Carola von Eschenbach, of his gray spats and the cutaway with braided lapels, and the deep red rose in his buttonhole. Her sobs were like music to my ears. Sobbing away for a little sympathy she was, and not a drop of sympathy in the house. It was pathetic. The more hysterical she grew the more deaf I became. It was like listening to the boom and sizzle of surf along the beach on a summer's night: the buzz of a mosquito can drown out the ocean's roar. Anyway, after she had worked herself up to a state of collapse, when the neighbors couldn't stand it any longer and there were knocks on the door, then her aged mother would come crawling out of the bedroom and with tears in her eyes would beg me to go in there and quiet her a bit. «Oh, leave her be,» I'd say, «she'll get over it.» Whereupon, ceasing her sobs for a moment the wife would spring out of bed, wild, blind with rage, her hair all down and tangled up, her eyes swollen and bleary, and still hiccoughing and sobbing she would commence to pound me with her fists, to lambast me until I became hysterical with laughter. And when she saw me rocking to and fro like a crazy man, when her arms were tired and her fists sore, she would yell like a drunken whore —«Fiend! Demon!»—and then slink off like a weary dog. Afterwards, when I had quieted her down a bit, when I realized that she really needed a kind word or two, I would tumble her on to the bed again and throw a good fuck into her. Blast me if she wasn't the finest piece of tail imaginable after those scenes of grief and anguish! I never heard a woman moan and gibber like she could. «*Do anything* to me!» she used to say. «Do what you want!» I could stand her on her head and blow into it, I could back-scuttle her, I could drag her past the parson's house, as they say, any goddamn thing at all—she was simply delirious with joy. Uterine hysteria, that's what it was! *And I hope God take me,* as the good master used to say, *if I am lying in a single word I say.*

(God, mentioned above, being defined by St. Augustine, as follows: «An infinite sphere, the center of which is everywhere, the circumference nowhere.»)

However, *always merry and bright!* If it was before the war and the thermometer down to zero or below, if it happened to be Thanksgiving Day, or New Year's or a birthday, or just any old excuse to get together, then off we'd trot, the whole family, to join the other freaks who made up the living family tree. It always seemed astounding to me how jolly they were in our family despite the calamities that were always threatening. Jolly in spite of everything. There was cancer, dropsy, cirrhosis of the liver, insanity, thievery, mendacity, buggery, incest, paralysis, tapeworms, abortions, triplets, idiots, drunkards, ne'er-do-wells, fanatics, sailors, tailors, watchmakers, scarlet fever, whooping cough, meningitis, running ears, chorea, stutterers, jailbirds, dreamers, storytellers, bartenders—and finally there was Uncle George and Tante Melia. The morgue and the insane asylum. A merry crew and the table loaded with good things—with red cabbage and green spinach, with roast pork and turkey and sauerkraut, with kartoffel-klosze and sour black gravy, with radishes and celery, with stuffed goose and peas and carrots, with beautiful white cauliflower, with apple sauce and figs from Smyrna, with bananas big as a blackjack, with cinnamon cake and Streussel Kuchen, with chocolate layer cake and nuts, all kinds of nuts, walnuts, butternuts, almonds, pecans, hickory nuts, with lager beer and bottled beer, with white wines and red, with champagne, Kummel, malaga, port, with schnapps, with fiery cheeses, with dull, innocent store cheese, with flat Holland cheeses, with limburger and schmierkase, with homemade wines, elderberry wine, with cider, hard and sweet, with rice pudding and tapioca, with roast chestnuts, mandarins, olives, pickles, with red caviar and black, with smoked sturgeon, with lemon meringue pie, with lady fingers and chocolate eclairs, with macaroons and cream puffs, with black cigars and long thin stogies, with Bull Durham and Long Tom and meerschaums, with corncobs and toothpicks, wooden toothpicks which gave you gum boils the day after, and napkins a yard wide with your initials stitched in the corner, and a blazing coal fire and the windows steaming, everything in the world before your eyes except a finger bowl.

Zero weather and crazy George, with one arm bitten off by a horse, dressed in dead men's remnants. Zero weather and Xante Melia looking for the birds she left in her hat. Zero, zero, and the tugs snorting below in the harbor, the ice floes bobbing up and down, and long thin streams of smoke curling fore and aft. The wind blowing down at seventy miles an hour; tons and tons of snow all chopped up into tiny flakes and each one carrying a dagger. The icicles hanging like corkscrews outside the window, the wind roaring, the panes rattling. Uncle Henry is singing «Hurrah for the German Fifth!» His vest is open, his suspenders are down, the veins stand out on his temples. *Hurrah for the German Fifth!*

Up in the loft the creaking table is spread; down below is the warm stable, the horses whinnying in the stalls, whinnying and champing and pawing and stomping, and the fine aromatic smell of manure and horse piss, of hay and oats, of steaming blankets and dry cruds, the smell of malt and old wood, of leather harness and tanbark floats up and rests like incense over our heads.

The table is standing on horses and the horses are standing in warm piss and every now and then they get frisky and whisk their tails and they fart and whinny. The stove is glowing like a ruby, the air is blue with smoke. The bottles are under the table, on the dresser, in the sink. Crazy George is trying to scratch his neck with an empty sleeve. Ned

Martini, the ne'er-do-well, is fiddling with the phonograph; his wife Carrie is guzzling it from the tin growler. The brats are downstairs in the stable playing stinkfinger in the dark. In the street, where the shanties begin, the kids are making a sliding pond. It's blue everywhere, with cold and smoke and snow. Tante Melia is sitting in a corner fingering a rosary. Uncle Ned is repairing a harness. The three grandfathers and the two great-grandfathers are huddled near the stove talking about the Franco-Prussian war. Crazy George is lapping up the dregs. The women are getting closer together, their voices low, their tongues clacking. Everything fits together like a jigsaw puzzle—faces, voices, gestures, bodies.

Each one gravitates within his own orbit. The phonograph is working again, the voices get louder and shriller. The phonograph stops suddenly. I oughtn't to have been there when they blurted it out, but I was there and I heard it. I heard that big Maggie, the one who kept a saloon out in Flushing, well that Maggie had slept with her own brother and that's why George was crazy. She slept with everybody—except her own husband. And then I heard that she used to beat George with a leather belt, used to beat him until he foamed at the mouth. That's what brought on the fits. And then Mele sitting there in the corner—she was another case. She was queer even as a child. So was the mother, for that matter. It was too bad that Paul had died. Paul was Mele's husband. Yes, everything would have been all right if that woman from Hamburg hadn't shown up and corrupted Paul. What could Mele do against a clever woman like that—against a shrewd strumpet! Something would have to be done about Mele. It was getting dangerous to have her around. Just the other day they caught her sitting on the stove. Fortunately the fire was low. But supposing she took it into her head to set fire to the house—when they were all asleep? It was a pity that she couldn't hold a job any more. The last place they had found for her was such a nice berth, such a kind woman. Mele was getting lazy. She had had it too easy with Paul.

The air was clear and frosty when we stepped outdoors. The stars were crisp and sparkly and everywhere, lying over the bannisters and steps and window-ledges and gratings, was the pure white snow, the driven snow, the white mantle that covers the dirty, sinful earth. Clear and frosty the air, pure, like deep draughts of ammonia, and the skin smooth as chamois. Blue stars, beds and beds of them, drifting with the antelopes. Such a beautiful, deep silent night, as if under the snow there lay hearts of gold, as if this warm German blood was running away in the gutter to stop the mouths of hungry babes, to wash the crime and ugliness of the world away. Deep night and the river choked with ice, the stars dancing, swirling, spinning like tops. Along the broken street we straggled, the whole family. Walking along the pure white crust of the earth, leaving tracks, foot-stains. The old German family sweeping the snow with a Christmas tree. The whole family there, uncles, cousins, brothers, sisters, fathers, grandfathers. The whole family is warm and winey and no one thinks of the other, of the sun that will come in the morning, of the errands to run, of the doctor's verdict, of all the cruel, ghastly duties that foul the day and make this night holy, this holy night of blue stars and deep drifts, of arnica blossoms and ammonia, of asphodels and carborundum.

No one knew that Tante Melia was going completely off her nut, that when we reached the corner she would leap forward like a reindeer and bite a piece out of the moon. At the corner she leapt forward like a reindeer and she shrieked. «The moon, the moon!» she cried, and with that her soul broke loose, jumped clean out of her body. Eighty-six million miles a minute it traveled. Out, out, to the moon, and nobody could think quick enough to stop it. Just like that it happened. In the twinkle of a star.

And now I'm going to tell you what those bastards said to me....

They said—*Henry, you take her to the asylum tomorrow. And don't tell them that we can afford to pay for her.*

Fine! *Always merry and bright!* The next morning we boarded the trolley together and we rode out into the country. If Mele asked where we were going I was to say—«to visit Aunt Monica.» But Mele didn't ask any questions. She sat quietly beside me and pointed to the cows now and then. She saw blue cows and green ones. She knew their names. She asked what happened to the moon in the daytime. And did I have a piece of liverwurst by any chance?

During the journey I wept—I couldn't help it. When people are too good for this world they have to be put under lock and key. There's something wrong with people who are too good. It's true Mele was lazy. She was born lazy. It's true that Mele was a poor housekeeper. It's true Mele didn't know how to hold on to a husband when they found her one. When Paul ran off with the woman from Hamburg Mele sat in a corner and wept. The others wanted her to do something— put a bullet in him, raise a rumpus, sue for alimony. Mele sat quiet. Mele wept. Mele hung her head. What little intelligence she had deserted her. She was like a pair of torn socks that are kicked around here, there, everywhere. Always turning up at the wrong moment.

Then one day Paul took a rope and hanged himself. Mele must have understood what had happened because now she went completely crazy. The day before they found her eating her own dung. The day before that they found her sitting on the stove.

And now she's very tranquil and she calls the cows by their first name. The moon fascinates her. She has no fear because I'm with her and she always trusted me. I was her favorite. Even though she was a half-wit she was good to me. The others were more intelligent, but their hearts were bad.

When brother Adolphe used to take her for a carriage ride the others used to say— «Mele's got her eye on him!» But I think that Mele must have talked just as innocently then as she's talking to me now. I think that Mele, when she was performing her marriage duties, must have been dreaming innocently of the beautiful gifts she would give to everybody. I don't think that Mele had any knowledge of sin or of guilt or remorse. I think that Mele was born a half-witted angel. I think Mele was a saint.

Sometimes when she was fired from a job they used to send me to fetch her. Mele never knew her way home. And I remember how happy she was whenever she saw me coming. She would say innocently that she wanted to stay with us. Why couldn't she stay with us? I used to ask myself that over and over. Why couldn't they make a place for her by the fire, let her sit there and dream, if that's what she wanted to do? Why must everybody *work*—even the saints and the angels? Why must half-wits set a good example?

I'm thinking now that after all it may be good for Mele where I'm taking her. No more work. Just the same, I'd rather they had made a corner for her somewhere.

Walking down the gravel path toward the big gates Mele becomes uneasy. Even a puppy knows when it is being carried to a pond to be drowned. Mele is trembling now. At the gate they are waiting for us. The gate yawns. Mele is on the inside, I am on the outside. They are trying to coax her along. They are gentle with her now. They speak to her so gently. But Mele is terror-stricken. She turns and runs toward the gate. I am still standing there. She puts her arms through the bars and clutches my neck. I kiss her tenderly on the forehead.

Gently I unlock her arms. The others are going to take her again. I can't bear seeing that. I must go. I must run. For a full minute, however, I stand and look at her. Her eyes seem to have grown enormous. Two great round eyes, full and black as the night, staring at me un-comprehendingly. No maniac can look that way. No idiot can look that way. Only an angel or a saint.

Mele wasn't a good housekeeper I said, but she knew how to make fricadellas. Here is the recipe, while I think of it: a distemper composed of a humus of wet bread (from a nice urinal) plus horse meat (the fetlocks only) chopped very fine and mixed with a little sausage meat. Roll in palm of hands. The saloon that she ran with Paul, before the Hamburg woman came along, was just near the bend in the Second Avenue El, not far from the Chinese pagoda used by the Salvation Army.

When I ran away from the gate I stopped beside a high wall and, burying my head in my arms, my arms against the wall, I sobbed as I had never sobbed since I was a child. Meanwhile they were giving Mele a bath and putting her into regulation dress; they parted her hair in the middle, brushed it down flat and tied it into a knot at the nape of the neck. Thus no one looks exceptional. All have the same crazy look, whether they are half crazy or three-quarters crazy, or just slightly cracked. When you say «may I have pen and ink to write a letter» they say «yes» and they hand you a broom to sweep the floor. If you pee on the floor absent-mindedly you have to wipe it up. You can sob all you like but you mustn't violate the rules of the house. A bughouse has to be run in orderly fashion just as any other house.

Once a week Mele would be allowed to receive. For thirty years the sisters had been visiting the bughouse. They were fed up with it. When they were tiny tots they used to visit their mother on Blackwell's Island. The mother always said to be careful of Mele, to watch over her. When Mele stood at the gate with eyes so round and bright her mind must have traveled back like an express train. Everything must have leaped to her mind at once. Her eyes were so big and bright, as if they saw more than they could comprehend. Bright with terror, and beneath the terror a limitless confusion. That's what made them so beautifully bright. You have to be crazy to see things so lucidly, so all at once. If you're great you can stay that way and people will believe in you, swear by you, turn the world upside down for you. But if you're only partly great, or just a nobody, then what happens to you is lost.

Mornings a brisk intellectual walk under the screaming elevated line, walking north from Delancey Street toward the Waldorf where the evening before the old man had been lounging around in Peacock Alley with Julian Legree. Each morning I write a new book, walking from the Delancey Street station north toward the Waldorf. On the fly-leaf of each book is written in vitriol: *The Island of Incest*. Every morning it starts with the drunken vomit of the night before; it makes a huge gardenia which I wear in the buttonhole of my lapel, the lapel of my double-breasted suit which is lined with silk throughout. I arrive at the tailor shop with the black breath of melancholy, perhaps to find Tom Jordan in the busheling room waiting to have the spots removed from his fly. After having written 369 pages on the trot the futility of saying Good Morning prevents me from being ordinarily polite. I have just this morning finished the twenty-third volume of the ancestral book, of which not even a comma is visible since it was all written extemporaneously without even a fountain pen. I, the tailor's son, am now about to say Good Morning to Endicott Mumford's crack woolen salesman who stand before the mirror in his underwear examining the pouches under his eyes. Every limb and leaf of the family tree dangles before my eyes: out of the crazy black fog of the Elbe there floats this changing island of incest which produces the marvelous gardenia that I wear in my buttonhole each morning. I am just about to say Good Morning to Tom Jordan. It trembles there on my lips. I see a huge tree rising out of the black fog and in the hollow of the trunk there sits the woman from Hamburg, her ass squeezed tightly through the back of the chair. The door is on the latch and through the chink I see her green face, the lips set tight, the nostrils distended. Crazy George is going from door to door with picture post cards, the arm that was bitten off by a horse lost and buried, the empty sleeve flapping in the wind. When all the pages have been torn from the calendar except the last six Crazy George will ring the doorbell and, with icicles in his mustache, he will stand on the threshold, cap in hand, and shout—«Merry Christmas!» This is the craziest tree that ever rose out of the Elbe, with every limb blasted and every leaf withered. This is the tree that shouts regularly once a year—«Merry Christmas!» Despite the calamities, despite the flow of cancer, dropsy, thievery, mendacity, buggery, paralysis, tapeworms, running ears, chorea, meningitis, epilepsy, liverworts, et cetera.

I am just about to say Good Morning. It trembles there on my lips. The twenty-three volumes of the Domesday Book are written with incestuous fidelity, the covers bound in finest morocco, and a lock and key for each volume. Tom Jordan's bloodshot eyes are pasted on the mirror; they shudder like a horse shaking off a fly; Tom Jordan is always either taking off his pants or putting on his pants. Always buttoning or unbuttoning his fly. Always having the stains removed and a fresh crease put in. Tante Melia is sitting in the cooler, under the shade of the family tree. Mother is washing the vomit stains out of last week's dirty wash. The old man is stropping his razor. The Jews are moving up from under the shadow of the bridge, the days are getting shorter, the tugs are snorting or croaking like bullfrogs, the harbor is jammed with ice cakes. Every chapter of the book which is written in the air thickens the blood; the music of it deafens the wild anxiety of the outer air. Night drops like a boom of thunder, deposits me on the floor of the pedestrian highway leading nowhere eventually, but brightly ringed with gleaming spokes along which there is no turning back nor standing still.

From the shadow of the bridges the mob moves up, closer and closer, like a ringworm, leaving a huge festering sore than runs from river to river along Fourteenth Street. This line of pus, which runs invisibly from ocean to ocean, and age to age, neatly divides the Gentile world that I knew from the ledger from the Jewish world that I am about to know from life. Between these two worlds, in the middle of the pus line that runs from river to river, stands a little flower pot filled with gardenias. This is as far as the mastodons roam, where the buffaloes can graze no more; here the cunning, abstract world rises like a cliff in the midst of which are buried the fires of the revolution. Each morning I cross the line, with a gardenia in my buttonhole and a fresh volume written in the air. Each morning I wade through a trench filled with vomit to reach the beautiful island of incest; each day the cliff rises up more toweringly, the window-lines straight as a railroad track and the gleam of them even more dazzling than the gleam of polished skulls. Each morning the trench yawns more menacingly.

I should be saying Good Morning now to Tom Jordan, but it hangs there on my lips tremblingly. What morning is this that I should waste in salutation? Is it *good,* this morning of mornings? I am losing the power to distinguish morning from morning. In the ledger is the world of the fast disappearing buffalo; next door the riveters are sewing up the ribs of the coming skyscrapers. Cunning Oriental men with leaden shoes and glass craniums are plotting the paper world of tomorrow, a world made entirely of merchandise which rises box on box like a paper-box factory, f. o. b. Canarsie. Today there is still time to attend the funeral of the recent dead; tomorrow there will be no time, for the dead will be left on the spot and woe to him who sheds a tear. This is a good morning for a revolution if only there were machine guns instead of firecrackers. This morning would be a splendid morning if yesterday's morning had not been an utter fiasco. The past is galloping away, the trench widens. Tomorrow is further off than it was yesterday because yesterday's horse has run wild and the men with leaden shoes cannot catch up with him. Between the good of the morning and the morning itself there is a line of pus which blows a stench over yesterday and poisons the morrow. This is a morning so confused that if it were only an old umbrella the slightest sneeze would blow it inside out.

My whole life is stretching out in an unbroken morning. I write from scratch each day. Each day a new world is created, separate and complete, and there I am among the constellations, a god so crazy about himself that he does nothing but sing and fashion new worlds. Meanwhile the old universe is going to pieces. The old universe resembles a busheling room in which pants are pressed and stains removed and buttons sewn on. The old universe smells like a wet seam receiving the kiss of a red-hot iron. Endless alterations and repairs, a sleeve lengthened, a collar lowered, a button moved closer, a new seat put in. But never a new suit of clothes, never a creation. There is the morning world, which starts from scratch each day, and the busheling room in which things are endlessly altered and repaired. And thus it is with my life through which there runs the sewer of night. All through the night I hear the goose irons hissing as they kiss the wet seams; the rinds of the old universe fall on the floor and the stench of them is sour as vinegar.

The men my father loved were weak and lovable. They went out, each and every one of them, like brilliant stars before the sun. They went out quietly and catastrophically. No shred of them remained—nothing but the memory of their blaze and glory. They flow now inside me like a vast river choked with falling stars. They form the black flowing river which keeps the axis of my world in constant revolution. Out of this black, endless, ever-expanding girdle of night springs the continuous morning which is wasted in creation. Each morning the river overflows its banks, leaving the sleeves and buttonholes and all the rinds of a dead universe strewn along the beach where I stand contemplating the ocean of the morning of creation.

Standing there on the ocean's shore I see Crazy George leaning against the wall of the undertaker's shop. He has on a funny little cap, a celluloid collar and no tie; he sits on the bench beside the coffin, neither sad nor smiling. He sits there quietly, like an angel that has stepped outside of a Jewish painting. The man in the coffin, whose body is still fresh, is decked out in a modest pepper and salt suit just George's size. He has a collar and tie on and a watch in his vest pocket. George takes him out, undresses him and, while he changes his clothes, lays him on the ice. Not wishing to steal the watch he lays the watch on the ice beside the body. The man is lying on the ice with a celluloid collar around his neck. It is getting dark as George steps out of the undertaker's shop. He has a tie now and a good suit of clothes. At the corner drugstore he stops off to buy a joke book which he saw in the window; he memorizes a few jokes standing in the subway. They are Joe Miller's jokes.

At precisely the same hour Tante Melia is sending a Valentine greeting to the relatives. She has a gray uniform on and her hair is parted in the middle. She writes that she is very happy with her new-found friends and that the food is good. She would like them to remember however that she asked for some *Fastnacht Kuchen* the last time—could they send some by mail, by parcel post? She says that there are some lovely petunias growing up around the garbage can outside the big kitchen. She says that she took a long walk on Sunday last and saw lots of reindeer and rabbits and ostriches. She says that her spelling is very poor, but that she was never a good hand at writing anyway. Everybody is very kind and there is lots of work to do. She would like some *Fastnacht Kuchen* as soon as possible, by air mail if possible. She asked the director to make her some for her birthday but they forgot. She says to send some newspapers because she likes to look at the advertisements. There was a hat she saw once, from Blooming-dale's, she thought, and it was marked down. Maybe they could send the hat along with the *Fastnacht Kuchen?* She thanks them all for the lovely cards they sent her last Christmas—she still remembers them, especially the one with the silver stars on it. Everybody thought it was lovely. She says that she will soon be going to bed and that she will pray for all of them because they were always so good to her.

It's growing dusky, always about the same hour, and I'm standing there gazing at the ocean's mirror. Ice-cold time, neither fast nor slow, but a stiff lying on the ice with a celluloid collar—and if only he had an erection it would be marvelous ... too marvelous! In the dark hallway below Tom Jordan is waiting for the old man to descend. He has two blowsers with him and one of them is fixing her garter; Tom Jordan is helping her to fix her garter. Same hour, toward dusk, as I say, Mrs. Lawson is walking through the cemetery to look once again at her darling son's grave. Her dear boy Jack, she says, though he was thirty-two when he kicked off seven years ago. They said it was rheumatism of the heart, but the fact is the darling boy had knocked up so many venereal virgins that when they drained the pus from his body he stank like a shitpump. Mrs. Lawson doesn't seem to remember that at all. It's her darling boy Jack and the grave is always tidy; she carries a little piece of chamois in her handbag in order to polish the tombstone every evening.

Same dusky time, the stiff lying there on the ice, and the old man is standing in a telephone booth with the receiver in one hand and something warm and wet with hair on it in the other. He's calling up to say not to hold the dinner, that he's got to take a customer out and he'll be home late, not to worry. Crazy George is turning the leaves of Joe Miller's joke book. Down further, toward Mobile, they're practicing the St. Louis Blues without a note in front of 'em and people are getting ready to go crazy when they hear it yesterday, today, tomorrow. Everybody's getting ready to get raped, drugged, violated, soused with the new music that seeps out of the sweat of the asphalt. Soon it'll be the same hour everywhere, just by turning a dial or hanging suspended over the earth in a balloon. It's the hour of the kaffee-klatchers sitting around the family table, each one operated on for a different thing, the one with the whiskers and the heavy rings on her fingers having had a harder time than any one else because she could afford it.

It's staggeringly beautiful at this hour when every one seems to be going his own private way. Love and murder, they're still a few hours apart. Love and murder, I feel it coming with the dusk: new babies coming out of the womb, soft, pink flesh to get tangled up in barbed wire and scream all night long and rot like dead bone a thousand miles from nowhere. Crazy virgins with ice-cold jazz in their veins egging men on to erect new buildings and men with dog collars around their necks wading through the muck up to the eyes so that the czar of electricity will rule the waves. What's in the seed scares the living piss out of me: a brand new world is coming out of the egg and no matter how fast I write the old world doesn't die fast enough. I hear the new machine guns and the millions of bones splintered at once; I see dogs running mad and pigeons dropping with letters tied to their ankles.

Always merry and bright, whether north from Delancey Street or south toward the pus line! My two soft hands in the body of the world, ploughing up the warm entrails, arranging and disarranging, cutting them up, sewing them together again. The warm body feeling which the surgeon knows, together with oysters, warts, ulcers, hernias, cancer sprouts, the young kohlrabies, the clips and the forceps, the scissors and tropical growths, the poisons and gases all locked up inside and carefully covered with skin. Out of the leaking mains love gushing like sewer gas: furious love with black gloves and bright bits of garter, love that champs and snorts, love hidden in a barrel and blowing the bung-hole night after night. The men who passed through my father's shop reeked with love: they were warm and winey, weak and indolent, fast yachts trimmed with sex, and when they sailed by me in the night they fumigated my dreams. Standing in the center of New York I could hear the tinkle of the cowbells, or, by a turn of the head, I could hear the sweet sweet music of the death rattle, a red line down the page and on every sleeve a mourning band. By twisting my neck just a little I could stand high above the tallest skyscraper and look down on the ruts left by the huge wheels of modern progress. Nothing was too difficult for me if only it had a little grief and anguish in it. *Chez nous* there were all the organic diseases—and a few of the inorganic.

Like rock crystal we spread, from one crime to another. A merry whirl, and in the center of it my twenty-first year already covered with verdigris.

And when I can remember no more I shall always remember the night I was getting a dose of clap and the old man so stinking drunk he took his friend Tom Jordan to bed with him. Beautiful and touching this— to be out getting a dose of clap when the family honor was at stake, when it was *at par*, you might say. Not to be there for the shindig, with mother and father wrestling on the floor and the broomstick flying. Not to be there in the cold morning light when Tom Jordan is on his knees and begging to be forgiven but not being forgiven even on his knees because the inflexible heart of a Lutheran doesn't know the meaning of forgiveness. Touching and beautiful to read in the paper next morning that about the same hour the night before the pastor who had put in the bowling alley was caught in a dark room with a naked boy on his lap! But what makes it excruciatingly touching and beautiful is this, that not knowing these things, I came home next day to ask permission to marry a woman old enough to be my mother. And when I said «get married» the old lady picks up the bread knife and goes for me. I remember, as I left the house, that I stopped by the bookcase to grab a book. And the name of the book was—*The Birth of Tragedy*. Droll that, what with the broomstick the night before, the bread knife, the dose of clap, the pastor caught red-handed, the dumplings growing cold, the cancer sprouts, et cetera.... I used to think then that all the tragic events of life were written down in books and that what went on outside was just diluted crap. I thought that a beautiful book was a diseased portion of the brain. I never realized that a whole world could be diseased!

Walking up and down with a package under my arm. A fine bright morning, let's say, and the spittoons all washed and polished. Mumbling to myself, as I step into the Woolworth Building—«Good morning, Mr. Thorndike, fine morning this morning, Mr. Thorn-dike. Are you interested in clothes, Mr. Thorndike?» Mr. Thorndike is not interested in clothes this morning; he thanks me for calling and throws the card in the waste basket. Nothing daunted I try the American Express Building. «Good morning, Mr. Hathaway, fine morning this morning!» Mr. Hathaway doesn't need a good tailor—he's had one for thirty-five years now. Mr. Hathaway is a little peeved and damned right he is thinks I to myself stumbling down the stairs. A fine, bright morning, no denying that, and so to take the bad taste out of my mouth and also have a view of the harbor I take the trolley over the bridge and call on a cheap skate by the name of Dyker. Dyker is a busy man. The sort of man who has his lunch sent up and his shoes polished while he eats. Dyker is suffering from a nervous complaint brought on by dry fucking. He says we can make him a pepper and salt suit if we stop dunning him every month. The girl was only sixteen and he didn't want to knock her up. Yes, patch pockets, please! Besides, he has a wife and three children. Besides, he will be running for judge soon—judge of the Surrogate Court.

Getting toward matinee time. Hop back to New York and drop off at the Burlesk where the usher knows me. The first three rows always filled with judges and politicians. The house is dark and Margie Pennetti is standing on the runway in a pair of dirty white tights. She has the most wonderful ass of any woman on the stage and everybody knows it, herself included. After the show I walk around aimlessly, looking at the movie houses and the Jewish delicatessen stores. Stand awhile in a penny arcade listening to the siren voices coming through the megaphone. Life is just a continuous honeymoon filled with chocolate layer cake and cranberry pie. Put a penny in the slot and see a woman undressing on the grass. Put a penny in the slot and win a set of false teeth. The world is made of new parts every afternoon: the soiled parts are sent to the dry cleaner, the used parts are scrapped and sold for junk.

Walk uptown past the pus line and stroll through the lobbies of the big hotels. If I like I can sit down and watch other people walking through the lobby. Everybody's on the watch. Things are happening all about. The strain of waiting for something to happen is delirious. The elevated rushing by, the taxis honking, the ambulance clanging, the riveters riveting. Bellhops dressed in gorgeous livery looking for people who don't answer to their names. In the golden toilet below men standing in line waiting to take a leak; everything made of plush and marble, the odors refined and pleasant, the flush flushing beautifully. On the sidewalk a stack of newspapers, the headlines still wet with murder, rape, arson, strikes, forgeries, revolution. People stepping over one another to crash the subway. Over in Brooklyn a woman's waiting for me. Old enough to be my mother and she's waiting for me to marry her. The son's got T. B. so bad he can't crawl out of bed any more. Tough titty going up there to her garret to make love while the son's in the next room coughing his lungs out. Besides, she's just getting over an abortion and I don't want to knock her up again—not right away anyhow.

The rush hour! and the subway a free for all paradise. Pressed up against a woman so tight I can feel the hair on her twat. So tightly glued together my knuckles are making a dent in her groin. She's looking straight ahead, at a microscopic spot just under my right eye. By Canal Street I manage to get my penis where my knuckles were before. The thing's jumping like mad and no matter which way the train jerks she's always in the same position vis-a-vis my dickie. Even when the crowd thins out she stands there with her pelvis thrust forward and her eyes fixed on the microscopic spot just under my right eye. At Borough Hall she gets out, without once giving me the eye. I follow her up to the street thinking she might turn round and say hello at least, or let me buy her a frosted chocolate, assuming I could buy one. But no, she's off like an arrow, without turning her head the eighth of an inch. How they do it I don't know. Millions and millions of them every day standing up without underwear and getting a dry fuck. What's the conclusion—a shower? a rubdown? Ten to one they fling themselves on the bed and finish the job with their fingers.

Anyway, it's going on toward evening and me walking up and down with an erection fit to burst my fly. The crowd gets thicker and thicker. Everybody's got a newspaper now. The sky's choked with illuminated merchandise every single article of which is guaranteed to be pleasant, healthful, durable, tasty, noiseless, rainproof, imperishable, the *nee plus ultra* without which life would be unbearable were it not for the fact that life is already unbearable because there is no life. Just about the hour when old Henschke is quitting the tailor shop to go to the card club uptown. An agreeable little job oil the side which keeps him occupied until two in the morning. Nothing much to do—just take the gentlemen's hats and coats, serve drinks on a little tray, empty the ash trays and keep the matchboxes filled. Really a very pleasant job, everything considered. Toward midnight prepare a little snack for the gentlemen, should they so desire it. There are the spittoons, of course, and the toilet bowl. All such gentlemen, however, that there's really nothing to it. And then there's always a little cheese and crackers to nibble on, and sometimes a thimbleful of port. Now and then a cold veal sandwich for the morrow. Real gentlemen! No gainsaying it. Smoke the best cigars. Even the butts taste good. Really a very, very pleasant job!

Getting toward dinner time. Most of the tailors have closed shop for the day. A few of them, those who have nothing but brittle old geezers on the books, are waiting to make a try-on. They walk up and down with their hands behind their backs. Everybody has gone except the boss tailor himself, and perhaps the cutter or the bushelman. The boss tailor is wondering if he has to put new chalk marks on again and if the check will arrive in time to meet the rent. The cutter is saying to himself: «Why yes, Mr. So-and-so, why to be sure ... yes, I think it should be just a little higher there ... yes, you're quite right ... it was little off on the left side ... yes, we'll have that ready for you in a few days ... yes, Mr. So-and-so ..., yes, yes, yes, yes, yes, yes....» The finished clothes and the unfinished clothes are hanging on the rack; the bolts are neatly stacked on the tables; only the light in the busheling room is on. Suddenly the telephone rings. Mr. So-and-so is on the wire and he can't make it this evening but he would like his tuxedo sent up right away, the one with the new buttons which he selected last week, and he hopes to Christ it doesn't jump off his neck any more. The cutter puts on his hat and coat and runs quickly down the stairs to attend a Zionist meeting in the Bronx. The boss tailor is left to close the shop and switch out all the lights if any were left on by mistake. The boy that he's sending up with the tuxedo right away is himself and it doesn't matter much because he will duck round by the trade entrance and nobody will be the wiser. Nobody looks more like a millionaire than a boss tailor delivering a tuxedo to Mr. So-and-so. Spry and spruce, shoes shined, hat cleaned, gloves washed, mustache waxed. They start to look worried only when they sit down for the evening meal. No appetite. No orders today. No checks. They get so despondent that they fall asleep at ten o'clock and when it's time to go to bed they can't sleep any more. Walking over the Brooklyn Bridge.... Is this the world, this walking up and down, these buildings that are lit up, the men and women passing me? I watch their lips moving, the lips of the men and women passing me. What are they talking about—some of them so earnestly? I hate seeing people so deadly serious when I myself am suffering worse than any of them. *One* life! and there are millions and millions of lives to be lived. So far I haven't had a thing to say about my own life. Not a thing. Must be I haven't got the guts. Ought to go back to the subway, grab a Jane and rape her in the street. Ought to go back to Mr. Thorndike in the morning and spit in his face. Ought to stand on Times Square with my pecker in my hand and piss in the gutter. Ought to grab a revolver and fire point-blank into the crowd. The old man's leading the life of Reilly. He and his bosom pals. And I'm walking up and down, turning green with hate and envy. And when I turn in the old woman'll be sobbing fit to break her heart. Can't sleep nights listening to her. I hate her too for sobbing that way. The one robs me, the other punishes me. How can I go into her and comfort her when what I most want to do is to break her heart?

Walking along the Bowery ... and a beautiful snot-green pasture it is at this hour. Pimps, crooks, cokies, panhandlers, beggars, touts, gunmen, chinks, wops, drunken micks. All gaga for a bit of food and a place to flop. *Walking and walking and walking.* Twenty-one I am, white, born and bred in New York, muscular physique, sound intelligence, good breeder, no bad habits, etc., etc. Chalk it up on the board. Selling out at par. Committed no crime, except to be born here.

In the past every member of our family did something with his hands. I'm the first idle son of a bitch with a glib tongue and a bad heart.

Swimming in the crowd, a digit with the rest. Tailored and re-tailored. The lights are twinkling—on and off, on and off. Sometimes it's a rubber tire, sometimes it's a piece of chewing gum. The tragedy of it is that nobody sees the look of desperation on my face. Thousands and thousands of us, and we're passing one another without a look of recognition. The lights jigging like electric needles. The atoms going crazy with light and heat. A conflagration going on behind the glass and nothing burns away. Men breaking their backs, men bursting their brains, to invent a machine which a child will manipulate. If I could only find the hypothetical child who's to run this machine I'd put a hammer in its hands and say: Smash it! Smash it!

Smash it! Smash it! That's all I can say. The old man's riding around in an open barouche. I envy the bastard his peace of mind. A bosom pal by his side and . a quart of rye under his belt. My toes are blistering with malice. Twenty years ahead of me and this thing growing worse by the hour. It's throttling me. In twenty years there won't be any soft, lovable men waiting to greet me. Every bosom pal that goes now is a buffalo lost and gone forever. Steel and concrete hedging me in. The pavement getting harder and harder. The new world eating into me, expropriating me. Soon I won't even need a name.

Once I thought there were marvelous things in store for me. Thought I could build a world in the air, a castle of pure white spit that would raise me above the tallest building, between the tangible and the intangible, put me in a space like music where everything collapses and perishes but where I would be immune, great, godlike, holiest of the holies. It was *I* imagined this, I the tailor's son! I who was born from a little acorn on an immense and stalwart tree. In the hollow of the acorn even the faintest tremor of the earth reached

me: I was part of the great tree, part of the past, with crest and lineage, with pride, *pride.*
And when I fell to earth and was buried there I remembered *who* I was, *where* I came
from. Now I am lost, *lost,* do you hear? You don't hear? I'm yowling and screaming—don't
you hear me? Switch the lights off! Smash the bulbs! Can you hear me now? *Louder!* you
say. *Louder!* Christ, are you making sport of me? Are you deaf, dumb, and blind? Must I
yank my clothes off? Must I dance on my head?

All right, then! I'm going to dance for you! A merry whirl, brothers, and let her whirl
and whirl and whirl! Throw in an extra pair of flannel trousers while you're at it. And don't
forget, boys, I dress on the right side. You hear me? Let 'er go! *Always merry and bright!*

6. Jabberwhorl Kronstadt

This man, this skull, this music ...

He lives in the back of a sunken garden, a sort of bosky glade shaded by whiffletrees
and spinozas, by deodars and baobabs, a sort of queasy Buxtehude diapered with elytras
and feluccas. You pass through a sentry box where the concierge twirls his mustache *con
furioso* like in the last act of Ouida. They live on the third floor behind a mullioned
belvedere filigreed with snaffled spaniels and sebaceous wens, with debentures and
megrims hanging out to dry. Over the bell-push it says: «JABBERWHORL CRON-
STADT, poet, musician, herbologist, weather man, linguist, oceanographer, old clothes,
colloids.» Under this it reads: «Wipe your feet and blow your nose!» And under this is a
rosette from a second-hand suit.

«There's something strange about all this,» I said to my companion whose name is
Dschilly Zilah Bey. «He must be having his period again.»

After we had pushed the button we heard a baby crying, a squeaky, brassy wail like
the end of a horse-knacker's dream.

Finally Katya comes to the door—Katya from Hesse-Kassel—and behind her, thin as
a wafer and holding a bisque doll, stands little Pinochinni. And Pinochinni says: «You
should go in the drawing room, they aren't dressed yet.» And when I asked would they be
very long because we're famished she said, «Oh no! They've been dressing for hours. You
are to look at the new poem father wrote today—it's on the mantelpiece.»

And while Dschilly unwinds her serpentine scarf Pinochinni giggles and giggles, saying oh, dear, what is the matter with the world anyway, everything is so behind-time and
did you ever read about the lazy little girl who hid her toothpicks under the mattress? It's
very strange, father read it to me out of a large iron book.

There is no poem on the mantelpiece, but there are other things— *The Anatomy of
Melancholy,* an empty bottle of Pernod Fils, *The Opal Sea,* a slice of cut plug tobacco,
hairpins, a street directory, an ocarina ... and a machine to roll cigarettes. Under the
machine are notes written on menus, calling cards, toilet paper, match boxes ... «meet the
Cuntess Cathcart at four» ... «the opalescent mucus of Michelet» ... «deflux-ions ... cotyle-
dons ... phthisical» ... «if Easter falls in Lady Day's lap, beware old England of the clap»
... «from the ichor of which springs his successor» ... «the reindeer, the otter, the marmink,
the minkfrog.»

The piano stands in a corner near the belvedere, a frail black box with silver candle-
sticks; the black keys have been bitten off by the spaniels. There are albums marked
Beethoven, Bach, Liszt, Chopin, filled with bills, manicure sets, chess pieces, marbles, and
dice. When he is in good humor Kronstadt will open an album marked «Goya» and play
something for you in the key of C. He can play operas, minuets, schottisches, rondos, sara-

bands, preludes, fugues, waltzes, military marches; he can play Czerny, Prokofiev or Granados, he can even improvise and whistle a Provencal air at the same time. *But it must be in the key of C.*

So it doesn't matter how many black keys are missing or whether the spaniels breed or don't breed. If the bell gets out of order, if the toilet doesn't flush, if the poem isn't written, if the chandelier falls, if the rent isn't paid, if the water is shut off, if the maids are drunk, if the sink is stopped and the garbage rotting, if dandruff falls and the bed creaks, if the flowers are mildewed, if the milk turns, if the sink is greasy and the wallpaper fades, if the news is stale and calamities fail, if the breath is bad or the hands sticky, if the ice doesn't melt, if the pedals won't work, it's all one and come Christmas because everything can be played in the key of C if you get used to looking at the world that way.

Suddenly the door opens to admit an enormous epileptoid beast with fungoid whiskers. It is Jocatha the famished cat, a big, buggerish brute with a taupe fur and two black walnuts hidden under its kinkless tail. It runs about like a leopard, it lifts its hind leg like a dog, it micturates like an owl.

«I'm coming in a minute,» says Jabberwhorl through the sash of the door. «I'm just putting on my pants.»

Now Elsa comes in—Elsa from Bad Nauheim—and she places a tray with blood-red glasses on the mantelpiece. The beast is bounding and yowling and thrashing and caterwauling: he has a few grains of cayenne pepper on the soft lilypad of his nose, the butt of his nose soft as a dum-dum bullet. He thrashes about in large Siamese wrath and the bones in his tail are finer than the finest sardines. He claws the carpet and chews the wallpaper, he rolls into a spiral and unrolls like a corolla, he whisks the knots out of his tail, shakes the fungus out of his whiskers. He bites clean through the floor to the bone of the poem. He's in the key of C and mad clean through. He has magenta eyes, like old-fashioned vest buttons; he's mowsy and glaubrous, brown like arnica and then green as the Nile; he's quaky and qualmy and queasy and teasey; he chews chasubles and ripples rasubly.

Now Anna comes in—Anna from Hannover-Minden —and she brings cognac, red pepper, absinthe and a bottle of Worcestershire sauce. And with Anna come the little Temple cats—Lahore, Mysore, and Cawnpore. They are all males, including the mother. They roll on the floor, with their shrunken skulls, and bugger each other mercilessly. And now the poet himself appears saying what time is it though time is a word he has stricken from his list, time, sib to death. Death's the surd and time's the sib and now there is a little time between the acts, an oleo in which the straight man mixes a drink to get his stomach muscles twitching. Time, time, he says, shaking a little cayenne pepper into his cognac. A time for everything, though I scarcely use the word any more, and so saying he examines the tail of Lahore which has a kink in it and scratching his own last coccyx he adds that the toilet has just been done in silver where you'll find a copy of *Humanite*.

«You're very beautiful,» he says to Dschilly Zilah Bey and with that the door opens again and Jill comes forward in a chlamys of Nile green.

«Don't you think she's beautiful?» says Jab.

Everything has suddenly grown beautiful, even that big buggerish brute Jocatha with her walnuts brown as cinnamon and soft as lichee.

Blow the conch and tickle the clavicle! Jab's got a pain in the belly where his wife ought to have it. Once a month, regular as the moon, it comes over him and it lays him low, nor will inunctions do him any good. Nothing but cognac and cayenne pepper—to start the stomach muscles twitching. «I'll give you three words,» he says, «while the goose turns over in the pan: whimsical, dropsical, phthisical.»

«Why don't you sit down?» says Jill. «He's got his period.»

Cawnpore is lying on an album of Twenty-Four Preludes. «I'll play you a fast one,» says Jab, and flinging back the cover of the little black box he goes *plink, plank, plunk!* »I'll do a tremolo,» he says, and employing every finger of his right hand in quick succession he hits the white key C in the middle of the board and the chess pieces and the manicure sets and the unpaid bills rattle like drunken tiddledywinks. «That's technique!» he says, and his eyes are glaucous and rimed with hoarfrost. «There's only one thing travels as fast as light and that's angels. Only angels can travel as fast as light. It takes a thousand light years to get to the planet Uranus but nobody has ever been there and nobody is ever going to get there. Here's a Sunday newspaper from America. Did you ever notice how one reads the Sunday papers? First the rotogravure, then the funny sheet, then the sports column, then the magazine, then the theater news, then the book reviews, then the headlines. Recapitulation. Ontogeny-phylog-eny. Define your terms and you'll never use words like time, death, world, soul. In every statement there's a little error and the error grows bigger and bigger until the snake is scotched. The poem is the only flawless thing, provided you know what time it is. A poem is a web which the poet spins out of his own body according to a logarithmic calculus of his own divination. It's always right, because the poet starts from the center and works outward....»

The phone is ringing.

«Pythagoras was right.... Newton was right.... Einstein is right....»

«Answer the phone, will you!» says Jill.

«Hello! Oui, c'est le Monsieur Kronstadt. Et votre nom, s'il vous plait? *Bimberg?* Listen, you speak English, don't you? So do I.... *What?* Yes, I've got three apartments— to rent or to sell. *What?* Yes, there's a bath and a kitchen and a toilet too.... No, a regular toilet. No, not in the hall—in the apartment. One you sit down on. Would you like it in silver or in gold leaf? *What?* No, the toilet! I've got a man here from Munich, he's a refugee. *Refugee! Hitler! Hitler! Compris?* Yeah, that's it. He's got a swastika on his chest, in blue.... *What?* No, I'm serious. Are *you* serious? *What?* Listen, if you mean business it means cash.... *Cash!* You've got to lay out *cash. What?* Well, that's the way things are done over here. The French don't believe in checks. I had a man last week tried to do me out of 750 francs. Yeah, an American check. *What?* If you don't like that one I've got another one for you with a dumbwaiter. It's out of order now but it could be fixed. *What?* Oh, about a thousand francs. There's a billiard room on the top floor.... *What?* No ... no ... no. Don't have such things over here. Listen, Mr. Bimberg, you've got to realize that you're in France now. Yeah, that's it.... When in Rome.... Listen, call me tomorrow morning, will you? I'm at dinner now. *Dinner.* I'm eating. *What?* Yeah, *cash* ... 'bye!»

«You see,» he says, hanging up, «that's how we do things in this house. Fast work, what? Real estate. You people are living in a fairyland. You think literature is everything. You *eat* literature. Now in this house we eat goose, for instance. Yeah, it's almost done now.

Anna! Wie geht es? Nicht fertig? Merde alors! Three girls ... refugees. I don't know where they come from. Somebody gave them our address. Fine girls. Hale, hearty, buxom, sound as a berry. No room for them in Germany. Einstein is busy writing poems about light. These girls want a job, a place to live. Do you know anybody who wants a maid?

Fine girls. They're well educated. But it takes the three of them to make a meal. Katya, she's the best of the lot: she knows how to iron. That one, Anna—she borrowed my typewriter yesterday ... said she wanted to write a poem. I'm not keeping you here to write poems, I said. In this house *I* write the poems—if there are any to write. You learn how to cook and darn the socks. She looked peeved. Listen, Anna, I said, you're living in an imaginary world. The world doesn't need any more poems. The world needs bread and butter. Can you produce more bread and butter? That's what the world wants. Learn French and you can help me with the real estate. Yeah, people have to have places to live in. Funny. But, that's how the world is now. It was always like that, only people never believed it before. The world is made for the future ... for the planet Uranus. Nobody will ever visit the planet Uranus, but that doesn't make any difference. People must live places and eat bread and butter. For the sake of the future. That's the way it was in the past. That's the way it will be in the future. *The present?* There's no such thing as the present. There's a word called Time, but nobody is able to define it. There's a past and there's a future, and Time runs through it like an electric current. The present is an imaginary condition, a dream state ... *an oxymoron.* There's a word for you—I'll make you a present of it. Write a poem about it. I'm too busy ... real estate presses. Must have goose and cranberry sauce.... Listen, Jill, what was that word I was looking up yesterday?»

«Omoplate?» says Jill promptly.

«No, not that. Omo ... omo ...»

«Omphalos?»

«No, no. Omo ... omo ...»

«I've got it,» cries Jill. «*Omophagia!*»

«Omophagia, that's it! Do you like that word? Take it away with you! What's the matter? You're not drinking. Jill, where the hell's that cocktail shaker I found the other day in the dumbwaiter? Can you imagine it—a *cocktail shaker!* Anyway, you people seem to think that literature is something vitally necessary. It ain't. It's just literature. I could be making literature too—if I didn't have these refugees to feed. You want to know what the present is? Look at that window over there. No, not there ... the one above. *There!* Every day they sit there at that table playing cards—just the two of them. She's always got on a red dress. And he's always shuffling the cards. *That's the present.* And if you add another word it becomes subjunctive....»

«Jesus, I'm going to see what those girls are doing,» says Jill.

«No you don't! That's just what they're waiting for —for you to come and help them. They've got to learn that this is a *real* world. I want them to understand that. Afterwards I'll find them jobs. I've got lots of jobs on hand. First let them cook me a meal.»

«Elsa says everything's ready. Come on, let's go inside.»

«Anna, Anna, bring these bottles inside and put them on the table!»

Anna looks at Jabberwhorl helplessly.

«There you are! They haven't even learned to speak English yet. What am I going to do with them? *Anna ... hier! 'Raus mit 'em! Versteht?* And pour yourself a drink, you blinking idiot.»

The dining room is softly lighted. There is a candelabra on the table and the service glitters. Just as we are sitting down the phone rings. Anna gathers up the long cord and brings the apparatus from the piano to the sideboard just behind Kronstadt. «Hello!» he yells, and unslacking the long cord, «just like the intestines ... *hello!* Oui! Oui, madame ... je suis le Monsieur Kronstadt... et votre nom, s'il vous plait? Oui, il y a un salon, un entresol, une cuisine, deux chambres a coucher, une salle de bain, un cabinet ... oui, ma-dame.... Non, ce n'est pas cher, pas cher du tout ... on peut s'arranger facilement ... comme vous voulez, madame.... A quelle heure? Oui ... avec plaisir.... *Comment?* Que dites-vous? Ah non! Au contraire! Ca sera un plaisir ... un grand plaisir.... Au revoir, madame!» Slamming it up—«Kuss die Hand, madame! Would you like your back scratched, madame? Do you take milk with your coffee, madame? Will you ...?»

«Listen,» says Jill, «who the hell was that? You were pretty smooth with her. Oui, madame ... non, madame! Did she promise to buy you a drink too?» Turning to us—«Can you imagine it, he has an actress up here yesterday while I'm taking a bath ... some trollop from the Casino de Paris ... and she takes him out and gets him soused....»

«You don't tell that right, Jill. It's this way ... I'm showing her a lovely apartment—with a dumbwaiter in it—and she says to me won't you show me your poetry—*poesie* ... sounds better in French ... and so I bring her up here and she says I'll have them printed for you in Belgian.»

«Why Belgian, Jab?»

«Because that's what she was, a Belgian—or a Belgianess. Anyway, what difference does it make what language they're printed in? Somebody has to print them, otherwise nobody will read them.»

«But what made her say that—so quick like?»

«Ask me! Because they're good, I suppose. Why else would people want to print poems?»

«Baloney!»

«See that! She doesn't believe me.»

«Of course I don't! If I catch you bringing any prima donnas up here, or any toe dancers, or any trapeze artists, or anything that's French and wears skirts, there's going to be hell to pay. Especially if they offer to print your poems!»

«There you are,» says Jabberwhorl, glaucous and glowbry. «That's why I'm in the real estate business—Go ahead and eat, you people.... I'm watching.»

He mixes another dose of cognac and pepper.

«I think you've had enough,» says Jill. «Jesus, how many of them have you had today?»

«Funny,» says Jabberwhorl, «I fixed her up all right a few moments ago—just before you came—but I can't fix myself up....»

«Jesus, where's that goose!» says Jill. «Excuse me, I'm going inside and see what the girls are doing.»

«No you don't!» says Jab, pushing her back into her seat. «We're gonna sit right here and wait... wait and see what happens. Maybe the goose'll never come. We'll be sitting here waiting ... waiting forever ... just like this, with the candles and the empty soup plates and the curtains and ... I can just imagine us sitting here and some one outside plastering a wall around us.... We're sitting here waiting for Elsa to bring the goose and time passes and it gets dark and we sit here for days and days.... See those candles? We'd eat 'em. And those flowers over there? Them too. We'd eat the chairs, we'd eat the sideboard, we'd eat the alarm clock, we'd eat the cats, we'd eat the curtains, we'd eat the bills and the silverware and the wallpaper and the bugs underneath ... we'd eat our own dung and that nice new fetus Jill's got inside her ... we'd eat each other....»

Just at this moment Pinochinni comes in to say good night. She's hanging her head like and there's a quizzical look in her eye.

«What's the matter with you tonight?» says Jill. «You look worried.»

«Oh, I don't know what it is,» says the youngster. «There's something I want to ask you about.... It's awfully complicated. I don't really know if I can say what I mean.»

«What is it, snookums?» says Jab. «Say it right out in front of the lady and the gentleman. You know *him,* don't you? Come on, spit it out!»

The youngster is still holding her head down. Out of the corner of her eye she looks up at her father slyly and then suddenly she blurts out: «Oh, what's it all about? What are we here for anyway? Do we have to have a world? Is this the only world there is and why is it? That's what I want to know.»

If Jabberwhorl Kronstadt was somewhat astonished he gave no sign of it. Picking up his cognac nonchalantly, and adding a little cayenne pepper, he answered blithely: «Listen, kid, before I answer that question— if you *insist* on my answering that question—you'll have to first define your terms.»

Just then there came a long shrill whistle from the garden.

«Mowgli!» says Kronstadt. «Tell him to come on up.»

«Come up!» says Jill, stepping to the window.

No answer.

«He must have gone,» says Jill. «I don't see him any more.»

Now a woman's voice floats up. «Il est saoul ... completement saoul.»

«Take him home! Tell her to take him home!» yells Kronstadt.

«Man mari dit qu'il faut rentrer chez vous ... oui, chez vous"

«*Y'en a pas!*» floats up from the garden.

«Tell her not to lose my copy of Pound's *Cantos*» yells Kronstadt. «And don't ask them up again ... we have no room here. Just enough space for German refugees.»

«That's a shame,» says Jill, coming back to the table.

«You're wrong again,» says Jab. «It's very good for him.»

«Oh, you're drunk,» says Jill. «Where's that damned goose anyhow? Elsa! Elsa!»

«Never mind the goose, darling! This is a game. We're going to sit here and outlast 'em. The rule is, jam tomorrow and jam yesterday—but never jam today.... Wouldn't it be wonderful if you people sat here just like you are and I began to grow smaller and smaller ... until I got to be just a tiny, weeny little speck ... so that you had to have a magnifying glass to see me? I'd be a little spot on the tablecloth and I'd be saying—Timoor ... *Ti-moor!* And you'd say where is he? And I'd be saying—*Timoor,* logodaedaly, glycophos-phates, Billancourt, *Ti-moor* ... O timbus twaddle down the brawkish brake ... and you'd say....»

«Jesus, Jab, you're drunk!» says Jill. And Jabber-whorl glausels with gleerious glitter, his awbrous orbs atwit and atwitter.

«He'll be getting cold in a minute,» says Jill, getting up to look for the Spanish cape.

«That's right,» says Jab. «Whatever she says is right. You think I'm a very contrary person. *You»* he says, turning to me, *«you* with your Mongolian verbs, your transitives and intransitives, don't you see what an affable being I am? You're talking about China all the time ... *this* is China, don't you see that? *This* ... this what? Get me the cape, Jill, I'm cold. This is a terrible cold ... sub-glacial cold. You people are warm, but I'm freezing. I can feel the ice caps coming down again. A fact. Everything is rolling along nicely, the dollar is failing, the apartments are rented, the refugees are all refuged, the piano is tuned, the bills are paid, the goose is cooked and what are we waiting for? *For the next Ice Age!* It's coming tomorrow morning. You'll go to the window and everything'll be frozen tight. No more problems, no more history, no more nothing. *Settled.* We'll be sitting here like this waiting for Anna to bring in the goose and suddenly the ice will roll over us. I can feel the terrible cold already, the bread all icicled, the butter blenched, the goose gazzled, the walls wildish white. And that little angel, that bright new embryo that Jill's got under her belt, that'll be frozen in the womb, a glairy gawk with ice-cold wings and the lips of a snail. Jugger, jugger, and everything'll be still and quiet. Say something warm! My legs are frozen.

Herodotus says that on the death of its father the phoenix embalms the body in an egg made of myrrh and once every five hundred years or so it conveys the little egg embalmed in myrrh from the desert of Arabia to the temple of the sun at Heliopolis. *Do you like that?* According to Pliny there is only one egg at a time and when the bird perceives that its end is near it builds a nest of cassia twigs and frankincense and dies upon it. From the body of the nest is born a little worm which becomes the phoenix. Hence *bennu,* symbol of the resurrection. *How's that?* I need something hotter. Here's another one.... The firewalkers in Bulgaria are called *Nistingares.* They dance in the fire on the twenty-first of May during the feast of Saint Helena and Saint Constantine. They dance on the red-hot embers until they're blue in the face, and then they utter prophecies.»

«Don't like that at all,» says Jill.

«Neither do I,» says Jab. «I like the one about the little soul-worms that fly out of the nest for the resurrection. Jill's got one inside her too ... it's sprouting and sprouting. Can't stop it. Yesterday it was a tadpole, tomorrow it'll be a honeysuckle vine. Can't tell what it's going to be yet ... not eventually. It dies in the nest every day and the next day it's born again. Put your ear to her belly ... you can hear the whirring of its wings. Whirrrr... whirrrr. Without a motor. Wonderful! She's got millions of them inside her and they're all whirring around in there dying to get out. Whirrrr ... whirrrr. And if you just put a needle inside and punctured the bag they'd all come whirring out ... imagine it... a great cloud of soul-worms ... millions of them... and so thick the swarm that we wouldn't be able to see each other.... A fact! No need to write about China. Write about *that!* About what's inside of you ... the great vertiginous vertebration ... the zoospores and the leucocytes ... the wamroths and die holenlindens ... every one's a poem. The jellyfish is a poem too—the finest kind of poem. You poke him here, you poke him there, he slithers and slathers, he's dithy and clabberous, he has a colon and intestines, he's vermiform and ubisquishous. And Mowgli in the garden whistling for the rent, he's a poem too, a poem with big ears, a wambly bretzular poem with logamundiddy of the goo-goo. He has round, auricular daedali, round robin-breasted ruches that open up like an open barouche. He wambles in the wambhorst whilst the whelkin winkles ... he wabbles through the wendisb wikes whirking his worstish wights.... Mowgli ... owgli... whist and wurst....»

«He's losing his mind,» says Jill.

«Wrong again,» says Jabber. «I've just found my mind, only it's a different sort of mind than you imagined. You think a poem must have covers around it. The moment you write a thing the poem ceases. The poem is the present which you can't define. You live it. Anything is a poem if it has time in it. You don't have to take a ferryboat or go to China to write a poem. The finest poem I ever lived was a kitchen sink. Did I ever tell you about it? There were two faucets, one called Froid and the other Chaud. Froid lived a life *in extenso,* by means of a rubber hose attached to his schnausel. Chaud was bright and modest. Chaud dripped all the time, as if he had the clap. On Tuesdays and Fridays he went to the Mosque where there was a clinic for venereal faucets. Tuesdays and Fridays Froid had to do all the work. He was a bugger for work. It was his whole world. Chaud on the other hand had to be petted and coaxed. You had to say «not so fast,» or he'd scald the skin off you. Once in a while they worked in unison, Froid and Chaud, but that was seldom. Saturday nights, when I washed my feet at the sink, I'd get to thinking how perfect was the world over which these twain ruled. Never anything more than this iron sink with its two faucets. No beginnings and no ends. Chaud the alpha and Froid the omega. Perpetuity. The Gemini, ruling over life and death. Alpha-Chaud running out through all degrees of Fahrenheit and Reaumur, through magnetic filings and comets' tails, through the boiling cauldron of Mauna Loa into the dry light of the Tertiary moon; Omega-Froid running out through the Gulf Stream into the paludal bed of the Sargasso Sea, running through the marsupials and the foramini-fera, through the mammal whales and the Polar fissures, running down through island universes, through dead cathodes, through dead bone and dry rot, through the follicles and tentacles of worlds unformed, worlds untouched, worlds unseen, worlds unborn and forever lost. Alpha-Chaud dripping, dripping; Omega-Froid working, working. Hand, feet, hair, face, dishes, vegetables, fish washed clean and away; despair, ennui, hatred, love, jealousy, crime ... dripping, dripping. I, Jabberwhorl, and my wife Jill, and after us legions upon legions ... all standing at the iron sink. Seeds falling down through the drain: young canteloupes, squash, caviar, macaroni, bile, spittle, phlegm, lettuce leaves, sardines' bones, Worcestershire sauce, stale beer, urine, bloodclots, Kruschen salts, oatmeal, chew tobacco, pollen, dust, grease, wool, cotton threads, match sticks, live worms, shredded wheat, scalded milk, castor oil. Seeds of waste falling away forever and forever coming back in pure draughts of a miraculous chemical substance which refuses to be named, classified, labeled, analyzed, or drawn and quartered. Coming back as Froid and Chaud perpetually, like a truth that can't be downed. You can take it hot or cold, or you can take it tepid. You can wash your feet or gargle your throat; you can rinse the soap out of your eyes or drive the grit out of the lettuce leaves; you can bathe the new-born babe or swab the rigid limbs of the dead; you can soak bread for fricadellas or dilute your wine. First and last things. Elixir. I, Jabberwhorl, tasting the elixir of life and death. I, Jabberwhorl, of waste and H_2O composed, of hot and cold and all the intermediate realms, of scum and rind, of finest, tiniest substance never lost, of great sutures and compact bone, of ice fissures and test tubes, of semen and ova fused, dissolved, dispersed, of rubber schnausel and brass spigot, of dead cathodes and squirming infusoria, of lettuce leaves and bottled sunlight ... I, Jabberwhorl, sitting at the iron sink am perplexed and exalted, never less and never more than a poem, an iron stanza, a boiling follicle, a lost leucocyte. The iron sink where I spat out my heart, where I bathed my tender feet, where I held my first child, where I washed my sore gums, where I sang like a diamond-backed terrapin and I am singing now and will sing forever though the drains clog and the faucets rust, though time runs out and I be all there is of present, past and future. *Sing,* Froid, sing transitive! *Sing,* Chaud, sing intransitive! Sing Alpha and Omega! Sing Hallelujah! Sing out, O sink! Sing while the world sinks ...»

And singing loud and clear like a dead and stricken swan on the bed we laid him out.

7. Into the Night Life...

A Coney Island of the mind.

Over the foot of the bed is the shadow of the cross. There are chains binding me to the bed. The chains are clanking loudly, the anchor is being lowered. Suddenly I feel a hand on my shoulder. Some one is shaking me vigorously. I look up and it is an old hag in a dirty wrapper. She goes to the dresser and opening a drawer she puts a revolver away.

There are three rooms, one after the other, like a railroad flat. I am lying in the middle room in which there is a walnut bookcase and a dressing table. The old hag removes her wrapper and stands before the mirror in her chemise. She has a little powder puff in her hand and with this little puff she swabs her armpits, her bosom, her thighs. All the while she weeps like an idiot. Finally she comes over to me with an atomizer and she squirts a fine spray over me. I notice that her hair is full of rats.

I watch the old hag moving about. She seems to be in a trance. Standing at the dresser she opens and closes the drawers, one after the other, mechanically. She seems to have forgotten what she remembered to go there for. Again she picks up the powder puff and with the powder puff she daubs a little powder under her armpits. On the dressing table is a little silver watch attached to a long piece of black tape. Pulling off her chemise she slings the watch around her neck; it reaches just to the pubic triangle. There conies a faint tick and then the silver turns black.

In the next room, which is the parlor, all the relatives are assembled. They sit in a semicircle, waiting for me to enter. They sit stiff and rigid, upholstered like the chairs. Instead of warts and wens there is horsehair sprouting from their chins.

I spring out of bed in my nightshirt and I commence to dance the dance of King Kotschei. In my nightshirt I dance, with a parasol over my head. They watch me without a smile, without so much as a crease in their jowls. I walk on my hands for them, I turn somersaults, I put my fingers between my teeth and whistle like a blackbird. Not the faintest murmur of approval or disapproval. They sit there solemn and imperturbable. Finally I begin to snort like a bull, then I prance like a fairy, then I strut like a peacock, and then realizing that I have no tail I quit. The only thing left to do is to read the Koran through at lightning speed, after which the weather reports, the *Rime of the Ancient Mariner* and the Book of Numbers.

Suddenly the old hag comes dancing in stark naked, her hands aflame. Immediately she knocks over the umbrella stand the place is in an uproar. From the upturned umbrella stand there issues a steady stream of writhing cobras traveling at lightning speed. They knot themselves around the legs of the tables, they carry away the soup tureens, they scramble into the dresser and jam the drawers, they wriggle through the pictures on the wall, through the curtain rings, through the mattresses, they coil up inside the women's hats, all the while hissing like steam boilers.

Winding a pair of cobras about my arms I go for the old hag with murder in my eyes. From her mouth, her eyes, her hair, from her vagina even, the cobras are streaming forth, always with that frightful steaming hiss as if they had been ejected fresh from a boiling crater. In the middle of the room where we are locked an immense forest opens up. We stand in a nest of cobras and our bodies come undone.

I am in a strange, narrow little room, lying on a high bed. There is an enormous hole in my side, a clean hole without a drop of blood showing. I can't tell any more who I am or where I came from or how I got here. The room is very small and my bed is close to the door. I have a feeling that some one is standing on the doorsill watching me. I am petrified with fright.

When I raise my eyes I see a man standing at the doorsill. He wears a gray derby cocked on the side of his head; he has a flowing mustache and is dressed in a checkerboard suit. He asks my name, my address, my profession, what I am doing and where I am going and so on and so forth. He asks endless prying questions to which I am unable to respond, first because I have lost my tongue, and second because I cannot remember any longer what language I speak. «Why don't you speak?» he says, bending over me jeeringly, and taking his light rattan stick he jabs a hole in my side. My anguish is so great that it seems I must speak even if I have no tongue, even if I know not who I am or where I came from. With my two hands I try to wrench my jaws apart, but the teeth are locked. My chin crumbles away like dry clay, leaving the jawbone exposed. «Speak!» he says, with that cruel, jeering smile and, taking his stick once again, he jabs another hole through my side.

I lie awake in the cold dark room. The bed almost touches the ceiling now. I hear the rumbling of trains, the regular rhythmic bouncing of the trains over the frozen trestle, the short, throttled puffs of the locomotive, as if the air were splintered with frost. In my hand are the pieces of dry clay which crumbled from my chin. My teeth are locked tighter than ever; I breathe through the holes in my side. From the window of the little room in which I lie I can see the Montreal bridge. Through the girders of the bridge, driven downward by the blinding blizzard, the sparks are flying. The trains are racing over the frozen river in wreaths of fire. I can see the shops along the bridgeway gleaming with pies and hamburger sandwiches. Suddenly I do remember something. I remember that just as I was about to cross the border they asked me what I had to declare and, like an idiot, I answered: «I *want to declare that I am a traitor to the human race*» I remember distinctly now that this occurred just as I was walking up a treadmill behind a woman with balloon skirts. There were mirrors all around us and above the mirrors a balustrade of slats, series after series of slats, one on top of another, tilted, toppling, crazy as a nightmare. In the distance I could see the Montreal bridge and below the bridge the ice floes over which the trains raced. I remember now that when the woman looked around at me she had a skull on her shoulders, and written into the fleshless brow was the word sex stony as a lizard. I saw the lids drop down over her eyes and then the sightless cavern without bottom. As I fled from her I tried to read what was written on the body of a car racing beside me, but I could catch only the tail end and it made no sense.

At the Brooklyn Bridge I stand as usual waiting for the trolley to swing round. In the heat of the late afternoon the city rises up like a huge polar bear shaking off its rhododendrons. The forms waver, the gas chokes the girders, the smoke and the dust wave like amulets. Out of the welter of buildings there pours a jellywash of hot bodies glued together with pants and skirts. The tide washes up in front of the curved tracks and splits like glass combs. Under the wet headlines are the diaphanous legs of the amoebas scrambling on to the running boards, the fine, sturdy tennis legs wrapped in Cellophane, their white veins showing through the golden calves and muscles of ivory. The city is panting with a five o'clock sweat. From the tops of the skyscrapers plumes of smoke soft as Cleopatra's feathers. The air beats thick, the bats are flapping, the cement softens, the iron rails flatten under the broad flanges of the trolley wheels. Life is written down in headlines twelve feet high with periods, commas and semicolons. The bridge sways over the gasoline lakes below. Melons rolling in from Imperial Valley, garbage going down past Hell Gate, the decks clear, the stanchions gleaming, the hawsers tight, the slips grunting, the moss splitting and spelching in the ferry slips. A warm sultry haze lying over the city like a cup of fat, the sweat trickling down between the bare legs, around the slim ankles. A mucous mass of arms and legs, of half-moons and weather vanes, of cock robins and round robins, of shuttlecocks and bright bananas with the light lemon pulp lying in the bell of the peel. Five o'clock strikes through the grime and sweat of the afternoon, a strip of bright shadow left by the iron girders. The trolleys wheel round with iron mandibles, crunching the papier-mache of the crowd, spooling it down like punched transfers.

As I take my seat I see a man I know standing on the rear platform with a newspaper in his hand. His straw hat is tilted on the back of his head, his arm rests on the motorman's brass brake. Back of his ears the cable web spreads out like the guts of a piano. His straw hat is just on a level with Chambers Street; it rests like a sliced egg on the green spinach of the bay. I hear the cogs slipping against the thick stub of the motorman's toe. The wires are humming, the bridge is groaning with joy. Two little rubber knobs on the seat in front of me, like two black keys on a piano. About the size of an eraser, not round like the end of a cane. Two gummy thingamajigs to deaden the shock. The dull thud of a rubber hammer falling on a rubber skull.

The countryside is desolate. No warmth, no snug-ness, no closeness, no density, no opacity, no numerator, no denominator. It's like the evening newspaper read to a deaf mute standing on a hat rack with a palmetto leaf in his hand. In all this parched land no sign of human hand, of human eye, of human voice. Only headlines written in chalk which the rain washes away. Only a short ride on the trolley and I am in a desert filled with thorns and cactus.

In the middle of the desert is a bathhouse and in the bathhouse is a wooden horse with a log-saw lying athwart it. By the zinc-covered table, looking out through the cobwebbed window, stands a woman I used to know. She stands in the middle of the desert like a rock made of camphor. Her body has the strong white aroma of sorrow. She stands like a statue saying good-by. Head and shoulders above me she stands, her buttocks swoopingly grand and out of all proportion. Everything is out of proportion—hands, feet, thighs, ankles. She's an equestrian statue without the horse, a fountain of flesh worn away to a mammoth egg. Out of the ballroom of flesh her body sings like iron. Girl of my dreams, what a splendid cage you make! Only where is the little perch for your three-pointed toes? The little perch that swung backward and forward between the brass bars? You stand by the window, dead as a canary, your toes stiff, your beak blue. You have the profile of a line drawing done with a meat-ax.

Your mouth is a crater stuffed with lettuce leaves. Did I ever dream that you could be so enormously warm and lopsided? Let me look at your lovely jackal paws; let me hear the croaking, dingy chortle of your dry breath.

Through the cobwebs I watch the nimble crickets, the long, leafy spines of the cactus oozing milk and chalk, the riders with their empty saddlebags, the pommels humped like camels. The dry desert of my native land, her men gray and gaunt, their spines twisted, their feet shod with rowel and spur. Above the cactus bloom the city hangs upside down, her gaunt, gray men scratching the skies with their spurred boots. I clasp her bulging contours, her rocky angles, the strong dolmen breasts, the cloven hoofs, the plumed tail. I hold her close in the choked spume of the canyons under the locked watersheds twisted with golden sands while the hour runs out. In the blinding surge of grief the sand slowly fills my bones.

A pair of blunt, rusty scissors lies on the zinc-covered table beside us. The arm which she raises is webbed to her side. The hoary inflexible movement of her arm is like the dull raucous screech of day closing and the cord which binds us is wired with grit. The sweat stands out on my temples, clots there and ticks like a clock. The clock is running down with nervous wiry sweat. The scissors move between on slow rusty hinges. My nerves race along the teeth of the comb, my spurs bristle, the veins glow. Is all pain dull and bearable like this? Along the scissors' edge I feel the rusty blunt anguish of day closing, the slow webbed movement of hunger satisfied, of clean space and starry sky in the arms of an automaton.

I stand in the midst of the desert waiting for the train. In my heart there is a little glass bell and under the bell there is an edelweiss. All my cares have dropped away. Even under the ice I sense the bloom which the earth prepares in the night.

Reclining in the luxurious leather seat I have a vague feeling that it is a German line on which I am traveling. I sit by the window reading a book; I am aware that some one is reading over my shoulder. It is my own book and there is a passage in it which baffles me. The words are incomprehensible. At Darmstadt we descend a moment while the engines are being changed. The glass shed rises to a nave supported by lacy black girders. The severity of the glass shed has a good deal the appearance of my book—when it lay open on my lap and the ribs showed through. In my heart I can feel the edelweiss blooming.

At night in Germany, when you pace up and down the platform, there is always some one to explain things to you. The round heads and the long heads get together in a cloud of vapor and all the wheels are taken apart and put together again. The sound of the language seems more penetrating than other tongues, as if it were food for the brain, substantial, nourishing, appetizing. Glutinous particles detach themselves and they dissipate slowly, months after the voyage, like a smoker exhaling a fine stream of smoke through his nostrils after he has taken a drink of water. The word *gut* is the longest lasting word of all. «*Es war gut!*» says some one, and his *gut* rumbles in my bowels like a rich pheasant. Surely nothing is better than to take a train at night when all the inhabitants are asleep and to drain from their open mouths the rich succulent morsels of their unspoken tongue. When every one sleeps the mind is crowded with events; the mind travels in a swarm, like summer flies that are sucked along by the train.

Suddenly I am at the seashore and no recollection of the train stopping. No remembrance of it departing even. Just swept up on the shore of the ocean like a comet.

Everything is sordid, shoddy, thin as pasteboard. A Coney Island of the mind. The amusement shacks are running full blast, the shelves full of chinaware and dolls stuffed with straw and alarm clocks and spittoons. Every shop has three balls over it and every game is a ball game. The Jews are walking around in mackintoshes, the Japs are smiling, the air is full of chopped onions and sizzling hamburgers. Jabber, jabber, and over it all in a muffled roar comes the steady hiss and boom of the breakers, a long uninterrupted adenoidal wheeze that spreads a clammy catarrh over the dirty shebang. Behind the pasteboard streetfront the breakers are ploughing up the night with luminous argent teeth; the clams are lying on their backs squirting ozone from their anal orifices. In the oceanic night Steeplechase looks like a wintry beard. Everything is sliding and crumbling, everything glitters, totters, teeters, titters.

Where is the warm summer's day when first I saw the green-carpeted earth revolving and men and women moving like panthers? Where is the soft gurgling music which I heard welling up from the sappy roots of the earth? Where am I to go if everywhere there are trapdoors and grinning skeletons, a world turned inside out and all the flesh peeled off? Where am I to lay my head if there is nothing but beards and mackintoshes and peanut whistles and broken slats? Am I to walk forever along this endless pasteboard street, this pasteboard which I can punch a hole in, which I can blow down with my breath, which I can set fire to with a match? The world has become a mystic maze erected by a gang of carpenters during the night. Everything is a lie, a fake. Pasteboard.

I walk along the ocean front. The sand is strewn with human clams waiting for some one to pry their shells apart. In the roar and hubbub their pissing anguish goes unnoticed. The breakers club them, the lights deafen them, the tide drowns them. They lie behind the pasteboard street in the onyx-colored night and they listen to the hamburgers sizzling. Jabber, jabber, a sneezing and wheezing, balls rolling down the long smooth troughs into tiny little holes filled with bric-a-brac, with chinaware and spittoons and flowerpots and stuffed dolls. Greasy Japs wiping the rubberplants with wet rags, Armenians chopping onions into microcosmic particles, Macedonians throwing the lasso with molasses arms. Every man, woman, and child in a mackintosh has adenoids, spreads catarrh, diabetes, whooping cough, meningitis. Everything that stands upright, that slides, rolls, tumbles, spins, shoots, teeters, sways and crumble?, is made of nuts and bolts. The monarch of the mind is a monkey wrench. Sovereign pasteboard power.

The clams have fallen asleep, the stars are dying out. Everything that is made of water snoozes now in the flap-pocket of a hyena. Morning comes like a glass roof over the world. The glassy ocean sways in its depths, a still, transparent sleep.

It is neither night nor day. It is the dawn traveling in short waves with the flir of an albatross's wings. The sounds that reach me are cushioned, gonged, muffled, as if man's labors were being performed under water. I feel the tide ebbing without fear of being sucked in; I hear the waves splashing without fear of drowning. I walk amidst the wrack and debris of the world, but my feet are not bruised. There is no finitude of sky, no division of land and sea. I move through sluice and orifice with gliding slippery feet. I smell nothing, I hear nothing, I see nothing, I feel nothing. Whether on my back or on my belly, whether sidewise like the crab or spiral like a bird, all is bliss downy and undifferentiated. The white chalk breath of Plymouth stirs the geologic spine; the tip of her dragon's tail clasps the broken continent. Unspeakably brown earth and men with green hair, the old image recreated in soft, milky whiteness. A last wag of the tail in non-human tranquility; an indifference to hope or despair or melancholy. The brown earth and the oxide green are not of air or sky or sight or touch. The peace and solemnity, the far-off, intangible tranquility of the chalk cliffs, distils a poison, a noxious, croaking breath of evil that hangs over the land like the tip of a dragon's tail. I feel the invisible claws that grip the rocks. The heavy, sunken green of the earth is not the green of grass or hope but of slime, of foul, invincible courage. I feel the brown hoods of the martyrs, their matted hair, their sharp talons hidden in scabrous vestments, the brown wool of their hatred, their ennui, their emptiness. I have a tremendous longing for this land that lies at the end of the earth, this irregular spread of earth like an alligator basking. From the heavy, sexless lid of her batted eye there emanates a deceptive, poisonous calm. Her yawning mouth is open like a vision. It is as if the sea and all who had been drowned in it, their bones, their hopes, their dreamy edifices, had made the white amalgam which is England.

My mind searches vainly for some remembrance which is older than any remembrance, for the myth engraved on a tablet of stone which lies buried under a mountain. Under the elevated structure, the windows full of pies and hamburgers, the rails swiftly turning, the old sensations, the old memories invade me again. All that belongs with docks and wharves, with funnels, cranes, pistons, wheels, ties, bridges, all the paraphernalia of travel and hunger repeats itself like a blind mechanism. As I come to the crossroads the living street spreads out like a map studded with awnings and wine shops. The noonday heat cracks the glazed surface of the map. The streets buckle and snap.

Where a rusty star marks the boundary of the past there rises up a clutter of sharp, triangular buildings with black mouths and broken teeth. There is the smell of iodoform and ether, of formaldehyde and ammonia, of fresh tin and wet iron molds. The buildings are sagging, the roofs are crushed and battered. So heavy is the air, so acrid and choking, that the buildings can no longer hold themselves erect. The entrance ways have sunk to below the level of the street. There is something croaking and froglike about the atmosphere. A dank, poisonous vapor envelops the neighborhood, as if a marsh-bog underlay the very foundations.

When I reach my father's home I find him standing at the window shaving, or rather not shaving, but stropping his razor. Never before has he failed me, but now in my need he is deaf. I notice now the rusty blade he is using. Mornings with my coffee there was always the bright flash of his blade, the bright German steel laid against the smooth dull hide of the strop, the splash of lather like cream in my coffee, the snow banked on the window ledge, putting a felt around his words. Now the blade is tarnished and the snow turned to slush; the diamond frost of the window panes trickles in a thin grease that stinks of toads and marsh gas. «Bring me huge worms,» he begs, «and we will plough the minnows.» Poor, desperate father that I have. I clutch with empty hands across a broken table.

A night of bitter cold. Walking along with head down a whore sidles up to me and putting her arm in mine leads me to a hotel with a blue enamel sign over the door. Upstairs in the room I take a good look at her. She is young and athletic, and best of all, she is ignorant. She doesn't know the name of a single king. She doesn't even speak her own language. Whatever I relate to her she licks up like hot fat. She lards herself with it. The whole process is one of getting warm, of putting on a coat of grease for the winter, as she explains to me in her simple way. When she has extracted all the grease from my marrow bones she pulls back the coverlet and with the most astounding sprightliness she commences her trapezoid flights. The room is like a humming bird's nest. Nude as a berry she rolls herself into a ball, her head tucked between her breasts, her arms pinned to her crotch. She looks like a green berry out of which a pea is about to burst.

Suddenly, in that silly American way, I hear her say: «Look, I can do *this,* but I can't do *that!*» Whereupon she does it. Does what? Why, she commences to flap the lips of her vagina, just like a hummingbird. She has a furry little head with frank doglike eyes. Like a picture of the devil when the Palatinate was in flower. The incongruity of it sledges me. I sit down under a trip-hammer: every time I glance at her face I see an iron slit and behind it a man in an iron mask winking at me. A terrifying drollery because he winks with a blind eye, a blind, teary eye that threatens to turn into a cataract.

If it weren't that her arms and legs were all entangled, if she weren't a slippery, coiling snake strangled by a mask, I could swear that it was my wife Alberta, or if not my wife Alberta then another wife, though I think it's Alberta. I thought I'd always know Alberta's crack, but twisted into a knot with a mask between her legs one crack is as good as another and over every sewer there's a grating, in every pod there's a pea, behind every slit there's a man with an iron mask.

Sitting in the chair by the iron bedstead, with my suspenders down and a trip-hammer pounding the dome of my skull, I begin to dream of the women I have known. Women who deliberately cracked their pelvis in order to have a doctor stick a rubber finger inside them and swab the crannies of their epiglottis. Women with such thin diaphragms that the scratch of a needle sounded like Niagara Falls in their fallen bladders. Women who could sit by the hour turning their womb inside out in order to prick it with a darning needle. Queer doglike women with furry heads and always an alarm clock or a jigsaw puzzle hidden in the wrong place; just at the wrong moment the alarm goes off; just when the sky is blazing with Roman candles and out of the wet sparks crabs and star fish, just then always and without fail a broken saw, a wire snapping, a nail through the finger, a corset rotting with perspiration. Queer dogfaced women in stiff collars, the lips drooping, the eyes twitching. Devil dancers from the Palatinate with fat behinds and the door always on a crack and a spittoon where the umbrella stand should be. Celluloid athletes who burst like ping-pong balls when they shoot through the gaslight. Strange women— and I'm always sitting in a chair beside an iron bedstead. Such skilful fingers they have that the hammer always falls in the dead center of my skull and cracks the glue of the joints. The brain pan is like a hamburger steak in a steaming window.

Passing through the lobby of the hotel I see a crowd gathered around the bar. I walk in and suddenly I hear a child howling with pain. The child is standing on a table in the midst of the crowd. It's a girl and she has a slit in the side of her head, just at the temple. The blood is bubbling from her temple. It just bubbles—it doesn't run down the side of her face. Every time the slit in her temple opens I see something stirring inside. It looks like a chick in there. I watch closely. This time I catch a good glimpse of it. It's a cuckoo! People are laughing. Meanwhile the child is howling with pain.

In the anteroom I hear the patients coughing and scraping their feet; I hear the pages of a magazine closing and the rumble of a milk wagon on the cobblestones outside. My wife is sitting on a white stool, the child's head is against my breast. The wound in her temple is throbbing, throbbing as if it were a pulse laid against my heart. The surgeon is dressed in white; he walks up and down, up and down, puffing at his cigarette. Now and then he stops at the window to see how the weather looks. Finally he washes his hands and puts on the rubber gloves. With the sterilized gloves on his hands he lights a flame under the instruments; then he looks at his watch absent-mindedly and fingers the bills lying on the desk. The child is groaning now; her whole body is twitching with pain. I've got her arms and legs pinned. I'm waiting for the instruments to boil.

At last the surgeon is ready. Seating himself on a little white stool he selects a long, delicate instrument with a red-hot point and without a word of warning he plunges it into the open wound. The child lets out such a blood-curdling scream that my wife collapses on the floor. «Don't pay any attention to *her!*» says the cool, collected surgeon, shoving her body aside with his foot. «Hold tight now!» And dipping his crudest instrument into a boiling antiseptic he plunges the blade into the temple and holds it there until the wound bursts into flames. Then, with the same diabolical swiftness, he suddenly withdraws the instrument to which there is attached, by an eyelet, a long white cord which changes gradually into red flannel and then into chewing gum and then into popcorn and finally into sawdust. As the last flake of sawdust spills out the wound closes up clean and solid, leaving not even the suggestion of a scar. The child looks up at me with a peaceful smile and, slipping off my lap, walks steadily to the corner of the room where she sits down to play.

«That was excellent!» says the surgeon. «Really quite excellent!»

«Oh, it was, eh?» I scream. And jumping up like a maniac I knock him off the stool and with my knees firmly planted in his chest I grab the nearest instrument and commence to gouge him with it. I work on him like a demon. I gouge out his eyes, I burst his eardrums, I slit his tongue, I break his windpipe, I flatten his nose. Ripping the clothes off him I burn his chest until it smokes, and while the flesh is still raw and quivering from the hot iron I roll back the outer layers and I pour nitric acid inside—until I hear the heart and lungs sizzling. Until the fumes almost keel me over.

The child meanwhile is clapping her hands with glee.

As I get up to look for a mallet I notice my wife sitting in the other corner. She seems too paralyzed with fright to get up. All she can do is to whisper—«Fiend! Fiend!» I run downstairs to look for the mallet.

In the darkness I seem to distinguish a form standing beside the little ebony piano. The lamp is guttering but there is just sufficient light to throw a halo about the man's head. The man is reading aloud in a monotonous voice from a huge iron book. He reads like a rabbi chanting his prayers. His head is thrown back in ecstasy, as if it were permanently dislocated. He looks like a broken street lamp gleaming in a wet fog.

As the darkness increases his chanting becomes more and more monotonous. Finally I see nothing but the halo around his head. Then that vanishes also and I realize that I have grown blind. It is like a drowning in which my whole past rises up. Not only my personal past, but the past of the whole human race which I am traversing on the back of a huge tortoise. We travel with the earth at a snail-like pace; we reach the limits of her orbit and then with a curious lopsided gait we stagger swiftly back through all the empty houses of the zodiac. We see the strange phantasmal figures of the animal world, the lost races which had climbed to the top of the ladder only to fall to the ocean floor. Particularly the soft red bird whose plumes are all aflame. The red bird speeding like an arrow, always to the north. Winging her way north over the bodies of the dead there follows in her wake a host of angelworms, a blinding swarm that hides the light of the sun.

Slowly, like veils being drawn, the darkness lifts and I discern the silhouette of a man standing by the piano with the big iron book in his hands, his head thrown back and the weary monotonous voice chanting the litany of the dead. In a moment he commences pacing back and forth in a brisk, mechanical way, as if he were absent-mindedly taking exercise. His movements obey a jerky, automatic rhythm which is exasperating to witness. He behaves like a laboratory animal from which part of the brain has been removed. Each time he comes to the piano he strikes a few chords at random—plink, plank, plunk! And with this he mumbles something under his breath. Moving briskly toward the east wall he mumbles—«theory of ventilation»; moving briskly toward the west wall he mumbles—«theory of opposites»; tacking north-northwest he mumbles—«fresh air theory all wet.» And so on and so forth. He moves like an old four-masted schooner bucking a gale, his arms hanging loosely, his head drooping slightly to one side. A brisk indefatigable motion like a shuttle passing over a loom. Suddenly heading due north he mumbles—«Z for zebra ... zeb, zut, Zachariah ... no sign of b for bretzels....»

Flicking the pages of the iron book I see that it is a collection of poems from the Middle Ages dealing with mummies; each poem contains a prescription for the treatment of skin diseases. It is the Day Book of the great plague written by a Jewish monk. A sort of elaborate chronicle of skin diseases sung by the troubadors. The writing is in the form of musical notes representing all the beasts of evil omen or of creeping habits, such as the mole, the toad, the basilisk, the eel, the beetle, the bat, the turtle, the white mouse. Each poem contains a formula for ridding the body of the possessed of the demons which infest the underlayers of the skin.

My eye wanders from the musical page to the wolf hunt which is going on outside the gates. The ground is covered with snow and in the oval field beside the castle walls two knights armed with long spears are worrying the wolf to death. With miraculous grace and dexterity the wolf is gradually brought into position for the death stroke. A voluptuous feeling comes over me watching the long-drawn-out death deal. Just as the spear is about to be hurled the horse and rider are gathered up in an agonizing elasticity: in one simultaneous movement the wolf, the horse, and the rider revolve about the pivot of death. As the spear wings through the body of the wolf the ground moves gently upward, the horizon slightly tilted, the sky blue as a knife.

Walking through the colonnade I come to the sunken streets which lead to the town. The houses are surrounded by tall black chimneys from which a sulphurous smoke belches forth. Finally I come to the box factory from a window of which I catch a view of the cripples standing in line in the courtyard. None of the cripples have feet, few have arms; their faces are covered with soot. All of them have medals on their chest.

To my horror and amazement I slowly perceive that from the long chute attached to the wall of the factory a steady stream of coffins is being emptied into the yard. As they tumble down the chute a man steps forward on his mutilated stumps and pausing a moment to adjust the burden to his back slowly trudges off with his coffin. This goes on ceaselessly, without the slightest interruption, without the slightest sound. My face is streaming with perspiration. I want to run but my feet are rooted to the spot. Perhaps I have no feet. I am so frightened that I fear to look down. I grip the window sash and without daring to look down I cautiously and fearfully raise my foot until I am able to touch the heel of my shoe with my hand. I repeat the experiment with the other foot. Then, in a panic, I look about me swiftly for the exit. The room in which I am standing is littered with empty packing boxes; there are nails and hammers lying about. I thread my way among the empty boxes searching for the door. Just as I find the door my foot stumbles against an empty box. I look down into the empty box and behold, it is not empty! Hastily I cast a glance at the other boxes. None of them are empty! In each box there is a skeleton packed in excelsior. I run from one corridor to another searching frantically for the staircase. Flying through the halls I catch the stench of embalming fluid issuing from the open doors. Finally I reach the staircase and as I bound down the stairs I see a white enamel hand on the landing below pointing to—The Morgue.

It is night and I am on my way home. My path lies through a wild park such as I had often stumbled through in the dark when my eyes were closed and I heard only the breathing of the walls. I have the sensation of being on an island surrounded by rock coves and inlets. There are the same little bridges with their paper lanterns, the rustic benches strewn along the graveled paths; the pagodas in which confections were sold, the brilliant skups, the sunshades, the rocky crags above the cove, the flimsy Chinese wrappers in which the firecrackers were hidden. Everything is exactly as it used to be, even to the noise of the carrousel and the kites fluttering in the tangled boughs of the trees. *Except that now it is winter.* Midwinter, and all the roads covered with snow, a deep snow which has made the roads almost impassable.

At the summit of one of the curved Japanese bridges I stand a moment, leaning over the handrail, to gather my thoughts. All the roads are clearly spread out before me. They run in parallel lines. In this wooded park which I know so well I feel the utmost security. Here on the bridge I could stand forever, sure of my destination. It hardly seems necessary to go the rest of the way for now I am on the threshold, as it were, of my kingdom and the imminence of it stills me. How well I know this little bridge, the wooded clump, the stream that flows beneath! Here I could stand forever lost in a boundless security, lulled and forever rapt by the lapping murmur of the stream. Over the mossy stones the stream swirls endlessly. A stream of melting snow, sluggish above and swift below. Icy clear under the bridge. So clear that I can measure the depth of it with my eye. Icy clear to the neck.

And now, out of the dark-clustered wood, amidst the cypresses and evergreens, there comes a phantom couple arm in arm, their movements slow and languid. A phantom couple in evening dress—the woman's low-necked gown, the man's gleaming shirt studs. Through the snow they move with airy steps, the woman's feet so soft and dry, her arms bare. No crunch of snow, no howling wind. A brilliant diamond light and rivulets of snow dissolving in the night. Rivulets of powdered snow sliding beneath the evergreens. No crunch of jaw, no moan of wolf. Rivulets and rivulets in the icy light of the moon, the rushing sound of white water and petals lapping the bridge, the island floating away in ceaseless drift, her rocks tangled with hair, her glens and coves bright black in the silver gleam of the stars.

Onward they move in the phantasmal flux, onward toward the knees of the glen and the white-whiskered waters. Into the clear icy depths of the stream they walk, her bare back, his gleaming shirt studs, and from afar comes the plaintive tinkle of glass curtains brushing the metal teeth of the carrousel. The water rushes down in a thin sheet of glass between the soft white mounds of the banks; it rushes below the knees, carrying the amputated feet forward like broken pedestals before an avalanche. Forward on their icy stumps they glide, their bat wings spread, their garments glued to their limbs. And always the water mounting, higher, higher, and the air growing colder, the snow sparkling like powdered diamonds. From the cypresses above a dull metallic green sweeps down, sweeps like a green shadow over the banks and stains the clear icy depths of the stream. The woman is seated like an angel on a river of ice, her wings spread, her hair flown back in stiff glassy waves.

Suddenly, like spun-glass under a blue flame, the stream quickens into tongues of fire. Along a street flaming with color there moves a dense equinoctial throng. It is the street of early sorrows where the flats string out like railroad cars and all the houses flanked with iron spikes. A street that slopes gently toward the sun and then forward like an arrow to lose itself in space. Where formerly it curved with a bleak, grinding noise, with stiff, pompous roofs and blank dead walls, now like an open switch the gutter wheels into place, the houses fall into line, the trees bloom. Time nor goal bothers me now. I move in a golden hum through a syrup of warm lazy bodies.

Like a prodigal son I walk in golden leisure down the street of my youth. I am neither bewildered nor disappointed. From the perimeter of the six extremes I have wandered back by devious routes to the hub where all is change and transformation, a white lamb continually shedding its skin. When along the mountain ridges I howled with pain, when in the sweltering white valleys I was choked with alkali, when fording the sluggish streams my feet were splintered by rock and shell, when I licked the salty sweat of the lemon fields or lay in the burning kilns to be baked, *when was all this that I never forgot what is now no more?*

When down this cold funereal street they drove the hearse which I hailed with joy had I already shed my skin? I was the lamb and they drove me out. I was the lamb and they made of me a striped tiger. In an open thicket I was born with a mantle of soft white wool. Only a little while did I graze in peace, and then a paw was laid upon me. In the sultry flame of closing day I heard a breathing behind the shutters; past all the houses I wandered slowly, listening to the thick flapping of the blood. And then one night I awoke on a hard bench in the frozen garden of the South. Heard the mournful whistle of the train, saw the white sandy roads gleaming like skull tracks.

If I walk up and down the world without joy or pain it's because in Tallahassee they took my guts away. In a corner against a broken fence they reached inside me with dirty paws and with a rusty jackknife they cut away everything that was mine, everything that was sacred, private, taboo. In Tallahassee they cut my guts out; they drove me round the town and striped me like the tiger. Once I whistled in my own right. Once I wandered through the streets listening to the blood beating through the filtered light of the shutters. Now there's a roar inside me like a carnival in full blast. My sides are bursting with a million barrel-organ tunes. I walk down the street of early sorrows with the carnival going full blast. I rub my way along spilling the tunes I have learned. A glad, lazy depravity swinging from curb to curb. A skein of human flesh that swings like a heavy rope.

By the spiral-hung gardens of the casino where the cocoons are bursting a woman slowly mounting the flowerpath pauses a moment to train the full weight of her sex on me. My head swings automatically from side to side, a foolish bell stuck in a belfry. As she moves away the sense of her words begins to make itself manifest. *The cemetery,* she said. *Have you seen what they did to the cemetery?* Moseying along in the warm wine press, the blinds all thrown open, the stoops swarming with children, I keep thinking of her words. Moseying along with light niggerish fancy, bare necked, splayfooted toes spread, scrotum tight. A warm southern fragrance envelops me, a good-natured ease, the blood thick as molasses and flapping with condors' wings.

What they have done for the street is what Joseph did for Egypt. What *they* have done? No *you* and no *they* any more. A land of ripe golden corn, of red Indians and black bucks. Who *they* are or were I know not. I know only that they have taken the land and made it smile, that they have taken the cemetery and made of it a fertile, groaning field. Every stone has been removed, every wreath and cross has vanished. Hard by my home now there lies a huge sunken checkerboard groaning with provender; the loam is rich and black, the sturdy, patient mules sink their slender hoofs into the wet loam which the plough cuts through like soft cheese. The whole cemetery is singing with its rich fat produce. Singing through the blades of wheat, the corn, the oats, the rye, the barley. The cemetery is bursting with things to eat, the mules are switching their tails, the big black bucks are humming and chanting and the sweat rolls down their shanks.

The whole street is living now off the cemetery grounds. Plenty for everybody. More than enough. The excess provender goes off in steam, in song and dance, in depravity and recklessness. Who would have dreamed that the poor dead flat-chested buggers rotting under the stone slabs contained such fertilizing wisdom? Who would have thought that these bony Lutherans, these spindle-shanked Presbyterians, had such good fat meat left on their bones, that they could make such a marvelous harvest of corruption, such nestsful of worms? Even the dry epitaphs which the stonecutters chiseled out have worked their fecundating power. Quietly there under the cool sod these lecherous, fornicating ghouls are working their power and glory. Nowhere in the whole wide world have I seen a cemetery blossom like this. Nowhere in the whole wide world such rich, steaming manure. Street of early sorrows, I embrace you! No more pale white faces, no Beethoven skulls, no crossbones, no spindle shanks. I see nothing but corn and maize, and goldenrods and lilacs; I see the common hoe, the mule in his traces, flat broad feet with toes spread and rich silky loam of earth sloshing between the toes. I see red handkerchiefs and faded blue shirts and broad sombreros glistening with sweat. I hear flies droning and the drone of lazy voices. The air hums with careless, reckless joy; the air hums with insects and their powdered wings spread pollen and depravity. I hear no bells, no whistles, no gongs, no brakes grinding; I hear the clink of the hoe, the drip of water dripping, the buzz and quiet pandemonium of toil. I hear the guitar and the harmonica, a soft tam-tam, a patter of slippered feet; I hear the blinds being lowered and the braying of a jackass deep in his oats.

No pale white faces, thanks be to Christ! I see the coolie, the black buck, the squaw. I see chocolate and cinnamon shades, I see a Mediterranean olive, a tawny Hawaiian gold; I see every pure and every cross shade, *but no white.* The skull and crossbones have disappeared with the tombstones; the white bones of a white race have yielded their harvest. I see that everything pertaining to their name and memory has faded away, and *that,* that makes me wild with joy. In the buzz of the open field, where once the earth was humped into crazy little sods, I mosey along down the sunken wet furrows with thirsty tinkling toes; right and left I spatter the juicy cabbage loam, the mud pressed by the wheel, the broad green leaves, the crushed berries, the tart juice of the olive. Over the fat worms of the dead, squashing them back into the sod, I walk in benediction. Like the drunken sailor man I reel from side to side, my feet wet, my hands dry. I look through the wheat toward the puffs of cloud; my eye travels along the river, her low-laden dhows, her slow drift of sail and mast. I see the sun shooting down its broad rays, sucking gently at the river's breast. On the farther shore the pointed poles of wigwams, the lazy curl of smoke. I see the tomahawk sailing through the air to the sound of familiar bloodcurdling yells. I see painted faces, bright beads, the soft moccasin dance, the long flat teats and the braided papoose.

Delaware and Lackawanna, Monongahela, the Mohawk, the Shenandoah, Narragansett, Tuskegee, Oskaloosa, Kalamazoo, Seminole and Pawnee, Cherokee, the great Manitou, the Blackfeet, the Navaho range: like a huge red cloud, like a pillar of fire, a vision of the outlawed magnificence of our earth passes before my eyes. I see no Letts, Croats, Finns, Danes, Swedes; no micks, no wops, no chinks, no polacks, no frogs, no heinies, no kikes. I see the Jews sitting in their crows' nests, their parched faces dry as leather, their skulls shriveled and boneless.

Once more the tomahawk gleams, scalps fly, and out of the river bed there rolls a bright billowy cloud of blood. From the mountain sides, from the great caves, from the swamps and Everglades pours a flood of blood-flecked men. From the Sierras to the Appalachians the land smokes with the blood of the slain. My scalp is cut away, the gray meat hangs over my ears in shreds; my feet are burned away, my sides pierced with arrows. In a pen against a broken fence I lie with my bowels beside me; all mangled and gory the beautiful white temple that was stretched with skin and muscle. The wind roars through my broken rectum, howls like sixty white lepers. A white flame, a jet of blue ice, a torch-spray spins in my hollow guts. My arms are yanked from their sockets. My body is a sepulcher which the ghouls are rifling. I am full of raw gems that bleed with icy brilliance. Like a thousand pointed lances the sun pierces my wounds, the gems flame, the gizzards shriek. Night or day I know not which; the tent of the world collapses like a gasbag. In a flame of blood I feel the cold touch of a tong: through the river gorge they drag me, blind and helpless, choking, gasping, shrieking with impotence. Far away I hear the rush of icy water, the moan of jackals neath the evergreens; through the dark green forest a stain of light spreads, a vernal, prussic light that stains the snow and the icy depths of the stream. A pleasant, choking gurgle, a quiet pandemonium as when the angel with her wings outstretched floated legless under the bridge.

The gutters are choked with snow. It is winter and the sun glares down with the low bright glint of noon. Going down the street past the flats. For an hour or two, while the sun lasts, everything turns to water, everything flows, trickles, gurgles. Between the curbs and the snow banks a freshet of clear blue water rises. Within me a freshet that chokes the narrow gorge of my veins. A clear, blue stream inside me that circulates from my toes to the roots of my hair. I am completely thawed out, choking with an ice-blue gaiety.

Going down the street past the flats, an ice-blue gaiety in my narrow, choking veins. The winter's snow is melting, the gutters are swimming over. Sorrow gone and joy with it, melted, trickling away, pouring into the sewer. Suddenly the bells begin to toll, wild funereal bells with obscene tongues, with wild iron clappers that smash the glass hemorrhoids of the veins. Through the melting snow a carnage reigns: low Chinese horses hung with scalps, long finely jointed insects with green mandibles. In front of each house an iron railing spiked with blue flowers.

Down the street of early sorrows comes the witch mother stalking the wind, her wide sails unfurled, her dress bulging with skulls. Terrified we flee the night, perusing the green album, its high decor of frontal legs, the bulging brow. From all the rotting stoops the hiss of snakes squirming in the bag, the cord tied, the bowels knotted. Blue flowers spotted like leopards, squashed, blood-sucked, the earth a vernal stain, gold, marrow, bright bone dust, three wings aloft and the march of the white horse, the ammonia eyes.

The melting snow melts deeper, the iron rusts, the leaves flower. On the corner, under the elevated, stands a man with a plug hat, in blue serge and linen spats, his white mustache chopped fine. The switch opens and out rolls all the tobacco juice, the golden lemons, the elephant tusks, the candelabras. Moishe Pippik, the lemon dealer, fowled with pigeons, breeding purple eggs in his vest pocket and purple ties and watermelons and spinach with short stems, stringy, marred with tar. The whistle of the acorns loudly stirring, flurry of floozies bandaged in lysol, ammonia and camphor patches, little mica huts, peanut shells triangled and corrugated, all marching triumphantly with the morning breeze. The morning light comes in creases, the window panes are streaked, the covers are torn, the oilcloth is faded. Walks a man with hair on end, not running, not breathing, a man with a weathervane that turns the corners sharply and then bolts. A man who thinks not how or why but just to walk in lusterless night with all stars to port and loaded whiskers trimmed. Gowselling in the grummels he wakes the plaintiff night with pitfalls tuning left to right, high noon on the wintry ocean, high noon all sides aboard and aloft to starboard. The weathervane again with deep oars coming through the portholes and all sounds muffled. Noiseless the night on all fours, like the hurricane. Noiseless with loaded caramels and nickel dice. Sister Monica playing the guitar with shirt open and laces down, broad flanges in either ear. Sister Monica streaked with lime, gum wash, her eyes mildewed, craped, crapped, crenelated.

The street of early sorrows widens, the blue lips blubber, the albatross wings ahead, her gory neck unhinged, her teeth agibber. The man with the bowler hat creaks his left leg, two notches further down to the right, under the gunwales, the Cuban flag spliced with noodles and mock oranges, with wild magnolias and young palmetto shoots chaffed with chalk and green slaver. Under the silver bed the white geranium bowl, two stripes for the morning, three for the night. The castors crooning for blood. The blood comes in white gulps, white choking gulps of clay filled with broken teeth, with mucilage and wasted bones. The floor is slippery with the coming and going, with the bright scissors, the long knives, the hot and cold tongs.

In the melting snow outside the menagerie breaks loose, first the zebras with gorgeous white planks, then the fowling birds and rooks, then the acacias and the diamond backs. The greenery yawns with open toes, the red bird wheels and dives below, the scrumtuft breaks a beak, the lizard micturates, the jackal purrs, the hyenas belch and laugh and belch again. The whole wide cemetery safely sprinkled cracks its joints in the night. The automatons crack too with mighty suits of armor encumbered and hinges rusted and bolts unlocked, abandoned by the tin trust. The butter blossoms out in huge fan wreaths, fat, oleandrous butter marked with crow's feet and twice spliced by the hangman John the Crapper. The butter yowsels in the mortuary, pale shafts of moonbeam trickling through, the estuaries clogged, the freights ashudder, the sidings locked. Brown beagled bantams trimmed with red craw and otter's fur browse the bottom lands. The larkspur does a hemorrhage. The magnesia wells ignite, the eagle soars aloft with a cleaver through the ankle.

Bloody and wild the night with all hawk's feet slashed and trimmed. Bloody and wild the night with all the belfries screeching and all the slats torn and all the gas mains bursting. Bloody and wild the night with every muscle twisted, the toes crossed, the hair on end, the teeth red, the spine cracked. All the world wide awake twittering like the dawn, and a low red fire crawling over the gums. All through the night the combs break, the ribs sing. Twice the dawn breaks, then steals away again. In the trickling snow the oxide fumes. All through the street the hearses pass up and down, up and down, the drivers munching their long whips, their white crapes, their cotton gloves.

North toward the white pole, south toward the red heron, the pulse beats wild and straight. One by one, with bright glass teeth, they cut away the cords. The duck comes with his broad bill and then the low-bellied weasel. One after another they come, summoned from the fungus, their tails afeather, their feet webbed. They come in waves, bent like trolley poles, and pass under the bed. Mud on the floor and strange signs, the windows blazing, nothing but teeth, then hands, then carrots, then great nomadic onions with emerald eyes, comets that come and go, come and go.

East toward the Mongols, west toward the redwoods, the pulse swings back and forth. Onions marching, eggs chattering, the menagerie spinning like a top. Miles high on the beaches lie the red caviar beds. The breakers foam, snap their long whips. The tide roars beneath the green glaciers. Faster, faster spins the earth.

Out of black chaos whorls of light with portholes jammed. Out of the static null and void a ceaseless equilibrium. Out of whalebone and gunnysack this mad thing called sleep that runs like an eight-day clock.

8. Walking Up and Down in China

Now I am never alone. At the very worst I am with God!

In Paris, out of Paris, leaving Paris or coming back to Paris, it's always Paris and Paris is France and France is China. All that which is incomprehensible to me runs like a great wall over the hills and valleys through which I wander. Within this great wall I can live out my Chinese life in peace and security.

I am not a traveler, not an adventurer. Things happened to me in my search for a way out. Up till now I had been working away in a blind tunnel, burrowing in the bowels of the earth for light and water. I could not believe, being a man of the American continent, that there was a place on earth where a man could be himself. By force of circumstance I became a Chinaman— a Chinaman in my own country! I took to the opium of dream in order to face the hideousness of a life in which I had no part. As quietly and naturally as a twig falling into the Mississippi I dropped out of the stream of American life. Everything that happened to me I remember, but I have no desire to recover the past, neither have I any longings or regrets. I am like a man who awakes from a long sleep to find that he is dreaming. A pre-natal condition—the born man living unborn, the unborn man dying born.

Born and reborn over and over. Born while walking the streets, born while sitting in a cafe, born while lying over a whore. Born and reborn again and again. A fast pace and the penalty for it is not death simply, but repeated deaths. Hardly am I in heaven, for example, when the gates swing open and under my feet I find cobblestones. *How did I learn to walk so soon? With whose feet am I walking?* Now I am walking to the grave, marching to my own funeral. I hear the clink of the spade, the rain of sods. My eyes are scarcely closed, I have barely time to smell the flowers in which they've smothered me, when *bango!* I've lived out another immortality. Coming back and forth to earth this way puts me on the alert. I've got to keep my body in trim for the worms. Got to keep my soul intact for God.

Afternoons, sitting at La Fourche, I ask myself calmly: «Where do we go from here?» By nightfall I may have traveled to the moon and back. Here at the crossroads I sit and dream back through all my separate and immortal egos. I weep in my beer. Nights, walking back to Clichy, it's the same feeling. Whenever I come to La Fourche I see endless roads radiating from my feet and out of my own shoes there step forth the countless egos which inhabit my world of being. Arm in arm I accompany them over the paths which once I trod alone: what I call the grand obsessional walks of my life and death. I talk to these self-made companions much as I would talk to myself had I been so unfortunate as to live and die only once and thus be forever alone. *Now I am never alone. At the very worst I am with God!*

There is something about the little stretch from the Place Clichy to La Fourche which causes all the grand obsessional walks to bloom at once. It's like moving from one solstice to another. Supposing I have just left the Cafe Wepler and that I have a book under my arm, a book on Style and Will. Perhaps when I was reading this book I didn't comprehend more than a phrase or two. Perhaps I was reading the same page all evening. Perhaps I wasn't at the Cafe Wepler at all, but hearing the music I left my body and flew away. *And where am I then?* Why, I am out for an obsessional walk, a short walk of fifty years or so accomplished in the turning of a page.

It's when I'm leaving the Cafe Wepler that I hear a strange, swishing noise. No need to look behind—I know it's my body rushing to join me. It's at this moment usually that the shit-pumps are lined up along the Avenue. The hoses are stretched across the sidewalk like huge groaning worms. The fat worms are sucking the shit out of the cesspools. It's this that gives me the proper spiritual gusto to look at myself in profile. I see myself bending over the book in the cafe; I see the whore alongside me reading over my shoulder; I feel her breath on my neck. She waits for me to raise my eyes, perhaps to light the cigarette which she holds in her hand. She is going to ask me what I am doing here alone and am I not bored. The book is on Style and Will and I have brought it to the cafe to read because it's a luxury to read in a noisy cafe—and also a protection against disease. The music too is good in a noisy cafe—it augments the sense of solitude, of loneliness. I see the upper lip of the whore trembling over my shoulder. Just a triangular patch of lip, smooth and silky. It trembles on the high notes, poised like a chamois above a ravine. And now I am running the gauntlet, I and myself firmly glued together. The little stretch from the Place Clichy to La Fourche. From the blind alleys that line the little stretch thick clusters of whores leap out, like bats blinded by the light. They get in my hair, my ears, my eyes. They cling with bloodsucking paws. All night long they are festering in the alleyways; they have the smell of plants after a heavy rain. They make little plantlike sounds, imbecilic cries of endearment which make the flesh creep. They swarm over me like lice, lice with long plantlike tendrils which sponge the sweat of my pores. The whores, the music, the crowds, the walls, the light on the walls, the shit and the shit-pumps working valorously, all this forms a nebula which condenses into a cool, waking sweat.

Every night, as I head toward La Fourche, I run the gauntlet. Every night I'm scalped and tomahawked. If it were not so I would miss it. I come home and shake the lice out of my clothes, wash the blood from my body. I go to bed and snore loudly. *Just the right world forme!* Keeps my flesh tender and my soul intact.

The house in which I live is being torn down. All the rooms are exposed. My house is like a human body with the skin peeled off. The wallpaper hangs in tatters, the bed-steads have no mattresses, the sinks are gone. Every night before entering the house I stand and look at it. The horror of it fascinates me. After all, why not a little horror? Every living man is a museum that houses the horrors of the race. Each man adds a new wing to the museum. And so, each night, standing before the house in which I live, the house which is being torn down, I try to grasp the meaning of it. The more the insides are exposed the more I get to love my house. I love even the old pisspot which stands under the bed, and which nobody uses any more.

In America I lived in many houses, but I do not remember what any house was like inside. I had to take what was happening to me and walk the streets with it. Once I hired an open barouche and I rode down Fifth Avenue. It was an afternoon in the fall and I was riding through my own city. Men and women promenading on the sidewalks: curious beasts, half-human, half-celluloid. Walking up and down the Avenue half-crazed, their teeth polished, their eyes glazed. The women clothed in beautiful garbs, each one equipped with a cold storage smile. The men smiled too now and then, as if they were walking in their coffins to meet the Heavenly Redeemer. Smiling through life with that demented, glazed look in the eyes, the flags unfurled, and sex flowing sweetly through the sewers. I had a gat with me and when we got to Forty-second Street I opened fire. Nobody paid any attention. I mowed them down right and left, but the crowd got no thinner. The living walked over the dead, smiling all the while to advertise their beautiful white teeth. It's this cruel white smile that sticks in my memory. I see it in my sleep when I put out my hand to beg—the George C. Tilyou smile that floats above the span-dangled bananas at Steeplechase. America smiling at poverty. It costs so little to smile—why not smile as you ride along in an open barouche? Smile, smile. Smile and the world is yours. Smile through the death rattle— it makes it easier for those you leave behind. Smile, damn you! *The smile that never comes off!*

A Thursday afternoon and I'm standing in the Metro face to face with the homely women of Europe. There's a worn beauty about their faces, as if like the earth itself they had participated in all the cataclysms of nature. The history of their race is engraved on their faces; their skin is like a parchment on which is recorded the whole struggle of civi-lization. The migrations, the hatreds and persecutions, the wars of Europe —all have left their impress. They are not smiling; their faces are composed and what is written on them is composed in terms of race, character, history. I see on their faces the ragged, multicol-ored map of Europe, a map streaked with rail, steamship and airplane lines, with nation-al frontiers, with indelible, ineradicable prejudices and rivalries. The very raggedness of the contours, the big gaps that indicate sea and lake, the broken links that make the islands, the curious mythological hangovers that are the peninsulas, all this strain and erosion indi-cates the conflict that is going on perpetually between man and reality, a conflict of which this book is but another map. I am impressed, gazing at this map, that the continent is much more vast than it seems, that in fact it is not a continent at all but a part of the globe which the waters have broken into, a land broken into by the sea. At certain weak points the land gave way. One would not have to know a word of geology to understand the vicis-situdes which this continent of Europe with its network of rivers, lakes, and inland seas has undergone. One can spot at a glance the titanic efforts that were made at different periods, just as one can detect the abortive, frustrated efforts. One can actually feel the great changes of climate that followed upon the various upheavals. If one looks at this map with the eyes of a cartologist one can imagine what it will look like fifty or a hundred thousand years hence. So it is that, looking at the sea and land which compose the continents of man, I see certain ridiculous, monstrous formations and others again which bear witness to heroic struggles. I can trace, in the long, winding rivers, the loss of faith and courage, the slipping away from grace, the slow, gradual attrition of the soul. I can see that the frontiers are marked with heavy, natural boundaries and also with light, wavering lines, variable as the wind. I can feel just *where* the climate is going to change, perceive as inevitable that certain fertile regions will wither and other barren places blossom. I am sure that in certain quarters the myth will come true, that here and there a link will be found between the unknown men we were and the unknown men we are, that the confusion of the past will be marked by a greater confusion to come, and that it is only the tumult and confusion which is of importance and that we must get down and worship it. As man we contain all the elements which make the earth, its real substance and its myth; we carry with us everywhere and always our changing geography, our changing climate. The map of Europe is changing before our eyes; nobody knows where the new continent begins or ends.

I am here in the midst of a great change. I have forgotten my own language and yet I do not speak the new language. I am in China and I am talking Chinese. I am in the dead center of a changing reality for which no language has yet been invented. According to the map I am in Paris; according to the calendar I am living in the third decade of the twentieth century. But I am neither in Paris nor in the twentieth century. I am in China and there are no clocks or calendars here. I am sailing up the Yangtsze in a dhow and what food I gather is collected from the garbage dumped overboard by the American gunboats. It takes me all day to prepare a humble meal, but it is a delectable meal and I have a cast-iron stomach.

Coming in from Louveciennes.... Below me the valley of the Seine. The whole of Paris thrown up in relief, like a geodetic survey. Looking across the plain that holds the bed of the river I see the city of Paris: ring upon ring of streets; village within village; fortress within fortress. Like the gnarled stump of an old redwood, solitary and majestic she stands there in the broad plain of the Seine. Forever in the same spot she stands, now dwindling and shrinking, now rising and expanding: the new coming out of the old, the old decaying and dying. From whatever height, from whatever distance of time or place, there she stands, the fair city of Paris, soft, gemlike, a holy citadel whose mysterious paths thread beneath the clustering sea of roofs to break upon the open plain.

In the froth and bubble of the rush hour I sit and dream over an *aperitif.* The sky is still, the clouds motionless. I sit in the dead center of traffic, stilled by the hush of a new life growing out of the decay about me. My feet are touching the roots of an ageless body for which I have no name. I am in communication with the whole earth. Here I am in the womb of time and nothing will jolt me out of my stillness. One more wanderer who has found the flame of his restlessness. Here I sit in the open street composing my song. It's the song I heard as a child, the song which I lost in the new world and which I would never have recovered had I not fallen like a twig into the ocean of time.

For him who is obliged to dream with eyes wide open all movement is in reverse, all action broken into kaleidoscopic fragments. I believe, as I walk through the horror of the present, that only those who have the courage to close their eyes, only those whose permanent absence from the condition known as reality can affect our fate. I believe, confronted with this lucid wideawake horror, that all the resources of our civilization will prove inadequate to discover the tiny grain of sand necessary to upset the stale, stultifying balance of our world. I believe that only a dreamer who has fear neither of life nor death will discover this infinitesimal iota of force which will hurtle the cosmos into whack — *instantaneously.* Not for one moment do I believe in the slow and painful, the glorious and logical, ingloriously illogical evolution of things. I believe that the whole world—not the earth alone and the beings which compose it, nor the universe whose elements we have charted, including the island universes beyond our sight and instruments—but the whole world, known and unknown, is out of kilter, screaming in pain and madness. I believe that if tomorrow the means were discovered whereby we might fly to the most remote star, one of those worlds whose light according to our weird calculus will not reach us until our earth itself be extinguished, I believe that if tomorrow we were transported there in a time which has not yet begun we would find an identical horror, an identical misery, an identical insanity. I believe that if we are so attuned to the rhythm of the stars about us as to escape the miracle of collision that we are also attuned to the fate which is being worked out simultaneously here, there, beyond and everywhere, and that there will be no escape from this universal fate unless simultaneously here, there, beyond and everywhere each and every one, man, beast, plant, mineral, rock, river, tree and mountain *wills* it.

Of a night when there is no longer a name for things I walk to the dead end of the street and, like a man who has come to the end of his tether, I jump the precipice which divides the living from the dead. As I plunge beyond the cemetery wall, where the last dilapidated urinal is gurgling, the whole of my childhood comes to a lump in my throat and chokes me. Wherever I have made my bed I have fought like a maniac to drive out the past. But at the last moment it is the past which rises up triumphantly, the past in which one drowns. With the last gasp one realizes that the future is a sham, a dirty mirror, the sand in the bottom of the hourglass, the cold, dead slag from a furnace whose fires have burned out. Walking on into the heart of Levallois-Perret I pass an Arab standing at the entrance to a blind alley. He stands there under the brilliant arc light as if petrified. Nothing to mark him as human—no handle, no lever, no spring which by a magic touch might lift him out of the trance in which he is sunk. As I wander on and on the figure of the Arab sinks deeper and deeper into my consciousness. The figure of the Arab standing in a stone trance under the brilliant arc light. The figures of other men and women standing in the cold sweat of the streets—figures with human contours standing on little points in a space which has become petrified. Nothing has changed since that day I first came down into the street to take a look at life on my own account. What I have learned since is false and of no use. And now that I have put away the false the face of the earth is even more cruel to me than it was in the beginning. In this vomit I was born and in this vomit I shall die. No escape. No Paradise to which I can flee. The scale is at balance. Only a tiny grain of sand is needed, but this tiny grain of sand it is impossible to find. The spirit and the will are lacking. I think again of the wonder and the terror with which the street first inspired me. I recall the house I lived in, the mask it wore, the demons which inhabited it, the mystery that enveloped it; I recall each being who crossed the horizon of my childhood, the wonder that wrapped him about, the aura in which he floated, the touch of his body, the odor he gave off; I recall the days of the week and the gods that ruled over them, their fatality, their fragrance, each day so new and splendorous or else long and terrifyingly void; I recall the home we made and the objects which composed it, the spirit which animated it; I recall the changing years, their sharp decisive edges, like a calendar hidden away in the trunk of the family tree; I recall even my dreams, both those of night and those of day. Since passing the Arab I have traversed a long straight road toward infinity, or at least I have the illusion that I am traversing a straight and endless road. I forgot that there is such a thing as the geodetic curve, that no matter how wide the deviation, there where the Arab stands, should I keep going, I shall return again and again. At every crossroads I shall come upon a figure with human contours standing in a stone trance, a figure pitted against a blind alley with a brilliant arc light glaring down upon him.

Today I am out for another grand obsessional walk. I and myself firmly glued together. Again the sky hangs motionless, the air stilly hushed. Beyond the great wall that hems me in the musicians are tuning up. Another day to live before the debacle! Another day! While mumbling thus to myself I swing suddenly round past the cemetery wall into the Rue de Maistre. The sharp swing to the right plunges me into the very bowels of Paris. Through the coiling, sliding intestines of Montmartre the street runs like a jagged knife wound. I am walking in blood, my heart on fire. Tomorrow all this will perish, and I with it. Beyond the wall the devils are tuning up. Faster, faster, my heart is afire!

Climbing the hill of Montmartre, St. Anthony on one side of me, Beelzebub on the other. One stands there on the high hill, resplendent in his whiteness. The surface of the mind breaks into a choppy sea. The sky reels, the earth sways. Climbing up the hill, above the granulated lids of the roofs, above the scarred shutters and the gasping chimney pots....

At that point where the Rue Lepic lies over on its side for a breathing spell, where it bends like a hairpin to renew the steep ascent, it seems as if a flood tide had receded and left behind a rich marine deposit. The dance halls, the bars, the cabarets, all the incandescent lace and froth of the electrical night pales before the seething mass of edibles which girdle the base of the hill. Paris is rubbing her belly. Paris is smacking her lips. Paris is whetting her palate for the feast to come. Here is the body moving always in its ambiance—a great dynamic procession, like the temple friezes of Egypt, like the Etruscan legend, like the morning of the glory of Crete. Everything staggeringly alive, a swarm of differentiated matter. The warm hive of the human body, the grape cluster, the honey stored away like warm diamonds. The streets swarm through my fingers. I gather up the whole of France in my one hand. In the honeycomb I am, in the warm belly of the Sphinx. The sky and the earth they tremble with the live, pleasant weight of humanity. At the very core is the body. Beyond is doubt, despair, disillusionment. The body is the fundament, the imperishable.

Along the Rue d'Orsel, the sun sinking. Perhaps it's the sun sinking, perhaps it's the street itself dismal as a vestibule. My blood is sinking of its own weight into the fragile, glassy hemorrhoids of the nerves. Over the sorrow-bitten facades a thin scum of grease, a thin green film of fadedness, a touch of dementia. And then suddenly, presto! all is changed. Suddenly the street opens wide its jaws and there, like a still white dream, like a dream embedded in stone, the Sacre Coeur rises up. A late afternoon and the heavy whiteness of it is stifling. A heavy, somnolent whiteness, like the belly of a jaded woman. Back and forth the blood ebbs, the contours rounded with soft light, the huge, billowy cupolas taut as savage teats. On the dizzy escarpments the trees stick out like spiny thorns whose fuzzy boughs wave sluggishly above the invisible current that moves trance-like beneath the roots. Pieces of sky still clinging to the tips of the boughs—soft, cottony wisps dyed with an eastern blue. Level above level, the green earth dotted with bread crumbs, with mangy dogs, with little cannibals who leap out of the pouches of kangaroos.

From the bones of the martyrs the white balustrades, the martyred limbs still writhing in agony. Silk legs crossed in Kufic characters, maybe silk sluts, maybe thin cormorants, maybe dead houris. The whole bulging edifice with its white elephant skin and its heavy stone breasts bears down on Paris with a Moorish fatalism.

Night is coming on, the night of the boulevards, with the sky red as hell-fire, and from Clichy to Barbes a fretwork of open tombs. The soft Paris night, like a ladder of toothless gums, and the ghouls grinning between the rungs. All along the foot of the hill the urinals are gurgling, their mouths choked with soft bread. It's in the night that Sacre Coeur stands out in all its stinking loveliness. Then it is that the heavy whiteness of her skin and her humid stone breath clamps down on the blood like a valve. The night and Paris pissing her white fevered blood away. Time rolling out over the xylophones, the moon gonged, the mind gouged. Night comes like an upturned cuspidor and the fine flowers of the mind, the golden jonquils and the chalk poppies, are chewed to slaver. Up on the high hill of Montmartre, under a sky-blue awning, the great stone horses champ noiselessly. The pounding of their hoofs sets the earth trembling north in Spitsbergen, south in Tasmania. The globe spins round on the soft runway of the boulevards. Faster and faster she spins. Faster and faster, while beyond the rim the musicians are tuning up. Again I hear the first notes of the dance, the devil dance with poison and shrapnel, the dance of flaming heartbeats, each heart aflame and shrieking in the night.

On the high hill, in the spring night, alone in the giant body of the whale, I am hanging upside down, my eyes filled with blood, my hair white as worms. One belly, one corpse, the great body of the whale rotting away like a fetus under a dead sun. Men and lice, men and lice, a continuous procession toward the maggot heap. This is the spring that Jesus sang, the sponge to his lips, the frogs dancing. No trace of rust, no stain of melancholy. The head slung down between the crotch in black frenzied dream, the past slowly sinking, the image balled and chained. In every womb the pounding of iron hoofs, in every grave the roar of hollow shells. Womb and shell and in the hollow of the womb a full-grown idiot picking buttercups. Man and horse moving now in one body, the hands soft, the hoofs cloven. On they come in steady procession, with red eyeballs and fiery manes. Spring is coming in the night with the roar of a cataract. Coming on the wings of mares, their manes flying, their nostrils smoking.

Up the Rue Caulaincourt, over the bridge of tombs. A soft spring rain falling. Below me the little white chapels where the dead lie buried. A splash of broken shadows from the heavy lattice work of the bridge. The grass is pushing up through the sod, greener now than by day—an electric grass that gleams with horsepower carats. Farther on up the Rue Caulaincourt I come upon a man and woman. The woman is wearing a straw hat. She has an umbrella in her hand but she doesn't open it. As I approach I hear her saying—«c'est une combinaison!»—and thinking that *combinaison* means underwear I prick up my ears. But it's a different sort of *combinaison* she's talking about and soon the fur is flying. Now I see why the umbrella was kept closed. «*Combinaison!*» she shrieks, and with that she begins to ply the umbrella. And all the poor devil can say is— «*Mais non, ma petite, mais non!*»

The little scene gives me intense pleasure—not because she is plying him with the umbrella, but because I had forgotten the other meaning of «*combinaison*» I look to the right of me and there on a slanting street is precisely the Paris I have always been searching for. You might know every street in Paris and not know Paris, but when you have forgotten where you are and the rain is softly falling, suddenly in the aimless wandering you come to the street through which you have walked time and again in your sleep *and this is the street you are now walking through.*

It was along this very street that I passed one day and saw a man lying on the sidewalk. He was lying flat on his back with arms outstretched—as if he had just been taken down from the cross. Not a soul approached him, not *one*, to see if he were dead or not. He lay there flat on his back, with arms outstretched, and there was not the slightest stir or movement of his body. As I passed close to the man I reassured myself that he was not dead. He was breathing heavily and there was a trickle of tobacco juice coming from his lips. As I reached the corner I paused a moment to see what would happen. Hardly had I turned round when a gale of laughter greeted my ears. Suddenly the doorways and shopfronts were crowded. The whole street had become animated in the twinkling of an eye. Men and women standing with arms akimbo, the tears rolling down their cheeks. I edged my way through the crowd which had gathered around the prostrate figure on the sidewalk. I couldn't understand the reason for this sudden interest, this sudden spurt of hilarity. Finally I broke through and stood again beside the body of the man. He was lying on his back as before. There was a dog standing over him and its tail was wagging with glee. The dog's nose was buried in the man's open fly. That's why everybody was laughing so. I tried to laugh too. I couldn't. I became sad, frightfully sad, sadder than I've ever been in all my life. I don't know what came over me....

All this I remember now climbing the slanting street. It was just in front of the butcher shop across the way, the one with the red and white awning. I cross the street and there on the wet pavement, exactly where the other man had lain, is the body of a man with arms outstretched. I approach to have a good look at him. It's the same man, only now his fly is buttoned *and he's dead.* I bend over him to make absolutely sure that it's the same man and that he's dead. I make absolutely sure before I get up and wander off. At the corner I pause a moment. What am I waiting for? I pause there on one heel expecting to hear again that gale of laughter which I remember so vividly. Not a sound. Not a person in sight. Except for myself and the man lying dead in front of the butcher shop the street is deserted. Perhaps it's only a dream. I look at the street sign to see if it be a name that I know, a name I mean that I would recognize if I were awake. I touch the wall beside me, tear a little strip from the poster which is pasted to the wall. I hold the little strip of paper in my hand a moment, then crumple it into a tiny pill and flip it in the gutter. It bounces away and falls into a gleaming puddle. I am not dreaming apparently. The moment I assure myself that I am awake a cold fright seizes me. *If I am not dreaming then I am insane.* And what is worse, if I am insane I shall never be able to prove whether I was dreaming or awake. But perhaps it isn't necessary to prove anything, comes the assuring thought. I am the only one who knows about it. I am the only one who has doubts. The more I think of it the more I am convinced that what disturbs me is not whether I am dreaming or insane but whether the man on the sidewalk, the man with arms outstretched, was myself. If it is possible to leave the body in dream, or in death, perhaps it is possible to leave the body forever, to wander endlessly unbodied, unhooked, a nameless identity, or an unidentified name, a soul unattached, indifferent to everything, a soul immortal, perhaps incorruptible, like God—who can say?

My body—the places it knew, so many places, and all so strange and unrelated to *me.* God Ajax dragging me by the hair, dragging me through far streets in far places —*crazy places* ... Quebec, Chula Vista, Brownsville, Suresnes, Monte Carlo, Czernowitz, Darmstadt, Canarsie, Carcassonne, Cologne, Clichy, Cracow, Budapest, Avignon, Vienna, Prague, Marseilles, London, Montreal, Colorado Springs, Imperial City, Jacksonville, Cheyenne, Omaha, Tucson, Blue Earth, Tallahassee, Chamonix, Greenpoint, Paradise Point, Point Loma, Durham, Juneau, Aries, Dieppe, Aix-la-Chapelle, Aix-en-Provence, Havre, Nimes, Asheville, Bonn, Herkimer, Glendale, Ticonderoga, Niagara Falls, Spartan-burg, Lake Titicaca, Ossining, Dannemora, Narragan-sett, Nuremberg, Hanover, Hamburg, Lemberg, Needles, Calgary, Galveston, Honolulu, Seattle, Otay, Indianapolis, Fairfield, Richmond, Orange Court House, Culver City, Rochester, Utica, Pine Bush, Carson City, Southold, Blue Point, Juarez, Mineola, Spuyten Duyvil, Pawtucket, Wilmington, Coogan's Bluff, North Beach, Toulouse, Perpignan, Fontenay-aux-Roses, Widde-combe-in-the-Moor, Mobile, Louveciennes.... In each and every one of these places something happened to me, something fatal. In each and every one of these places I left a dead body on the sidewalk with arms outstretched. Each and every time I bent over to take a good look at myself, to reassure myself that the body was not alive and that it was not I but myself that I was leaving behind. *And on I went—on and on and on.* And I am still going and I am alive, but when the rain starts to fall and I get to wandering aimlessly I hear the clanking of these dead selves peeled off in my journeying and I ask myself— *what next?* You might think there was a limit to what the body could endure, but there's none. So high does the body stand above suffering that when everything has been killed there remains always a toenail or a clump of hair which sprouts and it's these immortal sprouts which remain forever and ever. So that even when you are absolutely dead and forgotten some microscopic part of you still sprouts, and be the past future so dead there's still some little part alive and sprouting.

It's thus I'm standing one afternoon in the broiling sun outside the little station at Louveciennes, a tiny part of me alive and sprouting. The hour when the stock report comes through the air—*over the air,* as they say. In the bistro across the way from the station is hidden a machine and in the machine is hidden a man and in the man is hidden a voice. And the voice, which is the voice of a full-grown idiot, says—American Can.... American Tel. & Tel.... In French it says it, which is even more idiotic. *American Can ... American Tel. & Tel....* And then suddenly, like Jacob when he mounted the golden ladder, suddenly all the voices of heaven break loose. Like a geyser spurting forth from the bare earth the whole American scene gushes up— American Can, American Tel. & Tel., Atlantic & Pacific, Standard Oil, United Cigars, Father John, Sacco & Vanzetti, Uneeda Biscuit, Seaboard Air Line, Sapolio, Nick Carter, Trixie Friganza, Foxy Grandpa, the Gold Dust Twins, Tom Sharkey, Valeska Suratt, Commodore Schley, Millie de Leon, Theda Bara, Robert E. Lee, Little Nemo, Lydia Pinkham, Jesse James, Annie Oakley, Diamond Jim Brady, Schlitz-Milwaukee, Hemp St. Louis, Daniel Boone, Mark Hanna, Alexander Dowie, Carrie Nation, Mary Baker Eddy, Pocahontas, Fatty Arbuckle, Ruth Snyder, Lillian Russell, Sliding Billy Watson, Olga Nethersole, Billy Sunday, Mark Twain,

Freeman & Clarke, Joseph Smith, Battling Nelson, Aimee Semple McPherson, Horace Greeley, Pat Rooney, Peruna, John Philip Sousa, Jack London, Babe Ruth, Harriet Beecher Stowe, Al Capone, Abe Lincoln, Brigham Young, Rip Van Winkle, Krazy Kat, Liggett & Meyers, the Hallroom Boys, Horn & Hardart, Fuller Brush, the Katzenjammer Kids, Gloomy Gus, Thomas Edison, Buffalo Bill, the Yellow Kid, Booker T. Washington, Czolgosz, Arthur Brisbane, Henry Ward Beecher, Ernest Seton Thompson, Margie Pennetti, Wrigley's Spearmint, Uncle Remus, Svoboda, David Harum, John Paul Jones, Grape Nuts, Aguinaldo, Nell Brinkley, Bessie McCoy, Tod Sloan, Fritzi Scheff, Lafcadio Hearn, Anna Held, Little Eva, Omega Oil, Maxine Elliott, Oscar Hammerstein, Bostock, The Smith Brothers, Zbysko, Clara Kimball Young, Paul Revere, Samuel Gompers, Max Linder, Ella Wheeler Wilcox, Corona-Corona, Uncas, Henry Clay, Woolworth, Patrick Henry, Cremo, George C. Tilyou, Long Tom, Christy Matthewson, Adeline Genee, Richard Carle, Sweet Caporals, Park & Tilford's, Jeanne Eagels, Fanny Hurst, Olga Petrova, Yale & Towne, Terry McGovern, Frisco, Marie Cahill, James J. Jeffries, the Housatonic, the Penobscot, Evangeline, Sears Roebuck, the Salmagundi, Dreamland, P. T. Barnum, Luna Park, Hiawatha, Bill Nye, Pat McCarren, the Rough Riders, Mischa Elman, David Belasco, Farragut, The Hairy Ape, Minnehaha, Arrow Collars, Sunrise, Sun Up, the Shenandoah, Jack Johnson, the Little Church Around the Corner, Cab Galloway, Elaine Hammerstein, Kid McCoy, Ben Ami, Ouida, Peck's Bad Boy, Patti, Eugene V. Debs, Delaware & Lackawanna, Carlo Tresca, Chuck Connors, George Ade, Emma Goldman, Sitting Bull, Paul Dressier, Child's, Hubert's Museum, The Bum, Florence Mills, the Alamo, Peacock Alley, Pomander Walk, The Gold Rush, Sheepshead Bay, Strangler Lewis, Mimi Aguglia, The Barber Shop Chord, Bobby Walthour, Painless Parker, Mrs. Leslie Carter, The Police Gazette, Carter's Little Liver Pills, Bustanoby's, Paul & Joe's, William Jennings Bryan, George M. Cohan, Swami Vivekananda, Sadakichi Hartman, Elizabeth Gurley Flynn, the Monitor and the Merrimac, Snuffy the Cabman, Dorothy Dix, Amato, the Great Sylvester, Joe Jackson, Bunny, Elsie Janis, Irene Franklin, The Beale Street Blues, Ted Lewis, Wine, Woman & Song, Blue Label Ketchup, Bill Bailey, Sid Olcott, In the Gloaming Genevieve and the Banks of the Wabash far away....

Everything American coming up in a rush. And with every name a thousand intimate details of my life are connected. What Frenchman passing me in the street suspects that I carry around inside me a dictionary of names? and with each name a life and a death? When I walk down the street with a rapt air does any frog know *what* street I'm walking down? Does he know that I am walking inside the great Chinese Wall? Nothing is registered in my face—neither suffering, nor joy, nor hope, nor despair. I walk the streets with the face of a coolie. I have seen the land ravaged, homes devastated, families uptorn. Each city I walked through has killed me—so vast the misery, so endless the unremitting toil. From one city to another I walk, leaving behind me a grand procession of dead and clanking selves. *But I myself go on and on and on.* And all the while I hear the musicians tuning up....

Last night I was walking again through the Fourteenth Ward. I came again upon my idol, Eddie Carney, the boy whom I have not seen since I left the old neighborhood. He was tall and thin, handsome in an Irish way. He took possession of me body and soul. There were three streets—North First, Fillmore Place and Driggs Avenue. These marked the boundaries of the known world. Beyond was Thule, Ultima Thule. It was the period of San Juan Hill, Free Silver, Pinocchio, Uneeda. In the basin, not far from Wallabout

Market, lay the warships. A strip of asphalt next to the curb allowed the cyclists to spin to Coney Island and back. In every package of Sweet Caporals there was a photograph, sometimes a soubrette, sometimes a prizefighter, sometimes a flag. Toward evening Paul Sauer would put a tin can through the bars of his window and call for raw sauerkraut. Also toward evening Lester Reardon, proud, princely, golden-haired, would walk from his home past the baker shop—an event of primary importance. On the south side lay the homes of the lawyers and physicians, the politicians, the actors, the firehouse, the funeral parlor, the Protestant churches, the burlesk, the fountain; on the north side lay the tin factory, the iron works, the veterinary's, the cemetery, the schoolhouse, the police station, the morgue, the slaughterhouse, the gas tanks, the fish market, the Democratic club. There were only three men to fear—old man Ramsay, the gospel-monger, crazy George Denton, the peddler, and Doc Martin, the bug exterminator. Types were already clearly distinguishable: the buffoons, the earth men, the paranoiacs, the volatiles, the mystagogues, the drudges, the nuts, the drunkards, the liars, the hypocrites, the harlots, the sadists, the cringers, the misers, the fanatics, the Urnings, the criminals, the saints, the princes. Jenny Maine was hump for the monkeys. Alfie Betcha was a crook. Joe Goeller was a sissy. Stanley was my first friend. Stanley Borowski. He was the first «other» person I recognized. He was a wildcat. Stanley recognized no law except the strap which his old man kept in the back of the barber shop. When his old man belted him you could hear Stanley screaming blocks away. In this world everything was done openly, in broad daylight. When Silberstein the pants maker went out of his mind they laid him out on the sidewalk in front of his home and put the strait jacket on him. His wife, who was with child, was so terrified that she dropped the brat on the sidewalk right beside him. Professor Martin, the bug exterminator, was just returning home after a long spree. He had two ferrets in his coat pockets and one of them got away on him. Stanley Borowski drove the ferret down the sewer for which he got a black eye then and there from Professor Martin's son Harry who was a half-wit. On the shed over the paint shop, just across the street, Willie Maine was standing with his pants down, jerking away for dear life. «Bjork» he said. «Bjork! Bjork!» The fire engine came and turned the hose on him. His old man, who was a drunkard, called the cops. The cops came and almost beat his old man to death. Meanwhile, a block away, Pat McCarren was standing at the bar treating his cronies to champagne. The matinee was just over and the soubrettes from The Bum were piling into the back room with their sailor friends. Crazy George Denton was driving his wagon up the street, a whip in one hand and a Bible in the other. At the top of his crazy voice he was yelling «Inasmuch as ye do it unto the least of my brethren ye do it unto me also,» or some such crap. Mrs. Gorman was standing in the doorway in her dirty wrapper, her boobies half out, and muttering «Tch tch tch!» She was a member of Father Carroll's church on the north side. «Good marnin' father, fine marnin' this marnin'!»

It was this evening, after the dinner, that it all came over me again—I mean about the musicians and the dance they are making ready. We had prepared a humble banquet for ourselves, Carl and I. A meal made entirely of delectables: radishes, black olives, tomatoes, sardines, cheese, Jewish bread, bananas, apple sauce, a couple of liters of Algerian wine, fourteen degrees. It was warm outdoors and very still. We sat there after the meal smoking contentedly, almost ready to doze off, so good was the meal and so comfortable the hard chairs with the light fading and that stillness about the rooftops as if the houses themselves were quietly breathing through the fents. And like many another evening, after we had sat in silence for a while and the room almost dark, suddenly he began to talk about himself, about something in the past which in the silence and the gloom of the evening began to take shape, not in words precisely, because it was beyond words what he was conveying to me. I don't think I caught the words at all, but just the music that was coming from him—a kind of sweet, woody music which came through the Algerian wine and the radishes and the black olives. Talking about his mother he was, about coming out of her womb, and after him his brother and his sister, and then the war came and they told him to shoot and he couldn't shoot and when the war was over they opened the gates of the prison or the lunatic asylum or whatever it was and he was free as a bird. How it happened to spill out this way I can't remember any more. We were talking about *The Merry Widow* and about Max Linder, about the Prater in Vienna—and then suddenly we were in the midst of the Russo-Japanese war and there was that Chinaman whom Claude Farrere mentions in *La Bataille.* Something that was said about the Chinaman must have sunk to the very bottom of him for when he opened his mouth again and started that speech about his mother, her womb, the war coming on and free as a bird I knew that he had gone far back into the past and I was almost afraid to breathe for fear of bringing him to.

Free as a bird I heard him say, and with that the gates opening and other men running out, all scot-free and a little silly from the confinement and the strain of waiting for the war to end. When the gates opened I was in the street again and my friend Stanley was sitting beside me on the little step in front of the house where we ate sour bread in the evening. Down the street a ways was Father Carroll's church. And now it's evening again and the vesper bells are ringing, Carl and I facing each other in the gathering gloom, quiet and at peace with each other. We are sitting in Clichy and it is long after the war. But there's another war coming and it's there in the darkness and perhaps it's the darkness made him think of his mother's womb and the night coming on, the night when you stand alone out there and no matter how frightful it gets you must stand there alone and take it. «I didn't want to go to the war,» he was saying. «Shit, I was only eighteen.» Just then a phono began to play and it was *The Merry Widow* waltz. Outside everything so still and quiet—just like before the war. Stanley is whispering to me on the doorstep —something about God, the *Catholic* God. There are some radishes in the bowl and Carl is munching them in the dark. «It's so beautiful to be alive, no matter how poor you are,» he says. I can just barely see him sticking his hand into the bowl and grabbing another radish. So beautiful to be alive! And with that he slips a radish into his mouth as if to convince himself that he is still alive and free as a bird. And now the whole street, free as a bird, is twittering inside me and I see again the boys who are later to have their heads blown off or their guts bayoneted—boys like Alfie Betcha, Tom Fowler, Johnny Dunn, Sylvester Goeller, Harry Martin, Johnny Paul, Eddie Carney, Lester Reardon, Georgie Maine, Stanley Borowski, Louis Pirosso, Robbie Hyslop, Eddie Gorman, Bob Maloney. The boys from the north side and the boys from the south side—all rolled into a muck heap and their guts hanging on the barbed wire. If only one of them had been spared! But no, not one! Not even the great Lester Reardon. The whole past is wiped out. It's so beautiful to be alive and free as a bird. The gates are open and I can wander where I please. But where is Eddie Carney? Where is Stanley?

This is the Spring that Jesus sang, the sponge to his lips, the frogs dancing. In every womb the pounding of iron hoofs, in every grave the roar of hollow shells. A vault of obscene anguish saturated with angel-worms hanging from the fallen womb of a sky. In this last body of the whale the whole world has become a running sore. When next the trumpet blows it will be like pushing a button: as the first man falls he will push over the next, and the next the next, and so on down the line, round the world, from New York to Nagasaki, from the Arctic to the Antarctic. And when man falls he will push over the elephant and the elephant will push over the cow and the cow will push over the horse and the horse the lamb, and all will go down, one before the other, one after the other, like a row of tin soldiers blown down by the wind. The world will go out like a Roman candle. Not even a blade of grass will grow again. A lethal dose from which no awakening. Peace and night, with no moan or whisper stirring. A soft, brooding darkness, an inaudible flapping of wings.

9. Burlesk

Now works the calmness of Scheveningen like an anesthetic.

Standing at the bar looking at the English cunt with all her front teeth missing it suddenly comes back to me: *Don't Spit On the Floor!* It comes back to me like a dream: *Don't Spit On the Floor!* It was at Freddie's Bar on the Rue Pigalle and a man with lacy fingers, a man in a white silk shirt with loose flowing sleeves, had just rippled off «Good Bye Mexico!» She said she wasn't doin' much now, just battin' around. She was from the Big Broadcast and she had caught the hoof and mouth disease. She kept running back and forth to the toilet through the beaded curtains. The harp was swell, like angels pissing in your beer. She was a little drunk and trying to be a lady at the same time. I had a letter in my pocket from a crazy Dutchman; he had just returned from Sofia. «Saturday night,» it said, «I had only one wish and that was that you could have sitten next to me.» *(Where* he didn't say.) «The only thing I can write you now is this—after having left the hustling noisy New York works the calmness of a town like Scheveningen as a anaesthetic.» He had been on a bust in Sofia and he had taken to himself the prima donna of the Royal Opera there. This, as he says, had given him just the right kind of rakish reputation to find grace with the public opinion of Sofia. He says he is going to retreat and start again a sober life—in Scheveningen.

I hadn't looked at the letter all evening but when the English cunt opened her mouth and I saw all her front teeth missing it came back to me—*Don't Spit On the Floor!* We were walking through the ghetto, the crazy Dutchman and I, and he was dressed in his messenger uniform. He had delivered all his messages and he was off duty for the rest of the evening. We were walking toward the Cafe Royal in order to sit down and have a beer or two in peace. I was giving him permission to sit down and have a beer with me because I was his boss and besides he was off duty and he could do as he pleased in his spare time.

We were walking along Second Avenue, heading north, when suddenly I noticed a shop window with an illuminated cross and on it it said: Whosoever Believeth In Me Shall Not Die.... We went inside and a man was standing on a platform saying: «Miss Powell, you make ready a song! Come now, brothers, who'll testify? Yes, Hymn No. 73. After the meeting we will all go down to call on our bereaved sister, Mrs. Blanchard. Let us stand while we sing Hymn No. 73: *Lord plant my feet on the higher ground.* As I was saying a moment ago, when I saw the steeplejack painting our new steeple bright and pure for us the words of this dear old hymn rushed to my lips: *Lord plant my feet on the higher ground.*»

The place was very small and there were signs everywhere—«The Lord is my Shepherd, I shall not want,» et cetera. The most prominent sign was the one over the altar: *Don't Spit On the Floor.* They were all singing Hymn No. 73 in honor of the new steeple. We were standing on the higher ground and I had a good view of the signs on the wall, especially the one over the pulpit—*Don't Spit On the Floor.* Sister Powell was pumping away at the organ: she looked clean and spiritual. The man on the platform was singing louder than the others and though he knew the words by heart he held the hymn book in front of him and sang from the notes. He looked like a blacksmith who was substituting for the regular preacher. He was very loud and very earnest. He was doing his best, between songs, to get people to testify. Every now and then a man with a squeaky voice piped up: «I praise God for his savin' and keepin' power!»

Amen! Glory! Glory! Hallelujah!

«Come now,» roars the blacksmith, «who'll testify? You, brother Eaton, won't you testify?»

Brother Eaton rises to his feet and says solemnly: «He purchased me with a price.»

Amen! Amen! Hallelujah!

Sister Powell is wiping her hands with a handkerchief. She does it spiritually. After she has wiped her hands she looks blankly at the wall in front of her. She looks as though the Lord had just anointed her. Very spiritual.

Brother Eaton, who was purchased with a price, is sitting quietly with hands folded. The blacksmith explains that Brother Eaton was purchased with the price of Christ's own precious blood shed on the cross, on Calvary, it was. He would like some one else to testify. *Some one else, please!* In a little while, he explains, we will all go down in a body to have a last look at Sister Blanchard's dear son who passed away last night. *Come now, who'll testify?*

A quaky voice: «Folks, you know I'm not much for testifyin'. But there's one verse very dear to me ... very dear. It's Colossius 3. *Stand still and see the salvation of the Lord.* Just stand still, brothers. Just be quiet. Try it sometime. Get down on your knees and try to think of him. Try to listen to him. Let him speak.

Brothers, it's very dear to me—Colossius 3. Stand still and see the salvation of the Lord.

Hear! Hear! Glory! Glory! Praise the Lord! Hallelujah!

«Sister Powell, you make ready another song!» He wipes his face. «Before we go down to take a last look at Sister Blanchard's dear son let us all join in singing one more hymn: *What a friend we have in Jesus!* I guess we all know that by heart. Men, if you're not washed in the blood of the Lamb it won't matter how many books your name is registered in down here. Don't put him off! Come to him tonight, men ... *tonight!* Come now, all together—*What a friend we have* ... Hymn No. 97. Let everybody stand and sing before we go down in a body to Sister Blanchard's. Come now, Hymn No. 97.... «*What a friend we have in Jesus....*«

It's all arranged. We're all going down in a body to look at Sister Blanchard's dear dead son. All of us— Colossians, Pharisees, snotnoses, gaycats, cracked sopranos—all going down in a body to have a last look. I don't know what has happened to the crazy Dutchman who wanted a glass of beer. We're going down to Sister Blanchard's, all of us in a body—the Jukes and the Kallikaks, Hymn No. 73 and *Don't Spit On the Floor!* Brother Pritchard, you put out the lights! And Sister Powell, you make ready a song!

Good-bye Mexico! We're going down to Sister Blanchard's. Going down to plant our feet on the higher ground. Here a nose missing, there an eye out. Lopsided, rheumy, bile-ridden, sweet, spiritual, wormy and demented. All going down in a body to paint the steeple pure and bright. All friends with Jews. All standing still to see the salvation of the Lord. Brother Eaton's gonna pass the hat around and Sister Powell's gonna wipe the spit off the walls. All purchased with a price, the price of a good cigar' *Now works the calmness of Scheveningen like M anesthetic.* All the messages are delivered. For those preferring cremation we will have a few very fine niches for urns. Sister Blanchard's dear dead son is lying on the ice, his toes are sprouting. The mausoleum provides a place where families and friends may lie side by side in a snow-white compartment, high and dry above the ground, where neither water, damp, nor mold can enter.

Moving toward the National Winter Garden in a yellow taxi. The calmness of Scheveningen is working on me. Letters like music everywhere and God be praised for his savin' and keepin' power. Everywhere black snow, everywhere lousy black wigs. WATCH THIS WINDOW FOR SLIGHTLY USED BARGAINS! MUST VACATE! Glory! Glory! Hallelujah!

Poverty walking about in fur coats. Turkish baths, Russian baths, Sitz baths ... baths, baths, and no cleanliness. Clara Bow is giving «Parisian Love.» The ghost of Jacob Gordin stalks the blood-soaked tundras. St. Marks-on-the-Bouwerie looks gay as a cockroach, her walls sweet minted and painted a tutti-frutti. BRIDGE WORK ... REASONABLE PRICES. Moskowitz is tickling the cymbalon and the cymbalon is tickling the cold storage rump of Leo Tolstoi who has now become a vegetarian restaurant. The whole planet is turned made out to make warts, pimples, blackheads, wens. The hospitals are all renovated, admission free, side entrance. To all who are suffering, to all who are weary and heavy-laden, to every son of a bitch dying with eczema, halitosis, gangrene, dropsy, be it remembered, sealed and affixed that the side entrance is free. Come ye one and all! Come, ye sniveling Kallikaks! Come, ye snot-nosed Pharisees! Come and have your guts renovated at less than the cost of ordinary ground burial. Come tonight! Jesus wants you. Come before it's too late— we close at 7:15 on the dot.

Cleo dances every night!!

Cleo, darling of the gods, dances every night. *Mommer, I'm coming! Mommer, I want to be saved!* I'm walking up the ladder, Mommer.

Glory! Glory! Colossius! Colossius 3.

Mother of all that's holy, now I'm in heaven. I'm standing behind the standees who are standing behind Z for zebra. The Episcopal rector is standing on the church steps with a broken rectum. It says—NO PARKING. The Minsky brothers are in the box office dreaming of the river Shannon. The Pathe News clicks like a hollow nutmeg. In the Himalayas the monks get up in the middle of the night and pray for all who sleep so that men and women all over the world, when they awake in the morning, may begin the day with thoughts that are pure, kind, and brave. The world passes in review: St. Moritz, the Oberammergau Players, Oedipus Rex, chow dogs, cyclones, bathing beauties. My soul is at peace. If I had a beer and a ham sandwich what a friend I would have in Jesus! Anyway, the curtain is rising. Shakespeare was right—*the show is the thing!*

And now, ladies and gentlemen, the curtain is rising on the cleanest, fastest show ever produced in the Western Hemisphere. The curtain is rising, ladies and gentlemen, on those portions of the anatomy called respectively the epigastric, the umbilical, and the hypogastric. These choice portions, marked down to a dollar ninety-eight, have never before been shown to an American audience. Minsky, the king of the Jews, has imported them especially from the Rue de la Paix. This is the cleanest, fastest show in New York. And now, ladies and gentlemen, while the ushers are busy squirting and fumigating, we will pass out a number of French post cards each and every one guaranteed to be genuine. With every post card we will also pass out a genuine German hand-made microscope made in Zurich by the Japanese. This, ladies and gentlemen, is the fastest, cleanest show in the world. Minsky, the king of the Jews, says so himself. The curtain is rising ... the curtain is rising....

Under cover of darkness the ushers are spraying the dead and live lice and the nests of lice and the egg lice buried in the thick black curly locks of those who have no private baths, the poor, homeless Jews of the East Side who in their desperate poverty walk about in fur coats selling matches and shoe laces. Outside it's exactly like the Place des Vosges or the Haymarket or Covent Garden, except that these people have faith—in the Burroughs Adding Machine. The fire escapes are crowded with pregnant women who have blown themselves up with bicycle pumps. All the poor desperate Jews of the East Side are happy on the fire escapes because they are eating ham sandwiches with one foot in the clouds. The curtain is rising to the odor of formaldehyde sweetened with Wrigley's Spearmint Chewing Gum, five a package. The curtain is rising on the one and only portion of the human anatomy about which the less said the better. In life's December when love is an ember it will be sad to remember the star-spangled bananas floating over the sheet-iron portions of the epigastric, hypogastric and umbilical sections of the human anatomy. Minsky is dreaming in the box office, his feet planted on the higher ground. The Oberammergau Players are playing somewhere else. The chow dogs are being bathed and perfumed for the blue ribbon show. Sister Blanchard is sitting in the rocker with a fallen womb. Age comes, the body withers—but hernia can be cured. Looking down from the fire escape one sees the beautiful, unending landscape, exactly as it was painted by Cezanne—with corrugated ash cans, rusty can openers, broken-down baby carriages, tin bathtubs, copper boilers, nutmeg graters and partially nibbled animal crackers carefully preserved in cellophane. This is the fastest, cleanest show on earth brought all the way from the Rue de la Paix. You have the choice of two things—one looking down, down into the black depths, the other looking up, up into the sunlight where the hope of the resurrection waves above the star-spangled banner each and every one guaranteed to be genuine. Stand still, men, and see the salvation of the Lord. Cleo is dancing tonight and every night this week at less than the price of ordinary ground burial. Death is coming on all fours, like a sprig of shamrock. The stage glitters like the electric chair. Cleo is coming. Cleo, darling of the gods and queen of the electric chair.

Now «works the calmness of Scheveningen like an anesthetic. The curtain rises on Colossius 3. Cleo advances out of the womb of night, her belly swollen with sewer gas. Glory! Glory! I'm climbing up the ladder. Out of the womb of night rises the old Brooklyn Bridge, a torpid dream wriggling in spume and moonfire. A drone and sizzle scraping the frets. A glister of chrysoprase, a flare of naptha. The night is cold and men are walking in lock step. The night is cold but the queen is naked save for a jockstrap. The queen is dancing on the cold embers of the electric chair. Cleo, the darling of the Jews, is dancing on the tips of her lacquered nails; her eyes are twisted, her ears filled with blood. She is dancing through the cold night at reasonable prices. She will dance every night this week to make way for platinum bridges. O men, behind the *virumque cano,* behind the duodecimal system and the Seaboard Air Line stands the Queen of Tammany Hall. She stands in bare feet, her belly swollen with sewer gas, her navel rising in systolic hexameters. Cleo, the queen, purer than the purest asphalt, warmer than the warmest electricity, Cleo die queen and darling of the gods dancing on the asbestos seat of the electric chair. In the morning she will push off for Singapore, Mozambique, Rangoon. Her barque is moored to the gutter. Her slaves are crawling with lice. Deep in the womb of night she dances the song of salvation. We are all going down in a body to the Men's Room to stand on the higher ground. Down to the Men's Room where it is sanitary and dry and sentimental as a churchyard.

Imagine now, while the curtain's falling, that it's a fine balmy day and the smell of clams coming in from the bay. You step out along the Atlantic littoral in your cement suit and your gold-heeled socks and there's the roar of Chop Suey in your ears. The Great White Way is blazing with spark plugs. The comfort stations are open. You try to sit down without breaking the crease in your pants. You sit down on the pure asphalt and let the peacocks tickle your larynx. The gutters are running with champagne. The only odor is the odor of clams coming from the bay. It's a fine balmy day and all the radios are going at once. You can have a radio attached to your ass—for just a little more. You can tune in on Manila or Honolulu while you walk. You can have ice in your ice water or both kidneys removed at the same time. If you have lockjaw you can have a tube put up your rectum and imagine you're eating. You can have anything you want for the asking. That is, if it's a fine balmy day and the smell of clams coming in from the bay. Because why? Because America is the grandest country God ever made and if you don't like this country you can get the hell out of it and go back where you came from. There isn't a thing in the world America won't do for you if you ask for it like a man. You can sit in the electric chair and while the juice is being turned on you can read about your own execution; you can look at a picture of yourself sitting in the electric chair while you are waiting to be executed.

A continuous performance from morn till midnight. The fastest, cleanest show on earth. So fast, so clean, it makes you desperate and lonely.

I go back over the Brooklyn Bridge and sit in the snow opposite the house where I was born. An immense, heartbreaking loneliness grips me. I don't yet see myself standing at Freddie's Bar in the Rue Pigalle. I don't see the English cunt with all her front teeth missing. Just a void of white snow and in the center of it the little house where I was born. In this house I dreamed about becoming a musician.

Sitting» before the house in which I was born I feel absolutely unique. I belong to an orchestra for which no symphonies have ever been written. Everything is in the wrong key, *Parsifal* included. About *Parsifal,* now —it's just a minor incident, but it has the right ring.

It's got to do with America, my love of music, my grotesque loneliness....

Was standing one night in the gallery of the Metropolitan Opera House. The house was sold out and I was standing about three rows back from the rail. Could see only a tiny fragment of the stage and even to do that had to strain my neck. But I could hear the music, Wagner's *Parsifal,* with which I was already slightly familiar through the phonograph records. Parts of the opera are dull, duller than anything ever written. But there are other parts which are sublime and during the sublime parts, because I was being squeezed like a sardine, an embarrassing thing happened to me—*I got an erection.* The woman I was pressing against must also have been inspired by the sublime music of the Holy Grail. We were in heat, the two of us, and pressed together like a couple of sardines. During the intermission the woman left her place to pace up and down the corridor. I stayed where I was, wondering if she would return to the same place. When the music started up again she returned. She returned to her spot with such exactitude that if we had been married it could not have been more perfect. All through the last act we were joined in heavenly bliss. It was beautiful and sublime, nearer to Boccaccio than to Dante, but sublime and beautiful just the same.

Sitting in the snow before the place of my birth I remember this incident vividly. Why, I don't know, except that it connects with the grotesque and the void, with the heartbreaking loneliness, the snow, the lack of color, the absence of music. One is always falling to sleep with the fast pace. You start out with the sublime and you end up in an alley jerking away for dear life. Saturday afternoons, for example, breaking chain in Bill Woodruff's accessory shop. Breaking chain all afternoon for a half-dollar. Jolly work! Afterwards we'd all go back to Bill Woodruff's house and sit and drink. Come dark Bill Woodruff would get out his opera glasses and we'd all take turns, looking at the woman across the yard who used to undress with the shade up. This business of the opera glasses always infuriated Bill Woodruff's wife. To get even with him she'd come out in a negligee studded with big holes. A frigid son of a bitch, his wife, but it gave her a kick to walk up to one of his friends and say—«feel my ass! feel how big it's getting.» Bill Woodruff pretended not to mind. «Sure,» he'd say, «go ahead and feel it. She's cold as ice.» And like that she'd pass herself around, each one grabbing her ass to warm her up a bit. A funny couple they were. Sometimes you'd think they were in love with each other. She made him miserable, though, holding him off all the time. He used to say: «I can get a fuck out of her about once a month—if I'm lucky!» Used to say it right to her face. It didn't bother her much. She had a way of laughing it off, as though it were an unimportant blemish.

If she had simply been cold it wouldn't have been so bad. But she was greedy too. Always clamoring for dough. Always hankering for something they couldn't afford. It got on his nerves, which is easy to understand, because he was a tight, scrounging bastard himself. One day, however, a brilliant idea occurred to him. «You want some more dough, is that it?» he says to her. «All right, then, I'm going to give you some dough—but first you've got to slip me a piece of tail.» (It never occurred to the poor bastard that he might find another woman who'd enjoy a bit of fucking for its own sake).

Well, anyway, the amazing thing about it was that every time he slipped her a little extra she'd manage to screw like a rabbit. He was astonished. Didn't think she had it in her. And so, little by little, he got to working overtime in order to lay aside the little bribe which would make the frigid son of a bitch come across like a nymphomaniac. (Never thought, the poor sap, of investing the money in another gal. Never!)

Meanwhile the friends and neighbors were discovering that Bill Woodruff's wife wasn't such a cold proposition as she had been cracked up to be. Seems she was sleeping around like—with every Tom, Dick, and Harry. Why the hell she couldn't give her own spouse a little piece on the side, *gratis,* nobody could figure out. She acted as though she were sore at him. It started out that way right from the beginning. And whether she was born frigid or not makes no difference. As far as he was concerned she was frigid. She'd have made him pay until his dying day for every piece she handed him if it weren't for the fact that somebody put him wise to her.

Well, he was a cute guy, Bill Woodruff. A mean, scrounging bastard if ever there was one, but he could be cute too when necessary. When he heard what was going on he didn't say a word. Pretended that things were just as always. Then one night, after it had gone along far enough, he waited up for her, a thing he seldom did because he had to get up early and she was used to coming in late. This night, however, he waited up for her and when she came sailing in, chipper, perky, a little lit up and cold as usual he pulled her up short with a «where were you tonight?» She tried pulling her usual yarn, of course. «Cut that,» he said, «I want you to get your things off and tumble into bed.» That made her sore. She mentioned in her roundabout way that she didn't want any of that business. «You don't feel in the mood for it, I suppose,» says he, and then he adds: «that's fine, because now I'm going to warm you up a bit.» With that he up and ties her to the bedstead, gags her, and then goes for the razor strop. On the way to the bathroom he grabs a bottle of mustard from the kitchen. He comes back with the razor strop and he belts the piss out of her. And after that he rubs the mustard into the raw welts. «That ought to keep you warm for tonight,» he says. And so saying he makes her bend over and spread her legs apart. «Now,» he says, «I'm going to pay you as usual,» and taking a bill out of his pocket he crumples it and then shoves it up her quim.... And that's that about Bill Woodruff, though when I get to thinking on it I want to add that light of heart he sallied bravely forth carrying the pair of horns which his wife Jadwiga had given him.

And the purpose of all this? To prove what has not yet been demonstrated, namely that

THE GREAT ARTIST IS HE WHO CONQUERS THE ROMANTIC IN HIMSELF.

Filed under R for rat poison.

And what by that? you say.

Why just this.... Whenever it came time to visit Tante Melia at the bughouse mother would do up a little lunch, saying as she laid the bottle between the napkins—«Mele always liked a drop of Kummel.» And when it came mother's turn to visit the bughouse and say to Mele well Mele how did you like the Kummel, and Mele shaking her head and saying what Kummel, I didn't see any Kummel, why I could always say she's crazy of course, I gave her the Kummel. What was the sense in pouring a drop of Kummel down Mele's throat when she was so goddamned disoriented as to swallow her own dung?

If it were a sunny day and my friend Stanley commissioned by his uncle, the mortician, to carry a stillbirth to the cemetery grounds, we would take a ferry boat to Staten Island and when the Statue of Liberty hove in sight overboard with it! If it were a rainy day we would walk into another neighborhood and throw it down the sewer. A day like that was a festive day for all the sewer rats; A fine day for the sewer rats scampering through the vestibule of the upper world. In those days a still-birth brought as high as ten dollars and after riding the shoot-the-chutes we always left a little stale beer for the morning because the finest thing in the world for Katzenjammer is a glass of stale beer.

I am speaking of things that brought me relief in the beginning. You are at the beginning of the world, in a garden which is boxed off. The sky is banked like sand dunes and there is not just one firmament but millions of them; the crust of every planet is carved into an eye, a very human eye that neither blinks nor winks.

You are about to write a beautiful book and in it you are going to record everything that has given you pain or joy. This book, when written, will be called *A Prolegomenon to the Unconscious.* You will dress it in white kid and the letters will be embossed in gold. It will be the story of your life without emendations.

Everybody will want to read it because it will contain the absolute truth and nothing but the truth. This is the story that makes you laugh in your sleep, the story that starts the tears flowing when you are in the middle of a ballroom and suddenly realize that none of the people around you know what a genius you are. How they would laugh and weep if they could only read what you have not yet written because every word is absolutely true and so far nobody has dared to write this absolute truth except yourself and this true book which is locked up inside you would make people laugh and weep as they have never laughed, never wept before.

In the beginning this is what brings relief—the true book which nobody has read, the book which you carry around inside you, the book dressed in white kid and embossed with letters of gold. In this book there are many verses *colossially* dear to you. Out of this book came the Bible, and the Koran, and all the sacred books of the East. All these books were written at the beginning of the world.

And now I'm going to tell you about the technical aspect of these books, *this* book whose genesis I am about to relate....

When you open this book you will notice immediately that the illustrations have a queer pituitary flavor. You will see immediately that the author has forsaken the optical illusion in favor of a post-pineal view. The frontispiece is usually a self-portrait called «Praxus» showing the author standing on the frontier of the middle brain in a pair of tights. He always wears thick-lensed spectacles, Toric, U-31 flange. In ordinary waking life the author suffers from normal vision but in the frontispiece he renders himself myopic in order to grasp the immediacy of the dream plasm. By means of the dream technique he peels off the outer layers of his geologic mortality and comes to grips with his true mantic self, a non-stratified area of semi-liquid character. Only the amorphous side of his nature now possesses validity. By submerging the visible I he dives below the threshold of his schizophrenic habit patterns. He swims joyously, ad lib., in the amniotic fluid, one with his amoebic self. But what, you ask, is the significance of the bird in his left hand?

Why, just this: the bird is purely metaphysical—a quaternary type of the genus dodo, having a tiny, dorsal aperture through which it delivers homilies on the nature of all things. As a species it is extinct; as an eidolon it retains its corporeality—but only if maintained in a state of equipoise. The Germans have immortalized it in the cuckoo clock; in Siam it is found on the coins of the Twenty-third Dynasty. The wings, you will observe, are almost atrophied—because in the pseudo-catalepsy of the dream it does not need to fly, it needs only to *imagine* that it is flying. The hinges of the bill are slightly out of order as the original ball-bearings were lost while flying over the Gobi desert. The bird is definitely not obscene and has never been known to foul its nest. It lays a speckled egg about the size of a walnut whenever it is about to undergo metamorphosis. It feeds on the Absolute when hungry, but it is not a carrion bird. It is exclusively migratory and, despite the vestigial wings, flies incessantly over great imaginary tracts.

If this is clear we can now go on to something else— to the peculiar object swinging from the author's left elbow, for example. With due humility I must admit that this is a little more difficult to explain, being an image of great subjunctive beauty haunting the scar tissues of the hind brain. In the first place, though contiguous to the elbow you will note that it is not suspended from the elbow. It lies at the junction of fore arm and upper arm asymptotally—that is, a symbol rather than a precise ideological concept. The numbers on the lowest pan correspond to certain Runic devices which have resulted in the pragmatic invention known as the metronym. These numbers lie at the root of all musical composition—as imponderable mathematic. These numbers lead the mind back to organic modalities so that structure and form may sustain the elegant perpetuity of logic.

This much clarified, let me add that the conical object in the background must necessarily be capable of only one interpretation: laziness. Not ordinary laziness, as the Pauline doctrine would have it, but a sort of spasmic phlegm induced by the leaden fumes of pleasure. It is hardly necessary to specify that the halo above the conical object is not a quoit nor even a lifesaver, but a purely epistemological phenomenon—that is, a phantastikon which has taken its stance in the melancholy rings of Saturn.

And now, dear reader, I wish that you would make ready to ask me a question before I file this portrait away under P *for petunia*. Won't somebody please testify before we go down to have another look at that dear dead face? Do I hear some one speaking or is that a shoe squeaking? It seems to me I hear some one asking something. Some one is asking me if the little shadow on the horizon line might be a homunculus. Is that right? Are you asking me, Brother Eaton, if that little shadow on the horizon line might be a homunculus?

Brother Eaton doesn't know. He says it might and again it might not.

Well, you are right and you are wrong, Brother Eaton. Wrong because the law of hypothecation does not permit of what is known as doing the duck; wrong because the equation is carried over by an asterisk whereas the sign points clearly to infinity; right because all that is wrong has to do with incertitude and in clearing away dead matter an enema is not sufficient. Brother Eaton, what you see on the horizon line is neither homunculus nor a plugged hat. It is the shadow of Praxus. It shrinks to diminutive proportions in the measure that Praxus waxes great. As Praxus advances beyond the pale of the tertiary moon he disembarrasses himself more and more of his terrestrial image. Little by little he divests himself of the mirror of substantiality. When the last illusion has been shattered Praxus will cast no shadow. He will stand on the 49th parallel of the unwritten eclogue and waste away in cold fire. There will be no more paranoia, everything else being equal. The body will shed its skins and the organs of man will hold themselves proudly in the light. Should there be a war you will please rearrange the entrails according to their astrologic significance. The dawn is breaking over the viscera. No more logic, no more liver mantic. There will be a new heaven and a new earth. Man will be given absolution. *Filed under A for anagogic.*

10. Megalopolitan Maniac

Imagine having nothing on your hands but your destiny. You sit on the doorstep of your mother's womb and you kill time—or time kills you. You sit there chanting the doxology of things beyond your grasp. Outside. Forever outside.

The city is loveliest when the sweet death racket begins. Her own life lived in defiance of nature, her electricity, her frigidaires, her soundproof walls. Box within box she rears her dry walls, the glint of lacquered nails, the plumes that wave across the corrugated sky. Here in the coffin depths grow the everlasting flowers sent by telegraph. In the vaults below the riverbed the gold ingots. A desert glittering with mica and the telephone loudly ringing.

In the early evening, when death rattles the spine, the crowd moves compact, elbow to elbow, each member of the great herd driven by loneliness; breast to breast toward the wall of self, frustrate, isolate, sardine upon sardine, all seeking the universal can opener. In the early evening, when the crowd is sprinkled with electricity, the whole city gets up on its hind legs and crashes the gates. In the stampede the abstract man falls apart, gray with self, spinning in the gutter of his deep loneliness.

One name branded deep. One identity. Everyone pretends not to know, not to remember any more, but the name is branded deep, as deep within as the farthest star without. Filling all space and time, creating infinite loneliness, this name expands and becomes what it always was and always will be—*God.* In the herd, moving with silent feet, in the stampede, wilder than the greatest panic, is God. God burning like a star in the firmament of the human consciousness: God of the buffaloes, God of the reindeer, man's God.... *God.*

Never more God than in the godless crowd. Never more God than in the early evening stampede when the spine rattling with death telegraphs the song of love through all the neurones and from every shop on Broadway the radio answers with megaphone and pick-up, with amplifiers and hook-ups. Never more loneliness than in the teeming crowd, the lonely man of the city surrounded by his inventions, the lost seeker drowning in the common identity. Out of desperate lonely love-lack is built the last stronghold, the webbed citadel of God formed after the labyrinth. From this last refuge no escape except heavenward. From here we fly home, marking the strange ether channels.

Done with his underground life the worm takes on wings. Bereft of sight, hearing, smell, taste he dives straight into the unknown. Away! Away! Anywhere out of the world! Saturn, Neptune, Vega—no matter where or whither, but away, away from the earth! Up there in the blue, with firecrackers sputtering in his asshole, the angel-worm goes daft. He drinks and eats upside down; he sleeps upside down; he screws upside down. At the maximum vitesse his body is lighter than air; at the maximum tempo there is nothing but the spontaneous combustion of dream. Alone in the blue he wings on toward God with purring dynamos. The last flight! The last dream of birth before the bag is punctured.

Where now is he who out of endless nightmares struggled up toward the light? Who is he that stands on the surface of the earth with lungs collapsing, a knife between his teeth, his eyes bursting? Vulcanized by sorrow and agony he stands aghast in the swift, corruptive flux of the upper world. With blood-soaked eyes how glorious it is to behold the world! How bright and gory the empire of man! man! Look, there he is rolling along on his little sledge, his legs amputated, his eyes blown out. Can't you hear him playing? He is playing the *Song of Love* as he rolls along on his little sledge. In the coffee house, alone with his dreams and a revolver under his heart, sits another man, a man who is sick with love. All the clients have gone, save a skeleton with a hat on. The man is alone with his loneliness. The revolver is silent. Beside him is a dog and a bone, and the dog has no use for the bone. The dog is lonely too. Through the window the sun streams in; it shines with a ghastly brilliance on the green skull of the lovelorn. The sun is rotting with ghastly brilliance.

So beautiful the winter of life, with the sun rotting away and the angels flying heavenward with firecrackers up their ass! Softly and meditatively we march through the streets. The gymnasiums are open and one can see the new men made of stovepipes and cylinders moving according to chart and diagram. The new men who will never wear out because the parts can always be replaced. New men without eyes, nose, ears or mouth, men with ball bearings in their joints and skates on their feet. Men immune to riots and revolutions. How gay and crowded the streets are! On a cellar door stands Jack the Ripper swinging an axe; the priest is mounting the scaffold, an erection bursting his fly; the notaries pass with their bulging portfolios; the klaxons going full blast. Men are delirious in their newfound freedom. A perpetual seance with megaphones and ticker tape, men with no arms dictating to wax cylinders; factories going night and day, turning out more sausages, more pretzels, more buttons, more bayonets, more coke, more laudanum, more sharp-edged axes, more automatic pistols.

I can think of no lovelier day than this in the full bloom of the twentieth century, with the sun rotting away and a man on a little sledge blowing the *Song of Love* through his piccolo. This day shines in my heart with such a ghastly brilliance that even if I were the saddest man in the world I should not want to leave the earth.

What a magnificent evacuation, this last flight heavenward from the holy citadel! Looking downward the earth seems soft and lovely again. The earth denuded of man. Unspeakably soft and lovely, this earth bereft of man. Rid of God-hunters, rid of her whoring progeny, the mother of all living wheels her way again with grace and dignity. The earth knows no God, no charity, no love. The earth is a womb which creates and destroys. And man is not of the earth, but of God. To God then let him go, naked, broken, corrupt, divided, lonelier than the deepest gulch.

Today yet a little while Progress and Invention keep me company as I march toward the mountain top. Tomorrow every world city will fall. Tomorrow every civilized being on earth will die of poison and steel. But today you can still bathe me in God's wonderful love lyrics. Today it is still chamber music, dream, hallucination. *The last five minutes!* A dream, a fugue without a coda. Every note rotting away like dead meat on the hooks. A gangrene in which the melody is drowned by its own suppurating stench. Once the organism feels death within its grasp it shudders with rapture. A quickening which mounts to triumphant agony—the agony of the death rattle, when food and sex are one. The whirlpool! and everything that is sucked into it going *down* with it! The wild, unknowing savage who began at the circumference in pursuit of his tail drawing in closer and closer in great labyrinthine spirals and now reaching the dead center where he whirls on the pivot of self with an incandescence that sends a blinding flood of light through every gutter of die soul: spinning there insane and insatiate, the ghoul and gouger of his soul, spinning in centrifugal lust and fury until he sputters out through the hole in the center of him; going down like a gas bag—vault, cellar, ribs, skin, blood, tissue, mind, and heart all consumed, devoured, blottoed in final annihilation.

This is the city, and this the music. Out of the little black boxes an unending river of romance in which the crocodiles weep. All walking toward the mountain top. All in step. From the power house above God floods the street with music. It is God who turns the music on every evening just as we quit work. To some of us is given a crust of bread, to others a Rolls Royce. All moving toward the Exits, the stale bread locked in the garbage cans. What is it that keeps our feet in unison as we move toward the shining mountain top? It is the *Song of Love* which was heard in the manger by the three wise men from the East. A man without legs, his eyes blown out, was playing it on the piccolo as he rolled through the street of the holy city on his little sledge. It is this *Song of Love* which now pours out of millions of little black boxes at the precise chronological moment, so that even our little brown brothers in the Philippines can hear it. It is this beautiful *Song of Love* which gives us the strength to build the tallest buildings, to launch the biggest battleships, to span the widest rivers. It is this Song which gives us the courage to kill millions of men at once by just pressing a button. This Song which gives us the energy to plunder the earth and lay everything bare.

Walking toward the mountain top I study the rigid outlines of your buildings which tomorrow will crumple and collapse in smoke. I study your peace programs which will end in a hail of bullets. I study your glittering shop windows crammed with inventions for which tomorrow there will be no use. I study your worn faces hacked with toil, your broken arches, your fallen stomachs. I study you individually and in the swarm—and how you stink, all of you! You stink like God and his all-merciful love and wisdom. God the maneater! God the shark swimming with his parasites!

It is God, let us not forget, who turns the radio on each evening. It is God who floods our eyes with shining, brimming light. Soon we will be with Him, folded in his bosom, gathered up in bliss and eternity, even with the Word, equal before the Law. This is coming about through love, a love so great that beside it the mightiest dynamo is but a mosquito buzzing.

And now I take leave of you and your holy citadel. I go now to sit on the mountain top, to wait another ten thousand years while you struggle up toward the light. I wish, just for this evening, that you would dim the lights, that you would muffle the loudspeakers. This evening I would like to meditate a bit in peace and quiet. I would like to forget for a little while that you are swarming around in your five-and-ten-cent honeycomb.

Tomorrow you may bring about the destruction of your world. Tomorrow you may sing in Paradise above the smoking ruins of your world-cities. But tonight I would like to think of one man, a lone individual, a man without name or country, a man whom I respect because he has absolutely nothing in common with you— MYSELF. Tonight I shall meditate upon that which lam.

Louveciennes;—Clichy;— Villa Seurat. 1934-1935.

Printed in the United Kingdom
by Lightning Source UK Ltd.
133300UK00002B/199/P